O F

L O V E

A N D

L I F E

O F
LOVE
AND
LIFE

Three novels selected and condensed
by Reader's Digest

The Reader's Digest Association Limited, London

The Reader's Digest Association Limited
11 Westferry Circus, Canary Wharf, London E14 4HE

www.readersdigest.co.uk

ISBN 0-276-42871-4

For information as to ownership of copyright in the material of
this book, and acknowledgments, see last page.

CONTENTS

Erica James
Paradise House

Running a bed and breakfast is not Genevieve Baxter's dream—it was her mother's. But when Serena Baxter leaves unexpectedly, the smooth running of Paradise House falls to Genevieve. Her shocked father is not much use and her sisters, Nattie and Polly, are too caught up in their own lives to offer much constructive help. But Genevieve is not afraid of hard work—it helps to keep the past at bay.

PART I

WHEN GENEVIEVE BAXTER was eleven years old, her family played a trick on her father; they organised a surprise fortieth birthday party for him. Nineteen years later, Genevieve and her sisters were planning to surprise him again.

The plan, once they'd given him his cards and presents after breakfast, was to make him think that they were all far too busy to spend the day with him (or to be up to anything behind his back) and to hint that perhaps he ought to take himself off for a long walk. To underline this, Genevieve had told him that she had a thrilling day of ironing and bookkeeping ahead, Polly had said that she had lessons to teach in St David's, and Nattie had kicked up a fuss that she would have to put in an appearance at the wine bar where, reputedly, she worked. This was perhaps the least convincing fib, as Nattie rarely worked if she could help it. She claimed a job wasn't compatible with being a single mother. Truth was, despite being all of twenty-eight, she still believed that money grew on trees. The rest of the family lived in hope that one day Lily-Rose, a sweet-natured four-year-old, would teach her mother the ways of the world. No one else had managed to.

Genevieve carried her tea and toast to her favourite spot in the garden (the private area, away from their guests) and thought of the one person who might give the game away: Granny Baxter, Daddy Dean's mother. The name Daddy Dean had been Gran's invention. She had started calling him this when Genevieve was born. The name had stuck and his daughters had subsequently followed their grandmother's example, as had Lily-Rose. Gran had always been a one-off, but these days she alternated between blithe confusion and sparkling lucidity, which made her as unpredictable as the weather.

Yesterday had been a typical example of the fickleness of the Pembrokeshire weather. The morning had started out pleasantly enough, but by the afternoon the wind had gusted in from the Atlantic and rattled the windows of Paradise House. Driving rain had sent all but the hardiest of coastal walkers fleeing for cover—straight into the teashops of Angel Sands and the only public house, the Salvation Arms. This May morning, though, the wind and rain had passed and a golden sun shone in a sky of misty apricot.

At eight o'clock, in an hour's time, Genevieve would be cooking and serving breakfast. Three couples and a single man were staying with them—all first-timers, which was unusual; a lot of their bed-and-breakfast guests had been coming for years.

Before moving to Angel Sands, Genevieve and her family had been regular visitors to this part of Pembrokeshire, spending every summer holiday in a cottage a mile out of the village. Then their father had decided to sell their home, Brook House Farm, a 450-acre dairy farm that had belonged to his father and his father before him. 'It's a new beginning,' he'd told the family, when he finally accepted an offer from the builder who had pestered him to sell up for more than three years.

The 'new beginning' had been mum's idea. Serena Baxter had never really taken to the role of farmer's wife. 'Whoever came up with the design for a cow deserves to be one,' she used to say.

Genevieve's parents had met at a church barn dance. It had been love at first sight when Serena had tripped over a bale of hay and fallen into the arms of an anxious-looking man five years older than her. The spirited youngest daughter of the local vicar was an unlikely match for the stolid only son of a farmer, but they were wed within the year.

The years passed. Genevieve arrived, her sisters following shortly after, and their father took on the running of Brook House Farm, his own parents deciding it was time to take it easy. But Serena began to dream of another life. She imagined a picturesque guesthouse by the sea, with breeze-filled bedrooms decorated in pastel shades; bowls of potpourri placed on polished antique furniture that she and Daddy Dean had lovingly restored together; linen as white and fresh as snow. And because their father was crazy about Serena, her dream became his.

The day they heard that a sizable property with ten bedrooms in Angel Sands had come onto the market, Daddy Dean made an offer for it. Paradise House, with its whitewashed walls and pantiled roof, stood imposingly alone on the hillside with magnificent views of the pretty bay. The previous owners had let the Edwardian house go. Water poured through missing roof tiles, broken windows were boarded up and gutters hanging off. It was going for a song.

Although more than ten years had passed, Genevieve could still recall the family's excitement the day they moved in. She suspected the removal men could remember it, too. The drive to the house was too steep and narrow for the large van to negotiate and the men had nearly killed themselves lugging furniture up to the house in the sweltering heat of an August afternoon.

And so 'the dream' became reality and they all lived happily ever after. Except it didn't quite work out that way.

Selling Brook House Farm had been the hardest thing their father had ever done, and Genevieve knew that he had never forgiven himself for taking this bold step. Not that he said as much—he was a man of few words and rarely expressed himself—but as the years went by and Serena eventually guessed what was on his mind, she too fell victim to a guilty conscience, for hadn't she been the one to instigate the change in their lives? Yet, instead of sitting down to discuss it—talking things through wasn't a Baxter trait, as Genevieve knew better than anyone— Serena turned the problem into an even bigger drama by running away from it. Literally.

'We need some time apart,' she told their father, as the taxi waited at the front door to take her to the station. 'I still love you, but I can't bear to see what I've done to you. Forgive me, please, and let me go.'

Unbelievably, he did just that, and Serena went to stay with her sister in Lincoln. 'I had to do as she asked,' Daddy Dean told Genevieve and her sisters. 'She'll be home soon. When she's ready. I know she will.' This apparent benign acceptance of the situation was so typical of their father. He was a stoic to the last. Genevieve was frequently maddened and frustrated by his behaviour, but she was just like him. Neither of them could cope well with confrontation.

Serena had been gone six months now. Initially she had phoned every other week and chatted about nothing in particular, but the calls had petered out and were replaced by letters. At the end of March, Genevieve and her sisters, plus little Lily-Rose, went to see Serena in secret, to try to persuade her to come back. But Serena had plans. An old schoolfriend, living in New Zealand, had invited her to stay. The so-called friend ran a winery in Hawkes Bay, and was, of all things . . . a *man*! She swore blind that there was nothing to read into the situation, but Genevieve and her sisters had been so appalled that they left early, Nattie driving like a lunatic and swearing she would never speak to their mother again. They never told their father about the visit, nor said anything when Serena wrote to him with the news that she was going to New Zealand to visit a friend. They pretended it was the first they'd heard of it and, by way of distraction, Genevieve suggested that he should throw himself into getting Paradise House into better shape.

Another father in another family might have been able to rely upon his grown-up children for practical help, but sadly this was not to be the case. Polly, the baby of the family and the only one still living at home, was undeniably the cleverest and the prettiest, but she was dreamily vague and languid, and her practical skills rated a big zero. She went in for what Genevieve called a 'vintage' look, wearing long forties-style flowery dresses she picked up from charity shops or jumble sales. She played the flute, violin and piano, and could have joined an orchestra if she'd put her mind to it. However, she opted to work as a peripatetic music teacher. She loved her subject and she loved children, probably because, though twenty-six, she still possessed a wide-eyed innocence and an endearing ability to think well of others.

As for Nattie, well, it was difficult to know where to start. She was the middle sister and lived in Tenby in a grotty bedsit. There was a tenuous boyfriend on the scene, but he wasn't Lily-Rose's father. Which was just as well because he was a feckless beach bum.

If Nattie excelled at picking appalling boyfriends, she also excelled at being rebellious and stubborn. As a child she had driven their parents mad with her tantrums. She was a loving mother to Lily-Rose, but she thought nothing of arriving at Paradise House and expecting someone to take care of her daughter while she went off on some crusade or other. Life for Nattie was one long fight against those who would abuse or exploit others. It never occurred to her that she did her own share of exploiting. No one rebuked her for her lack of consideration, for they enjoyed looking after Lily-Rose, who was blue-eyed and strikingly blonde with corkscrew curls, and a delight to have around.

It was partly because her sisters were so impractical that Genevieve had made the decision to come home to Paradise House during her mother's absence. She'd held off from doing so, knowing that like her mother she was running away, but it would only be for a while, until she knew what she wanted to do next. It wasn't Paradise House alone that needed a firm hand to steer its course; she did too.

Top of Genevieve's list of 'things to be done' at Paradise House had been to advertise for a cleaner. The only candidate to come forward was Donna Morgan, a cousin of Debs who ran Debonhair, the local hair salon. Donna had recently moved to Angel Sands to escape her bully of an ex-husband. She was in her mid-fifties with a touch of the Bonnie Tyler about her—lots of back-combed dyed blonde hair, husky voice, faded denim and high heels, and a heavy hand when it came to eye make-up. She worked part-time behind the bar at the Salvation Arms.

Genevieve had offered her the job but couldn't deny how uneasy she felt. Had it been her imagination, or had Donna looked at her father with more than passing friendliness? Since Serena had gone, there had been a surprising number of widowed or divorced female callers at Paradise House. They came bearing offers of help—did her father want his ironing done? Or maybe a casserole or two cooked? Gran said it was a biological fact that once a single woman got a whiff of a helpless and bewildered man, there was no stopping her. 'Heaven help him, for they'll keep banging on that door until Serena comes home.'

But any female attention invariably had Daddy Dean running in the opposite direction, usually to his workshop in the garden. Essentially he was a shy man who hated to be the focus of attention, but he was also a man who loved his wife as much as the day she'd tripped and fallen into his arms more than thirty years ago.

Her tea and toast finished, Genevieve walked back up to the house. She had seven breakfasts to cook, a birthday cake to ice and a surprise party to arrange. Donna would also be arriving for her first day at Paradise House, which meant her father would make himself conveniently scarce and perhaps go for that long walk she had suggested.

There had never been any question of leaving Granny Baxter behind in Cheshire when the family moved to Angel Sands. But she had surprised everyone by insisting that she didn't want to live with them at Paradise House. 'I want my own little place,' she'd said, 'like I have here.' For years Gran (and Granddad before he'd died) had lived in a bungalow on the farm. As luck would have it, a month after the Baxters had moved into Paradise House, a cottage had become available. Perfectly situated in the main street of the village, it was fifty yards from the shops and, in Gran's own words, within shouting distance of the rest of the Baxters.

Genevieve rang the doorbell at Angel Cottage. She had a key to let herself in, but she had promised to use it only in an emergency. She waited, then rang it several more times. Ten minutes to three wasn't the best time to come—Dick Van Dyke would be in the final stages of uncovering the guilty party in *Diagnosis Murder*. Gran was an avid follower of daytime telly. She was no slouch when it came to late-night viewing either. At eighty-two years old, she was embarrassingly up-to-date with all the latest trends.

At last the duck-egg-blue door was opened. 'I knew all along who the murderer was,' Gran said. 'It was that smart piece of work with the shoulder pads. She had spurned lover stamped all over her face.'

Genevieve followed her through to the sitting room. It was low-ceilinged and appeared even smaller than it was due to the quantity of furniture squeezed into it. Framed family photographs adorned every surface, and in pride of place on the television was a black and white picture of Gran and Granddad on their wedding day.

'I was about to make myself a snack,' Gran said to Genevieve. 'Do you want anything?'

'No, thanks. You haven't forgotten the party, have you? There'll be plenty to eat then.'

Her grandmother clicked her tongue. 'Of course I haven't forgotten!' She moved a cushion on the sofa and revealed a carefully wrapped present. 'I hid it there in case your father popped in.' She repositioned the cushion and said, 'If we're going to be drinking this afternoon, we ought to line our stomachs. I'll make us a quick sandwich.'

The tiny kitchen was just as cluttered as the sitting room. Genevieve's hands always itched to tidy it. The ironing board was out and the iron was hissing gently, sending little puffs of steam into the air.

'Shall I put this away for you, Gran?'

'Better still, finish those odds and ends for me.' With a flash of steel that made Genevieve step back, Gran used the bread knife to point to a pile of undergarments and dishcloths.

While Gran hacked at the wholemeal loaf, Genevieve pushed the nose of the iron into places other irons dare not go. She was conscious that if she didn't keep an eye on the time, and the reason why she was here—to fetch Gran and take her up to Paradise House—her father's party would never happen.

The sandwich made, Gran sat at the postage-stamp-sized table the other side of the ironing board. 'So how are you, Genevieve?'

Genevieve had wondered how long it would be before Gran seized her opportunity. She kept her eyes on the iron. 'I'm fine,' she said.

'Still taking the pills?'

'No.'

'That's good. Any more nightmares?'

'A few.'

'Eating properly?'

'Of course.'

'Mm . . . You should talk about it more, Genevieve. Bottling's for fruit, not people.'

'Coming from a Baxter, that's nothing short of pioneering stuff,' Genevieve said.

'We should learn from our mistakes. It's time you and your parents did the same. You're not depressed, are you?'

'No. I told you, I'm fine.'

Gran went to change for the party, her sandwich scarcely touched. Genevieve knew the last fifteen minutes had been nothing but a ruse to ensure some time alone. Listening to her grandmother moving about upstairs, Genevieve tidied the kitchen, or tidied what she could without incurring Gran's fury at being interfered with.

The interrogation hadn't been as bad as it could have been. Gran was right, though; Genevieve *should* talk about it more. But each time she did, she ended up reliving the experience, and for days afterwards felt anxious and unable to sleep at night. She pushed the memories away and put the iron on the windowsill to cool, then went through to the sitting room to wait for Gran.

The local paper was on the coffee table. She picked it up and read the lead story slowly. It wasn't until she was twelve that she had been diagnosed as dyslexic. Up until then, while she'd been at primary school, she had learned to blend into the background and hope the teacher wouldn't ask her to read anything out. By the age of twelve it was getting harder to cover up her embarrassment at never being able to copy correctly from the blackboard. Embarrassment then turned to shame as she was classed as a 'slow learner'. Finally, an English teacher had suggested to her parents that Genevieve be tested for dyslexia. Tests showed that while the language part of her brain didn't work properly, her IQ was surprisingly high. This, Genevieve and her parents were told, explained why she'd managed to cover her tracks so successfully. But the harm had been done: the label of 'lazy and thick' had been applied to her for so many years, subconsciously it would never leave her.

One of her biggest regrets was that when she was seventeen, due to what became known as 'that time when she wasn't well', she'd dropped out of school and taken a variety of jobs—cinema usherette, shop assistant, even a stint as a kennel maid. Then from nowhere she got the idea to become a cook, and found a part-time job in a restaurant. Before long, by attending the local technical college twice a week, she proved herself both competent and quick to learn. But just as things seemed to be coming together for her, her father sold the farm in Cheshire and they moved down to Pembrokeshire. She applied for a post at a hotel in Cardiff, where Nattie was doing a Media Arts degree at the university. The two of them shared a poky one-bedroomed flat.

It was a disaster. Genevieve lasted ten months working in the kitchen from hell, putting up with ridiculous hours and a foul-mouthed, hard-drinking chef, before she decided enough was enough. Then she found another job in an up-market restaurant specialising in overpriced nouvelle cuisine, but soon realised she was out of the frying pan and into the fire. She was only twenty-two, but felt more like ninety-two. Trainee chefs, she had come to realise, were treated as little more than cannon fodder. It wasn't for her.

A spate of jobs followed, then clever old Gran came up with a novel career move for her. 'Why don't you keep house for some la-di-da family? I bet there's plenty of folk willing to pay through the nose for someone who can cook as well as you do and keep them organised.'

As daft as it sounded, Genevieve pursued the suggestion and found to her astonishment that there was quite a market for housekeepers. So long as she was prepared to be flexible and take anything on, plenty of opportunities were on offer. The work was varied and not badly paid. It also came with live-in accommodation and occasionally the opportunity to travel, when the families took her on holiday with them.

The sweetest of all the people she'd worked for had been George and Cecily Randolph, an elderly couple who had treated her more as a granddaughter than an employee. But just thinking of them brought on a stab of pain, and she was glad to hear Gran coming down the stairs singing 'Mine Eyes Have Seen the Glory'.

Good old Gran. She could always be relied upon to chase away a maudlin thought.

To Genevieve's relief, everything had gone according to plan and the surprise party was well into its stride.

Their friends were mostly what the born-and-bred locals referred to as 'newcomers', but when it came down to it, there were very few in the village who could lay claim to being a true local. Stan and Gwen Norman, who'd taken over the mini-market in the village five years ago, were laughing and chatting with Huw and Jane Davies who, a short while after the Baxters had moved to Angel Sands, had given up the rat race in Cardiff, bought the former blacksmith's cottage and workshop and converted it into a pottery and art gallery.

Over by the conservatory and sitting in the shade, Ruth Llewellyn was nodding her head to whatever Gran was saying. Ruth and her husband, William, recent arrivals, ran Angel Crafts, a gift shop in the centre of the village. On the other hand, the Lloyd-Morris brothers, Roy and David, had been butchers in Angel Sands for as long as anyone could remember and, once tasted, their Welsh spring lamb and homemade sausages could never be forgotten.

Genevieve had thought about holding the party in the evening, but then Huw and Jane wouldn't have been able to make it, along with Tubby Evans—real name Robert. So late afternoon it had to be. The only other guest was Adam Kellar. Everyone knew that Adam had an enormous crush on Nattie, and, predictably, the object of his desire was ignoring him. She stood barefoot, wearing a pair of dungarees rolled up to her knees, and was lecturing Tubby on the perils of pesticides.

Tubby, so called because of his short legs and rotund shape, drove the mobile fruit and veg van and had access to anything newsworthy in the area; houses had been bought and sold via him in a single afternoon.

A flash of white across the lawn caught Genevieve's attention. It was Polly, dressed in an ankle-length white cotton dress that was practically see-through. She was drifting through the orchard in the dappled sun-light, clutching a bunch of bluebells. Lily-Rose was following closely in her footsteps, quite a feat in the long grass, given that she was wearing her mother's multicoloured clogs. Trailing behind her was a cardboard box containing a collection of favourite dolls and teddy bears.

Seeing that Adam was standing on his own, Genevieve carried a tray of canapés over to him. 'How's it going?' she asked. She was fond of Adam and couldn't help but feel sorry for him. Ever since he'd arrived in Angel Sands, he'd been hopelessly smitten with Nattie. But Nattie refused to have anything to do with him. Genevieve thought her sister was a fool. Adam was warm-hearted and endlessly generous. Endlessly forgiving, too, especially with Nattie.

'But how could I consider him as a potential date?' she would say. 'I mean, for pity's sake, he wears a gold bracelet!'

Adam helped himself to a miniature Yorkshire pudding topped with a sliver of rare beef and horseradish sauce, the movement causing the offending piece of jewellery to slide down his tanned forearm. 'Everything's just cracking,' he said. 'I've bought another caravan park. At Nolton Haven. It needs wads of cash throwing at it, but by the time I've finished, I'll have turned it into another of my premier sites.'

This was how Adam had made his money, buying run-down caravan parks and turning them around. He owned five in Pembrokeshire, three in Devon, five in Cornwall and another two near Blackpool. He was thirty-three but had been a bona fide millionaire since the age of twenty-six, after selling everything he had and borrowing heavily to buy his first site in Tenby. He'd cashed in on a changing market, he'd once explained to Genevieve. Nowadays they were called executive holiday homes and he provided excellent on-site facilities in the form of club-houses, swimming pools, play areas, gyms, spa centres and evening entertainment.

Genevieve admired him for his enterprise and sheer hard work. He'd left school in Wolverhampton when he was sixteen and had worked tirelessly ever since. Now, he had a lot to enjoy: a beautiful house in Angel Sands he'd had built eighteen months ago, a choice of flashy cars to drive, and an apartment in Barbados. All that was missing was the right person to share it.

Genevieve offered Adam another canapé. His gaze was fixed on Nattie across the lawn. 'She's not worth it, Adam. You're better off without her.'

He smiled and for a split second looked almost handsome. Still staring at Nattie, he said, 'She's unique, Gen, and I'm a patient man.' He chewed on the miniature Yorkshire pudding. 'You know, these aren't bad. Ever thought of setting up your own catering business? You could do really well; small business functions, wedding parties, anniversaries. That's if you're going to stick around Angel Sands.'

Genevieve laughed. 'What? On top of running Paradise House?'

'You can do it, Gen. You know you can. It's a matter of organisation, which I know you're good at. All you have to do is decide what you want, then go for it. If capital's a problem, I could fund you initially. You know, just to get you up and running.'

'Adam Kellar, you are the sweetest man alive. But I'm OK for money.'

The theme tune from *The Great Escape* had him reaching into his jacket pocket for his mobile phone. Leaving him to answer his call, Genevieve wandered over to Polly. She was sitting on the old rope swing in the orchard, humming softly and looking out to sea, her long, baby-fine blonde hair lifting on the warm breeze.

'Everything OK, Poll?'

Her sister turned; her face both beautiful and sad. 'I was just thinking of Mum. She should be here.'

Genevieve sat on the grass beside the swing and gazed at the turquoise sea glittering in the bright sunshine. A lone seagull wheeled overhead, its cry adding a poignant echo to the moment.

She should be here.

It was a simple but true statement. Serena hadn't forgotten their father's birthday—she had sent a card from New Zealand—but she was very much the missing guest.

It was when Daddy Dean was holding Lily-Rose aloft so she could help him blow out the candles on the cake, all fifty-nine of them, and Tubby had teased him for being two and a half years older than him, that a surprise guest appeared.

'I hope it's not too late for me to wish you a happy birthday,' said a vision in faded denim and sparkly rhinestone gems. Donna Morgan looked very much as though she'd turned up at the wrong party, in her phenomenally tight jeans, fringed and bejewelled jacket and white cowboy boots.

'I don't want to intrude, but I wanted to give you a little something,' she said. With her strong Caerphilly accent and husky voice, the words directed at Daddy Dean came out loaded with sing-songy innuendo.

Holding Lily-Rose as though she were a human shield, Daddy Dean took a step backwards. Right onto Gran's foot. She let out a yelp and spilt her glass of Madeira down the front of her dress. Adam was instantly on hand with a paper napkin, but Gran was more worried about her empty glass. 'I hadn't even had a sip of it!' she muttered. Once it was refilled and Donna had apologised, calm and order were restored. Donna looked around for the intended recipient of her present, but there was no sign of him.

Genevieve had to bite back a smile. 'I'll go and see if I can find him,' she said.

Nattie caught up with her in the conservatory. 'The bloody nerve of that woman! Just who does she think she is, coming on to Dad like that? Tell me you didn't invite her, Gen.'

'Of course I didn't.'

'So how did she know it was his birthday?'

'I let it slip this morning.'

They found their father upstairs in his and their mum's bedroom. He was sitting in the rocking chair he'd bought and restored for their mother when Polly was born. Lily-Rose was bouncing on the bed, beaming happily because no one was stopping her, but Dad was staring wretchedly at the card in his hands; it was the one Serena had sent him.

Genevieve and Nattie knelt on the floor, one either side of the chair. Neither spoke. What could they say? Every time a woman showed the slightest interest in him, it made him think of Serena and how much he longed for her to come home.

'I'm sorry,' he said, his words catching in his throat. 'Silly of me.'

'Not silly at all,' said Genevieve, stroking his arm.

'Absolutely not,' agreed Nattie, and gave him a hug.

'But would it really be so bad if Donna did fancy Daddy?' asked Polly later that night.

They were alone in her bedroom at the top of the house where they'd always slept in what had been the attic rooms, while their parents and guests slept on the floor below. Nattie and Lily-Rose were stopping over. Genevieve and her sisters were sitting crosslegged on Polly's double bed with a tray of leftovers between them. An empty bottle of wine stood on the bedside table. Polly's question had taken Genevieve by surprise. Surely it mattered. He was their father.

Nattie said, 'Poll, I'm warning you, don't you dare go all Pollyanna on me, imagining good in everyone. Donna Morgan is bad news.'

Polly tilted her head and frowned. 'But how do we know that?'

'Because it's obvious. The woman is clearly after husband number two and sees Dad as a sitting target. She'd have him for breakfast.'

'You have no way of knowing that,' Genevieve said. 'And it strikes me the only crime she's committed so far is to overdress and wear too much make-up.'

They fell silent until Nattie said, 'But what you're both losing sight of is that Dad won't ever be interested in her. Or any other woman for that matter. It's Mum he wants.'

'In that case, what are we worrying about?' Genevieve said. 'Donna will soon get the message and leave him alone.'

A week had passed since her father's birthday. After hanging out the washing—sheets, pillowcases, duvet covers, towels and bath mats—and leaving a bowl of bread dough to rise, Genevieve decided to go for a walk. Dad was down at Gran's fixing a leaky tap and Polly was playing the piano in the guest sitting-room.

Not wanting to disturb her sister, Genevieve wrote a brief note saying when she would be back. She propped the piece of paper against the jug of wild flowers on the table and listened to her sister belting out a piece of explosive music. To look at Polly you'd never expect her to play with such energy. Hidden depths, thought Genevieve, as she shut the door behind her and stepped outside into the sunshine.

Instead of going round to the front of the house, she walked the length of the garden and climbed over the low wall to join the coastal path in an easterly direction. The path was steep and narrow, lined either side with golden-yellow gorse bushes. She paused to catch her breath and looked back the way she had come, to Angel Sands. It was a close-knit and traditional little community, with its roots in limestone quarrying. But the quarrying had stopped a long time ago; nowadays tourism was the staple. Visitors relished the peace and quiet and beauty of the coastline, as well as the warmth of those who welcomed them.

There were plenty of stories, some even true, about the rugged coastline. One tale told that the timber used in the building of some of the older cottages in Angel Sands had come from a ship that had been smashed on the rocks in the neighbouring bay, aptly named Hell's Gate.

Angel Sands had acquired its name because of these treacherous rocks. Centuries ago, if a storm blew up and an unfortunate ship found itself being pushed towards the mouth of Hell's Gate, the sailors knew their only chance of escape was to hold fast against the wind and hope to sail into the calmer waters of the bay around the headland.

Unsurprisingly, a myth was soon established, that the bay was guarded by an angel and it would only come to your aid if you prayed hard enough and loud enough. There were a few fanciful people in the village who believed that if you listened carefully on a wild and stormy night you could hear, rising up from the swelling waters, the agonised cries of those whose prayers hadn't been answered.

Genevieve started walking again, enjoying the warm, salty breeze against her face: it was good to be out in the fresh air. It had been a hectic morning. The guests had been down early for breakfast. They were keen walkers and she'd made packed lunches for them all. She liked to think that running a successful bed and breakfast was down to being flexible and offering the guests these little extras.

If she stayed—and she might have to if her mother didn't come back—she would want to make some changes at Paradise House. It would be nice to offer an evening meal. Only yesterday, Donna had been less than flattering about the meals at the Salvation Arms.

It was working well, having Donna to help with the cleaning. But for all her efficiency, there was still the problem of her and Dad. Whenever she was around, he would instantly make himself scarce. Gran was seeing a lot more of him these days, much to her irritation—with every visit, he claimed to find something wrong with her little house, something that required his immediate attention.

'What's got into him?' Gran had asked Genevieve and her sisters. 'Just as I'm settling down to watch the telly, he knocks on the door.'

They hadn't told Gran what was going on, that Dad was hiding from Donna, because the last thing they needed was her involvement.

In fairness to Donna, she was showing no sign of intensifying her attack on their father. Maybe she knew she was backing a loser. Nattie wasn't convinced, though, and was sure she was just changing her tactics. 'When we're least prepared for it, she'll strike,' was her opinion.

But no matter how negative Nattie was, Genevieve wasn't prepared to lose Donna, especially if she was going to start cooking evening meals. And then there was Adam's suggestion that she should start a catering business . . .

It was good having so much to think about. It gave her less time to dwell on the real reason she had come back home, to the place where she had always felt safe. No one knew better than she did that it was the easiest thing in the world to slip into a downward spiral. But real fear was difficult to shake off, and since that dreadful night when two masked men had broken into George and Cecily's home, she had known exactly what fear was.

It had been a perfectly ordinary evening. She had cooked George and

Cecily their supper and, after she'd cleared away, they had all settled down to watch the television together. 'We don't like the thought of you upstairs on your own,' they had said when she first went to work for them as their housekeeper. 'Please sit with us. Unless, of course, you'd rather not.' She had agreed all too readily. They had travelled the world and were a fascinating couple to talk to. Right away she felt at home with them. They lived in a beautiful sixteenth-century manor house in Surrey. It was far too big for them, but it had been their home for nearly forty years and they couldn't imagine living anywhere else.

The two masked men had got in through a French window in the library and had crept into the drawing room while Genevieve was making George and Cecily a cup of tea during an advert break. When she returned with the tea tray, the robbers had tied up the couple and were threatening George with a hunting knife.

Genevieve dropped the tray and tried to make a run for the telephone in the hall. But the men grabbed her by the hair and dragged her back into the room, where they pushed her to the floor, covered her mouth with tape, strapped her hands behind her back and then tied her ankles. While the men ransacked the house, she willed her employers to cooperate with them, but when the robbers demanded George give them the code to open the safe in the main bedroom, and he refused, they went mad and seized Cecily . . .

Genevieve sat down on the grass, her heart pounding. The memory of the terror in Cecily's eyes would never leave her. Neither would the look on George's face when he realised what he'd allowed the men to do to his wife. Never had Genevieve felt so helpless. Or so frightened.

The robbers were never caught. If they had been, they'd have been charged with Cecily's murder. George had died in hospital soon afterwards, as a result of the attack. Three months later, Genevieve was still having nightmares and couldn't face being on her own at night. That was why she'd come home to Paradise House and her family.

Only Gran had an inkling of what she'd gone through—she'd deliberately underplayed it with the rest of her family. But Gran had a nose for these things.

There was one inescapable truth about life at Paradise House. Nothing stood still; the moment your back was turned, things happened. When Genevieve returned home after her walk, she found that Nattie and Lily-Rose had moved in, bringing with them a wealth of clutter that filled the hall and stairs. They'd also brought a donkey, which was tethered to a wooden stake on the front lawn. While the donkey honked and brayed and Lily-Rose went berserk with delight at the prospect of riding him as soon as she'd had lunch, Tubby's van rolled up the drive.

'Well, look you see, you'll never guess what,' he said, stepping down from the van, his Llanelli accent as bright and jolly as his face. 'At long last, Ralph Griffiths has got planning permission for that dilapidated old barn of his and has agreed to sell it.'

This *was* big news. The sale of any property in the area caused ears to flap and tongues to wag.

'Who, what, when and name your source,' demanded Nattie.

Tubby wiped his hands on the front of his apron. 'Well, *cariad*, I just heard it down at Debonhair, so it's got to be on the button.'

Both Nattie and Genevieve nodded. The gospel according to St Deb was always to be believed.

'But the bit you girls are going to like is who Ralph's selling to. He's selling to an eligible young man. He lives in Buckinghamshire,' Tubby informed them, 'and the barn's to be a holiday home for him. Debs says his name's Jonjo Fitzwilliam and he's only thirty-three but has made a bundle of money out of health and fitness centres.'

'So why's he coming here?' Genevieve asked. 'If he's got money, why isn't he buying a holiday home somewhere more glamorous?'

'Perhaps he's a man of discernment! Debs also said he's bringing his own architect to turn the barn into something really special.' Tubby smiled. 'Apparently this young architect boyo spent part of his child-hood here. So, with a bit of luck, he'll do a sympathetic job of the con-version.' Then, rubbing his hands on his apron again and bringing the gossip session to an end, he said, 'Now then, girls, what can I get you from the van?' He chuckled and glanced over towards the donkey. 'How about some carrots for your hairy friend?'

'Are they organic?'

But Genevieve wasn't listening. She walked back into the house, up the stairs to her bedroom. Only when she had closed the door behind her and leaned against it, did she let her brain receive the information her heart had registered the moment Tubby had described the man who would be coming to Angel Sands with Jonjo Fitzwilliam . . . *this young architect boyo spent part of his childhood here . . .*

It had to be Christian.

There were questions that needed answering. Why had a donkey taken up residence at Paradise House? Why had Nattie and Lily-Rose upped sticks from Tenby? How was Genevieve going to find out if Jonjo Fitzwilliam's architect was indeed who she thought he was?

Although it was this last question that dominated her thoughts, it seemed the donkey was destined to be the focus of conversation while

she prepared lunch for everyone, including Gran, who Dad had brought
back with him after fixing a loose stair rod.

'In case you were wondering,' announced Nattie as she put Lily-Rose
onto her booster seat, 'his name's Henry.'

'That's a nice name,' said Gran. 'Solid and reliable. What does he do?'

'The usual kind of thing, I guess, if he's given the chance; a romp in
the sun, plenty of juicy green stuff to nibble on and a regular supply of
carrots. I just had to give him the opportunity of a better life.'

'I should think you did. But he won't last two minutes with a girl like
you unless he gets some good red meat down him.'

Everyone stared at Gran, and gave up the struggle not to laugh.

Genevieve said, 'Gran, Henry's a donkey.'

Utterly unfazed, Gran said, 'Well, I still think Henry's a good name.
Even for a donkey. After all, they're solid and reliable, aren't they?
Certainly more reliable than any of the young men you've dallied with
in the past, Natalie.'

'So how did you come by him?' asked Genevieve.

'Huw and Jane told me about him. He'd been cooped up in a filthy
yard with nothing but a bucket of dirty water and a bag of mouldy hay.'

Dad glanced up from his paper, an eyebrow raised. 'And where's he
going to stay, love?'

Nattie turned on the charm. 'Well, I was rather hoping you might like
to have him here. Just think, you wouldn't have to bother mowing the
grass any more. And there'd be an endless supply of organic fertiliser for
the garden. Go on, what do you say? Please can Henry stay?'

Her father folded his newspaper and put it down. 'I suppose there's a
chance he might redress the balance around here. It'll be two males to
five females if he stays.'

Nattie jumped up from her chair and went to hug him.

Genevieve smiled. As if there'd be any doubt of Henry staying. Their
father was incapable of turning anyone or anything away. 'So what
about you and Lily-Rose?' she asked, sounding worryingly like the only
responsible adult at the table. 'Why have you decided to move back?'

'Call it a run of bad luck. They don't want me at the wine bar any
more and the tenancy on the bedsit's come to an end, leaving your wee
niece and penniless sister without a home.'

'What will you do?' Again the boring, responsible adult.

'Do?' echoed Nattie, with just a hint of sarcasm. 'Why, stay here of
course. Home sweet home. There's nothing like it.' She paused, as if
sensing there had been more to Genevieve's question than at first
appeared. Which there was. Genevieve knew her sister of old—Nattie
wouldn't lift a finger to help at Paradise House. She would actually

make more work for everyone. 'If coming home's good enough for you, Gen,' Nattie added, 'it's certainly good enough for me.'

Genevieve wasn't averse to taking Nattie on, but she knew when to back off. She wasn't in the mood for an argument over her sister's legendary slothfulness.

Daddy Dean took up his paper again and Polly, who hadn't yet uttered a word, chewed slowly on a piece of bread and cheese, her attention absorbed in the book she was reading: *Little Women*. Every now and then, Polly reread all her favourite classic children's novels. Very likely it would be *The Secret Garden* next week.

While Polly continued to turn the pages, Nattie and Gran egged on Lily-Rose's noisy farmyard impressions. But a dispute broke out when Gran started encouraging her to hiss like a snake. Challenged by Natalie about the likelihood of such a species being found in a farmyard, Gran retaliated, 'It's well known that there were adders in Pembrokeshire. Everyone knows that.'

'OK,' conceded Nattie. 'Now I come to think of it, there are plenty of snakes in the grass hereabouts. Adam, to name but one.'

Dad rattled his throat from behind his paper, registering his disapproval. He had a soft spot for Adam.

'And I bet any money you like,' Nattie went on, 'that this Jonjo Fitzwilliam will turn out to be just as awful. More money than sense and with terrible taste.'

Looking up from her book, Polly interrupted, 'Gen, have you thought who the architect might be?'

All eyes suddenly turned on Genevieve, apart from Lily-Rose's—she was carefully unwrapping a triangle of Dairylea and mooing.

'It's crossed my mind that it could be Christian,' said Genevieve. 'But it's only a guess. After all, there have to be any number of architects who holidayed here when they were children.'

Daddy Dean looked at her, concerned. 'And if it is him?'

'Then . . . then I'll look forward to meeting him again. Think how much we'll have to catch up on.'

Nattie leaned back in her seat and snorted. 'Yeah, I can picture the two of you. "How are you, Genevieve?" "Oh, not so bad. How about you, broken anyone else's heart recently?"'

'For goodness' sake, all that's in the dim and distant past. I put it behind me years ago. I suggest you do the same.'

Nice try, she told herself later that afternoon as she walked Gran home.

'Come in for a cup of tea,' Gran said, putting her key in the lock and pushing against the door. It had begun to swell in the warmer weather.

Genevieve edged away, afraid to cross the threshold. It wasn't PG Tips

Gran was offering, but another of her open-heart-surgery-minus-the-anaesthetic sessions.

'I ought to be getting back,' Genevieve murmured. 'You know what it's like, new guests arriving.'

It was rude and cowardly of her, but she kissed the old lady's cheek and turned to leave. Instead of going back up the hill to Paradise House—the new guests wouldn't be arriving for another two hours—she headed for the footpath that led west along the coastal path towards the next headland. Her destination was Tawelfan beach, where she and Christian had met. It was also where they had done a lot of other things.

They say you never forget your first kiss. Well, amen to that! She could still remember hers quite vividly, and as the path dropped down the grassy slope towards the sandy bay where Christian had first kissed her, she pictured the scene. She had been fifteen and Christian seventeen. They had been sitting in the shelter of the sand dunes, warming themselves after a swim and eating hamburgers from the kiosk in the car park. There was a smear of ketchup on her lip, so he later claimed, and he'd tilted his head towards hers and kissed it away.

He was from Ludlow in Shropshire and his family had been coming on holiday to Pembrokeshire for years. They owned a pretty, stone-built house in the next village. She'd met him when she was twelve. She'd been standing at the water's edge, letting the waves swoosh and swirl around her feet, when a voice cut through the squeals of other children playing nearby.

'You're not afraid to go in, are you?' The voice had a strange, almost unconnected tone. She turned to see who had spoken, thinking that perhaps he was foreign. A tall, angular boy in cut-off denim shorts was smiling at her. Or was he taunting her?

'I'm not afraid of anything,' she retorted, turning away and running into the shallow water, trying not to gasp at its numbing coldness. She kept going until it was deep enough to fling herself in and swim. There, that would show him! She looked back to the shore to see if he was watching. She was surprised to see him just a couple of yards behind her.

'You're a good swimmer,' he said, coming alongside. Again, that peculiar awkward tone to his voice. Definitely foreign.

'I swim for my school,' she said, not meeting his gaze.

He frowned. 'What did you say?'

'I said I swim for my school.'

The frown was replaced with a wide smile. 'Me too.'

It was the first thing they found they had in common and it set the tone of their friendship.

But the kiss, coming several years later, changed all that.

A light, drizzly rain was falling and the churning sea was as grey as the sky. It was a chilly and inhospitable day for the end of May. Inside the cosy kitchen at Paradise House, Genevieve was doing what she liked best, spending the afternoon baking. The comforting smell of syrup and allspice filled the kitchen—a fruitcake was in the oven, a treacle tart cooling on the wire rack—and now she was trying out a new recipe for meringues, carefully whisking glossy egg whites and icing sugar over a pan of simmering water.

When the mixture was the right texture, she switched off the electric whisk and turned to check on her niece, who earlier had been sitting at the table playing with some leftover pastry. Lily-Rose was now under the table, her face daubed with flour as she 'read' to her collection of dolls and teddies. They were neatly lined up and were being told to listen carefully. She couldn't read yet, but this was a favourite game.

Genevieve smiled and left her to it. Her niece was easy to look after; a confident little girl who enjoyed her own company.

Back with her meringues, Genevieve removed the bowl from the pan of water and whisked the mixture some more. When it had cooled, she reached for the piping bag. 'It's time to do the piping now,' she told Lily-Rose. 'Do you still want to help me?'

Lily-Rose shot out from under the table. 'Where's my pinny?'

'Here. But first we'd better wash your hands.'

Lily-Rose was in the process of dragging a chair across to the sink when there was a knock at the back door.

It was Adam, and by the look of him he'd recently had his hair cut. He was smartly dressed in a dark blue suit with a cream shirt. He would have looked great if it hadn't been for the novelty tie.

'If it's Dad or Nattie you're looking for, you're out of luck. They're not here. It's just Lily-Rose and me.'

'That's OK. It was you I wanted to see anyway.'

'I'll be with you in a minute. Sit down and make yourself at home.' Looking at the amount of flour her niece had got everywhere, she said, 'You'd better be careful where you put yourself. Where've you been, dressed like the cat's whiskers?'

Instead of answering her, he closed his eyes and breathed in deeply.

'You haven't taken up meditation have you?' she asked him.

He opened his eyes and laughed. 'No. For a moment there, I was a small boy. My mum was a great cook just like you.'

Adam freely admitted that part of his success was attributable to his upbringing. His father left home when he was a baby and when he was sixteen his mother was killed in a car crash: he learned from an early age to stand on his own two feet. After leaving school he went to work in a garage as a trainee mechanic. His employers soon realised that he was a natural salesman, so they took him out of his overalls and put him in a suit. In no time he was easily outperforming the other salesman. From cars he turned to caravans, and then to caravan parks.

'Genvy, will you help me wash my hands?' Lily-Rose was standing on the chair at the sink, her arms outstretched towards the taps.

'Of course, darling.'

Lily-Rose smiled shyly at Adam. 'You could help us make the cakes.'

'I don't think he's wearing the right kind of clothes,' Genevieve said.

'If you gave him a pinny he'd stay clean.'

'That's all right, Rosy-Posy, I'm just fine watching you two.'

While Lily-Rose giggled at the pet name he used for her behind Nattie's back, he removed his jacket, hung it on the cleanest chair and made himself at home by putting the kettle on. Genevieve liked that about him; he was easy to have around. By the time he'd made a pot of tea and found some juice for Lily, she had two trays of bite-sized meringues ready for the oven, along with a special one of Lily-Rose's oddly shaped efforts. She took out the fruitcake, lowered the oven temperature and slid in the trays.

'So, what did you want to see me about?'

But her question went unanswered. From the garden came an unearthly groaning.

'What the dickens is that noise?' Adam joined them at the window above the sink, where Genevieve was once again helping Lily-Rose to wash her hands.

Genevieve pointed towards the orchard and explained about Henry. 'He's been with us for two weeks now, another of Nattie's crusades. Recently he's started braying like a thing possessed. Once he gets going nothing will stop him.'

'He's lonely,' Adam said knowledgeably.

'How do you know?'

He went back to the teapot and poured out their tea. 'When I was little, the local neighbourhood nutter kept a pair. Then, when one of them died, we were kept awake all night. The din was horrendous. But as soon as a replacement was found, the lovesick donkey perked up.'

Genevieve groaned. 'As if I didn't have enough to do. Now I have to find Henry a soul mate.' Since being back at Paradise House it seemed each day brought her yet another responsibility.

He passed her a mug. 'I could help you if you like. I know a bloke in Saundersfoot—'

She interrupted him with a laugh. 'Just how many *blokes* do you know, Adam? You seem to have one for every occasion.'

He shrugged. 'I'm just a fixer. A go-between. Which leads me nicely on to the reason I'm here.'

'Oh? And there was me thinking it was my irresistible company, that you were seeing me behind Nattie's back to make her jealous.'

A faint hue of red appeared on Adam's face. He could take any amount of teasing about his professional life, or even his gold bracelet, but Genevieve knew his feelings for Nattie were not to be made fun of. Hiding his discomfort by helping Lily-Rose off the chair, he said, 'I've got a proposition for you. A business proposition,' he added hastily, letting Lily-Rose climb onto his lap as he sat down.

Genevieve took a chair opposite him. 'Go on, I'm listening.'

'I've just had lunch with my accountant and his daughter's getting married next weekend. The thing is, they've been let down by the hotel where they were going to have the reception.'

'And you want to know if we've any spare rooms that weekend.' She went to fetch the bookings diary she kept by the phone.

'No. Accommodation isn't the problem; everyone's more or less local. It's the buffet.'

She sat down again. 'Oh, I get it; I've just become one of your magical *blokes*, haven't I?'

'All I said was that I'd have a word with you. Nothing more than that.'

'And how many would I be cooking for? Twenty? Twenty-five?'

He looked down at Lily-Rose. 'Um . . . the guest list is quite big.'

'How big?'

'Eighty-odd.'

'*What?*'

'You can do it, Gen. I know you can.'

'Feeding eighty hungry people, that's a lot of cooking. And a lot of stuff to ferry about.'

'That's where the second part of my proposition comes in. Is there any chance the reception could be held at Paradise House? You have to admit, if the weather's good, it's a great spot.'

She had to admire his gall. 'And if the weather is like it is today?'

They both turned and looked outside; the drizzle had become a downpour.

'To be on the safe side, I'll tell Gareth and Gwenda to organise a marquee and tables and chairs. That way all bases will be covered.'

'You've put an awful lot of thought into this,' she said, amused he'd taken her consent as a foregone conclusion.

'No more than any problem I'm confronted with.'

'OK,' she conceded. 'I'll do it. Although I'll have to check with Dad. It's his house, after all.'

Again Adam lowered his gaze to the top of Lily-Rose's curly blonde hair. 'Don't be cross, but I had a quick word with him earlier. He said it was your decision.'

Sliding off Adam's lap, Lily-Rose said, 'Can I have another drink, please?'

Adam reached for the carton before Genevieve had put down her mug of tea. Then, putting his hand into his jacket pocket, he produced a phone number and a cheque. 'Gareth hoped you'd say yes, so he wrote this out in advance. When the job's done, there'll be that much again.'

When Genevieve took the cheque, she did a double take. 'Good grief. You haven't made out I'm better than I am, have you?'

'All I've done is tell Gareth the truth. I reckon if you do exactly what you did for your father's birthday party, you'll be a huge success. And once word goes round, I guarantee you'll have more offers of work.'

Genevieve turned from tucking the cheque into her bag. 'Adam,' she said slowly, 'it sounds suspiciously like you've engineered this.'

He put a hand to his chest. 'Hand on heart, there's been no skulduggery; this has fallen right into your lap.' Then, switching his attention from her to Lily-Rose, he said, 'Your auntie isn't very trusting, is she? I wonder why that is, Rosy-Posy.'

Lily-Rose giggled, put down her plastic mug and wandered out of the kitchen. As Genevieve eased the fruitcake out of its tin and onto a wire cooling rack, she reflected how her instinct was always to question, even if it meant doubting the kindest of people, like Adam.

Her thoughts were interrupted by Adam saying, 'Gen, there's talk down in the village. It's about this Jonjo Fitzwilliam character who's bought Ralph's barn. Or more precisely, about the architect who'll be doing the conversion. Is it true you used to be childhood sweethearts?'

Thwack! There it was. She plonked herself with a heavy thump in the chair opposite. 'What else are the good folk of Angel Sands saying?'

'That he broke your heart. That you've never got over it.'

She stared open-mouthed at him. 'But that's rubbish.'

He shook his head. 'You can always tell me to mind my own business, but did he really break your heart?'

She nodded. 'And some.'

'Do you want to discuss it?'

'So that I can satisfy your curiosity?'

'No,' he said firmly. 'To put us on an equal footing. You know everything there is to know about me, but you're guarded about yourself.'

He was right, of course. She preferred to keep things to herself. So how to tell Adam what had gone on? She decided to go right back to the beginning, to that first day, when she met Christian.

PART II

THEY SWAM IN SILENCE, away from the splashing and squealing. The tide was going out and Genevieve knew they had to be careful. 'We'd better not go too far,' she said.

He nodded and pointed to the nearest rocks, which formed the right-hand spur of the bay. For a few seconds he swam on ahead, his arms cutting through the water cleanly, effortlessly. She followed suit and was soon level with him. Neither was out of breath when they climbed up onto the smooth, flat rocks that were warm from the sun.

'I love it here,' she said, 'it's the best place in the world.'

When he didn't respond she wished she hadn't said anything. He probably thought it was a silly thing to say. She squeezed the water from her ponytail and sat down.

He sat down too, and looked directly at her. 'It's great here, isn't it? It's my favourite place,' he said, in his strange, off-key voice.

She frowned, wondering why he'd as good as repeated what she'd just said. 'Yes,' she agreed. 'My family come here every year. How about you?'

There was a pause before he answered, during which she realised he was making her feel uncomfortable.

'We've been coming since I was eight,' he said. 'How old are you?'

'Twelve. And you?'

Another pause, followed by the same feeling of discomfort.

'Fourteen,' he replied.

And then she understood why he was making her feel so weird. He was staring at her too closely, his gaze too penetrating. She shifted away from him and turned her head to look back towards the beach and her parents. She stood up and waved to her father. When eventually he caught sight of her and waved back, she sat down again, although part of her didn't want to. This strange boy might be an excellent swimmer, but he wasn't the easiest person to talk to. She didn't want to get saddled with him for the rest of the time they were here, not if he was always going to be so odd. She dangled her feet into the water and felt the tickly touch of swaying fronds of seaweed. 'Do you have any brothers or sisters?' she said.

Once again he ignored her question. That's it, she thought. I'm not

31

having anything more to do with him. She turned her head. 'Don't you know it's bad manners to ignore people?' She was about to slip back into the water and swim away when he laid a hand on her forearm.

'You have to look straight at me when you speak. If you don't, I can't read your lips. I'm deaf.'

Never had Genevieve felt so rude or cruel. Why hadn't she realised that that was why he spoke in that odd way? That he had looked at her so intently because he was trying to read her lips. Mortified, she murmured an apology.

He tapped her on the leg. 'What did you say?'

'I'm sorry,' she repeated, this time looking straight at him and stupidly raising her voice.

His mouth curved into a soft smile. 'Why are you sorry I'm deaf?'

'I'm not. I mean . . . well, I *am* sorry you're deaf, but what I meant was, I'm . . . I'm sorry I was so horrible to you.'

'And if I could hear properly, would you be so apologetic?'

He was twisting her words, just like Nattie did sometimes. Holding her ground, she said, 'If you weren't deaf I wouldn't have needed to apologise because I wouldn't have been so nasty.'

'So what you're saying is that you make a special case of being rude to the deaf. Or do blind people get the same treatment?'

Shocked that he could accuse her of something so awful, she opened her mouth to defend herself but then saw he was laughing at her. Annoyed, she shoved him hard. She caught him off-balance and with great satisfaction, watched him topple into the water.

When he surfaced, he slicked back his wet hair and rubbed his face. 'What was that for?'

'For being a pig and teasing me!' she shouted.

'You'll have to speak up,' he yelled with a grin, 'I can't hear you.'

His name was Christian May and they arranged to meet for a swim the following day, same place, same time. But the weather wasn't so nice, so they went for a walk along the coastal path instead. They walked for nearly an hour, stopping only to refer to the map and compass he'd brought. It was obvious from looking at the contents of Christian's tidily packed rucksack—map, compass, cagoule, camera, can of Coke and Mars bars—that he was as thorough as he was talkative. Now that she'd got the hang of remembering to look at him when she spoke, and to give him time to take in the shapes her mouth made, there was no stopping the flow of chatter between them.

To her surprise, she shared things with him that she wouldn't ordinarily discuss. She told him she had been diagnosed as dyslexic, something

she usually preferred to keep quiet for fear of people automatically class-
ing her as stupid.

'Does that mean you have fits?'

Thinking he must have misread her lips, she exaggerated her pronun-
ciation to help him. 'Dyslexic, not epileptic.' The slight twist to his own
lips told her that once again he'd caught her out. 'You're too sharp for
your own good,' she muttered.

'At least you're cottoning on to the fact that just because I can't hear
properly it doesn't necessarily mean I'm thick.'

And that was the bond between them. In their different ways, they
were both striving to convince the world they were as capable as the
next person, and three days into the holiday they were inseparable.

And insufferable, if Nattie was to be believed. 'You never want to do
anything with me any more,' she complained bitterly at breakfast one
morning when Genevieve reminded her mother that she was spending
the day with Christian again and would need a packed lunch. Mum was
miles away, drinking her cup of tea and staring out of the window.
'You're always off with that *boy*.' Nattie spat out the word 'boy' with as
much disgust as she could muster.

Genevieve felt a pang of guilt. Maybe she was being selfish by going
off with Christian yet again. 'I suppose you could come with us,' she
offered. 'I'm sure Christian wouldn't mind.'

But the invitation was thrown back at her. 'I'd rather eat a plate of
maggoty cabbage.'

'Who wants a plate of maggots?' asked Daddy Dean, glancing up from
his newspaper.

'Nobody's eating maggots, Dad,' Genevieve reassured him. 'It's only
Nattie being silly.'

Across the table Nattie stuck out her tongue. Genevieve returned the
gesture and got up to make herself a cheese-and-pickle sandwich. She
no longer felt guilty for deserting her sister.

When it was time to go home to Cheshire, Genevieve left her packing
to the last minute, more reluctant than usual to return to Brook House
Farm and the start of the autumn term. She was going to miss more
than just the happy sense of freedom she always enjoyed in Angel
Sands; she was going to miss Christian. They had swapped addresses
with the intention of staying in touch. But she knew that wouldn't
happen. They would go home, pick up the lives they'd left behind, and
forget each other.

She was proved right. Every morning for three whole weeks she
watched for the postman, but there was no letter for her. And although

she enjoyed telling her best friend at school, Rachel, all about the good-looking boy she'd met on holiday—conscious that she was boasting, and, to her shame, omitting to say he was deaf—she couldn't bring herself to write to Christian. Not when there was the risk he might not write back. How humiliating would that be? There was also the small matter of her appalling handwriting and embarrassing spelling to consider. No. It was better all round to put him completely out of her mind.

The following summer, Genevieve and her family arrived in Angel Sands on a chilly, wet evening, to find that it hadn't stopped raining for over a week and the roof of their rented cottage had sprung a leak. The sloping ceiling in Genevieve's bedroom, with its pretty eaves and dormer window overlooking the cornfields, was bulging ominously and dripping onto the sodden carpet. Always at his best when confronted with a DIY challenge, their father threw himself with gusto into the project, instructing them to fetch buckets and pans.

Mercifully the ceiling didn't give way, but that night Genevieve lay awake listening to the steady plop, plop, plop of rainwater filling the circle of pots and pans on the floor. Her parents had wanted her to sleep with Nattie and Polly, but she'd said she'd be OK where she was. She wanted to be on her own. She had a full night ahead of her to prepare herself for the possibility of seeing Christian tomorrow.

If he was staying in Tawelfan again, and if she saw him, she was going to play it very differently from last summer. She was thirteen, a whole twelve months wiser than the silly girl who'd hoped he'd write. Her disappointment had been short-lived, but it still rankled that his words had been so empty.

The worst of it had been putting up with Nattie's teasing. 'What else did you expect?' she'd crowed. 'Boys always lie.' During the long journey down, in the back of the car, Nattie hadn't been able to resist a sly goad every now and then. 'I bet you he's found some other girl to hang around with,' she muttered. 'He won't even remember you.'

Her sister was probably right, but Genevieve was quick to remind herself that it didn't matter. Hadn't she only started to think of him again because there was the chance of bumping into him?

All true. But equally true was the hope that they *would* bump into each other so she could show him how changed she was. She'd got rid of her childish ponytail and had her hair cut shorter, to look more grown-up. It had been her best friend Rachel's idea and they'd gone to the hairdresser's together. Like her best friend, she was now allowed to wear a bit of make-up. Except she couldn't really be bothered. But Rachel could sit for hours in front of a mirror, happily messing about with her collection of lipsticks, eye-shadow compacts and wands of mascara. Occasionally Genevieve applied some nail varnish to her nails, but try as she might she could never get them to grow as long as Rachel's.

'You need to eat more jelly,' her friend would advise, 'that's the way to strengthen your nails. And put Vaseline on them before you go to bed.' Rachel was an expert on most matters these days; she read all the magazines and kept some of the more explicit ones hidden from her mother.

Genevieve had been friends with Rachel Harmony since they'd both started at the local high school. Before the end of the first week, they were best friends. Rachel knew all the right things to wear, could sing all the latest pop songs and knew exactly which bands were in and which were out, but Genevieve was not so well informed. She had been brought up on a nostalgic diet of Judy Garland and Broadway musicals. Thanks to her mother's sentimental taste in music, she knew all the words to 'Some Enchanted Evening', 'Meet Me in St Louis' and 'Zing! Went the Strings of My Heart'. Rachel was mad about Simon le Bon and Tony Hadley and had pictures of them on her bedroom walls.

Although Genevieve's bedroom was large, it was, she'd come to realise, shamefully old-fashioned. Beneath a threadbare rug were floorboards that creaked, and its furniture included a bed with a rattly old brass bedstead and a chest of drawers from a secondhand shop. The wallpaper, coming away in places, was ancient and flowery and had been chosen by Gran when she and Granddad had run the farm and lived in the 200-year-old farmhouse.

In contrast, Rachel lived on a recently built development of houses and her bedroom was a vision of colour coordination and honey-gold pine. Fitted cupboards housed Rachel's many clothes, and in front of the window stood a proper dressing table with a three-way mirror. There were shelves for her magazines, record player and growing collection of records. But if Genevieve had to name one thing of Rachel's that she truly envied, it would be the television in her friend's bedroom.

Two years ago Serena had declared the box that stood in the corner of the sitting room was one of the great evils of the modern age, and had banished it to the loft. But the wonderful thing about Mum was that she was never afraid to do a U-turn, and on Valentine's Day last year she had got their father to dig out the television set so she could watch Torvill and Dean win the gold medal at the winter Olympics in Sarajevo. With a deadpan face she justified her actions by saying it was a one-off event, a moment in sporting history that she didn't want her children to miss.

But Genevieve knew it wasn't sport or history her mother was interested in; she was an incurable romantic and wanted to see for herself the are-they-aren't-they? chemistry between the two skaters. 'Of course they're madly in love with each other,' she sniffled when the couple got up from the ice and the audience went berserk, throwing flowers and applauding wildly. 'Only love could produce something as magical as that.' She reached out to Daddy Dean and gave him a soppy look. He squeezed her hand in unspoken agreement.

The next day Serena insisted the television was returned to the loft, and Genevieve hungered for it. So whenever she stayed at Rachel's house, she binged on what her mother would have condemned 'mind-rotting trash'. Often she watched the telly while lying on Rachel's bed, as her friend, indifferent to what was on since she was never denied it, flicked through her magazine collection. Genevieve was sometimes glad she was dyslexic; some of the articles in Rachel's magazines were too embarrassing for words, page after page of mushy relationship stuff. And sex. But Rachel lapped it up and relished reading the articles aloud.

'Listen to this,' she'd say, swinging round from her dressing table. '"Think of the happiest and most incredibly satisfying moment of your life and times it by a thousand and that's how good an orgasm feels."'

Genevieve had tried to imagine sinking her teeth into a doughnut, tasting the dusty crust of sugar, feeling the sweet swell of soft dough roll around her mouth, jam oozing from the corner of her lips: a perfect explosion of heavenly sweetness. She then tried to imagine the experience increased by a factor of a thousand, as instructed, but could only imagine feeling sick. Would sex make her feel sick too?

The next morning, the first proper day of the holiday, she awoke to brilliant sunshine and a roof that had stopped leaking. Before breakfast was over, her father had borrowed a ladder from the neighbours and was investigating the damage.

'Nothing to it,' he announced, coming back into the kitchen to finish off his mug of cold tea, 'a couple of slates. Now then, let me fetch my tool kit from the car.' Their father never went anywhere without his red plastic tool box.

'You think more of that tool box than you do of me,' Mum would say. 'If the house was on fire and you had to choose between me and that wretched box, I wouldn't come out alive.'

'Nonsense, darling,' he'd argue good-humouredly. 'I'd sling you over my shoulder and carry the box in my other hand.'

'You see! I get *slung* over your shoulder, the box is lovingly carried.'

Their arguments were playful, never vindictive.

'OK if I go for a walk?' ventured Genevieve.

Everyone looked at her.

'What?' Genevieve asked. 'What did I say?'

Nattie sneered—she had sneering down to a fine art these days.

'I suppose you could run a few errands at the shop for us,' her father said. 'Some sausages for breakfast tomorrow morning would be nice.'

'Um . . . I wasn't thinking of going in that direction.'

'I bet you weren't.'

'Oh, don't be so cruel to your sister, Nattie. You too, Dean.' Her mother put down the pan she was washing and turned to Genevieve. 'If you want to catch up with that young man, then off you go.'

'Thanks, Mum!' She escaped before she could be forced to endure another of her sister's gibes.

The day was fresh and bright, the deepening blue of the sky a welcome sight after the rain. A warm, salty wind raced across the cornfields, rippling it like the sea in the distance. She walked happily down the lane towards the village. Either side of her, quaint little cottages, trim and whitewashed, stood to attention, their doors and window frames painted cheerful colours, their small gardens pretty and well-tended. Some of them had window boxes full of tumbling flowers; vivid scarlet geraniums mixed with blue and white lobelia and orange nasturtiums. She came to a small junction and took the road that led up the steep hill out of Angel Sands, towards Tawelfan beach.

Reluctantly she tugged off her sweatshirt. It was chosen because it hid her chest, which to her increasing horror seemed much too big.

'Wow!' Rachel had said before the end of term, when they'd been changing for gym. 'When did your breasts get so big? I wish mine would get a move on like yours.'

Her friend was right. Overnight her breasts had decided to grow. Genevieve draped the sweatshirt round her shoulders, using the sleeves to hide the cause of her embarrassment.

Thirty minutes later she was looking down onto Tawelfan beach and could see that only a handful of people had staked a claim to the curving stretch of sand. There was no direct access by car, which meant it was never very crowded. It was the main reason why Christian's parents had bought Pendine Cottage, less than a mile away.

Genevieve made for her favourite spot in the sand dunes that backed the beach, with the broad expanse of heath behind. Removing her sweatshirt from her shoulders, she folded it into a makeshift pillow and lay back, her eyes closed against the sun. Perfect.

Lost in thought, she felt a shadow pass over the sun. She snapped open her eyes. At first she didn't recognise him, not with the sun directly behind him. It was his voice, though, that clinched it.

'Hello, Genevieve, I hoped I might find you here.'

Oh, that was casual of him! He'd lied about staying in touch, and now he was expecting her to believe that he hoped she'd be here.

She sat up. 'Really? Why's that?'

He frowned, then sat down beside her, his long legs stretched out in front of him. 'Because I've been looking forward to seeing you again.'

She noticed his voice was deeper than last year and he looked thinner in the face, which made him seem more grown-up, and just visible through his wavy brown hair, longer and thicker than last summer, was a hearing aid tucked behind his left ear. She didn't know why, but the sight of this quelled her antagonism towards him.

When she didn't say anything, he said, 'How are you, Genevieve?'

'Fine. I'm fine.'

He touched her on the arm and said, 'I can't see what you're saying.'

She felt herself colour and apologised, looking him self-consciously in the eye. 'Sorry, I forgot about that.'

'The same way you forgot to write to me?'

'It was *you* who never wrote to *me*.'

He shook his head. 'I lost your address. I waited for you to write.'

He was lying, just as Nattie said all boys did. 'I don't believe you—' But seeing the earnest expression on his face, she faltered. 'Did you really lose my address?'

'Yes. I threw it away by accident. Why didn't you write to me?'

'I decided to wait for your letter to come first. And when it didn't . . . well, I thought the same as you, that you hadn't meant to write, that it was just a polite thing to say.'

His face broke into a slow smile. 'So now we've got that straightened out, does that make us friends again?'

'I think it does,' Genevieve said shyly. She scooped up a handful of sand, let it trickle through her fingers, and wondered why her stomach felt so odd.

It was proving to be Genevieve's best holiday ever. She met up with Christian almost every day and together they followed the same routine: a swim at Tawelfan beach, followed by a walk along the clifftop until they found a suitable spot for a late picnic lunch.

Today they had climbed down onto a sheltered ledge where spongy cushions of thrift, pink and bright, grew in the cracks of the rocks. They were eating egg-and-cress sandwiches that Christian's mother had made. When they'd finished lunch, they both leaned against the rock and closed their eyes. Sitting companionably in the bright sun, she touched his arm and said, 'When you found me on Tawelfan beach last week, you were wearing a hearing aid. Why haven't I seen you using it since?'

He shrugged. It was another of the changes she'd noticed. Just as she'd grown taller and changed her hair, so had he. He was still thin, didn't quite fill out his clothes, and his shoulders, broad and angular, reminded Genevieve of a coat hanger. He was quieter too. In answer to her question, he said, 'It's new. Some piece of state-of-the-art technology that's supposed to help.'

'And does it?'

Another shrug. 'A bit. Depends on the situation. But I still instinctively rely on lip-reading.'

Before she could ask what kind of situation, he added, 'I'm so used to being without a hearing aid, I feel kind of weird with one.'

'How long have you had it?'

'Just a few weeks.'

'Then maybe you need to persevere.'

'You sound just like my parents. Next you'll be telling me to get my hair cut.'

She surveyed his thick hair that had a hint of New Romantics about it. 'Looks fine to me. I like it.'

Sensing that this was as personal as they'd ever got, she was suddenly shy. Almost as shy as she'd felt the first day they'd gone swimming together last week. Short of wearing a sweatshirt, there was simply no way to hide what was trying to appear over the top of her swimsuit. She had plunged into the chilly water, hoping against hope that Christian hadn't noticed anything different about her. But gradually she had relaxed and was happy to lie on the sand beside him in nothing but her swimsuit and not worry what he might be thinking.

'Boys think of sex every ninety-five seconds,' Rachel had told her. It had occurred to Genevieve that maybe her friend thought of it more often. Rachel's encyclopedic knowledge on the subject of sex included the dos and don'ts of flirting. 'Forget all that old-fashioned stuff about fluttering your eyelashes,' she'd told Genevieve. 'All you need to do is comment on a bloke's appearance and he'll know you're interested.'

Flirting had been the last thing on Genevieve's mind just now when she'd remarked on Christian's hair, and she hoped he wouldn't read anything into her words.

'By the way,' he said suddenly, 'I meant to say how much I liked your hair. It suits you. What made you get it cut?'

Help! Was he flirting with her?

They had walked farther than usual, so it took them longer to get home. They always parted at Tawelfan beach, he to go inland to Pendine Cottage, she to follow the coastal path to Angel Sands. On this occasion, while they were arranging to meet the following morning, he took her by surprise; he held her hand for the last few yards. Nervously, she let her hand rest in his.

A big smile accompanied her back to Thrift Cottage, but when she let herself in, the smile was instantly wiped from her face. Back home, at Brook House Farm, Granddad had suffered a heart attack. He was in intensive care and they were driving home at once. Genevieve's first thought wasn't that she might not see her grandfather alive again, but that she wouldn't see Christian tomorrow. The shameful selfishness of this thought haunted her for a long time afterwards.

Genevieve had always thought of Granny Baxter as a big, strong woman. But seeing her stooped over the cooker as she stirred the ancient jam pan, she revised her opinion. Granny Baxter had shrunk.

Four weeks had passed since Granddad's funeral, the first Genevieve had attended. When their mother's parents had died the girls had been too young to attend. But they'd all been there this time round, neatly lined up in the front pew of St Augustine's. Before setting off, their mother had given each of them one of their father's freshly laundered handkerchiefs. 'Just in case,' she'd murmured.

After the service, when they were outside in the hot August sunshine, and the time came to lower the coffin into the ground, Genevieve had clutched her father's handkerchief, trying to keep herself from thinking of Granddad's dead body just feet away.

Four weeks on and Genevieve still had her father's handkerchief, carefully folded just as it had been the morning of the funeral. Now it was in her jeans pocket as she sat at the kitchen table, thinking how frail Granny Baxter looked as she stirred the damson jam. She felt for the 'just in case' handkerchief, just in case she might cry.

Everyone except her had cried when Granddad died. Even her father. That had shocked her, but not enough to bring on her own tears. You're nothing but a selfish cow, she'd told herself, willing the tears to appear. But they wouldn't come, despite the harsh words she scourged herself with: *How could you think of Christian when Granddad was dying in agony? What kind of a granddaughter are you? The worst kind! That's what you are.*

She didn't know for sure if Granddad had died in agony, but she needed to believe he had, to worsen the crime she'd committed. Now all she had to do was find a suitable punishment to fit it.

She dabbed at the crumbs and the smear of butter icing on her plate and licked her finger clean. She looked at the remains of Gran's home-made Victoria sponge cake in the middle of the table, and was tempted to ask for another slice. She couldn't recall a day when there wasn't something 'fresh out' of the oven when she called on Gran.

Egg-custard tart had been Granddad's favourite, and it had been a long-standing joke in the family that nobody had a sweet tooth like he did, or the same appetite. He was a big man, but not what you'd call fat. To Genevieve, when she was little, he'd been a giant of a man, and wonderfully warm-hearted. 'Come on, my bonnie girl,' he'd say, 'climb up here on my lap and I'll read you a story. We'll have a bun too, shall we? And maybe a mug of hot chocolate.'

Since his death, Genevieve had expected her grandmother to stop baking completely. But, if anything, she was cooking twice as much and the pantry was filling up fast.

They filled the jars that had been drying in the warm oven, and Genevieve was given the job of sealing them with circles of waxed paper, while Gran wrote out the stick-on labels. When the last one had been labelled, sealed and carried through to the pantry, Genevieve said, 'It doesn't seem right that all this goes on without Granddad. He should be here.' She swallowed, not quite sure what had made her say such a thing. 'I'm sorry, Gran. I shouldn't have said anything.'

'Nonsense, if that's how you feel, that's just what you should have said.'

'But does it make it worse for you? Hearing people talk about him?'

Gran put down the pan she'd been about to carry to the sink. 'Genevieve, I'd much rather hear you talk about your grandfather than hear nothing from you at all. In fact, I'd go so far as to say you've been much too quiet these last four weeks.'

Genevieve knew it had been a mistake to start the conversation. She could feel the backs of her eyes prickle. Needing something to provide a diversion, she said, 'Here, let me wash that pan for you.'

'No,' Gran said. 'I have a much better idea. Why don't I cut you another slice of cake and make us some mugs of hot chocolate?'

The comforting reminder of her grandfather was too strong for Genevieve, and she fought hard to hold back the stinging tears. But it wasn't working. She yanked the 'just in case' handkerchief from her pocket and pressed it to her eyes. She cried and cried, for what felt like for ever, her head resting on her grandmother's shoulder. She sobbed for all those times she'd curled up on Granddad's lap and had been made to feel so special.

But if she had thought the stream of tears would bring her some relief, she was wrong. The world still felt horribly black and empty to her, with nowhere for her to hide her shame.

Easter was early the next year and brought with it a letter from Christian.

There had been others. The first, with its Pembrokeshire postmark, had arrived the day before the funeral, and had told her how sorry he was to hear of her grandfather's death. They had left Angel Sands so hurriedly there had been no opportunity for her to explain. But word had soon gone round the village—everyone knew the Baxters who stayed at Thrift Cottage—and by lunchtime the following day, after he'd given up waiting for her on Tawelfan beach, he had knocked on the door of the cottage. A neighbour told him they'd gone, and why. Genevieve had read the letter again and again, until she concluded that he was genuine in his need to let her know he was thinking of her.

But she had thrown the letter away. She didn't want to think of him. Not when it reminded her of her selfishness.

A month passed and another letter arrived. It contained some photographs, two of her alone, and one of the pair of them. Then a Christmas card came, asking if she'd received his last letter with the photographs. She sent one in return, his name at the top of the card, hers at the bottom. She wanted to deny all knowledge of receiving the photos but she didn't want to lie, so she wrote a few words of thanks.

Now, five months later, a third letter had arrived. She sat in the garden beneath her favourite cherry tree, blossom drifting down in the breeze, and caught the sound of her father driving the tractor across the top field. She opened the envelope, her mind made up. This time she would write a proper letter back to Christian. She had deliberately hurt someone who'd gone out of his way to be nice to her. It wouldn't be long before summer was upon them and she didn't want to turn up in Angel Sands with things unsaid. Christian deserved an apology from her.

She opened his letter, her heart racing a little as she anticipated his words, that he was looking forward to seeing her again in Angel Sands.

But her happy anticipation skittered away. She read the letter through several times. He was going on a student exchange trip to Madrid for the whole of the summer holiday. He didn't know how he was going to manage lip-reading in a language he couldn't speak, but his parents had decided that going to Spain would broaden his horizons.

No! It wasn't fair. She didn't want him to go to Spain. She suddenly remembered the way he'd held her hand, and wished she could turn back the clock. She'd give anything still to be on the beach at Tawelfan and for her grandfather to be fit and well.

She folded the letter, slipped it into the envelope and went inside. She needed something to eat. Something sweet and comforting.

Almost a year later, Rachel suggested to Genevieve that she needed to lose weight. Her friend's exact words were, 'Don't think I'm being rude, Gen, and I'm only saying this for your own good, but I've heard some of the girls at school calling you names behind your back.'

They were in Genevieve's bedroom, Rachel lying on her front on the bed with her legs in the air, Genevieve sitting on the ledge by the open window. Her friend's words caused a coldness to grip Genevieve and her insides drained away.

'What names?' she asked, turning from the window.

'Oh, you know, the usual kind of drivel: Fatso Baxter and wobble wobble, here comes jelly Gen.' Rachel's voice was matter-of-fact.

Genevieve's heart slammed. The coldness became a burning heat that seemed to swallow her up whole.

'Tell you what,' Rachel continued, 'I'd been thinking of going on a diet myself. We could do it together if you want.'

The offer was absurd. Rachel was stick thin; never in a million years would anyone call her Fatso Harmony. She had the kind of graceful body Genevieve could only dream of. The only trouble she had in buying clothes was finding a pair of jeans tight enough for her minuscule bum. But in that moment Genevieve loved her friend for her thoughtfulness. 'You'd do that for me?' she said, her voice small and croaky.

'Of course. Why wouldn't I?'

'Because you don't need to. You're . . . you're perfect as you are.'

Rachel turned over and sat up, her back as straight and poised as a ballerina's. 'You must be blind, Gen. Look at me!' She lifted the blouse of her school uniform and revealed a stomach that was enviably smooth and taut. She pinched the skin—what she could get hold of—and said, 'That can go for starters.'

Genevieve wasn't convinced. Yet aware that her friend was trying to help and encourage her, she said, 'What sort of diet shall we go on?' She knew nothing about dieting, but was confident Rachel would know.

Rachel was on her feet now, standing in front of the full-length mirror on the wardrobe door. 'We'll cut out all carbohydrates,' she said.

Well, that sounded easy enough. No potatoes or pasta. Or rice.

'That means no cakes or biscuits,' Rachel said with stern authority.

No cakes or biscuits. That wasn't so easy. Especially as Gran had invited the two of them for tea that afternoon.

They took the short cut to Gran's bungalow, along the footpath that circled the field known as Solomon's Meadow, where the newborn lambs were put because it was so sheltered. It was late afternoon and clouds of dizzy gnats danced in the warm May air. Normally Genevieve would have enjoyed the walk; she would have ambled along spotting birds' nests in the hedgerow or hoping for the first sighting of a particular wild flower. Today, having been told by Rachel that exercise and dieting went hand in hand, she set off at a cracking pace, hardly noticing her surroundings. Now, marching on ahead of Rachel, Genevieve wondered when she had started piling on the pounds. She suspected it had begun some time after last summer.

Angel Sands hadn't felt the same without Christian. She had missed their swims together, and their long walks. But most of all she'd missed what might have been between them. More holding hands. Maybe even a kiss. She was plagued with visions of him meeting an attractive Spanish girl in Madrid. What hope for a plain girl such as Genevieve Baxter? How could she ever compete?

Three weeks after driving home from Angel Sands, a postcard had arrived from Madrid—it was the only communication she'd had from Christian since the spring when he'd written to say he'd be spending the summer in Spain. She'd taken it upstairs to read in her bedroom, away from Nattie's prying eyes. She'd unwrapped a Twix, hidden inside an old shoebox at the bottom of her wardrobe. Perched on the window ledge—and only when she'd eaten the two sticks of chocolate—she ventured to read the card.

> Hi, Genevieve,
>
> As you can imagine, Madrid is very different from Angel Sands. It's much hotter, for a start. The family I'm staying with are nice, but it's a nightmare trying to understand them! I have to rely on my phrase book and gesture a lot.
>
> Miss you, Christian

She rummaged around inside the shoebox again and pulled out a packet of Rolos, then returned to her seat to read the card once more. There wasn't much to go on, but the connection, small as it was, gave her a tingly feeling, a tiny glow of happiness.

Miss you.

She put a Rolo in her mouth, sucked it for a moment, then rolled it gently round her teeth and tongue until the chocolate melted. Then came the taste of softening toffee; its smooth sweetness spreading through her mouth. All too soon it was gone.

Miss you.

Had he written that because he genuinely missed her? Or was it just one of those meaningless signing-off things you said, like, 'See you soon'?

By the time she'd finished the packet of Rolos, Genevieve had convinced herself that 'Miss you' meant nothing more than a polite 'Best wishes'. Even so, to be equally polite, she composed a brief letter in return so that it would be waiting for Christian when he came home. As the months passed, the number of letters exchanged between them increased, as did her weight. She didn't dare weigh herself, but she

44

reckoned she'd put on a stone and a half. Perhaps more.

Granny Baxter was waiting for them. Ushering the girls inside, she pointed in the direction of the sink and told them to wash their hands.

'I've done your favourite, Genevieve,' the old lady said. 'Egg, sausage, beans and chips. And there's treacle tart and custard for afters.'

Rachel threw Genevieve a look of eye-rolling horror. Their backs were to Gran as they stood at the sink. 'There are enough calories in that lot to kill us. Tell her you're not hungry,' she hissed.

'But I *am* hungry.'

'We're on a diet, Gen. Remember?'

'What are you two whispering about over there?'

'Nothing, Gran.'

But Genevieve couldn't do as Rachel said. She couldn't hurt Gran's feelings by refusing to eat what she'd gone to so much trouble to cook. So she ate. Later that night, when everyone had gone to bed, she thought of what Rachel had told her as they'd walked back through Solomon's Meadow, that all the famous models threw up to keep slim. She crept along to the bathroom and made herself sick. It was the most revolting thing she had ever done. But it was also strangely consoling.

In their last exchange of letters, Genevieve and Christian had arranged to meet on Tawelfan beach, even if it was raining.

It was. As Genevieve waited for Christian to appear, heavy raindrops pattered noisily against the hood of her cagoule, making her feel as though she were inside a tent. She pressed herself into the hollow of the rocks, glad that the tide was out and had provided her with a place of relative refuge. The beach was deserted and a strong wind was gusting, whipping up the sea and adding a salty taste to the rain. Doubt seized hold of her. Maybe Christian wouldn't show up.

There had been much made of her meeting Christian again. Nattie, now thirteen going on twenty-three, had discovered horses and boys (in that order) and seldom talked about anything else. She was of the opinion that Christian definitely had the hots for Genevieve. 'Why else would he have kept writing to you?' she'd said.

Genevieve was desperate for him to view her as more than a friend. She hadn't seen him for two years, which, as Gran said, was a long time in which to re-create a person, to turn him into something he probably wasn't. But at least Gran listened and didn't make fun of Genevieve when she told her how her feelings for Christian had changed. She had confided in her grandmother while helping to pick the first crop of raspberries. In response, Gran had said, 'You know, your grandfather wasn't the first man I fell in love with.'

This was news to Genevieve, a revelation on the scale of Gran suddenly confessing that she used to be a stripper. 'Really?'

'Oh, no. There was Hugh before him. And John, and of course, there was Igor too.'

'Oh, Gran, surely you never went out with someone called Igor?'

'I did, as a matter of fact. And we called it courting in those days.'

Genevieve did the sums. 'You must have been very young when you went out—sorry, when you were *courting* with those men.'

'A little bit of experience never did anyone any harm, my girl. Remember that. Too many eggs in the one basket is rarely a good idea. Some get broken. Some tip out.'

'Are you referring to Christian?'

She patted Genevieve's hand. 'Let's just say that Christian is all very well for the here and now, but there's a whole world out there for you to explore and enjoy. What's more, there are many different kinds of love.'

Genevieve knew what Gran was getting at, but her grandmother was wrong. What she felt for Christian really was love. OK, she was only fifteen—sixteen in September—but she knew, as she stood waiting for him with the rain dripping off her hood and splashing onto her face, that it was the real thing.

Her biggest fear was that he'd met someone else, but wouldn't he have told her that in one of his letters? 'Oh, by the way, I've met this really great girl. You'd love her, she's funny, intelligent and so very slim.'

Just over two months had passed since she'd first made herself sick, and though she hated herself for doing something so disgusting, the weight had dropped off. She'd lost a stone already and intended to lose another. But rather than show off her slimmer self, she kept her clothes baggy, not wanting to attract attention to what she was doing.

She knew Mum would go ballistic if she discovered the truth and she had to be careful that she was seen to be eating normally. It was easy to miss meals, though. There were plenty of times when she was able to get out of tea, usually just saying she was in a hurry to get to Rachel's, or that she'd already eaten at Rachel's, was enough. Occasionally, when she was feeling low, if she'd had a bad day at school, she would binge on a comforting boost of crisps and chocolate bars in her room. And of course, there was always something to eat at Gran's. But so long as she had her secret weapon, she could do what she'd previously thought was impossible: she could eat *and* make herself slimmer and more attractive. For the first time she could remember, she felt in control of her life.

What with the noise of the wind and rain, and being deep in thought, she didn't hear footsteps approach. Not until he was standing right next to her did she look up and see Christian. Like her, he was dressed for the awful weather, and all she could see of him was his smiling face peering through the porthole of his hood. 'It's great to see you, Genevieve.'

Then, unbelievably, he threw his arms round her and actually hugged her. And it didn't stop there. He kissed her on each wet cheek.

'Come on,' he said, 'let's walk. You don't mind the rain, do you?'

She shook her head. She didn't care what they did. He could ask her to paddle across the Atlantic in a cardboard box and she'd do it. He helped her clamber over the rocks, and they headed across the beach, to the other side of the bay and the steeply wooded path that would take them up towards the clifftop. When they reached the grassy headland they stopped to catch their breath. Miraculously, the rain stopped. They flung back their hoods and simultaneously took a moment to see how changed they were.

'You've grown your hair,' he said.

Immediately she put a hand to her head, self-conscious of the mess it must be with all the wind. 'And you're—' And what? What was Christian, other than perfect? He'd definitely grown more handsome. Had filled out too and easily looked older than seventeen. He was a man now. With her mousy brown hair and nondescript features, she felt incredibly plain beside him, the kind of girl no one would look at twice. She noticed that he wore no hearing aid and realised that there had been little trace of that characteristic 'hollowness' in his voice. He stared at her, his gaze fixed intently on her mouth as he waited for her to finish what she'd started. 'And you're taller than ever,' she managed.

He laughed. 'I was warned that if I ate my greens I'd grow.'

They walked on, the strong wind tearing the clouds apart until at last the sun broke through. They stripped down to their T-shirts and tied the unwanted clothing round their waists. Genevieve could see how muscular Christian had become; his angular, coat-hanger shoulders were no more. *Bet he looks a real hunk in his swimming shorts*, she imagined Rachel whispering in her ear. Then, noticing the pair of scruffy old walking boots he was wearing, Rachel's whisper turned scornful. *What a turnoff!*

Christian had caught the direction of her glance. 'I spend most weekends tramping the hills. I was hoping you and I would get the chance to do some really long walks together.'

Her heart swelled. 'I'd like that,' she said.

He eyed her trainers doubtfully. 'Do you have any proper boots?'

'I'll get some. '

Now there was no Granddad to help on the farm, Dad couldn't get away for as long as he'd like. But Mum, being Mum, insisted that it was no reason for her and the girls to lose out.

'We only go on one holiday a year,' she complained. 'I don't see why we should have to forgo it.'

So Dad came for just one week, leaving 'his girls' plus Gran to enjoy a further two weeks without him. It was strange having Gran on holiday with them. It made it feel more like home. A home from home, in fact. After their father had set off for Cheshire that time, Mum started to talk about how nice it would be to live in Angel Sands permanently.

'It's not so daft,' Christian said when Genevieve told him of Serena's lunatic plan, to sell up the farm and buy a house to run as a bed and breakfast. 'You can pick up property relatively cheaply round here.'

They were on their way to St Govan's Chapel and were having lunch at a café in Stackpole Quay, a pretty little harbour which, until today, Genevieve hadn't given much thought to. Certainly she'd never considered its history or geography. But Christian made it come alive. He told her how the quay had been constructed in the eighteenth century to land cargoes of coal, which were then taken to Stackpole Court. Instead of the boats going away empty, they were then filled up with limestone. He knew all about Stackpole Court, a huge house built in 1735 but demolished in the sixties by its then owner, the fifth Earl of Cawdor.

'If I'd had a history teacher half as good as you, I might have carried on with it,' she said, stirring her glass of Coke with a straw and wondering if she dare eat the rest of her bacon bap. Her stomach was longing for it, but the slim, attractive girl inside her was telling her it was poison.

'It's a difficult subject to teach well,' he said. 'I've been lucky, I've had some brilliant teachers. Really inspiring. Are you going to leave that?'

Saved! 'I'm full. You have it.' She pushed the plate across the wooden bench table, wanting to please her constant companion, the slim, attractive girl. 'So how come you know so much about property prices round here? Thinking of becoming an estate agent?'

'No. But I am interested in houses. Or more particularly, their design. I'm going to study architecture at university next year. Or maybe do a gap year first then go to college.'

She was impressed. Doubly impressed because, against all the odds, he'd made it through mainstream education. 'You've got it all worked out,' she said.

As they climbed the steep steps up the hill to St Govan's Chapel, and looked back onto the tiny harbour, Christian rested his arm on her shoulder. Just like the time he'd held her hand two years ago, it seemed the most natural thing in the world. And that, she decided, was what she liked—loved—about Christian. There was no pretence to be anything other than what he was.

Why can't my life be as perfect as this all the time? she thought that night, lying in bed, for once not thinking guiltily about how much she'd eaten, and whether or not she should creep along to the bathroom.

The first time Gran met Christian, she made the mistake of forgetting he was deaf—or had 'impaired hearing' as he now preferred to call it. It was an easy mistake to make. He was so good at lip-reading, even Genevieve forgot sometimes. But once Gran had realised her gaffe, she made the further mistake of talking to Christian with her voice raised to the rafters.

'Genevieve tells me you want to be an architect,' she bellowed across the sitting room at Pendine Cottage, where the entire Baxter family (minus their father) had been invited for tea. Genevieve wanted to die. While Gran listened to Christian's reply, Genevieve tried subtly to attract her grandmother's attention by clearing her throat several times, in the hope that she might realise her mistake and lower her voice. Christian's mother, Ella, passed Genevieve a plate and a napkin and whispered, 'Don't worry, we're quite used to it. A ham sandwich?'

Genevieve took the offered sandwich, dainty and crustless. Hardly any calories at all, she told herself happily. *Don't you believe it*, Constant Companion warned her. She cleared her throat.

Gran threw her a sharp look. 'Genevieve, whatever is the matter with you? I'm trying to talk to Christian and all I can hear is rattle, rattle. Are you ill?'

Genevieve didn't know what to say. But Nattie did. 'She's not ill, Gran, but unless you keep your voice down, we'll all end up deaf.'

When tea was over, at Philip May's suggestion they all went out to the garden to play croquet.

'You don't know what you're taking on,' she told Christian. 'We Baxters are experts at this game.'

'Yes, but we Mays cheat to win.'

'And you think we don't?'

It wasn't long before the game disintegrated into a raucous shambles. Leaving Nattie and Polly to supervise the adults, Genevieve and Christian found themselves a quiet spot elsewhere in the garden. Unlike Thrift Cottage, the Mays' holiday home had an enormous garden. They lay on a tartan blanket on the soft grass and Genevieve couldn't remember ever feeling so happy. Floating between that state of not quite awake, yet not fully asleep, she pictured herself drifting away on a magic carpet with Christian. As she was floating high above the rooftops, she felt something tickling her cheek. An annoying fly. She flicked it away, but it came back. Irritated, she opened her eyes, and saw that Christian, raised up on one elbow, was leaning over her with a blade of grass.

'Caught red-handed,' he said with a smile. Then, very gently, he stroked her cheek some more.

She didn't stop him.

'It must be love,' declared Serena with embarrassing enthusiasm from the front of the car as they set off to Tenby to have a look round the shops. 'That's why you're not eating.'

Defences up, Genevieve was instantly on the alert. Squeezed in between Gran and Nattie—it was Polly's turn to sit in the front passenger seat—she leaned forward. 'What do you mean, I'm not eating?' Too late she realised she shouldn't have reacted so quickly.

'Don't look so serious, darling, I was just the same at your age. The weight simply dropped off me. It's called lovesickness.' Serena sighed. 'I remember the day I met your father . . .'

Genevieve almost sighed with relief too. She was off the hook. For the rest of the journey, with the windows down and the wind blowing at their hair, Serena told them the story of how she and Daddy Dean had fallen in love. It was a story they knew by heart, but never tired of.

When they arrived in Tenby, and Serena had found a parking space, they were allowed to split up and go their separate ways. Polly had run out of books to read, so Mum said she'd take her to the bookshop. Nattie wanted to go to the amusement arcade and took Gran by the arm, sure in the knowledge that their grandmother, equally addicted to slot machines, would step in with a purse full of pennies. Which left Genevieve happy to wander the narrow streets and cobbled alleyways on her own. It being August, the town was packed with holidaymakers. Genevieve enjoyed the hustle and bustle, the pretty shops and cafés decked out with colourful flower boxes and hanging baskets. Rachel wouldn't approve of it, though; the shops weren't fashionable enough for her. Rachel and her family went to America for their summer holiday, as well as at half-term in the autumn, and she always came back with tons of new clothes.

It was funny, but it was as though there were two Genevieves: the cautious, uptight one who lived at Brook House Farm, and who was best friends with Rachel Harmony, and the other one who was relaxed and carefree at Thrift Cottage, and was best friends with Christian May. When she thought about it, the two were incompatible. While Rachel was obsessed with not just her own appearance but everyone else's, Christian didn't give a hoot about what people thought of him. He wore exactly what he wanted, and did exactly what he wanted. But Rachel, for all her rigidity, was the best friend ever.

Buoyed up with a sense of well-being, Genevieve paused for a moment to look at the display of clothes in a shop window. Her gaze was distracted by a girl staring back at her. She was smiling, her long hair tucked behind her ears, her cheekbones forming a heart-shaped face. She was dressed in a T-shirt that was drab and too big for her, but there was no mistaking the curvy outline of the body beneath it.

Genevieve noted all this in less than a split second, then she was brought up short by the realisation that the girl was *her*. She knew she wasn't anywhere near as slim as Rachel but, and this took her breath away, she wasn't the Incredible Hulk she'd believed herself to be.

To celebrate, she shoved open the shop door. Mentally counting out her holiday money—five pounds that she'd saved, five pounds from Mum and Dad and another two pounds fifty from Gran—she started sliding a row of garments along the rail. A woman about the same age as her mother appeared at her side.

'Can I help you?'

'Um . . . I'd like to try one of these, please.' She pointed to the rail.

The woman hesitated. She looked at Genevieve, then back at the row of T-shirts. 'I'm not sure we have any of your size left.'

Genevieve's heart sank. She should have known the reflection in the window had been a cruel illusion.

'Everything on this rail is much too large for you,' the woman carried on. 'How about these over here? Do you see anything you like?'

Clutching her carrier bag and its size ten strappy top—*size ten!*—Genevieve left the shop in a giddy state of euphoria. Nothing in the whole wide world could make her feel any happier.

But she was wrong.

If Christian had thought it odd that she hadn't wanted to go swimming before now, he'd never said anything. He'd probably put it down to a 'girl thing', though why it had extended over two weeks may have given him cause to wonder. But today, twenty-four hours after the outing to Tenby, with her confidence at an all-time high, Genevieve had suggested they go for a swim.

Now, on Tawelfan beach, she and Christian had stripped down to their swimwear. She wasn't prepared for the sight of him in his swimming shorts. He was all muscle; his legs looked firm and toned, presumably from all that walking. He looked so good she had to turn away and catch her breath. When she'd recovered, and risked a glance back at him, she saw his eyes on her. She flinched, and Constant Companion whispered, *I warned you!*

'Ready for that swim?' he said.

ERICA JAMES

They picked their way through the sunbathers, playing children and windbreaks, and dipped their toes in the water.

'It's freezing!' she gasped.

He smiled. 'It's the Atlantic. What did you expect? Race you in!'

Suddenly she was that twelve-year-old girl again, the one who had met Christian on the beach and had defiantly risen to his challenge. And before she could think of a reason not to, she was in the water. He came in after her, dived beneath the waves when it was deep enough, then surfaced beside her, his shaggy hair plastered to his head and neck. He stood up—the water came to his chest—and pushed his hair back.

'The tide's coming in,' he said, 'so it'll be safe to swim round the headland. Do you fancy doing that?'

She did. By the time they'd swum all the way into the next bay, then returned to Tawelfan beach, they were starving.

'How about a burger?' Christian asked, towelling his hair dry.

Constant Companion materialised in a flash. *Oh, that's a good one! A burger. One hundred per cent pure unadulterated poison.*

'Maybe a sandwich,' she compromised.

But as they joined the queue at the kiosk, the temptation of a sizzling, big, fat, juicy burger was too much for her. She told herself that she had just swum nearly a mile, so she'd earned it.

They took their burgers and cans of Coke back to the dunes and found themselves a sheltered spot. It was there, quite unexpectedly, that Christian kissed her. She had imagined this moment for so long, but nothing could have prepared her for the real thing. The softness of his mouth against hers, so light and fleeting, lasted for no more than a few seconds, but it was enough to make the world stop spinning, for a fluttering warmth to spread through her and for her senses to become aware of everything that was going on around them. Music was playing close by on a radio, Elvis Presley singing one of her mother's favourite songs, 'The Wonder of You'. Looking into Christian's eyes—soft brown flecked with green and gold—she could only think, with painful poignancy, how appropriate the lyrics were: *'When no one else can understand me, when everything I do is wrong, you give me hope and consolation, you give me strength to carry on.'*

'What are you thinking?' Christian asked her.

She pointed to the radio. 'There's a song playing and it's …' Her voice trailed away.

'And it's what?'

She lost her nerve, unable to share with him that the lyrics summed up how he made her feel.

Later, when they still hadn't moved from the dunes and he was kissing

52

her again, she knew that there would never be anyone else for her. So full of happiness she thought she might burst, she smiled to herself. Just as her parents had 'Zing! Went the Strings of My Heart' as their song, she and Christian would have 'The Wonder of You'.

Genevieve didn't know why, but Rachel was in a strange mood; nothing she said or did seemed to help. But Genevieve didn't care; she had a letter from Christian in her blazer pocket.

They were on the school bus, and with another ten minutes to go before they'd be at school, Genevieve's hands itched to pull out the letter and read it through one more time: Christian had invited her to stay with him in Shropshire for the autumn half-term. 'If the weather's nice,' he'd written, 'Dad says we might drive down to Angel Sands for a few days.' Half-term was only three weeks away and Genevieve was fidgety with excitement. She wanted to show Rachel the letter, then run up and down the packed bus telling everyone the brilliant news. She found herself smiling broadly at the thought of seeing Christian again.

'Oh, for crying out loud, Gen, give it a rest, won't you!'

'What? What have I done?'

Rachel shifted in her seat and looked out of the window, her shoulder to Genevieve. 'You know jolly well,' she muttered.

Genevieve frowned. 'Have I done something to annoy you?'

Silence.

'Rachel?'

The shoulder turned a few degrees. 'If you must know, yes. Yes, you have. You're always going on about bloody Christian this, and bloody Christian that. Ever since the summer holidays you've been a real pain. I thought I was supposed to be your best friend.'

Genevieve was stung. 'But you *are* my best friend.'

'Yeah. That's why you're running off down to some godforsaken place in Shropshire for the whole of half-term. What about me? What am I supposed to do while you're away?'

'But I thought you were going to Florida, like you always do?'

The shoulder was back in place, the face turned even more to the glass. 'We're not going. Mum and Dad have changed their minds.'

'But you always go.'

Rachel whipped round. 'Don't you think I know that, you big fat moron!'

Appalled at the strength of her friend's attack, Genevieve stared straight ahead, concentrating on the neatly plaited hair of the girl in front. They completed the rest of the journey without another word. At school they avoided each other, and during the bus ride home at the end of the day, they sat together, but in tightlipped silence.

Genevieve got off the bus and walked home with her sisters. They were all at the same school now, but there was an unspoken agreement between them: they were never to sit near each other. Genevieve and Nattie sat upstairs, and twelve-year-old Polly downstairs, usually at the front, lost in whatever book she was reading. Nattie and Genevieve frequently had to drag her off the bus before she missed their stop.

'So what's up with you, Gen?' asked Nattie, stopping to roll down the waistband of her skirt so Mum wouldn't know how short she wore it for school. 'You look as miserable as—'

'I've had a horrible day, so please don't make it any worse.'

'Have you had a fight with Rachel?' This was from Polly.

'What makes you say that?' Genevieve said warily.

'I noticed you didn't sit next to her during lunch. She was with Katie Kirby and Lucinda Atkins.'

Nattie whistled. 'You must have had a bust-up if that's the case. Why else would she set up camp with the school she-devils? So what's been going on between you two?'

Genevieve gave in. She told her sisters about Rachel's behaviour on the bus that morning.

'She's jealous,' Nattie said. 'Jealous as hell.'

More kindly, Polly said, 'Perhaps she's frightened of losing you as a friend.'

Genevieve had worked out as much for herself. Question was, why?

Gran had the answer when Genevieve called in to see her after finishing her homework and told her what had happened.

'What's annoyed that girl most is you've done something without her approval.'

'Oh, that's just silly, Gran.'

'All I'll say, Genevieve, is this. Rachel's not as clever or as confident as she makes out. I suspect that she needs you as a friend more than you need her. And because of that, she'll soon make it up with you. Now then, how about a piece of cake?'

'No, thank you.'

'A slice of treacle tart perhaps?'

After feeling so low as a result of Rachel's hurtful outburst, nothing would have suited Genevieve more than to gorge herself on several slices of Gran's butter-rich treacle tart. But she fought the temptation.

You . . . big . . . fat . . . moron!

How could Rachel have said that? She, of all people, knew how hard Genevieve had worked to lose weight.

After returning from Angel Sands, back in the summer, Genevieve had rushed to see her friend, and the first thing she had done was to take off her jacket and show Rachel the top she'd bought in Tenby. 'Look,' she'd laughed. 'It's size ten. Can you believe it?'

Rachel looked up from her magazine. 'Really?'

'Yes! Isn't it amazing? I must have lost at least a stone.'

'Haven't you weighed yourself to check?'

'No. I can't bring myself to do it.'

Sliding off her bed, Rachel said, 'Well, let's do it now.' She pulled some scales out from under the bed and said, 'On you get.'

Genevieve stepped onto the scales. She watched the needle, saw it wobble, then hover into place. 'Eight stone and . . . and six pounds. And that's with my jeans on.' She smiled and hopped off the scales. 'I was right, I've lost a whole stone. Isn't that great?'

'It is. Well done. Now you don't have to bother any more, do you?'

'Oh, no, this is just the start. I want to lose another stone at least.'

Rachel went back to lying on the bed. 'Believe me, Gen, you've lost all the weight you need to. If you get any thinner you'll look stupid.' She twirled a lock of hair between her fingers. 'So what's your secret? How did you lose the weight?'

It was then that Genevieve told Rachel all about her and Christian. 'Mum keeps going on about me losing weight because I'm in love. I know it sounds silly, but I think she might be right.'

Rachel rolled her eyes.

Now, as Genevieve waved goodbye to her grandmother and walked home through Solomon's Meadow in the dusky twilight, she thought of Rachel's reaction when she'd told her that Christian was her boyfriend.

'But you're not really going out with him, are you?' she'd said. 'It's not like it's a proper relationship.'

'Yes, it is. We've kissed and everything!'

Rachel had laughed. 'That means nothing. He's probably just using you as a holiday fling. What's more, he might be lying to you. I bet there's a girlfriend at home he's not telling you about.'

'There isn't. I know there isn't. He isn't that sort of boy.'

'Yeah, well, you might be right. But you didn't throw yourself at him, did you?'

'Certainly not!'

'Good. Otherwise you'll just end up feeling cheap.'

But Christian never made Genevieve feel cheap. Special was how she felt. Uniquely special. He'd even told her he thought she was beautiful. He'd said it when they'd been lying on the beach one hot, sunny day. Opening her eyes, she'd found him staring down at her.

'What are you thinking?' she'd asked.

'I'm thinking how beautiful you are,' he'd said simply. For days and weeks afterwards, she spent long, dreamy moments recalling his words.

Saying goodbye at the end of the holiday had been horrible, though. He'd come to Thrift Cottage to wave them off and while no one was looking they had sneaked a final kiss and promised to write.

'I'll miss you,' she'd said, still in his arms, but pulling back so that he could see her lips.

'And I'll miss you too. Let's try and meet up some time soon.'

'I'd like that.'

Without fail they wrote every week. On her sixteenth birthday he sent her the most romantic present ever: a bunch of red roses. It seemed so grown-up. And because she'd plucked up the courage to tell him about the song that had been playing on the radio when he'd first kissed her, he also gave her a CD of Elvis songs, including 'The Wonder of You'. She hadn't the heart to tell him she couldn't play the CD because they didn't have a CD player at Brook House Farm. Rachel had a CD player, but Genevieve hadn't wanted to play it in front of her friend.

Thinking about it now, perhaps she *had* treated Rachel badly. She shouldn't have talked about Christian so much, or been so happy whenever a letter arrived. It had been insensitive of her. She would call Rachel to say she was sorry, that she wanted to be friends again.

She apologised again on the bus in the morning, and any coolness that had remained on the phone last night was gone. Rachel accepted her apology with good grace. She even managed to say sorry herself.

'I shouldn't have called you what I did. I don't ever want you to think that I'm jealous of you having a boyfriend, Gen,' she added. 'I'm not. You haven't slept with him, have you?'

'*No!*'

'Good. And even if he says he loves you, don't believe him. They all say that just so they can get you into bed. It's all they ever want to do.'

Keen to please her friend, Genevieve nodded and changed the subject. She asked how Rachel had got on with the English essay they had to hand in that morning.

But, perversely, Rachel seemed eager to discuss Christian. 'What I don't get is why he never rings you. Why does he only write?'

Genevieve still hadn't got round to telling Rachel about Christian's deafness—her friend could be cruel sometimes and she couldn't bear the thought of Rachel making fun of Christian. Deciding to answer her friend's question, and to hell with what she might say, Genevieve said, 'I would have thought it was obvious why he doesn't ring me. He's deaf. Don't you remember me telling you?' She stared out of the window, and hoped she wouldn't be struck down for such a blatant lie.

'*Deaf*! You mean, deaf as a post?'

'Yes.'

Rachel poked Genevieve with her elbow, to make her look at her. 'You never told me he was deaf. I'd have remembered a thing like that.'

Genevieve met her friend's gaze, ready to defend Christian should she have to. 'Maybe I forgot to tell you. Either way, it's no big deal.'

'But *deaf*, Gen. Now that's what I call weird. I mean, how do you communicate with him? Hand signals?'

'We talk as normally as you and I are doing right now.'

'How?'

'He reads my lips.'

'Pardon?'

'I said, he reads my—'

Rachel burst out laughing. 'Got you!'

She was still laughing to herself when they got off the bus, and for the rest of the day Genevieve was subjected to countless I-beg-your-pardon-you'd-better-speak-up jokes. By the end of it, Genevieve was ready to slap her friend's face.

'I'm afraid we all have to make allowances for Rachel,' Mum said through a cloud of steam as she thumped the iron down. 'She's going through a tough time. It's not easy for her.'

Over by the sink, Gran looked up from the new potatoes she was scrubbing and said, 'If Genevieve were to bend any further backwards for that girl, she'd be a contortionist!'

'I agree with Gran. Rachel's a complete pain in the backside. Just because her parents have split up, it doesn't give her the right to be such a bloody awful bitch.'

'Natalie Baxter, I've told you before about swearing!'

'Mum, I'm nearly fifteen. I'm a mass of hormonal angst; swearing is a vital outlet for my pent-up emotion.'

'Then I'll thank you to do it elsewhere. Now put your angst on hold and pass me your father's shirt to iron.'

Genevieve listened to her family discussing her friend, who was upstairs using the last of the hot water. Again.

It was five months since Rachel's mother had discovered her husband had been living a double life. All the times he'd said he was away chasing deals for his construction business, he'd been down in Kent seeing the other woman in his life. He'd even taken her on holiday. That was when he'd been spotted by one of his wife's closest friends in a hotel in Paris. Mrs Harmony had kicked him out, sworn vengeance on his wallet and refused to let him see Rachel, until he hit back with the law on his side and claimed his right to see his daughter. It was horrible for Rachel, Genevieve could see that, caught between her parents and expected to take sides.

'Mum's using me to punish Dad,' Rachel told Genevieve on the bus one morning, 'and I hate her for that, almost as much as I hate him for what he's done.'

Overnight, Rachel's behaviour at school changed. She became moody, rude and surly, even to the teachers. She disregarded all the rules, dyed her lovely blonde hair a dirty shade of black and teased it about a foot high, then hardened it with gel and hairspray. She had several more holes pierced in her ears, and was constantly late with handing in her homework, if she bothered to do it at all. She also started smoking, and then began to skip school altogether. Her parents were 'invited' to discuss the matter with the headmistress, as Rachel's class were only weeks away from sitting their GCSEs. Things picked up a bit as a result of the meeting and Rachel got through her exams—the last one for them both had been two weeks ago.

Then, at the weekend, she had arrived at Brook House Farm with yet more shocking news. Sitting on the fence behind the Dutch barn where no one would see them, she had lit up the first of many cigarettes after knocking back a large mouthful of vodka from the bottle in her bag. She told Genevieve she never wanted to see her father again.

'He's a lying, cheating, bastard and I hope he rots in hell.'

'What's he done now?'

'I don't want to talk about it. Can I doss down here with you for a while?' Taking a long drag on the cigarette, she flicked the glowing stub of it into the air. It landed several yards away in the sun-dried grass.

Genevieve leapt down from the fence and stamped it out. 'You mustn't do that, Rachel, you could start a fire.'

Rachel shrugged and raised the vodka to her mouth. 'Lay off, Gen, I get enough nagging from Mum at home. If she isn't screaming at Dad on the phone, she's having a go at me. So can I stay?' She held out the bottle.

Genevieve took it but didn't drink any. In her friend's current mood she wasn't sure she wanted her around full-time. Pushing this selfish thought aside, she said, 'I'll ask Mum.'

Minutes passed as they sat in the gathering dusk. After striking a match for another cigarette, Rachel said, 'Apparently I have a sister.' She snatched the vodka out of Genevieve's hands. 'My father has another child, with that woman.'

Imagining this was a recent event, Genevieve said, 'When was it born?'

'That's the good bit. Five years ago.'

'*Five years!* You're kidding?'

'Oh, yeah, like I'd go round joking about a thing like that. Her name's Christine,' Rachel said bitterly, 'and my father says she looks just like me.' She slipped down from the fence and swayed unsteadily. 'How can he compare the two of us? He always said I was special. That I was his . . .' Her voice trailed away and she slumped over the fence, her shoulders heaving with angry sobs.

Genevieve put her arm round her friend. She knew exactly what Rachel had been going to say, that her father had always called her his Special Little Princess. Poor Rachel, her crown had been taken from her a long time ago and she'd never even known it.

But remaining sympathetic towards Rachel wasn't easy. She had been staying with them for five days now and so far she'd argued with Nattie at least once a day; she'd been rude to Mum about her cooking; and, in Genevieve's eyes, had committed the cardinal sin of laughing at Gran behind her back.

Later that evening, when Genevieve heard the bath water running away, she went upstairs. It was time for some plain speaking. Rachel needed to be told she'd outstayed her welcome.

'Hi, Gen,' Rachel said, appearing on the landing just as Genevieve reached the top of the stairs. She was wearing a towel fashioned into a turban on her head. 'I've just had this great idea. Why don't I come on holiday with you? I can't face Dad this summer, and Mum's turned into a right psycho. What do you say?'

Despite Genevieve saying she didn't think it would be a good idea, Rachel went behind her back and asked Genevieve's parents if she could join them on holiday. And because Mum and Dad both felt sorry for her, they'd said she was more than welcome to join them, but warned her that it would be a bit of a squash.

After the longest, hottest journey Genevieve had ever known, they'd arrived and were unpacking. There were four bedrooms—one for Gran, one for her parents, one for Nattie and Polly, and the smallest, the room that had always been Genevieve's, was home for her and her friend.

'When your mum and dad said it would be small, I didn't think they meant doll's house small,' Rachel said rudely, still with half a case to unpack. 'The place is tiny. Where on earth shall I put all my clothes?'

'I told you not to bring so many. Put them in the cupboard. I'll use the shelves.'

Genevieve wasn't at all sure she'd survive the holiday. Or that her happy memories of the place would remain intact. Driving through the centre of the village, she had tried to look at it through Rachel's eyes. But what she'd seen before as quaint and relaxed, now seemed backward and old-fashioned. The only saving grace was that the hot weather had brought out the holidaymakers and the beer garden in front of the Salvation Arms was packed, as was the beach. A deserted, rain-sodden Angel Sands would never have survived Rachel's scorn and ridicule.

Their father was keen to try out the barbecue the owners of the cottage had supplied, and after they'd finished their unpacking, Nattie and Polly were sent to the village to buy chops and sausages. 'And you two,' their father said, looking at Genevieve and Rachel, 'can go over to Pendine Cottage, and see if Christian and his parents would like to join us.'

This, then, was the moment of truth. And as they set off in the late-afternoon sun, Rachel taking the opportunity to smoke, Genevieve knew that if Rachel said one disparaging word about Christian she would never speak to her again.

She had written to Christian to let him know that she would be bringing her friend with her, and warned him to ignore anything rude she said when they met. Last year, in October, when Genevieve had spent half-term with Christian, she had kept from him the falling-out that she and Rachel had had. But later, during the February half-term, when she was invited to go down to Shropshire again, she told him that Rachel had been jealous of her having a boyfriend. Putting an arm round her, he'd said, 'Then she ought to find one of her own and stop worrying about yours.'

It was only then that Genevieve wondered why Rachel didn't have a boyfriend. All those magazines teaching her how to have the perfect relationship and she hadn't even come close to one . . .

'You never said it would be so pretty,' Rachel said, as they looked down onto Tawelfan beach, where the sea glistened in the sunlight.

Genevieve checked her friend's face for signs of sarcasm—she was, after all, used to the glamorous beaches of Florida. To her surprise she saw that Rachel was smiling. Perhaps Mum and Dad had been right to bring her with them, and a relaxing, no-frills holiday away from her warring parents was just what she needed.

As it turned out, Christian and his parents couldn't come to Thrift Cottage that evening as they were going to meet some friends.

'So at last I meet Genevieve's mystery boyfriend,' Rachel said, when Mr and Mrs May left them alone in the garden to talk. 'Mind if I smoke?'

'I'd prefer it if you didn't,' Christian said.

Unsure how her friend would react to such directness, Genevieve watched Rachel put the packet of cigarettes back inside her bag. She was relieved when Rachel's lips curled into a smile and she said, 'I like a man who speaks his mind. Shows he knows what he wants in life.'

Sitting on the grass and looking up to where Genevieve and Rachel were sitting on a wooden bench, Christian smiled too. Genevieve's heart gave a sudden lurch; she'd never seen him look more attractive .

'So what's this about me being Genevieve's mystery boyfriend?' he said.

Rachel turned to Genevieve and laughed. 'Shall I tell him or will you?'

Frowning, Genevieve said, 'I would if I knew what you were talking about.' She glanced at Christian as if to say, please, just humour her.

'Well, the mystery to me is why Genevieve kept your disability such a big secret.'

Genevieve froze. She felt the colour drain from her face.

Christian's face altered too. Gone was the smile. 'And what disability would that be?'

Rachel switched her gaze from Christian to Genevieve. She slapped a hand over her mouth. 'Oh God, Gen! Have I said the wrong thing?' Then looking back to Christian, 'I'm so sorry. All I meant was; it was only recently that Gen told me you were deaf and I don't know why she did that. Kept it a secret, I mean.'

When neither Christian nor Genevieve spoke, Rachel puffed out her cheeks and said, 'I'm going for a walk. I need a fag.'

They watched her go. When she was out of earshot, Genevieve spoke. 'I'm sorry for what she said.'

He got up and joined her on the bench. 'It's OK. You did warn me.'

'But you're not disabled. It was an awful thing to say.'

'Clumsy maybe, but not awful.' He put his arms round her. 'Technically I am disabled. So let's leave it at that. Don't suppose you'd like to get your lips a bit nearer so I can read them better?'

Seeing that he was smiling again, she moved so that her face was just inches from his. 'Close enough?'

He shook his head. 'Closer, please.'

She pressed her mouth against his. His lips parted, and with her eyes closed, her heart thumping in her chest, she opened her mouth and welcomed the soft, slow movement of his tongue against hers. The feel of his hands round her neck made her skin tingle and a dizzying warmth flooded through her. They were still kissing when Rachel returned. Neither of them noticed her until she was almost upon them.

'Bloody hell, you two! It's a good thing I'm here or the pair of you would be at it.'

On their way back to Angel Sands, Rachel slipped her arm through Genevieve's. She had started doing this recently and Genevieve wished she wouldn't; people often stared at them.

'Sorry about putting my huge foot in it,' Rachel said. 'Am I forgiven?'

Still high on kissing Christian, Genevieve said, 'Of course. Although you must never use that word again in front of him.'

'What word?'

'The D word: disability.'

'Oh, that. He was fine about it. Especially once you got your tongue down his throat.'

Trying to hide her embarrassment, Genevieve said, 'You shouldn't have been watching.'

'What else could I do? You were in full view of me. But I'll say this. Your taste isn't bad. He's totally dee-luscious. He looks much older than eighteen. More like twenty-two. And that deaf thing really isn't a problem, is it? I love the way his eyes flickered over my mouth whenever I said anything. Very sexy. I could even fancy him myself.'

Genevieve's heart swelled, any earlier misgivings over her friend's blunder now gone from her mind. 'You really thought he was nice?'

'Get real! He's a drool object! A heartbreaker too, I shouldn't wonder.'

'Oh, no,' Genevieve said, 'Christian's not like that.'

'Gen, you sweet little innocent. *All* men are like that.'

Thinking of Rachel's father, Genevieve didn't argue. Instead, she took pleasure in her friend's approval of something so important to her.

September was a month of enormous change that year. Genevieve and Rachel were settling into the sixth form, Christian was preparing to go to university at the end of the month, and his parents were selling Pendine Cottage to buy a place in the Dordogne to do up. It set Serena off again about them doing a similar thing, finding a house in Pembrokeshire and running it as a bed and breakfast. She spoke of little else, and very soon their father began seriously to consider the offer made by a large building firm for Brook House Farm and its land.

Despite finding her A-level work even harder than she'd anticipated, Genevieve's confidence was rock steady. At last everything seemed to be going well for her. The weekend before Christian was due to take up his place at Exeter University, it was Genevieve's seventeenth birthday and her parents suggested he came to stay, and they'd throw a party.

Christian arrived on the afternoon of the party. To have some time alone together, Genevieve took him for a guided tour of the farm. First, she showed him the milking parlour, explained how the machinery worked, and how her father would have to computerise it if he was going to make it more economical.

'That's if we stay,' she added, as she led him outside and across the yard to the old hay barn.

'You think you won't?' Christian asked, taking hold of her hand.

'Mum's become obsessed with us moving down to Pembrokeshire.'

He smiled. 'It would be nearer Exeter.'

'It would, wouldn't it?'

The barn was warm and stuffy, the air heavy with the sweet smell of hay. Climbing the ladder up to the loft, where Genevieve and her sisters had often played as children, they sat on the dusty floor. 'This would make a fantastic house,' Christian said, taking off his sweatshirt and glancing round at the space. 'I'd love to convert old buildings into houses when I'm qualified as an architect.'

But for once Genevieve wasn't interested in what Christian had to say. Since the moment he'd arrived she'd wanted to kiss him, and suddenly feeling light-headed and breathless, she pushed him onto his back. She kissed him slowly on the lips, wanting so much for him to know what he meant to her. He returned her kiss, his mouth deliciously soft and tender. She slipped a hand under his T-shirt, wanting to touch the smooth hardness of his stomach. His hands, too, began to work at her clothes and when she sat up and took off her top, he stared at her, his eyes shining, his breath huskily audible in the stillness. She had never felt more sure of anything, but when she put her hands behind her back to undo her bra, he suddenly looked nervous.

'Gen, don't. Please don't.'

'It's OK. I want to.'

He put out his hands to stop her. 'I want to as well. But . . . but not here. Not now.'

Her heart slammed in her chest. 'Don't you love me?'

'It's not that. It's . . .' His voice broke off.

'You don't fancy me? Is that it?'

He smiled and put his arms round her neck. 'Oh, I fancy you all right. But I don't want to take any chances. You know, doing it without protection. I don't have any condoms.'

Condoms! Of course. How stupid she'd been. Relief flowed through her. She tilted her head back so that he could see her face. 'Another time, perhaps?'

He stroked her cheek. 'You better believe it.'

Rachel was the last guest to arrive, and she was fabulously overdressed in a slinky white dress that showed off her perfect figure and, if Genevieve's suspicions were right, the lack of a pair of knickers. On her head was a pink baseball cap with the words 'Spoilt Rotten' written in sparkly fake diamonds.

'A present from my father,' she said, catching Genevieve's glance. 'The dress too. It's his way of saying sorry and I'm quite prepared to take advantage of him.' She handed over an expensively wrapped package. 'For you. Happy seventeenth birthday, Gen.'

'Thanks, Rachel. It looks gorgeous before I've even unwrapped it.'

'Think nothing of it; it's more guilt money extracted from my father. The well is deep and given the chance, I'm going to run it dry.' She took in the other guests. 'There are a lot of people here. Where's Christian?'

'He's helping Dad with the barbecue.'

Serena breezed through just then, carrying a large bowl of salad, the smell of spring onions and peppers filling the air. She looked at Rachel. 'Hello, dear, I do hope you'll be warm enough.'

Rachel laughed. 'Oh, I expect I'll find some way to keep warm. Gen could always lend me something if I get desperate.'

'She might even lend you some knickers if you're nice. Now, if you'll excuse me, I must get this salad on the table.'

When they were getting ready to cut the cake—the Baxters liked nothing better than a good drum-rolling, cake-cutting moment—Genevieve went to look for Christian.

'Have you seen Christian?' she asked Polly. 'Mum wants to take some photographs of us all together.'

'I saw Rachel talking to Christian earlier,' Polly said, and a chill crept into Genevieve's heart. 'Do you want me to help you find them?'

'No. It's OK. You tell Mum and Dad to hold back the cake for a few minutes more. I won't be long.'

I'm being irrational, she told herself, but the chill took a stronger hold on her. She checked the house. No sign of them there. She tried the hay barn and that was where she found them. She didn't need to climb the ladder up to the loft, where only hours ago she and Christian had lain—where she'd been rejected—to know what they were doing. It was obvious. Rachel was gasping loudly and Christian was breathing hard, the floorboards creaking rhythmically.

She stumbled outside and ran, blinded by tears, across the yard to the house. She didn't stop running until she was upstairs and had thrown herself onto her bed. How could he? How could he betray her like that, and with Rachel of all people?

She was sobbing so hard into her pillow, she only realised Gran was in the room when she felt the mattress dip. She opened her eyes, plunged her head into her grandmother's lap and sobbed even harder.

'Oh, Gran,' she gulped, 'I . . . I saw them . . . they were together . . . in the barn . . . and they were . . . he was . . . I hate them both!'

'It's all right, sweetheart,' her grandmother soothed. 'You cry for as long as you need.' She rocked her gently, and the tears flowed as though they would never stop.

PART III

'I BET YOUR FATHER wanted to beat the little sod to a pulp! I hope he did.'

Genevieve smiled at Adam. 'You should know Dad better than that. Nattie, on the other hand, slapped his face so hard, she knocked him clean off his feet.'

'That's my girl!' Adam laughed heartily, jiggling Lily-Rose on his lap. She was back in the kitchen again, quietly helping herself from the packet of raisins on the table. 'So what happened next?'

'Heavens! Haven't you heard enough?'

'Sorry, am I being insensitive?'

'No. Not at all. But I guess the straight answer is, I recovered from a broken heart and grew up.'

'And the complicated answer?'

'Ah, well. I made myself ill, gave up on school and drifted aimlessly until I finally got my act together.'

He looked thoughtful. 'How ill, Gen?'

'Oh, you know; the full works. Depression. Anxiety. And starving myself in the belief that Christian had betrayed me because I was a big, fat, unlovable moron. All I could think of was making myself slowly disappear, taking all my problems with me.'

Adam reached across the table and laid his hand on top of hers. He didn't say anything, just shook his head. Lily-Rose, thinking it was a game, added her small hand to the pile. Giggling, she got back to the packet of raisins, eating them steadily, one by one.

'Why have you never mentioned any of this before?' Adam asked quietly. 'Or for that matter, why haven't your parents or sisters ever spoken of it?'

'It's called shame. Plus that well-known Baxter trait, an inability to talk about anything really important. Let's face it, it's why Mum's currently swanning around some winery in New Zealand and Dad refuses to get his head out of the sand.'

'But there's nothing to be ashamed about.'

Genevieve shook her head. 'Look at it from Mum and Dad's point of view. The first thing I remember Mum saying when I was taken into hospital, was, "Where did we go wrong?" You see, with nothing tangible to blame, they blamed themselves. They thought they should have been better parents. Then when I recovered, we all started to push my illness under the carpet, and before long it became known as "that time when she wasn't well". A tidy euphemism for something we wanted to put behind us.'

'So what happened to Rachel? After you'd torn her limb from limb.'

'She stayed on at school, though I never spoke to her again. The last I heard—this was years ago—was that she went to live with her father.'

'And Christian. Did he ever say he was sorry?'

'I didn't give him much of a chance to apologise. He wrote to me, but I returned all his letters unopened. After his parents sold Pendine Cottage, he never showed up in Angel Sands again.'

'And now the dirty love-rat is about to appear on the scene again. How do you feel about that?'

She got up to make some fresh tea. 'For a start, I don't view him as a dirty love-rat. Don't forget, we were little more than children. Teenage love isn't designed to last. My mistake was to take it too seriously.'

'A very pretty speech, Gen. How about you answer my question?'

With her back to him, staring out of the window, the rain still coming down, Genevieve tried to think what her answer really was.

'I'm curious,' she said at last, turning to face Adam. 'Curious to see if I still think he's as perfect as I once thought he was.'

Adam left Lily-Rose to her raisins, and came over to Genevieve, his expression serious. 'I'd have thought he settled that matter in the barn that night.'

She smiled. 'Are you worried I might still be carrying a torch for him?'

'And aren't you?'

'I told you, I'm intrigued. Nothing more.'

From outside came the sound of Henry kicking up an almighty row again. Adam switched his gaze from her to the garden.

'The sooner you find that donkey a pal, the better. Now then, I'd better get going. You won't forget to give Gareth and Gwenda a call about the wedding buffet, will you?'

With eighty-five wedding guests due to arrive at Paradise House, Genevieve was making her final round of checks. She looked in on the marquee in the garden, to see if the florist had arranged the flowers on the buffet tables. Yes. They were all there, beautifully displayed; baskets of yellow roses and creamy white irises.

Going out into the blazing June sunshine, she pondered why Adam was so determined to make her start up her own catering business. Since last week, he'd been on at her almost daily to consider his offer to back her. In the end, just to silence him, she'd told him about George and Cecily Randolph and the money George had left her in his will.

'You've been so good to me,' George had said, as he lay dying in hospital, 'and I'm sure Cecily would have wanted you to have the money. It's such a small amount, please don't refuse it.'

'So you see,' she'd told Adam, 'you don't have to take pity on me. But please don't mention the money to anyone.'

'Mr Discreet, that's me. But if you have the wherewithal, why don't you get stuck in to something?'

'Because if I'm going to do it, I'll do it when I'm good and ready. I won't be bullied by anyone, not even you, Adam.'

He'd looked hurt at that. 'I've never bullied anyone in my life, Gen.'

'You're a dear friend,' she'd told him, giving him a hug.

Inside the house, the sound of laughter was coming from the kitchen. Nattie, who was helping to serve along with Donna, had decided to dress for the part and was wearing a French maid's outfit. Genevieve wondered what Adam would make of his beloved parading herself so provocatively.

The bride and groom, Gwenda and Gareth, plus parents, were the first to arrive. They all looked with relief at the pretty garden with its dramatic backdrop of sparkling blue sea.

Polly was playing her part, too, providing background music. Last night, Adam had helped Daddy Dean to move the piano from the guest sitting-room to the conservatory, so that music would flow into the garden. Now, as the guests began to arrive, Polly struck up with 'Love Changes Everything'. Catching her eye from across the lawn, Gareth and Gwenda gave Genevieve the thumbs up.

Genevieve went outside again to make sure everyone had a drink. The guests, glasses in hand, were circulating well, some openly admiring the garden. Pots of begonias and geraniums lined the terrace, and against the south-facing wall of the house the palm trees were bathed in golden sunlight. Genevieve felt a satisfying glow of pride.

Echoing her thoughts, a voice said, 'You've done a fantastic job, Gen.'

It was Adam, dressed immaculately in a lightweight suit, its effect sadly marred by a tie depicting a pink flamingo.

'Thanks,' she said. 'But I didn't do it all alone.'

He sighed. 'Just take the credit and have done with it, will you?'

Genevieve laughed. 'OK, if you say so.' More seriously, she said, 'Have you seen Nattie yet?'

'No. Why do you ask?'

'Oh, no reason.' Changing the subject, she said, 'By the way, I had a word with that man you recommended over in Saundersfoot.'

'And?'

She pointed towards the far end of the orchard. 'See, or rather, listen. It's worked. Henry's been as good as gold, not a peep out of him. He hasn't left Morwenna's side since Dad fetched her this morning.'

'Morwenna?'

'Nattie's choice. It's Welsh for maiden. But she's cute, isn't she, with that light sandy face and chocolate body?'

'I can't honestly say that donkeys do it for me, Gen, but— What the hell does she think she's doing?'

Adam's gaze, no longer directed towards the orchard, had swung round to the middle of the lawn and was fixed on the object of his desire. Carrying a tray of canapés, Nattie had made her appearance, her skirt hitched up to reveal stocking tops and suspenders.

He wasn't the only one to stare. 'Why?' Adam said simply. 'Why does she do it?'

'Because she loves to stand out. It's why you're mad about her, Adam. Now if you'll excuse me, I still have a hundred and one things to do.'

Before heading back to the kitchen, Genevieve popped into the conservatory to see how Polly was getting on. She had company. Lily-Rose was sitting on the floor under the piano, stirring a bowl of ice cream.

'I thought Gran was supposed to be looking after Lily-Rose,' Genevieve said.

Her fingers still moving expertly over the keys, Polly replied, 'I think she may have got the wrong end of the stick.' She inclined her head towards the marquee.

There was Gran, a glass of champagne in one hand and a canapé in the other. She looked every inch the wedding guest, and not the handy baby sitter she had offered to be.

Genevieve bent down and held out her arms to her niece. 'OK, little missy. Out you come.'

Her words had no impact at all on Lily-Rose, who suddenly pointed through the open conservatory door and let out a cry of delight. '*Adam!*'

The man in question heard her squeal and turned round. She wriggled out from under the piano and ran helter-skelter towards him.

'Hello, Rosy-Posy,' he laughed, 'how's my best little girl?'

'We've got a new donkey. Do you want to come and see her? Her name's Morwenna.'

'In a moment, maybe.'

'I know it's a cheek, Adam,' said Genevieve, when she'd caught up with her niece, 'but I don't suppose you would keep an eye on her, would you?'

'No problem.' He bent down and lifted Lily-Rose onto his shoulders.

Wide-eyed with delight, the little girl beamed and grabbed hold of his ears. 'Giddy-up, giddy-up!'

'Thanks, Adam,' Genevieve said. 'What would we do without you?' She leaned in to kiss him. But the sight of two men appearing round the side of the house caught her eye, and she froze.

She had a pretty good idea who the taller and darker of the two was, but the other . . . the other, without doubt, was Christian.

As though a spell had been cast, everything around Genevieve became a muffled blur while, across the lawn, Christian was picked out in sharp focus. He'd changed, of course. As much as anyone would in thirteen years. He'd filled out more and his hair was cut shorter than she remembered. His eyes were hidden behind sunglasses, but she could tell from his stance that he was scanning the garden, searching for someone.

His gaze fell on her. His body stiffened and his hand reached for his sunglasses, then he turned to his companion, said something, and started to walk towards her.

Suddenly, the spell was broken. Next to her, Adam said, 'Gen, what's wrong? You look like you've seen a ghost.'

She moved closer to him. 'I have,' she whispered. 'It's Christian.'

'*What*? Where?'

'He's heading this way,' she murmured. 'Don't leave me.'

'Anything you say.' Adam lowered Lily-Rose from his shoulders and set her on the grass.

It felt as though an eternity passed before Christian was standing in front of her.

'Genevieve.'

'Hello, Christian.' She forced herself to look him dead in the eye. 'I was wondering when you'd show up.'

He looked puzzled. 'You were? I don't understand.'

'I live here,' she said, in answer to his question. 'At the moment we all do, Dad, Nattie, Polly and me. This is our home.'

'Paradise House?'

'We run it as a bed and breakfast . . . just as Mum always wanted. Remember her dream?'

'I didn't know. Really I didn't.'

'Why would you?' Her voice was sharp. 'Why are you here, Christian? I don't mean, in the area; everyone knows about Ralph's barn being sold and some architect doing it up—we had a feeling it might be you. But why are you here at Paradise House?'

He turned away, stared at some distant point out to sea, shifted his feet, then looked back at her. 'You're not going to believe this, but we were pointed in this direction and told that Paradise House was the best place to stay.' He paused. 'But given the circumstances . . . I'll tell Jonjo we'll try somewhere else.'

Then, as though only just noticing them, he glanced at Adam and Lily-Rose. 'Look,' he said, more to Adam than to Genevieve, 'I'm sorry for barging in. I'd better go.' He turned to leave, but hesitated, and just stood there staring at her. 'It's . . . it's good to see you again, Genevieve.'

She watched him walk away, back to find his companion, presumably their neighbour-to-be, Jonjo Fitzwilliam. She felt a hand on her shoulder.

'You OK, Gen?'

Still watching Christian's retreating figure, she nodded. 'I'm fine, Adam. Thanks.'

It soon became clear that Christian had lost his friend among the wedding guests. Soon he was approaching Genevieve once more.

'Sorry about this,' he said, 'but I can't find Jonjo. It's so typical of him. He has the attention span of a goldfish.'

'Do you always speak so highly of your friends?'

Adam's comment went unnoticed by Christian—he'd been looking at Genevieve for a response. 'I'll help you find him.'

'Thanks,' he said. 'Then I promise we'll get out of your way.'

They didn't have far to go before they found Jonjo. He was in the conservatory with Polly. They looked like a pair of Jane Austen characters, for he was leaning over the piano, watching her. Even Christian stood and stared at Polly. The last time he'd seen her she'd been a child.

As if the moment couldn't get any more unreal, a strident voice burst into the conservatory.

'I'll tell you this for free, if one more bloke asks me to bend down for his napkin, I'll poke a cocktail stick up his bum! *Bloody hell!* What're you doing here?'

Not even Polly could maintain her professionalism in the face of so many distractions. She caught sight of Christian and stopped playing.

In the silence that followed, Jonjo said, 'Christian, you never told me what my neighbours would be like in Angel Sands. Not a word did you say about musical angels or even fallen angels.' He eyed Nattie's outfit.

Genevieve saw that Nattie was dangerously armed with a plate of used cocktail sticks. 'Seeing as you're here, Christian, perhaps you and your friend would like a drink?' she said.

'Are you completely off your head, Gen?' demanded Nattie. 'How can you even *think* of allowing him to stay?'

They were in the kitchen, grabbing more trays of food to take outside to the guests.

'It's called acting civilly. Something you should try.'

'I'd rather take up growing bamboo shoots through my toes than be polite to that pig of a man. What he did to you was beyond—'

'Oh, shut up, will you! Now pass me that chilli and garlic dip for the prawns. OK, that's it. Out we go. Go on. People are waiting.'

Jonjo had eagerly accepted the offer of a drink, blind to Christian's discomfort. As Genevieve passed round a tray of canapés, she observed the two men sitting on the stone steps outside the conservatory. She had the feeling that neither was much interested in listening to the other. Jonjo, who she would bet didn't know the history between his friend and the Baxters, was being pulled like a magnet to stare at Polly. Christian was picking absently at the moss on the steps, his glass of wine untouched.

Having attended to the guests, and with only a few canapés left on her tray, Genevieve went over to Christian and Jonjo. 'Any takers for Thai prawns with chilli and garlic?'

Christian was instantly on his feet. 'Genevieve?'

'Yes?'

'I don't think this is a good idea.'

'Oh. Well, why don't you try one first?'

He brought his eyebrows together then looked at the tray. 'No, I didn't mean that. I meant me being here.'

Jonjo was now on his feet too, brushing away any dust that might have been clinging to the back of his linen trousers. He'd taken off his jacket, hooked it over the handle of the conservatory door, and Genevieve could see just how finely toned his body was. His black T-shirt clung to his broad chest and shoulders, the perfect advertisement for the health and fitness centres he ran.

'But we can't go yet, Christian,' Jonjo said. 'I haven't had a chance to talk to the future Mrs Fitzwilliam. May I?' He helped himself to a couple of canapés. 'Now tell me, Genevieve, when does your enchanting sister get time off? How can I propose to her if she's chained to the ivories?'

Christian rolled his eyes. 'Jonjo, give it a rest. We're leaving. Take no notice of him, Genevieve. He's only allowed out at weekends.'

For the first time since the two men had appeared, she smiled.

Jonjo reached for his jacket and threw Polly one last dazzling smile through the open door. 'Where exactly are we going, Christian? As far as I'm aware, we still don't have a place to rest our weary heads tonight.'

'You could try the Salvation Arms,' Genevieve said.

He pulled a face. 'Is that as bad as it sounds? A flea-ridden doss-house?'

'It's the local pub, you idiot,' snapped Christian. He turned to Genevieve. 'Thanks for the recommendation. We'll try there next.'

The following morning, Genevieve was up early. She had ten breakfasts to cook. It was also Sunday, which was often a complete changeover day—every room vacated and reoccupied within a matter of hours.

With her usual breakfast of tea and a slice of toast and marmalade, Genevieve wandered out to the garden. It was going to be another beautiful day. She settled herself on the wooden bench that overlooked the bay and sipped her tea. She was exhausted. Not surprisingly, sleep had eluded her for most of the night. Turbulent dreams of Christian staying at Paradise House had merged with nightmares of the robbery.

Soft footsteps behind her made her turn. 'Mind if I join you?' her father asked, a mug in his hand.

She made room for him on the bench. 'You're up early.'

'Not as early as you. Things on your mind?'

'A few.' She knew exactly what was on *his* mind. Knew also that he wouldn't come right out and say it. 'It went well yesterday,' she hedged. 'Thanks for your help. I couldn't have done it without you all.'

'Every commander in chief needs his foot soldiers.'

'I'd hardly describe myself as a commander in chief.'

'Then you should. Adam says you should do more of this specialised catering lark.'

'Adam says a lot of things.'

Her father slurped his tea. 'Was it very much of a shock seeing him again?' She noticed he couldn't bring himself to say Christian's name.

'At first, yes. But then I began to feel almost sorry for him.'

'Your mother would have given him what for, had she been here. I was tempted myself.'

Genevieve smiled. 'Liar. You're the biggest pacifist going, Dad.'

'And perhaps that isn't something I should be proud of. But I'll tell you what I am proud of, Gen, and that's you.'

She shrugged off the compliment with a shake of her head. 'Now you're being silly.'

He placed his mug on the armrest. 'It's true. I'm more proud of you than I can say. You know how I dry up when it comes to putting things into words.'

'But words aren't always necessary, Dad,' she said. She thought of all the school prize-givings, when he'd given each of his daughters a single red rose, whether they'd gone up on the stage to collect a prize or not.

'I disagree,' he said. 'Words stay with a person.'

'So is there something special you want to say to me?' Genevieve asked, almost dreading what he might say.

He cleared his throat. 'Yes. Your gran told me about the robbery.'

She turned and faced him. 'But *I* told you about it.'

'No, Genevieve. You told me what you wanted to tell me. That's not the same. Why did you tell your grandmother the robbery had been so brutal, but not me?'

She sighed, glad she hadn't told Gran everything. 'Because I didn't want to worry you. You had enough to think about with Mum going.'

'I don't understand. I'm your father. I'm supposed to worry about you.'

'Perhaps I feel I've given you sufficient worry over the years.'

She could see he wasn't buying it, but he let it go. 'You're all right, though, aren't you? I mean . . .'

She switched on the reassuring smile she knew he needed to see. 'Dad, I'm fine. Really. I get the occasional bad dream, but that will go with time.' Apart from last night's glitch, she had started to sleep better, and the fear of being alone had passed. Turning the spotlight onto him, she said, 'You didn't seem so nervous around Donna yesterday.'

A ghost of a smile passed across his face and he picked up his mug of tea. 'That's because I think I'm off the hook.'

'Really? How's that?'

'Donna's switched horses, you could say. I pointed her in Tubby's direction. I mentioned several times during the day that he'd been on his own for too long and that, though he'd never admit it, what he needed was someone to take care of him.'

'You sneaky old matchmaker, Dad! So is that why Tubby turned up towards the end of the party?'

'Yes. I invited him for a drink, then got them together.'

'I'm impressed.'

She truly was. In his own quiet way, her father had resolved matters better than she and her sisters could have done.

Noticing the time, Genevieve said, 'I'd better go inside and make a start on breakfast.'

Her father got to his feet with her. 'I'll help you.'

'There's no need. I can manage.'

'But I'd like to.'

'You never helped Mum.'

His face dropped. 'Maybe I should have.'

Trying to undo the harm she'd done, Genevieve said, 'Oh, you know what Mum was like, she had some daft notion that the kitchen was no place for a man.'

'Is, Gen. What Mum is like. Please don't put her in the past tense.'

Gran appeared after lunch. She swooped on Genevieve and offered to help peg out the third load of that day's washing.

'That's OK, Gran. Why don't you sit down and enjoy the sun. There should be some newspapers somewhere, unless the guests have taken them.' She hid behind a large duvet cover, anxious not to be left alone with her grandmother. Genevieve had wondered how long it would be before she showed up.

Ignoring her, Gran stooped to pick out a pillowcase from the laundry basket. She pegged it alongside the duvet cover that was flapping in the breeze. 'I saw him this morning,' she said.

'Saw who?'

Her lips compressed, Gran looked at her for a long, uncomfortable moment. 'Don't be obtuse with me, Genevieve Baxter. You know jolly well who I'm talking about. Now, stop fiddling with that washing and come and talk to me. In the absence of your mother, I'm taking it upon myself to look out for you.'

'Gran, I'm thirty years old! I don't need looking out for.'

'Age doesn't come into it. I don't think I would ever forgive myself if I stood back and allowed you to make yourself ill again.'

'Oh, Gran. You really think that because Christian's here in Angel Sands I'm going to revert to being a confused teenager?'

'It's possible, isn't it?'

'Gran, I'm touched, but really, there's no need for you to worry.'

'But seeing him again might stir up all those old memories . . . remind you of things you thought you'd put behind you.'

Genevieve took hold of her grandmother's hands and squeezed them gently, forcing her to look her in the eye. 'I'm stronger than you think, really. I know you see Christian as a trigger, but he isn't. I'm not that precariously balanced, Gran. Honestly.'

Withdrawing her hands, Gran said, 'Good. So you won't be cross when I tell you I've arranged for you to meet Christian.'

'*What?*'

'You heard. He said there were things he wanted to say to you. He mentioned the word apologise.'

'But I still don't understand why you've changed your stance. For years you wouldn't even call him by his name.'

'It's called disclosure, Genevieve. They were talking about it on *Kilroy* the other day.'

Genevieve frowned. Then smiled. 'I think you mean closure.'

Gran shrugged. 'Any which way, I told him to come here at four.'

Christian rang the doorbell on the stroke of four. A walk seemed appropriate, so they set off the way he'd just come, to the centre of the village, and then up the hill towards Tawelfan beach.

When they'd emerged from the steep path through the woods and were looking back down onto Angel Sands, she touched his arm to attract his attention. 'So, what was it you wanted to talk to me about?'

'Do you mind if we sit down? We'll be able to talk better that way.'

She nodded, and they wandered away from the main path and found a patch of soft, dry grass to sit on.

'When did you and your family move here?' he asked, removing his sunglasses and slipping them into his shirt pocket.

Genevieve gave him a brief potted history.

'And the wedding party yesterday, is that a regular thing?'

'No. That was Adam's idea. He's a terrible bully sometimes, but his heart's in the right place. He's the son my father never had and gets away with more than he should.'

'From the little I saw of him, he looks like he fits in well.'

'So how about you? You obviously became the architect you always wanted to be. Where are you living these days?'

'In a little place you've probably never heard of. Stony Stratford—'

'In Buckinghamshire.'

He bowed his head. 'I stand corrected.'

'And do you live in an amazing house you've designed yourself?'

'No. I'm still waiting to find the time. Clients keep getting in the way.'

'Clients like Jonjo?'

'He keeps me pretty busy with the fitness centres, and now there's this barn to do as a personal project for him. So yes, he's currently the most time-consuming client, for sure. But he's also a good friend. And as we all know, friends take the most enormous liberties. They rob us blind.' He lowered his gaze as they both took in his blunder. 'Well, that's as good a way as any to broach the subject,' he said. 'Genevieve, I know it's been a long time, but did you ever . . . did Nattie ever tell you about the letter she sent me?'

'Nattie? When?'

He swallowed and stared intently at the grass between his legs. 'When you were unwell.' His eyes slid back to her face.

'You knew I was ill? But how?' Then very slowly the penny dropped. Nattie had written to him behind her back. Annoyed, the colour rose in her face. 'What exactly did my sister tell you?'

'That it was my fault for making you so ill you very nearly died. Oh, Genevieve, I'm sorry. I'm sorry I did that to you.'

'You didn't.' Her voice was firm. '*I* did it. I don't blame anyone for my anorexic days. And just for the record, I had my bulimic moments as well.' She paused, realising that she had raised her voice, was practically lecturing him. 'Look, it all started well before my seventeenth birthday,' she continued, and less heatedly, 'not long after my grandfather died.

So you see, you have no cause to blame yourself.'

Again she could see him piecing together what she'd said. When he'd caught up, he didn't look like he believed her. 'I'm still sorry about . . . about that night in your father's barn.'

Her tone softened. 'It's OK, you can say her name. Rachel.'

But he didn't register what she'd said. 'To this day, I don't know what the hell I thought I was doing. It shouldn't have been her. It should have been you. But the night of your party, she told me you'd been seeing someone else, that you had been stringing me along for over a year.'

Genevieve was horrified. 'So you thought you'd get your own back and shag my best friend? Is that it? Asking for my side of the story was out of the question, I suppose?'

'I was angry and wanted to hurt you.'

'Trust me, it worked.'

They fell silent, the cry of a gull filling the space between them as they both stared out at the sea.

She touched him lightly on the arm. He turned. 'Why did you believe her, Christian? Why did you think I'd be capable of doing that to you?'

He fiddled with his watch, running his finger under the steel strap as if it was irritating his skin. At length, he said, 'Put it down to insecurity.'

'You! Insecure? Never.'

He tilted his head and frowned. 'You always thought I was so confident, didn't you? But think about it. I was an outcast, a swotty deaf kid totally lacking in any street cred.' He smiled ruefully. 'You were the nearest thing I had to a best friend in those days. You accepted me without question. From the moment you pushed me into the water, the day we met, I knew we were on the level.'

Picturing the scene, and the grin on his face when he yelled at her to speak up, she smiled and relaxed a little. 'I didn't ever see it that way. I used to wish I had your confidence. Do you remember that day when we were in the sand dunes and . . .'

'Go on.'

'No. I was going to say something silly. Something I'd regret.'

'You were thinking of that day when we first kissed, weren't you?'

She nodded.

'And later you told me about the song that was playing on the radio at the time—"The Wonder of You".'

She cringed. 'Please don't make me squirm.'

'"*When no one else can understand me, when everything I do is wrong, you give me hope and consolation, you give me strength to carry on.*"'

She looked at him. 'You remember the words?'

'Course I do. They came to mean as much to me as they did to you.'

There didn't seem anything Genevieve could add. She got to her feet. 'I ought to be making tracks. There are guests arriving soon.'

As they retraced their steps, Christian said, 'Genevieve, you haven't asked why I didn't try to get in touch with you again after Nattie wrote to me. I did write back to her, asking her to pass on a message to you, but she returned the letter, just as you'd done with all the others. She said I was never to get in touch with you, that any contact might make you ill again. I felt so responsible for what had happened, but had no way of helping you. So I kept away in the hope you'd get better, telling myself it was the right thing to do.'

Genevieve didn't know whether to be furious with Nattie for meddling or touched that she'd been so concerned. 'Well, all's well that ends well, I guess. Come on, I really need to get home.'

When they were standing outside the Salvation Arms, Christian said, 'Would you like to come and see Jonjo's barn tomorrow? If the weather's nice, and you have the time, we could walk and take a picnic.'

'I'm sorry, but it'll have to be another time. I've promised Lily-Rose I'll do something special with her tomorrow.'

'Oh.' He looked disappointed. But then his face brightened. 'Why don't you bring her? If you think she'd enjoy it.'

When Genevieve returned to Paradise House, all thoughts of Nattie's meddling were forgotten. Sitting in the garden with Polly, his arm on the back of the wooden bench they were sharing, was Jonjo. A dangerous mixture of adoration and sparkling mischief lit up his handsome face. There was no denying what a striking couple they made. Polly's delicate fairness seemed all the more ethereal next to Jonjo's dark good looks.

In contrast to the charming shade of pink that Polly had turned on seeing Genevieve, there was no awkwardness to Jonjo. 'How was your walk with Christian?' he asked. 'I hope you left him buried in the sand up to his neck. He's been such an edgy devil since yesterday afternoon. No chance of you shedding some light on what's giving him the hump?'

Genevieve got the feeling that Jonjo seldom expected an answer to any of his questions. She was about to ask if he or Polly would like a drink, when he pre-empted her.

'I've been trying to persuade your lovely sister to see my new home tomorrow. Do you think you could help me twist her arm? I know, why don't you come too?'

She explained about Christian's invitation. And that Lily-Rose was also included in the outing.

He turned to Polly, like a small boy who'd just been told he could stay up late. 'There! It's as good as settled. Now you'll have to come.'

Ralph's barn was situated half a mile inland from Tawelfan beach, a stone's throw from Pendine Cottage. As Jonjo drove his Land Rover Discovery down the bumpy track, Genevieve asked Christian if he'd ever been back to see the house.

'No. Never.'

'What about when you came here with Jonjo to view the barn?'

'He came alone. I saw the place for the first time two days ago.'

When they arrived, they had to negotiate rampant nettles and brambles, before Jonjo moved an old milk churn to one side and swung open one half of the wide double doors. 'What do you think?'

Genevieve went and stood in the middle of the gloomy barn. Beams of sunlight filtered through the holes in the roof. In among the cobwebs and shadows there was a graveyard of rusting old farm implements, rubber tyres and ripped tarpaulins. It was far from inspiring, but when Jonjo suggested they explore outside, the view from the rear was as perfect as she'd known it would be. All that separated them from the sea was a sloping, narrow stretch of heath and the sand dunes that backed the unspoilt beach. It was beautiful. She turned to Christian, standing beside her, and saw from his expression that he thought the same.

'I'm going to design it with the living area of the house upstairs,' he said, looking back at the barn. 'Each of the bedrooms will have a door leading out onto the garden. The main bedroom will catch the rising sun and the sitting room will have a fantastic view of the setting sun.'

'It sounds good.'

'Thanks. It'll mostly be open plan. I want to take full advantage of the natural light as well as bring the landscape inside.'

'Do you wish you were designing it for yourself?' she asked, when they were returning to the car to fetch the picnic. Jonjo and Polly were walking on ahead, while Lily-Rose, who'd been unusually quiet since leaving home, was holding Genevieve's hand and sliding occasional sideways glances in Christian's direction.

He came to a stop and looked the way they'd come. 'Yes. It's pretty much what I'd like for myself.'

They carried on walking and Genevieve glanced at Polly, who seemed quite at ease in Jonjo's larger-than-life company. She touched Christian's arm lightly to make him turn. 'I get the feeling that Jonjo doesn't know our history? Am I right?'

'Yes.'

'Why's that?'

He pushed his hands into his trouser pockets and frowned. 'Because it's none of his business.'

It wasn't a very satisfactory answer, but she didn't pursue it.

They had their picnic in the dunes, in a quiet, sheltered spot where a gentle breeze rustled the marram grass. Any wariness Lily-Rose had shown previously towards Jonjo and Christian seemed to be disappearing now. She sat crosslegged between them, slyly adding more crisps to her plate when she thought no one was watching. Even Christian seemed to be relaxing now and was telling Polly how he and Jonjo had got to know each other.

'And do you run your own practice?' asked Polly.

'No, more's the pity. I keep thinking about it, but the time never seems quite right to take the plunge.'

Jonjo tutted. 'I keep telling him to get on and go it alone, like I did, but he's too cautious for his own good. Now, Polly, how about another glass of bubbly and then we go for a walk?'

'I want to go for a walk as well,' piped up Lily-Rose. She tossed aside her plate and leapt to her feet.

'Not so fast, sweetheart,' said Genevieve. 'Have something more to eat. All you've had so far is a few crisps.'

She shook her head and rested her hands on her hips.

'It's OK, Gen,' said Polly. 'I'm sure Jonjo won't mind the company.'

Smart move, thought Genevieve, as she watched her sister take her eager little chaperone by the hand. If Jonjo was at all disappointed to be denied a romantic stroll along the beach, he didn't show it. Instead, he took hold of Lily-Rose's other hand and said, 'Christian, make sure you behave yourself while we're gone.'

'You must be very proud of her,' Christian said, when they were alone.

Thinking he was referring to Polly, she said, 'I am. Polly may be the least worldly-wise Baxter, but she's definitely the prudent one.'

He frowned. 'I didn't mean Polly. I meant your daughter. She's really cute. How old is she?'

It was Genevieve's turn to frown. 'Oh, no! No, you've got it wrong, I'm not her mother. Nattie is.'

'Nattie? But you . . . at the party . . . you and Adam, and Lily-Rose . . . You and Adam . . . you are married, right?'

She laughed. 'Absolutely not.' She told him about Adam being hopelessly in love with her sister.

'But you seemed,' he paused, as if conjuring up the right words, 'such a couple. I was convinced you were married.'

'As cheesy as it sounds, we're just good friends.'

'And you're not . . . remotely interested in him?'

'What is this? Are you trying to fix me up?'

He laughed now, and at last seemed relaxed. 'I wouldn't dream of it. How about some more of Jonjo's champagne while he isn't looking?'

She held out her wine glass. 'This is very decadent, isn't it?'

'You can always depend on Jonjo for the grand gesture.'

'Well, here's to many more of his grand gestures.'

He chinked his wineglass against hers, 'And . . . to old friends.'

His words hung in the air as they both sipped their drinks.

Christian said, 'Jonjo and I are leaving tomorrow. But we'll be back.'

'That sounds worryingly like a threat.'

He tilted his head and looked puzzled. 'It wasn't meant to be.'

Another silence followed. And then, 'Genevieve, you won't hold the past against me, will you? I'd hate to be forever defined by a mistake I once made.'

Unable to answer him, she turned away.

It was a week and a half since the day of the picnic. This morning, after their father had intercepted the postman, he had handed her a letter with a Buckinghamshire postmark. It was so reminiscent of years gone by that she had taken the letter outside to the garden to read.

The gist of Christian's letter was that he had really enjoyed catching up with her. Would she, he wondered, like to go for a proper walk the next time he was down?

In contrast to the one brief communication she'd had from Christian, Polly had been the subject of numerous calls from Jonjo. Often Polly wasn't around when he phoned and Genevieve ended up chatting with him instead.

'By the way,' he said during one conversation, 'Christian's told me everything. He's hardly the saint I had him down as, but it's not too late to exact revenge. I'd willingly do it myself on your behalf.'

'Or we could be very dull and just let sleeping dogs lie.'

'Spoilsport!'

Hearing the sound of Tubby's van coming to a stop at the front of the house, Genevieve roused herself and went to greet Tubby.

As a result of her father's intervention, romance was very much in the air. Tubby was positively glowing with it, bursting to share his happiness. It didn't come as a surprise, though. Donna had not been shy in sharing her own new-found happiness with Genevieve.

'Donna cooked me supper last night,' Tubby announced, while Genevieve helped herself to some tomatoes and passed them to him. 'And not just some trifling little snack. A feast fit for a king!'

'Well,' said Genevieve with a smile. 'Who'd have thought it? Old Tubby Evans falling in love.'

He blushed and reached for a paper bag, then shook it open. 'I tell you what, *cariad*, a man could get used to it.'

An hour later, Genevieve's father appeared in the kitchen, where Genevieve was taking advantage of the peace and quiet to get on with some bookkeeping.

'All alone, Genevieve?' he asked.

'Looks like it,' she said. 'Nattie and Lily-Rose are still down at Gran's and Polly's not due back until after seven.'

He sat down in the chair opposite her. 'Have you got a minute?'

She took off her glasses. 'Of course I have. What's up?'

'It's your mother.' He pulled out a letter from his back pocket and placed it on the table between them. 'It came this morning.'

They hadn't heard from Serena since their father's birthday and it seemed to Genevieve that the gap their mother's absence had initially created at Paradise House was slowly closing. She hated the thought that they would all eventually get so used to Serena not being around, that one day they'd get on with their lives as though she'd never existed.

'What does Mum say?' she asked.

'You can read it if you like.'

She put on her glasses again.

My dearest Dean,

I know it's unforgivable of me to have left it so long before writing again, but I just don't know where the time goes. As you know, it's winter here and Pete and I have been spending time away from the winery and staying in Wellington, visiting old friends of his who used to be neighbours. It is such a sophisticated place—so many art galleries, coffee-houses and trendy bars. Don't laugh, but I've developed quite a taste for vodka martinis!

I miss you and the girls and often think of you. Give my love to your mother and a special hug and a kiss to little Lily-Rose (if she hasn't already forgotten who I am).

All my love, Serena.

PS. I expect you've become quite used to me not being there. Sometimes it feels as though Paradise House was where someone else—not the real me—used to live.

Giving herself time to think, Genevieve pretended she was reading the letter again. On the face of it, it looked like Serena was rubbing their noses in it, telling them what a thoroughly enjoyable time she was having. But was it possible that Serena was trying to make Dad jealous? Until now the name of the friend in New Zealand had never been divulged. Genevieve felt sure that Serena had deliberately slipped in a bombshell guaranteed to make their father sit up and take notice. She removed her glasses, refolded the letter and pushed it across the table. She met her father's gaze.

'Who's this Pete character?' he asked. 'Where's he sprung from?'

'He's the old schoolfriend you were supposed to think was a woman,' she answered truthfully.

His eyes widened. 'You knew? You knew all along?'

She tried not to flinch at the pained disbelief in his voice.

'I'm sorry,' she murmured. 'But we thought it would hurt you too much to know the truth.'

'*We?* Your sisters knew as well?'

She nodded. 'We kept it from you because we never thought there'd be anything in it.'

He bent over the table and raked his hands through his hair. 'I've lost her,' he groaned. 'What an idiot I've been.'

Genevieve wasn't her grandmother's granddaughter for nothing. 'Dad,' she said, summoning up her most authoritative voice, 'look at me. And listen hard. You haven't lost Mum. But you will if you don't do something to get her back. Whoever this old friend is, you have to prove to Mum that he's nothing compared to you. It's time for action. Right?'

He blinked back tears and managed a nod. 'Right,' he repeated, but with a lot less conviction than Genevieve would have liked.

She wasn't entirely sure she was doing the right thing, but Genevieve decided to talk to Gran. Other than Serena, Gran was the only person who could make their father do something he didn't want to do, so after lunch, Genevieve set off for Angel Cottage. The air was fresh and tangy, and save for a few hearty souls, the beach was almost deserted. Passing the first of Angel Sands's teashops, Genevieve saw that it was packed. Next door was Debonhair. Scissors and comb poised, Debs smiled at her through the window. Genevieve gave her a small wave and continued on her way as briskly as the wind that tugged at her hair.

Gran opened the door to her knock, and immediately turned her back on Genevieve. 'Put the kettle on, dear, I'm watching *Murder, She Wrote.*' Nothing new in that, Genevieve thought with a smile. But what was new was the state of Gran's kitchen. Was her grandmother having a spring-clean? As far as Genevieve could see, Gran must have emptied every cupboard and drawer and stacked the tins and packets of food, crockery, pans and cutlery wherever she could find space on the small table and work surfaces.

Genevieve unearthed the kettle, filled it, then hunted through the toppling mess on the table for some tea bags. Once she'd located them, she joined her grandmother in the sitting room. 'What's going on in the kitchen, Gran?'

'Ssh!'

Genevieve looked at the television screen and saw that Jessica Fletcher was in the final throes of showing the confused cop how the crime was committed. When the credits rolled, Gran said, 'I've seen it before but I was hoping someone else would have done it this time.'

Genevieve was used to her grandmother's unfathomable logic. 'Are you having a major spring-clean, Gran?' she said.

Her grandmother looked at her as though she were mad. 'Now why would I be doing that in the middle of June?' She rose from her chair. 'I thought you were making some tea.'

'I am. The kettle's on.'

'Good. I'm parched. Now come with me; I need your help.'

Thinking Gran wanted a hand with putting everything away, Genevieve followed her back into the kitchen. The kettle was boiling, producing its customary rumbling noise, but the sound was amplified by the emptiness of the cupboard beneath it.

Gran suddenly grabbed hold of her arm, making her jump. 'There! Did you hear it?'

'What?'

'There it is again!'

But all Genevieve could hear was the kettle clicking off. Puzzled, she made the tea and watched Gran.

'Are you sure you can't hear it, Gen?' The old lady was peering into the cupboard beneath the sink.

Genevieve got down on the floor with her. 'What does it sound like?'

Gran backed out from the cupboard. 'What a silly girl you are. Since when has a mouse sounded like anything other than a mouse?'

Ah.

'Have you got any traps?' Genevieve asked. 'I could set them for you.'

Gran shook her head vehemently. 'I don't approve of setting traps.'

'So how are you hoping to get rid of them? Shake them by the paw and ask them to set up home elsewhere?'

A withering glance told her to be quiet and pour the tea. Genevieve wondered when the mouse problem had started. Dad hadn't said anything when he'd come back after visiting Gran two days ago.

'How long's this been going on, Gran?' she asked, at the same time inspecting the sugar bowl for mouse droppings.

'Since last night. I couldn't sleep and came down to warm some milk, and I heard the little blighters. But they're cunning so-and-sos, they wait till I'm not looking, then start to squeak and patter about the place.'

Genevieve was just passing Gran her mug when the old woman whipped round and nearly knocked it out of Genevieve's hand. 'Look, it's coming from there!' Once more on her hands and knees, Gran peered round the back of the cooker. 'I'm just not fast enough!'

'Are you sure you've got mice, Gran? I didn't hear anything.'

Gran stood up with a creak of joints. 'I hope you're not insinuating that I'm becoming vague and dotty, young lady.'

Genevieve laughed. 'You've been vague and dotty all your life. Now drink your tea and let me talk to you. I need your advice.'

Back in the sitting room, with the television switched off in order to have Gran's full attention, Genevieve filled her in on Serena's letter.

Gran was furious. 'The little madam. I'll give her cocktails!'

'What Mum's drinking isn't the point,' Genevieve said firmly. 'It's what she's trying to make Dad do that we have to focus on. I'm convinced she wants him to nail his colours to the mast. What do you think is the best way to tackle Dad? We have to make him realise he's the one to change things. He keeps saying Serena has to make her choice. That he can't *make* her come home. But I don't think that's what Mum wants. If she's the woman I think she is, she wants a husband to sweep her off her feet. A husband worth coming home to.'

Gran stirred her tea, her back ramrod straight with obstinate reproach. 'If it's drama she's after, I know just the thing. It's been on my mind for a while that they're both behaving like a couple of idiotic children. What they need is their bottoms spanking.'

Genevieve gave up. Gran wasn't in the best of moods to offer constructive advice. She set off home, disappointed.

A shout from the other side of the road, outside Roy and David's butcher shop, made her look up.

'Gen, it's me!' With a bulging carrier bag in each hand, Adam waited for a car to pass, then crossed the road. 'I was calling and calling to you, but you must have been in another world.'

She smiled. 'I was. A very strange place; my head.'

'Ooh, scary. How about you recover from the ordeal by having dinner with me tonight? My treat.' He indicated the bags of shopping. 'Roast lamb's on the menu.'

Adam was on the phone when Genevieve rang his doorbell that evening. He ushered her in, pointed at the open bottle of wine in the kitchen and disappeared to finish his call.

Whereas Paradise House was Edwardian and possessed a comfortable faded charm, Cliff View was all-singing, all-dancing, brand spanking new. Adam had spent a fortune on kitting out the eighteen-month-old house with black leather sofas, subdued oatmeal carpets, glass-and-marble units and remote-controlled lighting. If it weren't for the delicious smell of roast lamb coming from the oven, the kitchen, which was a high-gloss black and chrome affair with gleaming granite surfaces, might easily have been nothing more than a film set.

When he joined her in the kitchen, Genevieve saw that Adam was in casual mode, wearing a rugby shirt tucked into belted jeans. Watching him carve, Genevieve itched to pull out the shirt and loosen him up.

'I hope you don't mind having a tray supper?' Adam said, adding another slice of meat to one of the plates.

'Not at all. Much more relaxing.'

They carried their plates through to the sitting room, where Adam refilled their glasses of wine. He looked thoughtful as he sat down on the sofa opposite Genevieve.

'Actually, it's a bit awkward,' he said, chewing what was in his mouth. 'But I want to talk to you about something.'

'I don't ever recall a conversation between us being awkward.'

'Well, this is different.' He took a sip of his wine. 'It's about your sister. The thing is, I've come to an important decision. I have to get her out of my head, or she'll drive me nuts.' He sighed. 'I've reached a crossroads. I want to settle down, to share my life with someone special.'

'Adam, you're only thirty-three. Now that you've decided to untangle yourself from Nattie, the opportunity to meet the right person will probably arise of its own accord.'

He reached for the bottle of wine and topped up their glasses again. 'Now you're just being kind. You may not have noticed but I'm butt-ugly, and odds on the only reason a girl's ever going to be interested in me is because I've got a buck or two.' He swirled his wine round and stared into the glass.

Genevieve leaned forward in her chair. It was time for some straight talking. 'First thing,' she said, 'you're not butt-ugly, although you could benefit from some—' Her voice broke off. Could she tell him? Could she really suggest that if he spruced up his wardrobe he might attract the right sort of girl?

'Go on,' he said, 'finish what you were going to say.'

She cleared her throat. 'I don't mean this unkindly, Adam, but I think you might do better if you . . . if you took a closer look at what you wear. Your clothes are a little . . .' The baffled expression on his face stopped her from continuing. She wished she'd never started.

'A little what?' he prompted.

She took a large gulp of wine and steeled herself. 'Confusing,' she said. 'Your clothes give out the wrong sort of messages.'

He stared at her, dumbfounded. 'What's wrong with them?' He glanced down at his jeans. 'These weren't cheap, you know, they're Armani. Not market-stall tat.'

'I didn't think for one moment that they were. But have you ever thought maybe you try too hard?'

He pushed his plate away and seemed to contemplate what she'd said. She hoped she hadn't gone too far.

'OK,' he said slowly, 'if that's what you really think, why don't we go upstairs and you can explain where I'm going wrong?'

She laughed. 'If that's one of your chat-up lines, you might like to work on it.'

He laughed too and pulled her to her feet. 'I was referring to my clothes, not my mind-blowing skills in bed. Though, who knows, maybe that's my real problem.'

They went upstairs to his bedroom, which was directly above the sitting room with a view across the sea. Adam flung open the doors on the bank of wardrobes.

She whistled. 'Look at all those suits! And so many shirts!'

He smiled, proudly. 'And a different tie for each one of them.' He pulled open a drawer and revealed rows of neatly laid out ties.

This was when she knew she had to be cruel to be kind. She held up a particularly awful specimen—Goofy blowing smoke from the barrel of a gun—and said, 'Now there's no gentle way to break this to you, Adam, but believe me when I say that novelty ties are a huge turnoff.'

'But women are always saying they want a man with a sense of humour. GSOH, it's there in the personal ads. Not that I read them. Well, not much.'

She smiled at his embarrassment. 'We all read them, Adam, there's no shame in it. But back to the ties.' She picked out another one, a toothy mouse nibbling on a wedge of cheese. 'This shouts from the rooftops that you haven't grown up yet, that you're as sexy and sophisticated as Donald Duck. Which anyone who knows you properly, knows isn't true.'

He took the ties from her and threw them on the bed. 'Anything else?'

'Yes. Let your personality show you're warm and funny, not your clothes.' She caught sight of his gold bracelet on the bedside table. 'And you need to lose some of the flash, be more understated. Understated equals classy. Trust me.'

He smiled. 'I do. Completely.' To her surprise, he came over and hugged her. 'You know what? You're the perfect friend.'

Seeing as he'd taken his medicine so painlessly, she went for one last piece of advice. 'Right, this is going to hurt you a lot more than me, but raise your arms to your sides.'

Puzzled, he did as she said, and she untucked his rugby shirt. 'There, that's better. Don't you agree?' She turned him round to look at his reflection in the full-length mirror.

With a doubtful frown, he said, 'It looks untidy.'

'It looks *better*,' she replied. 'Now get used to it.'

'I feel like I've been through the wringer several times over,' he said later, when they were downstairs in the kitchen and he was playing with an expensive coffee machine. 'I had no idea you could be so tough.'

'A mistake other people keep making,' she said.

'Anyone in particular?'

'Not really. It's just that ever since Christian showed up, I get the feeling I'm being watched, in case I have a bad reaction to him.'

He passed her a large cup of frothy cappuccino. 'I did hear you'd been to see Ralph's barn with him.'

'Yes, but did you also hear that Jonjo, Polly and Lily-Rose were with us?'

'No. That minor detail was conveniently omitted. But how did it feel, seeing him again?'

She dipped her finger into the creamy froth of her coffee, then licked it. 'In the end it was fine. I've agreed to see him again when he makes a return trip to look at the barn. He's good company, just as he always was.' Changing the subject, she raised her cup and took a sip. 'Mm . . . this is delicious. Ten out of ten for the perfect cup of coffee.'

He put down his own drink, moved in close, and with his thumb, gently stroked her top lip. 'I like you better without the moustache.'

She lowered her gaze. But when he didn't step back, she suddenly found it difficult to look up at him again. Something weird had just happened and she wasn't sure she understood it. What she was sure of, though, was the overwhelming need to feel Adam touch her again, and a tremor of pure lust ran through her. Fearing the wobbling cup in its saucer would give her away, she put it down on the counter.

A body starved of touch for too long does the craziest of things, she told herself. Trying to keep calm, she forced herself to look up. When she did, she found he was staring at her in a way she'd never seen before. The blueness of his eyes had darkened and they were fixed intently on her own. She cleared her throat and said, 'It's getting late—'

But she got no further. As though the very air between them had imploded and sucked them in, they were suddenly in each other's arms. His mouth was warm, and when he pushed her against the counter and pressed his body against hers a thrill of excitement shot through her. Old friend or not, it didn't matter. She wanted him and he wanted her.

The next morning, breakfast was a shambles. Toast was burnt, eggs were dropped, orders were mixed and tempers lost. And it was all Genevieve's fault. She couldn't even blame Nattie, who was waiting on the tables in the dining room with polished professionalism.

'What the hell's the matter with you?' Nattie demanded, bursting through the kitchen door with a tray of rejected food. 'Table four ordered poached eggs, not scrambled!'

Daddy Dean was hot on Nattie's heels, a plate in his hands. 'You've forgotten the beans,' he said, more reasonably.

When at last the guests had left the dining room, her father asked if she was OK.

'I'm fine,' she lied.

'The hell you are!' disagreed Nattie. 'I've never seen you so disorganised.' She ripped off her apron and threw it on the table. 'Right then, that's me done for the day. Do you think Polly would mind looking after Lily-Rose a bit longer? Only there's something I need—'

'Oh, why bother asking?' Genevieve rounded on her. 'Do what you always do, just leave us to take care of your daughter!'

'Oo-er. Listen to who got out of bed the wrong side this morning.'

The telephone ringing prevented the row from developing further. Glad of the diversion, Genevieve pushed past her sister and snatched up the receiver.

It was Adam.

Her face and body burned with shame.

All Genevieve could think to do was go for a walk. The longer the better. A thick sea mist had rolled in during the night, and it had a calming effect on her.

Oh, but what had she done? What had possessed her to act in such a way? And now Adam wanted to see her, to talk it through. How could she face him when she couldn't even face herself in the mirror? She had told him she'd ring back when she had a free moment. Now all she had to do was contrive to be busy for the rest of time.

Wrapping her arms around herself, she recalled how they'd scrambled upstairs to his bedroom, ripped off the last of their clothes and fallen onto the bed, crushing the ties he'd earlier discarded from his wardrobe. Desperate to get on with it, Adam had reached for his bedside drawer. 'Better play safe,' he'd said. But the moment she heard him rip open the small packet, the reality of what they were doing crashed in on her. She pulled away from him, sat up straight.

'Gen?' he'd said.

But she couldn't speak. She lowered her head and pulled the duvet under her chin. He sat up too, put his arm round her.

'Gen?' he repeated. 'What is it?'

Still she said nothing.

He must have realised then what the problem was. He slid off the bed, and disappeared to the bathroom, leaving her to get dressed. She threw on what she could find—her knickers were nowhere to be seen—and vanished into the night before Adam could follow her downstairs. She had behaved badly, she knew. Atrociously. And to a dear friend.

The mist was clearing at last and ahead of her, with a clear view of the headland and Tawelfan beach beyond, she could see a figure in a bulky waxed jacket coming towards her. As the figure drew nearer, she realised it was Christian.

He waved to her. Something made her want to run to him, like in one of those old films her mother loved so much, but she forced herself to walk slowly.

When he was close enough to read her lips, she said, 'You're the last person I expected to see out here. When did you arrive?'

'Eight o'clock this morning, having got up at the crack of dawn. I had a free day and thought I'd do a lightning visit. I needed to take some more photographs of the barn. I also thought I'd walk as far as Angel Sands, knock on your door and invite you for a cream tea.'

She was tempted, but the thought of going back to Angel Sands, where all and sundry would observe them, made her say, 'You know what, I'd prefer to walk on to Tawelfan and grab a hot dog at the kiosk.'

A breeze had sprung up, the mist had gone, and patches of delicate blue had broken through the clouds. They'd taken off their jackets and were using them to sit on as they tucked into two enormous hot dogs—onions, mustard and tomato sauce oozing from both ends.

Christian picked up one of the polystyrene cups of tea they'd bought at the kiosk, removed the lid and handed it to her. 'This feels good,' he said. 'It's great seeing you again.'

'Likewise.'

There was no need to say it, but it was just like old times. They drank their tea companionably, watching the antics of a family nearby as they set up a windbreak, the father issuing instructions to his wife while the children, three of them, fought over the contents of a large cool bag.

Following her gaze, Christian said, 'Having made the mistake of marrying you off to Adam, with a child into the bargain, would I be making another mistake to assume you aren't, or haven't been married to anyone else?'

She faced him. 'I haven't even come close to it. Oh, there have been one or two men I thought had potential, but when push came to shove, they got a hearty shove.'

Laughing, he said, 'And I've been meaning to ask you, I haven't seen your mother. How is she?'

'For a woman going through a midlife crisis, she's having a ball.' Genevieve told him about Serena needing time out, and about the most recent letter from New Zealand. 'How are your parents? Did they ever buy that house in France?'

'They did, but Mum sold it when Dad died three years ago. Mum's health has gone downhill ever since. She's had one thing after another.'

Remembering that Christian had always been close to his parents, Genevieve said, 'I'm sorry about your dad. Will you give your mother my best wishes, when you see her next?'

'I will.' He checked his watch and said, with a sigh, 'I'm afraid I ought to be going.'

They got to their feet and Genevieve walked to Ralph's barn with Christian, where his car was parked. He threw in his jacket and exchanged his walking boots for a pair of dusty Timberlands.

'Hop in and I'll give you a lift home.'

'There's no need,' she said.

'I know there's no need, but I'd like to.'

She held her ground. 'The walk back will do me good.'

He tilted his head. 'What are you scared of, Genevieve? Get in the car and stop worrying about what other people will think.'

She squared her shoulders. 'I don't know what you're talking about.'

He held the door open. 'Yes, you do. Now get in.'

Slumping into her seat, Genevieve glanced sideways at Christian and saw he was smiling as he put the car into gear and drove off. 'How did you know?' she asked.

'That you didn't want to be seen with me? Oh, just a hunch.'

'You must think me very silly.'

'No. I'm just sorry you feel like that.'

For the rest of the short journey up to Paradise House, neither of them said anything. When they arrived, Christian switched off the engine and turned to face her. For a moment she thought he was going to kiss her. When he leaned towards her and pushed her hair away from her cheek, she said, 'Do you think that would be a good idea?'

His hand stayed where it was, pressing gently into the hollow of her neck, until slowly he lowered it. 'You're right,' he said. 'It would be a mistake, and not just because of our history.'

'What other reason could there be?'

'A very good one. Her name's Caroline.'

Nattie had been in the kitchen with Lily-Rose when Genevieve had come in from waving Christian off. Perhaps because she needed to confide in someone—even her hostile sister, who was still bristling from

Genevieve's earlier loss of temper—she had stupidly blurted out what he had just shared with her.

'And if he has a girlfriend,' Nattie continued now, in the utility room, 'why has he been down here sniffing round you?' Behind her, Lily-Rose was sitting at the kitchen table waggling a paintbrush in a jam jar of cloudy water.

'You have such a way with words, don't you?' Genevieve said quietly, conscious she didn't want her niece to hear their conversation. 'All we've been doing is catching up with one another. Nothing more.'

'He hurt you once before, Gen, I'd hate to see it happen again. And I notice you haven't answered my question. If he has a girlfriend, why would he want to be so pally with you?'

Genevieve picked up a laundry basket full of towels, to rest it on her hip. 'Oh, don't be ridiculous. Just look at Adam and me. Sometimes I think you live in a totally different world from the rest of us. Now, I have things to do, like putting these towels on the line. Unless you'd like to do it.' She was almost out of the door, wishing the reference to Adam hadn't proved her sister's point exactly, when Nattie called after her.

'By the way, Adam called for you. Twice in fact. I told him to lay off, that the last thing you needed was a nuisance caller.'

Eleven o'clock the next morning, following breakfast, Genevieve was tidying the dining room with Donna's help.

'I came here looking for a new life,' Donna said, gathering the pots of homemade jam and marmalade and adding them to her tray, 'but I never thought I'd fall in love. Not at my age.'

'So it's love, then, is it? You and Tubby?'

'Either that or we're both in lust!' She let rip with a husky laugh.

Whatever misgivings Genevieve might have had about Donna working at Paradise House had long since been replaced with a real fondness. She hadn't had an easy life, but she was always cheerful and positive.

Some time later, when they were halfway through making the beds and cleaning the bathrooms, Genevieve heard the doorbell. She ran downstairs to answer it. It was the florist, Rhys Williams, who had twice delivered flowers for Polly. He greeted Genevieve warmly, while handing over a bouquet of pale pink roses.

'Seems like I'm always here. Whoever the admirers are, keep them coming; I'll be able to retire early at this rate.'

Genevieve took the flowers through to the guest sitting-room and put them on the piano. They had to be for Polly. But she couldn't resist a peep at the label. *Dear Genevieve, sorry for what I very nearly did. Please forgive an old friend . . . if you can.*

Well, that did it! Now she *had* to apologise to Adam. It was only right to summon every scrap of her courage and face him.

That evening, when she could see the lights on in Adam's house across the bay and knew he was at home, Genevieve told her father she was slipping out for a few minutes.

She took with her a gift of her own making; a lemon meringue pie, which she knew was one of Adam's favourite desserts. He looked as awkward as she felt when he opened the door to her. She thrust the foil package towards him.

'It should be humble pie, but I thought you'd prefer lemon meringue laced with a double helping of whipped apologies.'

He closed the door after her. 'Come on through to the kitchen and I'll make us some coffee.'

'Actually, a large glass of wine would be better.'

It was warm enough to sit and have a drink outside. The sky had grown darker, insects hovered in the air and the sea surged in the bay.

'I'm glad you felt able to see me, Gen. I'd hate for anything to come between us.'

'I know; I feel exactly the same.'

He shook his head. 'I bet you don't. I bet you feel used. As though I tried to take advantage of you the other night.' He took a large gulp of wine. 'It . . . it's difficult to explain, but it sort of felt right with you. It made me realise how good it must be to have sex with someone you really care about. You know, to experience the whole package.'

She reached out and touched his arm. 'Oh, Adam. I'm sorry that it turned out the way it did. But for the sake of our friendship, we have to put it behind us.'

He looked up. 'I can, if you can.'

'Good,' she said resolutely. 'So no more embarrassment?'

'And no more hiding from me?'

'It's a deal.' Relieved, she said, 'By the way, you're looking good this evening. Have you been shopping?'

'I took your advice. I had to go to Swansea this afternoon, so I scooped up a load of new shirts and trousers.'

'The blue shirt looks great. The colour matches your eyes.'

He drained his glass and looked glum. 'And for whose benefit?'

'Hey, that doesn't sound like the Adam I know and love.'

'Yeah, well, it's been a strange couple of days, one way or another. Anyway, no more feeling sorry for myself.' A smile appeared on his face. 'I reckon I might never be allowed the opportunity again, so I'm going to say it now, Gen. You've got a great body, you know. *Very* sexy. I had no idea you had such good legs, either.'

He'd nearly knocked the breath out of her. She blushed and sat back in her chair, arms folded.

'Don't scowl at me, Gen. It's true. I don't think you have any idea how attractive you are. I can quite understand why your old boyfriend couldn't keep his eyes off you when he was down here. And why he's come back so soon. I saw the pair of you on the cliff path yesterday morning.'

'Adam Kellar, have you nothing better to do than spy on your neighbours? And what about all that mist? You couldn't possibly have seen us.'

'Binoculars are a wonderful invention. You should try them.' Then leaning forward to top up her wine, he said, 'So how's it going between the two of you? The old magic still there?'

'I think I preferred it when you were miserable and contrite,' she muttered. 'At least you didn't poke and pry.'

'Answer the question, Miss Huffy-Pants. Which reminds me, you left a pair here the other night. They're washed and ready for you to take home. Unless you want me to keep them as a souvenir?'

She blushed again. 'You realise that you're being quite insufferable?'

'Another few glasses of this Merlot and I might show just how insufferable I can be. Now, tell me, has he made a move on you?'

Genevieve pictured the scene in Christian's car. She decided to be honest with Adam. 'I think it did occur to him to try to kiss me, just to see what it would be like, but fortunately he thought better of it.' She explained about the girlfriend back home.

'And how did you feel when he said that? Were you disappointed? Relieved? Hurt? Or maybe plain old angry?'

'A bit of all those things,' she said, after taking a sip of wine. 'But I'm a big girl now and if there's a girlfriend on the scene, he's out of bounds.'

'And if the girlfriend becomes history? Does that bring him within range?'

'As I said, I'm a big girl. I can handle the likes of an old flame curious to take a trip down memory lane. I'm not in the least bit interested in pursuing that myself.' It was time to change the subject. 'Now then,' she said, 'before I forget why I came, I must thank you for the flowers.'

He gave her a blank look. 'Sorry, I'm not with you. What flowers?'

'You know, the roses. They came this morning.'

The blank expression was replaced with a slow smile. 'Remind me what the card said.'

Annoyed that he was playing games with her, she said, 'The wording went something like, "Dear Genevieve, sorry for what I very nearly did. Please forgive an old friend . . . if you can."'

Adam looked at her steadily. 'Like I said, the guy couldn't keep his eyes off you.'

Granny Baxter seemed intent on turning Angel Cottage on its head and giving it a good shake. Convinced that the mice plaguing her kitchen had now taken up residence in the dusty confines of the under-stairs cupboard, she was issuing orders to Genevieve and her father.

'Careful where you stand, you might step on one!' And, 'Try not to make too much noise; we need to take them by surprise.'

The 'mouse thing', as it had become known, was close to being an obsession with Gran. Every conversation anyone had with her was punctuated with some new complaint. The mice were either keeping her awake at night with their squeaky cacophony in the chimney breast, or they were shredding her nerves with their prolonged silences. Either way, their presence was driving Gran mad. Yet it was difficult to use the word 'presence' because, as yet, no one had had an actual sighting. Other than Gran, no one had even heard so much as a squeak.

Deep down, Genevieve was concerned. If Gran was beginning to imagine things, then perhaps it was their responsibility to find out why. Right now Genevieve would give anything to see a family of mice trotting across the sitting-room carpet.

She was just wondering which one of them would be brave enough to broach the subject, when her grandmother said, 'And I hope you're going to do exactly what Genevieve thinks you should do.'

Uncertain which way the conversation was about to go, Genevieve looked anxiously at her father.

'And what would that be?' he said.

'Doing something about you and Serena, of course.'

It should have been a relief to see Gran revert so quickly to her normal self, but Genevieve flinched on her father's behalf.

'And if you leave it much later, Daddy Dean, you'll go to rack and ruin. No, don't look like that. I'm only speaking the truth. Which reminds me, you're beginning to bear an uncanny resemblance to that silly man on the television.'

'And which silly man would that be?' Dad's voice was tight.

'Oh, you know. The one who waves his arms about a lot.' Gran screwed up her eyes. 'Oh dear, whatever is his name? It sounds like dog. Something dog. Dog. Ken Dodd! That's who you remind me of.'

Genevieve stifled a laugh but her father looked offended.

'You do!' Gran persisted. 'When was the last time you had your hair cut? Look at it; it's sticking up all over your head. You need to make an appointment with Debs and get yourself tidied up, my boy. Or what will Serena think when you fly to Australia to sweep her off her feet?'

'Serena's in New Zealand, Mum. And I don't know where you've got this notion that I'm setting foot on any kind of an aeroplane.' He got to his feet and looked at his reflection in the mirror above the fireplace. 'I don't look anything like Ken Dodd.'

Gran made a small grunting sound. 'If you don't go and see her, it might well turn out to be the biggest mistake of your life. It's time you brought that wife of yours home where she belongs.'

Taking her cue, Genevieve said, 'Gran's right, Dad. You can't go on as you are. I really think you should go and see Mum. If you don't, she might start to think you don't want her back.'

In a gesture of despair, he raked his hands wildly through his hair. 'But how can I compete with this old friend who's giving her such a new and exciting time? What have I got to offer?'

'There!' cried Gran. 'Now you really do look like Ken Dodd.'

By the middle of July, no one needed a weather forecaster to tell them they were experiencing a heatwave. In the garden at Paradise House, Genevieve stood looking down onto the crowded beach. 'Who needs to go abroad when the weather's like this?' all their guests were saying.

She had now started cooking evening meals for those who wanted them and, after a two-week trial period, it was proving to be a success. And Adam had been on at Genevieve again about putting her supposed skills to better use.

'But if I take on too much, I won't be able to run Paradise House.'

'And is that what you want to do for the rest of your life?' he'd asked.

Christian had asked her much the same question during one of their email exchanges. It was three weeks since she had penned a note to him, thanking him for the roses, and he'd written back a week later, giving her his email address. Her answer to his question had been vague. Paradise House had been her parents' dream or, more specifically, her mother's, but sometime soon she knew she would have to chase her own. She did have something in mind, but until the right opportunity arose, she didn't want to tell anyone about it.

Walking back up the garden and into the house, Genevieve switched on her computer. The flashing white envelope on her screen showed that she had just one email waiting for her: it was from Christian. His mother was in hospital. Cancer. 'Mum's having all the treatment, but I know her heart's not in it. It makes me so angry that I can't do anything to stop the pain or the inevitable.' Genevieve wished she was better with words and could say something incisive and helpful. She wrote back immediately, offering what words of encouragement she could.

The house was empty so, switching on the answering machine, she walked through the village to Angel Cottage, to see if there was any shopping Gran needed doing.

After the 'mouse thing', to Genevieve's astonishment, her father had broached the subject of Gran seeing a doctor. Her reaction, unsurprisingly, was to hit the roof and tell anyone who would listen that there was nothing wrong with her.

'It's so embarrassing,' Nattie complained. 'She's making out that we're trying to have her put away.'

'But no one would believe it,' said Polly. 'Everyone knows that's the last thing we'd do.'

'Don't you be so sure,' their father muttered from behind his newspaper. 'The way I feel, I might just lock her up myself.' He was still smarting from the Ken Dodd comparison.

Now, Genevieve knocked on Gran's front door.

She knocked again. And again. And still Gran didn't appear. Nothing for it, Genevieve thought, and took the unprecedented step of using the key she'd been entrusted with.

'Gran?' she called out anxiously, shutting the door behind her. 'It's me, Genevieve.'

The house was refreshingly cool and still after the heat outside. It was also unnaturally quiet. She poked her head round the sitting-room door, then went through to the kitchen. Still no sign of Gran.

When she stood on the small landing, she thought she heard something. 'Gran?' She strained to hear the noise again.

Yes. There it was. It was coming from the bathroom. A faint moaning noise. She pushed open the door.

Her first thought was that subconsciously this was what she'd always dreaded . . . finding Gran dead.

The doctor saw himself out, leaving them to hover round the bed like actors in a second-rate television drama.

'If you're trying to annoy me,' Gran grumbled, 'you're doing a good job of it.'

'Good, I'm glad we're annoying you,' said Nattie, 'because you scared the hell out of us!'

'That's enough, Natalie,' her father murmured. Pale-faced and anxious, he dropped into the chair nearest Gran's bed. He rubbed his hands over his face. 'You're sure you're OK?' he said.

The old lady drew her eyebrows together. 'Please, I wish you'd all stop fussing. I'm as fit as a fiddle. Now, is there any chance of a cup of tea, or am I denied that basic human right?'

Genevieve and Polly volunteered for the job. In the kitchen, while they put together a tray of tea things, Genevieve said, 'She's at her most imperious when she's hiding from the truth, isn't she?'

'You're right. Beneath it all, she must be as shocked as the rest of us. But how are *you* feeling? It must have been awful finding her like that.'

'I'm fine,' Genevieve said, conscious that she was lying in the same glib way her grandmother just had. When she'd found Gran slumped in a heap on the bathroom floor—her hand still clutching a J-cloth and a puddle of pine fresh cleaner on the carpet—she'd turned the old lady over, seen the gash where she must have cracked the side of her head on the basin as she fell, and was about to rush downstairs to phone for an ambulance, when Gran had opened her eyes.

'Gran! Can you hear me?'

Her grandmother had winced and raised a hand to her head. 'Why are you shouting, Genevieve?' Then, looking about her, 'What are we doing here? Why are we on the bathroom floor?'

The calmness in her voice told Genevieve an ambulance wasn't necessary, but a doctor was. After she'd helped her grandmother to her feet and got her to sit on the edge of the bed—lying *in* bed was out of the question: 'Don't be absurd, Genevieve, you're making such a drama out of it!'—she phoned the local surgery. Then, remembering she'd put the answering machine on, she called her father on his mobile.

Dad arrived within minutes, followed hotly by Polly and Nattie with Lily-Rose. Finally Dr Shepherd joined the throng and, after a few minutes alone with Gran, he pronounced his patient shaken but in reasonably good health.

'From what she says, it seems she had a blackout,' he told them. 'Her blood pressure's a little higher than I'd like, but I don't see any point in causing alarm by whisking her into hospital for exhaustive tests. I suggest we leave things be and see how she gets on over the coming days.'

Part of Genevieve had wanted to disagree with the doctor and demand that the exhaustive tests he dismissed so lightly were carried out. But now, pouring boiling water into Gran's old brown Betty teapot, she saw that perhaps it would be better to keep an eye on her at home.

Polly went ahead of her to open the bedroom door, while Genevieve carried the tea upstairs. As she set the tray on Gran's bedside table her father said, 'Despite a difference of opinion, your grandmother will be having a guest to stay. Me.' Ignoring Gran's scowl, he added, 'It seems the easiest way, so long as you can handle things, Genevieve?'

'I'll manage perfectly.'

During breakfast the following morning, Genevieve had to give Nattie her due; without their father around, she was definitely trying to be more helpful. Her first negative comment of the day came now as she stood by the back door trying to escape the heat of the kitchen.

'It beats me how that lot can still tuck away a fry-up in this weather. You'd think they'd want nothing more than a chilled glass of orange juice and half a grapefruit.' Then turning back to Lily-Rose, who was sitting at the table and eating paper-thin slices of apple, she said, 'Pumpkin-Pie, how about a little paddle down at the beach when your Auntie Genvy's finished with me?'

Poking her finger through one of the slices of apple, Lily-Rose looked at Genevieve. 'Will you come as well?'

'I'd love to,' Genevieve said, spooning hot oil over the eggs in the spitting pan, 'but I need to go to the supermarket to do a big shop.'

'Mummy could help you.'

Before Genevieve could think of a suitable reply, the phone rang. She lifted the receiver.

'Genevieve, is that you?'

She hadn't spoken to him in a while, but recognised Jonjo's voice at once. 'Hello, Jonjo. If you're hoping to speak to Polly, she's left for work.'

'I know; I've just spoken to her on her mobile. She said I needed to speak to you. The thing is, I know it's last-minute stuff, but is there any chance of a couple of rooms being available this coming weekend? Christian and I are planning to come down to meet the builders and it's the only time we can both make it, assuming of course that Christian's mother doesn't get any worse.'

Genevieve checked the diary to make sure no one else had taken a booking without letting her know. 'If you don't mind sharing, we've just had a cancellation.'

'That's brilliant! But tell me it's not a double bed. The thought of sleeping with Mr May doesn't appeal.'

'No, it isn't. You're quite safe, it's a twin-bedded room.'

'Better and better. Now, depending on the traffic, we aim to be with you around lunchtime, is that OK?'

'Yes. One of us should be here to meet you. Probably me.'

'Oh, and before I forget, Christian says "Hi".'

'How's he doing, Jonjo? He was always so close to his parents.'

'He's coping pretty well, but I think the change at the weekend will do him good. Splitting up from his girlfriend hasn't helped either.'

This was news to Genevieve. 'When did that happen? He never mentioned anything in his emails.'

There was a silence and for a second Genevieve thought they'd been cut off. 'Are you still there, Jonjo?'

'Er . . . yes. Look, forget I said anything. If Christian hasn't mentioned it to you, it's certainly not my place to talk about it behind his back. See you on Saturday. Thanks so much, Genevieve.'

Putting the receiver down, Genevieve was left with Adam's words echoing in her ears: *And if the girlfriend becomes history? Does that bring him within range?*

It might do, her treacherous heart whispered.

But her head had other ideas. No! She told herself firmly. She would not fall in love with Christian all over again.

That afternoon, she took a quiche and some ready-made salad she'd bought at the supermarket down to Gran's so that her father wouldn't have to worry about cooking an evening meal.

'How's she behaving?' Genevieve asked when he let her in at Angel Cottage.

'Like a badly behaved child. I'm nearly out of patience. I've threatened her with another visit from Dr Shepherd if she doesn't do as she's told. Any news from up the hill?'

She told him about the conversation she'd had with Jonjo, about him and Christian booking in.

'And you're happy with that, for . . . for Christian to stay?'

She was touched her father still had difficulty saying Christian's name. 'Christian and I have moved on, Dad.'

'Good! Well, I've been doing some thinking and have reached an important decision. As soon as I think your gran can be trusted to be on her own again, I'm going to New Zealand to see your mother.'

'You are? Really?'

'Yes, I'm going to do what I should have done weeks ago. I'm going to try to make her come home. I've buried my head, because I couldn't bear the thought of losing her altogether. But it's a risk I have to take. I see that now. Some people say we only have one chance to get things right. Well, I disagree. I think if we're lucky, we get two.'

This was nothing short of radical stuff coming from her father. She never dreamed she'd hear him talk so openly. Her hunch that he might resolve matters himself had been right, after all.

Above their heads, as if to add a musical flourish to his words, came a noise followed by the tinkling of a bell.

'Let me go to Gran,' Genevieve said. 'You've earned a break.'

When she stood in the doorway of Gran's bedroom, she saw that the old lady, head slumped to one side on the pillows, was asleep—the sound had been the bell falling out of her hand and landing on the floor. Genevieve crept into the room and was just placing the bell on the bedside table when her grandmother stirred.

'Sorry, Gran, I didn't mean to disturb you.'

Gran straightened her neck and looked at Genevieve through sleepy eyes. 'It's a bit late to be sorry, Serena. But it's better late than never.'

'Gran, it's me, Genevieve.'

'Genevieve? Oh, I've no idea where she is. She's always so busy these days.' The old lady yawned and, closing her eyes, she leaned back against the pillows. 'Would you mind closing the door after you, Serena? I think I'll snatch a quick forty winks. I can't think why I'm so tired.'

When she joined her father down in the kitchen and saw the look on his face—the upbeat look of a man who had, at last, decided to act—Genevieve knew she couldn't tell him of the conversation she'd just had. He would put off going to see Serena. Later, as she walked home in the bright sunshine, she consoled herself with the thought that Gran was just tired. It was perfectly understandable that she could be confused.

The next morning, in a hurry to get all the chores done, Genevieve found herself thwarted at every turn. The telephone kept ringing and Donna was in one of her turbo-charged chatty moods.

'So what do you think, Genevieve? Is it a good idea that will go down well in the village? If we make a reasonable fist of it, Tubby reckons it might become an annual event. A tradition.'

Realising she hadn't been paying attention to Donna, Genevieve looked up from the pillow she was knocking into shape. 'I'm sorry, Donna, what were you saying?'

'You OK? You seem sort of distracted. Still worried about your gran?'

'A bit,' she said noncommittally. In fact, she'd lain in bed for hours last night worrying about her grandmother. 'But tell me what you were saying. What does Tubby think might become an annual event?'

'We've had this idea of putting on a charity talent contest at the Salvation Arms. You know the kind of thing, *Stars In Their Eyes*, people dressing up and belting out tunes we all know and love. There'd be an entrance fee and any money we raise, after giving out some prizes, will go to a local charity. What do you think? Will people go for it?'

'Oh, I should think there are any number of people in Angel Sands who'd go for it like a shot.'

'So what about you? Will you take part?'

'Me? Good Lord, no! I can't hold a note to save my life.'

Donna laughed. 'That's the point. People would pay good money to hear you try.'

'No way! Absolutely not.'

'Is that your final word?'

'Yes. But I'll help in any other way you want.'

When she walked down into the village an hour later, she was doing her usual eyes-fixed-on-the-pavement routine as she passed Debonhair, when a loud tap-tap-tap on the glass forced her to glance up. Brandishing her scissors and comb, Debs was standing over a man sitting in the chair nearest the window. It was a moment before Genevieve recognised her father. She went inside. The tiled floor around him was covered with a mat of thick grey hair.

He said, 'I only asked for a trim and look what she's done!'

'Get on with you!' Debs laughed. 'I'm giving him a make-over, just what he needs.' Then to Genevieve, she said, 'Has Donna told you about the talent contest she and Tubby want to put on? I've offered to do everyone's hair, and if they want wigs, I can get hold of them, no problem. How about you, Gen? Are you going to kick up your heels and show us the real you?'

'Oh, I think you all know the real me,' Genevieve said.

Debs winked. 'A bit of loosening up never hurt anyone.' Her voice was silky smooth. 'By the way, how's that young man of yours? I hear he's coming here again at the weekend. Staying up at your place, too. That'll be cosy for you, won't it?'

When, finally, Genevieve managed to get away, she walked on to Angel Cottage and let herself in. The sound of the television told her that Gran wasn't where she ought to be.

'I thought you were supposed to be in bed,' she chastised her grandmother, at the same time glad to see that there was plenty of colour back in her face. 'I've just spoken to Dad, and he said you'd promised to be good while he was having his hair done.'

'Your father, baloney! That man is getting above himself and if he doesn't watch his step . . . oh, be quiet a minute, it's *Bargain Hunt* and the auction's about to start. Come and sit down with me, Genevieve. Then I'll make us a nice cup of tea.'

Genevieve. Not Serena! So it had only been a one-off memory lapse. All the anxiety of last night faded, and Genevieve sat on the sofa with her grandmother. She put her arm round the old lady and kissed her.

'What's that for?'

'For being your usual self.'

'And who else would I be?'

The strain of cooking an evening meal and then getting up early to cook breakfast was taking its toll on Genevieve. During peak season, there was no chance of a lie-in, something she felt she badly needed right now. But given the choice, she'd rather be working long hours in Angel Sands than anywhere else.

She was making the most of a lull, relaxing on the steps outside the guest sitting-room, watching Nattie read to Lily-Rose on the lawn. Polly was playing the piano. It was a restful, harmonious piece she'd heard her sister play before. Despite being so tired, she felt calm: Gran was back to normal, bossing them all about with renewed vigour, and Dad, sporting his new haircut, was making arrangements to go and see Mum.

And on top of that, she was looking forward to seeing Christian and Jonjo. They wouldn't be arriving for another two hours, but she had everything ready.

Stretching her legs in front of her and lifting her long cotton skirt above her knees, she thought of what Adam had said about her having great legs. For years she had envied Polly her long, graceful legs and delicate features, and Nattie her straight up-and-down, tomboy shape. Now, eventually, she had come to terms with the way she looked. She took after her mother, with what Serena called a golden-age Hollywood hourglass figure.

Behind her, in the sitting room, Polly had started playing something else, something brisk and robust. She closed her eyes, and before long, she slept. She dreamed she was floating on her back in the sea, the waves lapping around her, caressing her lightly, but best of all, her mother was there too, at her side. It was a lovely dream and when the sound of an approaching car shooed it away, she opened her eyes reluctantly. Then she heard footsteps and a familiar voice.

'Hel-*lo!* Anyone at home?'

Jonjo and Christian? Already? She checked her watch. It was almost twelve. She stood up in time to see them coming round the corner.

'You're very early. Was there less traffic than you expected?'

'We decided to set off earlier than planned,' said Jonjo, 'in case the roads ground to a halt.' He cocked his ear and smiled. 'Is that the light of my life serenading my arrival?' Without giving Genevieve a chance to respond, he walked the length of the terrace and stepped inside the house to the guest sitting-room. The music stopped abruptly.

'If I start apologising for him now,' Christian said with a weary shrug, 'I could end up spending the entire weekend doing it. Can you just accept that he's a lunatic and humour him?'

'Come off it, Christian, he fits in perfectly with us Baxters. Anyway, officially you're both guests so I have to humour the pair of you.'

While Polly showed Christian and Jonjo up to their room, Genevieve prepared baguettes filled with smoked mackerel pâté and fresh crab, and reflected on Christian's appearance. Fatigue was etched around his eyes. The strain of his mother's illness was clearly affecting him deeply.

'I thought we'd eat in the garden,' Genevieve said, when Polly came into the kitchen. 'How are our guests settling in?'

'Jonjo loved the view.'

'I bet he did! Now, will you give me a hand taking the lunch outside? Oh, and where are Nattie and Lily-Rose?'

'They've gone down to see Gran.'

'And Dad?'

'Helping Tubby to creosote his garden fence.'

Genevieve wrinkled her nose. 'What a revolting job for a day like today. OK, you take the plates and cutlery and I'll manage the tray.'

They ate their lunch in the private area of garden in the shade. Jonjo did most of the talking. He raved about Christian's designs for his new home and boasted that it would be the best house in the area. Occasionally Christian would roll his eyes and exchange a smile with Genevieve, but his input to the conversation was minimal. When they'd finished eating, he offered to help Genevieve clear away.

'There's no need, there's hardly anything to do,' she said.

'But if I don't move, I'll nod off. Besides, I'm under orders from the boss to make myself scarce.' He nodded in Jonjo's direction.

Leaving Polly and Jonjo alone, they went inside the house. They worked in silence at first, then she asked him about his mother.

'She's had a run of good days,' he said, 'which is why I agreed to come down. But it won't last, the doctor says. The prognosis is weeks rather than months.'

'Oh, Christian, I'm so sorry. I don't know how I'd cope if I were in your shoes.' She told him about Gran and how worried she'd been over her fall. 'I know it's nothing compared to what you're going through.'

He disagreed. 'You're probably as close to her as you are to your parents. She's always been there for you. You know, I always envied you your family.'

'And I always envied you your self-contained unit of three.'

He turned and looked out of the window. She heard him say, 'And then there was one.'

At six o'clock Christian and Jonjo returned from Ralph's barn after a lengthy but successful meeting with the builder.

Jonjo asked Polly to go out with him for the evening and Christian said he'd eat whatever Genevieve wanted to cook, on the condition he ate in the kitchen with her.

'Not a good idea,' she said, 'Nattie will be around. Tell you what; we'll eat after everyone else, in the garden. Agreed?'

Smiling, he said, 'I don't remember you driving such a hard bargain.'

She cooked him sea bass with polenta and a salad with sweet balsamic dressing. At midnight, they were still sitting in the garden. The night air was heavy and soft, a faint breeze skimmed her bare arms, and the incoming tide, slowly creeping up the moon-washed shore, rattled the loose pebbles in the sand.

'This is so good,' Christian said simply, gazing out at the moon trailing its silvery reflection across the flat sea. He turned to look at her, his eyes dark and intense.

'It's one of the reasons I came back,' she replied.

'What were the others?'

'You don't want to know.'

She could have told him about the robbery, about George and Cecily, but decided against it. She didn't want to think of anything that would spoil the moment.

The next morning, Jonjo was off as soon as he'd finished his breakfast, and Genevieve sat with Christian while he ate the Paradise Special— eggs, bacon, sausage, black pudding, fried bread, tomatoes, mushrooms, and waffles to finish.

'I feel very rude eating in front of you,' Christian said. 'Why don't you have something to keep me company?'

'If it makes you feel better, I'll pinch one of your waffles.'

'Is that all? How about a sausage? Or some bacon?'

'No. You need building up. You've lost weight, Christian.'

'It's not been deliberate, I just haven't had time to eat. I've been working all day, then spending every evening with Mum. I've arranged for the hospital to text me on my mobile if . . . if there's an emergency.'

'How is she?'

'She says she's OK. But we both know that's a lie. She tells me what she thinks I want to hear. But I'm lousy at pretence. I like to be honest and play it straight.'

'You should be more like us Baxters. We've mastered the art of denial.'

'Is that what you did when you were . . . ' He stopped stirring his tea and looked awkward.

'It's OK, Christian, you can refer to my starve, binge or bust days without embarrassing me.' Then, changing the subject, she said, 'Did you know Jonjo's planning a picnic today?'

The guest list for the picnic kept growing.

Eventually they set off, picking up Gran on the way, and drove in two cars to Tawelfan beach, chosen above Angel Sands by Gran, who insisted that Jonjo show her where he'd be living, even though she was perfectly well acquainted with Ralph's barn. Polly's comment that Gran was quite taken with Jonjo was a massive understatement; she was utterly enamoured.

'Such a delightful young man,' she whispered in Genevieve's ear, after they'd bounced along the rutted, sun-dried track towards the barn and were unloading the boot of Jonjo's Discovery. 'So handsome. If Polly has any sense she'll hang on to him. They'd have the most beautiful children.'

Apart from Gran, they all carried something—lightweight chairs, the hamper, the cool bag of drinks, towels, two parasols, a fishing net, a bucket and spade and an inflatable dolphin, which Lily-Rose carried like an enormous baby in her arms. As they made the trek through the sand dunes to the beach, Genevieve was reminded of long-ago picnics with their father leading the way. On this occasion he was at the rear of the group, walking slowly with Gran, a supporting hand discreetly resting under her elbow.

As they'd expected, the beach was busy. They found themselves a suitable plot and began setting up camp. Quick as a flash, Lily-Rose stripped down to her fluorescent pink bikini bottoms and said she was going for a paddle.

'Oh, not yet,' yawned Nattie. 'Can't you wait ten minutes?'

'That's OK,' Genevieve said, 'I'll take her. Where's the suncream?'

Her sister tossed her the bottle. 'Thanks, Gen. I owe you.'

Slipping off his deck shoes and pulling his T-shirt over his head, Christian said, 'Mind if I come along?' He left his mobile with Jonjo and the three of them set off for the distant water's edge, Lily-Rose scampering on ahead, a castle-shaped plastic bucket swinging like a handbag from her wrist. They soon caught up with her and, holding her wrap-around skirt above her knees, Genevieve ventured into the first rush of shallow water.

'Look! *Look!*'

Both Genevieve and Christian bent down to see what Lily-Rose was pointing at: it was a starfish, about the size of the little girl's hand. 'Can I have it? Can I put it in my bucket to take home?'

It was obviously dead. 'I don't see why not,' Genevieve said.

The little girl picked it up and carefully put it into her bucket. 'I'm going to show Mummy my lucky starfish,' she said proudly. She ran off excitedly, hopping skilfully round the pebbles and the people on the beach. They watched her until she was safely with the family.

'Shall we walk to the rocks?' Christian said.

They walked along the shore. As they approached the rocks, a group of girls who had been sunbathing on them, swam off. Dangling their legs over the side of the sun-warmed rocks, Genevieve touched his arm lightly. He turned to face her.

'This is where I pushed you into the water, isn't it, the day we met?'

'It's also where I thought you were the nicest, prettiest girl I'd ever met.'

'Your memory must be playing tricks. I was never a pretty child.'

He shook his head. 'I'm not going to argue with you, Genevieve, so be quiet and accept the compliment.'

His words, said so forcibly, amused her. She swirled the water round with her feet, enjoying the sensation of her toes being pushed apart.

'Genevieve?'

She turned back to him. 'Yes?'

'Do you remember me saying at breakfast that I like to be honest and play it straight?'

'I do.'

'Well, the thing is,' he continued, 'I'm not in a relationship any more. Caroline and I . . . well, I've ended things with her. I just wanted you to know that.'

Genevieve didn't bother to feign surprise. Instead, she said, 'And the reason?'

He took a deep breath. 'It wouldn't have been fair to go on seeing her, not when—' He broke off and swallowed. 'Genevieve, you must have realised that ever since our paths crossed again, I haven't been able to get you out of my head.' He turned away. 'I promised myself I wouldn't say anything, but I guess I'm being selfish. I want you to know how I feel. More than that, I want to know how you feel, too.'

She touched his leg to make him look at her. 'Perhaps it's nothing more than a desire to relive the past.'

'No. It's more than that. There's something between us. Something that will always link us.'

She was surprised by his vehemence, and by her calm reaction.

'So where does that leave us?' he said. He looked and sounded wretched.

'Precariously placed, I'd say.'

He frowned and stared hard at her lips. 'What placed?'

'Precariously,' she repeated, trying to speak more distinctly. 'We either do nothing and go on wondering for the rest of our lives what might have been, or we throw caution to the wind and you try kissing me.' So much for her head ruling her heart!

His face softened instantly. 'I think I favour the second choice.'

'Me too.'

He had just raised his hand to her neck, and tilted his head to lean into her, when he hesitated and drew back. Following his gaze, over her shoulder, she turned to see Jonjo hurrying towards them, waving Christian's mobile.

'I'm sorry, Christian,' he said, 'but it's your mother. The hospital's just been in touch. We need to get going.'

PART IV

CHRISTIAN'S MOTHER DIED three days later. She spent the last thirty-six hours of her life in a coma with Christian at her side. Saddened by his loss, Genevieve was touched when Jonjo phoned to say that Christian wanted her to be at the funeral. Polly too, to keep her company. 'There are plenty of ageing rellies he hardly knows,' Jonjo had told her, 'but no one who really matters to him.'

Now, as Genevieve headed towards Ludlow, happy memories of staying with Christian all those years ago, came flooding back. Following the directions Christian had emailed, Genevieve turned into a country lane. The house was just as Genevieve remembered it: a pretty, half-timbered, thatched cottage. Genevieve parked the car and nudged Polly.

'We're here, Polly. Wakey, wakey.' Having been up since five, Genevieve would have liked the opportunity to doze as well. Determined in some small way to help Christian, she had offered to take care of feeding the funeral guests and had put together a modest buffet, which was in the boot.

Leaving Polly to stir herself, Genevieve got out of the car and went round to the boot, but before she'd got it open, she heard footsteps. Christian was coming towards her, dressed in a dark suit with a white shirt, open at the neck. She had never seen him in a suit before and at once thought how dazzlingly handsome he looked. Her heart fluttered and she felt a tightening in her chest. Without a word passing between them, they embraced.

The funeral was to be held in a small local church. The procession of cars moved sedately along the narrow country lanes. Following behind in Jonjo's Discovery, Genevieve sat in the back and stared out at the flowering hedgerows; she left Polly and Jonjo to their murmured conversation in front.

By the time Jonjo had found somewhere to park, they were the last to arrive. They slipped in at the back of the crowded church, but within seconds Christian appeared and said he'd saved them a seat at the front.

'Please,' he said, taking hold of Genevieve's hand, 'I don't want to be alone.'

The service was much the same as any other funeral she had been to:

hymns were sung, prayers were spoken, emotions were strained. But then the vicar asked Christian to step forward to say a few words about his mother. From his jacket pocket, he pulled out a piece of paper.

'All mothers have an extraordinary capacity to love and to encourage,' he began, 'and mine was no exception. She taught me to love and respect others as I would want to be loved and respected. She—' His voice cracked and he briefly closed his eyes. Genevieve's throat clenched and she willed him to carry on. 'She was a constant beacon of love and hope. I shall miss her more than I can say.'

Genevieve felt, rather than saw, Christian take his seat beside her. She turned to face him and mouthed the words, 'That was beautiful.'

He nodded and squeezed her hand. 'Thank you.'

He thanked her again when they were back at the house and the last of the guests were leaving.

'You've been such a help,' Christian said as she moved round the sitting room with a tray, gathering up plates and glasses.

'It's nothing,' she said. 'Canapés aren't difficult to make.'

He took the tray. 'But you must have been up so early to make them.'

'I was. But I shall sleep well tonight.'

'You are staying, aren't you?'

'If the offer's still on. Yes.'

Jonjo and Polly came into the room. Jonjo said, 'I blame you, Genevieve. If the food hadn't been so good, we would have been shot of that lot hours ago.'

Christian smiled—the first time he had that day—and said, 'I don't know about the rest of you, but I've had enough. I vote we leave the rest of the tidying up till later. Let's go and sit in the garden with a bottle of wine.'

It was only ten o'clock when Genevieve started to yawn. 'It's no good,' she apologised, stifling yet another yawn, 'I have to go to bed.'

Everyone else agreed that they were tired too, that it had been a long day. After locking up and turning out the lights, they went upstairs. Christian opened the door of the first room and told Polly that it was hers. Next door was Jonjo's room, and going farther along the landing, missing out his parents' room, he said to Genevieve, 'I thought you'd like to sleep in the room you stayed in before. If you need anything, I'm in the room the other side of the bathroom.'

She didn't know how long she'd been asleep, but she awoke with a start. Footsteps. She could hear footsteps. Someone was in the house. A burglar! Her heart began to beat faster and she tried hard to keep calm. She pushed back the duvet and crept out onto the landing.

Not knowing quite how she'd got there, she found herself at the bottom of the stairs. But she couldn't hear anything other than her pulse banging like a drum inside her head. This is madness, she thought. I shouldn't be doing this. Yet still her body betrayed her and she reached for a heavy vase on the hall table as her feet carried her forward.

To the sitting room. She pushed open the door and stepped in. The French windows were open, the curtains billowing. She was right! A gust of cool air rushed at her and she knew what she had to do. She had to fetch help. She couldn't do this alone.

She turned to retrace her steps, but the sight of a shadowy figure coming into the room rooted her to the spot. The vase slipped from her hands and she screamed. But no sound came out of her mouth. The blood drained from her, her legs buckled and she fell to the ground.

Genevieve came to with a painful jolt of panicky fear and let out a cry.

Arms held her and a voice said, 'Genevieve, it's OK. It's me, Christian.'

Confused and light-headed, she tried to focus. She looked around, took in that she was lying on the sofa, that there was a lamp on, and that Christian was kneeling in front of her. She sat up with a jerk.

'Have you called the police? Did he get away?'

'No, Gen. There's no need. It was me you saw. I'm so sorry I frightened you. I couldn't sleep and—'

'No. I would have recognised you. It wasn't you. It was . . .'

He took her hands in his and rubbed them gently. 'It was dark, Gen. You couldn't see properly.'

She forced herself to listen to him, to believe what he was saying. Looking at the broken bits of china, she slowly realised that the only intruder had been the one inside her head. She covered her face with her hands. 'Oh God. I'm so sorry. I feel so—' Stupidly she began to tremble. When he took her in his arms she started to cry.

'It's OK,' he murmured. 'It's my fault, I shouldn't have scared you.' He held her close, and she cried all the more.

She had had to tell the policemen all about that dreadful night with George and Cecily, but she'd told no one else exactly what had gone on. She'd told Gran the most, but each time she had been tempted to unburden herself fully, the thought of reliving the robbery was too much and she was almost physically sick.

Now she knew that the time had come to tell someone. She didn't want to be haunted by the memories any longer. Wrapped in Christian's arms, she felt safe enough to relive the trauma. In the end, the relief at having unburdened herself was so great that Genevieve began to cry.

Christian sat with her for more than an hour, holding her, reassuring her, finally making her a drink and helping her upstairs to bed.

When she woke in the morning, feeling groggy from all the crying, she looked across the room to where Christian was sleeping soundly in a chair, covered by a blanket. She studied his face, the face she'd memorised as a teenager, the face she'd thought she'd always love. Was it possible to love him again? Was that what he wanted? More to the point, was it what *she* wanted?

Genevieve had thought for a long time that the most momentous events in her life had all taken place during the summer months.

She thought this now as she and Polly were driving home to Paradise House. Polly hadn't said anything but, judging from her radiant looks, Genevieve didn't have to be a genius to work out that her sister had spent the night with Jonjo. There had been no sign of the two of them at breakfast. After Genevieve and Christian had given up waiting for them, Christian had suggested they make the most of the early-morning sun.

'Come with me,' he said. 'There's something I want to show you.'

He led her to the bottom of the garden, to the summerhouse, the roof of which was almost hidden beneath a fairy-tale drift of pastel-pink climbing roses. Swollen flowers tumbled gloriously, their fragrance sweet on the morning air. When Christian opened the door of the summerhouse, a further fusion of smells greeted them—sun-warmed cedar wood, mildewed canvas seats, musty old garden tools. Genevieve couldn't spot anything especially worth looking at in among the clutter, but when he closed the door and came towards her, she realised exactly why he'd brought her here.

At long, long last, his face inches from hers, his hands placed either side of her face, he kissed her. It was thirteen years since they'd kissed, but everything about the soft warmth of his lips, the feel of his body pressing into hers, was the same, and she kissed him back with a desire that made him strengthen his hold on her.

'You have no idea how much I've been longing to do that,' he said, when he released her.

'Is that why we're hiding in here?'

He smiled. 'Yes. To be sure of not being interrupted.'

'I think Polly and Jonjo have got other things on their minds.'

'In that case, I'd say we owe it to ourselves to make the most of their preoccupation with each other.'

They kissed and kissed, and would have gone on doing so if the summerhouse hadn't been so hot and airless, and if Genevieve hadn't promised her father she'd get back to Paradise House that afternoon.

In the days that followed, Genevieve was filled with longing to be with Christian. In the same way that as a teenager she'd devoted hours to daydreaming of him, she was constantly distracted by thoughts of the two of them in the summerhouse.

She knew from Christian's emails that there was no chance of seeing him for the foreseeable future; he was snowed under with work as well as sorting through his mother's things. He had asked if there was any way she could get away from Paradise House so they could spend some time together, but it was peak season and everything was happening at once. The big news was that Dad was leaving immediately for New Zealand. Polly was travelling to Heathrow with him—unsurprisingly, she had agreed to go to Hong Kong with Jonjo on a business trip—and their flights were only an hour apart.

Nattie, not to be left out, had received an invitation to a school reunion and was going away for a couple of days. As usual she was expecting Genevieve to step into the breach and not only hold the fort single-handedly, but take care of Lily-Rose as well. 'Oh, please, Gen,' she wheedled. 'I can hardly take Lily-Rose with me, can I? Please say you'll have her? Now that Gran's back to normal, she could help you.'

After kissing Polly goodbye and hugging her father, Genevieve watched him climb into his Land Rover; he looked like a man on a mission, jaw set firm, shoulders squared. He was at last embarking on what had to be the most important journey he would ever make. She hoped his nerve would hold out. Thank goodness he had Polly with him.

Not long after they'd left, Nattie took Lily-Rose down to the beach and Tubby stopped by with a delivery of fruit and veg and an update on the talent contest. To his delight, tickets were flying out of the door and it was going to be a night to remember. Genevieve would have liked to talk more with him about her own contribution to the event, but she didn't have time. She had an appointment.

An hour later she was in Tenby. It took a while to find somewhere to park, then she set off for the centre of the town. Loans, Adam had told her, were two a penny. She was about to discover if that was true.

She pushed against the door of the bank and went inside. After a short wait, she was shown through to a small office where Mrs Hughes, the loans manager, would see her. A crisp-haired woman in a lightweight suit rose from the other side of the desk.

'Please, sit down. Now then, what can I do to help you, Miss Baxter?'

Genevieve opened her folder and leaned forward in her seat. She spent the next ten minutes setting out her plans in as businesslike a manner as she could manage, remembering all that Adam had told her.

An hour later, as she let the bank door close slowly behind her,

Genevieve stood on the pavement and awarded herself a small pat on the back. Things looked promising. Her next stop was just off St Julian's Street, where she had arranged to see a solicitor, Mr Saunders. Not long afterwards, she emerged from his offices and stood on the pavement in the bright sunshine. Across the busy street she saw a familiar smiling face. She waited for a break in the traffic and crossed the road.

'Adam Kellar, are you stalking me?'

'I prefer to see myself as your guardian angel. So come on, future Businesswoman of the Year, shall I take you for a celebratory drink and you tell me how it went?'

'Or, why don't we have an ice cream down on the beach.'

He looked doubtfully at his suit. 'No chance. Not even for you.'

'OK then, we'll find a nice clean bench for you to sit on.'

When they reached the harbour, they bought two 99s with all the trimmings and Adam spotted a free bench. Genevieve held his ice cream while he took off his jacket and laid it on the back of the bench.

'Why are you wearing a suit on a day like this, Adam?'

'The same reason you're dressed to impress in your cute little power number.' He indicated the skirt and jacket that Genevieve was wearing. 'Only difference is, my business was conducted over lunch.'

'So what are you up to now? Another caravan park?'

'No.' His expression serious, he said, 'Look, this is strictly between you and me, but I'm thinking of selling up.' He licked his ice-cream. 'The truth is, I need a new challenge.'

'What do you have in mind?'

'Mm . . . too soon to say. Anyway, tell me about *your* plans.'

'Nothing's definite, but I've set the wheels in motion.'

'A done deal, I'd say. If you want any help, just give me a shout.'

When Genevieve was driving home, it struck her that if Adam moved somewhere new, she would lose her closest friend.

The next morning, as soon as Genevieve had cooked the last plate of bacon and eggs and Nattie had served it, her sister was upstairs throwing a bag together for her school reunion in Cheshire.

As Genevieve scrubbed the grill pan at the sink, feeling distinctly like Cinderella, a knock at the back door announced the arrival of Gran.

'Mark my words,' she said, flopping into the nearest chair, 'we're in for an almighty storm. Probably tonight. I can feel it in my bones.' Fanning herself with one hand and wiping her forehead with the other, she added, 'There's not a breath of air out there.'

'Gran, Nattie was going to fetch you in the car. You shouldn't be rushing around in this weather, it's much too hot.'

'I'm not completely daft, Genevieve. I got a lift from . . . oh, you know, what's-his-name?' She stopped fanning herself and stared into the middle distance. 'Oh, Adam. Now then, where's Lily-Rose?'

'She's upstairs with Nattie, helping her to pack. And talking of packing, where are your overnight things? If you can manage the stairs, I thought you could have Nattie's room.'

Gran gave her a withering look. 'Of course I can manage the stairs. Really, Genevieve, I'm growing tired of being treated like an old dear. Ever since I bumped my head you've done nothing but—'

Making a noisy entrance, Nattie came into the kitchen with Lily-Rose on her back and a large holdall in her hand. 'Hello, Gran. I thought I was supposed to be fetching you?'

'I got bored waiting and hitched a ride with Adam. As I've just been telling your foolish sister.' She looked reproachfully at Genevieve.

Nattie dropped her holdall with a thump, then leaning to one side, carefully manoeuvred her daughter to the floor. 'You'd better be careful, Gran. That man is determined to have one of us Baxter girls.'

Gran chortled. 'Did you hear that, Lily-Rose? I'm going to be Adam's new girlfriend. Wouldn't that be the funniest thing?'

Wrinkling her nose, the little girl came to her great-grandmother. Burying her elbows in the old lady's lap, she stared up into her face. 'Mummy says I have to look after the donkeys while she's away. Do you want to help me feed them?'

Gran cupped Lily-Rose's face in her hands. 'I will, just as soon as Mummy's gone. We need to give her a proper wave goodbye, don't we?'

Genevieve stood at the back door, taking in the storm-damaged garden. The weather had broken during the night, and the lawns and flowerbeds were untidy with a confetti of crushed petals; fuchsias were toppled, lavatera branches had been snapped off by the weight of drenched foliage, and flower heads on the hydrangea bushes looked weary and sodden. It was a far cry from the glorious sight of yesterday, when it had been bathed in hot late-July sunshine. It was raining now, but at least the air was fresh and clear.

As she suspected, breakfast took longer to get through that morning. Guests were in no hurry to embrace the day—these weren't the hardy year-round variety who walked the coastal path no matter what the weather. They had trickled down to the dining room, having treated themselves to a lie-in and a prolonged soak in the bath or shower.

After an apologetic call from Donna to say she wasn't feeling well enough to work, Genevieve made a start on cleaning the guest rooms. Gran had offered to help, but Genevieve suggested she read to Lily-Rose instead. 'If you can keep her entertained for as long as possible, I'd be really grateful,' Genevieve told her grandmother.

'But what about Henry and Morwenna?' Lily-Rose asked. 'I haven't fed them. Mummy said I had to.'

'Just as soon as the rain stops you can go to see them,' Genevieve said firmly. 'I'll be upstairs if you need me, Gran.'

She attacked her morning's work with determined energy, and was soon back downstairs loading the washing machine. With no sign of Gran or Lily-Rose in the kitchen, she made herself a cup of tea and sat down. Five minutes, she told herself, and then she'd tackle the ironing. After that, she'd have a long, revitalising shower to wash away her lethargy. She couldn't remember the last time she'd felt so bone-tired.

She yawned, and to taunt herself some more, she pictured herself in the summerhouse with Christian, in particular that moment when she knew he was going to kiss her. Within seconds, she had lowered her head to the kitchen table and dozed off. The next thing she knew, she was being jolted awake by the jangling ring of the telephone.

Except it wasn't the phone. It was someone at the front door. She went to see who it was. She hoped it wasn't anyone she knew. Dressed in a grubby T-shirt, her tattiest jeans with holes in the knees and her hair tied back with a rubber band, she looked and felt a mess.

She pulled open the door.

Christian!

For what felt like for ever, she held on to the door and stared at him. Was she still dreaming? Without speaking, he stepped over the threshold, kissed her politely on the cheek and then a lot less politely on the mouth. She breathed in the fresh, clean smell of him and felt her body go limp with longing. Still kissing her, holding her tight, he then manoeuvred her up against the wall and, tilting his head back, said, 'Please tell me there's no one else in the house?'

'I don't know. There might be some guests around.'

He kissed her again, then she took him by the hand and led him upstairs. Once they were in her bedroom, with the door shut and their bodies pressed against each other, all her earlier tiredness flew from her mind. When his hands circled her waist, then slid under her T-shirt and brushed against her breasts, she steered him towards the bed, at the same time unbuttoning his shirt. But suddenly she froze. She cocked her ear towards the door. 'What was that?'

Her gave her a half-smile. 'I didn't hear a thing.'

'There! There it is again. Oh God, it's probably Gran and Lily-Rose.'

He groaned and held her close. 'I suppose it's pointless trying to pretend we're not here?'

'We could try.'

Smiling, he said, 'No, the thought of your grandmother bursting in on us is hardly the erotic scenario I imagined when I drove down here this morning.'

She was straightening her hair while watching Christian do up the buttons of his shirt, when she heard the thumpty-thump-thump of small feet approaching. The bedroom door flew open and Lily-Rose burst in. Breathless and crying, tears streaming down her cheeks, she threw herself at Genevieve.

'Genvy, Henry and Morwenna have gone!'

Gran greeted Christian as though him showing up out of the blue at Paradise House was an everyday occurrence. Immediately they got down to the business of finding the missing donkeys. Leaving Lily-Rose with Gran, Genevieve and Christian set off on foot to knock on doors in the village, but no one had seen or heard so much as an *ee-aw*. They stood in front of the Salvation Arms, figuring out what to do next.

'Should we go farther afield?' Christian asked. 'We could drive along the coast. Let's go back up to the house and pick up my car.'

Genevieve fell in step with him. 'I bet you're wishing you'd never come down here, just for a wild donkey chase.'

He put his arm round her shoulders. 'I wouldn't have missed it for the world. At least I can say I got as far as your bedroom on this visit. Who knows, next time I might actually get you into bed.'

She leaned into him happily.

The house was unnaturally quiet when they let themselves in.

'That's odd,' Genevieve said, after she'd called to Gran and Lily-Rose and got no answer. 'I wonder where they've gone.'

'To your gran's, perhaps?'

'Mm . . . maybe.' She was suddenly annoyed. 'Why does my family do this to me? I spend all my time keeping an eye on them. These are Nattie's donkeys, she should be here to find them. Sometimes I wish I'd never come home.'

He looked at her hard, then took her in his arms. 'I'm glad you did, or we might never have met again.'

They spent the next hour trawling the coast road, stopping every now and then to ask if anyone had seen a pair of roaming donkeys. When it started to rain again, they drove home. The house was still empty, save for two guests who were reading in the conservatory. Genevieve had just served them tea when the phone rang.

'Hi there, Genevieve.' Tubby's jolly voice boomed down the line. 'Have you lost anything recently? Like a couple of absconding donkeys?'

'Tubby! Do you know where they are?'

He chuckled. 'Yes, and I'm keeping them as hostage until I receive five thousand pounds in used banknotes in the post. Oh, and you can throw in a Ferrari as well.'

'I'll throw in Nattie too, if you're not careful. Where did you find them?'

'I was down at that new pottery and tearoom near Stackpole, dropping off some strawberries, when I saw the pair of them in a field.'

'But that's miles away.'

'Not really. Anyway, I tethered them up, so they're safe for now. I can get hold of a horsebox and trailer if you like?'

'Thanks, Tubby, but we'll leave them there until Nattie gets back.'

She rang off and told Christian the good news.

'So, panic over? We can call off the air-sea rescue team?'

She laughed. 'For the time being, yes.' She glanced at her watch. 'I've just realised, you haven't had anything to eat since you arrived. You must be starving. What would you like?'

'Some of those scones would be good.' He indicated the open tin on the table, the pot of homemade jam and dish of whipped cream.

'Tell you what, help yourself while I give Gran a ring and see how she's getting on with Lily-Rose. I don't want her wearing herself out.'

There was no answer from her grandmother's telephone.

'Maybe she's nipped to the shops with Lily-Rose,' Christian suggested.

She shrugged. 'I know it seems silly, but something's not right. And why didn't she leave a note saying where she was going?'

'Does she always let you know what she's up to?'

'No. But—'

He put down his half-eaten scone. 'OK, then. Let's go.'

'Let's go where?'

'To your gran's, of course.'

'But she's not there, is she? If she was, she'd have answered the phone.' He started leading her towards the back door. 'Christian, what are you doing?'

'I know you well enough to understand that if we don't check on your grandmother, you'll just sit here worrying. Go on. Out you go.'

It was still raining, so they drove the short distance and parked directly in front of Angel Cottage. Genevieve knocked on the door, then knocked again. There was no sound, so she peered in at the window, her hands cupped round her eyes. Gran was on the sofa, her face turned towards the television. But she wasn't watching it, she was fast asleep. Genevieve tapped on the window, but got no response. She was just berating herself for forgetting her key when Christian joined her.

'Is there a way in at the back?' he asked.

They went round the side of the house to the back garden and found the kitchen door open. Genevieve went on ahead to the sitting room.

'Gran,' she said softly, not wanting to make her start. The memory of finding her grandmother on the bathroom floor was still fresh in her mind and her heart was beginning to pound. 'Gran, wake up!'

Her grandmother stirred. By the time she was fully awake and asking if Genevieve would put the kettle on, Christian had joined them.

'Genevieve,' he said, taking her aside, 'I've searched the house and garden, but there's no sign of Lily-Rose. She's not here. Where do you think she could have gone?'

'I've no idea. She's never wandered off before. Oh God, Christian, suppose someone's taken her?'

'Let's get out there and start looking.'

Hauling herself to her feet, Gran said, 'What are you two muttering?'

Genevieve broke the news to her grandmother as gently as she could, not wanting her overly alarmed. But Gran *was* alarmed. She clutched hold of Genevieve.

'It's all my fault,' she cried frantically. 'Lily-Rose kept wanting to look for Henry and Morwenna, and to distract her I brought her down here. I said if she was a good girl and played quietly so I could have a short nap, I'd take her to buy some sweets afterwards.'

'Then that's where she must be,' Genevieve said decisively, trying to allay her grandmother's distress—the old lady was now pacing the floor fretfully. 'You stay here, Gran. Christian and I will go round the shops.'

But no one had seen the little girl.

'Don't mess about, Genevieve,' Debs said. She was the first person not to pull her punches. 'Call the police. Go on. Do it now.'

'Perhaps I should just go and check Paradise House. She might have gone back there.'

'OK, but meanwhile I'll ring a few people and alert them.'

Alone, Genevieve ran all the way up the hill. Christian had offered to go back to Angel Cottage to check on Gran. After frantically searching every room at Paradise House, she drew yet another blank. Drenched to the skin, she stood in the kitchen and phoned the police. She gave the duty officer all the details she could, desperately trying to remember what Lily-Rose had been wearing. Then she made a second call; the one she was dreading. She had to tell Nattie her daughter was missing. But there was no answer from Nattie's mobile. She must have switched it off.

Grabbing a jacket, she dashed back down the hill to Gran's, scanning the now-deserted beach for any sign of a child, praying that when she reached Angel Cottage, Christian would tell her that Lily-Rose, all smiles and laughter, had just shown up. Passing the salon, Debs came out to her. Donna was with her. They both looked anxious.

'Any sign of Lily-Rose?' Debs asked.

Genevieve shook her head. 'No. But I've called the police. They're on their way.'

Christian opened the door to her, but his concerned expression, together with Gran still pacing the floor, flustered and muttering to herself, told her that Lily-Rose hadn't appeared. Shrugging off her wet jacket, Genevieve told Christian she'd phoned the police. 'They said they'd send someone as soon as they could.'

'Good. I'll get my jacket from the car.' He stopped for a moment and took her by the shoulders. 'Genevieve, we'll find her.'

While he went to fetch his jacket, Genevieve led Gran into the sitting room. Her concern for her grandmother was almost as strong as it was for her niece: the old lady was breathless and trembling. She sat with her on the sofa.

'Gran, you mustn't upset yourself.'

'How can you say that when it's no one's fault but my own that Lily-Rose's missing? I'll never know a moment's peace if something's happened to that poor little girl.' Distraught, her eyes brimmed with tears.

Trying not to let her apprehension show, Genevieve said, 'Gran, I need you to be rock steady. I can't get hold of Nattie, but I'm going to leave you her mobile number so you can keep trying it. You must tell her what's happened.' From her jeans pocket, she pulled out a piece of paper with the number clearly written on it; she handed it to her grandmother. 'Can you do that for me?'

With shaking hands, Gran took the piece of paper.

Joining Christian back out in the hall, where he was rummaging through a small rucksack, Genevieve pulled on her jacket. A knock at the door made her jump.

'What is it?' asked Christian.

'The door,' she said. 'It'll be the police.'

But it wasn't. A crowd of people stood outside: Tubby and Donna, Debs, Stan, Huw and Jane from the pottery, William and Ruth, the Lloyd-Morris brothers, Adam, and some of the regulars from the Salvation Arms. They were all dressed in boots and waterproofs.

'We're here to help,' Adam said, his face grim. 'Where do you want us to start looking?'

Their kindness was almost too much. Genevieve swallowed hard and took a deep, optimistic breath. With so much help, she told herself, they were bound to find Lily-Rose.

Donna offered to go up to Paradise House, in case Lily-Rose appeared there, while the rest split into pairs. Christian produced an Ordinance Survey map and the immediate area was divided and distributed accordingly. No one voiced the fear that if Lily-Rose had been taken by someone in a car she could be forty miles away by now.

The other unspoken fear Genevieve had was that Lily-Rose might have fallen into the sea. She told everyone how upset the little girl had been when Henry and Morwenna had gone missing, and how Gran might have put the idea into her head that they could have strayed along the coastal path in the dark during the storm.

'It's possible,' she said, 'that Lily-Rose went to look for them and got too close to the edge.'

An uneasy murmur went round the group. They exchanged mobile phone numbers and dispersed. There was an odd number of people, so Genevieve and Christian teamed up with Adam. The three of them skirted the headland and followed the coastal path in an easterly direction. The rain was coming down harder, making the ground slippery, and the wind, which had grown wild, whipped at the hoods on their jackets. They walked in silence, stopping occasionally to peer down the side of the cliff. Genevieve was beginning to fear the worst.

They walked as far as Hell's Gate. After pausing to look at Christian's map, the wind almost ripping it out of his hands, the three of them stood staring out at the rough, churning sea. The horizon was lost in the murky rain. The weather was getting worse.

Christian walked away from them, towards the edge of the path, and Genevieve watched him anxiously. Suddenly, he bent down, put a hand on a rock to take his weight and was gone. Genevieve rushed after him, Adam following behind. Below them, they could see Christian carefully picking his way over the jagged rocks towards a narrow ledge, where gulls were sheltering from the wind and spray. He stooped to pick something up. He turned, looked back to where they were standing, and waved a small, bright yellow Wellington boot.

'It's Lily-Rose's,' Genevieve cried. At once she and Adam were scrambling down the rock face. But the first signs of hope were tinged with fear. How could Lily-Rose have survived if she'd fallen?

Standing on the ledge together, they scanned the area beneath them, staring down into what was effectively a deep bowl cut into the rocks. The tide was coming in, and as the waves slapped and swirled, the wind roared with an animal-like baleful cry. Adam motioned for them to stay where they were, and pushed forward to a shallow cutting in the rock face. He'd had to wade into the menacing water.

Genevieve chewed on her lower lip as she watched Adam. Then, to her horror, she realised there was a lethal undercurrent where the water rushed into the bowl and couldn't get out. The next moment, Adam was sucked under. Genevieve screamed. Pulling off his jacket and shoes, Christian threw himself into the water. She watched in an agony of suspense for him to bob to the surface again. He did, but then dived back down again. When he surfaced, he was holding Adam. Christian dragged him over the side of the bowl and the two of them clung on to the rocks. Genevieve could see blood was flowing from Adam's temple. After they'd caught their breath, they swam across the bowl to the shallow cutting that, when the tide was out, would have seemed to an inquisitive child like an interesting cave to play in. But with the tide coming in, it was a deathtrap.

Holding the yellow boot Christian had found, she watched Adam disappear inside the dark hole. She willed their search to be over, that somehow, miraculously, Lily-Rose was safe inside the cave. She stared hard at the opening, and suddenly she saw Adam emerge, and . . . and he had Lily-Rose in his arms. Wet through and shivering, she was clinging to Adam as he carried her to safety. But to get to the ledge where Genevieve was standing, Adam and Christian had to make it back across the bowl. Genevieve suddenly wished it was Christian who was carrying Lily-Rose; he was clearly the stronger swimmer. Then, as if reading her mind, Christian exchanged a word with Adam and took the little girl from him.

Very slowly, they lowered themselves into the dangerous vortex of water. As a huge, swelling wave reared up and almost covered them, Lily-Rose screamed and thrashed her arms and legs about. Christian had to work hard to keep her in his arms. More agonising minutes passed, until finally he and Adam made it to the ledge.

Genevieve reached down, scooped up Lily-Rose and, wrapping the petrified little girl inside her jacket, gave thanks that the day hadn't ended in tragedy.

Once they'd climbed back up to the path and were heading for home, Adam took Christian's mobile—his own had been in his jacket pocket and was now useless—and phoned Donna at Paradise House with the good news, asking her to ring round and call off the search. He also asked her to phone the doctor's surgery so that Lily-Rose could be thoroughly checked over.

Dr Shepherd was waiting for them when they crashed, exhausted but triumphant, through the kitchen door.

To Genevieve's enormous relief, while Donna poured them all shots of brandy and fussed for them to get out of their wet clothes—her father's wardrobe was raided for Adam and Christian—Dr Shepherd gave Lily-Rose a clean bill of health.

'She's had an amazingly lucky escape,' he said. 'Best to get her into a nice warm bath and then bed. She'll be as right as rain come the morning.' Switching his attention from Lily-Rose to Adam and the cut to his head, he said, 'Looks like a few stitches wouldn't go amiss there. Sit down and I'll see to it now.'

When Dr Shepherd had finished with Adam, and Genevieve was seeing him out, she thanked him for coming so promptly and joked that, hopefully, it would be a while before they saw him again.

Back in the kitchen, dressed in her pyjamas and wrapped in a blanket, Lily-Rose was sitting on Adam's lap, telling him and Christian what had happened. While Gran was sleeping she'd decided, as Genevieve had suspected, to go and look for Henry and Morwenna.

'Mummy told me I had to make sure they were all right,' she said, 'and I promised her I would.' She explained how she had quietly opened Gran's back door, slipped through the gate at the end of the garden and gone down onto the cliff path. 'It was very windy. There was a funny noise, like Henry and Morwenna calling to me.'

The rest was easy to imagine. She'd mistaken the strange-sounding wind for braying and had gone to explore. She'd found the cave and discovered somewhere to play for a while. But then the tide had started to come in, cutting her off.

'Will Mummy be cross with me?' Lily-Rose asked anxiously.

It was then that Genevieve remembered Gran was supposed to be getting hold of Nattie.

'Donna,' she said, 'when you called the search off, did you ring Gran?'

'Oh, Gen, I'm sorry, I forgot all about that, what with the excitement. Shall I ring her now?'

'No, that's OK, I'll go down and see her.'

Adam shifted Lily-Rose off his lap and stood up. 'I'll walk down with you. I need to go home and change.' He glanced at Christian. 'I could lend you something if you like? Not that any of it will fit you properly.'

'Thanks,' Christian said.

Lily-Rose was happy enough to be left with Donna, so the three of them walked down the hill. Outside the Salvation Arms, Adam suggested Christian went with him up to his house to shower and change.

'Shall I meet you at your gran's?' Christian suggested.

'If you like. I'll probably be there a while. I'll leave the door on the latch for you.'

It was becoming a habit, Genevieve thought, as once again she was knocking on Gran's door and getting no answer. After another rap, Genevieve gave up and let herself in with her key, which she'd remembered this time.

'Gran, it's me,' she called out. She closed the door and went through to the sitting room, bursting to share the good news with her grandmother, wanting to be the one to put her mind at rest. 'Get the kettle on, Gran, we've found Lily-Rose and a celebratory cuppa's just what we need.'

Genevieve stood very still in the echoing silence. In an instant she knew that her grandmother couldn't hear. Her head leaning back against the sofa cushion, lips dried and slightly parted, she was completely motionless. There was no fall and rise to her chest. No little throaty grunt Gran often made when she was napping. Very slowly, almost reverently, Genevieve bent down and knelt beside the old lady. 'Oh, Gran,' she murmured. 'You never even said goodbye.' Tears filled her eyes and, letting them stream down her cheeks, she held her grandmother's cool, still hand. Never had that knotty, age-spotted hand been more precious to her.

The day had ended in tragedy, after all. But the real tragedy was that Gran's last moments before she died would have been so tormented. She would have left this world not knowing that Lily-Rose was safe. It broke Genevieve's heart that her grandmother had died thinking she'd let them down.

She didn't know how long she'd been kneeling on the floor sobbing, but she was suddenly conscious that Christian was beside her. She felt the steady pressure of his hand on her shoulder and, turning her tear-stained face to his, she said, 'How will we all manage without her? She was always there for us.'

He lifted her to her feet, took her through to the kitchen and cradled her, stroking her back. Eventually, she was able to think straight. There were things she had to do. Dr Shepherd would have to be sent for. Yet again. Then there was her family to notify—her parents in New Zealand and Polly in Hong Kong. And, of course, Nattie. Had Gran managed to ring her? She almost turned to go to the sitting room to ask Gran if she had, when . . . when she remembered.

The pain slapped at her. Never again would she be able to talk to her beloved grandmother. She reached for another tissue and blew her nose.

'This is when I feel so bloody useless,' Christian said.

Not understanding, she said, 'How do you mean?'

'I can't ring anyone for you. Do you want me to fetch Adam?'

Her first instinct was to say no, that she could manage. But the thought of Adam, decisive and always reassuring, made her say yes. 'But before you do that,' she said, 'could you send a text to Jonjo? I think I'd prefer it if Jonjo was the one to tell Polly about Gran. At least then she'll be told face to face by someone who cares about her.'

After everything had been done, including the formality of Gran's death certificate, they returned to Paradise House.

Donna had put a comfortable armchair from the sitting room into the kitchen for Lily-Rose, and the little girl was fast asleep in it, the head of a pink, long-eared rabbit sticking out from the blanket. Keeping her voice low, Genevieve thanked Donna for all her help and told her there was nothing else to be done just now. 'Go home, Donna,' she said, 'you've been wonderful.'

Thinking guiltily that she felt better for there being one less person around, and that she wouldn't mind being alone, Genevieve looked at Christian and wondered if this was how he'd felt after his mother had died. Fond as she was of both him and Adam, and deeply grateful for everything they'd done, she wished they'd go. It was a selfish, unworthy thought, because if it weren't for them Lily-Rose would be dead.

Dead.

Her thoughts returned to Gran. But the sound of hurried footsteps, followed by the back door flying open, didn't put a stop to them. It was Nattie, her face as white as chalk. She took one look at her daughter, curled up in the armchair, and burst into tears. She cried so hard that Lily-Rose stirred, and when she saw her mother, she too started to cry.

Genevieve signalled to Christian and Adam to give her sister some privacy, and led them to the conservatory.

Perhaps sensing her mood and that it was time to leave, Adam said, 'You know where I am, Gen, just give me a ring if you need anything.' He rested his hand on her arm.

She kissed him gratefully.

After he'd gone, Christian said, 'Do you want me to go as well?'

'Don't be offended, but yes. I think Nattie and I need some time alone.' She saw the disappointment in his face and felt a prickle of misgiving. It had been a long day for him and now he had a lengthy journey ahead of him.

'Are you sure you'll be all right?' he said.

'We'll be fine.'

But they weren't fine. Not really. Nattie was as devastated about Gran as she was. 'I know it's ridiculous,' her sister said late that night, 'but a part of me always believed Gran would live for ever.'

They were in Genevieve's room, sitting on her bed, and all they wanted to do was talk about Gran. To remember her.

Nattie was silent for a while, then said, 'I wish Mum and Dad were here. When did Dad say his flight would arrive?'

'He wasn't really making a lot of sense when I spoke to him the second time, but I checked online, and it looks like he should get to

Heathrow Airport at breakfast time the day after tomorrow.'

'And you're sure Mum isn't coming back with him?'

'He said they couldn't get another ticket. The flight was full. He got the last remaining seat. He was lucky to get that.'

Staring into the middle distance, Nattie said, 'He wasn't the only one who was lucky today.' Then, hugging herself, she looked back at Genevieve. 'I was in such a state earlier I didn't thank Adam and Christian for what they did. You too.'

'I'm sure they understood. Anyway, you can go and thank Adam tomorrow. And, Nattie,' she said, 'just for once, try to be nice to him. He risked his life trying to rescue Lily-Rose.'

Nattie reached for another tissue, her eyes filling with tears. 'Don't you think I realise that?' she said gruffly. 'Here I am practically suicidal with guilt and you're lecturing me on being nice to a man who saved Lily-Rose's life. Get real, Gen!'

The next day, they had a picnic lunch on the lawn, despite the grass still being damp. The sun was shining again and it felt good to be outside, to feel the uplifting warmth on their faces. Lily-Rose had wanted the picnic. 'A proper picnic,' she'd said, 'with a blanket and a basket.' Neither Genevieve nor Nattie felt inclined to refuse her. And it was now that Nattie chose to tell her daughter about her great-grandmother.

In response to her mother's explanation why they couldn't go and see Gran, and breaking off from trying to fit a Hula Hoop onto each of her fingers, Lily-Rose looked solemnly at Nattie. She didn't say anything. Then, just as her hands drooped and a Hula Hoop slipped off one of her fingers, a timely cry from a gull sitting high up on the chimney pot filled the silence and provided the distraction they needed.

'Do you remember how Gran was always putting bread out for the birds,' Genevieve said to Lily-Rose, 'but she'd chase the big gulls away?'

Lily-Rose nodded. 'She shook her broom at them.'

Nattie smiled. 'When I was a little girl, she shook her broom at me sometimes.'

'Because you were naughty?'

'Oh, Lily-Rose, I was the naughtiest girl in the whole world.'

Removing the remaining Hula Hoops from her fingers, and scattering them on the blanket, Lily-Rose stood up. She put her arms round her mother's neck and kissed her smack on the lips. Nattie hugged her tight and pressed a noisy kiss on Lily-Rose's cheek; it made her squeal and wriggle. As though the conversation about Gran had never taken place, she said, 'When can Henry and Morwenna come home?'

Genevieve was about to suggest they take up Tubby's offer of help, when she heard a noise coming from the front of the house. 'Look who's here, Lily-Rose,' she said.

Lily-Rose's face lit up. 'Henry! Morwenna!' Before anyone could tell her to slow down, she was off, dashing across the lawn to where Adam and Tubby were leading the donkeys out of a ramshackle horsebox.

'They look pleased as punch to be home,' Adam said, when the animals had been led to the orchard and were grazing contentedly on familiar grass. 'And before you accuse us of interfering, Nattie, we thought you and Gen had enough on your plates without worrying about these two.'

Genevieve went inside to fetch two ice-cold beers. When she rejoined them in the garden, they, with Nattie, were watching Lily-Rose feed handfuls of grass to the donkeys.

'If she carries on spoiling them like that,' Tubby said, 'they'll forget how to graze altogether. They'll be tapping on the window waiting to be invited inside.'

Tubby left when he'd finished his beer but at Nattie's invitation Adam stayed. Genevieve took it as her cue to leave them alone. She joined Lily-Rose in the orchard, and suggested they walk down to the shops. 'Let's buy some sweets to cheer us up, shall we?'

Back at Paradise House, Nattie was sitting on the terrace. It was obvious she was crying.

Lily-Rose put a hand on her mother's arm. 'Mummy, why are you crying? Would you like a sweet?'

Nattie raised her head and sniffed loudly. She tried to speak, but couldn't. She put her arms round Lily-Rose and held her tightly, as if she'd never let her go.

'Sorry about all that in the garden.' Nattie said later, when she was helping Genevieve get dinner ready. All but two guests had opted to eat in and, on reflection, a busy evening was just what they needed. Lily-Rose was watching a Disney video on the television in the corner of the kitchen.

'Don't be stupid, Nats, there's no need to apologise for crying.'

'It was Adam's fault, of course.'

Genevieve, her head in the oven as she checked on a main course of braised lamb shank in a Madeira sauce, stopped what she was doing. She looked at her sister sharply. 'How did you reach that conclusion?'

Nattie fiddled with the stubby remains of a root of ginger. 'If you must know, he'—she glanced over to Lily-Rose, and lowered her voice—'he told me he would have done anything to save Lily-Rose. That she really matters to him.'

'And you have a problem with that?' Genevieve closed the oven. 'I've been telling you for ages what a genuine guy he is.'

'It made me realise what a'—again she glanced over to Lily-Rose—'what a bitch I've been to him. He says he's moving out of the area. He told me there's nothing to keep him here. But what am I going to tell Lily-Rose?' Nattie continued. 'She adores Adam. She's lost her great-grand-mother, and to all intents and purposes her grandmother, and now Adam is deserting her. I've a good mind to make him tell Lily-Rose himself.'

'Oh, for goodness' sake, Nats, stop being so selfish and always think-ing of number one. Ask yourself the obvious question: why does Adam think there's nothing to keep him here?'

It was almost midnight when Polly arrived home. She was exhausted, having hardly slept during the long flight and then driven herself from Heathrow in a hire car that Jonjo had arranged. Seeing how shattered Polly was, Genevieve made her get ready for bed and then she and Nattie took Polly a mug of tea. As they were about to say good night and close the door, Polly yawned and said, 'Oh, I nearly forgot, Jonjo's asked me to marry him.'

They came back into the room, almost tripping over each other.

'What was your answer?' asked Genevieve.

'I said I'd think about it.'

'But you hardly know him,' said Nattie.

'That's what makes the prospect of marrying him so exciting. Who wants to marry someone they know completely? Where's the fun in that?' Yawning hugely, Polly closed her eyes. 'Good night.'

Shutting the door behind them, Genevieve thought how wonderfully simple Polly made life seem. It was good having her home again.

The morning brought a sky of brilliant blue and a sea that was as still and shiny as glass. After breakfast had been served and tidied away, Genevieve took the post out into the garden. There was a handful of With Deepest Sympathy cards from neighbours and friends, and a brief note from Christian to say how much he wished he could be with her.

'Me too,' she sighed.

She opened the rest of the mail, including a formal-looking envelope from the bank in Tenby. She held her breath as she ripped it open. She read the letter twice to be sure of its content, then put it back inside the envelope and wondered if she really dare go ahead.

She stood up to go back inside to help Donna. As she was crossing the lawn, she heard a car. She checked her watch. Could it be Dad? Still clutching the pile of mail, she went round to the front of the house and found her father stepping down from the driver's side of his Land Rover. She quickened her step to greet him.

She was almost upon him when she realised he wasn't alone. Pushing open the door on the passenger's side was Serena Baxter.

'But we thought you couldn't get a seat on the flight with Dad?' They were standing in the kitchen: Daddy Dean, Serena, Nattie, Lily-Rose and Genevieve.

'So did we. But they put me on standby at the airport. At the very last minute there was a cancellation.'

'Why didn't you tell us you were coming?' This was from Nattie and there was a distinct accusatory tone to her words.

'Oh, darling, there wasn't time. It's been such a mad rush. We just wanted to get back as soon as possible, to be with you all. Where's Polly?'

'Actually, I'm right here. Hello, Daddy. Hello, Mum! What a brilliant surprise! I thought I could hear your voices.' Rubbing the sleep from her eyes and still dressed in her nightie, Polly stepped into the room. Her sunny presence instantly took the edge off the atmosphere Nattie had generated. She kissed their father first, who had Lily-Rose in his arms, then their mother. 'You look different, Mum. Have you lost weight?'

Serena smiled. 'A little. I've taken up yoga. I'll tell you about it later. I've so much to share with you. Now then, shall I make us a drink?'

'Why don't I put the kettle on and make some lunch while you and Dad freshen up?' suggested Genevieve.

After lunch, while their father, who had scarcely uttered a word since arriving home, got on the phone and started organising the funeral, Serena asked Genevieve and her sisters to go for a walk with her. They didn't walk far, just down to the beach, where they picked their way through the stretched-out bodies and playing children till they found themselves a place to sit on the pebbles. After kicking off her sandals, Lily-Rose took her fishing net and went to play in a nearby rock pool.

Serena was wearing a simple, sleeveless, olive-coloured shift dress that suited her new shape. Her hair was cropped short, and where before it had been shot through with dowdy grey, it was now high-lighted with a flattering mixture of copper and nut-brown. She was wearing a pair of star-shaped earrings with a matching necklace and bracelet. Genevieve could see that the change had done her mother good. But what if it wasn't just the change of scene that was responsible for the new Serena? What if this old friend Pete was the cause?

'I've missed this so much,' Serena said, her arms embracing the shore and looking up to Paradise House.

Genevieve shot Nattie a warning glance, knowing it was on her tongue to say, 'Then why did you leave it so long before coming home?'

'I felt exactly the same when I came back,' Genevieve said, taking on the familiar role of mediator. 'I kept thinking I had to make the most of it in case it disappeared.'

'Oh, please,' cut in Nattie, not for a second put off by Genevieve's warning look, 'let's cut the deep and meaningful crap and get to the point. Mum, are you, or are you not, home for good?'

Serena placed a hand on Nattie's arm. 'Still the same old Natalie, then? Looking for a clear-cut answer to every question?'

'There you go again,' Nattie said angrily, 'avoiding the question. Is that what you've been learning to do while we've been consoling Dad? I don't think you have any idea how much you hurt him. What's more, I don't think you even care.'

'But, Nattie, I do. I care deeply. And not just about your father. About all of you. But did any of you stop and think about why I went?'

Nattie picked up a stone and brought it down hard on another. 'As far as I can see, you went because, selfishly, you wanted to indulge yourself in a stupid midlife crisis. You're a woman with . . . responsibilities. You're not supposed to go off when the whim takes you.'

Quietly, Serena said, 'Maybe I'm wrong, Nattie, but I think the reason you're so angry with me is that you're jealous. What would you give, right now, to be able to go off on your own? To go this very minute without a backward glance for any responsibilities you have? No, don't look so indignant. I know you love Lily-Rose, but I bet there's a part of you that would love to be able to do what I've done.'

Nattie gave their mother a ferocious stare. 'That's not true! And how can you say that after what nearly happened to Lily-Rose? How can you be so bloody insensitive?' She got to her feet and marched off, her shoes grinding the stones underfoot as she went over to the rock pools.

Serena sighed, and suddenly looked tired. 'I knew this would happen. It's one of the reasons I dreaded coming home.' She turned to Genevieve and Polly. 'I did miss you all, you know. I badly wanted to see you again, but as the weeks and then the months passed by I began to worry if you'd want me home.'

'But our letters! We told you how much we wanted you here.'

'Yes, but for my sake? Your father's? Or your own?'

Genevieve couldn't meet Serena's eyes. 'A mixture of all three,' she said truthfully.

'What about you, Polly?'

'I just wanted you to be happy, Mum. And if that meant you had to stay away, then sooner or later we would have come to terms with it. Are you going to divorce Dad?'

'Perhaps that's a question you should be asking your father. After all, I've given him every reason to want to divorce me.'

'Oh, Mum,' said Genevieve, 'how could you even think that? He's mad about you. Haven't you had a chance to talk things through yet?'

'Not really. Your gran's death has put *us* on hold for the time being. Your father has to want me home for all the right reasons.'

'What about Pete?' Genevieve asked. The question came out more snappily than she'd intended. 'Where does he fit in?'

'He doesn't.'

'Come off it, Mum. You've been living with him all these months. Of course he fits in.'

'I've been *staying* with Pete, not living with him, Genevieve. There's a big difference. There's also the small matter of him being gay.'

'*Gay?*' Genevieve had to repeat the word, to make sure she'd heard right. 'Why didn't you say? Why did you leave us to suspect the worst?'

'Because . . . because I needed to. I needed to shake your father up. To see how badly he wanted me. And not just as cook, cleaner and general dogsbody at Paradise House.'

It was as Genevieve had suspected. Her mother had grown tired of always being there for everyone. She couldn't blame her for that. Being taken for granted, as she'd come to know, was soul-destroying.

'And do you know what makes it worse?' Serena said. 'It's knowing that it was all my own fault. I encouraged your father to sell the farm and live out my dream of running a cosy b. and b. by the sea. But in the end it turned into something I didn't want any more. Can you imagine how guilty that made me feel?'

'But you still love him, Mum, don't you?'

Serena turned to Genevieve. 'As you grow older, Gen, you come to realise that it's not just love that keeps a marriage alive.'

'What, then?' But before her mother got the words out, Genevieve knew exactly what she was going to say.

'The unexpected. The thrill of not knowing what's going to happen next. Being stuck in a rut is what kills most marriages. I suppose what I'd come to realise was that without a zing in my heart, I felt dead.'

'You need to talk to Dad,' Genevieve said.

Serena nodded. 'I will. When your grandmother's funeral is over.'

It was a beautiful day.

'Your gran will have ordered the sun especially,' Tubby said to Genevieve as he put his arm round Donna, steering her out of St Non's Church. 'I bet she's looking down and wishing she was here with us.'

A painful lump of grief rose in Genevieve's throat. She wandered away from the main group of mourners and went to stand in the shade of a large yew tree that was supported on one side by a pair of sturdy oak props. She and Christian had sheltered here once from a sudden downpour. Disappointed that he hadn't been able to make it for the funeral—he'd emailed yesterday to say he was inundated with work—she thought how little contact there had been between them since Gran had died. She sensed something had changed between them, but couldn't put her finger on what it was.

Standing under the tree, she had never felt so alone or isolated. She hadn't just lost a grandmother, she'd lost an irreplaceable lifelong friend. And now Adam was thinking of moving away.

From across the graveyard, where he was standing on his own, Adam turned and caught her eye. He smiled and raised his eyebrows, as if to say, 'You OK?' She nodded, then stepped out of the shadows and into the sunlight to join him.

It was just as Gran would have wanted. Everyone, now that they had made a start on Genevieve's buffet, had loosened up, and the wine was flowing freely. The villagers were pleased to see Serena back within the Baxter fold and were all making the assumption that she was here to stay.

Genevieve had been desperate to talk to her father, to give him some kind of hint of what was expected of him, but her mother had made her promise, along with Polly, that they were not to say anything.

'It has to come from him,' Serena had said. 'If there's to be any chance of us staying together, your father has to work things out for himself.'

But was it fair to test him in this way?

Most people were now retreating to the tables placed in the shade, but Genevieve was sitting on the steps of the conservatory, enjoying the sun. She was now onto her third glass of wine.

'Room for a friend?' It was Adam, with a bottle of wine in his hand.

She moved along the step to make room for him.

'You look knackered,' he said, giving her glass a top-up.

'I'm fine.'

'You always say that.' He put his arm round her. 'You need a holiday, Gen.'

She let her head rest on his shoulder. 'You might be right. Where shall I go? I hear New Zealand is particularly good for putting the spring back into one's step.'

'Alaska or the Antipodes, you name it and I'll take you there.'

She lifted her head. 'Adam? You . . . you don't fancy me, do you?'

He laughed. 'Now what made you ask a daft question like that?'

Sober enough to blush, she hid her face in his shoulder. When she'd recovered, she said, 'So what's this I hear from Nattie about you abandoning us?'

'Do you Baxter girls tell each other everything?'

'Very little. That's half the problem with our family. Anyway, answer my question.'

'Ooh, scary. Genevieve gets tough!'

She dug him in the ribs with her elbow, spilling some of her wine onto the step, but he just pulled her closer, making her laugh.

'For heaven's sake, you two! Do you really think that's appropriate behaviour on a day like this?' Standing in front of them, hands on her hips, was Nattie, and she looked like thunder.

But all Genevieve could do was laugh even harder. How good it felt to let the tension of the last few days flow out of her.

Gran's will was very precise. Instead of leaving everything to Daddy Dean, she'd left it to Genevieve and her sisters. But whereas Genevieve and Polly were bequeathed an equal share of money, Nattie had been given Angel Cottage.

This is to provide my granddaughter and great-granddaughter with a home. And to ensure that it can never be got hold of by some feckless man Nattie gets involved with, the house is to be put in Lily-Rose's name until her eighteenth birthday. Only then will it legally belong to Natalie, by which time she might have achieved the unthinkable and settled down with a reliable man she can trust.

Nattie's response was to laugh out loud. 'Good on you, canny Gran!'

Later in the day, though, Genevieve found her in the orchard with Henry and Morwenna, tears streaming down her cheeks.

Rubbing the heels of her hands into her eyes to stem the flow of tears, Nattie said, 'I wish Gran was here for me to thank her properly. I miss her so much.'

That had been a week ago, and since then Nattie had undergone a dramatic change: she was talking about getting a job. It seemed that canny Gran had been exactly that.

'It's like she's growing up at last,' Genevieve said to Adam. He paid for their drinks and they took them outside, to sit in the evening sun at the Salvation Arms.

'You mean she's going to get off her bum and do a decent day's work?'

'She says she'll take the first job offer that comes, so long as it pays enough for a childminder for Lily-Rose, and then when Lily-Rose goes to school, she might go back to school herself to complete the degree she dipped out of.'

Adam nodded approvingly. 'Good for her. But I guess finding a reliable childminder for Lily-Rose won't be easy, or cheap.'

'It won't, but I'm sure I'll be able to help out now and again.'

Adam turned his beer glass round on the wooden table. 'And what about *your* plans? How do you think you'll have the time to take care of Lily-Rose if your own plans take off?'

She shrugged. 'These things have a way of sorting themselves out.'

He didn't look convinced and, after they'd finished their drinks, he went up to the bar for another round. She watched him chatting with Donna and thought about what he'd said. He was right, of course: babysitting Lily-Rose would be difficult. But as things stood, she'd heard nothing back from the solicitors in Tenby who were handling the sale, despite ringing them several times. All she wanted to do, with the help of a loan and the money George had left her, was to buy a modest-sized property to convert into a teashop-cum-restaurant.

It had been Tubby who had unwittingly alerted her to the possibility, and the property stood right here in the village, two doors up from Angel Crafts. For years the pretty little end-of-terrace house had been owned by a family in Cardiff, but now they wanted to sell up. Before they'd bought the house, it had been the village bakery, and one of the original bread ovens was still in place in what was now the kitchen. Planning permission to return the property to commercial use was a mere formality, so her solicitor had told her, but now Genevieve wasn't so sure. Perhaps this was proving to be the stumbling block.

'You look glum,' Adam said, when he returned with their drinks. 'I leave you for five minutes and come back to a face like a mullet.'

She grinned inanely. 'That better?'

'Marginally.'

'So what's the latest news from the bar?'

He took a long sip of his beer. 'According to Donna, the talent contest next Saturday night is a total sellout.'

'I know, she told me this morning. She also told me she's trying to persuade you to participate. Has she won you over?'

'Err . . . no comment.'

'She has, hasn't she? You're going to sing!'

He winked. 'Again, no comment.' After another mouthful of beer, he said, 'What's the latest on your parents?'

'As you might expect, nothing's been decided.'

He frowned. 'I don't get it. Your mother seems genuinely glad to be back. I can't imagine her leaving again.'

'It's not as simple as that. Mum's been home for nearly two weeks and as far as I know, she and Dad still haven't talked properly.'

'You'd think they'd both be desperate to clear the air and see how they stand. Especially your father.'

'I think Gran's death has taken precedence. And maybe they're both hiding behind it a little. Particularly Dad.'

'It wouldn't do any harm to give your father a nudge in the right direction. Your mother need never know.'

'I could, but in a way I agree with her. She needs to know that Dad wants her home for the right reasons. The sad thing is, if Gran were still alive, she would have knocked their heads together by now and got them to see how committed to each other they really are.'

Adam gave a short laugh. 'Commitment! Now that's a concept you and Nattie could do with familiarising yourselves with.'

'What do you mean?'

'Just look at Nattie. She deliberately chooses all the wrong boyfriends so she doesn't have to connect with them and get seriously involved. She's either terrified of being tied down or of being hurt.' Adam shrugged. 'Now tell me about you and lover-boy. How's it going? I can't remember the last time you mentioned him.'

She sank back into her seat. 'Difficult to say.'

'In what way?'

'Something's changed between us. Maybe it's because he's there and I'm here.'

'Are you saying it's fizzling out between the two of you?'

'I don't know. I really don't. Perhaps if we could actually speak to each other it would help. Long-distance relationships just aren't my thing. It doesn't seem to be enough for me.' She raised her eyes and looked at Adam. 'I sound selfish and greedy, don't I?'

'Not at all. There's nothing selfish in wanting to be with someone.'

Holding the stem of her empty wine glass, she twirled it round on her lap and thought of Polly and her long-distance relationship. Since coming back from Hong Kong, Jonjo had upped the ante in his bid to win Polly's heart. Polly hadn't told their parents that Jonjo had proposed to her, and she'd asked Genevieve and Nattie to keep quiet about it until she'd made up her mind whether or not to accept. Genevieve had confided in Adam, but had made him promise not to breathe a word.

'I wish I had what Polly's got,' she said suddenly. 'I don't mean I want Jonjo, nothing like that. I'd just like a bit more romance.'

He smiled. 'Do you think Polly will marry Jonjo?'

'You know, I have a feeling she just might. But in her own time. I've never known Polly to make a decision she's regretted.'

After last orders had been called, Adam walked her home. Remembering what he had said about her and Nattie being afraid of commitment, Genevieve asked him what she was supposed to be too scared to connect with.

'That's easy. You're afraid to connect with yourself, Gen. And until you do, no one else will be able to get really close to you.'

She came to a stop.

'Oh, Genevieve, don't tell me I've stunned you with my powers of deductive reasoning.' He slipped his arm through hers and made her walk on.

With the last of the breakfast guests gone, Nattie was helping Genevieve to clean the dining room. Across the hall, where Polly and Donna were tidying the guest sitting-room, Genevieve could hear Donna trying to press-gang her sister into lending a hand with the talent show; apparently the services of a musical director were now required.

'Everyone seems to be taking the talent show very seriously,' Genevieve remarked to Nattie, as she shook out a white cloth and laid it over a table. 'I hope it's the success Donna and Tubby want it to be.'

'That's typical of you,' said Nattie. 'Anxious on everyone else's behalf.'

'I just like things to go well. Anything wrong in that?'

'And if it's a disaster? What then?'

'Nothing, I suppose. But I don't like people to be disappointed.'

'But, Gen, it's *their* disappointment. Not yours. Oh, and talking of disappointments, Adam phoned to say he wanted to call in for a quick chat before going on to Tenby.'

'Did he say what he wanted?'

'No. And if you ask me he sounded distinctly furtive.'

Genevieve laughed and shook out another tablecloth. 'That's probably the nicest thing you've ever said about him.'

Nattie looked affronted. 'Hey, Adam and I are like this these days.' She held up a hand, the first two fingers crossed.

'So why did you just refer to him as a disappointment?'

Nattie laughed. 'Because he's taking all the fun out of my life. What's he done to his clothes? They're so normal. And have you noticed he doesn't wear that tacky bracelet any more?'

Genevieve kept her face straight. 'Really? I can't say I've noticed. And frankly, I'm surprised you have. What's got into you?'

Nattie ignored the question. 'I reckon there's some new girl on the scene we don't know about. Whoever she is, she's obviously taking him in hand. Do you suppose we ought to keep an eye on him?'

'Whatever for?'

'Oh, come on, Gen. Adam's just ripe for the plucking. All that money's bound to attract the wrong sort of girlfriend.'

'And you care?'

'Now look, Gen, I'm getting sick of your cynicism. He saved Lily-Rose's life, so in my book, I owe him. Which means the least I can do is save him from some money-grabbing, high-maintenance madam.'

'Wow! He'll sleep easy from now on, knowing you're on the case.'

Nattie was out in the garden tidying up after Henry and Morwenna when Adam arrived. He was in full suit mode.

'Another business lunch in Tenby?' Genevieve asked.

'Another lunch, another dime.'

'Well, come on through to the kitchen and you can fill me in. Nattie said you were acting distinctly furtive on the phone.'

'Actually, it was Nattie I wanted to speak to. I thought I'd made that clear on the phone to her.'

'Oh. Oh, right. I'll go and find her.'

Adam smiled. 'I'll go and find her myself if you're busy.'

It had rained overnight and Genevieve looked at his expensive shoes. 'Dressed like that? I don't think so. Put the kettle on and I'll go.'

Nattie threw down her shovel and muttered crossly when Genevieve told her that it was her Adam wanted to talk to. 'Don't you dare leave me alone with him,' she said as she stomped back up to the house. 'I don't want him taking advantage of our new-found relationship.'

Seconds later she was in the kitchen with Genevieve and Adam.

'So what's this about, Adam? You've not come here to propose, have you?'

Adam laughed good-humouredly. 'No, it's not a proposal of marriage, but it is a proposal of sorts.'

Putting their drinks down on the table, Genevieve said, 'You probably don't need me hanging around, I'll just go—'

'It's all right, Gen, there's no need to make yourself scarce. Unless, of course, Nattie would prefer it?' He turned to look at her.

Nattie shrugged. 'Always good to have a witness. Spit it out, then.'

'Right,' he said, 'first off, I hear you're looking for a job. One that will provide you with the means to pay for a good childminder?'

'Spot on.'

'Excellent. Because I have a job for you.'

Nattie straightened the straps of her dungarees. 'What kind of a job?'

'A nine-to-five job, working in the office of one of my caravan parks.'

'In one of your caravan parks? You must be bloody joking!'

Reaching for his mug of coffee, his voice casual, Adam said, 'This job comes with a ready-made crèche for Lily-Rose; the one the holiday guests put their own children in. I only employ fully qualified girls, so

135

you'd know Lily-Rose was being well looked after. What's more, it's free.'

Nattie switched her gaze from Adam to Genevieve. 'Did you cook this up between the two of you at the pub last night?'

'No! This is the first I've heard of it.'

'She's right,' said Adam. 'I only thought of it this morning.'

'I don't believe you.'

'Well, get over your disbelief and give me an answer. I need someone to answer the phones and deal with guests' queries. It'd be a challenge for you, Nattie, because you'll have to be pleasant.' This last comment was said with a smile.

'Watch it, mate. You push your luck at your peril. Anyway, I thought you were selling the parks?'

'I am, but these things take for ever. Meanwhile, I need someone to do the job for the rest of the season, or however long it takes. The girl who's been doing it for the last two years has just handed in her notice.'

'Why? Didn't she like the boss?'

'This might come as a surprise to you, but people generally like me. I'm a pretty fair employer, too.'

Nattie grunted. 'OK then, when do you want me to start? But I'm warning you, one wisecrack about a perk of the job being that I get to sleep with the boss and I'll have you for sexual harassment.'

A smile twitched at his mouth. 'Don't flatter yourself, Nattie. Moreover, I never mix business with pleasure.' He finished his coffee and got to his feet. 'I'll be in touch with all the relevant details.'

'The man's insufferable,' said Nattie, minutes later when Adam had left them.

'How can you say that when he's being so helpful?'

She smirked. 'I was going to add, he's insufferably generous. He'll be handing out blankets to the homeless next.'

Two days later, Genevieve received bad news. The estate agent in Tenby who had been handling the sale of the property in Angel Sands wrote to say that the owners had received and accepted a higher offer. There was no hint that, were she to come in with a higher offer, she would be successful. Anyway, she didn't want to play that game. Though the letter knocked her back, she kept its contents to herself. Besides, everyone was preoccupied with their own affairs. Adam was away checking out his parks down in Cornwall, Polly was on a visit to Buckinghamshire to stay with Jonjo and to meet his parents and, with Mum and Dad's help, Nattie was preparing to move in to Angel Cottage.

Angel Cottage was almost unrecognisable. The bulky furniture Gran had squeezed into the little house had either been sold or moved up to

Paradise House. The biggest transformation, so far, was the smallest bedroom at the back of the house, the one Gran had used as an apple store. The apple room, as Lily-Rose called it, was now hers. Serena and Daddy Dean had redecorated it and had replaced the ancient carpet.

It might have seemed that they were acting with indecent haste, doing up Angel Cottage so soon after Gran's death, but Genevieve felt sure her grandmother would approve. It did mean that while her parents were spending so much time down at Angel Cottage, they were continually in each other's company, which had to be a good thing.

She had mentioned this to Christian in an email and he'd replied that maybe what her parents needed was a new project. 'It sounds like they've grown bored of Paradise House and not of each other,' he wrote.

It was the last message she'd had from Christian and in the following days she'd steeled herself for what she now realised was inevitable; neither of them was suited to a long-distance relationship. Washing the mud from the potatoes she'd dug up from the vegetable patch, she thought how much better she was with friendships than love affairs. She thought of Adam and what he'd said about her being afraid to connect with herself. It was true: time and time again she had withdrawn from a relationship because, subconsciously, she didn't want that person to see the old Genevieve who had never gone away. The fat, ugly Genevieve who had convinced herself she didn't deserve a boyfriend like Christian.

Was she doing it all over again, then? Deliberately talking herself out of a chance of happiness in yet another act of self-destruction? Staring at the garden—it was raining again—and wondering if she would ever change, her attention was caught by a familiar song on the radio. It was Judy Garland singing 'Over the Rainbow'. Genevieve hoped that her parents had the radio on down at Angel Cottage—they were emulsioning the kitchen today. She pictured her mother on the stepladder, brush in hand, streaks of paint in her hair as she sang along, maybe even using the brush as a microphone, like she used to when they were little. Then, very slowly, a different picture appeared in Genevieve's head. It was a picture of her father. Holding her breath, frightened the faint glimmer of inspiration would fade, she held on to the image, right until the very last poignant note of the song.

It was the perfect answer.

But would her father have the nerve to carry off her idea? And who would be the best person to persuade him?

Adam and Genevieve had cornered Daddy Dean at Angel Cottage as he was jet-blasting the patio.

'What have you got to lose?' Adam had asked, after Genevieve had outlined what she'd thought was a stroke of pure genius on her part. 'It's the perfect way to prove how much you love her. And because she knows you so well, she'll know exactly how much courage it took. Trust me; you have to do it.'

'But I've never sung in public before.'

'Nor have I, but it's not stopping me,' said Adam.

Slowly coming round to the idea, Daddy Dean had said, 'You're sure it would work?'

'Yes, Dad.'

'But what shall I sing?'

'How about the King? Elvis.'

Daddy Dean looked doubtful. 'Would I have to dress up like him?'

'Yes,' said Genevieve. 'It's got to be a show-stopping moment to bring a tear to Mum's eye.'

There were tears in Genevieve's eyes now: she was slicing onions for a vegetable lasagne. It was the afternoon of the *Stars in Their Eyes* talent contest and overnight the extent of Genevieve's input for the event had grown dramatically. Two members of the kitchen staff at the Salvation Arms had gone down with a bout of laryngitis, so instead of just lending a hand in the kitchen, she was now in charge of cooking and serving a massive lamb and ham carvery with trifle and fresh strawberries to follow. She had decided to throw in a vegetarian option just in case, a mushroom and aubergine lasagne.

Genevieve slid the onions into the large frying pan on the hob, lowered the flame, added some crushed garlic and thought of her father, who should now be on his way home from Swansea with an Elvis outfit.

'Where's your father gone?' Serena had asked earlier.

'He's with Adam,' Genevieve had said.

Serena had looked at her suspiciously. 'Something's going on, isn't it? What's your father up to? And why does he always seem to be huddled in a corner with that woman?'

'Which woman?' Although, of course, Genevieve had known exactly who her mother was referring to.

'I'm talking about Donna,' Serena said impatiently. 'Has something been going on between those two while I've been away?'

Nattie had walked in at that moment. 'And what's it to you, Mum, what Dad gets up to? You didn't give a jam fig all those months you were away. Why be concerned now?'

There was no hostility in her voice, just a matter-of-fact tone that had made their mother drop her line of interrogation. 'Do you still want to go shopping in Tenby?' she'd asked.

Adding the salted and rinsed slices of aubergine, Genevieve stirred the pan and glanced across the kitchen to where Donna was peeling a mound of potatoes. It looked very much as though, without meaning to, their father had made his wife jealous. Serena's comment that he was always huddled up in a corner with Donna was an exaggeration, but it did contain an element of truth. The most professional singer in Angel Sands other than Polly, who was arriving home with Jonjo that afternoon, Donna was giving Dad singing lessons up at Adam's place.

'Do you think that's enough potatoes?' asked Donna.

Knowing that Donna had a hundred and one things to do, Genevieve said, 'That's plenty. And thanks for your help. But feel free to disappear if you want.'

'You sure?'

'Absolutely. It's not fair of me to monopolise the star of the show.'

Donna smiled. 'I think you might change your opinion when you hear your father tonight.'

Knowing she was responsible for putting her father through this ordeal, Genevieve said, 'People won't laugh at him, will they?'

'Trust me. He'll knock everyone dead. I wouldn't be surprised if there was a drop or two of Welsh blood in him.' Washing her hands, she said, 'Now, if you're sure there's nothing else I can do, I'll be off. See you later.'

Encouraged by Donna's words, Genevieve thought of the others, apart from Donna, who knew about the surprise. Tubby and Adam, her sisters and Christian had all said the same when she'd told them about it. 'It's inspired, Genevieve,' Christian had replied to her email. 'I just wish I could be there with you to enjoy the moment.'

The disappointment that once again Christian couldn't spare the time to drive down hit Genevieve harder than she'd expected. There was no reason why he should want to witness an entire village making a fool of itself, but she'd invited him because, if nothing else, it would give them the opportunity to talk things through. Surprised how hurt she felt, she'd replied to his email with a businesslike update on everything, then told him how she'd been gazumped on the teashop.

'If it's any consolation, you did the right thing in not increasing your offer,' he'd answered. 'They could have strung you along trying to get even more out of you.'

It was exactly what Adam had said when Genevieve had shared her setback with him. He'd hugged her hard and said, 'And what will you do if the agent calls you because the current deal has fallen through?'

'I shall tell him to go to hell. Then offer less than I did first time round.'

'Well done, Gen, you're learning fast.'

It didn't really feel like she was learning anything fast, but maybe Adam was right. He usually was.

Polly and Jonjo arrived home not long after Adam had dropped Dad at the front door, giving Serena no time to cross-examine him on where he'd been or what he'd been doing. She was too busy anyway, what with meeting Jonjo for the first time and throwing all her energy into interrogating him. What Serena didn't know, and nor did their father, was that Jonjo was a serious contender for the role of son-in-law. Polly still hadn't mentioned anything to their parents about Jonjo's proposal and as far as Genevieve was aware, she still hadn't given him an answer.

Then the line of questioning took an unexpected turn.

'Genevieve tells me you're an old friend of Christian May,' Serena said.

Instantly Genevieve was on the alert and regretting she'd told her mother about seeing Christian again. Like Nattie and her father, she hadn't been exactly thrilled by the news.

'That's right,' Jonjo said, without looking Genevieve's way. 'I got to know Christian several years ago when he boasted he could have made a better job of designing my first fitness centre.'

'Really? That doesn't sound like the Christian we used to know,' Serena said. 'Perhaps he's changed. Which might not be such a bad thing,' she added under her breath.

Genevieve cringed. But Jonjo, still not looking in Genevieve's direction, kept his tone even. 'I can't vouch for what he was like as a child. Apart from that one excusable blag, I'd say he's one of the most modest blokes I know. And completely reliable. Professionally as well as personally.' He put his glass down, before skilfully steering Serena off course. 'If you've got time, why don't I take you to look at the barn? The builders have made a start and I'm keen to see what they've done so far.'

Genevieve was grateful for his charm and quick thinking. 'That's a great idea, Jonjo.' She shot her sister a glance, hoping for back-up. 'Polly, why don't you go with Mum and Dad?'

Amid the kerfuffle of decision making—could they really spare the time?—Genevieve leaned towards Jonjo and whispered her thanks.

'No problem,' he said. 'By the way, Christian sends his love. He said to be sure I got the message right. Not best wishes. Not regards. His *love*.'

Genevieve felt the colour rush to her cheeks. All she could think to say was, 'I was hoping he might make it down for the weekend.'

Everyone was on their feet now. Jonjo took Genevieve aside. 'Things are OK between you and Christian, aren't they? He hinted that he thought there was someone else in the background.'

'What? But that's absurd. He knows perfectly well there isn't. No, the trouble is we don't see—'

But there was no time to finish their conversation. Serena was bearing down on them.

After waving them off, Genevieve hurried back to the kitchen to finish preparing the food for that evening.

There was only one person who could open the show and that was Donna. She looked as spectacular as she sounded—shoulder-length blonde hair backcombed to within an inch of its life, legs wrapped in the tightest jeans Genevieve had ever seen, and wearing her own body weight in lip gloss and eye make-up. She tottered around on the small makeshift stage on her six-inch, baby-pink stiletto heels, a death-defying act of pure bravery. She gave a magnificent, gutsy rendition of Bonnie Tyler singing 'Holding Out For a Hero' and had the place in an uproar when she finished. Tubby looked on proudly.

The plan for the evening was an hour of performances followed by a break for supper and then a further hour of performances. Daddy Dean was booked to do his slot towards the end of the evening, after Adam. Mum was still in the dark, as he'd sworn all those who knew to secrecy.

'But expect things to run over a bit,' both Tubby and Donna had warned Genevieve.

Standing with her mother and sister, Genevieve looked across the crowded pub to where the panel of judges sat with their pieces of paper. She didn't envy them their job. The obvious outright winner would be Donna, no question. But who would make second and third? Perhaps not the visitor currently on his feet doing an appalling impression of Tom Jones singing 'Sex Bomb'.

Nattie groaned. 'I know this is for charity, but there are limits.'

'Gran would have loved all this,' Genevieve said.

Serena smiled. 'She would have done a turn herself.'

By the time Tubby called half-time and announced that supper was served, they'd witnessed a Shania Twain, a warbling Mariah Carey, two Frank Sinatras—one singing 'My Way' and the other stumbling through 'Strangers in the Night'—a leather-clad Ricky Martin, and a bursting-at-the-seams Dolly Parton. Queuing for their food, everyone was in high spirits, talking and laughing about the performances. Those who had yet to sing were not allowed to show themselves, and Donna was currently ferrying trays of food up and down the stairs for them. Serena had been amazed when Dad had told her he'd volunteered to help Debs get the performers down to the stage on time.

'Let me take that for you,' she said to Donna, as once more Donna came into the kitchen for a tray of food. 'You can't possibly manage the stairs in those shoes again.'

Gripping the tray of food, Donna laughed. 'That's OK, Mrs Baxter, my feet are as tough as old coal scuttles.'

'Here, Mum,' Genevieve intervened—no way could they afford for Serena to go near the green room. 'Will you take this over to the judges? They look like they could do with a second helping of trifle.'

The first performer to take to the stage in the second half was Huw Davies. He got a massive cheer when Tubby introduced him as 'the cheeky lad from Stoke, Robbie Williams'.

'I had no idea Huw could sing so well,' Nattie said, at the end of his performance. 'It makes you look at these people in a whole new light.'

Genevieve knew that Adam was on next, and she wondered if Nattie might make the same observation of him afterwards. There was a short lull in the proceedings while Huw left the stage, then Adam appeared—hair brushed back from his forehead, fake whiskers applied to his chin and a black leather jacket turned up at the collar. He stepped onto the small stage and exchanged a quick, nervous glance with Polly who was sitting at the piano to accompany him.

Tubby introduced Adam. 'Put your hands together for none other than Mr Joe Cocker.'

A whistling, whooping round of applause went up, but when Adam leaned into the microphone and exchanged another look with Polly, the crowd fell quiet. The opening notes were Polly's and then Adam came in, his eyes closed, his voice low and husky.

'*You are so beautiful,*' he sang.

After all the raucous singing and booming backing tracks that had gone before, the audience was stunned into silence.

'*You're everything I hoped for,*' Adam sang on, his voice cracking with a rich, heartbreaking resonance.

Genevieve could hardly bear to listen. She felt weak all over, and all at once she realised that this was what she wanted from Christian. She wanted him to take her breath away.

Adam's performance was mesmerising, and when he sang the words, '*You're my guiding light,*' he slowly opened his eyes and looked over to where Genevieve, her mother and Nattie were grouped in the doorway. For a heart-stopping moment Genevieve thought he was looking at her, but then she realised it was Nattie, standing just behind her, who he was staring at. There was no mistaking that he was singing to her, and for her alone. She risked a glance at Nattie and saw that she was transfixed.

Only when the audience leapt to its feet, yelling its appreciation, did Adam look away from Nattie and take his bow.

What happened next had the entire pub in an uproar of hysterical approval. Nattie pushed through the crowd, leapt up onto the stage and grabbed hold of Adam. She kissed him full on the mouth, and just as

Genevieve was wondering if she'd have to fetch a crowbar to prise them apart, Nattie pulled away. Grinning into the microphone, she said, 'Guess what, folks, he kisses as well as he sings!'

'And about time too,' said Serena. 'That poor man's waited long enough for her to come to her senses. *Good God!* Is that your father? Oh, tell me it isn't!'

Despite the trademark Presley white fringed catsuit, the black wig, the sideburns, and the silver-framed sunglasses, the man now up on stage was unmistakably Daddy Dean.

'Tell me he's not going to sing,' murmured Serena. She was white-faced. 'He's never sung in public before. Never!'

Hiding her own anxiety, and reminding herself what Donna had said that afternoon, Genevieve said, 'Well, he's singing now, Mum.'

This time it wasn't Polly providing the musical accompaniment. The video CD up on the wall began with the backing track and 'Always On My Mind' started. Dad's eyes sought out Serena's face in the crowd.

'Maybe I didn't treat you quite as good as I should have . . . maybe I didn't love you quite as often as I could have.'

He was singing from the heart and it was the sincerity in his voice that brought a lump to Genevieve's throat. That and the choice of song.

'If I made you feel second best, girl, I'm so sorry I was blind . . .'

Genevieve had never been more proud of her father. Had he known all along that this was how Mum had been feeling? When the music stopped and he took his bow to earsplitting applause, she looked at her mother. Serena was sobbing openly, her face wet with tears.

Genevieve put her arms round her mother. 'Now do you see how much he loves you, Mum?'

'But he only had to say.'

'It wouldn't have been enough, would it? You know as well as I do, you wanted something big from him. A grand, over-the-top romantic gesture.'

After Tubby had introduced the next act, Genevieve asked if he knew where her father was. 'I think Elvis has left the building,' Tubby joked. 'From the look of him, I'd say he went for some fresh air.'

Squeezing through the crowds, Genevieve and her mother made it to the door and outside. It was still light and easy to spot him. Down on the beach, dressed in his white Elvis suit, he looked a lonely, incongruous figure. Genevieve nudged her mother.

'Go to him, Mum. Put him out of his misery.' She watched Serena walk away, then, knowing she'd done as much as she could, Genevieve turned and went back inside the pub to make a start on the washing-up.

The unexpected sight of Jonjo in the kitchen brought a smile to her lips: he was standing at the sink up to his elbows in soapy water.

'Seeing as you've been abandoned, Polly thought you might like the extra help,' he said. 'There's a hell of a lot to get through, isn't there? Beats me why a pub of this size doesn't have a dishwasher.'

She picked up a tea towel. 'There is one, but it's not working.'

'Oh, well, not to worry, you've got me instead.'

From the other side of the door, the music had changed tempo and an unknown woman's voice screeched out the theme to *Titanic*.

'I'm glad we're this side of the door,' Jonjo said. 'The punters in there could end up with blood pouring out of their ears if they're not careful.'

'You shouldn't criticise what you're not prepared to have a go at yourself,' she said good-humouredly.

'Some of us aren't as fair-minded as you, Genevieve. I haven't known you long, but I can't recall you ever saying a harsh word about anyone.'

'You haven't seen me when I'm rattled. I can turn nasty.'

He laughed. 'Yeah, about as nasty as Polly. You're two of a kind. No, make that three of a kind; you're both like your father.'

'Leaving Nattie out in the cold?'

'I don't think she currently feels out in the cold. The last time I saw Nattie, she and Adam looked decidedly hot. But never mind them, tell me about you and Christian. You have such an amazing history, you owe it to yourselves to work things out.'

She reached for a clean tea towel. 'Who said we have anything to work out?'

Jonjo was rinsing a plate under the tap, but stopped what he was doing. 'You need to talk to him. He needs your reassurance.'

'But we never get to spend any time together. Not like you and Polly.'

He frowned. 'It's seldom a good thing to make comparisons. Not when Christian isn't as lucky as me. I can take time off whenever I want, to be with Polly. Christian's problem is that he's bloody good at what he does and is in high demand. He's also lousy at delegating and saying no. Which leaves him precious little free time.'

She looked away uncomfortably. 'Stop lecturing me, Jonjo.'

'All I'm saying is, go easy on him. Who knows, he might just surprise you one of these days. He's not entirely lacking in sensitivity. After all, some of my perfection must have rubbed off on him along the way.'

She smiled. 'There's only the cutlery left to do. Let's take a break and go and watch some of the acts.'

He glanced at the clock. 'The job's almost done. Ten minutes' more and then we'll venture back into the fray.'

Surprised at his willingness to stick it out, she found another dry tea towel and scooped up a handful of knives and forks, grateful that in Nattie and Serena's absence she had him to help her.

Jonjo was true to his word, and exactly ten minutes later he pulled the plug out from the bottom of the sink. 'That's it. We're done here for now. Let's see if we can mount an attack on the bar for a drink. We've definitely earned it. You especially.'

There was no chance of getting a drink, the bar was much too busy, but Genevieve didn't mind. She was just happy to be out of the kitchen.

Tubby bounced back onto the stage. 'Well, ladies and gentlemen,' he boomed, 'that was to be our last performance of the contest, but we've had a late entry, one we simply couldn't refuse. So, if you'd like to put your hands together and give a warm welcome to this act, a very special person is in for a treat. Ladies and gentlemen, the Angel Sands Choir!'

'Angel Sands Choir?' repeated Genevieve. 'Who's that?'

Jonjo shrugged. 'Just do as the man says and put your hands together.'

She did, and watched with interest to see who would emerge through the curtain of sparkly red tinsel. But before anyone appeared, the backing track started. It was 'The Wonder of You'.

Genevieve turned to Jonjo to tell him how this particular song was her all-time favourite. But he wasn't there. Mystified, she looked round for him, but he'd vanished into thin air.

Back on the stage, the curtain moved and people began to appear, first . . . first Polly, and then . . . Nattie with Adam, his hand on her shoulder. Next came her parents, hand in hand, followed by Donna with a crowd of other performers. Including Jonjo! How on earth had he got there so quickly? He flashed her a grin and a wave. Then, with one fantastic voice that made the hairs on the back of her neck stand on end, they all looked at her and sang the words she knew by heart.

She knew who was behind this: Polly. Dear, sweet Polly. No one else in her family would have known what the song meant to her. A flicker of sparkly red tinsel at the back of the stage caught her attention, and someone else appeared on the stage. Her heart leapt.

It was Christian. And while everyone else swayed to the music and sang, he stepped down from the stage and came slowly towards her. And when he was standing right in front of her, he brought a hand forward and presented her with a single red rose.

'I couldn't serenade you in the way I'd have liked,' he said, leaning in to speak in her ear, 'so I roped in a few who could.'

She tilted her head back. 'You arranged all this yourself?'

'With a little help.'

The remains of the song was lost to her. Not minding that everyone was staring, she held the rose between her fingers and threw her arms round his neck and kissed him.She wasn't letting go of him for the rest of the night!

Gran used to say that miracles happen every day of our lives. 'And the reason we don't realise it,' she would explain, 'is that most of the time we are in too much of a rush to notice the angels going about their business.' After what had happened at the Salvation Arms, and what was happening to her now, Genevieve was inclined to agree with her.

Catching their breath outside the pub, Christian told her he was kidnapping her for the rest of the night. He led her to his car, which was parked outside Gran's house, and told her he wouldn't answer a single question until the time was right.

'Am I allowed to ask where we're going?' she said.

'It'll be obvious,' he said enigmatically. She thought he was taking her to Tawelfan beach, but soon realised she was wrong when he turned off down the narrow track to Ralph's barn. Or rather, Jonjo's barn. Parking alongside a large skip and a cement mixer, he switched off the engine and got out. He was round to her side of the car before she'd put a foot on the ground. 'You have to close your eyes,' he said, his face close to hers so that he could see her clearly. Producing a torch from the back of the car, he offered her his arm.

She heard a door scrape and guessed they were going inside the barn. After a few steps, he said, 'Now turn round, put your hands over your ears and keep your eyes tightly closed.'

She was tempted to sneak just one tiny glance. But she didn't. Then, feeling his hands on hers, he uncovered her ears and said, 'You can open your eyes and turn round now.'

She could hardly believe what she was seeing. The far end of the barn looked like something out of the Arabian Nights—a magical canopied palace strewn with sumptuous rugs and cushions. And everywhere there were candles sparkling like brightly polished jewels.

She turned to Christian. 'It's beautiful. But what's it doing here?'

'It's for you, Genevieve. Somewhere I can have you all to myself.' He took her hand. 'Come and sit down.'

In a daze, she did as he said. When she was settled on a low stool, he poured her a glass of chilled champagne.

'Courtesy of Jonjo,' Christian said. 'He told me he'd never forgive me if I stinted on what we drank.'

She took the glass from him. 'Jonjo never said anything. Not a word.'

He clinked his glass against hers. 'That was the general idea. The surprise was meant to take your breath away.'

'Any more surprises like this and I shall die of asphyxiation. When did you get here and arrange all this?'

'Around lunchtime with Polly and Jonjo. I followed them down and they helped get the main structure up.'

'I don't believe it. My sister was in on it as well?'

'Your parents, too. Jonjo brought them to see it this afternoon. It was also the perfect opportunity, after all these years, to meet your mother properly. And maybe convince her I'm not the bastard she remembers.'

Genevieve saw now how she'd been thoroughly tricked. Jonjo hadn't offered to show Serena the barn to silence her mother's questions, it had all been part of a much bigger picture.

'Do you have any other surprises up your sleeve?'

In the candlelight, he suddenly looked serious. 'I might. But first I have to ask you something. I want to know what your feelings are for Adam.'

'For Adam? What's he got to do with anything?'

'Genevieve, he has everything to do with it. Don't you see that?'

Confused, she said, 'No, I don't. He's a friend. A really good friend.'

'But you're so close to him. And it's him you always turn to, isn't it?'

She hesitated. 'Only because he's always there.'

'Like he was the day your grandmother died.'

'You were there, too.'

'Yes, but when we were in the conservatory at Paradise House, while he was saying goodbye, I saw the way the two of you connected. And believe me, I felt you didn't want or need me there.'

Genevieve thought back to that day and picked her way through the jumble of events and emotions. With a flash of recall, she pictured the way Adam had touched her arm in the conservatory, and how she'd kissed him goodbye, and the moment shortly after when she had told Christian she wanted to be alone with Nattie. Shocked, she saw the conclusion Christian must have reached.

'Is that why your emails tailed off?'

'Yes. I couldn't work out how you really felt about me.'

'But why didn't you just ask me what I felt?'

He put his glass down. 'You Baxters aren't the only ones afraid to open up, you know. I was worried that if I put you on the spot, I'd get the answer I didn't want to hear, and I'd lose you.' He paused. 'But I'm asking the question now. I need to know, Genevieve. I know Adam is mad about your sister, but are you secretly in love with him?'

She put her glass next to his. It was time to be completely honest with him. And with herself. She moved in close, so there could be no mistaking her words. 'Christian, I do love Adam, I admit that. But I love him affectionately, like a brother. The only man I've ever truly loved and desired is you. There's never been anyone else who made me feel the way you do. I loved you as a teenager, and I probably started to love you all over again that day you showed up at Paradise House looking for somewhere to stay. There, is that clear enough for you?'

A smile lightened the solemn expression that had clouded his face. 'Crystal clear,' he said. And when he kissed her, she knew that whatever doubts he'd been feeling, had now passed. He moved her to the soft-carpeted ground and put a cushion under her head.

They made love slowly, neither of them wanting to rush what they'd waited so long for. Afterwards, lying in his arms, bathed in the wash of golden candlelight, as he told her how beautiful she was, she did indeed feel beautiful. And loved.

In the weeks that followed, it was open season on the Baxter family. They had only themselves to blame, as Tubby was the first to say.

'If you must be so public in nailing your colours to the mast,' he teased Genevieve, 'what else do you expect, but for everyone to gossip about you?'

But for once, Genevieve wasn't bothered that her private life, a contradiction in terms these days, was being discussed so openly. Adam had just commented on this very point. They were up at St Non's, where she was changing the flowers on Gran's grave and he, at Lily-Rose's request, was helping gather daisies to make a daisy chain.

Genevieve brushed away a fly that had landed on the angel on her grandmother's headstone. 'It all depends what people are saying. But luckily I'm not the only one they're talking about. I reckon you're of more interest to everyone.'

He went over to Lily-Rose, sitting crosslegged in the shade of the yew hedge, and gave her the daisies he'd picked. Joining Genevieve again, Adam said, 'Any particular reason I'm the centre of attention?'

'Well, it's not every man who'd be brave enough to take on Natalie Baxter, is it?'

'At least they think I'm brave and not stupid.'

Genevieve smiled. 'So how's it going? Not regretting it, I hope.'

'No chance.' He hesitated. 'But how about Nattie? Has she said anything to you?'

'Well, it's not a big deal, and you must promise not to tell her I said anything, but'—she paused to glance at Lily-Rose—'the thing is, she thinks you're holding out on her.'

Adam's face broke into an enormous grin, then he looked serious again. 'I don't want to hurry things. I'm not interested in an easy-come, easy-go fling with Nattie. I want the real thing. Love.'

'Then you're doing exactly the right thing. I doubt any man's ever given her this much consideration. The fact that she's worrying why you haven't got her into bed yet means she cares. Something she hasn't had a lot of experience of doing in the past.'

Two days after the contest, after Christian had left to go back to work, Adam had called Genevieve to say he wanted to talk to her in private.

'You must have thought it very odd what I did,' he said to her, 'singing that song for Nattie after everything I'd shared with you.'

'Just a little. But only because you seemed to have got her out of your system.'

'I gave it my best shot, but in the end, I couldn't do it.'

'And what about selling up and moving away? Is that still going to happen?'

Shamefaced, he'd admitted that it had been a lie. 'I hoped it would make her think what it would be like if I wasn't around any more.'

Breaking into her thoughts now, Adam said, 'Nattie thinks you're avoiding me, Gen. Are you?'

'Yes,' she said, quite matter-of-factly. She didn't want to lie to Adam. 'Why?'

'Because you don't need an old chum like me hanging around and getting in the way.'

He looked at her sternly. 'You couldn't ever be in the way, Gen. I don't want things to change between us.'

But, despite his words, Genevieve knew that their friendship had already begun to change.

With Lily-Rose wearing a daisy-chain crown and carrying a matching one for her mother, Adam hoisted her onto his shoulders and they walked back down into the village.

After several days of grey skies and frequent showers, it was glorious again. The hot midday sun was high and bright in a flawless blue sky. The narrow streets were packed with smiling visitors—small, flush-faced children peering out from beneath sunhats and waving fishing nets at one another, middle-aged couples strolling slowly arm-in-arm, and groups of teenagers browsing the shops. They passed Angel Cottage but didn't stop. Nattie, along with everyone else, would be waiting for them at Paradise House where Serena was preparing a special lunch.

'What do you think this lunch is all about?' Adam asked as they waved at Debs through the open door of the crowded salon.

'I've a feeling Mum and Dad are going to make an announcement.'

'Any idea what it is?'

'If you'd asked me that a month ago I'd have said their divorce, but since you and Donna did such a good job of turning Dad into Elvis, they've barely let each out of their sight. Mum got her grand gesture of love from Dad that night, and Dad got a surprise—the realisation that the limelight's no bad place to be now and then.'

'Everything your father did that night was his own work,' Adam said.

'Donna and I had very little to do with his performance. When it's from the heart, it needs no extra encouragement.'

'In that case, the same must apply to your own performance. I've said it before, but you were show-stoppingly brilliant. It was a shame you couldn't have won joint first prize with Donna instead of making do with second.' To her amusement, a faint hue of red coloured his face.

It was early days, but Genevieve hoped her sister wouldn't disappoint Adam. Nattie had been her usual self, of course, taking on the chin the flak dished out by Tubby and their father.

'So what if I've changed my mind about Adam,' she told them. 'I was biding my time. I was being selective.' She told Genevieve and Polly that she had no intention of changing, though. 'Just because I'm going out with him, it doesn't mean I'm going to turn into something I'm not.'

'I think he'd be upset if you did, Nats,' said Polly.

'Yes,' agreed Genevieve. 'Goodness knows why, but it's the head-strong, difficult, stroppy you he's worshipped all this time, not some shallow, pliable girl without a thought in her head.'

But what amazed them most was Nattie sticking to her word and working for Adam. 'I made a promise and I'll see it through,' Nattie told them. 'Even if the job is as boring as hell.'

Lily-Rose, on the other hand, was full of all the fun things she had to do each day: playing on the climbing frame, winning several swimming races in the pool, and having her face painted. It was obvious she was having the time of her life.

As was Polly. Much to Jonjo's delight, the night after the talent show, Polly had agreed to get engaged. Embellishing the story with infuriat-ingly little detail, Polly had told them the following morning, while he was upstairs in the shower, how he'd taken her down to the beach and, in the moonlight, had produced a ring he'd bought in Hong Kong. They'd all crowded round her hand to get a closer look at the cluster of diamonds, and had let out a collective whistle.

Now, as Genevieve led the way round to the back door, she realised she couldn't imagine Paradise House without her youngest sister's benign presence in it.

Lunch was an alfresco affair. Dad had set up two tables end to end in the dappled shade of the orchard. Mum had covered them with a couple of large white cloths, and then had artfully flung handfuls of rose petals in between the plates and glasses. It bore all the hallmarks of a grand Baxter celebration. But what exactly were they celebrating?

Luckily there were no guests hanging around. With the answering machine switched on so lunch wouldn't be spoiled by having to run to the phone every five minutes, Mum instructed them to sit down.

'Adam and Nattie, you sit with Lily-Rose between the two of you. Jonjo, you sit opposite Polly and next to Nattie, and Genevieve, you go at the top of the table, next to your father, and, well, Christian, I think it's fairly obvious where you should go, next to Genevieve. There now, that's everyone sorted. Well, Daddy Dean, let's get these glasses filled!'

Looking happier than Genevieve could ever remember seeing him, her father moved slowly round the table, pouring out their wine. Across the table, she caught Nattie's eye as Adam showed Lily-Rose how to turn her paper napkin into a swan. Nattie smiled at Genevieve and rolled her eyes in Adam's direction. But there was no scorn or malice to the gesture, just a look of happy indulgence. Had she come to realise that Adam would make the most wonderful father for Lily-Rose? And a devoted husband into the bargain? Even Nattie must have figured that one out for herself. Not that Genevieve could talk. Look how she'd misread Christian's feelings towards her.

A slight squeeze on her leg under the table had her turning to Christian. 'You OK?' he mouthed.

She reached for his hand and mouthed back, 'I'm fine.' There it was again. *I'm fine.* Yes, but this time she really was.

'Hey, you two!' said Nattie from across the table, 'no secret conversations. We had enough of that when we were children. The pair of you were always leaving the rest of us out.'

Serena raised her glass. She waited for them all to follow suit. She looked down the length of the table to where her husband was sitting.

'Here's to us all and what lies ahead.'

They responded to the toast and Lily-Rose, gulping down her apple juice too fast, let out an enormous burp and made them all laugh.

'Do you think we ought to tell them what does lie ahead?' asked Daddy Dean.

'I suppose we ought to,' Serena said, 'seeing as it affects them so directly.'

'Come on, you two,' demanded Nattie. 'It's time to tell us what this lunch is all about.'

Serena looked at their father. 'Go on, then. You do the honours.'

With all eyes on him, Daddy Dean said, 'Your mother and I have decided we need some time away together and . . . and if it's OK with all of you, we want to go on an extended second honeymoon.'

'What a wonderful idea,' said Polly. 'For how long?'

'We haven't decided exactly. But it'll definitely be longer than our first.'

'Perhaps a month, maybe two,' Serena added more assuredly.

Nattie whistled. 'Now that's some second honeymoon.'

'Where are you thinking of going?' asked Genevieve.

'New Zealand. Your mother wants to show me where she's been staying and then we'll go exploring somewhere new. Australia seems a likely bet. I've always been fascinated by the idea of Alice Springs.'

'Then perhaps you'd better make it two to three months,' suggested Jonjo.

'But what about us? And Paradise House?' Nattie's voice had taken a turn for the worse.

Serena said, 'You'll be fine without us, Nattie. You have a lovely new house to live in, a job, a gorgeous daughter and'—she cast a look in Adam's direction—'a man who adores you. I'd say you'll have everything a girl could wish for. And as to Paradise House, well, that's slightly more complicated.'

She turned to Genevieve, who braced herself to hear the words she didn't want to hear. If there was one thing she was sure of, she didn't want to go on running Paradise House as it was. It was too exhausting.

'Genevieve,' her father said, 'your mother and I owe you a huge debt of gratitude for all the hard work you've put in since you came home, so before I say anything else, I just want to thank you. I, personally, don't know what I would have done without you.' Clearing his throat, he carried on. 'It's entirely up to you, but we wondered if you would want to take on the full responsibility of running Paradise House, but not as it is. So, we've come up with an idea we want you to consider. It would mean a total revamp of the place, someone to help oversee the work, and more importantly, someone special to put it on the map. And we think that special someone is you.'

Still holding Christian's hand beneath the table, Genevieve took a gulp of her wine and listened to what her parents had to say.

Christian and Genevieve were standing outside the Salvation Arms, looking down onto the beach. It was early evening, and only a handful of powerboat enthusiasts were left, making their noisy exit, winching boats onto trailers, yelling and slamming doors.

'Do you fancy a drink in the pub, or a walk?' she asked Christian.

'Let's walk to Tawelfan.'

They walked hand in hand along the coastal path, in an easy, comfortable silence. Taking the steep path down to Tawelfan, they found they had the beach to themselves. The dunes were also deserted, and they sat on the warm, dry sand, staring out at the horizon. Faint strands of clouds had formed in the sky around the setting sun and a chain of gulls flew along the shore, their wings hardly moving as they glided into the distance. In the perfect quiet of the moment, Genevieve thought of all that had been discussed that afternoon. Her parents going away for a second honeymoon; Jonjo saying he didn't want a long engagement—'If I give Polly too much time to think about it, she might change her mind,' he'd said—and Polly admitting that she'd already applied for several teaching jobs in Buckinghamshire so she could be with Jonjo. And lastly, there was her parents' idea to turn Paradise House into a smart, up-market country house hotel, with a gourmet restaurant.

They'd clearly put a lot of thought into it—they'd even been to the bank to see about a loan—and wanted her to do the same. 'We want to semi-retire,' her father said. 'We'll help as much as you want us to, but we want officially to sign over Paradise House to you three girls.'

What they had in mind was for Genevieve to have the larger share, because she would be the one responsible for making it work. Initially, Genevieve was unsure. Would this be her dream? Or would it still be her parents'? She would need proper full- or part-time staff. Donna had now moved in with Tubby and was the ideal candidate to be in charge of housekeeping. With someone so reliable on hand, Genevieve would be left to do what she enjoyed most—cooking.

The more she thought about it, the more excited she began to feel. There would be candlelit dinners, with cocktails beforehand on the terrace if the weather was warm, and roaring log fires in the winter.

But to achieve any of that, there would have to be a great deal of upheaval. As her father had said during lunch, 'The worst bit will be living here while the work is being carried out.'

'Sounds to me like you need an architect,' said Jonjo. 'A decent architect who comes with impeccable references.'

Turning from the sea, now, and looking at Christian, Genevieve said, 'You know that architect I might be in need of?'

'Yes.'

'Do you suppose he might be too busy with all his other commitments to help at Paradise House?'

'He might be. But on the other hand, he might not.' He reached for her hands, entwining his fingers through hers. 'I've come to an important decision, one that requires your approval before I take it any further. How would you feel if I lived here in Angel Sands?'

'That's quite a commute. You'd have to be up early to be in the office for nine each morning.'

'True. Although it would depend where the office was. If, say, I worked for myself, I could work wherever I wanted.'

'Are you saying what I think you're saying?'

He stroked her cheek. 'I love you, Genevieve, and I want to give *us* a real chance of working. We can't do that if we live so far apart.'

'You'd really do that?'

'In the blink of an eye. All I need to know is that you feel the same; that it's worth a go. But I'll warn you now, I've got it all planned. For the time being, I'm going to rent out my parents' house in Shropshire, sell my flat and rent a cottage near you. That way we won't be rushing things. Oh, and as to work, to begin with I reckon I can make a living from all the barns in the area that are ripe for conversion. And there are always holiday homes to renovate. What do you think? Will it work?'

A euphoric surge of happiness filled her. 'I think it will work *fine*, Christian. But just to be sure, this isn't a double bluff, is it? You're not threatening commitment in the hope I'll do a runner?'

He laughed out loud. 'You're not running anywhere. You're staying right here.' He pushed her back onto the warm sand and kissed her.

As Genevieve closed her eyes, she caught sight of a faint ghost of a cloud floating directly above their heads. She was probably imagining it, but it looked just like one of Gran's angels gazing down on her.

ERICA JAMES

When her marriage broke down and Erica James was struggling to make ends meet, a friend gave her some very good advice. 'He told me to view my situation as an opportunity to do something new, something I'd always wanted to do,' says Erica. 'As a hobby, I'd been dabbling with writing a novel and, for my sanity, it seemed now was the right time to start. It was hard but it became my lifeline during the really grim times.' *Paradise House* is Erica's ninth novel and what the author does so successfully is to vividly re-create people and places that she knows well. 'I set *Paradise House* in Pembrokeshire because that was where I went when my sons, Edward and Samuel, were at the toddler stage. There were lots of days spent on the beach playing for hours in rock pools and building sand castles, then running for cover when the rain started. I loved it and think I have an affinity with beaches because I grew up by the sea on Hayling Island. It seemed perfectly natural to me, at the age of twelve, to slip out of school at lunch time and cycle down to the beach for a quick swim. I can remember swimming in the sea during March one year—but you wouldn't catch me doing it now. I'd freeze to death!'

In *Paradise House*, Erica's heroine, Genevieve, suffers from dyslexia and her hero, Christian, is deaf. 'A friend of my eldest son is dyslexic and she was very helpful, as were the people I spoke to at a centre for the deaf in Cheshire,' said Erica. 'The idea for Christian's character came

to me some time ago when I was on holiday and met a young guy who was deaf. Initially I had no idea his hearing was impaired to the extent it was because he had worked so hard at perfecting his speech and his lip-reading skills. I was really impressed by this and I always knew he'd turn up in one of my books!'

Erica James went on to tell me that she also wanted to explore the reasons why a mother walks out on her family. 'So much is spoken about the male midlife crisis, I thought it was time the boot was on the other foot. Women always have an abundance of common sense and usually roll up their sleeves and work through any problems. But Serena Baxter just wasn't that sort of woman and so I decided to let her do what so many women would love to do: she simply walked away when the going got tough. I'm not saying it was the right thing to do, but it achieved the right result—her family sat up and gave her more thought.'

So is Erica James thinking of treating herself to some time out? 'Well, actually, I am planning a trip to Italy on my own next year,' she laughs. 'I want to go to Venice towards the end of the summer and not just as a holiday. I want to pretend to be Venetian for a while. I can just see myself sitting on a balcony overlooking the canal while working on the next book. The trouble is, I may not want to come home!'

Jane Eastgate

A SPECIAL
RELATIONSHIP
DOUGLAS
KENNEDY

When Sally Goodchild first meets Tony
Hobbs in war-torn Somalia, she is instantly
attracted to him. Both assigned as foreign
correspondents on different newspapers,
they know that in their line of work
relationships rarely last long-term. But then
Tony is recalled to London and Sally finds
out that she is expecting his baby.
It seems fate has dictated that they should
make a life together.

ONE

ABOUT AN HOUR after I met Tony Hobbs, he saved my life.

I know that sounds just a little melodramatic, but it's the truth. Or, at least, as true as anything a journalist will tell you.

I was in Somalia—a country I had never visited until I got a call in Cairo and suddenly found myself dispatched there. It was a Friday afternoon, the Muslim Holy Day. Like most foreign correspondents in the Egyptian capital, I was using the official day of rest to sun myself beside the pool of the Gezira Club. Even though the sun is a constant commodity in Egypt, it is something that correspondents based there rarely get to see. Especially if, like me, they are bargain basement one-person operations, covering the entire Middle East and all of eastern Africa. Which is why I got that call on that Friday afternoon.

'Is this Sally Goodchild?' asked an American voice.

'That's right,' I said, sitting upright and holding the cellphone close to my ear. 'Who's this?'

'Dick Leonard from the paper. I'm new on the Foreign Desk.'

'The paper' was my employer. Also known as the *Boston Post*.

'I'm sure you've heard about the flood in Somalia?' Leonard asked.

Rule one of journalism: never admit you've been out of contact with the world at large. So all I said was, 'How many dead?'

'No definitive body count so far, according to CNN.'

'Where exactly in Somalia?'

'The Juba River Valley. At least four villages have been submerged. The editor wants somebody there. Can you leave straight away?'

So that's how I found myself on a flight to Mogadishu, where we

159

landed just after midnight. After four hours' sleep at the Central Hotel, I managed to make contact with the International Red Cross in Somalia, and talked my way onto one of their helicopters that was heading for the flood zone. There were no seats inside the helicopter, and I sat with three Red Cross staffers on its cold steel floor. As it left the ground, the chopper lurched dangerously to the starboard side and we were all thrown against the thick webbed belts, bolted to the cabin walls, into which we had fastened ourselves before take-off. Once the pilot regained control and we evened out, the guy seated on the floor opposite me smiled broadly and said, 'That was a good start.'

Though it was difficult to hear anything over the din of the rotor blades, I did discern that he had an English accent. Then I looked at him more closely and figured that this was no aid worker. It wasn't just his tanned face—which, coupled with his blond hair, leant him a certain weather-beaten appeal; no, what really convinced me that he wasn't Red Cross was the slightly flirtatious smile he gave me after our near-death experience. At that moment, I knew that he was a journalist.

Just as I saw that he was looking me over, appraising me, and also probably working out that I too wasn't relief-worker material. Of course, I was wondering how I was being perceived. I have an angular face, a little gaunt, with a fair complexion that hasn't much in the way of wrinkles, and my light brown hair isn't yet streaked with grey. So though I may be crowding middle age, I can pass myself off as just over the thirty-year-old frontier.

These banal thoughts were abruptly interrupted when the helicopter suddenly rolled to the left as the pilot went full throttle and we shot off at speed to a higher altitude. Accompanying this abrupt ascent was the distinctive sound of antiaircraft fire. Immediately, the Brit was digging into his daypack, pulling out a pair of field glasses. Despite the protestations of one of the Red Cross workers beside me, he unbuckled his straps and peered out of one of the porthole windows.

'Looks like someone's trying to kill us,' he shouted over the din of the engine. But his voice was calm, if not redolent of amusement.

'Who's "someone"?' I shouted back.

'Usual militia bastards,' he said, eyes still fastened to the field glasses.

'But why are they shooting at a Red Cross chopper?' I asked.

'Because they shoot at anything foreign and moving. It's sport to them.'

That's when he flashed me a deeply mischievous smile, making me think: The guy's actually enjoying all this.

I smiled back. That was a point of pride with me: to never show fear under fire. A further three stomach-churning rolls to the right, followed by one more rapid acceleration, and we seemed to leave the danger zone. Ten nervous minutes followed, then we banked low. I craned my neck, looked out of the window and sucked in my breath. There before me was a submerged landscape—Noah's Flood. The water had consumed everything. Houses and livestock floated by. Then I spied the first dead body, face down in the water, followed by four more.

Everyone in the chopper was now peering out of the window, taking in the extent of the calamity. In the distance, we could see three white jeeps flying the Red Cross flag. There were around fourteen aid workers standing by the jeeps, frantically waving to us. There was a problem, however. A cluster of Somalian soldiers was positioned within a hundred yards of the Red Cross team, and they were simultaneously making beckoning gestures towards us with their arms.

'This should be amusing,' the Brit said.

'Not if it's like last time,' one of the Red Cross team said.

'What happened last time?' I asked.

'They tried to loot us,' he said.

We overflew the soldiers and the Red Cross jeeps. But the aid workers on the ground seemed to know the game we were playing, as they jumped into the jeeps, reversed direction, and started racing towards the empty terrain where we were coming down.

'Looks like there's going to be a little race to meet us,' the Brit said.

I peered out of my window and saw a dozen Somalian soldiers running in our direction.

'See what you mean,' I shouted as we landed with a bump.

With terra firma beneath us, the Red Cross man next to me was on his feet, yanking up the lever that kept the cabin door in its place. The others headed towards the cargo bay at the rear of the cabin, undoing the webbing that held in the crates of medical supplies and dried food.

'Need a hand?' the Brit asked one of the Red Cross guys.

'We'll be fine,' he said. 'But you better get moving before the army shows up.'

'Where's the nearest village?'

'It *was* about a mile due south of here.'

'Right,' he said. Then he turned to me and asked, 'You coming?'

I nodded, turned to the Red Cross man and said. 'Thanks for the lift.'

The Brit and I headed out of the cabin. As soon as we hit the ground, he tapped me on the shoulder and pointed towards the three Red Cross jeeps. Crouching low, we ran in their direction, not looking back until we were behind them. This turned out to be a strategically smart move, as we had managed to dodge the attention of the Somalian soldiers, who had now surrounded the chopper, guns trained on the Red Cross team.

'See that clump of trees over there?' the Brit said, pointing towards a small patch of gum trees about fifty yards away from us.

I nodded. After one final glance at the soldiers, who were now ripping into a case of medical supplies, we made a dash for it. It couldn't have taken more than twenty seconds to cover the fifty yards, but God did it seem long. I knew that, if the soldiers saw two figures running for cover, their natural reaction would be to shoot us down. When we reached the woods, we ducked behind a tree.

'Well done,' the Brit whispered. 'Think you can make it over there without getting shot?'

I looked in the direction he was pointing—another meagre grove of trees that fronted the now-deluged river. I turned back and met his challenging smile. 'I never get shot,' I said. Then we ran out of the trees, making a manic beeline for the next patch of cover. The Brit was ahead of me. But as soon as he reached the trees, something brought him to a sudden halt. I stopped in my tracks as I saw him walking backwards, his arms held high in the air. Emerging from the trees was a young Somalian soldier, his rifle trained on the Brit. Suddenly the soldier saw me—and when he turned his gun on me, I made a desperate error of judgment. Instead of putting my hands above my head, I hit the ground, certain he was going to fire. This caused him to roar at me, as he tried to get me in his sights.

Then, suddenly, the Brit tackled him, knocking him to the ground. He swung a clenched fist, slamming it into the soldier's stomach, knocking the wind out of him. The kid groaned, and the Brit brought his boot down hard on the hand that was clutching the gun. The kid screamed and released the weapon, which the Brit quickly scooped up and had trained on the soldier in a matter of seconds.

The kid now began to sob, curling up into a foetal position, pleading for his life. I turned to the Brit and said, 'You can't . . .'

But he just looked at me and winked. Then, turning back to the child soldier, he said, 'Did you hear? She doesn't want me to shoot you.'

The kid said nothing. He just curled himself tighter into a ball, crying like the frightened child he was.

'I think you should apologise to her, don't you?' said the Brit.

'Sorry, sorry, sorry,' the kid said, the words choked with sobs.

'Apology accepted?' the Brit asked me. I nodded.

He turned back to the kid and said. 'You can go now.'

The kid, trembling, got to his feet, certain he was going to be shot.

'It's all right,' the Brit said quietly. 'Nothing's going to happen to you. But you have to promise me one thing: you must not tell anyone in your company that you met us. Will you do that?'

The soldier nodded.

'Good. Are there any army patrols down river from here?'

'No. Our base got washed away. I got separated from the others.'

'How about the village near here?'

'Nothing left of it.'

'All the people washed away?'

'Some made it to a hill.'

'Where's the hill?'

The soldier pointed towards an overgrown path through the trees.

The Brit looked at me and said, 'That's our story.'

'Sounds good to me,' I said, meeting his look.

'Run along now,' the Brit said to the soldier. 'And remember, you never saw us. Understood?'

The boy soldier nodded and dashed out of the trees in the general direction of the chopper. When he was out of sight, the Brit shut his eyes, drew in a deep breath and said, 'Fucking hell.'

'And so say all of us.'

He opened his eyes and looked at me. 'You all right?' he said.

'Yeah—but I feel like a complete jerk.'

He grinned. 'You *were* a complete jerk—but it happens. Especially when you get surprised by a kid with a gun. On which note . . .'

He motioned with his thumb that we should make tracks. Which is exactly what we did—finding the overgrown path, threading our way on to the edge of swamped fields. We walked nonstop for fifteen minutes, saying nothing. Then the Brit pointed to a couple of large rocks positioned near the river. We sat down, but didn't say anything for a moment as we tried to gauge the silence. After a moment, he spoke.

'The way I figure it, if that kid had told on us, his comrades would be here by now.'

'You certainly scared him into thinking you would kill him.'

'He needed scaring. He would have shot you without compunction.'

'I know. Thank you.'

'All part of the service.' Then he proffered his hand and said, 'Tony Hobbs. Who do you write for?'

'The *Boston Post*.'

An amused smile crossed his lips. 'Do you really?'

'Yes,' I said. '*Really*. We do have foreign correspondents, you know.'

'So where do you correspond from?' he asked.

'Cairo. And let me guess. You write for the *Sun*?'

'The *Chronicle*, actually.'

I tried not to appear impressed. 'You based in London?'

'Cairo. I arrived ten days ago.'

There was a sound of nearby footsteps. We both tensed. Tony picked up the rifle he had leaned against the rock. Then we heard the steps grow nearer. As we stood up, a young Somalian woman came running down the path, a child in her arms. The mother was gaunt; the child chillingly still. As soon as the woman saw us, she began to scream, making wild gesticulations at the gun in Tony's hand. Tony twigged immediately. He tossed the gun into the rushing waters of the river, adding it to the flooded debris washing downstream. The gesture seemed to surprise the woman. But as she turned to me and started pleading with me, her legs buckled. Tony and I both grabbed her, keeping her upright. I glanced down at her lifeless baby, still held tightly in her arms. I looked up at the Brit. He nodded in the direction of the Red Cross chopper. We each put an arm round her emaciated waist, and began the slow journey back to the clearing where we'd landed earlier.

When we reached it, we escorted her past the soldiers and made a beeline for the Red Cross chopper. Two of the aid workers from the flight were still unloading supplies.

'Who's the doctor around here?' I asked. One of the guys looked up, saw the woman and child, and sprang into action, while his colleague politely told us to get lost.

'There's nothing more you can do now.'

Nor, it turned out, was there any chance that we'd be allowed back down the path towards that washed-out village. The Somalian Army had now blocked it off. When I found the head Red Cross medico and told him about the villagers perched on a hill around two miles from here, he said, 'We know all about it. And we will be sending our helicopter as soon as the army gives us clearance.'

'Let us go with you,' I said.

'It's not possible. The army will only allow three of our team and we need to send medical men.'

'Send two,' Tony said, 'and let one of us—'

But we were interrupted by the arrival of an army officer. He tapped Tony on the shoulder. 'You—papers.' Then he tapped me. 'You too.'

We handed over our respective passports. 'Red Cross papers,' he demanded. When Tony started to make up some far-fetched story about leaving them behind, the officer said one damning word, 'Journalists.'

Then he turned to his soldiers and said, 'Get them on the next chopper back to Mogadishu.'

We returned to the capital under virtual armed guard. When we landed on the outskirts, I fully expected us to be arrested. But instead, one of the soldiers asked me if I had any American dollars.

'Perhaps,' I said. And then, chancing my arm, I asked him if he could arrange a ride for us to the Central Hotel for ten bucks.

'You pay twenty, you get your ride.'

He even commandeered a jeep to get us there. En route, Tony and I spoke for the first time since being placed under armed guard.

'Not a lot to write about, is there?' I said.

'I'm sure we'll both manage to squeeze something out of it.'

We found two rooms on the same floor, and agreed to meet after we'd filed our respective copy. Around two hours later—shortly after I'd dispatched by email 700 words on the general disarray in the Juba River Valley, the sight of floating bodies in the river, the infrastructural chaos and the experience of being fired upon in a Red Cross helicopter by rebel forces—there was a knock at my door.

Tony stood outside, holding a bottle of Scotch and two glasses.

'This looks promising,' I said. 'Come on in.'

He didn't leave again until seven the next morning, when we checked out to catch the flight back to Cairo.

'Have you ever been married?' Tony asked, as we got tipsy on the flight.

'Foreign correspondents aren't the marrying kind. You?'

'You must be joking.'

'Never come close?'

'Everyone's come close once.'

We talked nonstop all the way back to Cairo. There was an immediate ease between us, not just because we had so much professional terrain in common, but also because we seemed to possess a similar worldview: slightly jaded, fiercely independent. We also both acknowledged that foreign corresponding was a kid's game, in which most practitioners were considered way over the hill by the time they reached fifty.

'Which makes me eight years away from the slag heap,' Tony said somewhere over Sudan.

'You're that young?' I said. 'I thought you were at least ten years older.'

He shot me a cool, amused look. 'You're fast.'

'I try.'

I could tell that he enjoyed repartee—not just for its verbal gamesmanship, but also because it allowed him to retreat from the serious, or anything that might be self-revealing. Every time our in-flight conversation veered towards the personal, he'd quickly switch into badinage mode. This didn't disconcert me. After all, we'd just met and were still sizing each other up. But I still noted this diversionary tactic, and wondered if it would hinder me from getting to know the guy—as, much to my surprise, I realised that I wanted to get to know Tony Hobbs.

Not that I was going to reveal that fact to him. So, when we arrived in Cairo, we shared a cab back to Zamalek (the relatively upmarket expatriate quarter where just about every foreign correspondent lived). As it turned out, Tony's place was only two blocks from mine. As the taxi slowed to a halt in front of my door, he reached into his pocket and handed me his card.

'Here's where to find me,' he said.

I pulled out a business card of my own, and scribbled a number on the back of it. 'And here's my number.'

'Thanks,' he said, taking it. 'So call me, eh?'

'No, you make the first move,' I said.

'Old-fashioned, are we?' he said, raising his eyebrows.

'Hardly. But I don't make the first move. All right?'

He leaned over and gave me a very long kiss. 'Fine,' he said.

As soon as I was upstairs in my empty, silent apartment, I kicked myself for playing the tough dame. *No, you make the first move*. What a profoundly dumb thing to say. Because I knew that guys like Tony Hobbs didn't cross my path every day.

Still, I could now do nothing but put the entire business out of my mind. So I spent the better part of an hour soaking in a bath, then crawled into bed and passed out for nearly ten hours—having hardly slept for the past two nights. I was up just after seven in the morning. I made breakfast. I powered up my laptop and turned out my weekly 'Letter from Cairo'. When the phone rang around noon, I jumped for it.

'Hello,' Tony said. 'This is the first move.'

He came by ten minutes later to pick me up for lunch. We never made it to the restaurant.

Much later, in bed, he turned to me and said, 'So who's making the second move?'

It would be the stuff of romantic cliché to say that, from that moment on, we were inseparable. Nonetheless, I do count that afternoon as the official start of us. What most surprised me was this: it was about the easiest transition imaginable.

'You know, I always end up cutting and running out of these things,' I told Tony about a month after we started seeing each other.

'Oh, so that's what this is—a thing.'

'You know what I'm saying.'

'That I shouldn't get down on one knee and propose, because you're planning to break my heart?'

I laughed and said, 'I really am not planning to do that.'

'Then your point is . . . what?'

'My point is . . . I'm happy with you, and the fact that I feel this way is surprising the hell out of me, because I haven't felt this way for a long time, and I'm just hoping you feel this way, because I don't want to waste my time on someone who doesn't feel this way, because—'

He cut me off by leaning over and kissing me deeply. When he finished, he said, 'I'm very pleased you're not cutting and running.'

Was that a declaration of love? I certainly hoped so. At that moment, I knew I was in love with him. Just as I also knew that my bumbling admission of happiness was about as far as I'd go in confessing such a major emotional truth. Such admissions have always been difficult for me. Just as they were also difficult for my schoolteacher parents, who were deeply reserved when it came to public displays of affection.

'You know, I can only once remember seeing our parents kiss each other,' my older sister Sandy told me shortly after they were killed in an automobile accident.

At which point Sandy broke down completely and wept so loudly that her grief sounded something like keening. My own displays of raw public grief were few in the wake of their death. Perhaps because I was too numb from the shock of it all to cry. The year was 1988. I was twenty-one. I had just finished my senior year at Mount Holyoke College and was going to graduate magna cum laude. My parents couldn't have been more pleased. When they drove up to the college to see me get my degree that weekend, they were in such unusually ebullient form that they actually went to a big post-commencement party on campus. I wanted them to spend the night, but they had to get back to Worcester that evening for some big church event the next day. Just before they got into the car, my father gave me a big uncharacteristic hug and said that he loved me.

Two hours later, he nodded off at the wheel on the Interstate. The car veered out of control and crashed through the centre guard rail into a Ford station wagon carrying a family of five. Two of the occupants—a young mother and her baby son—were killed. So were my parents.

In the wake of their death, Sandy kept expecting me to fall apart (as she was doing constantly). Then again, Sandy has always been the emotional roller coaster in the family. Just as she's also been the one fixed geographic point in my life—someone to watch over me. But we couldn't be more disparate characters. Whereas I was always asserting my independence, Sandy followed my parents into high-school teaching, married a teacher, moved to the Boston suburbs and had three children by the time she was thirty. She even managed to keep her life together after her husband walked out on her three years ago.

She's also been the one person with whom I've always been open about everything going on with me—with the exception of the period directly after the death of my parents. All accidental deaths are simultaneously absurd and tragic. As I told Tony during the one and only time I recounted this story to him, when you lose the most important people in your life—your parents—through the most random of circumstances, you come to realise that everything is fragile.

'Is that when you decided you wanted to be a war correspondent?' he asked, stroking my face.

'Got me in one.'

Actually, it took me a good six years to work my way up at the *Boston Post* from the City Desk to Features to a brief stint on the Editorial page. Then, finally, I received my first temporary posting to Washington and assorted mad parts of the world.

'If I hadn't become one, I wouldn't have had a quarter of the adventures that I've had.'

'And you wouldn't have met me,' Tony said.

'That's right,' I said, kissing him. 'I wouldn't have fallen in love with you.' Pause. I was even more dumbfounded than he was by that remark.

'Now how did that slip out?' I asked.

He kissed me deeply. 'I'm glad it did,' he said. 'I feel the same way.'

I was in love and astonished to have that love reciprocated.

Two weeks later, completely out of the blue, Tony asked, 'Feel like running off to London for a few days?' He explained that he'd been called back for a meeting at the *Chronicle*. 'Nothing sinister—just my annual lunch with the editor. Fancy a couple of days at the Savoy?'

It didn't take any further persuasion. I had been in London only once before, for four days in the eighties, so my vision of the place was selective, to say the least. I was just a little impressed by the suite we were given at the Savoy overlooking the Thames, and the bottle of champagne waiting for us in an ice bucket.

'Is this how the *Chronicle* usually treats its foreign correspondents?' I asked.

'You must be joking,' he said. 'But the manager's an old friend. We became chummy when he was running the Intercontinental in Tokyo.'

'Well, that's a relief,' I said.

'What?'

'That you didn't violate one of the cardinal rules of journalism— never pay for anything yourself.'

He laughed, and poured me a glass of champagne.

'No can do,' I said. 'On antibiotics.'

'Since when?'

'Since yesterday, when I saw the embassy doctor for a strep throat.'

'You should have told me.'

'Why? It's just a strep throat.'

'Well, I have to say I am disappointed. Because who the hell am I going to drink with over the next few days?'

Actually, that was something of a rhetorical question, as Tony had plenty of people to drink with over the three days we spent in London. He'd arranged for us to go out every night with assorted journalistic colleagues and friends. Even though Tony hadn't seen these people in about a year, work was only lightly mentioned ('Haven't been shot by Islamic Jihad yet, Tony?', that sort of thing), and never at great length. Whenever the talk veered towards the personal, it was swiftly deflected back towards less individual matters. I quickly sensed that to speak at length about anything private in a gathering of more than two people was considered just not done. Yet I rather liked this conversational style, and the fact that whenever serious events were broached, they were always undercut by a vein of acerbity and absurdity. No one embraced the kind of earnestness that so often characterised American dinner- table debate. Then again, as Tony once told me, the great difference between Yanks and Brits was that Americans believed that life was serious but not hopeless, whereas the British believed that life was hopeless, but not serious.

Tony remained pretty close-lipped about his lunch with the editor—except to say that it went well. But then, two days later, he gave me further details of that meeting. We were an hour into our flight back to Cairo when he said, 'I need to talk to you about something.'

'That sounds serious,' I said, putting down the novel I'd been reading.

'It's not serious. Just interesting.'

'By which you mean?'

'Well, during my lunch with the editor, he offered me a new job. Foreign Editor of the paper.'

This took a moment to sink in.

'Congratulations. Did you accept it?'

'Of course I didn't accept. I wanted to speak with you first.'

'Because it means a transfer back to London?'

'That's right.'

'Do you want the job?'

'Put it this way: His Lordship was hinting that I should take it. He was also hinting that, after nearly twenty years in the field, it was time I did a stint at HQ. And, the foreign editorship isn't exactly a demotion . . .'

A pause. I said, 'So you are going to take it?'

'I think I have to. But . . . uhm . . . that doesn't mean I have to come back to London alone.'

Another pause as I thought about that last comment. Finally, I said, 'I have some news too. And I have an admission to make.'

He looked at me with care. 'And what's this admission?'

'I'm not on antibiotics. Because I don't have a strep throat. But I still can't drink right now . . . because I happen to be pregnant.'

TWO

TONY TOOK THE NEWS WELL. He didn't shudder, or turn grey. There was a moment of stunned surprise, but then he took my hand and squeezed it and said, 'This is good news.'

'You really think that?'

'Absolutely. And you want to keep it?'

'I'm thirty-seven years old, Tony. Which means I've entered the realm of now or never. But just because I might want to keep it doesn't mean you have to be there too. I'd like you to be, of course. However . . .'

He shrugged. 'I want to be there,' he said.

'You sure?'

'Completely. And I want you to come to London with me.'

Now it was my turn to go a little white.

'You all right?' he asked.

'Surprised.'

'About . . . ?'

'The course this conversation is taking.'

For the rest of the flight to Cairo, Tony informed me that he thought this pregnancy was a very good thing; that, coupled with his transfer back to London, it was as if fate had intervened to propel us into making some major decisions. Though it might be something of an adjustment for both of us to be setting up house together—and for us to be at desk jobs (he was certain I could talk my way into the *Post*'s London bureau)—wasn't it time we finally surrendered to the inevitable and settled down?

'Are you talking marriage here?' I asked him after he finished his spiel.

He didn't meet my eye, but still said, 'Well, yes, I, uh, suppose I am.'

I was suddenly in need of a large vodka, and deeply regretted not being able to touch the stuff. 'I'm going to have to think about all this.'

Much to Tony's credit, he let the matter drop. Nor did he, in any way, pressure me over the next week. During the first few days after we got back from London, he gave me some thinking time. Yes, we spoke on the phone twice a day, and even had an amusing lunch together, during which we never mentioned the big question hanging over us . . . though, at the end of it, I did ask, 'Have you given the *Chronicle* your decision?'

'No, I'm still awaiting an update from someone. But the editor does need to know my decision by the end of the week.' And he left it at that.

Besides doing a lot of serious thinking, I also made several key phone calls—the first of which was to Thomas Richardson, the editor-in-chief of the *Post*. I was completely direct with him, explaining that I was marrying a journalist from the *Chronicle* and was planning to move to England. I also said that the *Post* was my home, and I certainly wanted to stay with the paper, but the fact that I was also pregnant meant that I would eventually need a twelve-week period of maternity leave, commencing about seven months from now.

'But that's wonderful news, Sally,' he said, sounding genuinely pleased.

'The thing is, we won't be moving to London for three months.'

'Well, I'm certain we can work something out at our London bureau. One of our correspondents has been talking about coming back to Boston, so your timing couldn't be better.'

There was a part of me that was alarmed about the fact that my boss had so eased my professional passage to London. Now I had no reason not to follow Tony. But when I informed him that my transfer to the London bureau of the *Post* seemed certain, his reply was reassuring. 'If the whole thing gets too overwhelming, then we'll find jobs somewhere cheap and cheerful, like *The Kathmandu Chronicle*.'

'Damn right,' I said laughing.

'Anyway, we're not the sort of people to become each other's jailers, now are we?' he said.

'Not a chance of that,' I said.

'Glad to hear it,' he said. 'So, I don't suppose it will be the end of the world if we get married in the next few weeks, now will it?'

'Since when did you get so damn romantic?' I asked.

'Since I had a conversation with our consular chap a few days ago.'

What this 'chap' told Tony was that my passage into Britain—both professionally and personally—would be far more rapidly expedited if we were husband and wife, whereas I would be facing months of immigration bureaucracy if I chose to remain single. Once again, I was astounded by the rate at which my life was being turned around. Destiny is like that, isn't it? You travel along, thinking that the trajectory of your life will follow a certain course. But then, you meet someone, you find yourself tiptoeing across that dangerous terrain called 'love'. Before you know it, you're on a long-distance phone call to your sister, telling her that not only are you pregnant, but you're also about to . . .

'Get married?' Sandy said, sounding genuinely shocked.

'It's the practical thing to do,' I said.

'You mean, like getting pregnant for the first time at thirty-seven?'

DOUGLAS KENNEDY

'Believe me, that was completely accidental.'

'Oh, I believe you. You're about the last person I'd expect to get intentionally knocked up. I'm thrilled for you. And I can't wait to meet Tony.'

'Come to Cairo for the wedding next week.'

'Next week?' she said, sounding shocked. 'Why so fast?'

I explained about wanting to sidestep working and residency permits before we moved to London in just under three months' time. I knew that Sandy wouldn't be able to make it over for the wedding—she did not have the money or the time.

'You know I can't come,' she told me. 'And hey, after all those war zones you've covered, motherhood won't seem much different.'

I did laugh. And I also wondered: Is she telling the truth?

But the next few weeks didn't allow me much opportunity for extended ruminations about my soon-to-be-changed circumstances. Especially as the Middle East was up to its usual manic tricks: a cabinet crisis in Israel and a ferry boat that overturned on the Nile.

'You know what I'll miss most about the Middle East?' I told Tony on the night before our wedding. 'The fact that it's so damn extreme, so completely deranged.'

'Whereas London is going to be nothing but day-to-day stuff?'

'I didn't say that.'

'But you are worrying about *that*.'

'A little bit, yes. Aren't you?'

'It *will* be a change.'

'Especially as you'll have additional baggage in tow.'

'Well, I'm happy about the additional baggage.'

I kissed him. 'Well, I'm happy that you're happy . . .'

'It will be an adjustment, but we'll be fine. And, believe me, London has its own peculiar madness.'

I remembered that comment six weeks later when we flew north to Heathrow. Courtesy of the *Chronicle*, we were being put up for six weeks in a company flat near the paper's offices in Wapping while we house-hunted. Courtesy of the *Chronicle*, all our belongings had been shipped last week from Cairo and would be kept in storage until we found a permanent place to live. And courtesy of the *Chronicle*, a large black Mercedes car collected us from the airport and began the slow crawl through evening rush-hour traffic towards central London.

As the car inched along the motorway, I reached over and took Tony's hand—noticing the shiny platinum wedding bands adorning our respective left hands, remembering the hilarious civil ceremony at which we were spliced in the Cairo registry office—a true madhouse without a roof, and where the official who joined us as husband and wife looked

172

like an Egyptian version of Groucho Marx. Now, here we were, only a few short months after that crazy twenty-four hours in Somalia, rolling down the M4 towards Wapping.

The driver pulled up in front of a modern building, about eight storeys tall. We took the elevator up to the fourth floor and came to a wood veneered door. The driver fished out two keys.

'You do the honours,' Tony said.

I took the keys and opened the door, stepping into a small, boxy one-bedroom apartment. It was furnished in a generic Holiday Inn style, and looked out onto a back alleyway.

'Well,' I said, taking it all in, 'this will make us find a house fast.'

It was my old college friend, Margaret Campbell, who was living in London with her lawyer husband, who expedited the house-hunting process. With her two kids off at school all day, and with my job at the *Post* not starting for another month, Margaret assumed the role of property adviser, working the phones and, after seeing close to twenty properties in that first week, deciding that an area called Putney was our destiny. As we drove south in her BMW, she pitched it to me.

'Great housing stock, all the family amenities you need, it's right on the river; and the District Line goes straight to Tower Bridge, which makes it perfect for Tony's office. Now, there are parts of Putney where you need over one-point-five to get a foot in the door, but where I'm taking you is just south of the Lower Richmond Road. Cute little streets that go right down to the Thames. The house may be a little small—just two bedrooms—but there's the possibility of a loft extension . . .'

'Since when did you become a realtor?' I asked with a laugh.

'Ever since I moved to this town. I tell you, the Brits might be all taciturn and distant when you first meet them, but get them talking about property, and they suddenly can't stop chatting.'

'Did it take you a while to fit in here?'

'The worst thing about London is that nobody really fits in. And the best thing about London is that nobody really fits in. Figure that one out, and you'll have a reasonably OK time here.'

The house in Sefton Street was distinctly cottagey, with two small reception rooms downstairs. But a kitchen extension had been built on to the back, and though all the cabinets were outdated, I was pretty certain that a ready-made kitchen from somewhere like IKEA could be installed without vast cost. The two bedrooms upstairs were papered in a funeral-home print, with an equally gruesome pink carpet covering the floor. But the estate agent, who showed us round, assured me that there were decent floorboards beneath this polyester veneer (something a surveyor confirmed a week later), and that the woodchip paper in the hallways could be stripped away and the walls replastered. The bathroom had a lurid salmon-pink suite, but at least the central heating and the wiring were new throughout. There was also substantial space for an attic study. For the first time in my transient life, I found myself thinking a surprisingly domesticated thought: this could actually be a home.

Margaret and I said nothing as we toured the house. Once we were outside, however, she turned to me and asked, 'So?'

'Bad clothes, good bones,' I said. 'But the potential is fantastic.'

'My feeling exactly. They're asking four-thirty-five . . .'

'I'm offering three-eighty-five . . . if Tony gives it the thumbs-up.'

Later that night, I spent the better part of my half-hour phone call with Sandy waxing lyrical about the cottage's possibilities and the genuine pleasantness of the neighbourhood—especially the towpath fronting the Thames, which was just down the street.

'Good God,' she said. 'You actually sound housebroken.'

'Very funny,' I said. 'Believe me, I keep shocking myself. Like I never thought I'd be poring over Dr Spock as if he was Holy Writ.'

'You reach the chapter where he tells you how to flee the country during colic?'

'Yeah—the stuff about false passports is terrific.'

'And wait until you experience your first broken night . . .'

'I think I'll hang up now.'

'Congrats on the house.'

'Well, it's not ours yet. And Tony still has to see it.'

'You'll sell it to him.'

'Damn right I will.'

But Tony was so wrapped up in life at the *Chronicle* that he could only make it down to Sefton Street five days later. When we reached the house, and met the estate agent, and started walking through every room, I watched Tony taking it all in and tried to gauge his reaction.

'Looks exactly like the house I grew up in,' he finally said, then added, 'But I'm sure we could improve on that.'

I launched into a design-magazine monologue, in which I painted extensive verbal pictures about its great potential once all the postwar tackiness was stripped away.

It was the loft conversion that won him over. Especially after I said that I could probably raid a small stock-market fund I had in the States to find the £7,000 that would pay for the study he so wanted, to write the books he hoped would liberate him from the newspaper that had clipped his wings.

Or, at least, that's what I sensed Tony was thinking after our first two weeks in London. Maybe it was the shock of doing a desk job after nearly twenty years in the field. Or maybe it was the discovery that newspaper life at Wapping was an extended minefield of internal politics. Whatever the reason, I did get the distinct feeling that Tony wasn't readjusting at all to this new office-bound life. Any time I raised the issue, he would insist that all was well; that he simply had a lot on his mind and was just trying to find his feet amid such changed circumstances.

'Hey, everyone gets a little moody, right?' Sandy said when I told her. 'And when you think of the changes you guys are having to deal with . . .'

'You're right, you're right,' I said.

'And he doesn't have fangs or sleep in a coffin?'

'No. But I am keeping a clove of garlic and a crucifix handy underneath the bed.'

'Good marital practice. But, hey. It sounds like you're basically not doing badly for the first couple of months of marriage, which is usually the time when you think you've made the worst mistake of your life.'

I certainly didn't feel that. I just wished Tony could be a little more articulate about what he was really feeling.

Only I suddenly didn't have enough time on my hands to consider my feelings about our newfangled life together, because our offer on the house was accepted. After we paid the deposit, it was I who organised the housing survey, and arranged the mortgage, and found a contractor for the loft and the extensive decorative work, and chose fabrics and colours, and did time at IKEA and Habitat and Heals, and also haggled with plumbers and painters. In between all these nest-building endeavours, I also happened to be dealing with my ever-expanding pregnancy, which, now that my morning sickness was long over, had turned into less of a discomfort than I had expected.

Once again, Margaret had been brilliant when it came to answering my constant spate of questions about the state of being pregnant. She also explained the workings of the National Health Service and how to register myself at my local doctor's office in Putney. It turned out to be a group practice, where the receptionist made me fill out assorted forms and then informed me that I had been assigned to Dr Sheila McCoy.

Dr McCoy—a pleasant woman in her forties—saw me a few days later, asked a lot of thorough, no-nonsense questions, and informed me that I would be under the care of an obstetrician named Hughes.

'Very senior, very respected, with rooms in Harley Street, and he does his NHS work at the Mattingly, one of the newest hospitals in London.'

When I met Mr Desmond Hughes a week later at an office in the Mattingly Hospital, I was immediately struck by his beak-like nose, his crisp, practical demeanour, and the fact that, like all British consultants, he was never referred to as Dr (as I later learned, all surgeons were traditionally called Mr Hughes) was also a testament to the excellence of British tailoring, as he was dressed in an exquisitely cut pinstripe suit, a light blue shirt with impressive French cuffs, and a black polka-dot tie. Our first consultation was a brisk one. He ordered a scan, he requested blood, he felt around my stomach, he told me that everything seemed 'to be going according to plan'.

I was a little surprised that he didn't ask me any specific questions about my physical state (beside a general: 'Everything seem all right?'). So, when we reached the end of this brief consultation, I raised this point. Politely, of course.

'Don't you want to know about my morning sickness?' I asked.

'Are you suffering from it?'

'Not any more.'

'Then morning sickness isn't an issue now.' He patted me on the hand. 'Anything else troubling you?'

I shook my head, feeling gently (but oh-so-firmly) chastised.

'Very good, then,' he said, shutting my file and standing up. 'See you again in a few weeks. And . . . uhm . . . you're working, yes?'

'That's right. I'm a journalist.'

'That's nice. But you do look a little peaky—so don't overdo it, eh?'

Later that evening, when I related this conversation to Tony, he laughed. 'Now you've just discovered two general truths about Harley Street specialists: they hate all questions, and they always patronise you.'

Still, Hughes rightly observed one thing: I was tired. This wasn't merely due to the pregnancy, but also to the pressures of trying to find the house, arrange all the building work, and simultaneously feel my way into London. The first four weeks evaporated in a preoccupied blur. Then, my initial month in London over, I had to start work again.

The *Boston Post's* office was nothing more than a room in the Reuters building on Fleet Street. My fellow correspondent was a twenty-six-year-old guy named Andrew DeJarnette Hamilton, who signed his copy A.D. Hamilton, and was the sort of ageing preppie who somehow managed to lace every conversation with the fact that he'd been to Harvard. I quickly decided to avoid him and, as soon as Tony and I moved into Sefton Street, I started filing most of my stories from home, using my advanced pregnancy as an excuse for working from Putney. Not that *chez nous* was the most ideal place to write, as the interior of the house was under construction. All the new cabinets and appliances had been installed in the kitchen, but the living room was a catastrophe, and the attic conversion was delayed, as the contractor had been called away to Belfast. At least the decorators had made the nursery their first priority, finishing it during our second week of residency. And thanks to

Margaret and Sandy, I had found out which crib and carry-chair to buy, not to mention all the other baby paraphernalia. So the stripped-pine crib (or 'cot' as they called it here) toned in well with the pink starry wallpaper, and there was a changing mat and a playpen already in position, ready for use. Though our bedroom had been painted, we were still waiting for the wardrobes to be fitted, which meant that the room was cluttered with assorted clothes rails.

In other words, the house was a testament to builders' delays and general domestic chaos, and possibly one of the reasons why I wasn't seeing much of Tony right now. Mind you, he was fantastically busy. He never seemed to get his pages to bed before eight most evenings and, in this early phase of his new job, he was also having to stay out late schmoozing with his staff, or work the phones, talking with his assorted correspondents around the planet.

'Don't despair,' I told Tony after I saw him glancing around the builders' debris. 'This will be a wonderful house.'

'I'm sure it will be.'

'Come on, Tony. Things will get better.'

'Everything's fine,' he said, his voice drained of enthusiasm.

'I wish I could believe you mean that,' I said.

'I do mean it.' With that, he drifted off into another room.

But then, at five that morning, I woke up to discover that everything wasn't fine. Because my body was playing strange games with me.

And in those first few bewildering moments when the realisation hit that something was very wrong, I bumped into an emotion I hadn't encountered for years.

Fear.

THREE

IT WAS AS IF I HAD BEEN ATTACKED during the night by a battalion of bed-bugs. Suddenly, every inch of my skin felt as if it was inflamed by what could only be described as a virulent itch—which no amount of scratching could relieve.

'I don't see any rash,' Tony said after he discovered me naked in our bathroom, scraping my skin with my fingernails.

'I'm not making this up,' I said angrily, thinking that he was accusing me of falling into some psychosomatic state. 'I'm in real trouble here.'

He got me dressed. He helped me into the car and drove straight to the Mattingly Hospital. We were inside the casualty department within moments, and when Tony saw that the waiting room was packed, he had a word with the triage nurse, insisting that, as I was pregnant, I should be seen straight away.

'I'm afraid you'll have to wait, like everyone else here.'

Tony tried to protest, but the nurse was having none of it.

'Sir, please sit down. You can't jump the queue unless . . .'

At that very moment, I supplied the *unless*, as the constant itch suddenly transformed into a major convulsion. Before I knew what was happening, I pitched forward and the world went black.

When I came to, I was stretched out in a steel hospital bed, with several intravenous tubes protruding from my arms. I felt insanely groggy, as if I had just emerged from a deep narcotic sleep.

I managed to summon up enough strength to push the call button by the side of the bed. As I did so, I involuntarily blinked for an instant and was suddenly visited by a wave of pain around the upper half of my face. I also became aware of the fact that my nose had been heavily taped. I pressed the call button even harder. Eventually, an Afro-Caribbean nurse arrived at my bedside. I squinted to read her name tag—*Howe*.

'Welcome back,' she said with a quiet smile.

'What happened?'

The nurse reached for the chart at the end of the bed and read the notes. 'Seems you had a little fainting spell in reception. You're lucky that nose of yours wasn't broken.'

'How about the baby?'

'No worries. The baby's fine. But *you* . . . you are a cause for concern.'

'In what way?'

'You're suffering from a high-blood-pressure disorder. It could be pre-eclampsia—but we won't know that until we've done some blood work and a urine test.'

'Can it jeopardise the pregnancy?'

'It can . . . but we'll try to get it under control. Now I'm afraid I need a urine sample.'

I eased myself out of bed and into the bathroom, filling a vial with pee. Then, when I was back in bed, another nurse came by and drew a large hypodermic needle of blood. Nurse Howe returned to tell me that Tony had just called. She'd informed him that Mr Hughes would be here at eight tonight, and suggested that he try to be at the hospital then. Mr Hughes (having been alerted to my condition) had ordered an ultrasound. Alarm bells began to ring between my ears.

'If I'm just suffering from high blood pressure, why is he ordering an ultrasound?'

'It's just routine.'

This was hardly comforting. All during the ultrasound, I kept staring at the vague outline on the foetal monitor, asking the technician (an Australian woman) if she could see if anything was untoward.

'No worries,' she said. 'You'll be fine.'

'But the baby . . . ?'

'There's no need to get yourself so . . .'

But I didn't hear the last part of that sentence, as the itching suddenly started again. Only this time, the area most affected was my midsection and my pelvis . . . exactly where the ultrasound gel had been smeared. Within the space of a minute, the itch was unbearable, and I found myself telling the technician that I needed to scratch my belly.

'Not a problem,' she said, removing the large ultrasound wand which she had been applying to my stomach. Immediately, I began to tear at my skin. The technician looked on, wide-eyed.

'You're going to hurt yourself . . . and the baby,' she said.

I pulled my hands away. The itching intensified. I bit so hard on my lip that it nearly bled.

'Are you all right?' the technician asked.

'No.'

She reached for a phone and clasped my arm. 'Help's on the way.'

A nurse arrived, pushing a tray of medication. She cleaned off the ultrasound gel. Then, using what looked like a sterile paint brush, she covered my stomach with calamine lotion. It instantly alleviated the itch. She then handed me two pills and a small glass of water.

'What are these?' I asked.

'A mild sedative.'

'But I don't want to be groggy when my husband gets here.'

'This won't make you groggy. It will just calm you down.'

'But I *am* calm.'

The nurse said nothing. Instead she deposited the two pills in my open palm. I reluctantly downed them and allowed myself to be helped into a wheelchair and transported back to the ward.

Tony arrived just before eight with a grim bunch of flowers and tried to mask his disquiet at the state of me.

'You should've seen the other guy,' I said, then heard myself laugh a hollow laugh.

'After the way you pitched forward last night, I expected much worse,' he said, leaning over to give me a peck on the head.

'That's comforting to know. Why didn't you call me today?'

'Conferences, deadlines, my pages to get out. It's called work.'

'You mean, like me? I'm work to you now, right?'

Tony took a deep, annoyed breath; a way of informing me that he wasn't enjoying the route this conversation was taking. But despite my drug-induced state, I still continued to play vexed. Because, right now, I felt so completely furious at everything and everyone—most especially, at the diffident man sitting on the edge of my bed.

'You could ask me if the baby's all right,' I said, my voice a paragon of tranquillised calm.

Another of Tony's exasperated intakes of breath. 'I have been worried about you, you know,' he said.

'Of course I know. Because you so radiate worry, Tony.'

'Is this what's called "post-traumatic shock"? What the hell do they have you on?'

A voice behind Tony said, 'Valium, since you asked.'

Mr Desmond Hughes stood at the edge of the bed, my chart in his hand, his bifocals resting on the extreme edge of his nose.

I asked, 'Is the baby all right, Doctor?'

Mr Hughes didn't look up from the chart. 'And a very good evening to you, Mrs Goodchild. And, yes, all seems fine.' He turned towards Tony. 'You must be Mr Goodchild.'

'Tony Hobbs.'

'Oh, right,' Hughes said, the only acknowledgment of Tony's name being the slightest of nods. Then he turned back to me and asked, 'And how are we feeling tonight? Bit of a ropey twenty-four hours, I gather.'

'Tell me about the baby, Doctor.'

'From what I could see on the ultrasound scans, no damage was done to the baby. Now, I gather you were admitted suffering from cholestasis.'

'What's that?' I asked.

'Chronic itching. Not uncommon among pregnant women and it often arrives in tandem with pre-eclampsia, which, as you may know is . . .'

'High blood pressure?'

'Very good, though we prefer to call it a hypertension disorder. Now the good news is that pre-eclampsia is often characterised by a high level of uric acid. But your urine sample was relatively normal, which is why I consider you *not* to be suffering from pre-eclampsia. But your blood pressure is dangerously high. If left unchecked, it can be some-what treacherous for both the mother and the child. Which is why I am putting you on a beta blocker to stabilise your blood pressure, as well as an antihistamine called Piriton to relieve the cholestasis. And I would also like you to take five milligrams of Valium three times a day.'

'I'm not taking Valium again.'

'And why is that?'

'Because I don't like it.'

'There are lots of things in life we don't like, Mrs Goodchild . . . even though they are beneficial.'

'It's *Ms* Goodchild,' I said. 'He's Hobbs, I'm Goodchild.'

A quick exchange of looks between Tony and the doctor. *Oh God, why am I acting so weird?*

'So sorry, *Ms* Goodchild. And, of course, I can't force you to take a substance that you don't want to take. But I think it is advisable.'

'Noted,' I said quietly.

'But you will take the Piriton?'

I nodded.

'Well, that's something at least,' Hughes said. 'Oh, one final thing. You must understand that high blood pressure is a most dangerous condition, and one which could cause you to lose the child. Which is why, until you have brought this pregnancy to term, you must have complete bed rest. That is why we'll be keeping you in hospital for the duration.'

I stared at him, stunned. 'The duration of my pregnancy?' I asked.

'I'm afraid so.'

'But that's nearly three weeks from now. I can't just give up work—'

Tony put a steadying hand on my shoulder, stopping me from saying anything more.

'I'll see you on my rounds tomorrow, Ms Goodchild,' Hughes said. With another quick nod to Tony, he moved on to the next patient.

'I don't believe it,' I said.

Tony just shrugged. 'We'll deal with it,' he said. Then he glanced at his watch, and mentioned that he had to get back to the paper now.

'But I thought you'd already put your pages to bed?'

'I never said that. Anyway, while you were unconscious, a little war's broken out among rival factions in Sierra Leone.'

'You have a man on the scene?'

'A stringer. Jenkins. Not bad, for a lightweight. But if the thing blows up into a full-scale war, I think we'll have to send one of our own.'

'Yourself, perhaps?'

'In my dreams.'

'If you want to go, go. Don't let me stop you.'

'I wouldn't, believe me.'

His tone was mild, but pointed. It was the first time he'd directly articulated his feelings of entrapment. Or, at least, that's how it came over to me.

'Well, thank you for making that perfectly clear,' I said.

He placed his gift of wilting flowers on the bedside table. Then he gave me another perfunctory kiss on the forehead.

'I'll call you first thing in the morning, and see if I can get over here before work.'

But he didn't call me. When I rang the house at eight thirty, there was no answer. When I rang the paper at nine thirty, Tony wasn't at his desk. And when I tried his mobile, I was connected with his voicemail. So I left a terse message: 'I'm sitting here, already bored out of my mind, and I'm just wondering: where the hell are you? Please call me asap, as I really would like to know the whereabouts of my husband.'

Around two hours later, Tony phoned. He sounded as neutral as Switzerland. 'Hello,' he said. 'Sorry I wasn't available earlier.'

'I called you at home at eight thirty this morning, and discovered that nobody was home.'

'What's today?'

'Wednesday.'

'And what do I do every Wednesday?'

I didn't need to furnish him an answer, because he knew that I knew the answer: he had breakfast with the editor of the paper which always started at nine. Which meant that Tony left home around eight. *Idiot, idiot, idiot . . . why are you looking for trouble?*

'I'm sorry,' I said.

'Not to worry,' he said, his tone still so detached, almost uninvolved. 'How are you doing?'

'Still feeling like shit. But the itch is under control.'

'That's something, I guess. When are visiting hours?'

'Right now would work.'

'Well, I'm supposed to be lunching with the chap who skippers the Africa section at the F.O. But I can cancel.'

Immediately I wondered: now why didn't he tell me about this lunch yesterday? Maybe he didn't want to let me know, then and there, that he wouldn't be able to visit in the morning. Maybe the lunch was a last-minute thing, given the situation in Sierra Leone. Or maybe . . . oh God, I don't know. That was the growing problem with Tony: *I didn't know.*

'No need. I'll phone Margaret, see if she can visit this afternoon.'

'Anything I can bring you tonight?' Tony asked.

'Just pick up something nice at Marks and Spencer's.'

Naturally, Margaret was at the hospital within a half-hour of my call. She tried not to register shock when she saw me, but didn't succeed.

'I just need to know one thing,' she said.

'No. Tony didn't do this to me.'

'You don't have to protect him, you know.'

'I'm not, *honestly*.' Then I told her about my charming interaction with Hughes, and how I refused to become a citizen of Valium Nation.

'Damn right you should refuse that stuff,' she said.

'Trust me to get aggressive on Valium.'

'How did Tony handle all this?'

'In a very English, very phlegmatic kind of way. Meanwhile, I'm quietly beginning to panic . . . not just at the thought of three weeks' enforced bed rest in here, but also at the realisation that the paper isn't going to like the fact that I'm out of action.'

'Surely the *Post* can't let you go?'

'Want to put money on that? They're financially strapped, like every newspaper these days. And I'm certain that, with me out of the picture for the next few months, they'll evict me without a moment's thought.'

'You're jumping to conclusions.'

'No. I'm just being my usual Yankee realist self. Just as I also know that, between the mortgage and all the renovations, spare cash is going to be scarce.'

'Well, then, let me do something to make your life in hospital easier. Let me pay for a private room in here for the next couple of weeks. You need to be as stress-free as possible right now, and being in a room on your own will certainly aid the process.'

'True. But say my pride doesn't like the idea of accepting charity from you?'

'It's not charity. It's a gift. A gift before I kiss this city goodbye.'

This stopped me short. 'What are you talking about?' I asked.

'We're being transferred back to New York. Alexander only heard the news yesterday.'

'When exactly?' I asked.

'Two weeks. There's been a big shake-up at the firm and Alexander's been made the senior partner heading up the litigation department. And since it's mid-term at school, they're shipping us all back in one go.'

I now felt anxious. Margaret was my one friend in London.

'Shit,' I said.

'That's about the right word for it,' she said. 'Because as much as I complain about London, I know I'm going to miss it as soon as we're ensconced back in the 'burbs.'

By the time Tony arrived at the hospital that evening, I had been transferred into a perfectly pleasant private room. But when my husband asked me how the upgrade came about—and I told him of Margaret's largesse—his reaction was both abrupt and negative.

'And why the hell is she doing that?'

'It's a gift. To me. Her very kind way of helping me out.'

'I'm not accepting charity from some rich American—'

'This is not *charity*. She's my friend and—'

'I'll pay for it.'

'Tony, the bill is already settled. So what's the big deal?'

Silence. I knew what the big deal was: Tony's pride. Not that he was going to admit such a thing. Except to say, 'I just wished you'd talked this over with me.'

'Well, I didn't hear from you all day and until I was moved in here, where there's a phone by the bed, it was a little hard to get up to make calls. Especially when I've been ordered to hardly move.'

'How are you doing?'

'The itch is a little better. And there is a lot to be said for being out of that godforsaken ward.'

A pause. 'How long did Margaret pay for the room?'

'Three weeks.'

'Well, I'll cover anything after that.'

'Fine,' I said quietly, dodging the temptation to add, 'Whatever makes *you* happy, Tony.' Instead I pointed to the Marks and Spencer bag in his hand and asked, 'Dinner, I hope?'

Tony stayed an hour that night—long enough to watch me gobble down the sandwich and salad he brought me. He also informed me that he'd emailed Thomas Richardson, the editor-in-chief at the *Post*, to explain that I would be out of action until the arrival of the baby.

'I bet he'll fire me,' I said.

'Well, his reply said that he'd be in touch with you. Now, concentrate on feeling better. You're shattered.' He gave me a somewhat perfunctory kiss on the head and said he'd drop by tomorrow morning before work.

'Grab every book you can find,' I said. 'It's going to be a long three weeks in here.'

Time had suddenly ballooned. Removed from all professional and domestic demands, each day in hospital seemed far too roomy for my liking. There were no deadlines to make, no appointments to keep. Instead, the first week crept into the next. There was a steady stream of books to read. And I quickly became addicted to Radios Three and Four. There was a daily phone call from Sandy. Margaret—bless her—managed to make it down to the hospital four times a week. And Tony did come to see me every evening. His post-work arrival was one of the highlights of my otherwise prosaic hospital day. He'd always try to spend an hour— but often had to dash back to the office or head off for some professional dinner thing. If he didn't seem otherwise preoccupied, he was amusing and reasonably affectionate. I knew that the guy was under a lot of pressure at the paper. And though he wouldn't articulate this fact, I sensed that he was silently wondering what the hell he had landed himself in—how, in less than a year, his once autonomous life as a foreign correspondent had been transformed into one brimming with the same sort of domestic concerns that characterised most people's lives. But he wanted this, *right*? He was the one who made all the convincing arguments about coming to London and setting up house together. And after my initial doubts, I fully embraced those arguments. But now . . .

Around ten days after Tony had sent the email to Thomas Richardson at the *Post*, Richardson called me.

'We're all deeply concerned about your condition . . .' Richardson said, starting off with his usual paternalistic patter.

'Well, all going well, I should be back on the job in six months tops—and that's including the three months of maternity leave.'

There was a pause on the transatlantic phone line and I knew I was doomed. 'I'm afraid we've been forced to make a few changes in our overseas bureaus—our finance people have been insisting on some belt tightening. Which is why we're turning London into a single correspondent bureau. And since your health has put you out of the picture . . .'

'But, as I said, I *will* be back within six months.'

'A.D. *is* the senior correspondent in the bureau. More to the point, he *is* on the job now.'

'Does this mean you're firing me, Mr Richardson?' I asked.

'Sally, *please*. We're the *Post*. We take care of our own. We'll be paying you full salary for the next three months. Then, if you want to rejoin us, a position will be made available to you.'

'In London?'

Another edgy transatlantic pause. 'As I said, the London bureau will now be staffed by only one correspondent.'

'Which means if I want a job, I'll have to come back to Boston?'

'That's right.'

'But you know that's impossible for me right now.'

'Sally, I understand your situation. But you have to understand mine.'

I ended the call politely, thanking him for the three months' pay and saying that I'd have to think about his offer, even though we both knew that there was no way I'd be accepting it. Which, in turn, meant that I had just been let go by my employer of the last sixteen years.

Tony was pleased to hear that, at least, I'd be able to help with the mortgage for the next few months. But I quietly worried about how, after my *Post* money stopped, we'd be able to manage all our manifold outgoings on one income.

'We'll work it out,' was his less-than-reassuring reply.

Margaret also told me to stop worrying about the money problem.

'Given the number of newspapers in this town, I'm sure you can find some freelance work. But only when it becomes necessary. You're going to have enough to cope with once the baby arrives. On which note, I don't suppose I could interest you in a cleaner? Her name's Cha, she's been with us for the entire time we've been in London, she's completely brilliant at what she does, and is now looking for additional work.'

'Give me her number and I'll talk it over with Tony. I'll also need to review the domestic budget before . . .'

'Let me pay for her.'

'No way. I can't accept it.'

'Well, you'll have to. Because it's my going-away gift to you. Six months of Cha, twice a week. And there's nothing you can do about it.'

'Six months? You're crazy.'

'Nah—just rich,' she said with a laugh.

'I'll have to talk it over with Tony. Whether he accepts the gift or not, you've been the best friend imaginable.'

She left town two days later. That evening, I finally got up the nerve to inform Tony about Margaret's goodbye gift.

'You cannot be serious,' he said, sounding annoyed.

'Like I said, it was her idea. And *yes*, it is a far too generous one, which is why I said I wouldn't accept it until I talked it over with you. Because I had a little suspicion that you'd react exactly like this.'

Pause. He avoided my angry gaze.

'What's the cleaner's name?' he asked.

I handed him the piece of paper on which Margaret had written Cha's name and her contact number.

'I'll call her and arrange for her to start next week. At our expense.'

I said nothing. Eventually he spoke again. 'The editor would like me to go to The Hague tomorrow. Just a fast overnight trip to do a piece about the war crimes tribunal. I know you're due any moment. But it's just The Hague. I can be back here in an hour, if need be.'

'Sure,' I said tonelessly. 'Go.'

'Thanks.' He leaned over and kissed me. 'I'll call you from The Hague tomorrow. And remember, I'm on the mobile if . . .'

After he left, I must have spent the better part of an hour wondering if I had married someone with whom I didn't share a common language. Oh, we both spoke English. But this was something more profound, more unsettling—the worry that we would always be strangers, thrown in together under accidental circumstances.

'Who knows anyone?' Sandy said to me during our phone call that evening. 'I always considered Dean to be a nice, stable, slightly dull guy. And what happens? After ten years and three kids, he decides he hates everything about our staid, secure, suburban life. So he meets the Nature Girl of his dreams—a park ranger in Maine—and runs off to live with her in some cabin in Baxter State Park. So, hey, at least you realise you're already dealing with a difficult guy. Which, from where I sit, is something of an advantage.'

Maybe she was right. Maybe I just needed to let everything settle down, and enter the realm of *acceptance* and other optimistic clichés. As in *look on the bright side, forget your troubles, keep your chin up* . . . that sort of dumb, sanguine thing.

As I drifted off into a thinly veneered sleep, one strange thought kept rattling around my brain: Why is everything so soggy?

At that moment, I jolted back into consciousness.

I sat up, suddenly very awake. I frantically pulled off the duvet. The bed was completely drenched.

My waters had broken.

FOUR

I DIDN'T PANIC. I didn't succumb to trepidation or startled surprise. I just reached for the call button. Then I picked up the phone and dialled Tony's mobile. It was busy, so I phoned his direct line at the paper and left a fast message on his voicemail.

'Hi, it's me,' I said, still sounding calm. 'It's happening . . . so please get yourself to the Mattingly as soon as you get back to London. This is definitely it.'

As I put down the receiver, a midwife showed up. She took one look at the sodden bedclothes and reached for the phone. Two orderlies arrived shortly thereafter. They raised up the sides of my bed, unlocked its wheels and pushed me out of the room, negotiating a variety of corridors before landing me in the baby unit. En route, I began to feel an ever-magnifying spasm. By the time the doors swung behind me, the pain had intensified to such an extent that I felt as if some alien was gripping my innards with his knobbly fist, determined to show me new frontiers in agony. A midwife was on the scene immediately—a diminutive woman of Asian origin. She grabbed a packet of surgical gloves from a nearby trolley, ripped it open, pulled them on, and informed me that she was going to do a quick inspection of my cervix.

'You are experiencing severe discomfort, yes?' she asked.

I nodded. 'Is the baby all right?'

'I'm sure everything is . . .'

There was another maniacal spasm. I reacted loudly, then asked, 'Can I have an epidural now?'

'Until the doctor has examined—'

'*Please* . . .'

She patted my shoulder and said, 'I'll see what I can do.'

But ten godawful minutes passed until she returned with a porter.

'Where have you been?' I asked, my voice raw and loud.

'Calm yourself, please,' she said. 'We had three other women waiting before you for ultrasound.'

'I don't want ultrasound. I want an epidural.'

But I was whisked straight away into the ultrasound suite, where my belly was coated with gel and two large pads applied to the surface of the skin. A large fleshy man in a white jacket came into the room.

'I'm Mr Kerr,' he said crisply. 'I'm Mr Hughes's locum today. In a spot of bother, are we?'

But suddenly he was interrupted by the ultrasound technician who said that sentence you never want to hear a medical technician say to a doctor, 'I think you should see this, sir.'

Mr Kerr looked at the screen, his eyes grew momentarily wide, then he turned away and calmly sprang into action. He spoke rapidly to a nurse—and, much to my horror, I heard him utter the words, 'Baby resuscitator.'

'What is going on?' I asked.

'We need to perform an emergency Caesarean.'

Before I could react to that, Mr Kerr explained that the ultrasound had shown that the umbilical cord might be around the baby's neck.

'The foetal monitor is showing a steady heartbeat. However, we need to move fast, because . . .'

But he didn't get to finish that sentence, as the doors swung open and two orderlies with carts came rushing in. The first was pulled up next to me. Then a small Indian woman in a white coat arrived and walked over to the bed. 'I'm Dr Chaterjee, the anaesthetist', she said.

She swabbed the top of my left hand with a cotton-wool ball. 'Little prick now,' she said, as she inserted a needle into the top of my hand. 'Now start counting backwards from ten.'

I did as instructed, muttering '*Ten, nine, eig* . . .'

And then the world went black.

It's strange, being chemically removed from life for a spell. You don't dream under anaesthetic, nor are you even notionally aware of the passage of time. You've entered the realm of nothingness, where all thoughts, fears, worries cannot invade your psyche.

Until I woke up.

It took me a moment or two to realise where I was—especially as my first view of the world was a pair of glowing fluorescent tubes, lodged above me. Gradually, the jigsaw pieces began to fall into place: hospital, ward, bed, sore head, sore body, baby . . .

'Nurse!' I yelled, scrambling for the button by the side of the bed. As I did so, I realised that I had tubes coming out of both arms, while the lower half of my body was still numb.

'Nurse!'

After a few moments, a dainty Afro-Caribbean woman arrived by my bedside. 'Welcome back,' she said.

'My baby?'

'A boy. Eight pounds, two ounces. Congratulations.'

'Can I see him now?'

'He's in the intensive care unit. It's just a routine thing, after a complicated delivery.'

'I *want* to see him. Now.' And then I added, 'Please.'

The nurse looked at me carefully. 'I'll see what I can do.'

She returned a few minutes later. 'Mr Kerr is coming to see you.'

'Do I get to see my baby?'

'Talk to Mr Kerr.'

He arrived just then. 'How are you feeling now?'

'Tell me about my son.'

'Quite a straightforward Caesarean . . . And the cord around his neck wasn't as tight as I feared. So, all in all . . .'

'Then why is he in intensive care?'

'Standard postoperative care—especially for a newborn after a difficult delivery. We did have to immediately ventilate him after birth . . .'

'Ventilate?'

'Give him oxygen. He did arrive a little floppy, though he responded well to the ventilation . . .'

'So the cord around the neck might have caused brain damage?'

'As I said before, I was pleased to discover that the cord hadn't wound itself firmly around your son's neck. But we've already run an ultrasound to make certain there was no blood on the brain . . .'

'Was there?'

'No, it was completely negative. More to the point, his APGAR scores were completely normal.'

'His what?' I asked.

'APGAR is a sort of checklist we run on every newborn child, gauging things like their pulse, reflexes, respiration and overall appearance. As I said, your son easily scored within the normal range. And in a day or so, we will run an EEG and an MRI, just to make certain that everything in the neurological department is working properly. But, at this point, I would try not to worry about such things.'

'I need to see him.'

'Of course. But you do realise that his initial appearance may upset you. Paediatric ICUs are not the easiest of places, after all.'

'I'll handle that.'

'All right then. But do understand, you will have to take things very easy for the next week or so. You've just had a major operation.'

He turned and started walking away. But then he wheeled back and said, 'Oh, by the way—congratulations. Any sign of the father yet?'

'Didn't he ring the hospital?' I asked the nurse.

'Not that I've heard,' she said. 'I'll check with my colleagues. And if you write down his number, I'll call him again.'

I looked at the clock on the wall. Six fifteen.

'Couldn't I try to call him?' I asked.

But as I said this, two orderlies showed up, wheelchair in tow. This one was custom-built to accommodate a patient who was wired to assorted drips, as it featured a frame from which plasma and saline bottles could be suspended.

'Let me phone him for you,' the nurse said. 'These fellows are going to need the chair back soon.'

The nurse handed me a pad and a pen. I scribbled down Tony's work number, his mobile and our home phone. She promised me she'd leave messages on all three numbers if she couldn't reach him directly. Then the orderlies went to work lifting me off the bed and into the chair, while simultaneously keeping me attached to my assorted tubes.

They pushed me through the maternity ward, down a long corridor, and into the service lift. The lift rose two floors and then the doors opened and we were directly in front of a set of double doors, by which was a sign: PAEDIATRIC ICU.

One of the orderlies leaned over and whispered in my ear, 'If I was you, luv, I'd keep my eyes shut until we get up alongside your baby. Take it from me, it can be a bit distressing in there.'

I followed his advice, and shut my eyes as we crept through the ward. After about a minute, the chair stopped. The orderly touched me gently on my shoulder and said, 'We're here, luv.'

A part of me wanted to keep my eyes closed, and demand to be turned round and taken back to my own room. But I knew I had to see him, no matter how upsetting his condition might be. So I took a deep breath and opened my eyes. And . . .

There he was.

I knew he would be in an incubator. And I knew that there would be wires and tubes. But what shocked me was the sight of an entire network of wires and tubes running from every part of his body—including two plastic ducts that had been pressed into his nostrils. He looked alien, almost otherworldly—and so desperately vulnerable. But another terrible thought hit me: *could that really be my son*? They say that you should be swamped by unconditional love the moment you first see your child . . . and that *the bonding process* should begin immediately. But how could I bond with this minuscule stranger, currently looking like a horrific medical experiment?

Staring into the incubator, all I felt was fear. Sheer terror. Not just about whether he had suffered brain damage, but whether I would be able to cope with all this. I wanted to cry for him—and for myself. I also wanted to flee the room.

The orderly seemed to sense this, as he gently touched my shoulder and whispered, 'Let's get you back to your bed, luv.'

I managed to nod, and then found myself choking back a sob.

They took me back to my room, gently lifted me back into bed and reset my assorted bottles above me. I sank down against the hard, starchy hospital pillow. Then, out of nowhere, I started to cry. The crying had an almost animalistic rage to it—loud, vituperative, and unnervingly hollow. The nurse who came running must have thought I was reacting to the state of my baby. But the fact of the matter was, I didn't know what I was crying about. Because I couldn't feel anything. My emotional world had gone numb.

'Sally . . . Sally . . .'

I ignored the nurse, pushing away her hands, curling up into a foetal position, clutching a pillow next to my face and biting it in an attempt to stifle the howls. But though the pillow muffled the sound, it didn't end the crying. The nurse put a steadying hand on my shoulder, using her free hand to speak into the walkie-talkie she usually kept strapped to her belt. When she finished, she said, 'Just hold on—help should be here in a moment.'

The help was another nurse, pushing a trolley laden down with medical paraphernalia. She was accompanied by the doctor on duty. The nurse who had been keeping the bedside watch spoke quickly to her colleagues. The doctor picked up my chart, scanned it, spoke to the nurses again, then left.

After a moment, I felt a hand raising the sleeve of my nightgown, as

DOUGLAS KENNEDY

the first nurse said, 'The doctor thinks this might help you relax, Sally.'

I didn't say anything—because I was still biting the pillow. But then came the sharp jab of a needle, followed by a warming sensation cascading through my veins.

Then the plug was pulled, and the lights went out.

When I returned to terra firma, I didn't suffer the same convulsive shock that accompanied my re-awakening after the delivery. No, this was a slower fade-in—accompanied by a Sahara-dry mouth. The first thing I noticed was a small decanter of water by the side of the bed. The second thing I noticed was Tony.

I could see him looking me over—taking in my anaemic complexion, shell-shocked eyes, and general distrait condition.

'So how's our boy doing?' he asked me, kissing me on the head.

'Poorly,' I said.

'That's not what they told me last night.'

'You were here last night?'

'Yes. While you were sleeping. I arrived just before eleven—direct from the airport. And I came straight up to see you. But they told me—'

'—that I'd been sedated for excessive crying?'

'—that you'd been having a hard time of it, so they'd given you something to help you sleep.'

'But why weren't you here before eleven?'

'Because I was in the bloody Hague, as you bloody well know. Now can we talk about more important things . . . like Jack.'

'Who's Jack?'

He looked at me, wide-eyed. 'Our son.'

'I didn't realise he'd been given a name yet.'

'We talked about this four months ago.'

'No, we didn't.'

'That weekend in Brighton, walking along the promenade . . .'

I suddenly remembered the conversation. We'd gone down to Brighton for a 'get-away-from-it-all weekend' (Tony's words), during which it rained nonstop and Tony got hit with mild food poisoning. But before Tony started regurgitating his guts out in our freebie suite at The Grand, we did take a brief, soggy walk along the seafront, during which he mentioned that Jack would be a fine name if the baby turned out to be a boy. To which I said (and I remember this precisely): 'Yeah, Jack's not bad at all.' But that wasn't meant to be interpreted as tacit approval for the name Jack.

'All I said was—'

'—you liked the name Jack. Which I took as your approval. Sorry.'

'Doesn't matter. I mean, it not like it's legal and binding as yet.'

192

Tony shifted uneasily on the bed. 'Well, as a matter of fact . . .'

'*What?*'

'I went down to Chelsea Town Hall this morning and got the forms to register him. Jack Edward Hobbs . . . Edward for my father.'

I looked at him, appalled. 'You had no right. No right . . .'

'Keep your voice down.'

'Don't tell me to keep my voice down when you . . .'

'Can't we get back to the subject of Jack?'

'He's *not* Jack. Understand? I refuse to let him be called Jack.'

'Sally, his name's not legal until you co-sign the registration form. So will you please—'

'What? Be reasonable? Act like a stiff-upper-lip Brit when my son is upstairs, dying . . .'

'He is not dying.'

'He *is* dying—and I don't care. You get that? I *don't* care.'

At which point I fell back against the pillows, pulled the covers over my head, and fell into another of my extended crying jags. A nurse had arrived on the scene moments before my outburst, and I could hear a lot of rapid-fire whispering . . . and phrases like, '*we've seen this sort of thing before*', '*often happens after a difficult delivery*'.

Though the covers were over my head, I retreated back to my foetal position, once again biting deeply into the pillow in an attempt to stifle my screams. Like last night, I didn't struggle when someone rolled up my sleeve and pricked my arm with a hypodermic. I remained in a narcotic, blissed-out state until the following morning, when hard shafts of sunlight streaked through the windows and I felt curiously rested.

Then the world crashed in on me. I scrambled for the call bell. A Northern Irish nurse, Nurse Dowling, was on duty.

'Good morning, Ms Goodchild. You seemed to be sleeping awfully well. And have you seen what's arrived while you were sleeping?'

It took a moment or so for my eyes to focus on the three large floral arrangements that adorned various corners of the room. The nurse gathered up the gift cards and handed them to me. One bouquet from the editor of the *Chronicle*. One from Tony's team on the Foreign pages. One from Margaret and Alexander.

'They're beautiful, aren't they?' Nurse Dowling said.

I stared at the arrangements, having absolutely no opinion about them whatsoever. They were flowers, that's all.

'Could I get you a cup of tea now?' Nurse Dowling asked. 'Perhaps a little breakfast?'

I thanked the nurse, and asked her if she could just find out how Jack was doing.

'Oh, you've already chosen a name for him,' she said.

'Yes,' I said. 'Jack Edward.'

'Good strong name,' she said. 'And I'll be right back with the tea and any news of Jack.'

Jack. Jack. Jack.

Suddenly I felt the worst wave of shame imaginable.

'He is dying—and I don't care. You get that? I don't care.'

How could I have said that? Had I so completely lost it that I *actually* expressed indifference about whether or not my son lived? I was unfit to be a mother, a wife, a member of the human race. I deserved everything bad that would now happen to me.

But, most of all, yesterday's bizarre, out-of-kilter rage had vanished. All I could now think was: I need to be with Jack.

Nurse Dowling returned with a breakfast tray and some news.

'I gather your little one's doing just fine. They're really pleased with the progress he's making, and he can probably be moved out of ICU in a couple of days.'

'Can I see him this morning?'

'No problem.'

I picked at my breakfast—largely because whatever appetite I had was tempered by an equally urgent need to speak with Tony. I wanted to utter a vast *mea culpa* for my insane behaviour yesterday, to beg his forgiveness, and also tell him that he and Jack were the best things that had ever happened to me. And, of course, I'll sign the registration document naming him Jack Edward. Because . . . because . . . be . . .

The crying had started again. Another extended bout of loud, insufferable keening. Come on, knock it off, I told myself. But as I quickly discovered, this was an absurd idea because I fell apart once more. Only this time I was cognisant enough of this sudden breakdown to be genuinely spooked by it. Especially as I worried that the medical staff might start writing me off as mentally askew, and worthy of more intensive chemical treatment. So I stuffed the pillow back into my mouth, clutched it against me like a life preserver, and started counting backwards from one hundred inside my head, telling myself that I had to have myself under control by the time I reached zero. But during this countdown, Nurse Dowling showed up accompanied by the orderly. I felt her hand against my shoulder, calling my name, asking me what was wrong. When I couldn't answer, I heard her turn to the orderly and mention something about getting the unit sister. At which point I had just reached the number thirty-nine, and suddenly heard myself shout, *'Thirty-nine!'*

This threw everybody—most especially Nurse Dowling, who looked at me as if I had completely abandoned all reason.

'What's happened?' she asked. I didn't know the answer to that—so all I said was, 'Bad dream.'

'But you were awake.'

'No,' I lied. 'I fell asleep again.'

'Are you sure you're OK?' she asked.

'Absolutely,' I said, touching my very wet face and attempting to wipe away the remnants of all that crying. 'Just a little nightmare.'

The unit sister arrived at my bedside just in time to hear that last comment. She was a formidable Afro-Caribbean woman in her early forties, and I could tell that she wasn't buying a word of it.

'Perhaps you need another sedative, Sally.'

'I am completely fine,' I said, my voice nervous.

'I'd like to believe that,' the unit sister said, 'but your chart shows that you've already had two such incidents. Which, I must tell you, is not at all unusual after a physically traumatic delivery. But if it persists . . .'

'It won't,' I said. 'It was just a nightmare. It won't happen again.'

The unit sister shrugged. 'All right,' she said, 'we'll forgo medication right now. But if you have another incident . . .'

'I *won't*. But I would desperately like to see my son, Jack.'

'That should be possible after Mr Hughes comes by on his rounds.'

'I have to wait until then?'

'It's just another hour or so. And you mustn't worry too much about what's going on right now. You've been through a great deal.'

She smiled and touched my arm, then left. Nurse Dowling said, 'Anything else I can get you?'

'If you could just hand me the phone, please.'

She brought it over to the bed, then left. I dialled home. I received no answer, which bothered me just a little, as it was only eight thirty in the morning, and Tony was a notoriously late sleeper. Then I called his mobile and got him immediately. I was relieved to hear him in traffic.

'I'm sorry,' I said. 'I'm so damn sorry about . . .'

'It's all right, Sally,' Tony said.

'No. It's not. What I said yesterday . . .'

'Meant nothing. You were in shock. It happens.'

'It still doesn't excuse what I said about Jack.'

A telling pause. 'So you like the name now?'

'Yes, I do. And I like you too. More than I can say.'

'Now there's no need to go all soppy on me. What's the latest word on our boy?'

'I won't know anything until Hughes does his rounds. When will you be in?'

'Around tea-time.'

'Tony . . .'

'I have pages to get out.'

'And you have a deputy. Surely the editor was most sympathetic . . .'

'Did you get his flowers?'

'Yes. And a bouquet from Margaret, too. You called her?'

'Well, she is your best friend.'

'Thank you.'

'And I also spoke with Sandy. Explained that it had been a compli-cated delivery, that you were a bit under the weather, and told her it was best if she didn't ring you for a few days. Naturally, she's phoned me three times since then to see how you're doing.'

'What did you tell her?'

'That you were making steady progress.'

Sandy being Sandy, I was certain that she didn't believe a word of his reassurances, and was now frantically worried about my condition. But I was grateful to Tony for keeping her at bay. Much as I adored my sister, I didn't want her to hear how fragile I was right now.

'Listen, I have to run now,' Tony said. 'I'll try to be in by early evening.'

'Fine,' I said, even though I didn't mean it, as I really wanted him at my bedside right now for some necessary emotional support.

Mr Hughes arrived promptly at ten. He was accompanied by the unit sister. He nodded hello, but said nothing until he had perused the notes hanging on the bedstead clipboard.

'So, Mrs . . .'

He glanced back at the clipboard.

'. . . Goodchild. Not the most pleasant few days, I'd imagine?'

'How is my son?'

Hughes hated being interrupted. And he showed his displeasure by staring down at the chart while speaking with me.

'I've just been looking in on him at ICU. All vital signs are good. And I spoke to the attending paediatrician, Dr Reynolds. He told me that an EEG performed this morning indicated no neurological disturbance. But, of course, to make certain that everything is functioning properly, an MRI will be conducted around lunchtime today. He should have results by evening time and I know he'll want to see you then.'

'Do you think that brain damage did occur?'

'Mrs Goodchild . . . though I can understand your worry, I am simply not in a position to speculate about such matters. That is Dr Reynolds's territory. Now, would you mind if I looked at Mr Kerr's handiwork?'

The unit sister helped me raise my nightgown, then she pulled away the bandages. I hadn't seen my wounds since the delivery and they shocked me: a crisscrossing sequence of railroad tracks.

'I gather you've been having a bit of emotional disquiet,' Hughes said.

'It was nothing.'

'You know, there's absolutely no shame in going a little wonky after giving birth. Quite commonplace, actually, given that one's hormones are all over the place. A course of antidepressants . . .'

'I need nothing, Doctor, except to see my son.'

'Yes, yes. I do understand. I'm sure sister here can arrange it once we're done.' He scribbled some notes onto my chart, spoke quickly to the unit sister, then turned back to me with a farewell nod.

'Good day, Mrs Goodchild, and try not to worry.'

That's easy for you to say, pal.

Half an hour later, having had my surgical dressings changed, I was up in Paediatric ICU. Once again, I followed the advice of that benevolent orderly and kept my eyes firmly closed as I was wheeled in. When I finally opened them, the sight of Jack made my eyes sting. Not that there was any change in his condition. Only now I had a desperate need to hold him, to cradle him. Suddenly, I knew that whatever happened to him, whatever horrors were revealed by the MRI, I'd deal with it. The way you deal with life's most unexpected, fiendish cards. But, oh God, how I didn't want that to come to pass.

I started to weep again. This time, however, I didn't feel the undertow of emotional hollowness that had so characterised the past few days. This time, I simply wept for Jack—and for what might become of him.

The orderly kept his distance while I cried. But after a minute or so, he approached me with a box of tissues and said, 'It might be best if we head back now.' And he returned me to my room.

'Good news,' Nurse Dowling said after I was helped back into bed. 'Mr Hughes says you can come off those nasty drips. First steps towards freedom, eh? Now what can I get you for lunch?'

But I refused all food, refused a rental television, refused the offer of a sponge bath. All I wanted was to be left alone—to lie in bed with the blankets pulled up to my chin, shutting out the cacophony of the world.

Then it was six o'clock. Much to my surprise, Tony showed up exactly when he said he would, bearing a bouquet of flowers and a nervousness that I found endearing.

'Any news?' he asked, sitting down on the edge of the bed and kissing my forehead.

I shook my head and forced myself to sit up. 'You look tense.'

Tony just smiled a stiff smile and lapsed into silence. There was nothing to say until the paediatrician made his appearance. Our shared anxiety was so palpable that saying nothing was the smartest option.

Tony took my hand, trying to be supportive. In doing so, he was letting me know just how scared he was.

Fortunately, this silence only lasted a minute or so, as Dr Reynolds arrived. I tried to read his face, but he was giving nothing away.

'How are you feeling, Ms Goodchild?' he asked.

'Not bad,' I said quietly.

'How's our son, Doctor?' Tony asked.

'Yes, I was about to come to that. Now . . . after consultation both with the paediatric neurologist and the radiologist, we've all reached the same conclusion: the MRI film shows a perfectly normal infant brain. Which, in turn, means that, based on this MRI—and the recent EEG— we *sense* that there has been no brain damage.'

Tony squeezed my hand tightly, and didn't seem to mind that it was a cold and clammy hand. It was only then that I realised I had my head bowed and my eyes tightly closed, like someone expecting a body blow. I opened my eyes and asked, 'You just said that you *sense* there's been no brain damage. Doesn't the MRI offer conclusive evidence?'

A sympathetic smile from Reynolds.

'The brain is a mysterious organism. And after a traumatic birth, when there was initially a question about whether the brain was denied oxygen, you cannot be one hundred per cent definitive there was no damage. However, all clinical evidence points to a positive outcome.'

'So there *is* something to worry about,' I said, getting agitated.

'If I were you, I'd move forward optimistically.'

'But you're *not* me, Doctor. And because you're more than hinting that our son has been brain damaged—'

Tony cut me off. 'Sally, that is not what the doctor said.'

'I *heard* what he said. And what he said is that there is a chance our son was denied oxygen to the brain and is therefore . . .'

Again, Tony intervened. '*Enough*, Sally.'

'Don't tell me—'

'*Enough!*' His vehement tone silenced me. And I suddenly felt appalled by the illogicality of my rant, and by the irrational anger I had shown this very decent and patient doctor.

'Dr Reynolds, I am so sorry.'

He raised his hand. 'There's nothing to apologise about, Ms Goodchild. I do understand just how difficult things have been. And I'll be back here tomorrow if you have any further questions.'

Then he wished us a good evening and left. As soon as he was out of the room, Tony looked at me for a very long time. Then he asked, 'Would you mind telling me what the hell that was all about?'

I looked away. 'I don't know.'

FIVE

THEY KEPT ME IN THE HOSPITAL for another five days. Since Jack's birth I had been expressing milk for him, and the breast pump had become my nemesis. I had to perform this charming bit of plumbing several times a day, in order to keep my milk ducts cleared. During this time, I was allowed constant visits with Jack in Paediatric ICU, and then the moment came when the nurse on duty told us that Dr Reynolds had sanctioned Jack's move to my room the next morning. It was a prospect that terrified me, because he would be my responsibility now.

But the next morning, I was paid a visit by Dr Reynolds.

'Now I don't want to upset you,' he began, 'but it seems that Jack has developed jaundice.'

'He *what*?'

'It's a common postnatal condition which affects almost fifty per cent of all newborn babies. It occurs when there is a breakdown of red blood cells and you get a build-up of a yellow pigment called bilirubin.'

'But what causes this build-up up of . . . what was it again?'

'Bilirubin. Generally, it comes from breast milk.'

'You mean, *I* have made him jaundiced? I've poisoned him.'

That dangerous edge had crept into my voice, and though I was aware of its ominous presence, there was nothing I could do to curb it.

Dr Reynolds spoke slowly and with great care. 'Ms Goodchild, you simply must not blame yourself. Because—as I said before—it is such a common ailment in new babies.'

'Can jaundice be dangerous?'

'Only if the levels of bilirubin get too high.'

'Then what happens?'

'Then,' Dr Reynolds said, 'it can prove toxic to the brain. *But*—and I must emphasise this—such levels are extremely rare. And so far, your son is not showing any signs of . . .'

But I wasn't listening to him any more. Instead, another voice had taken up residence inside my head. A voice which kept repeating: *You've poisoned him . . . and now he's going to be even more brain-damaged. And there's no one to blame but you . . .*

'Ms Goodchild? Are you all right?'

I looked up and could see Dr Reynolds eyeing me with concern.

'I'm . . . all right,' I said.

'Your son's jaundice will clear up in around ten days. During that time, we will have to keep him in the ICU. But, once again, there's nothing particularly ominous about that. It's just standard procedure for any newborn with jaundice. Would you like to go up to see him?'

'All right,' I said, but my voice sounded flat, devoid of emotion. Once again, I could see Dr Reynolds studying me with concern.

The blue light of the ICU masked the yellowish tint that now characterised Jack's skin. But it didn't matter that I couldn't see the actual physical evidence of his illness. I knew how sick he was. And I knew that it *was* my fault.

Afterwards, I called Tony at work and broke the news to him. When I mentioned that Jack had become jaundiced because of my breast milk, my husband said, 'Sally, you're talking rubbish.'

By the time Tony arrived at the hospital that night, I had managed to pull myself out of my self-flagellation jag. We went up to the ICU together. Again, the blue fluorescent tubes cast the ward in a spectral light and also bleached out the yellowed pigment of our son's skin. When Tony asked the attending nurse just how bad the jaundice was, she reassured us that it would be cleared up in a matter of days.

'So there's nothing to worry about?' Tony asked, giving his question a certain *for-my-benefit* pointedness.

'He should make a full recovery, with no lasting side effects,' the nurse said.

'See?' Tony said, patting my arm. 'All is well.'

I nodded in agreement—even though I didn't believe it. I knew the truth. Just as that nurse knew the truth. My milk had poisoned him.

For the next thirty-six hours, I maintained a calm-and-collected front, showing a rational face to the doctors and nurses, visiting Jack several times a day at the ICU, and always nodding in agreement when they kept feeding me optimistic falsehoods about his progress.

Then, as expected, I was given the all-clear to go home. It was something of a wrench to leave Jack behind in the ICU, but I was glad for his sake that he was in a place where I could do him no harm.

Getting out of the hospital was, therefore, something of a relief. Especially as Tony not only had dinner waiting for me when I came home, but (as promised) he'd also drafted in Margaret's cleaner, Cha, to give the place a thorough going-over, which meant that it now looked like a moderately tidy building site. And he had a bottle of Laurent Perrier in the fridge. But when he handed me a glass, all I could think was: This is not exactly a triumphant homecoming.

Still, I clinked my glass against his and downed the French fizz in one long gulp. Tony immediately refilled it.

'You're thirsty,' he said.

'I think it's called "needing a drink".' I drained my glass again.

'You OK?'

I didn't feel that question needed answering, because it was so damn obvious what was wrong here. I had come home from hospital after having a baby, but without the baby . . . even though I knew that Jack was better off without me.

'Nice bit of domestic news today,' Tony said. 'The builders were in.'

'You could have fooled me.'

'Anyway, the foreman—what's his name? . . . Northern Irish guy . . . Collins, right? . . . he was asking for you. And when I mentioned you'd had the baby, but he was in intensive care . . . well, Jesus, you should have seen the guilt kick in. Said he'd get a full crew in in the next few days, and try to have all the work done within a fortnight.'

'It's good to know that a potentially brain-damaged baby can finally get a builder to . . .'

'Stop it,' Tony said quietly, pouring me yet another glass.

'Have I already drunk the last one?'

'Looks that way. Dinner's ready.'

'Let me guess. Curry vindaloo?'

'Close. Chicken Tikka Masala.'

'Even though you know I can't stand Indian.'

'If you can't stand Indian, you've come to the wrong country.'

'Yes,' I said. 'I have done just that.'

Tony got one of those uncomfortable looks on his face.

'I'll go and get things underway in the kitchen.'

'And I'll go and unblock a milk duct.'

When I returned from the bathroom, having coped with the torture pump, I discovered that we weren't eating Chicken Tikka Masala (that was Tony's idea of a joke). Rather, a wonderful Spaghetti alla Carbonara, with freshly grated Parmesan cheese, a green salad, and a decent bottle of Chianti Classico, all courtesy of Marks and Spencer.

It was pure comfort food, and I ate like a hostage on his first full night of freedom. Only I didn't feel free of anything.

'Thank you for this beautiful dinner,' I said.

'Ready-made food isn't exactly beautiful.'

'Still, it was very thoughtful of you.'

Another of his shrugs. We fell silent. Then, 'I'm scared, Tony.'

'That's not surprising. You've been through a lot.'

'It's not just that. It's whether Jack will turn out . . .'

He cut me off. 'Sally . . . everyone says Jack will be just fine. Do I have to keep repeating that over and over? Have you lost all reason?'

'You're saying I'm crazy?'

'I'm saying, you're being irrational.'

'I have a *right* to be irrational. Because . . .'

But then I applied the emotional brakes. I had been shouting. Suddenly, I found myself truly appalled (yet again) by such a temperamental overload. One moment, I was in full-throttle fury. The next . . .

'I think I need to lie down.'

Tony gave me another of his long, nonplussed looks.

I got up and left the kitchen, and went to the bedroom, and changed into my pyjamas, and fell into bed, and pulled the blankets up over my head, and waited for sleep to come.

But it didn't arrive. On the contrary, I was shockingly wide awake, despite a deep, painful fatigue. But my mind was in high-octane over-drive, ricocheting from thought to thought, worry to worry. Entire horrendous scenarios played themselves out in my head—the last of which involved Jack, aged three, curled up, ball-like in an armchair, unable to focus on me, or his general surroundings, or the world at large, while some hyper-rational, hyper-calm social worker said, 'I really do think that you and your husband must consider some sort of "managed care" environment for your son.'

'Tony!'

No answer. I glanced at the clock: 2.05. How did that happen? I hadn't been asleep, had I? I turned over. Tony wasn't next to me. Immediately I was out of bed and in the corridor. But before I headed downstairs to see if he was up, watching a late-night movie, I saw the light on the still uncarpeted stairs leading up to his study.

The attic conversion had been finished while I had been in hospital, and Tony had evidently expended considerable effort on putting it together. His fitted bookshelves were now stacked with a selection from his extensive library. Another wall was filled with most of his CDs. He had a small stereo system and a short-wave radio in easy reach of the large stylish desk that he had chosen with me at the Conran Shop. There was a new Dell computer on the desk, and a new orthopaedic chair, upon which Tony was now sitting, staring at a word-filled screen.

'This is impressive,' I said, looking around.

'Glad you like it.'

I wanted to mention something about how it might have been nice if he'd concentrated his energies on unpacking the more shared corners of the house . . . but thought it wise to hold my tongue. It had been getting me into enough trouble recently.

202

'What time is it?' he asked absently.

'Just a little after two.'

'Couldn't sleep?'

'Something like that. You too?'

'Been working since you went off to bed.'

'On what? Something for the paper?'

'The novel, actually.'

'Really?' I said, sounding pleased. Because Tony had been threatening to start his first foray into fiction when I met him in Cairo. At the time he had intimated that if he ever got transferred back to dreaded, prosaic London, he was finally going to try to write the Graham Greene-esque novel that had been rattling around his head for the past few years.

'That's great news,' I said.

Tony shrugged. 'It might turn out to be crap.'

'It might turn out to be good.' I came over to him and put my hand on his shoulder. 'I'm sorry about before.'

'I'm sure you'll feel better in the morning. If you can stop worrying.'

But when I woke at seven o'clock, Tony wasn't next to me in bed. Rather, I found him asleep on the new pull-out sofa in his study, a pile of printed pages stacked up by the computer. When I brought him a cup of tea a few hours later, my first question was, 'How late did you work?'

'Only till three,' he said, sounding half awake.

'You could have come down and shared the bed.'

'Didn't want to wake you.'

But the next night, he did the same thing. When I turned the bedside light off, he hadn't joined me. And when I came to at eight the next morning, the space next to me was empty. Once again, I climbed the stairs to his study, only to find him under the duvet on his sofa bed.

This time, however, I didn't bring him a cup of tea. Nor did I wake him. But when he staggered downstairs around ten, looking harassed, the first thing he said to me was, 'Why the hell did you let me sleep in?'

'Well, since we seem to be living separate lives, I don't have to be your alarm clock. I'm just wondering if you're trying to tell me something.'

'For God's sake, I was just working late. It's a good time to work.'

'And it also gives you the excuse not to sleep with me.'

I knew that my husband was shrewdly ensuring that, when Jack came home, he'd be able to sidestep all the sleepless nights by using his novel as an excuse, and the sofa bed in his study as his refuge.

'No doubt it will only be a matter of time before he starts working out ways to get transferred back to Cairo—alone,' Sandy said when she called me that morning.

'He's just quietly freaking,' I said.

'Yeah . . . responsibility is such a bitch.'

Of course, this hadn't been my first phone conversation with my sister since I'd been in hospital. Since I had come home, we'd spoken two to three times a day. Naturally, Sandy was horrified by my news.

'If that deadbeat ex-husband of mine hadn't just taken off for a month-long hike with his outdoorsy paramour, I'd be over in London like a speeding bullet. But there's no one else to look after the kids.'

'I really think it's going to be all right,' I told Sandy, in an attempt to get her off the subject of my contrary husband. 'They're moving Jack out of Paediatric ICU today.'

'Well, that's something. Are you better?'

'I'm fine,' I said carefully. Though I had mentioned my initial post-natal dive to Sandy, I didn't go into great detail. But Sandy, per usual, wasn't buying my calmness.

'I've got a friend—Alison Kepler—she's the chief nurse in the post-natal division of Brigham and Women's Hospital. And she told me that postnatal depression can come in a couple of waves.'

'But I'm *not* having a postnatal depression,' I said, exasperated.

'How can you be certain? Don't you know that most depressed people don't know they're depressed?'

'Because I find myself getting so damn pissed-off with Tony, that's how. And don't you know that most depressed people are unable to get really pissed off at their husband?'

The next day, I arrived for my morning visit at ten thirty, to be met by the usual morning nurse, who said, 'Good news. Jack's jaundice has totally cleared up and we've moved him to the normal baby ward.'

When I arrived there, the ward sister on duty was waiting. 'Your timing's perfect,' she said. 'Jack needs to be fed.'

It was extraordinary to see him free from all the medical apparatus that had mummified him for the past ten days. Before, he had looked so des-perately vulnerable. Now his face had shaken off that drugged look of shock that had possessed him during the first few days of his life. And though Sandy (through her platoon of experts) had reassured me that he'd have no received memories of these early medical traumas, I couldn't help but feel more guilt. And suddenly, that reproving voice inside my head started again: *You brought this on yourself. You did it to him . . .*

Shut up!

I found myself shuddering and gripping the sides of Jack's crib. The nurse on duty studied me with concern.

'Are you all right?' she asked.

'Just a little tired, that's all,' I said, noticing her name tag: *McGuire*.

'Ready to take him?' the nurse asked.

No, I am not ready. I'm not ready for any of this. Because I can't cope.

'Sure,' I said, my smile tight. I sat down.

She reached in and gathered him up. He was very docile until he was put into my arms. At which point, he instantly began to cry. It wasn't a loud cry, but it was certainly persistent. Like someone who felt instantly uncomfortable with the hands now holding him. And that admonishing voice inside my head told me: *Well, of course he's crying. Because he knows it was you who did him harm.*

'Is he your first?' the nurse asked.

'Yes,' I said, wondering if my nervousness was showing.

'Maybe if you tried feeding him . . .' the nurse suggested.

'I've been having problems extracting milk,' I said.

'Well, he'll clear that problem up straight away,' she said. 'Let me take him for a moment while you sort yourself out.'

I'm not going to sort myself out. Because I can't sort myself out.

'Thank you,' I said. As soon as she relieved me of Jack, he stopped crying. I pulled up my T-shirt and freed my right breast from the nursing bra I was wearing. My hands were sweaty. I felt desperately tense— in part, because my milk ducts had been blocked over the past few days. But also because all I felt was terror.

Once the breast was exposed, the nurse returned Jack to me. His reaction to my touch was almost Pavlovian: *cry when you feel Mommy's hands*. And cry he did. Profusely. Until his lips touched my nipple, at which point he started making greedy suckling noises.

'There he goes,' the nurse said, nodding approvingly as he clamped his gums around my nipple and began to suck hard. Immediately, it felt as if a clothespeg had been applied to my breast. Though his mouth may have been toothless, his gums were steel-reinforced. And he clamped down so hard my initial reaction was a surprised scream.

'You all right there?' the nurse asked.

'His gums are just a little—'

But I didn't get to finish the sentence, as he bit down so hard that I actually shrieked. Worst yet, the pain had been so sudden, so intense, that I inadvertently yanked him off my breast, which sent him back into screaming mode.

'Oh God, sorry, sorry, sorry,' I said.

The nurse remained calm. She collected Jack from me, settling him down moments after she had him in her arms. I sat there, my breast exposed and aching, feeling useless and desperately guilty.

'Is he all right?' I asked, my voice thick with shock.

'Just got a little fright, that's all,' she said. 'As did you.'

'I really didn't mean to . . .'

'You're grand, really. Happens all the time. Especially if you're having a little problem with the milk flow. Now, hang on there a sec. I think I know how we can sort this problem out.'

Using her free hand, she reached for a phone. About a minute later, another nurse arrived with the dreaded breast pump.

The pain was appalling, but after a minute of vigorous pumping, the dam burst. And, though I now had tears streaming down my face, the relief was enormous too.

'All right now?' the nurse asked, all cheerful and no-nonsense.

I nodded. She handed Jack back to me. God, how he hated my touch. I moved him quickly to the now-leaking nipple. He was reluctant to go near it again, but when his lips tasted the milk, he was clamped onto it like a vice, sucking madly. I flinched at the renewed pain, but forced myself to stay silent. I didn't want to put on another show for this exceedingly tolerant nurse. But she sensed my distress.

'Hurts a bit, does it?'

'I'm afraid so.'

'Well, of course it hurts,' Sandy said when I phoned her around noon that day. 'Hell, I used to dread every moment of it.'

'Really?' I said, grabbing on to this revelation.

'Believe me, it didn't give me a big motherly buzz. When are you going back to the hospital?'

'Tonight,' I said, my voice so flat that Sandy said, 'Sally . . . you don't sound good.'

'Just a bad day, that's all.'

'Are you sure about that?'

'Yes,' I lied. Because the truth was . . . *What*?

I had no damn idea what the truth here was. Except that I *didn't* want to go back to the hospital that night. As soon as I hung up the phone, I escaped from the workmen who were everywhere in the house, and took refuge in Tony's study. I unfolded the sofa bed, opened the wicker box where Tony kept the duvet and pillows, made the bed, pulled down the shade on the dormer window, turned the phone on to voicemail, took off my jeans, and got under the covers. Even though there was an excessive amount of hammering and sanding on the lower floors, I was asleep within minutes—a fast, blacked-out tumble into oblivion.

Then I heard a familiar voice. 'What are you doing here?'

It took a moment or two to work out where I was. Or to adjust to the fact that it was now night, and the room had just been illuminated by the big floor lamp that stood to the right of the desk, and that my husband was standing in the doorway, looking at me with concern.

'Tony?' I asked, my voice thick with sleep.

'The hospital has been trying to reach you.'

Now I was completely awake. 'They *what*?'

'Jack had a minor setback this afternoon. The jaundice returned.'

Now I was on my feet, grabbing for my clothes. 'Let's go,' I said, pulling on my jeans. Tony put a steadying hand on my arm.

'I've been there already. It's OK. The blood tests showed only a very minor overload of bilirubin, so there's nothing to worry about. However, they did move him back to Paediatric ICU . . .'

I shrugged off Tony's hand. 'Tell me in the car.'

'We're not going. It's nearly midnight.'

'What?' I said, sounding genuinely shocked.

'You've been asleep all day. The hospital has been trying to ring you at home since three this afternoon. And I must have left you ten messages on your mobile.'

'I was taking a nap after seeing Jack this morning.'

'A twelve-hour nap?'

'I'm sorry.' I gently shook off his grip and finished getting dressed. 'I'm going over there.'

He blocked my path to the door. 'That's not a good idea right now. Especially after . . .'

'After *what*?' I demanded.

'Especially after the difficulties you had this morning.'

That bitch, Nurse McGuire. She shopped me.

'It was just a feeding problem, that's all.'

'So I gather. But one of the nurses on duty said you nearly yanked Jack off your breast.'

'It was a momentary thing. He hurt me.'

'Well, I'm sure he didn't mean to.'

'I'm not saying that. Anyway, it wasn't as if I threw him across the room. I just had a bit of a shock.'

'Must have been quite a shock if the nurse reported it to her superior.'

I sat down on the bed. I put my head in my hands. I really did feel like grabbing my passport, running to the airport and catching the first plane Stateside.

You can't do this . . . you're a maternal disaster area . . .

Why should a catastrophe of a mother like me care about her child? Anyway, even if I did care, *they* (the doctors, the nurses, my husband) all knew the truth about me. They had the evidence. And they saw just how . . . How *what*?

How . . . I wasn't understanding any of this.

How . . . one moment, I was wracked with grief and guilt for what had befallen Jack . . . the next, I couldn't give a damn.

'Sally?'

I looked up and saw Tony staring at me in that quizzical, peeved way of his. 'You really should go to bed,' he said.

'I've just slept twelve hours.'

'Well, that was your decision.'

'No. That was *my body's* decision. Because my body's noticed something that you haven't noticed. The fact that I am completely run down after a little physical exertion called "having a baby". Which, I know, in your book, is just about up there with stubbing your toe . . .'

Tony gave me a thin smile and started stripping the sofa bed.

'Think I'll go to work now,' he said. 'No need to wait up for me.'

'You don't care what's going on, do you?'

'Excuse me, but who ran to the hospital this evening when our son's mother put herself out-of-touch with the world?'

His comment caught me like a slap across the face, especially as he said it in an ultra-detached voice.

'That is so unfair,' I said, my voice a near-whisper.

'Of course you'd think that,' he said. 'Now if you'll excuse me . . .'

'Fuck you.' I stormed out of his study, slamming the door behind me.

Marching downstairs, my initial reaction was to fly out of the door, jump into a taxi, tell the driver to floor it to the Mattingly, march straight into Paediatric ICU, demand to see Jack immediately, and also demand that they find that Irish stool pigeon, so I could confront that Ms Holier-Than-Thou with the lies she'd peddled about me. And then . . . I would be bound and gagged and dispatched to the nearest rubber room.

I started to pace the floor. And when I say pace, I *mean* pace. As in a manic back-forth motion: *here-there, here-there, here-there.* Only when the thought struck me—*look at you, treading up and down the room like a laboratory animal on amphetamines*—did I force myself to sit down.

All right, all right. Stay busy. Do something to make the hours pass.

That's how I ended up unpacking just about every box and crate still strewn around the house. The entire process took about six hours and I had to work around what remained of the builders' mess. By the time I was finished, dawn light was just making a tentative appearance, and I had the weary, but satisfied buzz that comes from finishing a major domestic chore that had been naggingly unfinished for months.

I ran a bath. I sat soaking in the tub for nearly an hour. I told myself: *You see . . . a little displacement activity, and the gods of balance and equilibrium land comfortably on your shoulders. Everything's going to be fine now.*

So fine that, after I got dressed, I felt fully energised, even though I hadn't been to bed all night. I peeped in on Tony in his study. He was crashed out on his sofa . . . but I did notice a stack of new pages on the ever-growing manuscript pile. So I tiptoed over to his desk, made certain his radio alarm was set for nine o'clock, then scribbled a fast note:

Off to the hospital to see our boy. Hope you like the clean-up job on the house. Dinner tonight on me at the restaurant of your choice?
Love you . . .

I went downstairs. I checked my watch. Just after seven o'clock. I opened the front door and noticed that someone on the far side of the road was in the middle of building work, with an empty skip out front for assorted debris. I glanced back at the stack of empty cardboard boxes and now-broken-down packing crates, and thought: This would save a trip to the dump. I also remembered how everyone in the street had emptied their attics into our skip during the first stage of our renovations. So I decided that there would be few objections if a few items from my house ended up intermingling with my neighbour's debris.

However, as I was in the process of dumping the second lot of boxes into this large bin, a house door opened and a man in his mid-forties came out. He was dressed in a dark grey suit.

'You know, that is *our* skip,' he said, his voice full of tempered indignation. Immediately I became apologetic.

'Sorry, I just thought that, as it was kind of empty . . .'

'You really should ask permission before tossing things into other people's skips.'

'But I just thought . . .'

'Now I'd appreciate it if you'd remove all your rubbish—'

However, he was interrupted by a voice that said, 'Oh, for God's sake, will you listen to yourself.'

The gent looked a little startled. Then he became sheepish, as he found himself staring at a woman in her late forties. She was blonde, big-boned, with a heavily lined face, but still striking. Equally eye-catching was the very large labrador she had by her side. She had been walking by us when she heard our exchange. The Suit avoided her accusatory gaze and said, 'I was simply making a point.'

'And what point was that?'

'I really do think this is between myself and—'

'When I was having my new kitchen put in last year, who filled up my skip one night with half the contents of his loft?'

The Suit now looked appalled. 'I was just trying to make a point.'

At which my Good Samaritan with the labrador gave him a knowing smile, and said, 'Of course you were.' Then she turned back to me and proffered her hand. 'Julia Frank. You live at Number 27, don't you?'

'That's right.' I said, and introduced myself.

'I'm just across the road at Number 32. Nice to meet you. Do you need a hand with the rest of the boxes?'

'I'll be fine. But I . . .'

The gent cleared his throat, then he hurried back into his house.

'Twit,' Julia said under her breath after he was gone. 'No wonder his wife walked out last month.'

'I didn't know.'

She shrugged. 'Just another domestic drama, like we've all had. And, by the way, I heard you're a new mother. How's life without sleep?'

'Well . . . he's not home yet.'

Then I explained, in the briefest way possible, what had befallen him.

'Good God,' she said quietly. 'You've really had a ghastly time of it.'

'Him more than me.'

'But are you all right?'

'Yes and no. Sometimes I can't really tell.'

'Got time for a cup of tea?'

'I'd love to, but I really need to be at the hospital early this morning.'

'Completely understood,' she said. 'Anyway, drop by whenever. And do throw as much rubbish in that fool's skip as you like.'

With a pleasant smile, she ended our little encounter.

I followed her instructions, and threw all the remaining empty boxes into the skip, along with four brimming bags of builders' debris. Then I walked to the tube, thinking, 'I actually have a friendly neighbour.'

At the hospital, I was on my ultra-best behaviour. And I was hugely relieved to discover that Jack's return to Paediatric ICU had been a brief one, as he was back on the normal baby ward. The usual unit sister was there as well, eyeing me up carefully, the way one does with anyone who's been labelled 'a loose cannon'.

I gave her a big smile and said, 'Is Nurse McGuire around? I think I owe her an apology for being so extreme yesterday.'

Immediately the unit sister relaxed. 'I'm afraid she's off on a week's holiday, but when she's back I'll tell her what you said.'

'And I am sorry I didn't make it last night. It's just . . . well, to be honest about it, I was so tired I simply passed out.'

'Don't worry about it. Every mother is exhausted after giving birth. And the good news is: that little relapse last night was nothing more than that. In fact, you might be able to take him home tomorrow.'

I was all smiles. 'That is great news.'

'Are you up for feeding him now?'

Doing my best to disguise my unease, I nodded, keeping the fixed smile on my face. The unit sister motioned for me to follow her. We walked down the ward to Jack's crib. He was lying on his side, crying loudly. I tensed, wondering if he'd really start bawling when I picked him up. But I tried to mask this by saying, 'He sounds really hungry.'

The unit sister smiled back. My hands were sweaty as I picked him up. And, yes, his squeals did amplify as I lifted him.

Keep your nerve, keep your nerve, I told myself.

I pulled Jack close to me, rocking him gently. His crying redoubled. I quickly settled down into the hard, straight-back chair by the crib, opened my shirt, released my left breast from the nursing bra. I gently directed Jack's head toward the nipple. When he found it he began to suck ravenously. I shut my eyes as the pain hit. But then his voraciousness suddenly paid off, as his vacuum-like suction cleared the ducts and milk poured forth. He was eating.

'Are you in a bit of pain there?' the unit sister asked.

'Nothing that can't be managed,' I said.

This was the correct response, as the sister nodded approvingly and said, 'I'll leave you to it.'

As soon as she was out of sight, I leaned over and whispered into Jack's ear, 'Thanks.'

After ten minutes, I transferred Jack to the other nipple and, once again, his hoover of a mouth cleared all obstructions within moments and milk flowed freely.

When I returned home that morning from the hospital, there was a note waiting for me from Tony, saying:

Your invitation declined with regret. US Deputy Secretary of State in town tonight. Just received last-minute invitation for dinner at the embassy. Will make it up to you.

Great, just great. But after last night's stupidity, I wasn't going to call him up and hector him for turning down my invitation. Instead, I'd put a positive spin on this situation. Rather than fall into bed now for a nap, I'd force my way through the day on no sleep, then go by the hospital around seven and would be back home in bed by ten, tired out enough to sleep straight through the night without interruption. Come morning, I'd be back on a normal schedule, ready to bring my son home.

Of course, by the time I reached the Mattingly that night, I had been up for twenty straight hours, and was starting to veer into numb-with-fatigue territory. The evening feeding session at the hospital went on longer than expected, as Mr Hughes made a surprise visit to the baby ward. He was showing a group of his students round this corner of the hospital, and, when he saw me feeding Jack, he led his entourage over towards me. I had my son at my breast and turned my wince into a look of maternal contentment as he approached us.

'Bonding well, are we?' he asked.

'No problems,' I said, all smiley.

'Splendid, splendid. I spoke with Dr Reynolds earlier today—and he feels that your son is ready to be discharged. So you can collect him tomorrow morning if that doesn't present any problems.'

'None at all.'

'Very good, then.'

Hughes started explaining in highly technical language about Jack's complicated delivery, and how he had to be ventilated after birth. He then explained about how I was suffering from high blood pressure throughout my pregnancy . . . to the point where he wondered whether it was best to deliver the child prematurely.

'You never told me that,' I said.

Suddenly, all eyes were upon me. Hughes gave me a frown.

'Something the matter, Ms Goodchild?' he asked.

'You never told me you were considering a premature delivery.'

'That's because your high-blood-pressure condition wasn't pre-eclampsic . . . and because it did eventually stabilise. But, truth be told, when you were first admitted with high blood pressure, you were a borderline case for an emergency Caesarean . . .'

'Well, thanks for the information, even if it is a little after the fact. I mean, if there was a danger to me and my baby, shouldn't I have been given that emergency Caesarean option at the time?'

'Curiously enough, it is always better for the child if it is carried to full term. And curiously enough, Ms Goodchild, we are rather up-to-date on modern obstetric practice on this side of the pond . . . which means that we did do what was medically best for you and your son.'

Ten minutes later, having settled Jack back in his crib, I was in a cab rolling down the Fulham Road, crying like an idiot, wildly overreacting to Hughes's disparagement of me. By the time we reached Putney, I had finally managed to get myself under a degree of control.

I walked into the empty house and bolted upstairs to the bedroom. I threw off my clothes, put on a T-shirt and climbed into bed. I pulled the covers over my head. I blocked out everything.

When I jolted awake again at eight the next morning, I was so pleasantly groggy from such an unbroken period of unconsciousness that it took a moment or so to realise: *I've actually slept.*

Tony had assured me that he would take the morning off to drive me to the hospital to collect Jack. But when I shuffled down to the kitchen, I found a Post-it on top of a couple of crumpled bank notes. *Emergency at the paper. Here's £40 for a cab there-and-back. Will try to get home asap this evening. T xxx.*

I grabbed the phone. I punched in the number of Tony's direct line. I got his voicemail. So I phoned his mobile.

'Can't talk right now,' he said.

'I don't care what *emergency* you have on your hands. You're meeting me at the hospital, understand?'

'I can't talk.'

Then he hung up.

Immediately I rang back. He had obviously turned off his phone after our last conversation, as I was put through directly to his voicemail.

'How dare you—*how dare you*—pull this. You get your sorry English ass over to the hospital, or I am not going to be responsible for what happens next. Do you get that?'

I hung up, my heart pounding, my head full of righteous indignation and genuine upset. He just couldn't stand me up on this one.

But he did. Because I didn't hear from him for the rest of the morning. Anyway, I didn't have time to think about this latest example of Tony's complete indifference, as I needed to be at the hospital on time or further darken my reputation. So I ducked into the shower, and slapped some make-up on my face, and was at the Mattingly by eleven.

'Is your husband with you this morning?' the unit sister asked, eyeing me over, evidently wondering just what my emotional temperature might be.

'I'm afraid he had a crisis at work.'

Jack still reacted with upset when I touched him. And it was a struggle to get him into his Babygro. He also hated being strapped into the carry-chair.

'I presume your health visitor will be calling on you soon. So if you have any postnatal questions, she's the person to ask,' the sister said.

'Thank you for that. In fact, thank you for everything.'

'I hope he makes you very happy,' she said.

One of the nurses helped me downstairs with the carry-chair. She asked one of the porters to call me a cab. When we reached Sefton Street, the driver got out of and helped me with Jack to the front door.

It was so strange entering my empty house with this tiny creature.

Like all of life's bigger passages, you expect a sense of profundity to accompany the occasion. And, like all of life's bigger passages, the event itself is a letdown. I opened the door, picked up the carry-chair and brought Jack inside. I closed the door behind me. And, all I could think was: This might have been an occasion if my husband had been here.

Jack had fallen asleep during the cab ride, so I hoisted him upstairs to the nursery and unfastened the straps. Exercising the utmost care, I lifted him gently into his crib. He pulled his arms tight against himself as I covered him with the little quilt that Sandy had sent me. He didn't stir. I sat down in the wicker chair opposite the crib, and looked at my son. I waited to feel rapture, delight, maternal concern and vulnerability. All those damn emotions that every writer of every motherhood guide promises you will inhabit in the days after your child's birth. But all I felt was a profound, terrible hollowness.

A ringing phone snapped me out of this desperate, vacant reverie. I was hoping it was Tony, sounding contrite and suitably humble. Or Sandy, with whom I could have bitched at length about my detached, taciturn husband. Instead, I received a call from a woman with a decidedly London accent, who introduced herself as Jane Sanjay and said that she was my health visitor. Her tone was surprising: breezy, pleasant, 'I'm here to help'. She wondered if she might drop by this afternoon.

'Is there any reason why you need to see me right away?' I asked.

She laughed. 'Don't panic, I'm not the baby police!'

Jane Sanjay was about thirty, with an easy smile and an unfussy manner. Having expected a real social-worker type, I was rather taken aback to see this quietly attractive Anglo-Indian woman, decked out in black leggings and electric silver Nikes. Her face-to-face manner echoed her phone style, and she put me at ease, making all the right jolly noises about Jack, asking me a bit about how an American ended up in London, and questioning me gently about my general postnatal state. Part of me wanted to put on a happy face and tell her that everything was just hunky-dory. But who doesn't want to take another person into their confidence? Especially someone who, though in an official capacity, seems to have a sympathetic ear.

'I guess I've been feeling a little up-and-down since his arrival.'

'Nothing uncommon about that.'

'And I'm sure things will be different now that he's home with us. But—' I broke off, wondering how to phrase what I was about to say. 'Let me ask you something directly,' I finally said.

'Of course,' she said.

'Is it unusual to feel as if you're not . . . bonding . . . with your child.'

'Unusual? You must be joking. In fact, just about every other new mum I see ends up asking me the same question. Because everyone expects that they're going to instantly bond with their baby. Whereas the truth is, it can take a considerable amount of time to adjust to this new creature in your life. So, really, it's nothing to sweat about, eh?'

But that night, there was plenty to sweat about. To begin with, Jack woke up around ten o'clock and then refused to stop crying for the next five hours. To heighten the awfulness of this nonstop bawling, both of my breasts became blocked again and, despite Jack's hoover-like jaws, milk refused to flow. So I rushed into the kitchen and frantically spooned several scoops of formula powder into a bottle, then poured in the specified amount of water, shook it up, popped it into the microwave, pulled a rubber teat out of the steriliser, attached it to the bottle, raced back to the nursery, where Jack was now wailing, picked him up, sat him on my knee, and plugged him into the bottle. But after three or four slurps of the formula, he suddenly became ill and vomited up milk all over me. Then the screaming really started.

'Oh Jesus, Jack,' I said, watching regurgitated formula dribble down my T-shirt. At which point, I heard Tony's voice behind me, saying, 'Don't blame him.'

'I'm not blaming him,' I said. 'I just don't like being covered in puke.'

'What do you expect, giving him a bottle. He needs your milk.'

'Who the hell are you, Dr Spock?'

'Any fool knows that.'

'Why don't you fuck off back to your eyrie.'

'With pleasure,' he said, slamming the door behind him with such force that it not only startled me, but also scared Jack. His crying redoubled in response to the loud bang. I suddenly had this absolute, immediate urge to punch out a window with my fist. Instead, I put Jack back in the crib, stripped off my vomit-drenched shirt, pulled up my bra, and, picking him up from the crib, attached him to the right nipple. But, when the breast unclogged and Jack began to feed greedily, my reaction wasn't one of relief. Rather, I entered a strange new terrain . . . a realm called hysteria.

Or, at least, that's what it felt like to me. Incessant sobbing, accentuated by a mounting internal scream. It was a most peculiar sensation, this silent wail. It was as if I had retreated into a corner of my skull, from where I could hear myself, at a distant remove, crying. But, gradually, these external tears were overwhelmed by a huge lunatic screech. When this howl reached such a magnitude that it threatened to deafen me, I had no choice but to lay Jack down in his crib and negotiate the corridor towards our bedroom. Whereupon I fell onto the bed, grabbed a pillow, and used it to block my ears.

Curiously, this seemed to have a salutary effect. Within seconds, the internal howling stopped. So too did my sobbing. But in its place came silence. Or what, at first, seemed like silence . . . but then, out of nowhere, turned out to be the absence of sound. So I lay there for what seemed to be only a few moments, luxuriating in this new-found deafness. Until the door flew open and Tony came in, looking agitated. Initially, I couldn't hear what he was saying. One moment, Tony was silent pantomime, the next, his voice came crashing into my ears. And underscoring his angry tone was the nearby sound of Jack crying.

'—don't understand how the hell you can just lie there when your son's—' Tony said, this sentence crashing into my ears.

'Sorry, sorry, sorry,' I said, jumping to my feet and brushing past him. When I reached the nursery, I retrieved Jack from the crib and had him back on my left nipple within seconds. Fortunately, the milk flowed immediately and Jack's cries were temporarily silenced.

I leaned back in the wicker chair as he fed. I shut my eyes and willed myself back into the realm of deafness. Instead, I heard Tony's voice.

'What happened there?'

I opened my eyes. I sounded calm. 'My ears . . . earache or something.'

'Should I call the doctor?'

'No need.'

'I really do think—'

'Everything's fine now,' I said, cutting him off. 'It was just a little temporary distress.'

Temporary distress. How bloody English of me.

Tony studied me carefully. 'If you say so,' he said, sounding unconvinced. 'Mind if I go back to work?'

'No problem.'

And he left.

You bastard. Spending a derisory moment with me and your new son (on the first day he's home), before retreating to your sanctum. No doubt, once Jack starts crying again, my husband will plead the need for sleep ('because somebody has to earn the money around here') and head for the silent comfort of his sofa bed, leaving me to walk the floors.

Which is exactly what happened. To make things even more maddening, I encouraged Tony to sleep elsewhere. Because, by the time he came downstairs again—it was sometime after one o'clock—Jack was back in bawling mode, the thirty-minute feed being his sole respite from a long evening's cry. So when Tony found me in the living room with Jack, occasionally stealing a glance at the television, while simultaneously trying to rock him to sleep, I tried to play nice.

'Poor you,' Tony said. 'How long has he been going on like that?'

'Too long.'

'Anything I can do?'

'Get some sleep. You need it.'

'You sure about that?'

'This can't go on all night. He's going to have to pass out eventually.'

Eventually was the operative word here, as Jack did not settle down again until 3.17 a.m., exactly. By this time, not only were both breasts unblocked, they had been wrung dry by his persistent feeding. After five hours of tears, he burped a milk-saturated burp and passed out.

I couldn't believe my luck, and swiftly got him upstairs into his crib, then stripped off my grungy clothes, took a very hot shower and crawled into bed, expecting sleep to hit me like a sucker punch.

But nothing happened. I stared up at the ceiling, willing myself to pass out. No sale. I got up and made myself a cup of camomile tea, and looked in on Jack (still conked out), and washed down two aspirins, and got back into bed, and waited for sleep to arrive, and . . .

Jack began to cry again. I went into the nursery. I removed his dirty nappy. I cleaned his dirty bottom. I dressed him in a clean nappy. I picked him up. I sat down in the wicker chair. I lifted up my T-shirt. He attached himself to my left nipple. I winced in anticipation of the forthcoming pain. And . . .

Miracle-of-miracle—a no-problem flow of milk.

'Well, that's good news,' Jane Sanjay said when she dropped by late that afternoon. 'How many feeds now without a blockage?'

'I've just done the third of the day.'

'Houston, it looks like we've got full flow,' she said.

I laughed, but then added, 'Now, if I can just get some sleep.'

'Was he up all night?'

'No. Just me.'

'Well, hopefully it's a one-off bad night. You seem to be holding up pretty well under the circumstances.'

However, by two the next morning, I was beginning to wonder if I was veering into craziness. Tony had been out all evening at some foreign correspondents' dinner, and rolled in drunk around two o'clock—to find me slumped in front of the television, with Jack on my lap, crying his eyes out, unable to settle after an extended one-hour feed.

'Still up?' Tony asked, attempting to focus his eyes on us.

'Not by choice. Still standing?'

'Just about. You know what a journos' night out is like.'

'Yeah . . . I vaguely remember.'

'Want me to do anything?'

'How about hitting me over the head with a club?'

'Sorry, a little too caveman for my taste. Cup of tea?'

'Camomile, please. Not that it'll do any good.'

I was right. It didn't do any good. Because Tony never got round to making the tea. He went into our bedroom to use the en-suite bathroom, then somehow managed to end up crashed out across the bed, fully clothed, out for the count. Had I wanted to sleep, this would have presented a problem, as there was no way I was going to get him to budge from his cross-bed sprawl. But I had no need of a bed—because, once again, I couldn't turn off my brain, even though Jack finally turned off his at three o'clock.

'Two nights without sleep?' Jane Sanjay said the next afternoon. 'This is worrying. Especially as your son seems to be conking out for around four hours a night, which, I know, isn't exactly a lot of sleep time for you, but is certainly better than *no* sleep. Has your husband been helping with some of the all-night duties?'

'He's been a little busy on the work front,' I said, not wanting to start complaining to a stranger about Tony's disinterest in most baby matters. 'But I'm sure I'll collapse tonight.'

But I didn't fall asleep. And it wasn't Jack's fault. On the contrary, the little gent went down around ten and didn't stir until four the next morning. This miraculous six-hour window should have been filled with deep comatose sleep. Instead I spent it drinking endless mugs of herbal tea, and stewing for an hour in a steaming bath (laced with assorted chill-out aromatherapy oils), and doing my best not to disturb my sleeping husband who was spending a rare night in our bed.

And then Jack was awake and the new day had begun.

Into the nursery. Remove his dirty nappy. Clean his dirty bottom. Dress him in a clean nappy. Pick him up. Sit down in the wicker chair. Lift up T-shirt. Offer nipple. And then . . .

By three that afternoon, my vision was starting to blur. Forty-eight hours of nonstop consciousness did that. I could handle the fact that everything was distended and fuzzy; what I couldn't cope with was the feeling of calamity that was seizing me—I was in a no-exit situation from which there was no escape. A life sentence of domestic and maternal drudgery, with a man who clearly didn't love me.

Then, as I mused even further on my total despair, Jack began to cry again. I rocked him, I walked him up and down the hallway, I offered him a pacifier, my withered nipple, a clean nappy, more rocking, a walk down the street in his buggy, a return to his crib, thirty straight minutes of more bloody rocking in his bloody rocking chair . . .

When we had reached hour three of this uninterrupted crying jag, I sensed that I was heading for a rapid crash landing, where the idea of tossing myself out of a top-floor window suddenly seemed infinitely preferable to another single minute of my son's bloody yelping.

Then I remember reaching for the phone and punching in Tony's office number and getting his secretary on the line. She said he was in a meeting with the editor. I said it was an emergency. 'Well,' she said. 'Can I tell him what it's about?

'Yes,' I said, sounding most calm. 'Tell him if he's not home in the next sixty minutes, I'm going to kill our son.'

SIX

I DIDN'T WAIT FOR TONY to return the call. Because, after five straight hours of nonstop bellowing, Jack had suddenly exhausted himself into sleep. So, once I settled him down in the nursery, I unplugged the phone next to my bed. Then I threw off my clothes, crawled under the duvet, and finally surrendered to exhaustion.

Suddenly it was one in the morning and Jack was crying again. It took a moment to snap back into consciousness, and work out that I had been asleep for five hours. But that realisation was superseded by another more urgent consideration—how in the hell could my son have slept so long without a nappy change, let alone food?

Dashing into the nursery, I quickly discovered that, yes, Jack did need a nappy change—but that, courtesy of the empty bottle I saw left on top of a chest of drawers, he had been fed sometime earlier. The sight of the bottle threw me, because the only time I had ever offered Jack this breast substitute, he'd utterly rejected it. But now . . .

'So you didn't kill him after all.'

Tony was standing in the door frame, looking at me with an exhausted middle-of-the-night wariness. I didn't meet his stare. I simply picked Jack up and brought him over to the changing mat and started to unfasten his nappy.

'I'm sorry,' I said.

'You had my secretary rather upset,' Tony said. 'She actually hauled me out of the meeting with the editor, saying it was a family emergency. Thankfully she had the nous to say nothing more in front of His Lordship—but once I was outside his office, she informed me of what you told her and then asked me if I wanted to call the police.'

I shut my eyes and hung my head, and felt something approaching acute shame. 'Tony, I didn't know what I was saying . . .'

'Yes, I did sense that. Still, I thought it best to make certain that you hadn't taken the infanticide option, so thought it worth coming home. And when I walked in the door, there you both were, conked out. So I unplugged the baby alarm in his room, to let you sleep on.'

'You should have woken me.'

Silence.

'You know, I'd never dream of hurting Jack . . .'

'I certainly hope not.'

'Oh Jesus, Tony . . . don't make me feel worse than I do.'

He just shrugged, then said, 'Jack will take a bottle, you know. Or, at least, he took it from me.'

'Well done,' I said, not knowing what else to say. 'And you changed him as well?'

'So it seems. Sorry to have plugged the baby alarm back in. But once he was settled down, I thought I'd get back upstairs to the book . . .'

'No need to apologise. I should be up anyway.'

'You sure you're all right?'

Except for an appalling case of guilt, I was just fine.

'I'm so sorry.'

Tony just shrugged. 'You've said that already.'

I finished changing the nappy. I closed up Jack's Babygro. I picked him up, settled us both down in the wicker chair, lifted up my T-shirt, and felt him clamp down hard on my nipple. I let out a small sigh of relief when the milk started flowing immediately.

'Oh, one other thing,' Tony said. 'I took the liberty of making an appointment for you with the GP, tomorrow afternoon at two.'

'Why?' I said, though I already knew the answer to that question.

'You're not sleeping well.'

'I'm sure it's just a passing phase.'

'Best to get it seen to, don't you think?'

I said nothing. Tony pointed his thumb in the direction of his study. 'Mind if I . . . ?'

'Work away,' I said.

As soon as he was gone, I pressed my head down against Jack, and sat there in silent shame, wondering how I could have said such a thing—and feeling, for the first time since his birth, this overwhelming need to protect Jack and ensure that he came to no harm.

But as soon as I thought that, another unsettling rumination hit me: Do I need to protect him against myself?

I didn't sleep for the rest of the night. Nor did I find time for a nap in the morning, as Jack was wide awake. So by the time Jack and I reached the doctor's surgery that afternoon, exhaustion was beginning to settle in on me again—something which my GP diagnosed immediately.

'Is he keeping you up at night?' she asked.

'It's me who's keeping me up at night,' I said, then explained my irregular sleep patterns over the past few days.

'You *must* sleep,' she said. 'It's crucial for your well-being, and for your baby. So what I'd like to propose is a mild sedative that should help knock you out, should the sleeplessness return. One important question: have you also been feeling a bit depressed or down?'

I shook my head.

'You sure about that?' she asked. 'Because it's not at all unusual to suffer from such things when you're unable to sleep.'

'Honestly, all I need is a couple of nights of decent sleep . . .'

'Well, these pills should help you. One important thing to remember: after you've taken one of the sedatives, you mustn't breastfeed for at least eight hours, as the drug will be in your system.'

That night, Jack managed to cease his nonstop crying just around the time that Tony walked in—smelling of six gin and tonics too many.

'Any reason why you're so drunk?' I asked.

'Sometimes you just have to . . .'

'Get drunk?'

'You read my mind.'

'That's because I know you so well, dear.'

'Oh, do you now?' he said, suddenly a little too loud.

'I was being ironic.'

'No, you weren't. You were being critical.'

'Let's stop this right now.'

'But it's fun. And long overdue.'

I left the room.

I retreated to the nursery and positioned myself in the wicker chair, and stared ahead, and found myself very quickly returning to the despondency zone. Time suddenly had no meaning for me. I was simply cognisant of sitting in a chair, staring ahead. Yes, I knew that there was a child asleep on the other side of the room. Yes, I knew that said child happened to be my son. But beyond that . . .

Nothing.

Then Jack started crying. Suddenly I was all action. Manic action. Go, go, go, I told myself. Get on with it. You now know the drill by heart.

Remove his dirty nappy. Clean his dirty bottom. Dress him in a clean nappy. Pick him up. Sit down in the wicker chair. Lift up T-shirt. Offer nipple. And then . . .

After the feed, he passed out. I staggered to my bedroom and found the bed empty (Tony—surprise, surprise—having taken his impending hangover up to his study). I curled up on top of the duvet, and . . .

Nothing.

An hour, two hours, three . . .

My bladder called—the one thing that would get me out of the near-foetal position into which I had entwined myself. In the bathroom, as I sat on the toilet, I saw the bottle of sleeping pills on the shelf above the basin. The key to the real emptiness I craved.

When I reached the basin, I resisted the temptation to start ingesting the bottle, five pills at a time, ten big gulps, ensuring permanent oblivion. Instead I popped three pills (one above the recommended dose . . . but I wanted the extra knock-out assistance), and got back into bed, and . . .

The baby alarm went off. This time, however, I didn't rise and shine. No, this time my head felt as if it had been filled with a sticky, glutinous substance that made all my actions seem molasses-slow and fuzzy. But, yet again, I followed the drill. Remove his dirty nappy. Clean his dirty bottom. Dress him in a clean nappy. Pick him up. Sit down in the wicker chair. Lift up T-shirt. Offer nipple. And then . . .

Back to bed. Back to sleep. Instantaneous sleep. Until . . .

Tony was shaking me with considerable force, telling me to get up.

But I didn't want to get up. Because getting up would mean regarding the disaster that was my life. Getting up would . . .

'It's Jack,' Tony said, sounding scared. 'He seems to be unconscious.'

'What?'

I was on my feet, even though everything was still a chemically induced blur. When I reached Jack's crib, it took several moments for my eyes to snap into focus. But when they did, I felt as if someone had just kicked me in the stomach. Because Jack appeared to be catatonic.

As I picked him up, he went all floppy—his limbs splaying like a rag doll, his head lolling, his eyes unfocused, blank. I pulled him towards me and shouted his name. No response. I brought my face to his and could feel his faint breath, which was a relief. Then I turned to Tony and told him to call an ambulance.

They arrived within five minutes. The paramedics took over. We rode in the back of the ambulance with Jack. He had been attached to a heart monitor, and my eyes roamed between his tiny body and the steady beat being registered on the monitor. The paramedic-in-charge kept throwing questions at us: any convulsions or seizures or episodes of breathlessness or previous catatonic incidents?

Nothing, nothing, nothing.

And then we were at a hospital called St Martin's. There were two doctors waiting for us in the ambulance bay. The paramedic spoke with them. Jack was wheeled directly into a consulting room filled with medical hardware. A woman doctor in her mid-twenties was in charge. As she checked all vital signs, she too ran through the same checklist that the previous paramedic had used, and then asked if he was on any specific medication.

At which point, I felt something close to horror. Because I knew what the next question would be.

'Are you yourself on any medication?' she asked me.

'Yes,' I said.

'What kind exactly?'

I told her.

'And might you have breastfed your son before the stipulated eight hours?'

I could feel Tony's stare on me. Had somebody handed me a gun right now, I would have happily blown away the top of my head.

'Jack woke me up out of a heavy sleep,' I said, 'and I was so fogged, I didn't think—'

'Oh, for God's sake,' Tony said. 'Where is your brain?'

The doctor slightly touched Tony's sleeve; a hint that he should stop. Then she said, 'Believe me, it happens all the time. Especially with very tired new mothers.'

'But will he be all right?' Tony asked.

'What time did you take the pills?' the doctor asked me.

'Middle of the night, I think.'

'You *think*?' Tony said, the anger now showing.

'May I handle this, please?' the doctor asked, then addressed me directly. 'Now—you took the pills around, what, midnight, one o'clock?'

'I suppose . . .'

'And then he woke you up and you fed him . . . ?'

'Don't know . . . but it was still dark.'

'And who found him in this state?'

'Me,' Tony said, 'around nine this morning.'

'Which was probably around three to four hours after you fed him?'

'I guess so.'

She turned to the nurse and spoke in a low voice, issuing instructions.

'Is he going to be all right?' Tony asked.

'I think so. I've asked the nurse to put your son on a saline drip to keep him hydrated, and we'll also keep him on a heart monitor, just to be absolutely sure that everything is fine. But, from my experience of this situation, the baby simply has to sleep the medicine off.'

'But will there be any long-term damage?' Tony asked.

'I doubt it. The fact is, the dosage of the drug he received in the breast milk was so nominal that . . .'

That was the moment that my knees gave way and I hung on to the side of the trolley containing Jack, like a passenger on a sinking cruise liner, not wanting to abandon ship, but not knowing what to do.

'Are you all right?' the doctor asked me.

'I just need to . . .'

A nurse helped me into a chair, and asked me if I'd like a glass of water. I nodded. Then I put my head between my legs and started to gag. But all that came up was watery spew.

'Oh Jesus,' Tony said as I continued to heave.

'Would you mind waiting outside?' the doctor asked him. After he left, the nurse cleaned me up and then helped me to a trolley opposite the one on which Jack was still strapped.

'When did you last eat?' the doctor asked me.

'Don't know. A couple of days ago, I think.'

'And how long have you been feeling depressed?'

'I'm not depressed.'

'If you can't remember when you last ate . . .'

'Just tired, that's all.'

'That's another sign of depression. And if you've been on sleeping pills, you obviously haven't been—'

'I tried to kill him.'

'No, you didn't.'

'I should die.'

'That's another sign of depression.'

'Leave me alone.' I put my face in my hands.

'Have you ever suffered from depression before?'

I shook my head.

'And this is your first child?'

I nodded.

'All right then . . . I'm going to admit you.'

I said nothing.

'Did you hear what I said?' the doctor asked, her tone still calm, considerate. 'You seem to be showing pronounced signs of postnatal depression. Under the circumstances, I think it wise to admit you for observation. You must understand that what you are going through is not uncommon. In fact, postnatal depression is . . .'

But I rolled over on to the trolley and started to cover my ears with a pillow. The doctor touched my arm, as if to say 'Understood', then I heard her mention something about going to have a word with my husband. I was left alone in the observation room with Jack. But I couldn't bear to look at him. Because I couldn't bear what I had done to him.

A few minutes later, the doctor returned.

'I've spoken to your husband. He's been informed of my diagnosis, and agrees that you should be kept in. He also understands that it's hospital policy to admit the mother and child together, which will also allow us, in the short term, to make certain that there are no side effects from Jack's mild . . .'

She stopped herself from using a clinical term, like *overdose*.

'Anyway, your husband said he had to dash off to work. But he will be back tonight.'

I pulled the pillow back over my ears again. The doctor saw this and stopped her monologue. Instead, she picked up a phone and made a fast call. Then, after hanging up, she came back to me and said, 'It's going to be all right. And you will get through this.'

That was the last time I saw her, as two orderlies arrived, flipped up the brakes on Jack's trolley and wheeled him off. As he disappeared out of the door, a nurse came in and said, 'Don't worry. You'll be following him in a moment.'

But I wasn't worried. I was feeling nothing. Just an all-purpose general numbness; a sense that, once again, nothing mattered.

The orderlies returned for me about ten minutes later. They strapped me down (but not too tightly), then wheeled me down a long grey corridor until we reached a set of fortified doors, with wire mesh covering the glass on both sides and a coded lock to the right of the door. A sign above the lock contained two words: PSYCHIATRIC UNIT.

One of the orderlies punched in a code, there was a telltale click and I was pushed inside, the doors closing behind me with a decisive thud.

Then the orderly opened a door and I was pushed inside.

I was in a room, about twelve feet by twelve, with a window (barred), a television bracketed to the wall and two hospital beds. Both were empty, but judging from assorted personal debris on the small locker beside one of them, I already had a room-mate. A nurse came into the room. She was in her late forties, with thin, beak-like features, old-style horn-rimmed glasses and a carefully modulated voice.

'Sally?'

I didn't answer. I just looked at her name tag: *Shaw*.

'Now, Sally, these gentlemen need the trolley, so I'd like you to sit up and we'll take care of the rest.'

I didn't react.

'Sally, I'm going to ask you again. Will you please sit up, or should these gentlemen give you assistance?'

A pause. I could discern the threat lurking behind her even-tempered voice. I sat up.

'Good, very good,' Nurse Shaw said. 'Now do you think you could get down off the bed?'

I hesitated. Nurse Shaw tilted her head slightly, and the two orderlies were on either side of me. One of them whispered, 'Come on, luv'—his voice uncomfortable, almost beseeching. I let them help me down and onto the bed. Then, without a word, they returned to the trolley and steered it out of the room.

'Right then,' Nurse Shaw said. 'Let me explain a few things about the unit . . .'

The unit.

'First of all, your baby is in the ward about ten paces down the corridor from here. So, you can have complete access to him whenever you want, twenty-four hours a day. And you can also bring him in here with you . . . though we do prefer if he sleeps in the ward, as it will allow you to get some much-needed rest.'

And it will allow you to keep him out of my clutches . . .

'Now, the next thing that's important to realise is that you're not a prisoner here. Because, unlike some individuals in the unit, you haven't been sectioned. So if you want to go for a walk, or leave the unit for whatever reason, there's no problem whatsoever. All we ask is that you inform the ward sister on duty that you're leaving . . .'

Because we don't want some ga-ga dame like yourself running off with the baby . . . especially since you want to do him so much harm.

'Any questions?'

I shook my head.

'Fine. Now you'll find a hospital nightgown in the locker by the bed, so if you wouldn't mind changing into that, I'll see to it that your clothes are given a good wash.'

Because I spewed up all over them.

'And then, I gather it's been a while since you've eaten, so I'll have some food sent up straight away. But before all that, would you like to check in on your son?'

I shook my head. Nurse Shaw was reasonableness itself.

'No problem whatsoever. But do remember—to see him, all you have to do is ring the call bell by the side of the bed.'

But why would he want to see me? I poisoned him.

'Oh, one final thing: the unit psychiatrist, Dr Rodale, will be in to see you in about two hours. All right?'

I can't wait.

'Well, then, that's everything. So I'll leave you to get changed, and then I'll have one of my colleagues come back with lunch very shortly.'

The hospital nightgown stank of bleach and felt scratchy against the skin. I rolled up my street clothes into a big ball and shoved them into the locker. Then I crawled in between the equally scratchy sheets, and shut my eyes, and hoped for sleep. Instead, the door opened. A plumpish young nurse came in, *Patterson* on her name plate.

'G'day.'

Australian.

'You all right?'

I said nothing.

'No worries. Lunch here.'

She was having a one-way conversation with a catatonic. But there was nothing I could do about it. I'd entered yet another facet of this strange landscape, in which mere speech suddenly seemed impossible.

The nurse placed the lunch tray on to the sliding table positioned next to the bed. She eased it over. I lay there and did nothing. The nurse smiled at me, hoping to get a response.

'You're going to tuck into this lunch, aren't you? Or, at least, have a drink of something.'

I reached out for the tray. I took the glass of water. I brought it to my mouth. I drank a little while still in a prone position, which meant that some of the water ran down my face and on to the bedclothes. Then I put the glass back on the tray.

'Atta girl,' the nurse said. 'Now, how about a little tucker?'

I wanted to smile at the use of bush jargon in a South London hospital. But I couldn't do a damn miserable thing except lie there, feeling like a general all-purpose idiot.

'Tell you what. Why don't I leave lunch here and come back in half an hour, eh? But, please, do yourself a favour and munch on something.'

Half an hour later, she was back. And she didn't like the sight of the untouched lunch tray.

'Oh come on,' she said, still sounding chirpy as hell. 'You've got to want something in your tum, don't you?'

No. I want nothing. Because I want to shrivel. Like a prune. Do everyone a huge service and disappear from view. Permanently.

She sat down on the bed and squeezed my arm.

'I know this is all really crap. But a word of warning: the doc is coming by to see you in about an hour. And she takes a really dim view of postnatal anorexia, eh? If you don't believe me, talk to your roomie when they bring her back from theatre. So do yourself a favour and at least take a bite out of the apple before the doc shows up.'

The doctor was a woman in her late forties. Very tall, very plain, with mid-length brown hair sensibly cut, wearing a sensible suit under her white hospital coat, with sensible bifocals on the end of her nose.

'Ms Goodchild—*Sally*—I'm Dr Rodale, the unit's psychiatrist.'

She pulled up a chair next to my bed, then reached into her briefcase for a clipboard and a pen. 'Let's try to make a start.'

It was she who made a start, asking me to verify my age, whether this was my first child, my first experience of depression and/or the first time I had ever gone silent like this. She had also gathered, from looking at Jack's chart, that his had been a traumatic delivery, and was wondering if this had impacted on my mental health . . . blah, blah, blah.

'Now, Sally,' she said finally, after getting nowhere on the answer front, 'if you feel that you simply cannot talk at the moment, so be it. Do understand, though, that in order for me to render a proper diagnosis, and prescribe an appropriate course of treatment, you will have to answer my questions. The choice is yours. For the moment, anyway.

'However, I do see from your notes that your GP prescribed a mild sedative. I am going to ask the nurse to administer the same dose to you this evening. When I return to see you again tomorrow, I do hope we will be able to make better progress than today. Good afternoon.'

Five minutes after she left, the doors swung open and I met my room-mate. Or rather, I didn't meet her, as she was in a state of postoperative coma. Though I was still lying prone on my bed, I could see that she was a black woman around my age. Nurse Patterson read her chart, checked her pulse, and rearranged her bedclothes. Then, seeing me staring at her, she said, 'Her name's Agnes. Her little boy, Charlie, is in the ward with your guy. You'll probably have a bit to talk about when she comes round, because she's been through what you're going through. In fact, she's *still* going through it, which is a real shame, but there you are. There's no rhyme or reason to the dance you're dancing. It's just a matter of bringing it under control before it dances you right into serious physical trouble, which is what happened with poor Agnes here. But hey, let her tell you all about it. If you need anything, just buzz.'

I needed nothing. Certainly not the arrival, an hour later, of Tony. He was bearing a copy of that day's *Chronicle* and a festive bag of Liquorice All-Sorts.

'How's it going?' he asked me.

I said nothing.

'Brought you . . .'

He placed his gifts on the bedside locker, then looked for a chair, wondering whether to sit down or not. He decided to stand.

'I've just been in to see Jack. Good news. He's awake again and, from what the nurse told me, he gobbled down two bottles he was so damn hungry. Which, she said, is a good sign that he's back to normal.'

Because he's out of my tender loving care.

'Anyway, the nurse also said that you can visit him . . .'

I pulled the pillow over my head.

'She also said you'd been doing a bit of this too.'

Finally, I heard him leave. I removed the pillow. And then I heard a voice opposite me. 'Who are you?'

It was my room-mate, Agnes. She was sitting up, looking unfocused.

'You here yesterday? Don't remember . . . You were here, right? But maybe . . .' She broke off, looking confused. 'Agnes—that's me. You always put a pillow over your head like that? Agnes . . . you got that?'

Nurse Patterson came in here. 'Sally's a woman of few words,' she said.

'Sally?' Agnes asked.

'That's what I said. S-A-L-L-Y. And she's got a little baby boy, like you.'

'He's called Charlie?' Agnes asked.

'No. Your son's called Charlie. He's called Jack.'

'And I'm . . . I'm . . .'

'A little scrambled, that's all,' Nurse Patterson said. 'Just like last time.' She then approached me with a glass of water and a plastic pill cup.

I sat up and took the pills. Then I pulled the bedclothes over me and waited for the pills to kick in.

Then it was morning. My head was somewhere high up in a vaporous stratospheric zone. When I began to work out the *'where am I?'* question, I noticed that there was a needle in my arm, and a feed bag suspended above me. My room mate was absent. There was a new nurse on duty who was positioning another delectable repast in front of me. She was short and Scottish.

'Good sleep?'

I responded by getting to my feet, taking hold of the trolley with my feed bag, and pushing it towards the bathroom. When I returned, the nurse helped me back into bed, repositioning the drip.

'Now, there's oatmeal, and toast, and some fried eggs, and some good strong builders' tea—'

I turned away. The nurse continued talking.

'—and after breakfast, I'm sure you'll want to go to visit your baby. So what do you want to start with first?'

I ate nothing. 'OK,' the nurse said. 'But I know that Dr Rodale will not be pleased.'

She left the breakfast by the bed. Agnes came back into the room. I could see she was a tall, elegant woman.

'You were here yesterday, right?' she asked, getting back into bed. 'Sally, right? Or are you someone new? My memory . . .'

Another of her fractured sentences. She peered at me quizzically.

'Why don't you talk? Baby got your tongue?'

She laughed hysterically. And I thought: Got it in one, sweetheart.

Then, abruptly, the laughter ceased. 'You've got to eat,' she said. 'It'll get you into trouble if you don't. I mean, big trouble. I know it. Because I had it. And you don't want it. *You don't want it.*'

Dr Rodale showed up around three that afternoon. My untouched lunch was by the bed.

'And how are you today, Sally?'

I stared at the wall.

'Right . . . I see from your chart that you refused dinner last night, as well as breakfast and lunch today. Once again, this is your prerogative. But do understand that we are keeping you on a drip. And within the next day or two, we will have to make a decision about how to assist you out of your current state.'

Tony arrived at eight that night. He had obviously been briefed by Nurse Patterson, who was now back on duty, because he eyed the untouched dinner tray with unease, and sat down on the bed, and looked at me with a mixture of hopelessness, distaste and worry. He didn't kiss me or touch my hand, and had a hard time looking at me straight on. But he did say 'Hello.' When that got him nowhere, he then said, 'Jack is good.'

And then, 'They're worried about you not eating or talking.'

And then, 'OK . . . I'll go now.'

Is that his way of saying: 'I know when I'm not wanted'?

Next day followed a similar pattern to the previous one. The Scottish nurse offered me breakfast. I remained silent. Agnes tried to engage me in conversation. I remained silent. She went off to play with her son Charlie. I squandered the morning staring at the ceiling.

Then it was lunchtime. And I didn't eat lunch, except courtesy of the tube in my arm. Then it was three o'clock, and Dr Rodale walked in. Like actors in a bad play, we knew our prosaic lines off by heart. Or, at least, she knew her lines, whereas I simply had to maintain my weak, silent stance. The interview went according to form . . . with the good doctor finally saying, 'I will be calling your husband to discuss your situation and the options open to us.'

Tony arrived around eight that evening. This time he did kiss me on the cheek. He did pull up a chair close to me. He did take my hand. And said, 'You have got to start eating.'

I just looked at the wall.

'Your doctor—Rodale, isn't it?—she called me at the paper and said, if you didn't start consuming solid food, she wanted to consider electro-convulsive therapy. As in shock treatment. She said it was the best way to bring you out of whatever place you are right now, but she'd need my consent to do it.'

Silence. He wasn't looking at me again.

'I don't want to give my consent. But I also don't want to see you continue in this state.'

I turned away.

'Sally, *please* . . .'

I pulled the covers over my head. *Oh, why do I pull infantile stuff like this?* Suddenly, he pulled the covers off me. Looking me straight on, he hissed, 'Don't force my hand.' Then he left.

After he was gone, Agnes got out of her bed and walked over to where I lay. Her gait was hesitant. So too the focus of her eyes. But she sounded lucid.

'My husband didn't want to sign the papers either. He begged me to eat something and act like I knew where I was. But I didn't. Just had my fifth ECT yesterday. Guess it's doing some good, 'cause I'm eating again, and I'm able to play a bit with Charlie. But . . .'

Pause.

'. . . they say you only suffer short-term memory loss. But that's not what I've been suffering. I think all that electricity ends up frying it right out of you. The doctor keeps saying, once the treatment's over, it'll all come back again. But I don't believe her. Not for a moment. 'Cause—'

Pause.

'Listen to me. You can avoid this. You can. Just one mouthful of food, eh? Just one. Here . . .'

She pulled over the table, on which sat the untouched dinner tray of food. She reached for a bread roll and pulled off a piece of it.

'. . . just a piece of bread. I'll even butter it for you.'

She did just that. And put it next to my face. I turned away. She used her spare hand to pull my head back.

'Come on, you can do this.'

I turned away again. She forced me back. I turned away. Suddenly she put the roll directly against my mouth. I turned away. She yanked me back, her grip tight now. This time, she forced the bread against my teeth. Which is when I snapped, and brushed it away, and spat in her face. Without stopping to think, she suddenly backhanded me across my face. The shock was ferocious. So too was the pain. And I heard myself shouting, 'Nurse!'

Nurse Patterson came into the room. 'So . . . you can talk after all.'

Of course, I retreated into silence. Of course, I didn't touch the dinner tray. Of course, I took my knock-out pills like a good girl, and then waited for sleep to club me. But, when I woke the next morning, for the first time in days I actually felt hungry. And when the Scottish nurse brought in the breakfast tray, I mumbled two words, 'Thank you.'

This made her look up at me, startled, but rather pleased as well.

'You're most welcome. Think you can eat?'

I nodded. She helped me sit up and rolled the table over the bed.

'Could you drink some tea, perhaps?' she said.

I nodded again.

'I'll be right back.'

Eating was not an easy process after nearly a week. But I did manage to ingest half a bowl of porridge. It was slow going and, once or twice, I felt distinctly queasy. But I kept at it. Because I knew I had to.

Halfway through breakfast, Agnes stirred awake. Like me, she too was on heavy knock-out pills, so it also took her a moment or two to work out where she was, and what she was doing here. But then she caught sight of me hovering over the breakfast tray, fork in hand.

To her credit, she said nothing. She just gave me a small nod, then got up and went to the bathroom.

When lunch arrived, I managed to eat half a chicken leg and the white goo that they passed off as mashed potatoes. But it was important that I make a good show of my lunch, because Dr Rodale was due in shortly and I wanted to be absolutely certain that my rediscovered appetite was noted for the record.

She certainly walked into our room with new-found pleasantness.

'I've just heard your good news, Sally,' she said. 'Breakfast *and* lunch. Most reassuring. Do you think you can speak a bit now?'

'I'll try,' I said, the words taking some time to form.

'No rush,' she said, clipboard and pen at the ready. 'But it would be helpful to know . . .'

And she ran through the checklist again. My answers were brief but with her coaxing, I was able to answer all her questions. When she was finished, she congratulated me on 'a job well done'.

'Of course, the road ahead is by no means certain—and it must be negotiated with prudence. For example, are you ready to see Jack yet?'

I shook my head.

'Perfectly understandable,' she said, 'and under the circumstances, probably sensible. You should see him when you feel ready to see him, which, we hope, will not be too far off.'

She then explained that what I was going through was undoubtedly horrible for me, but by no means unique. Now that I had started to place my feet back on terra firma, it was possible to treat my condition largely through the use of antidepressants. With any luck, I should start to see some significant improvement within six weeks.

Six weeks? In here?

Dr Rodale saw the shocked look on my face.

'I know that sounds like a horrible length of time, but, believe me, I've seen depressions that have dragged on for months. The good news is: if you start responding well to the antidepressants, we will be able to send you home as soon as you're judged fit to go home.'

You mean, when I'm no longer a danger to myself and my baby?

SEVEN

THE DOCTOR WAS RIGHT. Just as there is no such thing as a free lunch, so there is no instant cure for depression. No fizzy Alka-Seltzer evaporation of the black swamp into which you've plunged.

'At first, you'll possibly wonder if the antidepressants are doing anything,' Dr Rodale told me. 'They take a little time to bite; it never works the same way with everybody.'

I was eating again, but my progress back to something approaching an appetite was slow, due, in part, to the horrendous slop they served at the hospital. So Tony began to do a Marks and Spencer's run for me every day, picking up sandwiches and salads, and even conferring with the nurses about what I should be eating. His solicitousness surprised and pleased me, but I knew he'd never articulate the reasons why he was suddenly being so thoughtful and considerate.

'Does it matter what his motivations are?' Ellen Cartwright asked me. 'The important thing is: Tony is showing concern.'

Ellen Cartwright was the unit's resident therapist. She was in her early fifties, and favoured long, capacious skirts and big baggy linen shirts.

'You've switched countries, you've put your career on hold, you've become a mother, while all the time trying to adjust to married life with a man about whom you're frequently uncertain . . . and that's before we factor in the difficult birth of your child. Now, when you add up all that, can't you see that you're making too big a deal about all this?'

'What I see,' I said, 'is someone who threatened the life of her child.'

How I wanted to see things differently. But during the first two weeks on antidepressants, I still felt sheer, absolute terror about even just looking in on Jack. I articulated this fear on a regular basis both to Ellen and to Dr Rodale. And when Tony danced around this question all I could say was, 'I just can't see him yet.'

I kept taking the antidepressants, and I kept talking three times a week to Ellen, and I kept talking to Sandy, who phoned constantly. And when Tony had to skip a few visits because of the usual global crises, I was perfectly sanguine. By the end of week four, the crying fits that marked most days had stopped. Agnes had checked out, and I'd had a variety of short-term room-mates since then.

Finally, Dr Rodale let me give up the sleeping pills, because I was making it through the night without interruption. Every so often, whenever I felt myself edging towards that black fathomless swamp, I seemed able to skirt the edge and re-route myself back to more stable terrain.

Then, a few days into week five, I woke up one morning and took my pills and ate my breakfast and announced to the nurse on duty that I would like to see Jack. There was no sudden lifting of the cloud that made me make this decision. I just wanted to see him.

The nurse didn't slap me on the back and say, 'Great news . . . and about time too, thank God.' She just nodded for me to follow her.

The baby ward had a heavily reinforced steel door, with a substantial lock—a sensible precaution in a psychiatric unit. The nurse punched in a code, then pulled the door open. There were only four babies in residence. Jack was in the first crib. I took a deep breath and looked in.

He'd grown, of course—by a half-foot at least. But what struck me so forcibly, so wonderfully, was the way he had lost that initial premature, post-delivery amorphous quality, and was now such a distinctive little guy. He was also fast asleep, and though I initially hesitated about picking him up, the nurse gave me an encouraging nod. So, with extreme care, I reached for him and brought him up next to me. Instead of crying, he snuggled his head against mine. I kissed him and smelt that talc-like, new-baby smell. I held him for a very long time.

That evening, I asked Nurse Patterson if Jack could be moved into my room. When Tony arrived, he was genuinely taken aback to see me bottle-feeding Jack.

'Well then . . .' Tony said.

'Yes,' I said. 'Well then, indeed.'

Word spread fast about my reunion with Jack. Dr Rodale was all smiles the next day, informing me that 'this was very welcome news'.

They kept me in for another two weeks. The time passed quickly, especially as I was now spending my entire waking day with Jack. They moved him to the baby ward every night, but other than that, the only time I relinquished his company was during my sessions with Ellen.

'The general feeling is that you're ready to go home,' she said at the start of week seven. 'The question is: do you think yourself ready to get on with life again?'

'You mean, this isn't life?'

For the first time since we started our sessions, I actually managed to make my therapist laugh. Then she told me I could leave any time I was ready to leave.

And so, the next morning, Tony showed up with the car around ten. Nurse Patterson was off-duty, but I'd thanked her the night before. I also thanked Ellen and Dr Rodale, having agreed to see Dr Rodale in two weeks to discuss my ongoing relationship with antidepressants.

All credit to Jack: he behaved like the perfect gentleman during his first days in Putney. He slept for five solid hours at a go. He slurped down five bottles. He didn't complain about the service, or the newness of his bedding, or the strange surroundings. Tony seemed reasonably content in his company, just as he seemed content doing low-key solicitous things like sterilising and preparing several bottles, and even changing his nappy on two occasions. No, he didn't take the night shift when Jack woke at 3 a.m., but he did insist that I grab a nap the next afternoon while he kept an eye on the boy.

But then, after five days, Tony went back to the paper, and his return to work also marked the beginning of a distancing process. He was held up at the paper until nine or ten several nights a week, and, of course, the novel was still flowing (or so he said). Which meant that, around midnight most evenings, he'd excuse himself and vanish upstairs.

I didn't complain. I just travelled down the antidepressant path of least resistance, since it had numbed that part of the brain in which anger and resentment lurked. When he wanted to share our bed and have sex with me, I was pleased. When he 'needed' to stay out late at the *Chronicle* and/or hide upstairs, I accepted it. I was just grateful that we had silently negotiated a degree of familial stability.

More tellingly, I was now so enjoying my son. Gone was the terrible fear that I couldn't handle the basics of motherhood, let alone that terrifying postnatal fear that I would do him harm. On the contrary, I now delighted in his company, revelling in the way his hand closed round my finger, the way he nuzzled his head against mine as I held him, the fact that it was so wonderfully easy to make him laugh.

'Sounds like you guys really are an item now,' Sandy said to me after I mentioned the sheer pleasure I was getting from Jack's company.

'He's a terrific kid,' I said.

'It's great to hear you so up. You must be relieved.'

'Just a little,' I said with a laugh.

As I wasn't exactly on the lookout for great intellectual or professional stimulation right now, I accepted my new domestic routine with a certain degree of relief. Cha the cleaner was on hand from nine until midday every morning, and she proved herself to be highly capable with Jack. She kept him happy while I caught up with sleep or took myself off for a walk down the towpath.

One morning, sitting in Coffee Republic in the High Street, nursing a latte, looking at all the other moms with pushchairs around me, the thought struck me: This is my life now.

And it could be far worse—or marked by real misfortune.

Like my poor sister Sandy. She rang me late the next night in a state of convulsive shock. Her ex-husband, Dean, had been killed earlier that day in a climbing accident on Mount Kathadin in northern Maine.

'Dumb bastard,' Sandy said, weeping uncontrollably over the death of a man who, just a few weeks earlier, she was referring to as 'that scumbag ex-husband of mine'. But that's the nature of a divorce, isn't it? You find yourself loathing that person around whom your world once centred. Sometimes you cannot help but wonder if the reason you now despise him is because you still so desperately love him.

Sandy said that the funeral would be in three days' time. Immediately, I said, 'I'll be there.' She argued that I was in no fit state to cross the Atlantic; that she had the three boys to support her. But I knew that three kids under the age of twelve were going to need support of their own during this horrendous time. So I said, 'I think I can do this.' And I told her I'd get back to her within a few hours.

Tony was exceptionally sympathetic when I informed him of the news. He virtually insisted that I go, offering to get his secretary to book the ticket to Boston for me. I phoned Dr Rodale, who was confident enough about my current stability to OK me to travel the Atlantic.

That day, Cha was in working at the house. When I mentioned that I would be out of the country for seventy-two hours and would have to find a nanny, she told me she'd do the job for £100 a day. I hired her on the spot. I told Tony of this arrangement and he seemed pleased with it.

Having received the medical all-clear and having organised child care, I found myself two days later on a Virgin flight to Boston. When I got to the airport, I received something of a surprise—as it turned out that Tony had booked me into their better class of seat called Premium Economy. As soon as I checked in, I rang him and said, 'I'm so grateful.'

'Don't be. It's the least I . . .'

I couldn't tell if he'd been pulled away from the phone, or had suddenly gone quiet on me.

'Tony, you still there?' I asked.

'Sorry, sorry, got . . .'

Another odd pause.

'Listen, I've got to go,' he said.

'You OK?'

'Fine, fine . . . just being hauled into conference, that's all.'

'Look after our great guy,' I said.

'Have no fear. Love you,' he said.

Some hours later, halfway over the Atlantic, it struck me that that was the first time Tony had told me he loved me since . . .

Well, I couldn't really remember the last time he'd said that.

The next three days were a nightmare. My sister was a wreck. My three nephews were in various stages of incomprehension and grief. The entire day of the funeral was an ordeal, made around five times worse by the fact that, courtesy of my antidepressants, I was forbidden to touch even the smallest mouthful of alcohol.

When we got back to Sandy's house that evening, the children were so drained and exhausted that they fell into their beds and straight to sleep. At which point Sandy sat down on the sofa next to me and fell apart. I held her as she sobbed into my shoulder.

We sat up late that night, talking, talking. She'd received a call the day before from Dean's lawyer, informing her that everything in his estate (bar a life insurance policy worth around $250,000) had been left to his girlfriend. Which, in turn, meant that Sandy's already sizeable financial problems were even more severe—as Dean's small $750 per month child-support contribution was an important component of the household budget. I didn't know what to say, except that I wished I was well-heeled enough to give her a monthly cheque for that amount.

'You've got enough crap on your plate,' she said.

At that moment, as if on cue, Tony rang from London. I glanced at my watch. Seven p.m. in Boston, midnight in London. Much to my immense relief, all he wanted to do was see how I was doing, and to report that all was well with Jack. We'd spoken the previous nights, and on each occasion Tony expressed genuine concern about Sandy's welfare and also quizzed me on my own mental state. This time, he wanted to know everything about the funeral. His tone was easy, receptive. He took down the details of my return flight ('I'll have a minicab pick you up at Heathrow').

When the call ended, Sandy said, 'You guys seem to be in a good place.'

'Yes. It's amazing the effect antidepressants have on a rocky marriage.'

I popped the specified two capsules when I woke the next morning. Then I called home, hoping to touch base with Cha. No answer, making me speculate that she must have taken Jack out for a walk. So I called Tony on his mobile, just to say a quick hello, but received his voicemail.

'I am so looking forward to seeing you guys,' I said.

I spent the afternoon in a shopping mall with Sandy, buying a few baby clothes. I popped two more antidepressants at lunchtime, and dropped the final two tablets right after saying goodbye to my sister.

'You'll pull through this,' I told her. 'Because you have to.'

I boarded the flight and settled down into my Premium Economy seat, silently thanking Tony for such a spontaneous act of generosity.

When we were airborne, I screwed in a pair of earplugs, blacked out the world with an eyeshade, and let the tautness of the last few days give way to exhausted sleep.

Then we were in London, where, as Tony said, there was a minicab driver waiting for me at the arrivals gate. We made Putney in record time. The driver helped me to the front door with my bag. I took out my key and unlocked it, opening it as quietly as possible. I stepped inside. And immediately knew that something was wrong. The front hallway had been stripped of a collection of framed historical photographs of Old Cairo that Tony had brought back from Egypt.

Maybe he'd decided to put them elsewhere in the house . . .

But then, as I headed up the stairs towards the nursery, I glanced sideways into the living room. This stopped me dead. Almost all the bookshelves had been emptied, along with Tony's extensive collection of CDs, and the fancy overpriced stereo he'd treated himself to shortly after we moved in.

We'd been burgled.

I ran up the stairs, shouting for Tony. I threw open the nursery door. Nothing . . . by which, I mean: no crib, no playpen, no toys, no carry-chair, no Jack. I stood in the middle of the empty room—divested of all its furniture, all its toys, and every bit of clothing I'd bought for him.

I blinked in shock. This wasn't a burglary.

Then I dashed upstairs to Tony's study. It had been completely stripped bare. I rushed down to our bedroom and flung open the wardrobe. All his clothes were gone, but mine were still there.

I sat down. I told myself: This isn't making sense. My husband and my son have vanished.

EIGHT

IT TOOK ME SEVERAL MINUTES to force myself up off the bed. All I knew was: I had just walked into a nightmare.

I grabbed the phone and punched in the number of Tony's mobile. I was instantly connected with his voicemail. My voice was decidedly shaky as I spoke. 'Tony, it's me. I'm home. And I must know what's going on. Now. Please. *Now*.'

Then I rang his office, on the wild off-chance that he might be in at seven-something in the morning. Again I was connected to his voice-mail. Again I left the same message.

Then I rang Cha. A computer-generated voice informed me that the mobile phone I was ringing had been switched off.

I didn't know what to do next.

The front doorbell rang. I ran towards it, hoping against hope that Tony was outside with Jack in his arms. Instead, I found myself facing a large, beefy guy in his late twenties.

'Sally Goodchild?' he asked.

'Yes, that's me,' I said.

'Got something for you,' he said, opening his briefcase.

'What?'

'I'm serving you with papers,' he said, all but shoving a large envelope into my hand.

'Papers? What sort of papers?'

'An *ex parte* court order, luv,' he said. 'Get yourself a solicitor. He'll know what to do.' Job done, he turned and left.

I tore open the envelope and read. It was an order given by The Honourable Mr Justice Thompson, yesterday, at The High Court of Justice. I read it once, I read it twice. It didn't make sense. Because what it stated was that, after an *ex parte* hearing in front of Mr Justice Thompson the court had granted Anthony Hobbs of 42 Albert Bridge Road, London SW11, *ex parte* interim residence of his son, Jack Hobbs, until a further order was given.

I sat down at the kitchen table. I tried to re-read the court order again. Three sentences into it, I dropped it, clasped my arms round me, and felt a deep chill that sparked off a low-level internal tremor.

This can't be happening . . . this can't be . . .

The court has granted Anthony Hobbs of 42 Albert Bridge Road, London SW11 . . .

A wave of terror seized me.

After an ex parte hearing in front of Mr Justice Thompson . . .

Why did he need a hearing? What was he arguing? What did I do that merited . . . ?

I reached for the phone and called the local minicab company. They had a car at my front door in five minutes. I gave the driver the address: 42 Albert Bridge Road, SW11.

It took nearly an hour to negotiate the two-mile crawl to Albert Bridge Road. When we arrived, some instinct told me to ask him to wait for a moment while I got out of the cab and negotiated the ten steps up to the front door of an imposing Victorian town house. I used the brass door knocker to announce my arrival, whacking it frantically. After a moment, it was opened by a diminutive, olive skinned woman.

'Yes?' she asked, looking at me warily.

Peering over her shoulder, I got a glimpse of the entrance hall. Very minimalist. Very sleek. Very architect designed. Very expensive.

'Who lives here?'

'Miss Dexter.'

'Anyone else?'

'She has a friend.'

'What's his name?'

'Mr Tony.'

'And does Mr Tony have a little boy?'

'A *beautiful* little boy,' she said, actually smiling.

'Are they here now?'

'They've gone away.'

'Whereabouts.'

'I don't know. Miss Dexter has a place in the country.'

'Do you have a phone number, an address?'

'I can't give—'

She shut the door in my face.

I stood there, thinking: This is all too absurd. This is some horrible prank, some fantastical misunderstanding that has ballooned into . . .

I walked back to the cab, climbed in, told the driver to take me back to Sefton Street, then slumped down into the back seat. Halfway home, I realised didn't have enough money to pay him. I needed to stop at a cashpoint. We pulled up in front of a NatWest machine, where I fed in my card, hit the numbers, and was greeted with a message: *This Account has been closed.* Account closed? He couldn't have . . . I rifled through my wallet until I found an AmEx card, which I held jointly with Tony. I punched in the Pin number and read: *Card No Longer Valid.*

No, no, *no.* I saw the driver glance at me with concern. I tried my own account, which had been largely depleted since I was no longer employed by the *Post.* I requested £50. Bingo. Five ten-pound notes came sliding out towards me.

I was back home by ten. The silence of the house was huge. I glanced at the court order on the table, the stripped shelves, the bare nursery. I walked into the bathroom and popped two antidepressants. I lay down on the bed. I shut my eyes, opening them a moment later out of some strange hope that I would suddenly find myself back in my restored former life. But instead, I found myself dominated by one sole horrifying realisation: *They've taken Jack away from me.*

I reached for the bedside phone. I dialled Tony's mobile. Again, the voicemail came on. Again I left a message. I phoned the *Chronicle*, and asked to speak to Judith Crandell, Tony's secretary.

'Hello, Sally,' she said.

'What's going on?' I asked, my voice loud.

I could hear her take a deep drag off a cigarette. 'Tony's resigned from the paper.'

'You're lying!'

'I'm not lying. He showed up with his car and cleared his desk. Then he said goodbye and left.'

'Did he leave a forwarding address?'

'Albert Bridge Road in Battersea.'

I put down the phone, shaking, then picked it up and tried Cha again. This time I got lucky. She answered on the third ring. But when she heard my voice, she was immediately nervous.

'I cannot talk,' she said in her tentative English.

'Why not? What did they tell you?'

A hesitant pause. Then, 'They told me I shouldn't talk to you . . .'

'Cha, you've got to explain . . .'

'I have to go back to work.'

The line went dead. I hit re-dial, and was immediately connected with a recording, informing me that the mobile phone I had been speaking to had been switched off.

The doorbell rang. I raced downstairs. But when I answered it, I found myself facing a blond, smug-looking man in a black suit.

'Are you a lawyer?' I asked.

He laughed a bemused laugh. 'Graham Drabble from Playfair Estate Agents in Putney. We're here to measure up the house.'

'What are you talking about?'

'Well, I was instructed by a Mr Hobbs to sell your house.'

'Well, my husband didn't tell me,' I said and shut the door.

He's selling the house? But he can't do that, can he?

While there was one part of my brain that simply wanted to crawl upstairs into bed and pull the covers over my head, another more dominant voice overrode such fatalistic logic, insisting: *get a lawyer now*. But I hadn't a clue about London lawyers, or the English legal system, or *ex parte* orders. A year in this city, and I hadn't made a single real friend. Except for Margaret.

Margaret.

Not thinking, I dialled her number in New York. It rang and rang. Finally, Margaret answered—sounding groggy and half awake.

'Oh God,' I said, 'I've woken you up.'

'That's . . . uh . . . OK, I think . . .'

'Listen, I'll call back.'

'Sally?' she said, finally working out who I was. 'What's wrong?'

I told her everything, trying not to break down en route. When I was finished, she sounded genuinely shocked. 'That's crazy.'

'I wish it was.'

'But . . . he gave you no intimation that he was planning this?'

'Nothing. In fact, while I was in hospital, he was actually supportive.'

'And this woman . . .'

'I don't know who she is. Except that she lives in a very big house on a very desirable road opposite Battersea Park.'

'But he can't just snatch your child like that.'

'Well, there's a court order . . .'

'What was his rationalisation?'

'As he's completely gone to ground, I can't ask him. But the bastard's trying to sell the house from under me.'

'But it's in both your names, right?'

'Of course it's in both our names. But as I haven't a clue how the law works here . . .'

'Alexander's in Chicago on business right now. I'll wait an hour until he's up, then give him a call and try to find out the name of a good attorney in London. Meantime, you hang in there, hon.'

She called back two hours later. 'Alexander's found an excellent firm in London—Lawrence and Lambert. He doesn't know anybody there personally, but he said that they come highly recommended. And, of course, you can use Alexander's name when you call them.'

As soon as I finished the call, I phoned Lawrence and Lambert. The receptionist was brusque. 'Is there a party you wish to speak with directly?'

'I need to speak with someone who deals with family law.'

'We have five lawyers here who deal with family law.'

'Well . . . could you put me through to one of them, please?'

I was put on hold. Then, after a moment, a young woman answered. Her accent was seriously Essex. 'Virginia Ricks's office.'

'Uh . . . does Miss Ricks do family law?'

'Who is this?'

I told her my name and explained how I had been recommended by Alexander Campbell.

'Well, Ms Ricks is tied up most of the day in court.'

'It is rather urgent.'

'What's your name again?'

I told her, then gave her both my home and mobile number.

Once I was off the phone, I had to face up to a very large question: what should I do next?

I called Sandy and horrified her with a detailed account of my London homecoming.

'He's met some rich bitch,' she echoed. 'And the way he's set the whole thing up makes it pretty damn clear that he wanted you to find out about the whole set-up straight away. I mean, he could have used your own address in the court order. Why didn't he?'

'I don't know.'

'Maybe because he wanted you to know about his new life. I mean, imagine if he had just disappeared with Jack, without letting you have his new address. You'd have the cops on his tail. This way . . . you know exactly what's happened.'

'But not why it's happened.'

'To hell with why. He's taken Jack. You've got to get him back. But the first thing you've got to do is find a lawyer.'

'I'm waiting for someone to call me back.'

'Jesus, Sally. This is horrible,' she said, her voice cracking.

'Yes,' I said. 'It is.'

'And I wish I could jump a plane right now.'

'You've got enough to cope with.'

'You won't do anything stupid . . .'

'Not yet.'

'Now you have me scared.'

'Don't be.'

But the truth was: I had me scared too.

I called Virginia Ricks again that afternoon. I was connected to her voicemail. I left a message. I called back at 5 p.m. This time, I was connected to her secretary again.

'Like I told you before,' she said, 'she's out at court all day.'

'But it is absolutely imperative that you get Ms Ricks to call me back as soon as possible.'

But I received no further calls for the rest of the day. Or night. Except for Sandy who rang at 6 p.m. London time and then again at 10 p.m. to check up on me.

'No news at all?' she asked.

'Only what I didn't tell you before. That Tony has resigned from the *Chronicle*, closed our joint bank account and cancelled our credit cards.'

She gasped. 'How are you going to pay for a lawyer?'

'Remember the bonds Mom and Dad left each of us?'

'Mine were cashed in long ago.'

'Well, I'm about to do the same. They should be worth around ten thousand dollars now.'

'That's something, I guess. Did you try Tony's cellphone again?'

'Only about five more times. It's locked onto voicemail.'

'You should go to sleep.'

'It's an idea, yeah.'

I took two sleeping tablets with my end-of-the-day dose of anti-depressants. Around three that morning, I jerked awake, and the silence of the house seemed cavernous. I walked into the empty nursery. I could hear the voice of Ellen Cartwright, the hospital therapist, telling me over and over again: *It's not your fault . . . it's not your fault.*

But I knew better. I was the architect of my own disaster. I had nobody to blame but myself.

The lawyer finally called around nine thirty that morning. Her voice was crisply cadenced, plummy. 'Sally Goodchild? Ginny Ricks here. My secretary said you called yesterday. Something urgent, yes?'

'Yes, my husband's vanished with our son.'

'Vanished? Really?'

'Well, not exactly vanished. While I was out of the country, he got a court order giving him residence of my baby . . .'

'You know,' she said, cutting me off, 'this is probably best discussed face-to-face. How are you fixed at the end of the week . . . say Friday around four p.m.?'

'But that's two days from now.'

'Best I can do, I'm afraid. Lots of divorcing couples right now. So Friday it is then, yes?'

'Sure.'

She gave me an address in Chancery Lane.

The next forty-eight hours were hell. I tried to stay busy. I cleaned the house. Twice. I called my old bank in Boston, asked them to cash in my bonds and wire the entire amount over to me. I took my antidepressants with metronomic regularity—and often wondered if this pharmacological compound was keeping me in check; if, without it, I would have already descended into complete mania. Somehow I was managing to push my way through the day. I even called Tony's long-estranged sister, who I'd never met (they'd had a falling out over something he wouldn't discuss with me), and who lived in East Sussex.

'Haven't spoken to Tony in years—so why should he call me now?' Pat Hobbs said.

'It was just a long shot.'

'How long have you two been married?'

'About a year.'

'And he's already abandoned you? That's fast work, right enough. Mind you, I'm not surprised. He's the abandoning sort.'

'You mean, he's done this before?'

'Maybe.'

'That's not an answer.'

'Maybe I feel I don't need to give you an answer.'

And the line went dead.

I hit my hand against my forehead, congratulating myself on another tactical diplomatic victory. I vowed to be on my absolute best behaviour when I met Virginia Ricks the next day.

The offices of Lawrence and Lambert were in a narrow terraced town house, sleekly renovated inside. There was a security man on the door, who made me sign in and checked that I did have an appointment upstairs. Then I headed up in the lift to the third floor and stepped out into a pleasant, modern reception area, with chrome furniture and copies of all the daily papers on the coffee table. While the receptionist phoned Virginia Ricks, I sat down and absently glanced through them, deliberately shunning the *Chronicle*.

Virginia Ricks was in her late twenties. As I expected, she was blonde, slightly horsey in the face, but immaculately polished.

'Ginny Ricks,' she said, proffering her hand and hurrying us both into a conference room. 'Do sit down.' She settled herself into the chair opposite mine. 'It's Sally, right? You were recommended to us by . . . ?'

'Alexander Campbell.'

'Sorry, never heard of him.'

'He ran Sullivan and Cromwell's London office for three years.'

'But he never had business with our firm?'

'No. He just told me, through his wife, that you were the best divorce lawyers in London.'

'Quite right too,' she said. 'And I presume that, because you're here, you want to get divorced.'

'Not precisely,' I said. And then I quickly took her through the entire story, right up to the bombshell court order. Ginny Ricks asked to see the order. I handed it over. She speed-read it.

'Evidently your husband got his barrister to convince a sympathetic judge that you were an unfit mother, and to grant this temporary order. Which, in turn, raises the unpleasant, but most necessary question: were you, in your opinion, an unfit mother?'

I shifted uneasily in my chair, because I was aware that Ginny Ricks was now studying me carefully. 'I don't know,' I said.

'Well, let me ask you this: did you ever physically abuse your child? Shake it when it was crying, toss it across the room, that sort of thing?'

'No. I did get angry once or twice . . .'

'Nothing unusual there. Parents often get angry at children and say angry things. As long as you didn't physically harm your child, we're on strong ground here. And during your stay at St Martin's . . . you were never sectioned, were you?'

'No. It was a voluntary stay.'

'No problem, then. Postnatal depression is such a commonplace thing these days. Though we will investigate what evidence they used against you, the way I see it, your husband doesn't have much of a case.'

'Then how did he get this court order?'

'You were out of the country, and his legal team obviously put together a case against you in which it was argued that the safety of your child was at risk.'

'But does this mean that I'm barred from seeing Jack?'

'I'm afraid so. The good news, however, is that this *ex parte* order can come to an end at the next hearing, which is fixed for ten days' time. That means we have just five working days, not counting both weekends, to build our case.'

'Is that enough time?'

'It has to be. Now, just a little spot of housekeeping. My fees are two hundred pounds an hour, I'll need to put an assistant on to this to help me with the research, and she'll cost around fifty pounds an hour. Then we will also have to instruct a barrister for the hearing. So, say a retainer of two thousand five hundred pounds to get us started.'

I was prepared for such an initial sum, but I still blanched.

'Is that a problem?' she asked.

'No, I have it. But what about him trying to sell the house?'

'We'll search the Land Registry and check who owns the house. Anyway, if you put money into it, you'll get it back on divorce. And if you get to keep Jack, you'll probably get to keep the house . . . or, at least, until he leaves school.'

'And getting some sort of support from my husband?'

'That's Monday's job,' she said, glancing at her watch. 'So, on Monday morning we'll need the retainer and a list of assorted health-care professionals and people who know you who can vouch for your good character and your relationship with your son. That's critical.'

She pulled over a diary, opened it, and glanced down a page.

'Monday's rather ghastly . . . but shall we say four forty-five?'

'Isn't that late in the day, if we only have this week to build the case?'

'Sally. I am trying to fit you in at a time when I shouldn't be taking on any more clients. Now, if you feel you can do better elsewhere . . .'

'No, no, Monday afternoon is fine.'

She stood up and proffered her hand. I took it. 'Until Monday then.'

The weekend was endless. On Monday morning, I went to the bank. The American money had arrived. I bought a sterling bank draft for

£2,500. This left me with just under $6,000—around £4,000—which I could certainly live on for a bit, as long as my legal bills didn't spiral beyond the initial retainer fee.

I brought this concern up with Ginny Ricks later that afternoon, after I had been kept waiting more than half an hour.

'So sorry about that,' she said, breezing in to the room where I was waiting.

I showed her the list of contacts I'd drawn up. There were only four names: Dr Rodale, Ellen the therapist, my GP, and Jane Sanjay, the health visitor. I'd discovered from her voicemail that Ellen was out of town. 'Don't worry, we'll track her down,' Ginny Ricks said. She also wondered out loud if there was a friend in town—preferably English ('It will play better in front of the judge, show you've found a footing here, that sort of thing')—who could vouch for my good character.

'You see, Sally, before the Interim Hearing next week, we will already have submitted witness statements to the judge. So the more people who have positive things to say about you as a mother . . .'

'I've only been in the country a few months. I haven't really met many people . . .'

'I see,' Ginny Ricks said. 'Well . . . I'll have one of our researchers get cracking on the witness statements today. One last thing: you did bring the retainer, I hope?'

I handed over the bank draft and said, 'If there's any way we could keep costs within that amount, I would greatly appreciate it. My resources are fairly limited.'

'We'll do our best,' she said, standing up. 'And, no doubt, we'll be speaking in the next few days.'

But the next person I ended up speaking with from Lawrence and Lambert was one of her assistants. Her name was Deirdre Pepinster. She also spoke in the same horsey voice affected by Ginny Ricks—yet with a 'this is so boring' inflection that made me uneasy.

'I've been trying to reach Ellen Cartwright . . . turns out she's on some hiking trip in Morocco and is completely out of contact until the week after next. And Jane Sanjay, your health visitor, is on extended leave of absence. Canada, I think. Won't be back for four months at least.'

'Any chance of tracking them down?'

'It might run up the bill a little more. But leave it with me. I'll also find out about the woman who's now with your husband . . .'

I didn't hear from her again until the end of the week.

'Right,' she said. 'The woman in question is named Diane Dexter. Home address: 42 Albert Bridge Road, London SW11. She also owns a house in Litlington, East Sussex . . . very handy for Glyndebourne.'

'So, she's rich?'

'Quite. Founder and chairman of Dexter Communications—a mid-sized, but highly successful marketing company. Privately owned. Very highly regarded. She's fifty, divorced, no children.'

Until now, that is.

'Any idea how or when she met my husband?'

'You'd have to hire a private detective for that. All I've been able to find out is the basic details about her.'

'So you don't know where they are now?'

'That wasn't part of my brief. But I did get a witness statement from your GP and from Dr Rodale, who treated you at St Martin's.'

'What did she say?'

'That you had been suffering from "pronounced postnatal depression", but responded well to the antidepressants. That was about it, actually. Oh, and I found out what happened at the *ex parte* hearing. Seems you threatened the life of your son one evening . . .'

'But that was sheer exhausted anger.'

'The problem is, you said it to your husband's secretary. Which means that a third party heard it. Which, in turn, means that there's third party evidence. On the health-visitor front, it seems that Ms Sanjay just left the place she was staying in Vancouver and has hit the road, travelling around Canada.'

'Maybe she has an internet address?'

'You don't have it by any chance?'

I stopped myself from letting out an exasperated sigh.

'No. But if you call the local health authority . . .'

'Fine, fine, I'll follow it up,' she said, sounding bored.

'Could you ask Ginny to call me, please. The hearing's next Tuesday, isn't it?'

'That's right. All our witness statements have to be with the court by close of business on Monday.'

Which meant that she only had the weekend to track down Jane Sanjay by email . . .

I got up and went into the kitchen, to a small shelf in a cabinet where we kept assorted cookbooks and a London A-to-Z, and a UK road atlas. Litlington in East Sussex was about seventy miles from London, and an easy run from Putney. Before I could stop myself, I had phoned Directory Enquiries and asked if there was a listing for a Dexter, D. in Litlington, East Sussex. Sure enough, there was such a listing. I wrote it down. But it took an hour, and that evening's dosage of antidepressants, to screw up the courage to make the call. Finally, I grabbed the phone, punched in the number, covered the mouthpiece with my hand, and felt my heart play timpani as it began to ring. On the fifth knell, just as I was about to hang up, it was answered.

'Yes?'

Tony.

I hung up, then sat down in a chair. Hearing his voice was . . .

No, not heartbreaking. Hardly that. In the week or so since this nightmare began, the one thing I felt towards my husband was rage . . . especially as it became increasingly clear that he had been hatching this plot for a considerable amount of time. I kept reviewing the last few months in my mind, wondering when his liaison with this Dexter woman began. I thought back to all of Tony's late evenings at the paper, and that wonderfully extended window of opportunity when I was doing time in the psychiatric unit: all those weeks when he could do whatever he wanted, wherever he wanted.

The shit. That was the only word for him.

I had another bad, sleepless night. At seven the next morning, I rang Budget-Rent-A-Car and discovered that they had a branch in the parade of shops near the East Putney tube station. When they opened at eight, I was their first customer, renting a little Nissan for the day—£32.00 all-in, as long as I had it back by eight the next morning.

Traffic was light all the way south. Then I turned right at a sign marked Alfriston/Litlington, and found myself entering a picture post-cardy image of Elysian England. I had driven into a well-heeled fantasy, of the sort that only serious money could buy. I knew I was looking for a house called Forest Cottage. I got lucky. Driving down a particularly winding road, my eyes glancing at every small house sign, I noticed the plain painted marker half buried in some undergrowth. I braked and started to negotiate the steep narrow drive.

Halfway up this avenue, the thought struck me: What am I going to do when I get to her house? What am I going to say? I had no planned speech, no strategy or game plan. I just wanted to see Jack.

When I reached the top of the drive, I came to a gate. I parked the car and got out. I walked to the gate and looked up at the pleasant, two-storey farmhouse about a hundred yards away. It appeared as well maintained as the manicured grounds surrounding it. There was a newish Land Rover parked by the front door. I decided that I would simply open the gate, walk up the drive, knock on the door, and see what would happen. There was a delusional part of me that thought: All I need to do is show my face, and Tony and this woman will be so ashamed of what they've done, they'll hand Jack to me on the spot . . .

Suddenly, the front door opened and there she was. A tall woman. Very elegant. Short black hair, lightly flecked with grey. Dressed in expensive casual clothes: black jeans, a black leather jacket, a designer variation on walking boots and a grey turtleneck sweater. And strapped around her neck was one of those baby slings, in which sat . . .

I nearly shouted his name. I caught myself. Perhaps because I was just so stunned by the sight of this woman, this stranger, with my son slung across her chest, acting as if he were her own child.

She was heading towards her Land Rover. Then she saw me. As soon as she caught sight of me at the gate she knew who I was. She stopped. She looked genuinely startled. There was a long, endless moment where we simply looked at each other, not knowing what to say next.

My hands gripped the gate. I wanted to run up to her and seize my son and dash back to the car and . . . But I simply couldn't move.

She suddenly turned away from me, heading back to the house. 'Tony . . .' I heard her shout. And I was gone. Hurrying back to the car, throwing it into reverse, making a fast U-turn, and shooting back down the drive. When I glanced in the rearview mirror, I could see Tony standing beside her, watching my car disappear.

I drove nonstop out of Litlington and back to the main road, pulling over into a lay-by, cutting the engine, placing my head against the steering wheel, and not being able to move for a very long time.

After around ten minutes, I forced myself to sit back up in the seat, turn the ignition key, put the car into gear, and head back towards London. I don't remember exactly how I got there. Some basic autopilot took over. I made it back to Putney. I dropped the car back to Budget, garnering a quizzical look from the clerk behind the desk when I handed in the keys so early. An hour later, I was lying on my bed at home, having taken double the recommended dose of antidepressants, feeling it deaden all pain, rendering me inert, inoperative for the rest of the day. That night, I also took double the dose of sleeping pills. It did the trick—comatose for eight hours.

And then it was Monday, and the phone was ringing.

'It's Ginny Ricks here,' my lawyer said, sounding terse, preoccupied. 'Just to bring you up to speed on everything. Deirdre has finished all the witness statements, which we are lodging at court this afternoon. I'll be instructing the barrister today, and the hearing's at the High Court tomorrow morning at ten thirty. You know where that is, don't you?'

'Well . . . uh . . . I'm not . . .'

'The Strand. Can't miss it. Ask anyone. And I'll have Deirdre positioned just outside the main entrance to spot you coming in. We'll be outside the courtroom somewhere within the building. And I presume you have something smart, but simple to wear. A suit would be best. Black even better.'

'I'll see what . . . sorry, I . . .' I lost track of the sentence.

'Are you all right, Sally?' she asked, sounding a little impatient.

'Bad night . . .' I managed to say.

'I hope you'll ensure that you have a far better night tonight—because, though you will not be called upon to testify tomorrow, the judge will be looking you over, and should you seem somewhat out-of-it, that will definitely raise concerns.'

'I promise to be . . . there,' I said.

'Well, I should certainly hope so,' she said.

At ten fifteen the next morning, I approached the High Court and walked up the steps. A young woman—plain, bespectacled, in a black raincoat over a simple grey suit—was waiting by the entrance doors. She looked at me questioningly. I nodded.

'Deirdre Pepinster,' she said. 'We're this way.'

She led us through security to a large, high-vaulted marble hall. It was like being in a church, with shadowy lighting, the echo of voices, and a constant parade of human traffic. We walked through the hall and after several turns, came to a door, outside which were several benches. Ginny Ricks was already seated on one of them, in conversation with an anaemic-looking man in his forties, dressed in a very grey suit.

'This is Paul Halliwell, your barrister,' Ginny Ricks said.

He proffered his hand. 'I've just received the witness statements this morning,' he said, 'but everything seems to be in order.'

'What do you mean, you just received the statements?' I said.

'I meant to call you about this late last night,' Ginny Ricks said. 'The barrister I'd instructed fell ill . . . so I had to find a substitute. But really, not to worry. Paul is very experienced—'

'But he's just looking at the statements now—'

We were interrupted by the arrival of the other side. At first sight, they were like an identikit version of my team: a thin, grey man; a big-boned blonde woman, a few years older than Ginny Ricks. They all seemed to know each other, though, as I quickly realised, the grey man was Tony's solicitor, whereas the blonde woman was his barrister.

Paul Halliwell pulled me aside. 'You know that this is merely an Interim Hearing, which you are not obliged to sit through, as it can be a bit stressful.'

'I have to be there,' I said, wanting to add, Unlike my husband, who's sent others to do his dirty work for him.

'Fine, fine, it's obviously better, because the judge knows you really care about the outcome. Now, I'm just going to have a quick read of all this,' he said, brandishing the witness statements, 'but it does seem very straightforward. The report from the doctor at the hospital is the key here. Very encouraged by your progress, and so forth. About the fact that you threatened your baby . . . I presume you were tired, yes?'

'I hadn't slept in days.'

'And you never in any way physically harmed your son?'

'Absolutely not.'

'That's fine then. The key here is that there was nothing violently aberrant in your behaviour towards your baby that would convince the court you pose a risk to the child . . .'

'As I told Ginny Ricks . . .'

On cue, she poked her head into our conversation and said, 'I've just been told we're starting in five minutes.'

'Fear not,' Paul Halliwell said. 'It will all be fine.'

The courtroom was a panelled Victorian room with leaded windows. The judge had a large chair at the front. Facing him were six rows of benches. Tony's team sat on one side of the courtroom, his barrister in the first bench, the solicitors behind him. My barrister sat in the same bench as Tony's, but on the opposing side of the court. I sat in the second row with Ginny Ricks and Deirdre. They informed me that, at this sort of hearing, the barristers didn't have to wear wigs and the judge wouldn't be in robes.

The court clerk asked us to stand as the judge was due to arrive. A side door opened. He walked in. We all stood up. His name was Merton and he was noted for taking care of business in a no-nonsense manner.

He asked Tony's barrister to 'open' the case, which she did in about two minutes, telling the judge who the parties were and explaining the background to the first *ex parte* hearing. The judge then said that he'd read the statements and that he just wanted to hear submissions.

Paul Halliwell stood up first and from the moment he kicked off his submission with the words 'My Lord' he narrated my side of the story with straightforward clarity and no lapses of concentration. But the argument he presented was merely a repetition of the facts.

'As Ms Goodchild's attending psychiatrist, Dr Rodale, states in her deposition, Ms Goodchild responded well to treatment and re-bonded well with her child. As to the claim that she informed her husband's secretary that she would kill her son . . . uh . . .'

He had to glance at one of the statements.

'. . . her son Jack . . . the fact is that at no time did Ms Goodchild ever actually physically harm her son. And though her comment may have been somewhat extreme, and one which Ms Goodchild deeply regretted from the moment she uttered it, it is important to take into account the fact that, like any new mother coping with an infant, Ms Goodchild had been suffering from extreme sleep deprivation which, in turn, can cause anyone to say unfortunate things in exhausted anger. I would hope as well, My Lord, that the court will take into account the fact that this comment was made when my client was suffering from postnatal depression, which is a most common and fiendish medical condition, and which can make an individual temporarily behave in a manner completely out-of-character. Once again, I refer My Lord to the statement of Dr Rodale . . .'

A few sentences later, he wrapped it up with the comment that it struck him as cruel and unusual punishment that my son be taken away from such an eminently respectable woman like myself—'a former distinguished journalist'—because of one angry comment spoken while 'trapped within the horrendous mental labyrinth that is depression'; a labyrinth from which I had now emerged back to 'completely functional normality'. And surely, how could the court keep a child from its mother, given the lack of any violent behaviour on my part?

But then Tony's barrister stood up. Ginny Ricks had told me that her name was Lucinda Fforde, and little more.

'My Lord, my client, Mr Anthony Hobbs, would be the last to dispute the fact that his wife was once a distinguished journalist with the *Boston Post* newspaper. Nor would he dispute the fact that she has been through a serious psychological illness, through which he supported her with great sympathy and understanding . . .'

Oh, please.

'But the issue here is not about Ms Goodchild's one-time professional standing or the fact—clearly documented by her psychiatrist—that she is gradually responding to pharmacological treatment for her postnatal depression. No, the issue here is about the welfare of her son Jack—and the fact that, through her actions of the last few weeks, Ms Goodchild has raised severe doubts about both her ongoing mental stability and her ability to cope with a young infant without endangering its safety.'

And then she brought out the heavy artillery.

'Now, My Lord, you will note from the witness statement by Ms Judith Crandell, who was Mr Hobbs's secretary at the *Chronicle*, that Ms Goodchild rang her husband at the newspaper several weeks ago and said—and this is a direct quote—"Tell him if he's not home in the next sixty minutes, I'm going to kill our son". Thankfully, Ms Goodchild did not make good on this threat, and though her counsel can certainly argue that this heinous comment was made under pressure, the fact, My Lord, is that all women dealing with newborn children suffer from sleep deprivation and its attendant lassitudes, but the vast majority of women do not threaten to kill their children. More tellingly, though one might be able to forgive one such outburst made in exhausted anger, the fact that Ms Goodchild made such a comment twice . . .'

I heard myself saying, 'What?' Immediately, every eye in the court was upon me, most tellingly that of the judge who looked at me with care.

Ginny Ricks jumped in before he could say anything.

'Apologies, My Lord. That will not happen again.'

'I should certainly hope not,' he said. Then turning back to Lucinda Fforde, he said, 'You may continue.'

'Thank you, My Lord,' she said, calmness personified, especially as she now knew that she had me. 'As I was saying, Ms Goodchild's threat to kill her child was not simply a one-off event. Following the delivery of her son, Ms Goodchild was hospitalised in the Mattingly, during which time her postnatal behaviour became increasingly erratic, to the point where, when her son was in the paediatric intensive care unit of that hospital, she was overheard by one of the nurses, telling her husband—and this is another direct quote from one of the witness statements that My Lord has before him—"He is dying—and I don't care. You get that? I don't care."'

Ginny Ricks looked at me, appalled. I hung my head.

'However, not only did she publicly proclaim her lack of interest in whether her son lived or died, she also was seen by one of the nurses to physically yank her infant son off her breast while feeding him so that the nurse was concerned about whether or not she might hurl the child on to the floor. Once again, My Lord, this is documented in the witness statements, taken by the nurse in question, a Miss Sheila McGuire, who has worked in the Mattingly for the past five years.

'You will also note a witness statement from the eminent obstetrics consultant, Mr Desmond Hughes, who states, very clearly, that he became increasingly concerned by Ms Goodchild's mental condition and his concerns about her ability to cope with the postnatal care for her son.

'Sadly, the concerns of Mr Hughes and his colleagues proved justified, as shortly after her release from hospital with her son, she was prescribed sedatives by her general practitioner to help combat the insomnia she had been recently suffering. Her GP had specifically warned her not to breastfeed her child while taking these sedatives. Shortly thereafter, however, her son was rushed to hospital in an unconscious state, having ingested tranquillisers from his mother's breast milk. And upon arrival at St Martin's Hospital, the staff were so concerned about Ms Goodchild's mental state that they admitted her to the Psychiatric Unit, where she remained for nearly six weeks.'

She now moved in for the coup de grâce—talking about how Mr Hobbs was the distinguished foreign correspondent for the Chronicle, who had just resigned as Foreign Editor to look after his son full time.

Once again, I wanted to scream, *'What?'* but restrained myself.

She then explained that Ms Dexter was the founder and chairman of one of the most influential marketing companies in Britain. She listed her real-estate holdings, her chairmanships of assorted well-known companies, and the fact that she was planning to marry Mr Hobbs as soon as his divorce was finalised.

'There is no doubt that Mr Hobbs and Ms Dexter will provide the sort of loving, secure environment in which Jack will flourish. There is also no doubt that, though Ms Goodchild may be responding well to pharmacological treatment, there are still large question marks over her ongoing stability, as proven by the fact that just two days ago she arrived unannounced and uninvited at the gates of Ms Dexter's weekend home in East Sussex. A most disturbing visitation, and one which contravened the *ex parte* order issued against her a fortnight ago.

'In conclusion, may I emphasise that neither Mr Hobbs nor Ms Dexter wish Ms Goodchild ill. On the contrary, her estranged husband is deeply distressed by her current debilitated state. Nor was there any malicious or vengeful agenda behind his decision to seek an *ex parte* order against his wife . . . which was done *solely* to protect their child.'

And then, suddenly, it was all over. Or, at least, Lucinda Fforde had thanked His Lordship and sat down. The judge then said he would retire to consider his decision and asked us all to return within twenty minutes when he would give judgment. Deirdre Pepinster nudged me to stand up as he rose and left.

I sank down in the seat again. There was a long pause. Then Ginny Ricks said, 'You actually went to that woman's country house?'

I said nothing.

'And why didn't you tell us about the sleeping pills incident? Or the threats you made against your child? I mean,' I heard Ginny Ricks say, 'if you had been direct with us, we could have . . .'

I wanted to tell her what an incompetent, Sloaney little bitch she was. Remind her how she failed to garner all the necessary facts from me, how she treated my case like an addendum to her ultra-busy life, how she failed to instruct my barrister until ten minutes before the hearing, and how she was now trying to blame me for her complete slipshodness.

But I said nothing.

Then the court clerk announced the entry of the judge. We all stood up. The side door opened, the judge walked in. He sat down. So did we. He began to speak. He didn't look at me as he talked. But his crisp voice was aimed directly at me. His judgment was brief and to the point.

After due consideration, he saw no reason to change the initial *ex parte* order—and was allowing this Residence Order to stand for the next six months, until the 'Final Hearing' regarding residence could take place. However, he was adding a few provisos to the original order. Though he concurred that the safety of the child was paramount, he also ordered that 'the mother be allowed weekly supervised contact at a contact centre within the borough of her residence'. He also commissioned a CAFCASS report, to be filed five weeks before the Final Hearing, which he fixed for six months' time, 'at which time the matter will be decided once and for all'.

Then he stood up and left.

Lucinda Fforde leaned over and proffered her hand to Paul Halliwell. From the brevity of the handshake and the lack of conversation between them, I could sense that this was a mere end-of-hearing formality. Then she and her solicitor hurried off, a quick nod to Ginny Ricks, hearing finished, job done, on to the next human mess. My barrister had a similar approach. He packed up his briefcase, picked up his raincoat, and left hurriedly, muttering 'We'll be in touch' to my solicitor. Even though he had only been parachuted into the case today, he too looked decidedly embarrassed by the outcome. Nobody likes to lose.

Deirdre Pepinster also stood up and excused herself, leaving me and my solicitor alone in the court. Ginny Ricks sighed a heavy theatrical sigh and said, 'Well, that's about as bad as it gets.'

'I just need,' I said, my voice shaky, 'a translation of what the judge just said.'

Another weary sigh. 'A Residence Order is exactly what it sounds like. The court decides with whom the child should reside and, in this instance, the judge has decided to maintain the status quo of the last order. Which means that your husband and his new partner will have residence of your son for six months, which is when there will be what the judge called a Final Hearing, at which time you will be able to argue your case again and hopefully work out a more favourable custody arrangement.

'For the moment, however, as he said, you will be granted supervised contact at a contact centre, which essentially means a room in some Social Services office in Wandsworth, where you will have an hour to be with your child once a week, under the supervision of a social worker. CAFCASS stands for "Child and Family Court Advisory and Support Service". And the CAFCASS report, which he commissioned, means that, in the next six months, the court reporter will be investigating your background, and that of your husband and his new partner. And to be absolutely direct about it, given the case they have compiled against you, I honestly don't see how you will be able to change the court's opinion. Especially as, by that time, the child will be overwhelmingly settled with his father and his new partner. Of course, should you wish to instruct us to take the case . . .'

I raised my head and stared directly at her. 'There is absolutely no chance of that,' I said.

She stood up, gave me one of her supercilious shrugs, and said, 'That is your prerogative, Ms Goodchild. Good day.'

I was now alone in the courtroom. I had just lost my son.

I kept playing that phrase over and over again in my head. The enormity of its meaning was still impossible to grasp.

After ten minutes, the court usher came in and told me I would have to leave. I stood up and walked out into the street.

I made it to the Temple Underground station. When the train came hurtling down the platform, I forced myself against a wall and clutched on to a waste bin, to ensure that I didn't pitch myself under it. I don't remember the journey south, or how I got back to the house. What I do remember is getting to the bedroom, closing all the blinds, unplugging the phone, stripping off my clothes, getting under the covers.

Not having a clue what to do next, I stayed in bed for hours, the covers pulled up over my head, wanting the escape of oblivion, yet being denied it. This time, however, although I felt an intense, desperate grief, it wasn't overshadowed by a feeling of imminent collapse or a downward plunge. I was simply convulsed by sadness.

So I forced myself out of bed, and forced myself to take a hot-and-cold shower. I plugged the phone back in around four. It rang immediately. It was Sandy. From the sound of my voice, she knew the outcome. But when I detailed the findings of the judge, and the supervised access I would have to Jack, she was horrified.

'Jesus Christ, it's not like you're an axe murderer.'

'True. But they certainly gave their barrister enough ammunition to depict me as someone who was on the verge of catastrophe. And I certainly didn't make life easier for myself by . . .'

And then I told her about my weekend trip down the country, apologising for not informing her before now.

'Don't worry about that,' she said, 'though you should know you can tell me anything . . . like *anything*, and I won't freak. The thing is, surely the court must have been sympathetic to the idea that you just *had* to see your son—which isn't exactly an abnormal instinct, now is it? And, like, it's not as if you pounded on their door, wielding a twelve-gauge shotgun. You just stood at the gate and looked, right?'

'Yes . . . but also the barrister representing me hadn't been properly briefed.'

'What do you mean by that?'

I explained about the slapdash approach of my solicitor. Sandy went ballistic. 'Who recommended this bitch to you?'

'The husband of my friend Margaret Campbell . . .'

'She was that American friend living in London, now back in the States, right?'

Later that evening, the telephone rang and I found myself talking to Alexander Campbell.

'Hope this isn't a bad time,' he said. 'But your sister called Margaret at home today, and told her what happened, and how this woman— Virginia Ricks, right?—behaved. And I just want to say I am horrified. And I plan to call Lawrence and Lambert myself tomorrow—'

'I think the damage has been done, Alexander.'

Margaret then came on the line to commiserate, and to say how bad she felt. 'Did they fleece you, those lawyers?'

'Hey, you're married to a lawyer. You know they always fleece you.'

'How much?'

'A retainer of twenty-five hundred sterling. But I'm sure the final bill will come to more than that.'

In fact, the Lawrence and Lambert bill arrived the next morning. I was right about it running beyond the original retainer—a cool £1,730 above the initial £2,500, every expense and charge laid out in fine detail. I also received a phone call from Deirdre Pepinster. She was as laconic as ever.

'I checked the Land Registry. The house is in both your names . . .'

Well, that's something, I guess.

'But before the hearing yesterday, we heard from your husband's solicitors. Seems he wants to sell up straight away.'

'Can he do that?'

'According to the law, each party who co-owns a house can force a sale. But it takes time and the divorce courts can stop it. Now, if you'd had residence of your child, that would be a different matter. No court would allow the house to be sold under you. But in this situation . . .'

'I get it,' I said.

'They have made an offer—a settlement offer, I should say.'

'What is it?'

'Uh . . . Ginny Ricks said we won't be representing you from now on.'

'That's absolutely correct.'

'Well, I'll just fax it to you then.'

It showed up a few minutes later—a lengthy letter from Tony's solicitors, informing me that their client wanted to expedite the divorce, and to be as generous as possible under the circumstances. As their client 'would be retaining residence of his son', there were no child support issues to deal with. His client would argue that alimony was also not an issue here, as I was perfectly capable of earning a living for myself. And as their client had put eighty per cent of the equity into the house, he could also expect to receive eighty per cent of whatever profit the sale yielded. However, wanting to be generous in this instance, he was offering the following deal: as long as I didn't contest residence, I would, upon the sale of the house, receive not just the £20,000 equity I had invested in it, but the £7,000 for the loft conversion (as I had paid for this myself), plus an additional £10,000 sweetener, plus fifty per cent of whatever profit the sale yielded. If, however, I didn't accept this offer, they would have no choice but to take this matter to court.

I had to admire Tony's solicitors: their offer was ferociously strategic. Accept our terms and you come out with a little money to get your life re-started again. Turn us down and we will embroil you in a legal battle that you cannot afford, and which will end up having the same result: Jack stays with Tony and that woman.

'You don't sound as shaky as I'd expect,' Sandy said that night when she phoned me.

'Oh, I'm shaky all right,' I said. 'And I find myself crying spontaneously. But this time I'm also angry.'

Sandy laughed. 'Glad to hear it,' she said.

But my anger was also tempered by the *realpolitik* of the situation. Legally and financially, I'd been trumped. For the moment, there wasn't a great deal I could do about it . . . except attempt to present an exemplary face to the world.

So when a woman named Clarice Chambers phoned me from Wandsworth Social Services to suggest that my first supervised visit take place in two days' time, I agreed immediately.

The 'contact centre' was located in a grim, modern, breeze-block building, just off Garratt Lane in Wandsworth. After I had sat on a bench in the reception area for ten minutes, a woman appeared and said 'Sally Goodchild', then directed me to Room 4, straight down the corridor, second door on my right. Walking down towards the room, I felt fear. I didn't know how I'd react to the sight of my son.

But he wasn't there when I went in. Rather, I found myself face-to-face with Clarice Chambers—a large, imposing Afro-Caribbean woman with a firm handshake and a firm smile. The room was set up as a nursery, with soft toys, and a playpen, and animal wallpaper that looked forlornly incongruous under the harsh fluorescent lighting.

'Where's Jack?' I said, my nervousness showing.

'He'll be with us in a minute,' she said, motioning for me to sit down in a plastic chair. 'I just want to chat with you for a bit before you have your visit with your son, and to explain how this all works.'

'Fine, fine,' I said, trying to steady myself. Clarice Chambers gave me another sympathetic smile, and then said that I should now consider this day and hour—Wednesday, 11 a.m.—as my time with Jack. His father had been informed of this fact, and Jack's nanny would be bringing him here every week. She would not be present during these visits, only myself and Clarice. However, if I wished, I could nominate a friend or family member as the supervisor for these visits.

'I'm still new in London, so I don't really know anybody who could . . .' I broke off, unable to continue.

Clarice touched my hand. 'That's fine then. I'll be your supervisor.'

She continued, explaining how I could bring any toys or clothes I liked for Jack. I could play with him. I could hold him. I could simply watch him sleeping. I could also bottle-feed him, and Clarice would act as liaison between the nanny and myself to find out what sort of formula he was drinking, and what his feeding routine was right now.

'The only thing you cannot do is leave the room with him unaccompanied. Nor, I'm afraid, can you be left alone with him at any time. Supervised contact means just that. All right?'

I nodded.

'Right then,' she said, standing up. 'I'll be back in a moment.'

She disappeared into an adjoining room and returned a moment later, holding a familiar carry-chair.

'Here he is,' she said quietly, handing him over to me.

Jack was fast asleep. But what struck me immediately was just how much he'd grown in three weeks. He'd filled out a bit, his face had more definition, more character. Even his fingers seemed longer.

'You can pick him up if you want,' she said.

'I don't want to disturb him,' I said. So I placed the carry-chair on the floor beside me, reached down and, using my right index finger, stroked his clenched fist. His hand unclenched, his fingers wrapped round mine, and he held on to me, still sleeping soundly.

That's when I lost the battle I'd been waging ever since I arrived here. I started to cry, putting a hand across my mouth to muffle the sobs and not wake him up. Once I glanced up at Clarice Chambers and saw her watching me with a cool professional eye.

'I'm sorry,' I whispered. 'This is all a bit . . .'

'You don't have to apologise,' she said. 'I know this is hard.'

He didn't wake for the entire hour, though his fist did unclutch after around ten minutes. So I simply sat by him, rocking him in his chair, stroking his face, thinking just how serene he was, and how desperate I was to be with him all the time.

Then, before I knew it, Clarice quietly said, 'It's time, I'm afraid.'

I gulped, and felt tears sting my face. 'All right,' I said.

She gave me another minute, then walked over to us. I touched his face with my hand, then leaned over and kissed his head, breathing in his talcum powder aroma. I stood up and stared out of a grimy window as she picked up the carry-chair and left. When she came back, she approached me and asked, 'Are you all right?'

'I'm trying to be.'

'The first time is always the hardest.'

No, I thought. Every time will be hard.

The next six days were bleak. My sleep was broken, despite the ongoing use of knock-out pills. I had little appetite. I left the house only for the occasional foray to the corner shop or Marks and Spencer. I found myself devoid of energy; so much so that, when I did go down to St Martin's Hospital for a consultation with Dr Rodale, she immediately commented on my wan appearance.

'Well, it's not been an easy few weeks,' I said.

'Yes,' she said, 'I did hear about the court order. I'm very sorry.'

'Thank you,' I said.

At the end of our interview, she announced herself once again pleased with my progress, and appeared even more gratified by the knowledge that the antidepressants had proved so effective.

'Which is good news. So I see no need to alter the dosage for the time being. Have you been in touch with Ellen Cartwright?'

Actually, she called me the next day, apologising profusely for being incommunicado when my solicitor's assistant came chasing her for a witness statement.

'The message on my answerphone was a bit garbled,' she said, 'so I didn't exactly understand why she needed this statement from me. Something about a court proceeding . . .'

I informed her about that proceeding, and its outcome. She sounded appalled. 'But that's scandalous,' she said. 'Especially as I could have told them . . . Oh God, now I feel dreadful. But how are you feeling?'

'Horrible.'

'Would you like to start our sessions again?'

'I think that would be a good idea.'

'Fine then. One thing, though—you know that I just do NHS locums at St Martin's—and only for anyone who's resident in the unit. If you want to see me, it will have to be on a private basis.'

'And what's the charge?'

'It's seventy pounds per hour, I'm afraid. But if you have private health care . . .'

When I had finished speaking to Ellen, I called BUPA, only to be given confirmation of what I had suspected. When Tony had left his job, the policy had been cancelled. I did some maths. Even if I restricted myself to a session a week between now and the full hearing in six months' time, I would still end up paying £1,680 for Ellen's therapeutic service—an impossible sum, given that I didn't have a job. So it looked like I would simply have to make do with my antidepressants and my extended transatlantic phone calls with Sandy.

'You have to find a new lawyer,' she said that night. 'Especially as you're going to have to deal with the house thing very soon.'

'I can't afford another one right now.'

'You're going to have to go back to work, aren't you?'

'I *want* to go back to work. I *need* to go back to work.'

I articulated the same sentiment to a Ms Jessica Law, the CAFCASS reporter, who visited me at home for a preliminary interview. She was around my age, wearing subdued clothes and wire-rimmed glasses. From the moment I opened the door, I could see that she was sizing me up, taking in everything about my bearing, my manners, my dress sense (well-pressed jeans, a black turtleneck, black loafers), and my material circumstances. She noticed my collection of books and classical CDs, and the fact that I served her cafetière coffee.

'Now I know this can't be the easiest of situations for you . . .' she said, sugaring her coffee.

'No, it isn't,' I said, thinking: Just about everyone I've met in the Social Services have used that expression.

'I plan to see you two or three times in all before I submit my report. You're not on trial here. My goal is simply to give the court an overall picture of your circumstances.'

I was, without question, on trial here—and we both knew it.

'I understand,' I said.

'Very good,' she said. 'Now then . . . I note from your file that you moved to London just under a year ago. So I suppose a reasonable first question might be: how are you finding life in England?'

When I recounted this question to Sandy later that night, she said, 'You've got to be kidding me? She actually asked you that?'

'And they say Americans are deficient in the irony department.'

'Well, did you furnish her with the appropriate *ironic* answer?'

'Hardly. I was very polite, saying that it hadn't been the easiest of adjustments, but that I had also been ill for the past few months and therefore couldn't really judge the place from the standpoint of someone who wasn't yet a functioning part of it. Which is when she asked me if it was my intention to become "a functioning part of England" to which I said, "Absolutely"—reminding her that I had been a correspondent here until my high blood pressure bumped me out of my job.'

"'I should be able to find work here,' I said.

"'So, should you regain residence of your son,' she asked, 'or should the court agree to shared residence, you would plan to raise him in England?'

"'Yes,' I said, 'that would be the plan—because he would then have access to both parents.'

'Smart answer,' Sandy said. 'Did your interrogator approve?'

'I think so. Just as I also think she doesn't disapprove of me. Which is something of a start. Still, the critical thing now is to find work—and show that I can once again be a *functioning* member of society.'

But my attempts to find work were fruitless ones. I tried all the major American newspapers and networks, using my few contacts at NBC, CBS and ABC. No sale. I tried the *New York Times,* the *Wall Street Journal,* and even my old stomping ground, the *Boston Post.* But if the job search was bearing nothing, at least I seemed to be in the good books of my handlers from the Wandsworth contact centre. Clarice told me that I seemed to be bonding well with Jack, and he was happily awake for all our sessions, which meant that I could feed him, change his nappy, and try to get him interested in assorted infant toys, and hold him close, and wish to God that I didn't have to hand him back at the end of the hour.

I resolved not to cry any more during these sessions, deciding that I needed to show a certain stability and equilibrium in front of Clarice, to prove that I was dealing with the enforced separation from my son, even though it was agony. But as soon as the session was over I would walk slowly out of the building, my head bowed, and stumble out into the grey, litter-strewn shabbiness of Garratt Lane, and find the nearest wall, and put my head against it, and cry like a fool for a minute or so, and then collect myself and try to get through the rest of the day.

I didn't mention these cry-like-a-fool moments to Jessica Law. All I would tell her was, 'I find this situation desperately hard.'

She'd look at me with a mixture of professional coolness and personal compassion, and say, 'I am aware of that.'

What else could she say? That, like a massive migraine, it would eventually abate? It wouldn't. We both knew that.

'I do hope that you keep your expectations about a future with Jack realistic,' she said during our third 'chat'.

As I turned into Sefton Street after my fourth supervised visit with Jack, I saw a nanny loading her infant charge into the baby seat of a Land Rover, and remembered how Jack nuzzled his head against my cheek just ten minutes earlier. I stopped. And I suddenly lost all hope.

I sat down on the hood of a car parked outside my house, and started to cry again.

'Sally . . . are you all right?'

I looked up. There was my neighbour, Julia Frank. I wiped my eyes.

'Just a bad morning, that's all. I'll be OK.'

'Cup of tea?'

'Please.'

She led me into her house, and down a corridor to her kitchen. She put the kettle on. I asked for a glass of water. I saw her watching me as I pulled my bottle of antidepressants out of my jacket pocket, removed a pill and washed it down with the water. She said nothing. She just made the tea, then poured me a cup and said, 'I don't want to pry, but . . . has something happened?'

'Yes. Something's happened.'

'If you want to talk about it . . .'

I shook my head.

'Fine,' she said. 'Milk? Sugar?'

'Both, please.'

She poured in a dash of milk and one sugar. She handed me the cup. I stirred it, and said, 'They took my son away from me seven weeks ago.'

And then I told her everything. When I finished, the tea was cold. There was a long silence. Then Julia asked, 'Are you going to let them get away with it?'

'I don't know what to do next.'

She thought about this for a moment, then said, 'Well, let's find you someone who does know what to do next.'

NINE

FROM THE MOMENT I walked into his office, I didn't like the look of Nigel Clapp. Not that he appeared strange or threatening. Actually, what first struck me about him was his absolute ordinariness: a truly grey man who seemed like he was born at the age of forty, and had spent his life cultivating a grey functionary look, right down to the cheap grey suit he was wearing over a polyester white shirt and a grubby maroon knit tie.

I could have handled the bad clothes, the sallow countenance, the thinning black hair, the light sleety accumulations of dandruff on both shoulders, and the way he never seemed to look at you while talking.

No, what really bothered me about Nigel Clapp was his handshake: a brief placement of four damp, limp fingers into your right palm. Coupled with the permanently stunned expression on his face, he certainly didn't inspire confidence.

Which was something of a worry—considering that Nigel Clapp was my new solicitor, and my one hope of ever getting my son back.

He did stand up when his secretary showed me into his office. Then he offered me his limp hand, and motioned me into the cheap orange plastic chair opposite his steel desk, and started shuffling through papers, and avoided my gaze. He must have spent a good two minutes going through my file, saying absolutely nothing, the only noise in the office coming from the traffic on Balham High Road, and the stentorian voice of his secretary next door. When he finally spoke, he didn't look up from the documents.

'So your former solicitor,' he said in a voice so low and hesitant that I had to bend forward to hear him, 'never sought leave to appeal the order?'

'We parted company immediately after the hearing,' I said.

'I see,' he said, his voice noncommittal, his eyes still focusing on the papers. 'And this business with the house . . . can you remember the names of the solicitors who handled the conveyancing?'

I told him. He wrote it down. Then he reluctantly looked at me.

'Maybe you'd like to tell me the entire story now.'

'When you say "entire"?'

'From . . . uh . . . I suppose . . . when you first met your husband to . . . uh . . . this morning, I suppose. I would just like an overall picture.'

I could feel my spirits tumble even further into despair. This man had the personality of a paper cup.

But still I took him through the complete tale of my marriage—from Cairo to London, to the early problems with the pregnancy, to the post-natal depression, to my extended stay in hospital, and the nightmare that I had walked into upon returning from Boston. I was frank with him—telling him how I made angry verbal threats against my son, and my difficult behaviour in hospital after his birth, the sleeping pills incident, my absurd decision to seek out Diane Dexter's country home—in short, everything that Tony's solicitors could use against me.

As I spoke, Clapp showed no emotion, he didn't interrupt, he didn't react to any of the more dire aspects of the tale.

When I finally finished, there was another pause—as if he didn't get the fact that my narrative was finished. Then, when this dawned on him, he turned back to my file, shuffled the papers together, closed it and said, 'Uhm . . . right then. Well, uhm, emergency Legal Aid will be available right now, although a final certificate won't be authorised until the forms have been processed. Anyway . . . uhm . . . we'll be in touch.'

An hour later, I was in Julia's kitchen.

'This guy isn't just diffident; he's one of those people who seems to be missing-in-action while still sitting in the same room as you.'

'Are you certain he's just not a little shy?'

'A *little* shy? He came across as *pathologically* shy . . . to the point where I can't see how the hell he's going to make any inroads for me.'

'Don't you think you should give him a little time?'

'I don't have much in the way of time,' I said. 'Less than four months, to be exact. And they don't call that Final Hearing *final* for nothing.'

'I know what the stakes are, Sally. I really do. And even though Nigel is your lawyer, I gather that you can get permission from the Legal Aid authority to change your solicitor if you have a good enough reason. I'm sure the right person could dig up the right dirt on your husband's relationship with that Dexter woman, and how they set this whole thing up. Don't you have any mega-rich friends who could help you hire a private detective to snoop around on your behalf?'

The only people I knew with any substantial money were Margaret and Alexander Campbell. But I felt that, if I approached them now, it would seem as if I were demanding something back for referring me to Lawrence and Lambert.

'As I told you before, my only family is my sister. She's broke. My parents were schoolteachers. Their only asset was their house—and thanks to what lawyers like to call "bad estate planning" and the suddenness of their death, that one asset was largely consumed by the government. Then there was the law suit after their death.'

'What law suit?'

I paused for a moment. Then I said, 'The one against my dad. The autopsy report found that he was about two glasses of wine over the legal limit. Not a vast amount, but he still shouldn't have been driving on it. And the fact that he hit a station wagon with a family of five in it . . .'

Julia looked at me, wide-eyed. 'Was anyone killed?'

'The mother and her fourteen-month-old son. Her husband and their two other kids somehow managed to walk away.'

Silence. Then I said, 'Before he got into the car, my father was with my mom at a college graduation party for me. Late in the evening, I handed him a glass of shitty Almaden wine, and he said he really couldn't handle anything more, and I said—and I remember this so damn clearly—"You going middle-aged on me, Dad?" And he laughed and said "Hell, no," and downed it in one go. And—'

I stopped. 'I still can't get over it.'

'What did your sister say when she found out?'

'That's the thing—she never did. I couldn't bring myself to tell her.'

'But, hang on. You don't really believe that *you* were responsible?'

'I gave my dad the glass of wine that sent him over the limit.'

'No. You just *handed* him the glass and then gently teased him about being middle-aged. He knew he had to drive after the party.'

'Try telling my conscience that. Once this all happened, I was certain that this was some sort of cosmic retribution; that Jack had been taken away from me because I had given my father the drink that made him crash the car that killed a little boy.'

Julia reached over the table and put her hand on my arm. 'You know that's not true.'

'I don't know anything any more. Nothing makes sense.'

'Well, one thing *must* make sense. You are not receiving divine punishment for your father's accident—because you had absolutely no role in that accident, and because it just doesn't work that way.'

I thought about that later, as I decided to treat myself to an extended walk by the river. I had found my jacket, put on a pair of shoes, and was heading towards the kitchen bowl in which I always tossed my house keys, when the phone rang. Damn. Damn. Damn. A part of me wanted to let the answerphone take it, but being a glutton for punishment, I reached for the receiver.

'Uh . . . I'd like to speak with Ms . . . uh . . . Goodchild.'

Wonderful. Just wonderful. Exactly the man I wanted to hear from late on a Friday afternoon. But I maintained a polite tone.

'Mr Clapp?'

'Oh, it is you, Ms Goodchild. Is this a good time?'

'Sure, I guess.'

'Uhm . . . well . . . Ms Goodchild. I just want to say that the court hearing went fine.'

Pause. I was genuinely confused. 'What court hearing?'

'Oh, didn't I tell you about that? I applied for a court order this morning, insisting that your husband pay the mortgage on your house until the divorce settlement is finalised.'

This was news to me. 'You did?'

'I hope you don't mind . . . I obtained the order this afternoon at three. And the judge decreed that your husband must continue to pay the mortgage until you have worked out a mutually agreed financial settlement.'

I couldn't believe what I was hearing.

'Does this mean that the house can't be sold out from under me?'

'Uh . . . that's right. And if your husband doesn't make the mortgage payments, he will be considered in contempt of court. Which means that he could be imprisoned for failing to meet his commitments.'

'Good God,' I said.

'One other thing,' he said. 'His solicitor said that he wants to make an offer, vis-à-vis interim financial support for you.'

'He *did*? Really?'

'I think he was rather nervous about the idea that, under the circumstances, the judge might instruct his client to pay you a substantial sum a month. So they offered you a thousand pounds a month in interim maintenance.'

'You're kidding me?'

'Is that too low?'

'Hardly. I don't want a penny of it.'

'Oh, right. But how about the mortgage?'

'That's different. The house is a shared investment. But I certainly don't want to be supported by *her* money.'

'Well, uh, that's your choice. And if, uh, you want me to continue handling this matter, I will inform them of your decision.'

I paused for a second's worth of reflection, then said, 'I'm pleased to have you in my corner, Mr Clapp.'

'Oh . . .' he said. And then added, 'Uhm . . . thanks.'

After his success on the mortgage front, Nigel Clapp vanished for seven days. Then, out of nowhere, he made contact with me again.

'Uhm . . .' he said after I answered the phone.

'Mr Clapp?'

'Well . . . uhm . . . names. I need the name of everyone who's dealt with you from the Social Services.' He paused, as if the effort of getting that one sentence out without an *uhm* had been overwhelming.

'Fine, no problem. Shall I email you them today?'

'Yes, uhm, email is all right.'

'You know that my first lawyer took witness statements from just about everybody?'

'Yes. I know that. Because I obtained copies of all court documents. But I would just like to speak with them all again.'

'I see,' I said. 'Is that necessary?'

'Well . . . uhm . . . *yes*, in fact.'

Later that day, while reporting this conversation to Julia, I said, 'You know, I think that was the first assertive thing he's said to me.'

'You shouldn't worry about him. He seems to know what he's doing.'

Four days later, I was woken up by a phone call around one o'clock in the morning.

'Hello, Ms Goodchild . . . Sally?'

'Who's this?' I asked, half-awake.

'Jane Sanjay. Your health visitor, remember?'

'Of course. Hello, Jane. Aren't you supposed to be out of the country?'

'I *am* out of the country,' she said. 'In Canada. But listen, your solicitor, Mr Clapp, tracked me down.'

'Mr Clapp found you?'

'That's right. And he explained what you've been going through—and asked me if I'd be prepared to testify on your behalf. Which, of course, I'm most willing to do, especially as I'll be back working for Wandsworth Council in just over two months' time. But the reason I'm calling—and I can't talk for much longer, as my phone card's about to run out—is just to tell you that I am so shocked that they took Jack away from you. And I just wanted to let you know that I'm completely behind you, and will help in any way I can.'

The next day, I called Nigel Clapp to congratulate him on tracking down Jane Sanjay.

'Oh, right,' he said. 'Uhm, finding her was . . . well, it took two phone calls. The first to the Council and then to her mother. We talked. And she agreed to be a witness on your behalf at the Final Hearing. Oh, and . . . uhm . . . just in case she gets delayed in Canada, I contacted the Law Society of Canada, and found the name of a solicitor in the town of Jasper, and spoke with him yesterday. He'll be taking a sworn affidavit from Ms Sanjay later in the week—which he'll also have notarised, to make certain it's admissible in an English court of law. But that's just a precautionary measure on my part.'

He then also informed me that almost all the other people I had listed in my email had been interviewed by his secretary, Mrs Keating.

'Are you happy with the new statements?' I asked him.

'I think they're fine, yes. Now . . . uhm . . . I think you should write a letter. To your husband. I'd like to establish . . . uhm . . . that you want contact with him as regards your son's well-being in his new home . . . as regards how this Ms Dexter is treating him, and what his plans are for the future. I'd also like to suggest that you propose a face-to-face meeting . . . just the two of you . . . to discuss Jack's future.'

'But I really don't want to meet him right now, Mr Clapp. I don't think I could face him.'

'I can appreciate that. But . . . uhm . . . unless I am mistaken . . . and I could be mistaken. . . uhm . . . I don't think he'll want to see you. Guilt, you see. He'll feel guilty. Unless I am wrong . . .'

'No,' I said. Was he always so self-denigrating? 'I don't think you're wrong.'

That evening I wrote the letter.

Dear Tony,

I cannot begin to articulate the grief you have caused me. Nor can I fathom how you could have betrayed me and your son in such a ferocious, self-serving way. You used my illness—a temporary clinical condition, from which I am now largely recovered—as a means by which to snatch my son from me, and reinvent your life with a woman who you were obviously seeing while I was pregnant. The fact that you then manipulated the facts of my post-partum depression to claim that I was a danger to Jack is unspeakable, both in its cunning and its cruelty.

But it is another, more pressing matter that compels me to write you. I am troubled by the fact that, as Jack's mother, I have been deliberately kept in the dark as to who is looking after him, whether he is being properly cared for, and if he is getting the proper maternal attention that an infant needs. There are also questions about his upbringing, no matter what the final custody arrangements turn out to be, which we must decide together.

That is what I want to most emphasise now. The fact that, despite the desperate anguish I feel by being unfairly separated from my son, and despite my anger at your terrible betrayal, my primary concern is Jack's welfare and his future happiness. For this reason, I am willing to put aside my anguish to sit down with you for the first of what must be an ongoing series of conversations about our son and his future. For his sake, we should put all our animosities to one side and talk.

I look forward to hearing from you shortly, proposing a time and place when we should meet.

Yours, Sally

'My, you are clever,' Julia said after I showed her the final draft.
'You can thank Mr Clapp for that. He made me write three different drafts before he was happy with the letter.'
Three days later, I received a letter from Tony.

Dear Sally

Considering the threats you made against the life of our son, and considering your complete lack of maternal interest in him following his birth, I find it rather extraordinary that you write me now, speaking about how I betrayed you. Especially when it is you who so betrayed an innocent baby.

As to your accusation that I was betraying you while pregnant, you should know that Diane Dexter has been a close friend of mine for years. And I turned to her as a friend for support when your mental health began to decline during your pregnancy. Our friendship only turned into something else after your breakdown and your irresponsible, endangering behaviour against our son.

She could not be a better surrogate mother to my son, and has provided Jack the safe, calm environment he needs in these early days of his life. I am most certainly aware of the fact that you—as Jack's mother—should have an important input into decisions about his future. But until I am sure that you are no longer a danger to him, I cannot sit down with you to 'talk things out'. Do understand: I hold no grudge against you whatsoever. And I only wish you the best for the future.

Yours sincerely

Tony

c.c. Jessica Law, Wandsworth DHSS

The letter shook in my hands as I read it. I immediately faxed a copy to Nigel Clapp, who rang me later that afternoon.

'Uhm . . . about your husband's letter . . .'

'It has me worried,' I said.

'Oh, really?'

'Because it's allowed that bastard to refute everything I said in the first letter. And because it also allowed him to put on the record his contention that she "saved" my son . . .'

'I could see how . . . uhm . . . you might be upset by such a comment. But as regards the damage the letter might do . . . it's what I wanted.'

'You *wanted* this sort of reply?'

'Uh, yes.'

Then there was another of his signature pauses, hinting that he wanted to move on to another topic of conversation.

'May I ask you if you've had any further success finding work?'

'I've been trying, but I just don't seem to be having much luck.'

'I spoke with Dr Rodale, your . . . uhm . . . psychiatrist. She told me that she will write a report, stating that, in light of your . . . uhm . . . your depression, she considers you still unfit for full-time employment. That will, at the very least, cover us in case your husband's barrister raises the issue at the hearing. But if you could find some sort of job, it would reflect favourably on your recovery from the . . . uhm . . .'

'Depression.'

'That's the word.'

A couple of days later, I received a phone call from Julia. She explained that she was in the office of an editor friend.

'When my friend here said he urgently needed a proofreader for a big job, I immediately thought of you. If, that is, you're interested . . .'

'Oh, I'm interested . . .'

The next day, I took the tube to Kensington High Street and spent an hour in the office of an editor named Stanley Shaw, a thin, quiet, rather courtly man in his mid-fifties.

'Are you at all knowledgeable about classical music?' he asked me.

'I can tell the difference between Mozart and Mahler,' I said.

'Well, that's a start,' he said with a smile, then quizzed me about whether I could adjust to Anglicisms, and technical musical terminology, and an extensive number of abbreviations that were a component part of the guide. I assured him that I was a fast learner.

'That's good, because we're going to need the entire guide of fifteen hundred pages proofread within the next two months.'

'I can do it.'

We shook hands on it. The next day, a motorcycle messenger arrived at my house with a large, deep, cardboard box of proofs. I had cleared the kitchen table for this task, already installing an anglepoise lamp and a jam jar filled with newly sharpened pencils. There was a contract along with the page proofs. Before signing it, I faxed it over to Nigel Clapp. He called me back within an hour.

'You've got a job,' he said, sounding surprised.

'It looks that way. But I'm worried about something. Whether my fee will invalidate me for Legal Aid.' The hearing was in ten weeks' time, and I was down to the equivalent of £1,500. It would be insanely tight. 'Supposing I asked Stanley for just a third of the fee up-front?'

'Yes. That would still put you well within the Legal Aid threshold.'

Stanley Shaw was only too willing to re-jig the contract, pointing out that, 'In the thirty years I've been a publisher, this is the first time that a writer or an editor has asked for a delayed payment.'

That evening, I did a bit more simple mathematics. I had a total of sixty-one days to do the job. Three pages an hour, eight hours per day— the work broken up into four two-hour sessions, with a half-hour break between each period. Of course, I had to work this schedule round my weekly visit with Jack, my bi-monthly talk with Jessica Law, my bi-monthly consultations with Dr Rodale. Otherwise, the work defined my time. Just as it helped me mark time, and accelerate the agonising wait for the Final Hearing.

Seven weeks later, while reading the section covering all complete sets of Vaughan Williams symphonies, I received word from Nigel Clapp that we had an exact date for the Final Hearing—June 18.

'Uhm . . . the barrister I want to instruct . . . and who does this sort of case very well . . . and . . . uhm . . . is also on the Legal Aid register . . . well, her name is . . . Maeve Doherty.'

'Irish?'

'Uhm . . . yes. Born and raised there, educated at Oxford, then she was part of a rather radical chambers for a while. She's available. She does Legal Aid. She will respond to the predicament you are in.'

'And say she ends up facing a judge who can't stand her politics?'

'Well . . . uhm . . . one can't have everything.'

I didn't have time yet to dwell on this potential problem, as Vaughan Williams gave way to Verdi and Victoria and Vivaldi and Walton and Weber and Weekes and—twenty-four hours to go—I was still working on Wesley, and drinking nonstop cups of coffee, and assuring Stanley Shaw that he could have a courier at my door at nine tomorrow morning, and somewhere around midnight, I reached the last listing (Zwillich), and suddenly the sun was rising, and I tossed the final page on top of the pile, and smiled that tired smile that comes with having finished a job. I ran a bath, and was dressed and awaiting the courier when he showed up at nine, and received a phone call an hour later from Stanley Shaw congratulating me on making the deadline. An hour after that, I was holding my baby son under the increasingly less watchful eye of Clarice Chambers, who told me that she was going to leave us alone this morning, but would be down the corridor if we needed her.

'How about that, Jack?' I said after she headed off. 'We're on our own.'

But Jack was too busy sucking down a bottle to respond.

I crashed out that night at seven, and slept twelve straight hours. I woke the next morning, feeling less burdened than I had felt in months. This lightening of mood carried on into the next week, when Stanley Shaw rang me and asked, 'I don't suppose you're free to do another job?'

'As a matter of fact, I am.'

'Tremendous. It's another doorstopper of a book. Our film guide. Currently clocking in at one thousand five hundred and thirty-eight pages. It needs to be fully proofed in nine weeks. Same terms as before?'

'Sounds good to me.'

'Well, come by the office tomorrow about noon. I'll take you through the parameters of it, and then I can buy us both lunch, if that's agreeable.'

'You're on,' I said.

Two days later, I was back at work, slowly inching my way through this fat critical compendium. And when Sandy asked me how I could mentally handle long stretches of such detailed work, I said, 'I just fall into it and black everything else out for the next couple of hours. So it's a bit like a temporary, fast-acting anaesthetic, which keeps everything else numb for a short amount of time. The pay's not bad either.'

Three weeks into this job, I received a phone call from Maeve Doherty. She explained that Nigel Clapp had given her the brief. As she liked to be instructed well before the date of the hearing and always met the individuals she would be representing, she would like to meet me.

Four days later, I took an afternoon off. I hopped on the Underground to Temple, walked up to Fleet Street, and entered a passageway called

Inner Temple, which brought me into a small, calm enclave of the law, hidden away from London's continuous din. I came to a door, outside of which was a wooden board, upon which had been painted, in immaculate black letters, the names of the fifteen barristers who made up these chambers. *Miss M. Doherty* was near the top of the list.

Her office was tiny. So was she, with petite features to mirror her small stature. She wasn't pretty—in fact, she almost could be described as plain—but there was a hint of a deeply strong resolve that she had latched on to as a way of countering her diminutive size. Her handshake was firm and she looked me directly in the eye when talking to me.

'Let me say from the start that I do think you've been unfairly vilified.'

She then talked strategy for the better part of a half-hour, quizzing me intensely about my marriage to Tony, about his personal history, centring in on the way he shut himself away in his study all the time after the baby was born, the late nights out on the town, the fact that he was so evidently involved with Diane Dexter during my pregnancy.

'I saw that letter you wrote your husband just a few weeks ago, as well as his reply. Very adroit strategy—especially as it got him to state, in writing, that theirs was just a platonic relationship. And if Nigel Clapp's investigations into her background yield what we hope they'll yield, then we really should have an interesting case to present against them.'

'Nigel Clapp is having the Dexter woman investigated? By whom?'

'He didn't say. Then again, as you've probably gathered by now, Mr Clapp is someone who, at the best of times, has difficulty with compound sentences. But, whatever about his interpersonal skills, he just might be the best solicitor I've ever worked with: utterly thorough, conscientious and engaged. Especially in a case like this one, where he feels, as I do, that our client has been seriously wronged.'

'He told you that?'

'Hardly,' she said with a smile. 'But we've worked together often enough that I know there are times when he's passionately committed to seeing things set right. This is definitely one of those instances. Just don't expect him to admit that to you.'

Then, just two weeks before the date of the Final Hearing, I received a call from Nigel Clapp. It was nearly eight at night.

'Uhm . . . sorry to be phoning so late.'

'No problem. I was just working.'

'How's work?' he said, in an awkward attempt to make conversation.

'Fine, fine. Stanley is actually talking about another proofing job to follow this one. It looks like I might have a steady income soon.'

'Good, good,' he said, sounding even more distracted then ever.

'You need to tell me something, Mr Clapp?' I asked.

An anxious silence. 'It's not good news. It's two-fold difficult news, I'm afraid. The first part has to do with Ms Law's CAFCASS report . . .'

I felt a cold hand seize the back of my neck.

'Oh my God, don't tell me she ruled against me?'

'Not precisely. She actually reported herself very impressed with you, very impressed with the way you have handled yourself in the wake of being separated from your son, very impressed as well with your recovery from your depression. But . . . uhm . . . I'm afraid she was also very impressed with your husband and Ms Dexter. And although it isn't her business to make a recommendation, she has let it be known that the child is in very good hands with his father and surrogate mother.'

I felt the phone trembling in my hand.

'Do . . . uhm . . . understand that this doesn't mean she's advised that the child stay with Ms Dexter—'

'And the second piece of bad news?'

'Well, this only arrived around an hour ago and . . . uhm . . . I'm still trying to digest it. It's a letter to me from your husband's solicitor, informing me that your husband and Ms Dexter are professionally relocating to Sydney for the next five years, where Ms Dexter has been engaged to start up a major new marketing concern.'

'Oh God . . .'

'Yes . . . and their solicitor informs me they're planning to take Jack with them.'

I was now rigid with shock. 'Can they legally do that?

'If the hearing goes their way, then you will have no say in the matter. They can take your son wherever they want to take him.'

TEN

'THE ISSUE HERE,' Maeve Doherty said, 'comes down to one central question: where does the child best belong? That's what the court will be deciding. The problem here, however, is that two court orders have indicated that you could be considered an unfit mother, and that your alleged behaviour after the child's birth indicated that the child could potentially be harmed by you. Which is what they are going to argue again. Now we can certainly call a variety of professional witnesses who can both vouch for your mental stability, your fitness as a mother, and the fact that you were suffering from clinical depression at the time. How many statements do we have now, Nigel?'

'Eight altogether,' he said. 'And . . . uhm . . . they're all very favourably disposed towards Ms Goodchild.'

'Which means we can count on eight favourable witnesses. The big sticking point, however, is the CAFCASS report. The court *always* pays attention to this report. It inevitably wields a considerable amount of influence on the final decision. The problem here is not having any real ammunition against either Tony or his partner. Unless your "detective" has turned up something, Nigel.'

'Shall I bring her in to see what she's managed to uncover?' he said.

'Your detective's a *she*?' I asked.

Nigel started to blush. 'It's . . . uhm . . . my secretary, Mrs Keating. She's really rather good at it,' he said.

'Why don't you get her in here?' Maeve said.

Nigel reached for the phone and dialled a number. From next door, we could hear Mrs Keating answer her phone with a loud, 'Yeah?'

'Would you mind coming in here for a moment, Rose, and would you please bring the Goodchild file with you?'

'Oh, yeah, right.'

She showed up a moment later. 'Ms Goodchild and Ms Doherty would like to hear the results of your investigation into Ms Dexter.'

'Fine by me,' she said, parking herself in a chair and opening the file. 'Diane Dexter, born Leeds, January 15, 1953. She went to the local grammar school. Bright girl—won a place at Leeds University in Economics. Went to London after getting her degree. Ten years in advertising. Then got headhunted by Apple UK to run their marketing division. Five years with them. Branched into market research. Co-founded a company—Market Force Limited—in 1987 with a partner named Simon Chandler, with whom she was romantically linked for a time. When they broke up in 1990, he bought out her share of the firm. She used the money to set up Dexter Communications. She's now worth around ten million.

'Now, here's what little dirt I could find on her. Two months' hospital-isation in 1990 at the Priory for "psychotropic dependence", better known as cocaine misuse. The bad news is that there were no arrests for drug possession and she's been clean since the Priory stint. In fact, she's given talks to youth groups about her past addiction, and has also raised money for a charity who sponsor drug-education programmes.'

'The cocaine angle is an interesting one,' Maeve Doherty said. 'There might be something there. Anything else?'

'Besides the relationship with Simon Chandler, there have been two failed marriages: a two-year quickie to a chap she married out of university. Then there was a six-year stint with a television director named Trevor Harriman, which ended when she met Simon Chandler in '85. In fact, Chandler was named as co-respondent in the divorce petition. Since she and Chandler parted company in 1990, there have been a few affairs—but nothing solid. Until she met Tony Hobbs in 1999.'

I interrupted here. 'Tony insisted that they were just friends.'

'Well,' Rose Keating said, 'they may have been "just friends", but she took him on a South African holiday in '99, then the Great Barrier Reef the following year, then spent a month with him in Cairo in 2001.'

'What month in 2001?' I asked.

'November.'

'That makes sense. We first hooked up in October of that year.'

'Hate to tell you this, but it was she who dropped him in December, because he wouldn't come back to London to live with her.'

Maeve Doherty came in here. 'Did you manage to find out when they started seeing each other again?'

She nodded. 'About twelve months ago.'

I sucked in my breath. And asked, 'How do you know that?'

'Ms Dexter's ex-housekeeper told me. He came over one afternoon.'

Maeve Doherty asked, 'But did the ex-housekeeper state whether he was just visiting her or actually *visiting* her?'

'Oh, it was definitely the latter. He stayed with her until about one in the morning . . . and they didn't emerge from her bedroom until it was time for him to leave.'

. . . and to go home and tell me he'd been out boozing late with his chums.

Now I asked, 'And according to the housekeeper, was he regularly at her place after that?'

'According to the housekeeper, he was over there all the time.'

Maeve Doherty commented, 'I suppose Mr Hobbs's barrister could question the validity of the housekeeper's testimony . . . especially as she is an ex-employee.'

'That's right,' Rose Keating said. 'Fired for alleged stealing.'

'Oh, great,' I said.

'Yeah, but the housekeeper got legal advice and forced Ms Dexter's hand. Turns out not only did she receive a written apology from her, saying the whole charge was false, she also got a year's wages.'

'And is this housekeeper willing to testify?' Maeve Doherty asked.

'Oh, yes. She don't think much of Ms Dexter. She also told me where and when the two of them slipped out of town for a little romantic rendezvous over the past six months. Twice in Brussels, once in

Paris. The hotels confirm that Mr Hobbs had company on both occasions.

'Oh . . . one final important thing. Seems Ms Dexter miscarried a child when she was big into cocaine. The year afterwards, she tried IVF. Didn't take. Tried it again in '92 and '93, by which time she was forty, and the game was kind of over. The thing is—according to the ex-housekeeper—having a kid has become an obsession with her.'

I looked at Rose Keating, amazed. 'How did you find all this out?'

She gave me a coy smile. 'I've got my ways, dear.'

Maeve Doherty said, 'The fact that they were carrying on while he was married to you is good stuff. The fact that he has written that theirs was a friendship until your illness—and we have proof otherwise—is also good stuff. And the fact that she's been desperate for a baby all these years . . . well, we can certainly put two-plus-two together on that one.'

But then she looked at me directly and said, 'However, I have to be honest with you, Sally. While all this evidence is useful, it still doesn't contradict, or undermine, the dirt they have against you. Can you think of anything about your husband that might be useful?

'I don't know,' I said. 'His life was pretty much work and the occasional girlfriend before I came along. I can't say he told me much . . .'

At that moment, I heard a tiny little ping in the back of my brain; a single line of conversation that had been spoken to me around seven months ago. Something I hadn't picked up on at the time. Until now.

'Are you all right, dear?' Rose Keating asked me.

'Could I use your phone, please?'

I called Directory Enquiries for Seaford. The number I wanted was listed, but the person I needed to speak with wasn't there. I left a message, asking Tony's sister to call me at home in London urgently. Then I went back to Nigel's office and explained who I was trying to contact, what she had said to me some months earlier, and why it might prove useful.

'Uhm . . . do you think you could track her down and talk to her?' Nigel Clapp asked. 'We have just twelve days.'

Twelve days. I rushed home to Putney and re-dialled the Seaford number. Once again, I was connected to the answerphone. Once again, I left a message. Then I went back to work on the *Film Guide*. But I was unable to fall into the rabbit hole of work and cut off the outside world. I kept glancing at the phone, willing it to ring. Which it didn't.

So I called back and left another message.

By midnight, I must have called another eight times. I slept fitfully and eventually found myself at the kitchen table around five that morning, proofing some more pages. At seven, I tried the Seaford number. No answer. I tried again at ten, at three, at six. Then, when I phoned at eight thirty, the unexpected happened. It was actually answered. When Pat Hobbs heard my voice, she became indignant.

'Was that you calling me all the time yesterday?'

'Ms Hobbs . . . Pat . . . please hear me out . . . He's taken my child from me.'

Silence. Then, 'Who's taken your child from you?'

'Your brother.'

'You have a child with Tony?'

'A son. Jack. He's about nine months old now. And Tony has . . . he's run off with another woman. And they've taken my son . . .'

'I could have told you my brother was a bastard. A charming bastard, but a bastard nonetheless. So, what can I do about this?'

'Remember when we spoke some time ago, and I mentioned that Tony had just left me, and you asked me . . .'

I encapsulated the conversation for her, even though I remembered it, word for word.

'*How long have you two been married now?*' she asked me.

'*Around a year.*'

'*And he's already abandoned you? That's fast work, right enough. Mind you, I'm not surprised. He's the abandoning sort.*'

'*You mean, he's done this before?*'

'*Maybe.*'

'What did you mean by "maybe"?'

'I'll tell you—on one condition. You never heard this from me.'

I agreed. Now it was her turn to tell a story. When she reached the end of her tale, she gave me an address and said, 'You can contact this woman. She lives in Crawley. But understand: I am to be kept out of the picture.'

I assured her that I'd say nothing about her involvement, then thanked her profusely for helping me out.

I called Nigel Clapp, excitedly blurting out everything that I had just learned. When I finally concluded with the comment 'Not bad, eh?', he said, 'Yes, that is rather good news.'

This, from Nigel Clapp, ranked as high optimism. He also said he'd dispatch Rose Keating to the address in Crawley.

Maeve Doherty rang me two days later to say how pleased she was with my detective work. 'It is certainly very interesting testimony,' she said, sounding cautious and guarded. 'And if carefully positioned in the hearing, it might have an impact. I'm not saying it's the smoking gun I'd like, but it is, without question, most compelling.'

Then she asked me if I was free to drop by her chambers for an hour, so we could go through how she was planning to examine me when I gave evidence at the hearing, and what I should expect from Tony's barrister.

Once inside her chambers, she did a practice run of a potential cross-examination, terrorising me completely, coldly haranguing me, attacking all my weaknesses, and undermining all my defences.

'Now you have me scared to death,' I said after she finished.

'Don't be,' she said. 'Keep your answers brief and concise. Do not deviate from your story and you'll be just fine.'

I doubted that—but, thankfully, the terror of the hearing was briefly superseded by the more immediate terror of not making the *Film Guide* deadline. I was actually grateful for the pressure, as it did block out the fear I had. It also forced me to work fourteen-hour days for the last week. Bar the occasional trip to the supermarket for food, and a fast thirty-minute canter along the towpath by the river, I didn't leave the house. Except, of course, for my weekly visit with Jack. I had a job to finish, and I was determined to have it done before the hearing, in order to allow me a decent night's sleep before heading to the High Court.

The manuscript went off by motorcycle courier at 9 a.m. on the day before the hearing. I headed off to the public baths in Putney shortly thereafter and spent an hour doing laps in the pool. Then I had my hair done, and took myself to lunch, then crossed the road to the local cinema and sat through some romantic drivel starring Meg Ryan, then collected my one suit from the dry cleaner's, and was home by five, and received a phone call from Maeve Doherty—telling me that she had just been informed of the judge who would be hearing the case.

'His name is Charles Traynor.'

'Is he a reasonable judge?' I asked her.

'Well . . .'

'In other words, he's not reasonable.'

'I would have preferred someone else besides him. Very old school. Very play it by the book. Very traditional . . .'

'Wonderful. Did you ever argue a case in front of this Traynor guy?'

'Oh, yes. And I have to say that I completely respected him. He's scrupulously fair when it comes to the application of the law. So I certainly wouldn't fear him.'

I decided to put all such fears on hold for the night, because I knew they would all come rushing in at daybreak. So I forced myself into bed by nine and slept straight through until the alarm went off at seven.

I was outside the High Court just after ten fifteen. The court was already in full swing, with bewigged barristers walking by, accompanied by solicitors lugging hefty document cases and anxious-looking civilians, who were either the plaintiffs or defendants in the legal dramas taking place within this vast edifice. Nigel Clapp appeared, pulling one of those airline pilot cases on wheels. Maeve Doherty was with him, dressed in a conserv-ative black suit. She had explained during our meeting the previous week that, as at the Interim Hearing, there would be no wigs, no robes.

'Uhm . . . good morning, Ms Goodchild,' Nigel said.

I attempted a smile and tried to appear calm. Maeve immediately detected my anxiousness.

'Just remember that it will be all over soon, and we stand a good chance now of changing the situation. Especially as I spoke with your new witness yesterday on the phone. You did well, Sally.'

A black cab pulled up in front of us. The door opened—and for the first time in over eight months, I found myself looking at the man who was still, legally speaking, my husband. Tony had put on a little weight in the interim, but he still looked damnably handsome, and had dressed well for the occasion in a black suit and a dark blue shirt. When he caught sight of me, he gave me the smallest of nods, then turned away. I couldn't look at him either, and also deflected his glance. But in that moment, an image jumped into my brain: catching sight of Tony Hobbs seated opposite me on the floor in that Red Cross chopper in Somalia, giving me the slightest of flirtatious smiles. That's how our story started, and this is where it had now brought us: to a court of law, surrounded by our respective legal teams, unable to look each other in the eye.

Tony's barrister, Lucinda Fforde, followed him, along with the same solicitor she used for the Interim Hearing. And then Diane Dexter emerged from the cab. Viewed up close, she did not contradict the image I had of her: tall, sleek, elegantly dressed in a smart business suit, tight black hair, a face that was wearing its fifty years with relative ease. Having caught sight of me, she looked right through me. Then, en masse, the four of them walked by us into the building, the two barris-ters exchanging pleasantly formal greetings with each other.

'Well,' Maeve said, 'it looks like we're all here. So . . .'

She led us through the High Court's vast foyer. Court 43 was up two flights of stairs. It was a large chapel-like courtroom in bleached wood. There were six rows of benches. The judge's bench was positioned on a raised platform. The witness stand was to its immediate left. Beyond this was a doorway, which (I presumed) led to the judge's chambers. As before, we were on the left-hand side of the court; Tony and Co. to the right. A court stenographer and a court clerk were positioned at the front.

Maeve had already explained to me that, as Tony was making 'appli-cation' to retain residence of Jack, he had been (legally speaking) cast in the role of *Applicant,* and since I was being forced to 'respond' to this application, I would be known as the *Respondent.* Tony's team would be opening the case and presenting their evidence first. His barrister would have already submitted her skeleton argument to the judge (as Maeve had submitted hers). Witnesses would be called, largely to corroborate the statements they had made. After each 'examination in chief' Maeve would be permitted to cross-examine the witnesses, then Lucinda Fforde could re-examine, if she desired. After the applicant's case had been presented, we would give our evidence. Then, after our case was presented, there would be closing arguments. We'd go first, with Tony's barrister to follow. Then Maeve would be allowed to make a response, after which Tony's barrister would have the final word.

Maeve Doherty positioned herself in the front row of the courtroom. I sat with Nigel Clapp directly behind her. Tony's side had exactly the same seating arrangements. I glanced at my watch: 10.31 a.m. The judge had yet to arrive. I knew already from Maeve that the hearing would be closed to members of the public, so the visitors' benches at the back of the court would remain empty. But then, suddenly, I heard a familiar voice say my name.

The voice was that of my sister, Sandy. I turned round. There she was, looking tired and disorientated, and dragging a roll-on suitcase behind her. I stood up, stunned. I said, 'What are you doing here?'

My tone wasn't wildly enthusiastic, and she picked up on this immediately. 'I just thought I should be here. Aren't you pleased?'

I gave her a quick hug and whispered, 'Of course, of course. It's just a shock, that's all. Did you just arrive? Who's looking after the kids?'

But we were interrupted by the court clerk announcing: 'Please stand.' I motioned Sandy to find a bench, and I went racing back to my spot next to Nigel Clapp. He was already standing.

'My sister,' I whispered to him.

'Oh . . . uhm . . . right,' he said.

The rear door opened, and Mr Justice Charles Traynor walked in. He was in his early sixties. Large. Imposing. Well-upholstered. With a full head of steel hair and an imperial bearing. He took his place on the platform. He bowed to us, we bowed to him. He nodded for us to sit down. He removed a pair of half-moon spectacles from the breast pocket of his suit and placed them on his nose. He cleared his throat. The clerk called the court to order. Traynor peered out at us. I could see him catch sight of the lone visitor in the back row.

'And who might you be?'

Nigel quickly whispered an explanation to Maeve Doherty, who rose and said, 'My Lord, that is the sister of the respondent, who has just arrived from the United States to be with Ms Goodchild for the hearing. We ask the court's permission to allow her to stay.'

Traynor looked towards Lucinda Fforde.

'Does the applicant's counsel wish to raise any objections?'

'One moment, please, My Lord,' she said, then leaned back and had a quick *sotto voce* conversation with Tony and his solicitor. After a moment, she stood and said, 'We have no objections, My Lord.'

'Very well, then. The visitor may stay.' He cleared his throat and asked the applicant's barrister to begin presenting her client's case.

Lucinda Fforde stood up with a little bow of the head towards the bench, and began to speak. 'My Lord, having been in receipt of my statement, you are in no doubt aware that this is, without question, a desperately sad and tragic case . . .'

With that, off she went, painting a picture of an intensely successful professional man—Anthony Hobbs, 'one of the outstanding journalists of his generation'—who had found himself involved with a woman about whom he knew very little, and who became pregnant only a few short weeks into their liaison. Of course, Mr Hobbs could have played the cad and turned his back on this woman. Instead, upon learning of his transfer back to London, he asked if she would like to accompany him—and, in fact, regularise their situation through marriage. Now though there's no doubt that Ms Goodchild had a most difficult pregnancy, and also had to cope with a most severe postnatal depression, her behaviour became exceptionally erratic, to the point where . . .

And then, as in her opening at the Interim Hearing, she listed and embellished everything they had against me. I had to hand it to her: she was brisk. She was concise. She was tough. She left the listener in no doubt that I had turned infanticidal, and that, as horrible as it was to separate a child from its mother, there was no choice in this instance. Especially as the child was happily settled with his father and Ms Dexter.

It was now Maeve's turn to outline our case, and she did so with impressive lucidity and compactness—brevity (she told me) being one of the virtues that Traynor preferred. She began by reminding the judge of my journalistic background, my long-standing work as a foreign correspondent with the *Boston Post*, my ability to cope admirably as a journalist and a woman in the Middle East. She then detailed, in about three sentences, my whirlwind romance with Mr Hobbs, falling pregnant at the age of thirty-seven, deciding to come with him to London, and then being hit with a nightmare pregnancy.

She took him through my decline and fall—her language economic, rigorous and devoid of melodramatic pity for what had befallen me.

'Though Ms Goodchild has never denied that, while in the throes of a clinical depression, she once expressed lack of concern about the child's survival, and once uttered a threat against her son, she never carried out this threat, nor committed any violent action against him. She also openly admits that, while suffering from sleep deprivation and her ongoing postnatal depression, she did accidentally breastfeed her son while taking sedatives—an incident for which she still feels remorse.

'But those three incidents I've just outlined are the entire sum total of the "crimes and misdemeanours" that my client has been accused of committing by the applicant. And out of these three incidents, the applicant manipulated the facts to initially obtain an emergency *ex parte* order against Ms Goodchild. A hearing that conveniently took place while she was out of the country at a family funeral. The applicant has since further exploited these incidents to win the Interim order, granting him residence of the child, essentially condemning Ms Goodchild as an unfit mother, and, with the exception of one pitiful hour a week, separating my client from her infant son for the past six months. I say that the applicant has acted in a ruthless, opportunistic fashion against his wife . . . and all for his own gain.'

She sat down. There was a moment's pause. Then Lucinda Fforde stood up and called her first witness: Mr Desmond Hughes.

He stepped into the witness box and took the oath.

'Mr Hughes, you are considered, are you not, one of the leading obstetrics specialists in the country,' Ms Fforde began, and then reminded the court that his witness statement had been submitted earlier. But just to verify the details of this statement, was it his opinion that Ms Goodchild's behaviour was abnormally extreme while under his care at the Mattingly Hospital?

He launched into this subject with reasoned relish, explaining how, in all his years as a consultant, I was one of the most aggressive and extreme patients he had encountered. He then went on to explain how, shortly after the birth of my son, the nurses on the ward had reported to him about my dangerously 'capricious and volatile behaviour'.

'Desperate stretches of crying,' he said, 'followed by immoderate bouts of anger, and an absolute lack of interest in the welfare of her child in the paediatric intensive care unit.'

'Now, in your witness statement,' Lucinda Fforde said, 'you emphasise this latter point, noting how one of the nurses reported to you that Ms Goodchild said—and this is a direct quote: "He *is* dying—and I don't care. You get that? I *don't* care."'

'I'm afraid that is correct. After her son was recovering from jaundice, she became extremely unsettled in front of the entire maternity ward.'

'Now it has been clinically argued that Ms Goodchild was in the throes of a postnatal depression during this time. Surely, you have dealt before with other patients suffering from this sort of condition?'

'Of course. However, I have yet to deal with a patient who reacted in such a profoundly aggressive and dangerous manner.'

'Thank you, Mr Hughes. No further questions at this juncture.'

Maeve Doherty now stood. Her voice was cool, level.

'Mr Hughes . . . I'd like to ask you when you had Ms Goodchild bound to her hospital bed?'

He looked startled. 'I never ordered that,' he said, his tone indignant.

'And when did you have her heavily tranquillised?'

'She was never heavily tranquillised. She was on a modest anti-depressant to deal with the postoperative shock she suffered from her emergency Caesarean . . .'

'And when you had her committed to the psychiatric wing of the Mattingly . . .'

'She was never committed, she was never heavily tranquillised, she was never bound to her bed.'

Maeve Doherty looked at him and smiled.

'Well, sir, having stated that, how can you then say that she was a dangerous patient?'

'It is true that she did not commit acts of physical violence, but her verbal behaviour . . .'

'But, as you just said, she was suffering from postoperative shock, not to mention trying to cope with the fact that her son was in intensive care. And there was an initial worry about whether the child had suffered brain damage during the delivery. Now, surely, under such circumstances, one might expect the patient to be rather agitated?'

'There is a large difference between agitation and . . .'

'Rudeness?'

Traynor came in here. 'Please refrain from putting words in the witness's mouth.'

'Apologies, My Lord,' Maeve Doherty said, then turned back to Hughes. 'If we have agreed that Ms Goodchild wasn't violent or so extreme in her behaviour, then how can you justify your claim that she was one of the most extreme patients you have ever dealt with?'

'Because, as I was trying to say earlier, before you interrupted me, her verbal abusiveness was so immoderate.'

'In what way immoderate?'

'She was thoroughly rude and disrespectful . . .'

'Ah,' Maeve said. 'She was *disrespectful*. Towards you, I presume?'

'Towards me and other members of the staff, yes.'

'But specifically, towards you, yes?'

'She did act in an angry manner towards me.'

'Did she use obscene language, or hurl insults at you?'

'No, not exactly . . . But she did challenge my medical judgment.'

'And that is extreme verbal abuse, in your book?'

Hughes glanced at Lucinda Fforde, like an actor asking for a prompt.

'Please answer my question,' Maeve Doherty said.

'My patients usually don't question me like that,' he said.

'But this *American* one did—and you didn't like it, did you?'

But before he could reply, she said, 'No further questions, My Lord.'

The judge asked Lucinda Fforde if she'd like to re-examine.

'Please, My Lord,' she said, standing up. 'Mr Hughes, please repeat for me the comment that one of your nurses reported as being said by Ms Goodchild when told about her son.'

Hughes stared at me with cold ire. 'She informed me that Ms Goodchild said: "He *is* dying—and I don't care. You get that? I *don't* care."'

'Thank you, Mr Hughes. No further questions.'

He looked to the judge, who informed him he could step down.

Next up was Sheila McGuire—the ward nurse who had shopped me to Hughes about the breastfeeding incident. She seemed desperately nervous and ill at ease on the stand, but she still managed to recount the entire story about how I yanked Jack off my breast in anger while feeding him, and had to be restrained from throwing him across the room.

'Now, explain this to me clearly,' Maeve said. 'Ms Goodchild just suddenly yanked the child off her breast in fury at having been bitten . . .'

'Well, it wasn't exactly a *yank*.'

'By which you mean what?'

'Well, she yanked, but she didn't intentionally *yank* . . .'

'I'm sorry, I don't follow.'

'Well . . . Ms Goodchild had been suffering from acute mastitis . . .'

'Otherwise known as inflammation of the breast which can calcify the milk flow, yes?'

'It doesn't always calcify, but it can cause a painful blockage.'

'So her breasts were profoundly swollen and painful, and then her son clamped down on her swollen nipple, and she reacted the way anyone would react if suddenly subjected to sudden pain,' Maeve said.

'Do please desist from leading the witness,' Traynor said.

'Apologies, My Lord. I will rephrase. Nurse McGuire, would you say that Ms Goodchild jumped in pain after her son bit down on her nipple?'

'Yes, that's true.'

'So the yank you speak about—it wasn't a premeditated movement, was it? It was, in fact, nothing more than a shocked reaction?'

'That's right.'

'So if we agree that she had a shocked, instinctive reaction to pull her son off her breast, then can we also agree that, for a moment, it seemed like she was about to hurl the child.'

'Absolutely.'

'But she stopped herself, didn't she?'

'Well, we were there to . . .'

'Did you make a grab for the baby?'

'Uh . . . no.'

'So Ms Goodchild stopped herself. No further questions.'

The second half of the morning was taken up with testimony from two other nurses from the Mattingly, and the point was still made that, in the eyes of the hospital nurses and my consultant, I had been seriously bad news on the ward.

Then, Jessica Law, author of the CAFCASS report, let it be known that, though I was on the road to recovery, Tony Hobbs and Diane Dexter had provided an exemplary environment for Jack. She began to wax lyrical about Chez Dexter. How the Divine Ms D. stepped into the breach and 'magnificently' provided for Jack's needs. How Mr Hobbs appeared to her as a most caring and devoted father, who had put his career on hold to care for his son on a full-time basis, and was clearly most happy in his relationship with Ms Dexter. How there was also a full-time nanny to supplement Mr Hobbs's child care. How she could not find fault with this arrangement, and how she was certain that Jack was—and this was the killer comment—'in the best place he could be right now'.

I expected Maeve Doherty to take her apart, to make her reiterate her positive assessment of my condition, and then question her about the real workings of the Hobbs/Dexter household.

But, instead, she just posed one question. 'Ms Law, in your considered opinion, doesn't Jack Hobbs deserve to be raised by both his parents?'

'Of course he does. But . . .'

'No further questions.'

I was stunned by the brevity of this cross-examination, and by the way Maeve didn't look at me on the way back to her place. Then Lucinda Fforde rose to re-examine.

'And I too just have one question for you, Ms Law. Would you mind confirming that the last sentence you spoke during my examination-in-chief was: "I am certain Jack is in the best place he could be right now".'

'Yes, that is what I said.'

'No further questions, My Lord.'

And we broke for lunch.

Once Mr Justice Traynor was out of the room and Tony and Co. swept out, looking most pleased with themselves, I turned to Maeve and said, 'May I ask you why . . . ?'

She cut me off. 'Why I didn't try to pull Jessica Law apart? Because

Traynor immediately gets his back up if anyone attacks a CAFCASS report, or the author behind it. And yes, what she said just now was harmful to us. But it would have been more harmful if I had begun to question her judgment. Trust me.'

'But what about the damage she's done?' I asked.

'Let's see what this afternoon brings,' she said. Then she told me that she and Nigel needed to go over a few things during lunch.

So Sandy and I retreated to a nearby Starbucks.

'Just like home,' she said looking around. 'You know, I think your barrister did a great job with that awful doctor and that Irish idiot of a nurse. But I don't understand why she just let that social worker woman off with just—'

'Sandy, *please* . . .'

She looked at me with a mixture of jet lag, confusion and hurt.

'I shouldn't have come, should I?'

I took her by the hand. 'I am very pleased you're here.'

'You're not just saying that.'

'No, *really*. You couldn't have been a better sister to me during this entire horrible business. Without you, I would have gone under. But . . .'

'I know, I know. The tension's unbearable now.'

I nodded.

'That's why I decided I had to come over here,' she said. 'Because I would have found it absolutely unbearable to be sitting in Boston, wondering how the hell this was going.'

'Not good, is what I'm thinking right now.'

'All right, maybe she didn't score with the social worker, but look how she dismembered Mr Big Shot Consultant . . .'

'The "social worker", as you call her, counts for everything in this case because her report is court-commissioned. You heard what Maeve said—the judge takes her word more seriously than anyone else's. Which is why this is looking so bad.'

'Who's up next this afternoon?'

'My wonderful husband.'

'I can't wait.'

I had to hand it to Tony, his testimony was masterful—a true performance. Tony in the witness box became Anthony Hobbs of the *Chronicle*: erudite, serious, a man of gravitas, yet also one of great compassion, especially when it came to dealing with his tragically wayward wife. Encouraged to wax humanitarian by Lucinda Fforde, he took her through the entire story of my breakdown, how he tried so hard to help me through it, how I rejected his support, and how he still stuck by me even after I threatened the life of our son.

Then he went into his 'friendship' with Diane Dexter—that, yes, it had always been a flirtatious friendship, but it had never been anything other than that, until his marriage began to disintegrate and he began to fear for the safety of his son. And then he made an impassioned 'new man' spiel about how fatherhood had been the best thing that had ever happened to him, how he had never really understood the remarkable joy and pleasure that having a child could bring to your life, just as he could not ask for a more remarkable (yes, he used that word twice) partner than Diane Dexter (and he looked directly at her as he sang her praises), and he was desperately, *desperately* distressed by the fact he had no choice but to take Jack away from my 'self-destructive rampage', but he did hope that, once I found my equilibrium again, I could perhaps play a role in his life. For the moment, however, he was fully committed to being Jack's 'principal carer', which is why he had decided to give up his job on the *Chronicle,* and how, when they moved to Australia next month, he would also not be seeking full-time employment for at least another year or so, in order 'to be there for Jack'.

Then Maeve Doherty stepped up to the plate. She looked at him with cool detachment.

'Mr Hobbs,' she began. 'We've just heard your appreciation of the joys of fatherhood. Which, of course, is most commendable. Just out of interest, sir, why did you wait so long before having children?'

'My Lord,' Lucinda Fforde said, sounding truly annoyed. 'I really must object to this line of questioning. What on earth does this have to do with the matter at hand?'

'Let the witness answer the question,' Traynor said.

'And I'm happy to answer it,' Tony said. 'The reason I didn't have children until I met Sally was because I was a nomadic journalist—I simply never had the chance to meet someone, settle down. But then I met Sally—and her pregnancy coincided with my return to London and the foreign editorship of the *Chronicle.* So this seemed like the ideal moment to make a commitment both to her and to fatherhood.'

'And before this, you simply had no experience of fatherhood?'

'No, none whatsoever.'

'Now Mr Hobbs, let's turn to another pertinent issue here . . . your decision to leave the *Chronicle.* You worked for the *Chronicle* for over twenty years. Is that correct?'

'Yes, that's right.'

'One of their most distinguished foreign correspondents. And then, just over a year ago, you were recalled to London to become the Foreign Editor. Were you pleased about being recalled?'

'It was difficult to adjust at first to office life again. But I did settle in . . .'

'Even though, some months later, you not only quit the foreign editorship, but also resigned from the paper. And during this same week, you also decided to end your marriage to Ms Goodchild, to seek an emergency court order in order to gain residence of your son, and move in with Ms Dexter. Quite a number of life-changing decisions in just a matter of days, wouldn't you agree?'

'The decisions I made were all predicated on the danger I perceived my son to be in.'

'All right, let's say you did decide it was important that you be at home with Jack for a while. Surely the *Chronicle* has a reasonably enlightened management, and surely, had you gone to them and said you wanted a leave of absence for personal matters, they would have been sympathetic. But to quit your job just like that, after over two decades with the paper? Why did you do that?'

'It wasn't "just like that", it was a decision which had been building for some time because I had discovered other ambitions.'

'Literary ambitions, perhaps?'

'That's right. I was writing a novel.'

'Ah yes, your novel. In her witness statement, which you have undoubtedly read, Ms Goodchild reports that, after your son came home from hospital, you became increasingly preoccupied with your novel, locking yourself up in your attic study, sleeping up there as well, making your wife deal with the broken nights and the four a.m. feeds.'

Tony had anticipated this question and was completely prepared for it. 'I think that is a profoundly unfair interpretation of the situation. After Sally lost her job . . .'

'Didn't your wife have no choice but to give up work because of a medical condition that threatened her pregnancy?'

'All right. After my wife was forced to give up work, I was the family's only source of income. I was putting in nine- to ten-hour days at the *Chronicle,* a newspaper at which I was no longer happy, and I was also attempting to fulfil a long-standing ambition to write fiction. On top of that, I was also coping with my highly unstable wife who was in the throes of a major depression . . .'

'But who was still coping with all the difficult business of child care. And for someone in the throes of a major postnatal depression, she handled all that rather remarkably, wouldn't you agree?'

'She spent nearly two months in a psychiatric ward.'

'Where your son was looked after as well. Leaving you plenty of time to develop your friendship with Ms Dexter into something else . . .'

Traynor let out one of his exasperated sighs. 'Miss Doherty, please resist the temptation to conjecture.'

'Apologies, My Lord. Now when your wife did leave hospital—and it should be pointed out that, recognising she did have a problem, she remained in that psychiatric unit of her own accord—did you not find her a calmer, more rational person?'

'From time to time, yes. But she suffered from severe mood swings that made me fear that she might lash out.'

'But she didn't lash out, did she?'

'No, but . . .'

'Returning to your book. I gather you have received an advance for your novel?'

Tony looked surprised that she knew this information.

'Yes, I've recently signed a contract with a publisher.'

'Recently—as in four months ago?'

'That's right.'

'So, up until that point, what did you do for income?'

'I had very little income.'

'But you did have Ms Dexter . . .'

'When she knew that Jack was in danger, Ms Dexter . . . Diane . . . did offer to take us in. Then when I decided to look after Jack full-time, she offered to take care of our day-to-day running expenses.'

'Now you say you're looking after Jack "full-time". But isn't it true that Ms Dexter has hired a full-time nanny to look after Jack?'

'Well, I do need time to work on my book.'

'But you said the nanny is full-time. So how many hours a day do you write?'

'Four to five.'

'And so, after the four to five hours of writing, you're with your son?'

'That's right.'

'So you really didn't leave the *Chronicle* to look after your son full-time. You left the *Chronicle* to write your novel. And Ms Dexter was there to conveniently subsidise that endeavour. Now, Mr Hobbs: your advance for this novel of yours. It was twenty thousand pounds, if I'm not mistaken?'

Again, Tony looked thrown by the fact that she knew this sum.

'That's right,' he said.

'Not a vast sum, but average for a first novel. And if I'm not mistaken, Ms Dexter hired Jack's nanny from a firm called Annie's Nannies.'

'I think that was the name of the firm, yes.'

'You *think*? Surely a committed father like yourself would have been in on this nannying decision from the start. Now, I checked with Annie's Nannies, and it seems that the average cost of a full-time nanny is, before tax, around twenty thousand pounds per annum. Which means your advance just about covers the cost of your son's child care, but nothing else. Ms Dexter does all that, doesn't she?'

Tony looked at Lucinda Fforde for guidance. She indicated that he had to answer.

'Well . . . I suppose Diane does cover the bulk of the costs.'

'But you yourself bought your wife's air ticket to the United States when she had to rush back after her brother-in-law's death.'

'Yes, that's true.'

'Did you encourage her to return to the United States?'

'I thought her sister needed her, yes.'

'Did you encourage her, Mr Hobbs?'

'Like I said, it was a family emergency, so I thought that Sally should be there.'

'Even though she was very worried about being away from her son for several days?'

'We had child care . . . our housekeeper.'

'Answer the question, please. Was she concerned about being away from her son for several days?'

Another nervous glance towards Lucinda Fforde. 'Yes, she was.'

'But you encouraged her to go. You bought her a Premium Economy ticket. And while she was out of the country, you went to court and obtained the *ex parte* court order that temporarily granted you residence of your son. Is that the correct sequence of events, Mr Hobbs?'

Tony looked deeply uncomfortable.

'Please answer the question,' Traynor said.

'Yes,' Tony said, in a low voice, 'that's the correct sequence of events.'

'No further questions,' Maeve said.

Tony did not look happy. Though he'd managed to deflect a few of her attacks, he was also someone who hated to be wrong-footed. And I thought she'd done a rather good job of that.

'Re-examination?' Traynor asked in that slightly bored voice of his.

'Yes, My Lord,' Lucinda Fforde said. 'And it is just one question, Mr Hobbs. Please remind us again why you felt it necessary to seek an emergency order, taking residence of your son.'

'Because I feared that she might fall into one of her dangerous moods again and, this time, actually carry out her threat to kill him.'

I gripped my hands tightly together, trying to force myself to stay silent. I had to admire Lucinda Fforde's supremely clever tactical logic: after all the palaver of a cross-examination, return to just one central point and undermine all the other points scored earlier against her client by one reiteration of an absolute lie.

When Tony was told he could step down, he returned to his seat next

to the Dexter woman. She gave him a little hug and whispered something into his ear. Then her name was called to enter the witness box.

She looked very impressive, standing up there. Poised, assured, just a
little regal. I could understand what Tony saw in her. Just as she—a
woman who had recently edged into fifty—would have admired his
professional accomplishments, his sardonic wit, and the fact that he
came accompanied by a child . . .

But as Lucinda Fforde took her through a review of her witness statement, it was clear how she was playing this game: the great friend who
found herself falling in love with her great friend, but knew she couldn't
break up his marriage. But then, his wife had her 'mental crisis', Tony
was desperately worried about little Jack's safety, she offered a room in
her house, one thing led to another, and . . .

'I must emphasise,' she said, 'that this wasn't a *coup de foudre*. I think I
can speak for Tony when I say that we both had these feelings for each
other for quite a number of years. Only we never had the opportunity
for involvement before now.'

Then Lucinda Fforde took her through new-found maternal feelings:
how she felt completely committed to Jack, how she only wanted the
best for him, and how she was taking a considerable amount of time off
work to be with him.

Then, finally, she came round to the subject of me.

'I've never met Sally Goodchild. I certainly hold nothing against her.
On the contrary, I feel so desperately sorry for her, and can only imagine
the horror of the past few months. And God knows, I believe in rehabil-
itation and forgiveness. Which is why I would never bar her from Jack,
and would welcome an open visiting arrangement in the future.'

Maeve Doherty stood up and smiled at the woman in the witness
stand. 'You've been married twice in the past, haven't you, Ms Dexter?'

She didn't like that question and it showed. 'Yes, that's right,' she said.

'And did you try to have children during these marriages?'

'Yes, of course I tried to have children during these marriages.'

'And you did have a miscarriage around 1990?'

'Yes, I did. And I know what your next question will be and I'd like to
answer it . . .'

The judge came in here. 'But you must first let Ms Doherty *pose* the
question.'

'I'm sorry, My Lord.'

'But yes, I would be very pleased to know what you thought my next
question would be?' Maeve said.

Dexter looked at her with calm, steely anger: '"Did you, Ms Dexter,
miscarry the baby because of drug abuse?" To which my answer would

be: Yes. I was seriously abusing cocaine at the time, and it provoked a miscarriage. I sought professional help after this tragedy. I spent two months at the Priory Clinic. I have not used or abused drugs since then. And my charitable work on drug education in schools is well known.'

'And you also attempted several IVF treatments in 1992 and 1993, both of which failed?'

Again, Dexter was taken aback by the revelation of this information. 'I don't know how you found out those facts, but they are correct.'

'And since then, you did try to adopt in . . . when was it? . . . 1996, but were turned down because of your age and your single status?'

'Yes,' she said, her voice barely a whisper.

'And then Tony Hobbs appeared in your life again, now back in London, now a new father with an infant child, and a wife who was suffering from profound clinical depression.'

Dexter looked at Maeve with barely contained rage.

'Now let me ask you this, Ms Dexter: if an acquaintance was to run into you on the street where you live, and saw you pushing Jack along in his pram, and ask: "Is he your child?" how would you respond?'

'I'd say: "Yes, I'm his mother."'

Maeve said nothing, letting that comment fill the silence in the courtroom. A silence that the judge broke.

'But you are *not* his mother, Ms Dexter,' he said.

'Not his biological mother. But I have become his surrogate mother.'

The judge peered at her over his half-moon spectacles, and spoke in that half-weary voice he so preferred. 'No, you haven't. Because it has yet to be legally determined whether or not you will be assuming the role of surrogate mother. The child in question has a mother and a father. You happen to live with the father. But that does not give you the right to state that you are the child's mother, surrogate or otherwise. Any further questions, Ms Doherty?'

'No, My Lord.'

'Re-examination, Ms Fforde?'

She looked seriously disconcerted. 'No, My Lord.'

'Then we'll reconvene after a ten-minute adjournment.'

Once he was out of the court, Maeve sat down next to Nigel and myself and said, 'Well, that wasn't bad at all.'

'Why did the judge so jump on her comment about considering herself his mother?' I asked.

'Because if there's one thing Charles Traynor hates more than barristers who try to attack a CAFCASS report, it's the new partner of someone in a divorce dispute going on as if she's the new-found parent. It goes completely against his sense of propriety or familial fair play.'

'Which is why you walked her into it?'

'Precisely.'

'What now?' I asked.

'I . . . uhm . . . think that's it for the witnesses,' said Nigel. 'So I presume the judge will reconvene just to formally end the proceedings and tell us all to be here at nine tomorrow morning.'

But when the judge returned, Lucinda Fforde had a little surprise for us. 'My Lord, we have a last-minute witness we would like to call.'

Traynor didn't looked pleased. 'And why has this witness been called at the last minute?'

'Because he's resident in the United States. In Boston, to be specific.'

I turned round and looked at Sandy, wondering if she had any idea whom they were planning to call. She shook her head.

'We were only able to obtain his statement the day before yesterday and fly him in last night. We apologise to the court for the lateness of his arrival. But he is crucial to our case and—'

'May I see his statement, please?' the judge asked, cutting her off. 'And please give a copy as well to Ms Doherty.'

She handed the statement to Traynor and to Maeve. My barrister scanned the document and didn't look pleased. In fact, she noticeably stiffened. The judge looked up from his copy of the statement and asked, 'And is Mr . . .' He peered down at the document again. '. . . Mr Grant Ogilvy here now?'

Grant Ogilvy. The name rang a distant bell somewhere.

'Yes, My Lord,' Lucinda Fforde said. 'He can testify immediately.'

'Well, what say you, Ms Doherty? You can raise all sorts of objections to this, should you wish to . . . and I would be obliged to back you up.'

I watched Maeve, and could see her thinking fast. She said, 'My Lord, with your permission, I'd like a five-minute consultation with my client before I make a decision.'

'Five minutes is fine, Ms Doherty. Court will stand in recess.'

Maeve motioned for me and Nigel to follow her outside. She found a bench. We grouped around it. She spoke in a low voice.

'Did you ever see a therapist named Grant Ogilvy?' she asked.

I put my hand to my mouth. *Him*? They found *him*?

I suddenly felt ill. Now I was certain to lose Jack.

'Ms Goodchild,' Nigel said, his voice filled with anxious concern, 'are you all right?'

I shook my head and sat down on the bench.

'Can I read what he told them?' I asked.

'Read it fast,' Maeve said, 'because we need to make a decision in about four minutes.'

I read the statement. It was what I expected. Then I handed it to Nigel. He lifted his glasses and glanced right through it.

'Uhm . . . isn't there some sort of patient/doctor confidentiality agreement about this sort of thing?' he asked.

'Yes, there is,' Maeve said, 'except when—as in this case—there is a child protection issue. Then the cloak of confidentiality can be breached. But I'm sure we could challenge it, and hold things up for weeks, and incite Traynor's ire in the process. The problem here is that tomorrow, we want to spring our surprise witness on them—which I always thought was going to be a tricky manoeuvre, but which Traynor will more readily allow if we've already accepted their surprise witness. It is a gamble, but one which I think is worth taking, as our witness will have far more bearing on the case than theirs will have. But, it has to be your decision, Sally. And, you need to make it right now.'

I took a deep breath. I exhaled. I said, 'All right. Let him testify . . .'

'Good decision,' Maeve said. 'Now you have exactly three minutes to tell me everything I need to know about what happened back then.'

When we returned to the courtroom, Maeve explained our position to Mr Justice Traynor. 'In the interests of expediting the hearing, and not causing any further delays, we will accept this last-minute witness.'

'Very well,' Traynor said. 'Please call Mr Ogilvy.'

As he walked in, I thought: Fifteen years on and he still looks almost the same. He was in his mid-fifties now. A little heavier around the middle, somewhat greyer, but still wearing that same sort of tan gabardine suit that he was sporting in 1982. He kept his line of vision aloft as he walked to the witness stand, so as not to see me. But once he was on the stand, I stared directly at him. He turned away and focused his attention on Lucinda Fforde.

'Now, Mr Ogilvy. To confirm your statement, you have been a practising psychotherapist in the Boston area for the past twenty-five years.'

'That's right.'

'And after the death of her parents in a car accident in 1988, Ms Goodchild was referred to you as a patient?'

He confirmed this fact.

'Well then, could you also please confirm what Ms Goodchild told you in the course of one of her sessions.'

For the next ten minutes, he did just that—recounting the story in just about the same way I had recounted it to Julia. He didn't try to exaggerate anything. What he said was a reasonable, accurate rendering of what I had told him. But, as my eyes bore into him, all I could think was: You haven't just betrayed me, you have also betrayed yourself.

When he finished, Lucinda Fforde looked at me and said, 'So, put rather baldly, Ms Goodchild gave her father the drink that sent him over the limit and caused him to crash the car—'

'I thoroughly object to this line of questioning, My Lord,' Maeve said, genuinely angry. 'Counsel isn't simply surmising, she is writing fiction.'

'I concur. Please rephrase, Miss Fforde.'

'With pleasure, My Lord. Though Mr Goodchild informed his daughter that he was over the limit, she still gave him the glass of wine. Is that correct?'

'Yes, that's correct.'

'And later that night, he crashed his car into another vehicle, killing himself, his wife, a young woman in her thirties, and her fourteen-month-old son?'

'Yes, that's correct.'

'And did Ms Goodchild share this information with anyone else?'

'Not to my knowledge.'

'Not with her one sibling, her sister?'

'Unless she did so in the last two decades, no. Because, one of the central themes of her conversations with me was that she couldn't confess this fact to her sister. She couldn't confess it to anyone.'

Suddenly, I heard a choked sob behind me. Then Sandy stood and ran out of the back door of the court. I started to stand up, but Nigel Clapp did something very un-Nigel Clapp. He grabbed my arm and caught me before I could give pursuit, whispering quickly, 'You mustn't leave.'

Back up front, Lucinda Fforde said, 'No further questions, My Lord.'

Maeve Doherty stood up and simply stared at Grant Ogilvy. She held this glare for a good thirty seconds. He tried to meet her contemptuous gaze, but eventually turned away. Mr Justice Traynor cleared his throat.

'You won't be kept here much longer, Mr Ogilvy,' Maeve said. 'Because I really don't want to spend much time talking to you.' She paused. 'How old was Ms Goodchild when she saw you as a patient?'

'Twenty-one.'

'How old was her father when he died?'

'Around fifty, I think.'

'Ms Goodchild handed him a drink at that party, yes?'

'Yes.'

'He refused.'

'Yes.'

'She said, "You going middle-aged on me, Dad?" And he drank the drink. Is that right?'

'Yes.'

'And you believe, because of that, she should be held culpable for the fatal accident he had several hours later?'

'I have never been asked to comment on her culpability.'

'But you've been brought all this way across the Atlantic to sully her character, haven't you?'

'I was brought here simply to relate the information she told me.'

'While she was a patient of yours, yes?'

'That's right.'

'And what are they paying you for your trouble?'

'My Lord, I do hate to interrupt,' Lucinda Fforde said, 'but this is improper.'

'Oh, *please*,' Maeve hissed. 'He's obviously not over here for altruistic reasons.'

'We are running out of time, Ms Doherty,' Traynor said. 'Is this line of questioning likely to take matters further?'

'I have no further questions for this . . . *gentleman*.'

Traynor heaved a huge sigh of relief. He could go home now.

'The witness is dismissed. Court is adjourned until nine a.m. tomorrow.'

As soon as Traynor had left the court, I was on my feet, racing out of the back door in search of Sandy. I found her on a bench in the hallway, her eyes red, her face wet. I tried to touch her shoulder. She shrugged me off.

'Sandy . . .'

The door of the courtroom opened, and out came Grant Ogilvy, accompanied by Tony's solicitor. Before I could stop her, Sandy was in his face.

'I'm going back to Boston in two days,' she yelled, 'and I'm going to make certain everyone who counts in your profession knows what you did here today. You understand? I am going to ruin you.'

A court usher, hearing her raised voice, came running towards the scene. But Tony's solicitor shooed him away.

'It's over now,' he whispered, and hustled a wide-eyed and deeply distressed Grant Ogilvy out of the building.

I turned towards Sandy, but she walked away from me. Maeve and Nigel were at the door of the courtroom, looking on.

'Is she going to be all right?' Maeve asked.

'She just needs to calm down. It's a dreadful shock for her.'

'And for you too,' Nigel added. 'Are you all right?'

I ignored the question and asked Maeve, 'How much damage do you think he did?'

'The truth is: I don't know,' she said. 'But the important thing now is: go and deal with your sister, try to stay calm, and, most of all, get a good night's sleep. Tomorrow will be a very long day.'

I noticed Nigel had Sandy's roll-on bag beside him.

'She left this behind,' he said. 'Anything I can do?'

I shook my head. He awkwardly reached over and touched my arm.

'Ms Goodchild . . . Sally . . . what you were just put through was so dreadfully wrong.'

As I went off to find Sandy, I realised that that was the one time Nigel Clapp had ever called me by my first name.

ELEVEN

SANDY WAS WAITING outside the court, leaning against a pillar.

'Let's get a cab,' I said.

'Whatever.'

In the ride back to Putney, she didn't say a word to me. She just leaned against one side of the taxi, exhausted, spent, in one of those dark states that I had got to know during childhood. I didn't blame her for being in such a black place. As far as she was concerned, I had betrayed her. And she was right. And now I didn't have a clue about how I should (or could) make amends for such a huge error of judgment.

When we reached the house, I made up the guest bed and showed her where the bathroom was, and let her know that there was plenty of microwavable food in the fridge. But if she wanted to eat with me . . .

'What I want is a bath, a snack, and bed. We'll talk tomorrow.'

'Well, I'm going to take a walk then.'

What I wanted to do was knock on Julia's door and ask her to allow me to scream on her shoulder for a bit. But as I approached my front door, I saw a note that had landed on the inside mat. It was from her, saying:

Desperate to know how it went today . . . but had to go out to a last-minute business thing. I should be home by eleven. If you're still up then, do feel free to knock on the door.
Hope you got through it all.
Love, Julia

God, how I needed to talk to her, to anyone. But instead, I took what solace I could from a walk along the river. When I got back I found that Sandy had indeed eaten a Chicken Madras and had taken her jet lag and her anger to bed early.

I picked at a microwaved Spaghetti Carbonara, then ran myself a bath.

299

I took the necessary dose of antidepressants and sleeping pills. I crawled into bed. The chemicals did their job for around five hours. When I woke, the clock read 4.30 a.m., and all I could feel was dread. Dread about my testimony later today. Dread about yesterday's debacle with Sandy. Dread about the influence that Grant Ogilvy would have on the judge's decision. Dread, most of all, that I was now destined to lose Jack.

I went down to the kitchen to make myself a cup of herbal tea. As I walked by the living room, I saw that the light was on. Sandy was stretched out on the sofa, awake, lost in middle-of-the-night thought.

'Hi,' I said. 'Can I get you anything?'

'You know what really kills me?' she said. 'It's not that you gave Dad that last drink. No, what so upsets me is that you couldn't tell me.'

'I wanted to, but . . .'

'I know, I know. And I understand all your reasons. But to keep that to yourself for all these years . . . Jesus Christ, Sally . . . didn't you think I'd understand? Didn't you?'

'I just couldn't bring myself to admit . . .'

'What? That you've been carrying fifteen years' worth of guilt for no damn reason? I could have talked you out of your guilt in a heartbeat. But you chose not to let me. That's what really staggers me.'

'You're right.'

'I know I'm right.' She laughed a cheerless laugh and pushed herself up off the sofa. 'I think I'll try to get two more hours of sleep.'

'Good idea.'

But I couldn't sleep. I just took up her place on the sofa and tried to fathom why I hadn't been able to tell her what I should have told her.

Somewhere over the next few hours, I did nod off, and then found myself being nudged by Sandy, who had a mug of coffee in one hand.

'It's eight o'clock,' she said, 'and this is your wake-up call.'

I slurped down the coffee. I took a fast shower. I put on my good suit again. I did a little damage control with foundation and blusher. We were out of the door and on the tube by nine fifteen.

'Sleep all right?' Maeve asked me as we settled down in the front left-hand bench of the court.

'Not bad.'

'And how is your sister?'

'A bit better, I think.'

Just then Nigel showed up, accompanied by Rose Keating. She gave me a little hug.

'You didn't think I was going to miss this, did you?' she asked. 'Who's the woman in the back row?'

'My sister,' I said.

'All the way over here from the States to support you? Good on her. I'll sit with her.'

'How is our last-minute witness?' Maeve asked.

'Due here this afternoon, as requested,' she said.

Tony and Co. then arrived, his lawyers nodding with their counterparts on this side of the court. Then the court clerk stood up and asked us to do so as well. Mr Justice Traynor entered, sat down, greeted us with a brief 'Good morning', and called the hearing to order.

It was now Maeve's turn to present our case. And so she called her first witness: Dr Rodale.

Maeve got her to recite her professional qualifications, her long-standing association with St Martin's, the fact that she'd had more than two decades' experience of treating women with postnatal depression, and had written several medical papers on the subject. She then had her outline, briefly, the emotional and physiological roller-coaster ride that was this condition; how it sneaked up unawares on its victims, how it often caused those in its vortex to do uncharacteristic things like uttering threats, becoming suicidal, refusing to eat or wash, committing violent acts . . . and how, with rare exceptions, it was always treatable.

Then she detailed my clinical case.

When she had finished Maeve asked her, 'In your opinion, is Ms Goodchild fully capable of resuming the role of full-time mother?'

She looked straight at Tony and said, 'In my opinion, she was fully capable of that role when she was discharged from hospital.'

'No further questions, My Lord.'

Lucinda Fforde stood up. 'Dr Rodale, during the course of your twenty-five-year career, how many women have you treated for postnatal depression?'

'Around five hundred, I'd guess.'

'And, of these, how many documented cases can you remember of a mother threatening to kill her child?'

Dr Rodale looked most uncomfortable with this question. 'Well . . . to be honest about it, I only remember three other *reported* instances . . .'

'Only *three* other instances, out of five hundred cases. It's obviously a pretty rare threat to make then. And let me ask you this: of those three cases . . . actually four, if you include Ms Goodchild, how many of those actually went on to murder their child?'

Dr Rodale looked straight at Lucinda Fforde. 'Only one of those women went on to kill her child.'

A triumphant smile crossed the lips of Lucinda Fforde. 'So, given that, one of those four women actually killed her child, there was a twenty-five per cent chance that Ms Goodchild would have killed her child.'

301

'My Lord—'

But before Maeve could utter anything more, Lucinda Fforde said, 'No further questions.'

'Re-examination?'

'Absolutely, My Lord,' Maeve said, sounding furious. 'Dr Rodale, please tell us about the patient who killed her child.'

'She was suffering from extreme schizophrenia, and one of the worst cases of manic depression I've ever treated. She had been sectioned, and the murder happened on a supervised visit with her child, when the supervisor became physically ill and had to leave the room for no more than a minute to seek help. When she returned, the mother had snapped her child's neck.'

There was a long silence.

'How rare is this sort of case in postnatal depression?' Maeve asked.

'Rarer than rare. As I said, it's the one instance in five hundred or so cases I've treated. And I must emphasise again that, unlike all the other cases, this was one where the patient was essentially psychotic.'

'So there is absolutely no relation whatsoever with the condition suffered by the woman who killed her child, and that of Ms Goodchild?'

'Absolutely none whatsoever. And anyone who attempts to make that sort of comparison is guilty of a monstrous manipulation of the truth.'

'Thank you, Doctor. No further questions.'

Next up was Clarice Chambers. She smiled at me from the witness box and, under gentle, brief questioning from Maeve, told her how well I had 'bonded' with Jack, the grief I had displayed at our first supervised visit, and the way I had been able to establish a genuine rapport with him during our hourly visits each week. And then Maeve asked her virtually the same question she had posed to Dr Rodale.

'As you have been the one-and-only person to have watched the interaction of Ms Goodchild and her son over the past months, is it your professional opinion that she is a caring mother?'

'A *completely* caring mother, in whom I have the greatest confidence.'

'Thank you. No further questions.'

Once again, Lucinda Fforde played the 'I have just one question for you' game. And the question was, 'In your experience, don't all mothers who have been legally prevented from unsupervised contact with their child—due to worries about the child's safety—don't they always express terrible grief in front of you?'

'Of course they do. Because—'

'No further questions.'

'Re-examination?'

'Ms Chambers, is it true that, for the past six weeks, you have allowed

Ms Goodchild to have unsupervised contact with her child?'

'That is completely correct.'

'And why have you permitted this?'

'Because it's clear to me that she is a normally functioning person, who presents no danger whatsoever to her child. In fact, I've actually felt that way about her since the beginning.'

'Thank you very much, Ms Chambers.'

Moving right along, Jane Sanjay took the stand. She explained that she had been my health visitor, and had seen me several times after I had come out of hospital with Jack. She reported that she had no doubts about my competence as a mother. Maeve asked, 'However, this was before the full-scale effects of the postnatal depression had afflicted her, is that correct?'

'Yes, that's true. But she was, at the time, obviously suffering from exhaustion, postoperative stress, not to mention ferocious worry about her son's condition. The exhaustion was also exacerbated by sleep deprivation, and the fact that she had no help at home. So, under the circumstances, I thought she was coping brilliantly.'

'So there was nothing in her behaviour to indicate a woman who could not deal with the day-to-day business of child care?'

'Nothing at all.'

'You know, of course, that she did accidentally breastfeed her son while taking a sedative. Is that, in your experience, a rare occurrence?'

'Hardly. We must have a dozen of those cases a year in Wandsworth. It's a common mistake. The mother isn't sleeping, so she's on sleeping pills. She's told, "Don't breastfeed while taking the pills." The child wakes up in the middle of the night. The mother is befuddled. She breastfeeds the child. And though the child goes floppy for a bit, he or she simply sleeps it off. And in the case of Sally . . . sorry, Ms Goodchild . . . the fact that this happened didn't have any bearing whatsoever on my opinion that she was a thoroughly competent mother.'

'No further questions.'

Up came Lucinda Fforde. 'Now, Ms Sanjay, didn't the breastfeeding incident of which you speak happen *after* your dealings with Ms Goodchild?'

'That's right. She entered hospital for a time thereafter.'

'She *entered* a psychiatric unit thereafter . . . the breastfeeding incident being the event that brought her to hospital. So how can you say that you *know* that this incident was just a mistake if you weren't there?'

'Because I've dealt with these sorts of cases before.'

'But you didn't specifically deal with this one . . .'

'I dealt with Ms Goodchild . . .'

'But *before* the incident, is that not right?'

Pause. Jane was cornered and she knew it. 'Yes, that's right.'

'As for your claim that "though the child goes floppy for a bit, he or she just sleeps off the drugs", I have a clipping here from the *Scotsman*, dated March 28 of this year—a short news item, detailing a death of a two-week-old boy in a Glasgow hospital after his mother breastfed him while taking a similar sedative. No more questions.'

'Re-examination, Ms Doherty?'

'Yes, My Lord. Ms Sanjay, have you ever dealt with a death like the one just described?'

'Never. But I am certain it could happen. I'd be interested to know if that mother in Scotland had been a drug addict, because many addicts mainline high doses of the drug. And if you then breastfed a baby after mainlining an overdose of sedatives, well, a tragedy like that can happen.'

The judge came in here. 'Just out of interest, was the Glaswegian mother a drug addict, Ms Fforde?'

Ms Fforde looked profoundly uncomfortable. 'She was, My Lord.'

After Jane was dismissed, the moment I was dreading had arrived. Maeve Doherty called my name. I walked down the aisle, entered the witness box, took the oath. I looked out at the courtroom with sheer terror.

Maeve was brilliant. She stuck to the script. She didn't ooze sympathy ('That won't play with Traynor'), nor did she lead me by the nose. But, point-by-point, she got me to explain the whirlwind nature of my relationship with Tony, my feelings about falling pregnant in my late thirties, my difficult pregnancy, the horror of discovering that Jack was in intensive care after his birth, and the fact that I began to feel myself mentally slipping into a black swamp.

'You know, the expression, "In a dark wood"?' I said.

'Dante,' Mr Justice Traynor interjected.

'Yes, Dante. And an apt description of where I found myself.'

'And in those moments of lucidity when you re-emerged from this "dark wood",' Maeve asked, 'how did you feel about shouting at doctors, or making those two unfortunate comments about your son, or accidentally breastfeeding him while on sleeping pills?'

'Horrible. Beyond horrible. And I still feel horrible about it. I know I was ill at the time, but that doesn't lessen my guilt or my shame.'

'Do you feel anger towards your husband about how he has behaved?'

'Yes, I do. I also feel that what's happened to me has been so desperately unfair, not to mention the most painful experience in my life . . . even more so than the death of my parents. Because Jack is my son. The centre of my life. And because he's been taken away from me—and for reasons that haven't just struck me as unjust, but also trumped up.'

'No further questions, My Lord,' Maeve said.

Lucinda Fforde now looked at me and smiled. The smile of someone who wants to unnerve you, wants you to know they've got you in their sights and are about to pull the trigger.

'Ms Goodchild, after being told of your son's critical condition while at the Mattingly Hospital, did you say: "He *is* dying—and I don't care. You get that? I *don't* care"?'

I gripped the rail of the witness stand. 'Yes, I did.'

'Did you, a few weeks later, call your husband's secretary at work and say: "Tell him if he's not home in the next sixty minutes, I'm going to kill our son"?'

'Yes, I did.'

'Did you breastfeed your son while taking sedatives after being specifically told *not* to do so by your GP?'

'Yes, I did.'

'Did your son end up in hospital after this incident?'

'Yes, he did.'

'Were you hospitalised for nearly two months in a psychiatric unit after this incident?'

'Yes, I was.'

'In 1988, did your father attend your commencement party at Mount Holyoke College in Massachusetts?'

'Yes, he did.'

'Did you give him a glass of wine at that party?'

'Yes, I did.'

'Did he tell you that he didn't want that glass of wine?'

'Yes, he did.'

'But you made the comment, "You going middle-aged on me, Dad?" and he downed the wine. Was that the correct sequence of events?'

'Yes.'

'Did he then drive off later that evening, killing himself, your mother, and two innocent passengers in another car?'

'Yes, he did.'

'I thank you, Ms Goodchild, for confirming that all the major accusations against you are correct ones. No more questions, My Lord.'

'Re-examination, Ms Doherty?'

'Yes, My Lord. But before I begin, I would like to take issue with the fact that Counsel used the word "accusations" in the context of my client. It should be noted that Ms Goodchild is *not* on trial here.'

'Noted,' Traynor said, with a bored sigh.

'Ms Goodchild, did you mean what you said *when* you said: "He *is* dying—and I don't care. You get that? I *don't* care"?'

'No, I didn't mean it at all. I was suffering from postoperative shock.'

'Did you mean what you said when you threatened the life of your child?'

'No. I was suffering from clinical depression.'

'Did you ever commit any violent act against your child?'

'Never.'

'Did you ever breastfeed him again while taking sedatives?'

'Never.'

'Are you now over your postnatal depression?'

'I am.'

'Did you give a glass of wine to your father on the fateful June night in 1988?'

'Yes, I did.'

'Now even though you didn't force it down his throat—and, in fact, made nothing more than a flippant comment—do you still feel guilty about giving him that glass of wine?'

'Yes, I do. I've always felt guilty about it. And I've lived with that guilt, day-in, day-out, for all these years.'

'But do you think you deserve that guilt?'

'Whether or not I deserve it, it is there.'

'I think that's called having a conscience. Thank you, Ms Goodchild, for so clearly stating the *real* facts of this case. No more questions.'

I stepped down from the stand. I walked down the aisle. I sat down next to Nigel Clapp. He touched my shoulder and said, 'Well done.'

High praise from Mr Clapp. But I still thought that Fforde had scored serious points against me, and had pointed up, for Traynor, the fact that I had validated all the accusations against me.

There was one more witness before lunch. Diane Dexter's former housekeeper. Her name was Isabella Paz. In Ms Dexter's employ until four months ago. And she confirmed that Mr Hobbs had been a regular guest to her residence since 1998 . . . and no, they did not sleep in separate rooms during these occasional visits that occurred when he was back in London from assorted overseas postings. She confirmed that Ms Dexter had gone on holiday with him in 1999 and 2000, and that she had spent a month with him in Cairo in 2001. And yes, he had been regularly visiting Ms Dexter since then—and, in fact, all but moved into her house for around eight weeks this past year . . . which, as Maeve Doherty helpfully added, were the eight weeks when Jack and I were resident in the psychiatric unit of St Martin's.

'In other words, Mr Hobbs and Ms Dexter had been carrying on an occasional romance since 1999, and a rather steady romance since his return to London in 2002?'

'That was how I saw it, yes,' she said.

During her cross-examination, Lucinda Fforde said, 'Weren't you fired by Ms Dexter for theft?'

'Yes—but then she took back what she said, and paid me money.'

'And before Ms Dexter, didn't you work for a Mr and Mrs Robert Reynolds of London SW5?'

'Yes, I did.'

'And weren't you fired from that job as well? For theft again?'

'Yes, but—'

'No further questions.'

'Re-examination?'

'A very fast question, Ms Paz,' Maeve said. 'Were you ever charged with theft by Mr and Mrs Reynolds. Officially charged, that is?'

'No.'

'And if the court wanted proof of the dates of, say, the holidays Ms Dexter took with Mr Hobbs, how could they obtain proof?'

'She keeps a diary by the phone, writes everything in it. Where she's going, who with. Once the year is finished, she puts the diary in a cabinet under the phone. She must have ten years of diaries down there.'

'Thank you, Ms Paz.'

When we broke for lunch, Nigel and Rose shot off to find our last-minute witness. Maeve excused herself to prepare for her final examination. So Sandy and I took a walk by the Thames. We didn't say much—the pressure of the hearing and yesterday's revelations stifling any serious conversation. But my sister did suggest that the morning went well for me.

'But how well?'

'Tony and his rich bitch were caught out lying about the newness of their relationship, and about only being just friends until after he snatched Jack. And I thought you were impressive.'

'I hear a *but* coming on.'

'*But* . . . I did think that Tony's barrister nailed you in her cross-examination. Not that you did anything wrong. Just that all the question marks hanging over you were confirmed by you. But maybe I'm just being overly pessimistic.'

'No, you're completely spot-on.'

When we returned to the court after the two-hour recess, Maeve was sitting alone on our side of the court and told me that, in order to ensure that Tony and Co. didn't run into our surprise witness, Nigel and Rose were dawdling with her in a coffee bar nearby. And as soon as the other side were in place . . .

In they walked, Tony and I pretending that there was a Berlin Wall between us. Immediately, Maeve was dashing up the aisle, her mobile phone in her hand. She was back within a minute, breathless, just as the clerk was calling the court to order. Traynor came in, just as Nigel came rushing down the aisle to slide in next to me. Traynor didn't like this at all. 'A little late, are we, sir?' he asked.

Poor Nigel looked mortified. 'I'm . . . uhm . . . sorry, My Lord.'

'So, Ms Doherty,' Traynor said. 'We *are* going to finish up this after-noon, I hope?'

'Without question, My Lord. But I must inform the court that, like the applicant, we also have a last-minute witness.'

Traynor's lips tightened. He didn't like this news at all.

'And why is this witness last minute?' Traynor asked.

'We were only able to obtain her statement in the past day—and it was still being proofed this morning.'

'Is the witness here now?'

'She is, My Lord.'

'May we know her name, please?'

Maeve turned slightly to aim her statement in the direction of Tony. 'Of course, My Lord. Her name is Elaine Kendall.'

Tony immediately started whispering into the ear of Lucinda Fforde. His instantaneous panic was evident.

'And do you have the statement from Ms Kendall?' the judge asked.

'We do, My Lord.' She handed out copies of the statement to the judge, to Lucinda Fforde, and to her solicitor. I watched as Tony relieved the solicitor of his copy, and scanned it, becoming increasingly perturbed with each paragraph, then loudly saying, 'This is outrageous.'

Traynor peered at him over his half-moon specs and asked, 'Please refrain from disturbing this courtroom, Mr Hobbs.'

Lucinda Fforde put a steadying hand on his shoulder and said, 'My client apologises for that small outburst, My Lord. Might I have a minute to consult with him?'

'A minute is fine,' he said.

There was a very fast, agitated huddle in Tony's corner.

'So, Miss Fforde,' Traynor said when the minute was up. 'Do you object to this last-minute witness?'

'I do, My Lord.'

'Well,' he said, 'given that the respondent's counsel accepted your last-minute witness yesterday—and given that none of us wants to have this case part-heard—I am going to allow this witness to be examined.'

'My Lord, I wish to speak with my client for a moment about whether he wishes me to lodge an objection, and also ask for a suspension of this hearing until such time as . . .'

'Yes, yes, we all know how that sentence finishes, Ms Fforde,' Traynor said. 'And the ball is, as they say, firmly in your court. Either you accept Counsel's last-minute witness—as she accepted yours yesterday—or we all say goodbye until four months from now, as I am going on circuit after the summer recess. The choice is between yourself and your client.'

'Thank you, My Lord.'

There was another frantic huddle on Tony's side of the court. Only this time, the Dexter woman was very much involved in this whispered debate—and it was clear that she had a very forceful point of view.

As they continued their hushed discussion, Maeve leaned over to me and whispered, 'Australia.'

Suddenly, I saw the brilliant stratagem behind Maeve's gamble. Knowing full well that Diane Dexter needed to be in Sydney as soon as possible to get her new office up and running, she wagered that Dexter would raise major objections when our side threatened a suspension of the hearing. Because that would mean Tony and Jack wouldn't be able to join her for at least four months—if, that is, Traynor ruled in their favour at that future time.

Their debate continued for another minute, during which time Tony tried to raise an objection, but was hissed down by Dexter. He looked rather defeated.

'So, Miss Fforde,' Traynor said, interrupting this conclave. 'Have you and your client reached a decision?'

Fforde looked directly at Dexter, who nodded affirmatively at her. Then she turned to Traynor and said, 'With reluctance, but not wishing to delay the conclusion of these proceedings any further, we will accept the respondent's new witness.'

Traynor looked most relieved. So too did Maeve Doherty, who afforded herself the most momentary of smiles. Traynor said, 'Please call your witness, Ms Doherty.'

'Elaine Kendall, My Lord.'

Elaine Kendall was a small, rather tired-looking woman in her late forties, with a smoker's face and fatigued eyes. She entered the witness box and stared straight at Tony with a look of joyless disdain. She took the oath, she steadied herself, Maeve began.

'Ms Kendall, would you tell the court how you know Mr Tony Hobbs?'

She started telling her story in a slow, hesitant voice. She had grown up in Amersham, and at Christmas 1982 she was working at a local pub when in came 'that gentleman sitting over there'. They got chatting over the course of the evening ('I was serving him, you see'), and he explained he was back in Amersham visiting his parents, and that he was some big deal foreign correspondent for the *Chronicle*.

'Anyway, he was very charming, very sophisticated, and once I was finished work, he asked me out for a drink. We went to a club. We drank far too much. One thing led to another, and we woke up next to each other the following morning.

'After that, he vanished. A couple of weeks later, I discovered I was pregnant. I tried to contact him through the newspaper, but got nowhere. And my dad and mum being real Irish Catholic and all . . . well, there was no way I was not keeping the baby. But . . . that man . . . he was in Egypt or somewhere at the time, and though we kept trying to get in touch with him, there was just silence from his side.

'Eventually, we had to hire a solicitor, make a fuss with his paper. Way I heard it, his bosses told him he had to settle this somehow, so he finally agreed to pay me some sort of child support.'

'What was that amount?'

'Fifty quid a month back in '83. We managed to get another solicitor on the job around '91. He got him up to a hundred and twenty-five pounds a month.'

'And Mr Hobbs never showed the slightest bit of interest in you or your son . . . ?'

'Jonathan. He was called Jonathan. And no, that man didn't want to know. Every year, I'd send him a picture of his boy, care of the *Chronicle*. Never a reply.'

'And—although I know the answer to this question, and must apologise to you for raising such a painful subject—where is your son now?'

'He died in 1995. Leukaemia.'

'That must have been terrible.'

'It was,' she said.

'Did you write to Mr Hobbs, informing him of his son's death?'

'I did. And I called the paper too, asking them to contact him. Never a word. I thought, at the very least, he could have called me then. It would have been such a small, decent gesture.'

Maeve Doherty said nothing for a moment, holding the silence. Then, 'No more questions.'

Lucinda Fforde had a frantic huddle with Tony. I looked over at Dexter. She was sitting there, cold, impassive.

'Ms Fforde?' Traynor asked. 'Do you wish to cross-examine?'

'Yes, My Lord,' she said, but I could see that she was desperately trying to find an impromptu strategy, a damage limitation reaction. And God, was she fast on her feet. Because she said, 'Ms Kendall, as much as I appreciate the tragedy of your story . . . I must ask you this: do you really think a one-night fling constitutes a life-time commitment?'

'When the result is a son, yes, I do.'

'But didn't Mr Hobbs make an ongoing financial commitment to you and your son?'

'A measly commitment, which my solicitor had to fight for.'

'But . . . I presume you were a sexually active woman at the time. After all, you did sleep with Mr Hobbs after just one night. Surely he could have demanded a paternity test?'

'I wasn't the local mattress. It was his baby. I'd slept with nobody before him for about a year.'

'But did he demand a paternity test?'

'No . . . he didn't.'

'You received a sum of money from the man who fathered your child. And surely fifty pounds meant something in 1983. Just as a hundred and twenty-five pounds meant something in the early nineties. So he did meet his responsibilities to you. And in the matter of the death of your son . . . you must recognise the fact that, as tragic as that death may have been for you, he had absolutely no connection with the boy. So . . .'

Suddenly, Elaine Kendall began to sob. She struggled to control it, but couldn't. It took her nearly a minute to bring herself under control, during which time everyone in the court could do nothing but watch hopelessly. Watching her sob, I felt nothing but shame.

When she finally stopped crying, she turned to the judge and said, 'I must apologise, My Lord. Jonathan was my only child. And even now, it's hard to talk about it. So I am sorry . . .'

'Ms Kendall, you owe this court no apology. On the contrary, it is we who owe you an apology.'

Then, sending a dagger-like look in the direction of Ms Fforde, he asked, 'Have you any further cross-examination, Ms Fforde?'

'No, My Lord.'

He gave Maeve a similar withering look and asked, 'Re-examination, Ms Doherty?'

'No, My Lord.'

'Ms Kendall, you are free to leave.'

She left the witness stand.

Traynor said nothing for a few moments. It was clear that he had been affected by the sight of that poor woman sobbing in the witness box. As soon as Elaine Kendall was out of court, Traynor glanced at his watch and said, 'As that was the last witness for the respondent, I would now like to hear closing submissions.'

But I didn't hear those two arguments, let alone the responses, or Lucinda Fforde exercising her legal right (as counsel for the applicant) to have the final word. Though I didn't move from my seat and was in clear hearing range of both barristers, something in me shut off. I just sat there, staring at the floor, willing myself not to hear—and succeeding.

Then Nigel Clapp was nudging me. Traynor was speaking.

'As that concludes all evidence and submissions in this hearing, I am now going off to consider my judgment. And I shall return in two hours' time to deliver it.'

This snapped me back to the here and now. After Traynor took his leave, I leaned forward to Maeve and urgently asked, 'If he's giving his judgment in two hours, does it mean he's already written most of it?'

'Perhaps he has,' she said, sounding deflated. 'Then again, he might just want to avoid coming to work tomorrow. I know that sounds prosaic, but it's the truth. He's noted for getting things done quickly.'

'Especially when he's already decided what the outcome will be?'

'I'm afraid so.'

I glanced across the court. There, opposite us, sat Diane Dexter. Immobile. There, next to her, was Tony, frantically whispering to her, trying to bring her around, their relationship suddenly gone haywire after the revelation just disclosed. A revelation that only came out because they had tried to rob me of my child. Which had given me no option but to lash out and find something to undermine them. No one wins in a case like this. Everyone comes out looking shabby and squalid.

I put my hand on Maeve's shoulder. 'Whatever happens now, I cannot thank you enough.'

She shook her head. 'I'm going to be straight with you, Sally. I think it looks bad. I could tell that Traynor truly hated our final flourish. Especially poor Elaine Kendall.'

'That was my fault. My great proactive move.'

'No, it was the right move. And what she said needed to be said.'

'What are you going to do for the next two hours?'

'Go back to chambers. And you?'

I grabbed my sister from the back of the court. We walked across Waterloo Bridge and lined up for last-minute tickets to the London Eye. Up we went, the city stretched out on all sides of us. Sandy peered out west—past the Palace, the Albert Hall, the green lushness of Kensington Gardens, the high residential grandness of Holland Park, into the endless suburban beyond.

'You say this town has got its great moments,' she said, 'but I bet most of the time, it's just grim.'

Which kind of sums up so much of life, doesn't it?

Having been released from that massive ferris wheel, we bought ice creams like a pair of tourists temporarily freed from the day-to-day demands of life. Then we crossed the bridge back to The Strand, and entered the High Court for what I knew would be the last time.

When we reached the court, Sandy asked, 'Can I sit next to you for the judgment?'

'I'd like that.'

Tony and his team were already in place when we got back. But I noticed that Diane Dexter was now sitting next to their solicitor. Maeve was in the front row next to Nigel. No one greeted each other. No one said a thing. Sandy and I sat down. The aura of fear was everywhere.

Five minutes went by, then ten. Then the clerk entered. And we all stood up. Traynor walked slowly to the bench, a folder held between his long, elegant fingers. He bowed. He sat down. We bowed. We all sat down. He opened his file. He started reading.

'Let me say at the start that, in the two brief days of this Final Hearing, we have had much dirty linen washed in a most public way. We have learned that Mr Hobbs had a son, and that he forged no relationship with this child. We've learned that Mr Hobbs's new partner, Ms Dexter, had a drug addiction problem, which she courageously overcame after it caused her to miscarry a child. We've also learned that Ms Dexter has gone to extreme lengths to have children . . . to the point where, if the respondent's counsel is to be believed, she was willing to conspire with her partner to snatch his child away from its mother, on allegedly trumped-up charges of threatened child abuse.'

Sandy glanced at me. Traynor had just hinted that he hadn't bought our case.

'We have learned that, over twenty years ago, Ms Goodchild handed her father a drink which may—or may not—have put him over the legal limit, and may, or may not, have contributed to the fatal accident in which he was killed along with his wife and two innocent people.

'And we've also learned that Ms Dexter and Mr Hobbs weren't particularly honest about the actual duration of their relationship . . . though, in truth, the court can't really see the importance of whether they were first intimate three years ago or just three months ago.'

Another nervous glance between Sandy and myself.

'And I say that because, amidst all the evidence, the central issue has been obscured: what is best for the child? That is the one and *only* issue here. Everything else, in the opinion of the court, is extraneous.

'Now, without question, the relationship between a mother and her child is the most pivotal one in life. The mother brings us into life, she suckles us, she nurtures us in the most critical early stages of our existence. For this reason, the law is most reluctant to disturb, let alone rupture, this primordial relationship—unless the trust which society places in a mother has been profoundly breached.

'Earlier today, counsel for the applicant outlined the "accusations", as she called them, against the respondent. And it must be acknowledged that these accusations are most grave and serious. Just as it must also be acknowledged that the respondent was suffering from a severe clinical disorder that impaired her judgment, and also caused her to behave in a thoroughly irrational way.

'But while acknowledging said clinical condition, can the court risk jeopardising the child's welfare? This is the central dilemma that the court has had to address. Just as it has also had to study whether the child's welfare will be better served by being placed in the care of its father and his new partner—a woman who may claim to be his surrogate mother, but who will never, in the eyes of this court, be considered so.'

He paused. He looked up over his glasses in my direction.

'Threatening a child's life—even in delusional anger—is a most serious matter . . .'

Sandy reached over and clasped my hand, as if to say: I'll be holding you as he sends you over the edge.

'Doing so twice is profoundly worrying. So too is poisoning a child with sleeping tablets—even though it was the result of a befuddled accident. But are these actions enough to break that primordial bond between mother and child? Especially when questions must be raised about the ulterior motives of the child's father, and the real reasons for the legal action he took eight months ago to gain residence of the child?

'Ultimately, however, we turn, once again, to the heart of the matter: if the mother is granted sole or shared residence of the child, will she act on the threats she made earlier? Shouldn't we be prudent in this case, and thus breach that primordial maternal bond, in order to serve the best interests of the child?'

Traynor paused and sipped at a glass of water. In front of me, Nigel Clapp put his hand to his face. Because that last sentence had given the game away. We'd lost.

Traynor put the water down and continued to read.

'These are the questions that the court has had to ponder. Large, taxing questions. And yet, when all the evidence is carefully studied, there is a clear answer to all these questions.'

I bowed my head. Here it was now. Finally. The judgment upon me.

'And so, after due consideration, I find that the mother, Ms Goodchild, did *not* intend to harm her child, and was *not* responsible for her actions during this period, as she was suffering from a medically diagnosed depression.

'I also find that the father, Mr Hobbs, has done everything he can to sever the bond between the mother and the child. As such, I find that the motivations of Mr Hobbs—and of his partner, Ms Dexter—in claiming that the child was at risk were not wholly altruistic ones. And I also find that they manipulated the truth for their own gain.'

Sandy was now squeezing my hand so hard I was certain she was about to break several bones. But I didn't care.

'These are the reasons why it is the *decision* of this court that this child must see and spend substantial time with both parents . . .'

He stopped for just for a second or two, but it felt like a minute:

'. . . but that I grant residence of the child to the mother.'

There was a long, shocked silence, broken by Traynor.

'As I also find that there was malice directed against the respondent, I order that the applicant pay the respondent's costs.'

Lucinda Fforde was instantly on her feet. 'I seek leave to appeal.'

Traynor peered down at her. And said, 'Leave refused.'

He gathered up his papers. He removed his glasses. He looked out at our stunned faces. He said, 'If there is no further business, I will rise.'

TWELVE

SIX WEEKS LATER, London had a heatwave. It lasted nearly a week.

'Isn't this extraordinary?' I said on the fifth day of high temperatures.

'It'll break,' Julia said. 'And then we'll be back to the grey norm.'

'True—but I'm not going to think about that right now.'

We were in Wandsworth Park. It was late afternoon. Around a half-hour earlier, Julia had knocked on my door and asked me if I was up for a walk. I pushed aside the new manuscript I was working on, moved Jack from his playpen to his pushchair, grabbed my sunglasses and my hat, and headed off with her. By the time we reached the park, Jack had fallen asleep. Parking ourselves on a grassy knoll by the river, Julia reached into her shoulder bag, and brought out two wine glasses and a chilled bottle of Sauvignon Blanc.

'Figured we should celebrate the heat with a drop of drinkable wine . . . that is, if you can indulge just now?'

'I think I can get away with a glass,' I said. 'I'm down to two anti-depressants a day now.'

'That is impressive,' she said,

'Well, Dr Rodale hasn't pronounced me "cured" yet.'

315

'But you're certainly getting there.'

She uncorked the wine.

'Here you go,' Julia said, placing a glass beside me. I sat up.

'Here's to finished business,' she said.

We clinked glasses.

'Have you reached a settlement with Tony's solicitors yet?'

'Yes, we've just got there.'

Actually, it was Nigel Clapp who got us there, forcing their hand through his usual hesitant determination.

We would still own the house jointly, and would split the proceeds when and if it was ever sold. Tony would handle the full mortgage payment, in addition to £1,000 maintenance per month, which would cover our basic running costs, but little more.

Still, I didn't want any more. In fact, in the immediate aftermath of the hearing, my one central thought (beyond the shock of winning the case and getting Jack back) was the idea that, with any luck, I would not have to spend any time in the company of Tony Hobbs again. True, we had agreed joint custody terms: he'd have Jack every other weekend. Then again, the fact that he'd be spending all forthcoming weekends in Sydney ruled out much in the way of shared custody . . . though Nigel was assured, through Tony's solicitors, that their client would be returning to London on a regular basis to see his son.

Tony also assured me of this himself during our one conversation. This took place a week after the hearing, on the day both our solicitors had agreed upon for Jack to be returned to me. 'The hand-over' as Nigel Clapp called it—an expression that had a certain Cold War spy novel ring to it, but was completely apt. Because, on the morning before, I received a phone call from Pickford Movers, informing me that they would be arriving tomorrow at 9 a.m., with a delivery of nursery furniture from an address in Albert Bridge Road. Later that day, Nigel rang to say he'd heard from Tony's solicitors, asking him if I'd be at home tomorrow around noon, 'as that's when the hand-over will take place'.

'Did they say who'll be bringing Jack over?' I asked.

'The nanny,' he said.

The next morning, the movers arrived. Within sixty minutes, not only had they unloaded everything, but they'd also put Jack's crib, wardrobe and chest of drawers back together again in the nursery. Accompanying the furniture were boxes of clothes and baby paraphernalia. I spent the morning putting everything away, rehanging the mobile that had been suspended above his cot, repositioning the bottle steriliser in the kitchen, and setting up a playpen in the living room.

Then, at noon, the front doorbell rang. I went to the door, expecting some hired help to be standing there, holding my son. But when I swung it open, I found myself facing Tony. I blinked with shock, and then immediately looked down, making certain that he had Jack with him. He did. My son was comfortably ensconced in his carry-chair, a pacifier in his mouth, a foam duck clutched between his little hands.

'Hello,' Tony said quietly.

I nodded back, noticing that he looked very tired. There was a long awkward moment where we stared at each other.

'I thought I should do this myself,' he finally said.

'I see.'

'I bet you didn't think I'd be the one to bring him.'

'Tony,' I said quietly, 'I now try to think about you as little as possible. But thank you for bringing Jack home.'

I held out my hand. He hesitated for just a moment, then slowly handed me the carry-chair. I took it. There was a brief moment when we both held on to him together. Then Tony let go. The shift in weight surprised me, but I didn't place the carry-chair on the ground. I didn't want to let go of Jack. I looked down at him. He was still sucking away on his pacifier, oblivious to the fact that—with one simple act of exchange, one simple hand over the trajectory of his life had just changed.

There was another moment of awkward silence.

'Well,' I finally said, 'I gather the one thing our solicitors have agreed upon is that you're to have contact with Jack every other weekend. So I suppose I'll expect you a week from Friday.'

'Actually,' he said, avoiding my gaze, 'we're making the move to Australia next Wednesday.'

'Then I suppose I won't expect you a week from Friday.'

'No, I suppose not.'

Another cumbersome silence. I said, 'Well, when you're next in London, you know where to find us.'

'Are you going to remain in England?' he asked.

'At the moment, I haven't decided anything. But as you and I have joint responsibility for our son, you will be among the first to know.'

Tony looked down at Jack. He blinked hard several times, as if he was about to cry. But his eyes remained dry, his face impassive.

'I suppose I should go,' he said without looking up at me.

'Yes,' I said. 'I suppose you should.'

'Goodbye then.'

'Goodbye.'

He gazed at Jack, then back at me. And said, 'I'm sorry.'

His delivery was flat, toneless. Was it an admission of guilt or remorse? A statement of regret at having done what he'd done? Or just the fatigued apology of a man who'd lost so much by trying to win? Damn him, it was such a classic Tony Hobbs moment. Enigmatic, obtuse, emotionally constipated, yet hinting at the wound within. Just what I expected from a man I knew so well . . . and didn't know at all.

I turned and brought Jack inside. I closed the door behind us. As if on cue, my son began to cry. I leaned down. I undid the straps that held him in the carry-chair. I lifted him up. But I didn't instantly clutch him to me and burst into tears of gratitude. Because as I elevated him out of the chair—lifting him higher—to the point where he was level with my nose, I smelled a telltale smell. A full load.

'Welcome back,' I said, kissing him on the head. But he wasn't soothed by my maternal cuddle. He just wanted his nappy changed.

Half an hour later, as I was feeding him downstairs, the phone rang. It was Sandy in Boston, just checking in to make certain that the hand-over had happened. She was at a loss for words when I told her that it was Tony who had shown up with Jack.

'And he actually said sorry?' she asked, sounding downright shocked.

'In his own awkward way.'

'He can't expect you to forgive him.'

'No—but he can certainly *want* to be forgiven. Because we all want that, don't we?'

'Do I detect your absurd lingering guilt about Dad?'

'Yes, you most certainly do.'

'Well, you don't have to ask for my forgiveness here. Because what I told you back in London still holds: I don't blame you. The big question here is: can you forgive yourself? You didn't do anything wrong. But only you can decide that. Just as only Tony can decide that he did do something profoundly wrong. And once he decides that, maybe . . .'

'What? An open confession of transgression? He's English!'

'Well, in just a little while, you won't have to deal with Englishness again,' she said.

This was Sandy's great hope, and one that she had articulated to me a week earlier as we waited for her flight at Heathrow. The hearing had just ended. Tony and Co. had left hurriedly—Diane Dexter having all but dashed alone up the aisle of the court as soon as Traynor had finished reading his decision. Tony followed in close pursuit, with Lucinda Fforde and the solicitor finding a moment to shake hands with Maeve and Nigel before heading off themselves. Which left the rest of us sitting by ourselves in the court, still trying to absorb the fact that it had gone our way. Maeve eventually broke the silence. Gathering up her papers, she said, 'I'm not much of a gambler—but I certainly wouldn't have put money on that outcome. My word . . .'

Nigel was also suitably preoccupied and subdued as he repacked his roll-on case with thick files. I stood up and said, 'I can't thank you both enough. You really saved me from . . .'

Nigel put up his hand, as if to say: 'No emotionalism, *please.*' But then he spoke. 'I am pleased for you, Sally. *Very* pleased.'

Meanwhile, Sandy just sat there with tears running down her face—my large, wonderful, far too gushy sister, emoting for the rest of us. Nigel seemed both touched and embarrassed by such raw sentiment.

Maeve touched my arm and said, 'You're lucky in your sister.'

'I know,' I said, still too numb by the decision to know how to react. 'And I think what we all need now is a celebratory drink.'

'I'd love to,' Maeve said, 'but I'm back in court tomorrow and I'm really behind in preparation. So . . .'

'Understood. Mr Clapp?'

'I've got a house closing at five,' he said.

So I simply shook hands with them both, thanked Maeve again, and told Nigel I'd await his call once Tony's people wanted to start negotiating terms and conditions for the divorce.

'So you want to keep using me?' he asked.

'Who else would I use?' I asked. And for the first time ever in my presence, Nigel Clapp smiled.

When he left, Sandy said we should definitely down a celebratory drink . . . but at the airport, as she had a plane to catch. So we hopped the tube out to Heathrow, and got her checked in, and then drank a foul glass of red plonk in some departure lounge bar. That's when she asked me, 'So when are you and Jack moving to Boston?' One thing at a time, I told her then. And now, as she raised this question again on this first afternoon at home with my son, my answer was even more ambiguous. 'I haven't decided anything yet. For the moment, all I want to do is spend time with my son and experience a normal life.'

After a pause she said, 'There is no such thing as normal life.'

That was five weeks ago. And though I do agree with Sandy that normal life doesn't exist, since then I have certainly been trying to lead something approaching a quiet, ordinary existence. I get up when Jack wakes me. I tend to his needs. We hang out. He sits in his carry-chair or plays with his toys while I work. We go to the supermarket, the High Street. Twice since he's come home, I've entrusted him to a baby sitter for the evening, allowing me to sneak off to a movie with Julia. Other than that, we've been in each other's company nonstop. No doubt, there will come a point when such a routine needs to be altered. But for the moment, the everydayness of our life strikes me as no bad thing.

Especially since the sun has come out.

'Five pounds says it won't rain tomorrow,' I told Julia as she poured herself another glass of wine.

'You're on,' she said. 'But you will lose.'

'You mean, you've heard the weather forecast for tomorrow?'

'No, I haven't.'

'Then how can you be so sure it will rain?'

'Innate pessimism as opposed to your all-American positive attitude.'

'I'm just a moderately hopeful type, that's all.'

And, of course, late that night, it did start to rain. I was up at the time with my sleep terrorist son, feeding him a bottle in the kitchen. Suddenly, out of nowhere, a large heaving clap of summer thunder announced that the heavens were about to open. Then, around five minutes later, they did just that. A real tropical downpour, which hammered at the windows with such percussive force that Jack pushed away the bottle and looked wide-eyed at the wet, black panes of glass.

'It's all right, it's all right,' I said, pulling him close to me. 'It's just the rain. And we better get used to it.'

DOUGLAS KENNEDY

When I met Douglas Kennedy in London recently, I was desperate to ask him the one question that any woman who has read *A Special Relationship* wants to ask: how was he (a mere man) able to write so movingly and knowledgeably about how a new mother thinks and feels? 'Well, thank you,' he answered, with a charming smile. 'I am really pleased that you were moved by it. I don't find it that hard to write from the female perspective. The trick is not to think about how a *woman* would react to a certain situation, but to ask how my character, Sally Goodchild, would react.'

Douglas Kennedy then went on to describe the research for his novel, including his conversations with a woman who had suffered from postnatal depression. 'She was quite remarkable and was invaluable to me when it came to detailing—with arresting honesty—her own nightmarish descent into the dark room that is postnatal depression.' He also read about family law and spoke with a solicitor who told him about the CAFCASS report and supervised visits. 'Plus I must have been the first man ever to go online to look at how breast pumps work!' he laughs. 'But, seriously, there is a desperate myth in modern life that everything is great. And if you don't love your children immediately there is something wrong with you. I don't think that is true at all. Like all major events in

life, there is a lot of fear; people don't know what they are doing and they don't know how they are going to react to it. I think that should be acknowledged.'

Douglas Kennedy, like Sally Goodchild, is an American now living in London. Having grown up in New York, he crossed the Atlantic in the mid-seventies and after thirteen years in Ireland, where he met his wife, Grace, he moved to London fifteen years ago and has since had two children, Max and Amelia. 'I love London,' he told me. 'I am a culture junkie so I enjoy all London has to offer.' He also has a studio in Paris—he speaks fluent French—and a holiday home on the unspoilt island of Gozo, just off the coast of Malta. 'Writers have to get away to work,' he told me. 'I am lucky because my writing has been successful, so I've been able to buy more than one home. Life is short, so why not?'

After writing several travel books, Douglas Kennedy wrote three internationally acclaimed thrillers, *The Dead Heart*, *The Big Picture* and *The Job*. He then made a conscious decision to change genres and write a love story. 'I wasn't trying to show a sensitive side,' he told me. 'I was just on a roll, and I had a couple of ideas for stories that felt right, and if you are on a roll as a writer, you keep going—mainly because the prospect of stopping is too terrifying to contemplate.'

Jane Eastgate

Marcia Willett

The Children's Hour

In the big old house overlooking
the sea, five small children listened
as their mother read them a story—
for it was the children's hour.
Theirs was an idyllic childhood,
filled with simple pleasures as they
played together on the beach and
in the gardens.
Until war and personal tragedy
disrupted their lives.

Chapter One

EARLY AUTUMN SUNSHINE SLANTED through the open doorway in golden powdery bands of light. It glossed over the ancient settle, dazzled upon the large copper plate that stood on the oak table, and touched with gentle luminosity the faded silk colours of the big, square tapestry hanging on the wall beneath the gallery. A pair of short-legged gumboots, carelessly kicked off, stood just outside on the granite paving slab and, abandoned on the settle, a willow trug waited with its cargo of string, secateurs, an old trowel and twists of paper containing precious seeds.

The tranquil stillness was emphasised by the subdued churring of the crickets, their song just audible above the murmur of the stream. Soon the sun would slip away beyond the high shoulder of the cliff, rolling down towards the sea, and long shadows would creep across the lawn. It was five o'clock: the children's hour.

The wheelchair moved out of the shadows, the rubber tyres rolling softly across the cracked mosaic floor, pausing outside the drawing room. The occupant sat quite still, listening to voices more than sixty years old, seeing chintzes scuffed and snagged by small feet and sandal buckles, an embroidery frame with its half-worked scene . . .

Hush! Someone is telling a story. The children group about their mother: two bigger girls share the sofa with the baby propped between them; another lies upon her stomach on the floor, one raised foot kicking in the air—the only sign of barely suppressed energy—as she works at a jigsaw puzzle. Yet another child sits on a stool, close to her mother's chair, eager for the pictures that embellish the story.

'I'll tell you a story,' said the Story Spinner, *'but you mustn't rustle too much, or cough or blow your nose more than is necessary . . . and you mustn't pull any more curl-papers out of your hair. And when I've done you must go to sleep at once.'*

Their mother's voice is as cool and musical as the stream, and just as bewitching, so that the children are drawn into another world: the world of make-believe, of once upon a time.

In the hall, outside the door, Nest's eyes were closed, picturing the once-familiar scene, her ears straining to hear the long-silent words, her fingers gripping the arms of her wheelchair. The telephone bell fractured the silence, breaking the spell, a door opened and footsteps hurried along the passage. She raised her head, listening until, hearing the clang of the receiver in its rest, she turned her chair slowly so that she was able to survey the gallery. Her sister Mina came out onto the landing and stared down at her.

'At least the bell didn't wake you,' she said with relief. 'Were you going out into the garden? I could bring some tea to the summerhouse.'

'Who was it?' Nest was not deflected by the prospect of tea. Some deep note of warning had echoed in the silence, a feather-touch of fear had brushed her cheek, making her shiver. 'Was it Lyddie?'

'No, not Lyddie.' Mina's voice was bracingly cheerful, knowing how Nest worried about the family's youngest niece. 'No, it was Helena.'

Their eldest sister's daughter had sounded uncharacteristically urgent—Helena was generally in strict control of her life—and Mina was beginning to feel a rising anxiety.

She passed along the gallery and descended the stairs. Her navy tartan trews were tucked into thick socks and her pine-green jersey was pulled and flecked with twigs. Silvery white hair fluffed about her head like a halo but her grey-green eyes were still youthful, despite their cage of fine lines. Three small white dogs scampered in her wake, their claws clattering, anxious lest they might be left behind.

'I've been pruning in the shrubbery,' she told Nest, 'and I suddenly realised how late it was getting so I came in to put the kettle on. But I got distracted looking for something upstairs.'

'I should love a cup of tea,' Nest realised that she must follow Mina's lead, 'but I think it's too late for the summerhouse. The sun will be gone. Let's have it in the drawing room.'

'Good idea.' Mina was clearly relieved. 'I shan't be two minutes. The kettle must be boiling its head off.'

She hurried away across the hall, her socks whispering over the patterned tiles, the Sealyhams now running ahead, and Nest turned her chair and wheeled slowly into the drawing room. It was a long, narrow room with a fireplace at one end and a deep bay window at the other.

'Such a silly shape,' says Ambrose to his wife when she inherits the house just after the Great War. 'Hardly any room to get round the fire.'

'Room enough for the two of us,' answers Lydia, who loves Ottercombe House almost as much as she loves her new, handsome husband. 'We shall be able to come down for holidays. Oh, darling, what heaven to be able to get out of London.'

It was their daughter, Mina, who, forty years later, rearranged the room, giving it a summer end and a winter end. Now, comfortable armchairs and a small sofa made a semicircle round the fire while a second, much larger, sofa, its high back to the rest of the room, faced into the garden. Nest paused beside the French windows looking out to the terrace with its stone urns, where a profusion of red and yellow nasturtiums sprang up between the paving slabs and tumbled down the grassy bank to the lawn below.

'We'll be making toast on the fire soon.' Mina was putting the tray on the low table before the sofa, watched by attentive dogs. 'No, Boyo, sit down. Right down. *Good* boy.'

Nest manoeuvred her chair into the space beside the sofa and accepted her tea gratefully. 'So what did our dear niece want?'

Mina sank into the deep cushions of the sofa, unable to postpone the moment of truth any longer. She did not look at Nest in her chair but gazed out of the window, beyond the garden, to the wooded sides of the steep cleave. 'She wanted to talk about Georgie,' she said. 'Helena says that she can't be trusted to live alone any longer. She's burned out two kettles in the last week and yesterday she went off for a walk and then couldn't remember where she was. Someone got hold of Helena at the office and she had to drop everything to go and sort her out. Poor old Georgie was very upset.'

'By getting lost or at the sight of her daughter?' Nest asked the question lightly—but she watched Mina carefully, knowing that something important was happening.

Mina chuckled. 'Helena does rather have that effect on people,' she admitted. 'The thing is that she and Rupert have decided that Georgie will have to go into a residential nursing home. They've been talking about it for a while and have found a really good one fairly locally. They can drive to it quite easily, so Helena says.'

'And what does Georgie say about it?'

'Quite a lot, apparently. If she has to give up her flat she can't see why she can't live with them. After all, it's a big place and both the children are abroad now. She's fighting it, naturally.'

'Naturally,' agreed Nest. 'Although, personally, if it came to a choice between living with Rupert and Helena or in a residential home I know which I'd choose. But why is Helena telephoning us about it? She doesn't usually keep us informed about our sister's activities.'

'I think Helena has tried quite hard to keep Georgie independent, and not just because it makes it easier for her and Rupert,' Mina was trying to be fair, 'but if she needs supervision they can't just leave her at their place alone. Anyway, the reason for her call is to say that the home can't take Georgie just now, and would we have her here for a short stay?'

Nest thought: Why do I feel so fearful? Georgie's my sister. She's getting old. What's the matter with me? 'What did you tell Helena?' she asked.

'I said we'd talk it over,' answered Mina. 'Do you think we could cope with Georgie for a month or two?'

A month or two. Nest battled with her sense of panic. 'Since it would be you who would be doing most of the coping,' she answered evasively, 'how do *you* feel about it?'

'I expect I could manage. What I feel is,' Mina paused, took a deep breath, 'or, at least, what I *think* I feel is that we should give it a try.' She looked at her sister. 'But I suspect that you're not happy about it.' She hesitated. 'Or frightened of it? Something, anyway.' She didn't press the point but stroked Polly Garter's head instead, crumbling a little of her shortcake and feeding her a tiny piece. Nogood Boyo was up from his beanbag in a flash, standing beside her, tail wagging hopefully. She passed him a crumb and in a moment all three dogs were beside her on the sofa.

'You're hopeless.' Nest watched her affectionately as Mina murmured to her darlings. 'Utterly hopeless. But, yes, you're right. I've been feeling odd all day. Hearing voices, remembering things. I have this presentiment that something awful might happen. A hollow sensation in my stomach.' She laughed a little. 'But I can't think why poor old Georgie should be cast as a figure of doom, can you?'

She glanced at Mina, surprised at her lack of response. Her sister was staring into the garden, frowning slightly. For a brief moment she looked all of her seventy-four years, and Nest's anxiety deepened.

'Your expression isn't particularly reassuring,' she said. 'Is there something I don't know about Georgie after all these years?'

'No, no.' Mina recovered her composure. 'I'm simply wondering if I can cope with Georgie, that's all. I'm only a year younger. Rather like the blind leading the blind, wouldn't you say?'

'No, I wouldn't,' answered Nest sharply, not particularly comforted by Mina's reply. 'You don't burn out kettles or go for walks and forget where you are.'

'Just as well.' Mina began to laugh. 'There wouldn't be anyone to find me up on Trentishoe Down.' A pause. 'What made you think it was Lyddie?'

'Lyddie?' Nest looked at her quickly. 'How d'you mean?'

'The phone call. You asked if it was Lyddie. Has she been part of this presentiment you've had all day?'

'No.' Nest shook her head, grimacing as she tried to puzzle it out. 'It's difficult to explain. More like a very strong awareness of the past, remembering scenes, that kind of thing.' She hesitated. 'Sometimes I'm not certain if it's what I actually *do* remember or if it's what I've been told. You were always telling me stories, interpreting the world for me. Giving people names of characters in books. Well, you still do that.'

Mina smiled. 'Such fun,' she said, 'although a little bit tricky when you called Enid Goodenough "Lady Sneerwell" to her face. Poor Mama was horrified.'

'It was fright,' Nest excused herself, laughing at the memory, 'coming upon her unexpectedly after everything you'd said about her.'

'Lady Sneerwell and Sir Benjamin Backbite. What a poisonous pair the Goodenoughs were.' Other memories were connected with this thought and Mina bent to stroke Captain Cat, feeding him the final piece of shortbread. 'So what do we do about Georgie? Are we up to it? Perhaps we should ask Lyddie what she thinks about it?'

'Why not? Let's clear up first, though.'

'Good idea. By then she'll have finished work for the day and we won't be interrupting her.'

Lyddie made a final note on the typescript, fastened the sheets of the chapter into a paperclip and leaned both arms on the desk, hunching her narrow shoulders. Black silky hair, layered into a shiny mop, curved and flicked around her small, sweet face: ivory-skinned with a delicately pointed chin. Dressed warmly in a cloudy-soft mohair tunic, which reached almost to the knees of her moleskin jeans, nevertheless she was chilly. Her tiny study, the back bedroom, was cold, the light dying away, and she was longing for exercise. The large dog, crammed into the space between her desk and the door, raised his head to look at her.

'Your moment just might have come,' she told him. 'You just *might* get a walk. A quick one.'

The Bosun—a Bernese Mountain dog—stood up, tail waving expectantly, and Lyddie inched round her desk and bent to kiss him on the nose. He had been named, after consultation with her Aunt Mina, for Byron's favourite dog, Boatswain.

'You are very beautiful,' she told him, 'and good. Come on, then.' They descended together and he waited patiently while she collected a long, warm, wool jacket and thrust her feet into suede ankle boots. As they walked through the narrow alleys and streets that led into the lanes behind Truro, Lyddie's attention was concentrated on keeping the Bosun under restraint until, freed at last from the restrictions of the town, he was released from the lead. She watched him dash ahead, smiling to herself at his exuberance, remembering the adorable puppy that had been waiting for her on the morning of her first wedding anniversary: a present from Liam.

'You need company,' he'd said, watching her ecstatic reaction with amusement. 'Working away alone all day while I'm at the wine bar.'

It was just over two years since she'd given up her job as an editor with a major publishing house in London, married Liam and moved to Truro, to live in his small terraced house not far from the wine bar that he ran with his partner, Joe Carey. It was a trendy bar, near the cathedral, not sufficiently prosperous to employ enough staff to enable her and Liam to spend many evenings alone together. Usually he was at home for what he called the 'graveyard watch'—the dead hours between three o'clock and seven—but this week one of the staff was away on holiday and Liam was taking his shift. It made a very long day.

'Come in as soon as you've finished,' he'd said, 'otherwise I'll see nothing of you. Sorry, love, but it can't be helped.'

Oddly, she didn't object to going to The Place; sitting at the table reserved for staff in the little snug, watching the clients and joking with Joe; eating some supper and snatching moments with Liam.

'No fertiliser like the farmer's boots,' Liam would say. 'We have to be around. The punters like it and the staff know where they are. It's the secret of its success even if it means irregular hours.'

She never minded, though. After the silence and concentration of a day's copy-editing she found the buzz in The Place just what she needed. Liam's passionate courtship had come as a delightful, confidence-boosting shock after a three-year relationship with a man who'd suddenly decided that he simply couldn't commit to the extent of he and Lyddie buying a house together or having children, and certainly not to marriage. James had accepted the offer of a job in New York and Lyddie had continued to live alone for nearly a year, until she'd met Liam, after which her life had begun to change very rapidly. She'd missed her job and her friends, and the move had been a frightening rupture from all that she'd known, but she loved Liam far too much to question her decision—and her darling old aunts were not much more than two hours away, over on Exmoor.

Aunt Mina's call had caught her within minutes of finishing work. They were such a pair of sweeties, Mina and Nest, and so very dear to her, especially since the terrible car accident: her own parents killed outright and Aunt Nest crippled. Even now, ten years later, Lyddie felt the wrench of pain. She'd just celebrated her twenty-first birthday and been offered her first job in publishing. Struggling to learn the work, rushing down to Oxford to see Aunt Nest in the Radcliffe, dealing with the agony of loss and misery: none of it would have been possible without Aunt Mina.

Lyddie hunched into her jacket, pulling the collar about her chin, remembering. At weekends she'd stayed at the family home in Iffley with her older brother, Roger; but she and Roger had never been particularly close and it had needed Aunt Mina to supply the healing adhesive mix of love, sympathy and strength that bound them all together. In her own grief, Lyddie had sometimes forgotten that Aunt Mina was suffering too: her sister Henrietta dead, another sister crippled. How heavily she and Roger had leaned upon her; sunk too deeply in their own sorrow to consider hers. The small, pretty house had been left to them jointly and it was agreed that Roger, an academic like his father, should continue to live there until he could afford to buy Lyddie out. Until she'd met Liam, Lyddie had used the house as a retreat but, when Roger married Teresa, it was agreed that between them they could afford to raise a mortgage which, once it was in place, would give Lyddie the sum of £150,000.

Running the wine bar meant that she and Liam rarely managed to visit Oxford but Roger and Teresa had been to Truro for a holiday and, for the rest of the time, the four of them maintained a reasonable level of communication. Nevertheless, Lyddie felt faintly guilty that she and Liam had more fun with Joe and his girlfriend, Rosie—who worked at The Place—than they did with her brother and his wife.

'It's all that brain,' Liam had said cheerfully. 'Far too serious, poor loves. Difficult to have a really good laugh with a couple who take size nine in headgear.'

Lyddie had been embarrassed by his implication but Joe had intervened. They'd been sitting together in the snug and Joe, seeing her confusion, had aimed a cuff at Liam's head.

'Leave her alone,' he'd said, 'and get the girl a drink. Just because you can't understand true nobility of spirit when you see it . . .' and Liam, still grinning, had stood up and gone off to the bar, leaving Lyddie and Joe alone together.

As she paused to lean on a five-bar gate, watching the lights of the city pricking into the deepening twilight, Lyddie attempted to analyse her feelings for Joe. He was always very chivalrous towards her, unlike Liam's rough-and-tumble way of carrying on, and his evident admiration boosted her confidence which, because of Liam's popularity, could be slightly fragile. She'd been taken aback by the hostility she'd encountered from some of Liam's ex-girlfriends and it was clear that a few of them did not consider his marriage to be particularly significant. Two or three women continued to behave as if he were still their property: they treated Lyddie as an intruder. Liam tended to shrug it off and she quickly learned not to expect any particular public support from him: they were married and, having made this statement, he expected her to be able to deal with these women sensibly. This was not quite as easy as it sounded. Apart from the fact that her confidence had been seriously damaged by James's departure, her husband was extraordinarily attractive—hair nearly as black as her own silky mop, knowing brown eyes, lean and tough—and he knew it. Without his presence The Place was a little less exciting, the atmosphere less intimate. He had an indefinable magic that embraced both sexes, so that men called him a 'great guy' while their women flirted with him. Joe's quiet, appreciative glance, his protectiveness, helped Lyddie to deal with the competition and she rather liked to hear Liam protesting against Joe's attentions. Of course, there was Rosie to consider. Lyddie had hoped that she and Rosie might become intimate but Rosie held Lyddie at arm's length. Perhaps Rosie felt less secure in her relationship with Joe because of Lyddie's married status; maybe she slightly resented the special treatment that Joe, Liam and the other members of staff accorded Lyddie. At The Place, Rosie was one of the waitresses and that was all. Lyddie was careful never to respond too flirtatiously to Joe when Rosie was around but it was often hard, when Liam was chatting up an attractive female punter, not to restore her own self-esteem by behaving in a similar manner with Joe.

Lyddie turned away from the gate, called to the Bosun and headed back towards the town, thinking about the Aunts. It seemed rather unfair of Helena to ask Aunt Mina to cope with her sister for so long.

'Two months?' she'd repeated anxiously. 'It's an awfully long time, Aunt Mina, especially if she's being a bit dotty.'

She could hear that Aunt Mina was battling with several emotions and so she'd tried to be practical, pointing out the obvious problems of dealing with an elderly and strong-minded woman—who was probably in the grips of dementia or Alzheimer's—with no help except limited assistance from another sister who was confined to a wheelchair. At the same time, Lyddie was able to identify with Aunt Mina's need to help Georgie. 'She is our sister,' she'd said.

Lyddie had felt an onrush of sadness. 'You must do what you think is right,' she'd said, 'but do tell me if it gets tricky. Perhaps we could all club together for you to have some help if Helena and Rupert don't suggest it themselves. Or I could work at Ottercombe if necessary, you know.'

'I'm sure you could, my darling,' Mina had answered warmly, 'but we'll probably manage and it will be a change for us. Now, tell me about you. Is everything all right . . . ?'

'I'm fine,' she'd answered, 'absolutely fine. And Liam too . . .'

Later, in the scullery at Ottercombe, Mina was clearing up after supper. The routine was generally the same each evening: Mina prepared to wash up while Nest, sitting beside the draining board, would wait, cloth in hand. Once dried, each item would be placed on the trolley next to her chair and, when it was all done, Mina would push the trolley into the kitchen while Nest went away to prepare for the remainder of the evening's entertainment: a game of Scrabble or backgammon at the gate-leg table, a favourite television programme, or a video of one of Mina's much-loved musicals. She had never lost her talent for reading aloud and books were another mainstay of their amusement. Their simple diet included not only the well-loved classics—Austen, Dickens, Trollope—but also Byatt, Gardam, Keane and Godden and was interleaved with travelogues, a thriller or *The Wind in the Willows*, depending on their mood. Lyddie occasionally brought along a current best seller or the latest Carol Ann Duffy to liven up their appetites.

As she put the plates back on the dresser, Mina was making plans for Georgie's arrival. Although she'd known almost immediately that this visit couldn't be avoided—how could she deny her own sister?—nevertheless, she was deeply unsettled by the thought of it. Her own anxieties about whether she could cope had been overshadowed by Nest's form-less premonitions. Or were they formless? Every family had skeletons of one shape or another—and Georgie had always loved secrets. She'd used them as weapons over her siblings, to shore up her position as eldest, to make herself important.

'I know a secret'—a little singsong chant. Mina could hear it quite clearly. Her heart speeded and her hands were clumsy as she arranged the after-supper tray, lifted the boiling kettle from the hot plate of the Esse, made the tea. Was it possible that Georgie knew Nest's secret?

'Don't be more of an old fool than you can help.' She spoke aloud, to reassure herself. If Georgie had suspected anything she would have spoken up long since. And, if she'd kept silent for more than thirty years, why should she speak now? Mina shook her head and shrugged away her forebodings. There was no need for all this silly panic. Yet, as she refilled the kettle, her heart ached with a strange longing for the past and she thought she heard her mother's voice reading from *A Shropshire Lad*: Housman's 'blue remembered hills'.

Mina stood quite still, her head bowed, still holding the kettle. The land of lost content: those happy, laughter-filled years with Papa away in London for much of the time so that the children had Mama all to themselves, reading to them, taking them to the beach, for excursions on the moors; the rules belonging to the smart London house relaxed into permanent holiday. The tears had come much later . . .

Mina is eight years old when her mother, Lydia, is sent down to Ottercombe for a long rest. The youngest child, Josephine—for Timmie and Nest are not yet born—has just had her fourth birthday and in the last three years there have been two miscarriages. Ambrose believes that the sea air will do Lydia good, strengthening her, so that she will be able to give him the son for which he craves.

'All these women!' he cries—but she hears the irritation rasping beneath the geniality and feels the tiny tick of fear deep inside her. She has had twelve years in which to discover the seam of cruelty buried deep in Ambrose's bluff good temper. He is not physically cruel—no, not that—but he uses language to prick and goad so that Lydia learns that a voice can be both instrument and weapon.

Her own voice is an instrument: pure, sweet, controlled. She sings to her babies, lulling them with nursery rhymes, and reads to them.

'All these books,' says Ambrose. 'Oh, for a boy to play a decent game of cricket.'

Ambrose is an attractive man, with brown curling hair. His eyes are a bright, sparkling blue and he has an easy, confident approach which makes people, at first, feel very comfortable with him. It is he who names the children: Georgiana, Wilhelmina, Henrietta, Josephine. Only later does Lydia understand that these lovely names are related to his frustration at being the father of girls. He is not the type of man to be interested in babies, and she thinks it is just a joke when he asks after George or Will, but, as they grow, the joke wears thin. She hates to hear her pretty daughters addressed as George, Will, Henry and Jo.

'Don't be so sensitive, darling,' he says, the blue eyes a little harder now, less sparkling, as they look at her; she tells herself that she must be careful not to irritate him, and that it's simply, like most men, he longs for a son. She feels inadequate, as if she is failing him, and hopes for another child to follow Josephine; a little boy, this time. After her first miscarriage Lydia begins to suffer asthma attacks and during the winter of 1932, so as to avoid the London fog, she is despatched to Ottercombe. She cannot quite believe her luck. Since a child, Exmoor has been her idea of paradise and, although Ambrose has consented to summer breaks in the old house at the head of the cleave, he does not like to leave her behind when he returns to London. He is a senior civil servant and his delightful wife is a great asset to him. Lydia is beautiful, popular—and useful. So she is deeply touched when he announces that he is prepared to manage without her for as long as is necessary. Her health, however, is not the only reason for Ambrose's unexpected attack of philanthropy. Ambrose has made a new friend, a wealthy widow whose robust appetites and tough ambition match his own, and he seizes this opportunity to know her better. He drives the family down himself, in his handsome, much-cherished Citroën, and settles them at Ottercombe. The young local couple, who are glad to earn extra money to caretake the house, are given instructions to shop and clean and care for Lydia and her children so that the following morning, when Ambrose drives away, his thoughts are all directed towards a certain house in St John's Wood.

As the sound of the engine dies in the distance, Lydia gives a great sigh of relief. Her children run shouting and laughing on the lawn and Wilhelmina tugs at her arm.

'May we go to the beach, Mama? If we wrap up warmly?'

Lydia bends to hug her. 'Of course we shall. After lunch. Afternoons are the best times for the beach, even in the winter.'

'And we'll come back and have tea by the fire, won't we? Will you read to us?'

'Yes, my darling, if that's what you'd all like. I'll read to you.'

So it begins.

In her bedroom, which had once been the morning room, Nest was very nearly ready for bed. The room, adapted for her needs, was austere, simple and unadorned, no roads back to the past by way of photographs or knick-knacks; no possessions with which she might be defined. Only necessities stood on the small oak chest, although several books were piled up on the bedside table along with her Walkman. She was able to stand for short periods, to haul herself along using furniture and her stick as aids, but she tired quickly and the pain was always there, ready to remind her that she was severely limited. At first, in the dark months immediately following the accident, she hadn't wanted to move at all. Suffering was a penance for her guilt. She'd lie on her bed, staring at the ceiling above, reliving the appalling moment: Henrietta at the wheel, Connor beside her, head half-turned to Nest in the back seat. If only she hadn't spoken, hadn't cried out in frustration, maybe Henrietta wouldn't have been distracted for that vital, tragic moment.

It was Mina who had propelled Nest back into life, both physically and emotionally; bullying her into her wheelchair so as to push her into the garden, manhandling Nest and her chair into the specially adapted motor caravan, forcing her to live. 'I can't,' she'd mumbled. 'Please, Mina. I don't want to see anyone. I have no right . . .'

'Not even the deaths of Henrietta and Connor give you an excuse to wall yourself up alive. Anyway, Lyddie needs you . . .'

'No!' she'd said, head turned aside from Mina's implacability. 'No! Don't you see? I *killed* them.'

'Lyddie and Roger know only that Henrietta misjudged the bend, not why. They need you.'

Lyddie's love and sympathy had been the hardest burden to bear.

'I think you'll find,' Mina had said much later, 'that living and loving will be just as cruel as self-imposed seclusion could ever be. You'll be punished quite enough—if that's what you want.'

So Nest had given herself up to life as best she could, withholding nothing, accepting everything—nearly everything. She still refused to allow Mina to push her down to the sea. The sea was the symbol of freedom, of holiday; the reward after the long trek from London. Oh, the smell of it; its cool, silky embrace on hot hands and feet; its continuous movement, restless yet soothing.

Now, as she lay at last in bed, exhausted by the exertions of getting there, she could picture the path to the sea. Here, between Blackstone Point and Heddon's Mouth, the steep-sided cleave, thickly wooded with scrub oak, beech and larch, cuts a deep notch into the cliff. At the head of the cleave, a quarter of a mile from the sea, stands Ottercombe House, sheltered and remote in its wild, exotic garden. A rocky path, stepped with roots, runs beside the stream that rises on Exmoor, on Trentishoe Down. A tiny spring at first, it gathers speed, trickling from the heights, spilling down the rock face in a little waterfall behind the house, welling through the culvert in the garden and pouring along the narrow valley until, finally, it plunges into the sea.

Her eyes closed, Nest could picture each bend in the path to the beach; she could see the rhododendrons flourishing. In early May drifts of bluebells grow beneath the terraces of trees, a cerulean lake of falling, flowing colour. In August, when the heather is in flower, the shoulders of the moor, which hunch above even the highest trees, shimmer bluish-purple in the afternoon sun. The path itself holds tiny seasonal treasures: bright green ferns, a clump of snowdrops, yellow-backed snails. How the children dawdle, postponing that delicious moment when they can at last see the sea; the cleave widening out as if to embrace the crescent-shaped beach, the cliff walls descending steeply into the grey waters. The stream, which has been beside them all the way, tumbles into a deeply shelving, rocky pool and then travels on, carving a track across the shaly sand until it is lost in the cold waters of the Bristol Channel.

Nest and her brother, Timmie, learn to swim in the rock pool; they paddle there too, with shrimping nets and bright, shiny tin buckets, and share a passion for the wildlife on this rock-bound coast. 'We'll live here together when we grow up,' he tells her.

'But who will look after us?' The youngest of the family, it is beyond Nest's experience that she might one day do this for herself.

'Mina will,' he answers confidently. Nine years older than he, Mina at fourteen seems already adult.

'Yes,' she agrees contentedly. 'Mina will look after us.'

Stirring restlessly, Nest recalled this prophecy. Mina had, indeed, looked after her—and now she must look after Georgie too. Panic fluttered just below Nest's ribs, her fears returning—bringing memories with them—and she groaned. Sleep would elude her now, and she would become prey to those night-time terrors that left her exhausted and ill—but there was a tried-and-tested remedy at hand. She hauled herself up against the pillow, switched on the light and reached for Bruce Chatwin's *In Patagonia*.

In her bedroom upstairs, Mina was pottering happily. The dogs, curled ready for sleep in their baskets, watched her as she moved about, their ears cocked as she murmured to them, a quiet monotone—'Good dogs, good little persons. There then, settle down now'—and then that little exhalation, an explosion of air escaping from her lips in a descending scale, 'po-po-po', as she paused for a moment to brush her hair.

This room, which had once been her mother's bedroom, was a complete antithesis to Nest's cell. Here, freed briefly from the necessary disciplines of nearly a lifetime of caring first for her mother and then for Nest, Mina allowed her passion for vivid, visual drama full rein and, glad to see her creating something of her own, various members of the family had contributed by bringing her presents: prints, silk cushions, ornaments, even small pieces of furniture. Mina received them with delight. The walls were crammed with images; a chaise longue, loaded with cushions, reposed beneath the window facing a Lombok tallboy, exquisitely painted with exotic birds, which stood against the opposite wall beside a bucket-shaped cane chair. Odd, fascinating objects jostled on every polished surface: photographs in a variety of pretty frames, a pair of Chinese *cloisonné* vases, an amusing set of papier-mâché ducks.

The room brimmed with colour. A velvet throw covered the deep, high double bed, its jewel colours—amethyst, sapphire and ruby— repeated in the long, heavy curtains, and three long shelves creaked with books, stacked and piled together. A thick, plain grey carpet was almost completely covered by beautiful, ancient rugs and a high, lacquered screen half hid the alcove in the far corner.

After the glowing, extravagant display of textures and tints, the starkness of the small alcove was a shock. A simple shelf, containing a computer monitor with a keyboard and a printer, ran the length of the wall, a typist's swivel chair beside it. Mina came round the screen, switched on the computer and sat down, humming beneath her breath while the screen scrolled and flickered. She typed in her password and waited, watching eagerly, her grey-green eyes focused and intent. She was rewarded at last: 'You have four unread messages.' With a sigh of pleasure Mina began to open her mail.

Chapter Two

WHEN LYDDIE WOKE, Liam was already up. She could hear him in the bathroom, whistling beneath his breath. Pulling the pillows about her, she lay contentedly—half waking, half dreaming—until a gush of water in the waste pipe and a closing door announced Liam's presence.

'Not *still* asleep?' He sighed, shaking his head as he dragged on jeans and a sweatshirt. 'And me thinking that you'd be downstairs getting the coffee on. That poor dog will be crossing his legs, I should imagine.'

'You've let him out already. *And* had some coffee.' She was unmoved, too comfortable to feel guilty. 'What's the time?'

'Ten to eight. Of course, it's all very well for those of us who work at home . . .'

'Oh, shut up,' she said lazily. 'You'd hate to work at home. You can't go half an hour without needing to speak to someone.'

'Just as well in my job,' he answered cheerfully. He bent to peer at himself in the glass on the small pine chest as he dragged a comb through his thick, dark hair.

'Who's opening up today?' she asked, hands behind her head, watching him appreciatively. 'Isn't it Joe's turn?'

'It is, indeed. A nice slow start for us, although I need to go to the bank.' He turned to look at her, catching her glance and smiling to himself. 'You look very beautiful, lying there.' He bent over her, kissing her lightly, and she put her arms about him. 'And to think,' he murmured in her ear, 'if it hadn't been for that damn dog of yours, I wouldn't be up at all. And you feeling sexy this morning. Isn't it just my luck?'

She chuckled, releasing him. 'You don't do too badly. A doting wife and all that adulation from your female customers.' She was learning that a light touch earned approval. 'Most men would kill for the amount of attention you get.'

'Ah, there's safety in numbers,' he told her. 'And what about you and Joe, if it comes to that, canoodling together in the snug while I'm working like a dog? What do you talk about, the two of you?'

'Joe's nice.' There was a sweetness in the knowledge that he'd noticed. 'He's great company. He talks about things that you find boring, like books and films.'

'Ah, that's just his way of chatting you up, cunning fellow that he is. You'll need to watch yourself, I can see that. But he doesn't make you laugh the way I can.'

'No,' she admitted, almost reluctantly, a tiny frown appearing, 'no, he doesn't, but then he doesn't flirt like you do, either . . .'

He kissed the rest of the sentence away—until she forgot Joe entirely and the frown was smoothed into delight—and then gently detached himself. She clung briefly, though instinct warned her against any show of possessiveness, and sighing regretfully, she pushed back the duvet.

'Make me some coffee while I have a shower, would you, Liam? Tell the Bosun I'm on my way.'

'I'll do that.' He hesitated, watching her thoughtfully. 'If you were quick we could drive out to Malpas and give him a walk along the river. It's a fantastic morning. Would you like that?'

'Oh, I'd love it.' Her face was bright with anticipation. 'I'll be five minutes,' she promised. 'Well, ten.'

She fled to the bathroom and Liam went downstairs, frowning a little, to tell the Bosun about the treat in store for him.

'It's a glorious morning.' Mina opened the kitchen door to let the dogs out into the freedom of the garden. 'How about a little trip in the camper? Coffee at Simonsbath, on to Dunster and back over Countisbury. We might as well make the most of it.'

She didn't add 'before Georgie arrives' but it was implicit in the glance the sisters exchanged.

'Did you manage to get through to Helena just now?' Nest asked, trying to sound casual, almost indifferent.

'Yes.' Mina was now peering out of the door. 'Yes, I did. She was very relieved. And grateful. They're bringing Georgie down on Saturday.'

'On *Saturday*?' Nest exclaimed. 'Good grief! They're not wasting any time.'

Mina turned to face her; she looked uncomfortable. 'It seems they have the opportunity to sell her flat, d'you see?'

'I don't believe it. My goodness, they don't hang about, do they?' Nest began to laugh. 'I hope Georgie has agreed.'

'They need the money from the flat, so Helena says, to fund the nursing home.' Mina, as usual, was trying to be fair. 'They want her to have the best.'

'Sure they do!' said Nest drily. 'And what if we couldn't have had her here?'

Mina was silent for a moment. She knew that Helena had also contacted her cousin Jack, their brother Timmie's son, asking if he and his wife, Hannah, could take Georgie in, if necessary. Mina knew that Nest would disapprove of this but she suspected that the truth would out before too long—Jack was very fond of his two aunts and in constant contact—and she decided that Nest might as well know at once.

'Actually, I had an email from Jack last night saying that Helena had been in touch,' she admitted. 'If we'd refused she was going to ask him if he and Hannah could cope.'

'You must be joking?' Nest was incredulous. 'I should have thought that those two have quite enough on their plates already. They've just started a new term with a houseful of boys to organise, as well as two children of their own. I can just see Georgie in the middle of a boys' preparatory school. The mind boggles.'

'Jack would have done it,' said Mina, smiling a little.

'Jack would do anything for anyone. He's Timmie's son. And Hannah, bless her, would go along with it.'

'He was anxious about us managing. Goodness, I don't know what we'd do without that boy. Or Hannah, for that matter. And then there's Lyddie, always in touch and worrying about us. How blessed we are.'

'It's odd, isn't it,' began Nest slowly, 'that we don't have that same sense of . . .' she hesitated, feeling for the right word, '*satisfaction* about Lyddie and Liam that we have about Jack and Hannah.'

'Liam's fun,' said Mina quickly, 'and terribly attractive . . .'

'But?' prompted Nest. 'There has to be a "but" after that.'

'But it's as if Lyddie feels that she needs to live up to him. Of course, she was knocked sideways when James left her and I sense that she's vulnerable with Liam, as if she's afraid that it might happen again if she's not careful. I feel a kind of wariness on Lyddie's side. There's no . . . *serenity*. Not like there is between Jack and Hannah. I hope she doesn't do something silly.'

'What sort of thing?' Nest looked anxious.

'Oh, I'm being an old fool.' Mina tried to shrug away her imaginings. 'I was just remembering when we went to Truro and had lunch with them at The Place. I thought that she and Joe were very friendly. She seems quite at ease with him, there's no tension and she can be herself, but I had the feeling that Liam didn't care for it.'

'Joe and Liam have been friends since school,' said Nest, trying to reassure herself as well as Mina. 'I can't believe that Joe—'

'No, of course not. I told you, I'm being foolish. We're both on edge at the prospect of coping with Georgie.'

'I've had a thought.' Nest was smiling. 'Why don't we invite Jack down while Georgie's here? He'll sort us all out.'

Mina began to chuckle. 'That's an idea. Dear Jack. So like his father. Oh, poor old Timmie.' She gave a great sigh. '*How* I still miss him!'

'I never wanted him to be a soldier,' Nest said almost angrily. 'I remember pleading with Mama about it. She said, "He would be unhappy doing anything else," but then she never imagined what would happen in Northern Ireland.' Her face was bleak. 'I often imagine—' She broke off in distress. 'At least he can't have known anything about it.'

'He was such a tower of strength,' said Mina gently, 'although in a quiet way. It can't have been easy being the only boy among five girls.'

'Papa must have been delighted,' said Nest, 'when Timmie turned up. And Mama too, of course. I must have been a bit of a disappointment coming after him. Another girl . . .' A tiny silence. 'Anyway, I'll go and get myself ready. Can you manage with the breakfast things?'

'Of course I can,' said Mina. 'This won't take a moment. Away you go. And of course you weren't a disappointment. Of *course* you weren't.'

She watched Nest wheel across the hall, thinking of the secrets kept for so many years—and Georgie's singsong chant: 'I know a secret. Can you guess? We have a new baby brother. Do you think Papa will love us any more?'

Piling the plates beside the sink in the scullery, Mina found herself thinking of that year before Timmie was born, the year that Timothy Lestrange first arrived at Ottercombe House.

During that year of 1932, Lydia and the children spend only the term-time in London. When Ambrose arrives early in August for the summer break he has a tall, fair-haired stranger with him. 'This is Timothy Lestrange, darling. One of my oldest friends. He was halfway up some unpronounceable mountain when we got married and he's been abroad for most of the time since.'

Lydia, smiling at Timothy, taking his hand, senses at once that he is an ally. The apprehension she always feels when Ambrose is due at Ottercombe is dissipated by an inexplicable relief.

'Ambrose insisted that I would be welcome,' he says. 'I apologise for arriving unannounced.'

'He turned up last night,' says Ambrose, 'due for a long leave. We haven't seen each other for years. I couldn't just give him a drink and say goodbye, could I?'

'Of course you couldn't,' agrees Lydia.

'I explained that there's no telephone here so we weren't able to warn you.' Ambrose airs an old grievance. 'In fact there's not much here at all.'

'Not much?' Timothy's eyebrows are raised. 'Only glorious country-side, a lovely old house and your wife and children.'

'Well, if you put it like that . . . Where are the *Bandar-log*, Lydia?'

Ambrose is a great Kipling fan and Lydia and Timothy exchange another smile.

'The children are down at the sea. They'll be home for tea soon. Would you like to bring your luggage in while I make the guest room ready?' She watches them go out into the sunshine, standing for a moment to relish this new strange joyfulness, and then hurries upstairs.

The children immediately respond to Timothy's warmth; their father is less abrasive in his company, less critical, and instinctively they know that it is to Timothy that they owe this respite. He draws the sting from the genial brutality of Ambrose's remarks. It is Timothy who renames the children and so earns Lydia's gratitude.

'Here they are,' says Ambrose, as the children straggle up from the beach, 'here are the *Bandar-log*. This is the eldest, George. Then Will and Henry. And this is the youngest, Jo.'

Timothy shakes hands gravely with each child. 'But why such names?' he asks, puzzled. 'Such pretty children and so like their mother. Why boys' names?'

'It's the next best thing to having sons,' says Ambrose bluffly—and Lydia turns her head away, biting her lip.

Timothy sees how she is hurt and gradually, as he talks to the children and plays with them, he softens George into Georgie, renames Will as Mina, Jo becomes Josie—but Henry . . . 'is Henrietta,' says Lydia, 'because nothing else quite works.'

'I like my proper name,' says five-year-old Henrietta firmly.

The others, meanwhile, are enchanted with their new names and, made bold by Timothy's championship, refuse to answer their father if he doesn't use them.

'Mutiny,' says Ambrose, slapping Timothy on the back. 'Mutiny in my own home,' but he too accepts the change.

'Timothy is nice, isn't he, Mama?' says Mina. 'He's like a very kind magician. Like Merlin.' Lydia is reading from a book about King Arthur and the Knights of the Round Table. It is after tea, during the children's hour. 'He's put a spell on all of us, hasn't he?'

And Lydia, dreamy-eyed, answers, 'Yes, my love, I think he has.'

'Don't ask him what he does,' instructs Ambrose, as they change for dinner that first evening. 'It's all a bit hush-hush. He does all this exploring and so on but, in fact, he's attached to the army. He'll tell you a few yarns, I expect. Hell of a chap.'

As the weeks pass, Timothy becomes part of the family; yarning with Ambrose in his study; walking with Lydia in the woods; playing with the children on the beach. Lydia blossoms into radiant health, Ambrose loses his city pallor, growing bronzed and fit, and the children are happy and at ease.

By the time the holidays are over, and Ambrose and Timothy return to London, Lydia is pregnant again.

Mina woke to a gripping, formless panic. The bedroom was already filled with early sunshine and she lay for some moments, breathing deeply, watching the shift of light and shade on the wall. Slowly, this nameless terror formed and shaped itself into very real problems. How much longer would she remain fit and strong enough to look after Nest? Resolutely, and with an enormous effort, she turned her thoughts into happier, more positive channels and presently the anxiety attack passed. She sat up, reaching for her dressing gown, murmuring to the dogs, who stirred in their baskets, watching with bright eyes.

'Shall we go downstairs, my darlings? Shall we? A cup of tea for me and perhaps a bicky for you? Would you like that?'

Like the drawing room, the kitchen was long and narrow: the working half, with the Esse and white-painted shelves and cupboards, had a door to the scullery, but the other half was a cheerful, cosy area. The square pine table was set beneath the window and a wicker chair stood beside the glass-paned door, which opened into the little courtyard with its alpine garden. The whole space had been arranged to accommodate Nest's wheelchair without sacrificing the comfortable, intimate atmosphere that Mina had created in the latter years of her mother's life.

'Just right for two, but for *three* . . .?' wondered Mina anxiously—and then pulled herself together. There was plenty of room for Georgie; it was simply that there hadn't been more than two people living in the house for more than forty years. 'And it's only for a short while,' she said aloud, opening the door so that the dogs might go outside. 'A little holiday. It'll be fun.'

The dogs disappeared into the wild, exciting garden beyond the courtyard and Mina filled the kettle and put it on the Esse. She made her mug of tea, turned the wicker chair so that it stood in the sun and, sipping gratefully, watched the birds. The bird table was alive with movement and colour: the flick of tiny wings, a rippling of gold and blue, smooth-feathered heads darting and pecking. Mina finished her tea but continued to watch, dreaming and remembering in the sun.

It is Timothy who encourages the building of the rock garden. In the days long before tubs and pot plants, the courtyard is a rather dreary place with its rock wall and mossy flagstones. Lydia likes to cook, to grow herbs beside the kitchen door, and Timothy shows how she could build a miniature garden full of colour to delight her as she works. Ambrose is smilingly tolerant of anything that Timothy suggests and waves them off to search for appropriate plants at nurseries in Ilfracombe and Barnstaple.

Georgie and Mina struggle through the garden carrying between them shapely rocks, and even Henrietta toils back from the beach with pretty stones in her bucket. The rock garden becomes the main topic of conversation, the pinnacle of endeavour, while seed catalogues and reference books litter the morning room table, varieties of plants ringed with circles of red ink. After tea, as Lydia sews, and Henrietta and Josie crayon busily in their colouring books, Timothy tells stories of travelling in the Pyrenees and the Alps, describing the flowers he has seen, and throwing in a few bandits for the sake of Mina, who listens round-eyed. Georgie sits ostentatiously on her father's knee while Ambrose continues to smile paternalistically upon the whole group.

Later, when Lydia and the children are alone again, strange packages arrive: rare and pretty plants from other countries, destined for the rock garden. As the child grows within her, Lydia sings and plays with her daughters and waits for the spring when the white-bloomed hutchinsia will flower along with the yellow euryops daisy from South Africa. In the winter evenings, with the children tucked in bed, she takes the letters from her sewing box: sheets of thin, flimsy paper, in blue-lined envelopes bearing exciting foreign stamps, covered with a looping, inky scrawl. A rosy glow from the oil lamp's glass bowl informs the moment of intimacy as she shares her lover's adventures, his fears, and the precious outpourings of love.

In the light early evenings of a cold sweet spring, the lazy broken fluting of the blackbird's song fills her with a poignant restlessness and, after the children's hour, to their delight, she wraps them in warm clothes and takes them down to the beach. The sea's surging song, as it sweeps across the ridged and buckled sand, calms her longing and quietens her need. She watches her children play but her thoughts are far away. Georgie and Mina have races. Lydia waves to them, laughing, holding her hands high to clap as she keeps an eye on Josie scrambling beside the rock pool. Henrietta shows them her basket of shells and stones and, as the moon rises, they gather their belongings and set off for home in the gathering twilight. Moths flit beneath the trees as bats dart and swoop above their heads, causing Henrietta to scream.

'Tired,' says Josie, sitting down suddenly among the ferns beside the stream. 'Carry.'

'Oh, darling,' says Lydia anxiously. 'Can you manage just a few more steps?' She is weary too, and Josie is heavy. Lydia is fearful of losing the child, which she has managed—so far—to carry so successfully.

'Tired,' whimpers Josie, beginning to grizzle. It is Mina who hauls her up into her arms and staggers along with her.

Soon, even the walk to the sea is too much for Lydia and she is confined to the garden and the house. Jenna, the young woman who helps to shop and clean, cycles over to Ottercombe most days to assist with the younger children while Georgie and Mina are at the local school. One morning, soon after the Easter holidays have begun, Lydia doesn't get up at all; messages are sent to London and the doctor calls in his small, black Ford.

'I know a secret.' Georgie sidles behind Mina, one eye on Jenna, who is spreading a picnic lunch on the rocks. Henrietta helps her to weight down the cloth with stones while Josie peeps hungrily into the large wicker basket. The house has been in confusion for several days: their father is down from London, bringing a woman in nurse's uniform with him, and Mama remains in her bedroom. Georgie, who comes running down from the house to join the others on the beach, is breathless. Her skinny chest heaves beneath the fair-isle jersey she has been told she must wear, for the late April weather, though sunny, is cold.

'Is it Mama?' asks Mina, fearfully. 'Is Mama dead?'

'No,' answers Georgie scornfully. 'Of course she isn't, silly. We have a new baby brother.' A pause. A cloud covers the sun, and the wind is chill on their bare legs. Mina is too weak with relief to feel the discomfort but Georgie stares at Mina, her pose forgotten, her eyes frightened. 'A brother. Do you think Papa will love us any more?'

Lyddie carried the Jiffy bag up to her study. The bag contained the typescript for her next editing project, an historical saga. The editor, an old friend and a former employer, had already discussed certain points with Lyddie on the telephone.

'We've had to do quite a lot of revising so look out for the timing.'

She'd booked Lyddie for another project, for the first two weeks of December, had a gossip and hung up, but not before telling Lyddie how she envied her being able to work in Cornwall. Lyddie was not in the least deceived; most of her colleagues had been shocked at the idea of her giving up her job and working freelance from Truro. She'd known that they were anxious for her. Her story of how she'd met Liam while she was on holiday in Cornwall, the speed at which the relationship had warmed from attraction into love, sounded too much like fiction. The fact that he'd asked her to marry him went some way to allaying their fears but it was a huge step. It sounded wonderful, they'd agreed cautiously, but wouldn't she miss London?

It had been difficult to describe her love for Liam or explain her readiness to quit London for the old cathedral city of Truro. Once they'd met Liam, of course, those colleagues had been more understanding. Knowing that they could trust her, they were also very ready to offer her freelance work.

'I'd hate to give it up completely,' she'd told Liam, 'and the money will be useful.'

He couldn't deny it. The lease on The Place hadn't come cheap and he'd insisted that the refurbishment must be classy; nothing tacky. Joe had agreed with him; Liam knew the market, knew just what was needed—and he'd been right. The Place was hauling in the punters, filling a particular well-heeled niche. The mortgage with the bank, however, was a large one.

As she noted in red ink the date on her calendar when the typescript was due back to the publisher, Lyddie wondered whether she should offer the money from what could be raised on the house in Iffley, once the deal was completed. Liam hadn't mentioned it and, oddly, she felt a certain restraint in raising the subject. Liam was deeply possessive about his business—it was his child, his world, and, although he encouraged her to come in for supper or lunch, he never made her feel truly a part of it. He and Joe were partners; The Place was theirs. Neither of them ever sought her advice or opinion but continued to treat her as though she were a valued, very special guest. In the snug, after a day of copy-editing, she could simply relax; her meals were presented with all the courtesy given to any of their clients. Yet her particular association *did* make her more special, which was rather fun. Did she want to change the balance? Would she be capable of putting a large sum of money into a business that didn't encompass her, without wanting to become involved in any way? And why should it make any difference if she had no control? After all, she was already dependent on the business: it was her livelihood, as well as Liam's and Joe's. The proceeds provided for her, paid the mortgage of the little terraced house—but not completely. She had her own work, the results of which shared their own personal financial load.

She was afraid to change the status quo, yet unhappy at the idea of not contributing more substantially if she had the means. Perhaps she would speak to the Aunts about it before she suggested it to Liam. Tomorrow was a day off and she'd planned a trip to Exmoor; Lyddie felt a little glow of expectation. Sitting down at her desk, pulling on a fleece jacket, she settled down to work.

The dogs sat together at the end of the terrace, ears alert. Voices could be heard, rising and falling from inside the house, and then the three women emerged into the sunshine. The Bosun stood up, tail wagging wildly, and hurried to sit beside Lyddie's chair; Nogood Boyo examined the contents of the tray placed on the bamboo table; Captain Cat settled beside Nest. Only Polly Garter continued to lie dreaming in the sun.

Mina poured the coffee. 'We're all ready,' she told Lyddie cheerfully. 'Her room's looking very pretty—just the flowers to do. You know, we haven't seen Georgie for ages. Oh, more than a year at least. It'll be fun, won't it, Nest?'

Nest's eyelid flicked as Lyddie looked at her and she smiled as she took her mug. 'I'm sure it will,' she answered.

Lyddie slipped her arm round the Bosun's neck. 'But you would say, wouldn't you, if things got a bit . . . well, a bit out of hand?'

'Poor Georgie,' said Mina lightly. 'She's not some kind of lunatic, you know. Only getting rather old and forgetful. Well, aren't we all! I don't think we shall need physically to restrain her.'

'And if we do,' added Nest lightly, 'we'll knock her out with a treble dose of my tramadol hydrochloride and tie her to her bed.'

Lyddie chuckled, as Nest had intended she should. 'I wouldn't put it past you, either,' she replied. 'You're both very unscrupulous women.'

Mina raised her eyebrows. 'How exciting you make us sound. So how is Liam?'

The slight pause caused both women to glance at her.

'He's fine,' Lyddie said at last. 'Great. Everything's fine. But, actually, I did want to talk to you about something.'

She hesitated again, while Mina and Nest strove to contain their nervous impatience.

'Nothing too serious?' suggested Mina, unable to bear the tension any longer. 'Nothing . . .'

'No, no,' said Lyddie quickly. 'Of course not. It's simply that once

Roger has got his mortgage sorted out I should get a hundred and fifty thousand. Liam's never mentioned it but I know The Place has got a big mortgage. Do you think I should offer it to him to help pay it off?'

'No,' said Nest sharply and at once—and both Mina and Lyddie stared at her in surprise.

Lyddie gave a small embarrassed chuckle. 'Well, that's honest, anyway,' she said—but she looked worried.

'Sorry,' said Nest quickly. 'That was rather a knee-jerk reaction but probably an honest one. Sorry . . .'

'I asked you,' said Lyddie quickly. 'Don't apologise. But why do you say that? After all, it's my livelihood too, isn't it? And Liam's my husband. Shouldn't the whole thing be a partnership? Financially as well as emotionally and . . .' She shrugged. 'Well, you see what I'm getting at.'

'The money could perhaps be invested,' began Mina carefully, 'against hard times. The Place is a huge success, anyone can see that, but things can go wrong and it might be wiser—'

'But it's not just that,' interrupted Nest. 'Sorry, Mina, but I think this should be said. The Place is very much Liam's show. Well, his and Joe's. It seems to me that you're not really included in any way. Would you say that's a fair observation?'

'Perfectly fair.' Lyddie sat upright, her silk-black hair gleaming in the sunshine. Her small face looked sad, the wide, grey-green eyes thoughtful, and the two older women each experienced a clutch of fear. 'You've really put your finger on it,' Lyddie told Nest, after a moment or two. 'I'm not included in any aspect at all. It's almost weird but I can understand it. Liam can be very possessive. Possibly it might be different if he didn't have a partner.'

'But that's the point, isn't it?' Nest was quick to pick this up. 'He does. You'd be backing Joe too.'

'There might be some legal way of splitting it into three. Or into shares,' Mina was determined that all aspects should be considered, 'so that if Joe were to leave or ask to be bought out . . .'

'It's risky.' Nest was sticking with her gut reaction. 'And if Liam hasn't asked, why offer? He's a very independent man and he probably prefers to keep his business quite separate from his family life. It's a very wise decision. He and Joe can slug things out between them but two against one means trouble. I should think it would be almost impossible for you to put money into The Place and then manage to stay disinterested, especially should things begin to go wrong. At the moment it's Liam's problem. You don't have to question or argue or fall out over it. You might make it very difficult for him if you make him the offer.'

'I'm sure,' Mina agreed quickly, 'that if he were hoping for some financial assistance he would have mentioned it by now.'

'You could be right.' Lyddie was looking more cheerful. 'I'll think about it carefully but you've cleared my mind,' and she settled back in her chair to talk about books.

Much later, once Nest was in bed, Mina seated herself at the computer. It was her nephew Jack, Timmie's son, who had introduced her to the Internet. During the early months after the car accident, with Nest almost destroyed by pain and grief and guilt, Jack had shown Mina how to communicate with other people in a similar position to her own.

'You need something of your own,' he'd told her, 'otherwise your whole investment will be in Aunt Nest and that's dangerous. Surf the Net. Talk to other carers; exchange jokes and let off steam. Just don't sink yourself into becoming a slave like you did with Grandmama. Oh, I know you loved her, and that you were happy looking after her, but I've seen you doing your own thing for the last ten years: going off to the States to visit Aunt Josie and the boys, going to Oxford, buying puppies. I don't want you to disappear,' and he'd grinned at her and kissed her briefly on the lips.

It was odd that he should always do this—not a kiss on the cheek, or a hug, but a gentle salute on her withered lips. Afterwards, once he'd gone, she'd press them gently with her fingers, as if holding the kiss in place. Darling Jack! Tall and blond, just like his father, just like Timmie.

Ambrose, bursting with pride, insists that Timothy must be godfather to his new son and says to Lydia, 'Let's call him after old Timothy, shall we, darling?'

Lydia agrees gratefully, rocking her new baby boy, marvelling at his fairness after four black-haired girls. Ambrose returns to London in tearing spirits while Lydia and her daughters settle into a new pattern of living. Timmie—'Timothy' is quickly shortened by Josie is a contented, cheerful baby, and his sisters vie for the responsibility of watching over him and showing him off to their few neighbours.

'How strange,' murmurs Enid Goodenough, hanging over the cradle. 'So blond. Not like his sisters at all, is he?'

She glances with bright, malicious eyes at her brother, Claude. He titters a little, drooping an eyelid at Enid. 'Quite a changeling.'

Lydia pours the tea calmly. 'He takes after my father,' she tells them. 'He was very fair and very tall.'

'How *very* convenient,' murmurs Enid Goodenough, so low that Lydia does not quite catch the words.

But Mina, who is never very far from her new brother, hears what she says and is puzzled. Mama is restless after their visit, preoccupied as she holds the baby so that her cheek rests against his round blond head. Mina watches, longing to restore the harmony the Goodenoughs have destroyed.

'It's time for our story, Mama,' she says, knowing that the children's hour creates a special world of its own. 'Shall I call the others?'

Mama smiles, touching Mina's hair, and nods, the anxious lines smoothing from her face, and Mina sighs an unconscious gasp of relief as she runs away to find her sisters. At nine years old, books are her chief delight, her greatest comfort. Their created worlds are her reality and she peoples the cleave and the beach with these characters who are so well known to her. Soon they are ready: Georgie and Mina on the sofa, with Timmie supported carefully between them, Josie lying on the floor with her wooden jigsaw puzzle and Henrietta on the stool where she can see the pictures. The windows are open to the scents and birdsong of the summery garden and the scene is tranquil. Mina relaxes against the cushions, waiting for her mother's voice. The book is opened and Mama begins to read.

Mina, humming to herself as she scrolled about the screen, was wondering just how much her life had been defined and influenced by books. Sometimes she feared that she'd never left the sheltering walls of make-believe, living most of her life in this beautiful and peaceful backwater; and then she'd remind herself of her own shattered love affair, those war years in London and her marriage, followed by her young husband's death in Jerusalem after the war. What contrasts she'd experienced! Those few years, with their unique atmosphere combining daily tragedy and fear with a fervent, greedy desire for living, had been followed by the quiet, routine-driven world that invalids inhabit. Her love of books had saved her from boredom and frustration. It was because of her passion for literature that she'd met Elyot. His wife was disabled and he too used the Internet to keep in touch with the world beyond their small, restricted lives. He and Mina had visited a chatroom that was used as a literary forum and—both being enthusiastic about a particular book—had begun to exchange opinions and recommendations more directly. He was simply 'Elyot'. Gradually their correspondence had begun to deal with more than the contents of books, as carefully, without disloyalty, they began to describe their frustrations and fears, each encouraging the other, sympathising and boosting morale.

It was difficult not to allow themselves to become more intimate; certainly Mina longed to know more about this intelligent, witty man, although she was well aware that disappointment was bound to result if she were to probe too closely. Meanwhile, they enjoyed an intimacy of their own, which related to fictional characters, certain phrases and gentle badinage. He was without siblings, and was fascinated by her stories about her family and especially about the prospective visit from Georgie. His last email had been full of admiration.

From: Elyot
To: Mina
What a brave woman you are. I shall resist the temptation to use literary references that relate to three sisters but, seriously, I hope you won't be overwhelmed. I also hope you won't be too busy, my dear friend, to 'e' me.

Her heart had been foolishly warmed by that short phrase 'my dear friend' and, hoping to make him smile with her own passing reference to 'black and midnight hags', she'd assured him that she would stay in touch. Tonight, ready to distract herself from more pressing problems and Georgie's imminent arrival, Mina began to open her mail.

Chapter Three

'TEA,' SAID LIAM, putting the mug carefully among the papers on Lyddie's desk. 'Mother of God, it's cold in here!' he exclaimed. 'You'll be getting stiff, sitting there for hours with winter coming on.'

Lyddie shrugged, picking up her mug and holding it in both hands. 'It's lovely and cosy when the sun's shining,' she said. 'Anyway, the room's too small to have an electric fire with the Bosun in here. His coat would singe.'

'Wouldn't you rather have a fire?' Liam poked the Bosun teasingly with his toe, then he leaned both hands on the desk and reached across to kiss her. 'I have to be away into the town. I'll see you later at The Place.'

'Oh.' She was disappointed. 'I'll be finishing in an hour or so and I was hoping we might have time for a walk.'

He edged round the Bosun. 'Sorry, love. Maybe tomorrow.'

She felt foolishly forlorn, looking forward as she did to those few hours together when she finished at about five and he went to the wine bar at seven o'clock. Yet, as usual, instinct warned against making demands, expressing her need. 'So where are you off to?'

'Oh, here and there. I want to see a guy about advertising in a new local magazine. I have to pop into the bank. Just things. I'll see you.'

She heard him run lightly down the stairs. Lyddie sipped her tea; her concentration was shattered by his brief visit and his kiss had unsettled her. Liam had made several visits to the bank just lately, although he never discussed the outcome with her, and he was a trifle preoccupied. His lovemaking had an urgent, needy edge that excited and delighted her, yet she hated to think that he could not confide in her. One of the things that had attracted her to him was that there was nothing of the boy about him. He was attractive, tough, self-contained, and his choosing her from such a wide field had been terrifically good for her ego.

Closing her eyes she recalled the moment at which he'd paused beside her table during that lunchtime at The Place, looking down at her with a flattering concentration.

'Are you happy?' he'd asked, as if he really wanted to know.

She'd burst out laughing at such an odd approach.

'Nearly,' she'd answered with surprising insouciance—for she was usually rather shy with strangers—'very nearly but not quite.'

His face had lit into a disarming smile and the new look that slid into his brown eyes had caused her heart to bang unevenly.

'Well, now, and what can we do to make the difference?' he'd asked. 'Some more coffee? A brandy? It's a terrible thing to be nearly happy but not quite. Better to be entirely miserable.'

She'd pretended to muse over her answer, longing to be witty and original but knowing that she would fail. 'Oh, I don't think I agree with you,' she'd responded coolly. 'And I think, after such a delicious meal, that what I'd like most is a walk.'

Her smile had been very nearly dismissive, although it was a tremendous effort to look away from him, to pick up her bag and casually glance into it for her purse.

'And I'd say that you were right.' He was watching her thoughtfully. 'I know exactly the place I'd go on a lovely afternoon. I was just going out myself, and I'd be delighted to show you. Afterwards, you might like to come back for a cup of coffee to set you on your way?'

It had been a moment of pure, magical madness. A hush had fallen on the tables as he'd raised a hand to Joe and they'd gone out together, to walk beside the river.

'Why do you call it The Place?' she'd asked him.

'Because it's the best place to be, the only place to be, the place to be seen, where it all happens, why else?' he'd answered, shrugging, and she'd laughed.

'And are you entirely happy now?' he'd asked later, as they'd paused for a moment in the shadow of the cathedral.

'Entirely,' she'd answered recklessly—and so it had begun.

'I've never seen old Liam like this,' Joe had told her. 'You've really knocked him sideways. Mind you, I can't say I blame him.'

His glance was approving, envious, and she'd felt as if another woman had slipped inside her skin: confident, brave, sexy, clever. Liam loved her and he wanted to marry her; oh yes, she was entirely happy. Later, watching him weaving among the tables, seeing the slack, almost vacant expressions of the women who desired him, she'd felt the weakening shiver of vulnerability, yet it seemed to her that the real driving force in Liam's life was The Place; separate from his love for her but absolutely necessary to him. He would work for it, fight for it; it was his *raison d'être*. Might it be possible that its future was threatened?

After her visit to the Aunts she'd decided that she would not offer to put her money into the business unless Liam asked for it. If he did, then she would have to reassess her own position. It was horrid, however, to think of him worrying about the loan if she were in a position to help him but, until Roger got his act together with remortgaging the house in Iffley, she didn't have the money anyway. The whole question was, for the moment, academic.

Lyddie finished her tea, picked up her pencil and plunged back into the eighteenth century.

Mina, clearing up the leaves on the lawn, heard the car approaching. She dropped the rake and hurried across the grass with the dogs running ahead. Georgie was in the passenger seat, Helena driving, and for a moment the two sisters stared at each other through the glass of the window while Helena switched off the engine and began to climb out. Georgie sat quite still, her expression stubborn, resentful, almost secretive. Dressed very tidily in a hand-knitted brown jersey with the white collar of her shirt showing at the neck, and a brown plaid kilt, she had the appearance of an elderly—and very cross—child.

Mina thought: Oh dear. She looks so *old*.

She was moved with love and pity at the sight of her older sister's vulnerability and she hastened to open the door.

'Georgie,' she said warmly. 'This is fun. How nice to see you.'

Helena was hurrying round the back of the car, embracing Mina and bending to assist her mother from her seat.

'There!' she exclaimed brightly. 'Isn't this nice? We've had *such* a lovely trip across the moor, Aunt Mina, haven't we, Mother?'

Georgie allowed herself to be helped from the car, her glance sliding slyly over Mina's face, watching for a reaction. Mina, who knew that Helena could be intolerably patronising, grinned briefly at her sister, sending a tiny wink, and, for a moment, the years rolled back, uniting them in that inexplicable partisanship of siblings, of shared history. Georgie stood upright, shook off her daughter's arm and looked about.

'Where's Nest?' she asked.

Mina suppressed a smile: trust Georgie to require the full welcoming committee. 'She's probably asleep,' she answered. 'Poor Nest has bad nights, so she makes up for it by taking a nap after lunch.'

Georgie snorted contemptuously. 'If she didn't sleep all afternoon she'd probably sleep better at night.' She ignored the dogs, and turned towards the house.

'It's pain Nest suffers from, not insomnia.' Mina's feeling of sympathy was disintegrating into irritation. 'Do try to use your imagination.'

'Now, now! No squabbling,' cried Helena gaily. 'Of course, Mother's stamina is quite extraordinary. She'll wear you out, you'll see.'

Georgie turned her head away sharply, and Mina glanced at her curiously. It was clear that Georgie was suffering from humiliation; old and helpless, she was being passed round like a parcel. A chill struck deep into Mina's heart. How long before she and Nest would be unable to manage—and who would care then?

'Come and have some tea,' she said.

She saw now that sympathy from her younger sister would be unendurable to Georgie's dignity—such rags of it that remained—and she took pains to keep her voice unemotional. Georgie stumped ahead, refusing to accept the role of guest; determined to lay claim to equality.

'Nothing changes,' she said, looking around the hall with satisfaction. 'Where have you put me?'

'In our old room: the one we shared during the war.' Mina watched for a negative reaction. 'I thought you'd like to be back in it again.'

'Mmm.' Georgie was noncommittal, withholding approval. 'I need the loo.' She crossed the hall and disappeared upstairs.

Mina looked at Helena, eyebrows raised. 'She seems on good form?'

It was a question—and Helena responded defensively. 'She looks wonderful, I couldn't agree more. And she sounds perfectly lucid. But, you wait. There will be a gradual change. Loss of memory, fumbling for a word, that kind of thing.'

'Really?' Mina sounded sceptical.

'Yes, really!' Helena, beginning to lose her patience, suddenly remembered that it would be foolish to overdramatise Georgie's problems.

Mina watched her, amused by her dilemma, and saw her niece struggling to control her irritation.

'Look, Aunt Mina, I promise you that we're doing our best for her, as we see it. And our GP agrees with us. The home is absolutely lovely and she'll be much happier there than stuck in an extension, with some kind of minder, and me and Rupert out all day. After all,' Helena's face was suddenly despondent, 'it's not as if she's ever liked Rupert . . .'

'I know.' Mina was moved by such genuine hurt to a sudden sympathy. 'I understand your difficulties.'

'It *is* difficult.' Helena looked as if she might suddenly burst into tears, her managing, confident exterior abruptly crumbling. 'To be honest, we spend a great deal of time with her, we rarely get a moment to ourselves, and she's *utterly* ungrateful. She's rude to Rupert and nothing I do is ever right. At the same time I feel dreadfully guilty, putting her into a home. I know what you're all thinking but I don't know what else to do. We'd never find anyone who'd put up with her full-time and I don't see why I should give up my job when she never shows me the *least* affection . . .'

A door closed upstairs and Helena fell silent, biting her lips. Mina touched her niece lightly on the arm, shocked at such an outburst from the well-controlled Helena.

'I'm sure you're doing the right thing,' she said gently. 'We aren't judging you. Remember, I know Georgie better than any of you.'

Helena stared at her. 'Yes,' she said. 'Yes, of course you do. And it won't be for long, honestly.'

'Don't worry about it,' Mina said. 'We'll manage.'

Georgie descended the stairs and rejoined them, a secret smile on her lips. 'It looks very nice,' she said to Mina. 'Very comfortable. So what was that about some tea?'

Later, as the sisters waved Helena off, Mina felt panic fluttering under her ribs. Georgie was watching her, an odd expression on her face as the sound of the engine grew fainter, and Mina wondered what she should say to her older sister. Should she say: 'Welcome back?' or 'It's good to have you home again?' Instead, surprising herself, she said something quite different.

'Do you remember,' she asked, 'how we used to go to the top of the drive to wait for Papa or Timothy and ride down on the running board?' In the silence, the sunlit garden was suddenly full of memories and she saw Georgie swallow, her face crumpling. 'Come on,' Mina said, taking her arm. 'Let's walk down to the sea.'

After Nest's birth, it is Timothy, rather than Ambrose, who is the most frequent visitor to the house on Exmoor.

'Another girl,' says Ambrose, almost indifferently. The novelty of having a son is wearing a little thin in the face of his growing affection for the widow in St John's Wood. Well born, well placed in society, she has no children to distract either of them from their needs, and she is clever at choosing the right company to amuse him and further his ambition. Lydia and the children are encouraged to spend more and more time at Ottercombe and Nest's birth gives Ambrose the perfect excuse to send Lydia out of London for the long summer holiday, insisting upon the necessity of peace and rest for her health.

'We'll call her Ernestina, after my father,' he says—and it is Timmie, not yet two years old, who cannot frame the long word and renames her Nest. Pale-skinned and black-haired like her sisters, Nest grows up as Timmie's shadow: the Tinies. Lydia is content to allow Mina to play a large part in the mothering of the two youngest, while even six-year-old Josie considers herself grown-up in contrast with Timmie and Nest.

Timothy visits, bringing strange toys and delicious sweets, treating the children with a tenderness they have never been shown by their father. These visits are awaited with impatience and, when they hear the familiar toot-tooting of his horn echoing from the high coastal road, the children toil up the drive to meet him. Clinging like monkeys to the doors, they balance on the running boards, screaming with excitement as they bump down towards the house. He is dragged from the car, each child importunate in her—or his—demand to show the latest achievement or to hurry him down to the sea. But 'Mama first,' insists Timothy and they wait impatiently while he goes to greet Lydia in the morning room. Timothy is instinctively accorded Papa's privileges and he sees her alone while the children squabble in the hall about which should be the first treat on his agenda.

They all know, however, that it will be exactly, reassuringly, as it always is: first the long, rambling walk to the sea and games on the beach, then home again for tea in the drawing room, and finally the latest chapter of the current book. This is the time of quiet, the unravelling of the long day's cares; it is the children's hour.

'Hello. Sorry, who . . .? Oh, *Jack*! Sorry, I've just got in from a walk. How are you?' Clutching the telephone receiver, Lyddie dropped her coat on a kitchen chair. 'And how is my goddaughter?'

'Your goddaughter is a wild child,' answered her cousin, 'and if she wishes to live to see her second birthday she'll need to mend her ways. How are things in Truro?'

'Fine.' Lyddie chuckled. 'Poor Flora. What's she been up to now?'

'Poor *Flora*!' echoed Jack indignantly. 'What about us? Hannah and I are worn to a ravelling, Tobes is bullied and terrorised and you say "Poor Flora"! So when are you coming to see us?'

'Oh, Jack, I'd love to,' replied Lyddie longingly.

She visualised the old stone house in Dorset, set in the parklands of the school grounds, with the eight small boys who lived with Hannah and Jack for the first year of their prep-school life. Her cousin's wife was quick, capable, warm-hearted, a perfect foil for Jack's unflappable, rock-like strength, and the boys adored both of them equally. Four-year-old Toby had a ready-made family of elder brothers who spoiled Flora shockingly. A few days with Jack and Hannah was a tonic that restored Lyddie whenever she was low: a sanctuary where she could be herself.

'Half-term next week,' offered Jack temptingly. 'The boys will be gone and your goddaughter would love to see you.'

'Oh, it would be heavenly.' Lyddie calculated rapidly. 'Perhaps just for one night. I'll check with Liam. It would be great to see you. It's sweet of you to offer when you're probably both knackered.'

'Well,' Jack's voice was teasing, 'to be honest, it's the Bosun we really want to see but we know that he can't come without you. Seriously, though, how are the Aunts? Have you seen them?'

'Not since Aunt Georgie arrived.' Lyddie decided to overlook the insult. 'We've had speaks and Aunt Mina seemed OK. I'm hoping to go over on Sunday for an hour or two.'

'We were wondering whether to dash down to see them during half-term.' He sounded cautious. 'Would they be up to it, d'you think?'

'I think they'd love it. Come on, Jack! You know they would. You and Han and the kids are their favourite people.'

'You underestimate yourself,' he answered gently, 'but thanks. Yes, I know that Mina and Nest are always pleased to see us but I don't want to make problems for Aunt Mina. Four extra people to entertain and Flora, bless her heart, is a real handful at the moment.'

'They'll manage,' promised Lyddie confidently. 'So when were you thinking of going?'

'Well, that's why I've phoned. If you can manage a visit we'll fit it round that. I know you have deadlines to keep.'

'Yes, I do,' said Lyddie gratefully. 'Look, I need to check with my calendar and with Liam and I'll get back to you this evening.'

'Great. Speaks later, then,' he said, and hung up.

Lyddie replaced the receiver more slowly. It was odd—and worrying: that image of the old stone house and the reminder that, there, she was able to be herself. It implied a lack of honesty, of strain, in her life here in Truro with Liam. She picked up her coat, allowing herself to admit the element of fear in her relationship with her husband. Oh, not a physical fear, no, but a fear of losing him if she should confront him too openly with her own needs: the need to be part of his whole life and her growing longing for his child. Each tentative approach was cleverly fielded with a smile, a shrug, a caress, while she struggled to find a fingerhold in his smooth resistance to her cautious advances. Yet why should she be cautious? Why not speak out honestly? She knew the answer even while she instinctively refused to face it: Liam did not require her to be part of his whole life, nor was starting a family on his agenda. His was the strength of those who withhold some vital part of themselves, who can withdraw love at will, and some atavistic instinct warned her against the risk of making demands.

Lyddie shivered at the thought of losing him, remembering how James had left her because he was unable to commit to a serious relationship. Liam, at least, had been very ready to marry her—the rest would surely follow. She must be patient a little longer.

Georgie's arrival had done very little to assuage Nest's fears; rather, her sister's presence only increased her anxiety. It was clear, after a few days, that Georgie was walking a narrow path between normality and instability. She refused the role of guest with a confidence that was almost offensive, behaving as if they were still all young together and she, as eldest, had the most authority. Meals were altered—'Surely you eat more than cereal for breakfast?'—their quiet evenings disrupted—'Time for my soap. You don't mind if I switch the television on, do you?'—and the plans for each day were dictated by her particular needs.

'Barnstaple today,' she'd say at breakfast, spooning up her porridge and looking to see whether Mina was ready with the scrambled eggs. 'I need some wool and something new to read. Is the toast burning? You know I've always hated burnt toast.'

'I shall kill her,' vowed Nest after a particularly trying day. Georgie had retired early with a headache. 'My sympathies, I have to say, are now utterly with Helena and Rupert. Mind you, I shouldn't think the home will keep her for more than a week. They'll probably expel her. *Can* you be expelled from a nursing home?'

'Not at those fees,' said Mina cynically. 'The higher the fees, the greater the tolerance, that's my experience. But think how humiliating it is for her to be bundled off to us while Helena sells up her flat and arranges for her to be shipped off to a home. The powerlessness, for someone as control-minded as Georgie, must be terrible.'

'Given that she's treating you rather like a servant I think you're very noble.' Nest was almost irritated by Mina's compassion. 'After all, this *is* your house. Mama left it to you. Georgie's behaving as if we've all slipped back fifty years.'

'I think that's exactly what she's done. I expect—'

The door opened, very slowly and silently, and Georgie stood looking at them. Her sisters stared at her, startled into immobility, each wondering how long she'd been there, trying to remember what they'd said.

'I've come for a glass of water,' Georgie said.

She frowned a little, as if trying to get her bearings, and came farther into the kitchen. Her silvery white hair was rumpled into a fluffy crown and her eyes were vacant, staring sightlessly.

'I thought I'd given you one.' Mina's voice was calm. 'Never mind. Go back to bed and I'll bring it up.'

Georgie's face crumpled a little, her eyes filled with tears and she looked quite unbearably sad but, before either of her sisters could speak, her expression changed again, smoothing into an odd, listening look, distant and unearthly, as if she could hear a conversation that neither of them could detect.

'Where's Mama?' she asked plaintively. Her glance strayed between the two of them, puzzled, and Mina took her arm.

'Not here,' she said. 'Not at the moment. You must go back to bed. I'll come with you.'

They went away together, Georgie allowing herself to be led as though she were a child. Nest remained quite still, shocked, almost frightened, until Mina returned.

'Is she OK?' Nest asked fearfully.

'I think so.' Mina looked shaken. 'I think she's confused about where she is. For a moment she thought that I was Mama.'

'You look like her,' said Nest. 'We all do, but you most of all. Oh, Mina, she looked almost mad.'

Mina touched her arm comfortingly but looked preoccupied. 'Well, Helena warned me that she had these moments,' Mina said, 'but I didn't imagine them quite like that.'

'It was creepy.' Nest shivered. 'You don't think she might get up again and wander about?'

'I hope not,' answered Mina anxiously. 'I wouldn't dare to lock her in, even if I had a key. She could be perfectly normal five minutes from now and then think how embarrassing it would be.'

'Anyway, she might need to go to the loo.'

They stared at each other nervously, each quite suddenly on the point of hysterical laughter, and Mina took a deep breath. 'Get off to bed,' she said. 'I'll listen out for her while I undress. And take a sleeping tablet. It's your physio day tomorrow and you need to be as relaxed as possible.'

They embraced and Nest wheeled herself away to her bedroom. In bed, waiting for the tablet to take effect, dreams and memories merged into jumbled, confusing patterns until, at last, she slept.

'I know a secret,' says Georgie importantly. The afternoon is hot but tall beeches crowd about the lawn, giving shelter from gales and sun alike, and it is cool and shady in the corner where Timmie and Nest are giving a tea party for their toys.

'Bet you don't.' Eleven-year-old Josie turns cartwheels across the grass, the skirt of her cotton gingham frock falling over her ears.

The Tinies draw closer together, envious of Josie's indifference. Sometimes Georgie's secrets are frightening. Timmie's lips tremble but he presses them firmly into a smile and holds Nest's hand—for she is youngest. They draw closer together, gazing at Georgie.

'There's going to be a war,' she says.

They stare at her uncomprehending, almost relieved.

'What is war?' asks Timmie, who is six now. 'What does it mean?'

Before she can answer, Mina comes out of the house calling to the children to come in for tea.

'Don't say anything,' says Georgie to them quickly. 'It's a secret. Papa will be cross.'

But Timmie is beginning to learn that Georgie cheats, binding them by threats that are groundless. 'But what is it?' he asks in a louder voice, feeling brave now that Mina is in earshot. 'What is war?'

Georgie turns to face Mina, who is angry—which, oddly, frightens Timmie even more—and she and Georgie glare at each other across the pathetic remains of the little tea party.

'Mama told you not to tell them,' she says, her voice low and furious.

Georgie shrugs, pretending indifference, but she looks uncomfortable. Nest, upset by Mina's uncharacteristic rage, begins to cry so that Mina is distracted and Georgie is able to slip quickly away.

'But what is war?' Timmie is genuinely frightened now.

'It won't happen here.' Mina, comforting Nest, looks up at Timmie. 'It's nothing to do with here. It's to do with countries fighting over something they both want. Their rulers are arguing about land, and then fighting starts and everyone takes sides, d'you see?'

'I think so.' He frowns. 'Like Josie and Henrietta and the tennis shoes. Both wanting them but not really knowing whose they were.'

Mina smiles at him. 'Just like that only bigger. But nothing will happen here except that we shan't see Papa so much. We shall stay here but Papa will have to stay in London. He's needed there. He won't be actually in danger but the thing about war is that lots of people become involved in it, even if they aren't doing the fighting.'

Timmie reflects on this for a moment. 'But we don't see Papa much, anyway,' he points out, quite cheerfully. Another thought strikes him. 'Shall we see Timothy? Will he have to do fighting?' he asks anxiously.

'I don't know. We'll have to wait and see. But you and Nest are quite safe. Now come and have some tea.'

He nods, and they follow her in through the French windows while the toys remain ranged about the table, forgotten and forlorn, as the twilight deepens and shadows stretch across the lawn.

Mina had other memories as she settled the dogs, the bedroom door slightly ajar so that she could hear Georgie should she get up. The familiar, well-loved surroundings soothed her and by the time she was wrapped in her long fleece robe—a birthday present from Lyddie—she felt ready for her nightly session on the Net. She read an email from Josie, full of questions about Georgie, and sent a carefully edited report back. There was no point in worrying Josie, who was too far away to be able to help. With Elyot, however, she was much more honest.

From: Elyot
To: Mina
How are things with you? A truly bad day today with Lavinia. She doesn't recognise me and cries out in fear if I go near her. She's had times when she's confused me with other people but this was terribly distressing. She's in bed now but I shall sit up for a while and hope to have a chat with you, if you're around this evening.

The knowledge that he, too, was suffering anxiety in a similar condition filled Mina with a kind of grateful relief and she was far less cautious than usual as she described the evening's events. He was swift with his reply.

From: Elyot
To: Mina
It's the combination of helplessness and fear, isn't it? I feel like this. Sometimes I simply want to shout at her because it seems impossible that she doesn't know me or could believe that I would wish to harm her. I feel hurt and terribly, terribly lonely.

Mina sat staring at these words, her heart aching with a longing to comfort him, warmed by a sense of comradeship.

From: Mina
To: Elyot
Dear Elyot, if only I could really be of help to you. Do you have friends who could take the load occasionally or does Lavinia find them threatening? I know you've described certain—shall we say 'interesting'—scenes but you've made such light of them that I've probably underestimated how difficult it really is. Georgie is nothing to this. We had a

very chequered relationship throughout our childhood and we've seen very little of each other for the last forty years. You and Lavinia have lived together all that time and it must be appalling for you, not only to feel so outcast but to watch someone you love disintegrating. Having had one tiny experience of it tonight I can only be amazed at your courage.

His reply came quickly.

From: Elyot
To: Mina
Your experience has been a different one, dear old friend, but just as demanding. You were plunged into a shocking disaster to which you had instantly to adapt, not only dealing with Nest but also relied upon heavily by various other members of your family. There has been a violence to your whole experience that is missing in ours. I see now that we have been slowly advancing into a mist of muddle, 'Was I supposed to be back for lunch?', 'I simply cannot remember why I've come into this shop', 'I've forgotten what I was going to say', which was innocent enough until one realises that it has deepened into a thick fog through which neither of us can find our bearings. I have to remain cheerful or she becomes anxious.

This last sentence filled Mina with a terrible pity and reminded her, with an almost physical shock, of Mama during the war years at Ottercombe. She sat for some time, trying to come to a decision, and at last typed one more message to Elyot.

From: Mina
To: Elyot
I've never known you have a holiday away from Lavinia in all the time we've been corresponding. Might it be sensible to have a break? Is there anyone to whom you could entrust her? Although it might, at present, sound like a busman's holiday, you could always come here for a few days. Don't answer now. Think about it. We'll talk tomorrow. Good night, Elyot.

She closed down the computer, her heart knocking foolishly in her breast. Would he agree? Was it possible that she might, at last, meet the man who had been such a source of comfort to her?

'You're an old fool,' she muttered, listening one last time for a sound from Georgie's room before she closed her door. She paused beside the rosewood table to look at the small objects that had been kept on Mama's bedside table: a wooden rosary; a Wedgwood bowl; and the small silver case that held a green glass bottle.

Mina clipped open the silver top and held the bottle to her nose.

Even now, twenty years after Mama's death, the faint scent of the smelling salts had the power to carry Mina back to those last years of her mother's life, and beyond that, to the early years of the war.

'I want to go to London with Papa,' says Georgie, one July morning in 1940. 'I don't want to be stuck down here with a war going on. There must be something I could be doing and I can look after him until I decide what it is.'

Lydia slips the thin blue sheets of her letter into the envelope and looks at her eldest daughter. How pretty she is—and how determined. 'You haven't finished school,' she answers patiently but firmly, 'and you're barely seventeen . . .'

The Tinies watch anxiously, spoons suspended, as another battle of wills is joined across the breakfast table.

'There's no *point* in school any more,' cries Georgie, exasperated. 'If I wait another year I might have no choice in what I have to do. Papa says he can get me a job as a driver at the War Office.'

Lydia's fingers nervously smooth the letter folded beside her empty plate. 'In a year it might be over,' she tells her children.

'Oh, honestly!' Georgie rolls her eyes in disgust. 'That's what they said about the last one.'

Only Mina hears the almost pleading note in Mama's voice and sees her flinch at Georgie's reply. She watches her mother's restless fingers and notes the bistre shadows beneath her eyes.

'I think it would be a good idea for Georgie to go to London,' she says—and Georgie glances at her gratefully. 'She'll have to do something soon and it will be nice for Papa to have her with him. They can look after each other. I can understand that she wants to be useful. We all do . . .'

Lydia stares at her. 'Not you too?'

'No.' Mina smiles at her reassuringly. 'Not like that, anyway. I shall stay here and look after all of you. But Georgie's right. It's pointless going back to school and you can't cope with everything on your own, Mama. Not now, with Jean and Sarah and the babies as well as the Tinies.'

Lydia's two young cousins, with their children, have evacuated to Ottercombe. The two young mothers, with two babies and a toddler between them, take up a great deal of space and, with the younger children unable to go to school, a great deal of organisation is required.

'How fortunate,' says Enid Goodenough, who still visits with her brother but less often due to petrol shortages, 'that you have enough family to fill the house'—by this time evacuees from Bristol and Croydon are arriving on Exmoor—'so that you don't have to put up with strangers. And Ambrose? How does he manage all alone?'

She manages to invest the last two words with a subtle inference that alerts Mina and causes even Lydia to frown.

'He's very capable,' she answers calmly, 'and Mrs Ponting goes in every day. I feel quite sure that Ambrose has everything he needs.'

'Oh, I'm certain you can be confident about *that* . . .'

Now, remembering those words and the sneering smile that accompanied them, Lydia suddenly thinks that Georgie's idea is, perhaps, a good one. 'Very well,' she says. 'I will speak to Papa, I promise.'

'Thanks,' says Georgie to Mina later, in their bedroom, 'for sticking up for me. It seems a bit mean, though, leaving you to all this.'

'Oh, I don't mind a bit,' answers Mina honestly. 'I shan't go back next term either. I shall teach Henrietta and Josie and the Tinies. It'll be good practice if I want to be a teacher after the war. And Mama can't manage alone. You're not frightened about air raids?'

'Well, nothing's happening, is it?' Georgie shrugs and lies full-length on her bed. 'It'll be fun. Sally Hunter says she's having a terrific time. Lots of handsome young officers and parties and things. She drives an old general about, that's what made me think of it.'

'And did Papa really say that he could get you a job driving?'

Georgie nods. 'If you ask me he's got a bit fed up with being on his own so much. He took me around a lot when I went up to London last time. Showing me off. I liked it, rather. He's still very good-looking, isn't he? I hadn't realised how important he is and everyone was very nice to me. There was a woman who seemed to turn up everywhere we went who didn't seem to like it much. She was very offhand with me. Once I saw her crying and he was reasoning with her but he looked horribly uncomfortable.' Georgie frowns as she recalls her own reaction: distaste that her distinguished father should be obliged to look . . . well, shifty; undignified. 'It was a bit odd.'

The sisters exchange a glance, puzzled; on the edge of exposing some adult secret. Instinctively, each retreats from discussing it further.

'Well then, perhaps it's a good thing you're going,' says Mina. She watches as her elder sister swings herself off the bed, notices the silky pleated skirt clinging to her long legs. 'Isn't that Mama's skirt?'

'Mmm.' Georgie twirls. 'It's a Fortuny. She simply never wears it so I asked to borrow it. After all, there's not a lot of use for it down here, is there? Look at this jacket. It's vicuña.' Georgie twirls again, holding it against her. 'What d'you think?'

Mina, glancing down at her cotton frock, feels a twinge of pure envy. 'It's a bit mere,' she says casually.

Georgie shoots her sister a sharp glance. 'Mere' has been a favourite word ever since they rediscovered *The Young Visitors* on the bookshelf in the nursery, a code that they apply secretly, to people, places, events, and can reduce them to fits of giggles. Quite suddenly, Georgie feels a huge surge of love for Mina. 'You'll come to London, won't you?' she says. 'Sally's meeting simply loads of gorgeous men.'

'Course I shall,' says Mina. 'Hurry up and change, lunch will be ready soon.'

As she goes downstairs, she sees someone moving about in the drawing room and crosses the hall, wondering if it is one of the Tinies; but it is Lydia who sits on her heels before her sewing box, putting something away. She glances over her shoulder as Mina comes in and there is the sudden crackle of paper and the sharp little bang of a drawer closing.

'I thought it was Nest or Timmie,' Mina tells her. 'They have this game of hiding before lunch . . . Are you feeling unwell, Mama?'

Lydia straightens, holding on to the back of the sofa. 'No, no. Well, perhaps a little tired. The babies were crying again last night.'

Her face is thin and there is so much pain in her eyes that Mina is shocked: this is more than sleepless nights. She has never questioned Mama before, but she senses a shift in their relationship. 'Was your letter . . . ? I saw you reading it at breakfast. Did it have bad news?'

Mina's eyes are on a level with her own, her look is grave and compassionate, and Lydia longs desperately for the luxury of confession. She must trust someone and why not this, the dearest of her daughters?

'It was from Timothy,' she whispers. 'He is being sent on some secret mission. He can't speak of it . . . Only to let us know that he will be gone for some time.' Her eyes blur with tears, her lips tremble.

'Oh, poor Mama.' Mina instinctively puts her arms round her mother. We shall all miss him, shan't we? Will we be able to say goodbye to him?'

Her innocent acceptance soothes Lydia's guilt and gives her courage. It is heaven merely to be able to speak his name aloud. 'No, no,' she says. 'He can't possibly get away but I'm glad to share it with you, Mina. He makes light of it, naturally, but it's dangerous, I know it is . . .' She hesitates, looking anxiously into those clear, untroubled eyes. 'Perhaps we shouldn't mention it to the others?'

'Oh, no,' agrees Mina at once. 'They wouldn't understand and the Tinies might be frightened.'

'Yes,' says Lydia, weak with relief. 'That's what I thought. It's a secret between you and me, my dear child.'

Mina, feeling proud and very grown-up, kisses her mother lightly on the cheek. 'It's lunchtime,' she says. 'Go and make yourself pretty while I get the children organised.'

She hurries away, so as to intercept the children coming in from the garden, and Lydia goes upstairs, comforted.

Chapter Four

'OK, SO IT'S I WHO AM in the wrong entirely. I am at fault for taking exception to your opening a letter addressed to me. That's the way of it, is it?'

'Oh, for Heaven's *sake*.' Lyddie was trembling with anger and shock: Liam's reaction had been quite unexpectedly violent. 'It was a mistake. So I didn't look carefully at the address. So big deal. We *do* have a joint account at this bank, remember? Anyway, why all the secrecy? We're married, after all. Is it really so terrible that I should open one of your letters by mistake?'

He stopped pacing, so as to stare at her, and she was struck by the realisation that he was utterly unfamiliar to her; the flow of chemistry that connected and fused them into a special, unique entity had been switched off. Lyddie felt an odd combination of fright and loneliness.

'So that's fine, then,' he said, 'except, you see, that I don't believe that it was a mistake.'

Lyddie swallowed, looking away from his wholly unfriendly, penetrating stare. Unfortunately his suspicion was all too true. Liam's increasing edginess had begun to worry her to the extent that, when the letter arrived with the flap not quite stuck down, she'd given way to a terrible need to see what was happening at the bank. She was deeply ashamed of herself but, even so, had been quite unprepared for the scorching blast of Liam's fury.

'The letter was *not* closed properly,' she answered evenly, 'and I hadn't looked to see to which of us it was addressed, but, yes, OK, when I realised that it was about The Place and not us, I looked anyway. I've been very worried about you and I thought you'd been trying to protect me from . . . whatever.'

He smiled, not a pleasant smile. 'Ah, so you were worrying about me. What a devoted wife it is, imagine.'

Lyddie bit her lip, her cheeks burning. 'It's hard,' she told him, 'to keep myself completely cut off from the business you love so much and which supports us. You know all about *my* work and what I earn—'

'And you know all about The Place. Mother of God, you're in there every day and treated like the Queen of Sheba!'

She pleated her fingers together, trying to sort out her thoughts. 'I'm treated like an honoured guest,' she agreed at last. 'I know that—and I admit that I like it. But, at the same time, I know even less about it than . . . than Rosie does.'

'And what does Rosie know about anything?' he asked sharply.

She stared up at him, puzzled. 'You know what I mean. She's *involved*. OK, it's at a superficial level but it's more than I've got.'

'I imagined that as my wife you wouldn't be concerned about what the barmaids think they know,' he answered stingingly.

'I'm not. It's not *like* that— Oh, let's stop this, can we?'

He raised his eyebrows, watching her. 'I don't know. Can we?'

'Oh, Liam, I'm truly sorry.' She controlled her longing to move towards him: his whole body language warned her off. 'What would *you* do if you could tell something was worrying me but I wouldn't share it with you?'

'I'd imagine that you were adult enough to have the right to your privacy and honour it accordingly.'

He might just as well have slapped her.

'Yes,' she said on a deep breath. 'Well, there's no answer to that.'

'And so now you know all about my problems how do you plan to lift the burden from my shoulders?'

She was silent, still smarting with embarrassment.

'You see,' he continued after a moment or two, 'it's not just me, is it? It's Joe. He might not like you knowing all his secrets too.'

'But this wasn't to Joe, was it?' she replied miserably. 'I imagine the company correspondence goes to The Place. This was to you, personally. I know that you're going to increase the mortgage on this house. Why?' she pleaded. 'Why, Liam, when you know I can raise some money on the house in Iffley?' Her conversation with the Aunts and her subsequent resolution was so much dust and ashes now, in the face of his icy rejection. 'Why won't you let me help you?'

'I don't want to be "helped".' He spoke the word with distaste. 'I started this business and whether it stands or falls is up to me. Can you not understand that?'

'Yes, yes, I can understand it. But don't I come into this at all? This house is yours but we share it now. Suppose you put it at risk by increasing the mortgage on it? It's my home too.'

'So it is. But I shan't let you down. You'll have to learn to trust me.' A tiny pause; a light, very slight relaxation of his bunched muscles. 'Do you find that impossible?'

'No, of course not.' She felt too wretched to protest further; all she longed for was the old familiar harmony. 'It's clear that The Place is a terrific success . . .' She hesitated, afraid of endangering the faint warming of the arctic atmosphere between them. 'I'm truly sorry, Liam . . .'

'And so am I.' It wasn't clear whether he was referring to her misdemeanour or tendering an apology, but he touched her lightly on the head before moving to the door. 'I've an appointment in the town and I shall go straight on to The Place. See you later for supper, I expect.'

The door closed behind him: Lyddie sat quite still. It was terrible to be so much in love that almost nothing mattered except the beloved's kiss. She wrung her hands together, humiliated by the depth of her physical need for him, willing him to return, but only the Bosun appeared, padding gently, warily, to sit beside her, offering her the grateful, warming benefit of his love.

Later that afternoon, just as Jack and his family were assembling for tea, the telephone rang. With a resigned gesture, he hurried away to his study while Hannah groaned with irritation. Her energetic vivacity kept her as slender at thirty-three as she'd been at twenty, and she was pretty and stylish in a sharp, up-to-the-minute way. Despite looking after Jack and their children, as well as eight small boys during term-time, she still managed to keep her own catering business in operation. She was devoted to her children and adored Jack.

When he came back into the kitchen he looked preoccupied, but he smiled at Toby as he slid into the seat beside his daughter's highchair.

'Who was it?' demanded Hannah.

'Honey,' said Flora. '*Not* jam. No, no, no . . .'

'Is there some resonance about the word "no",' mused her father, moving the honey-pot with a practised thrust beyond Flora's sticky reach, 'which lends itself to the childish imagination? Why not "yes" or "please"? Wasn't "no" the first word our darling daughter uttered?'

'Actually,' answered Hannah, putting Marmite soldiers on Toby's plate, 'it was "Bog off!" courtesy of young Jackson.'

Toby made round eyes and mouthed 'Bog off!' at his father, who winked back at him.

'What a lovely boy he was,' he said, with a reminiscent sigh. 'We owed so much to him by the time he went.'

'Yes,' agreed Hannah grimly. 'Tobes's vocabulary was startlingly improved. OK, Flora, if you don't want it I shall give it to Caligula.'

Flora stared down at the enormous tabby cat and sniffed pathetically, eyes wet with frustrated tears. Toby watched sympathetically. 'It's new jam,' he told her encouragingly. 'Not the old one. It's really, really nice.'

Flora's lower lip resumed its normal size and her arched limbs relaxed a little. She allowed, grudgingly, a tiny portion of bread and jam to be inserted into her mouth. When none of it reappeared her parents breathed deeply, as if some great object had been achieved.

'Tobes is destined for the diplomatic corps,' observed Jack, 'if we've still got one in twenty years' time.'

'Possibly,' agreed Hannah, 'but who was it on the phone?'

'Oh, yes!' Remembering, Jack's face fell. 'It was Lyddie. She can't get over to see us after all.'

'Oh, no!' Hannah stared at him in disappointment. 'Why not?'

He hesitated. 'I'm not absolutely sure. She just said that everything was a bit on top of her and she couldn't get away.'

'Rats!' said Hannah crossly. 'I was really looking forward to it.'

'I wanted to show her how I could ride my new bicycle,' said Toby sadly. 'And I'd done a picture.'

'And Flora wanted to show off her new word,' said Jack, trying to raise their spirits a little. 'Didn't you, my darling?'

Flora scowled at him, cheeks bulging.

'What new word?' asked Toby, interested.

'Jack!' warned Hannah. 'That will do. It's not like Lyddie to stand us up. Are you sure she's OK?'

'Not really,' admitted Jack. 'I couldn't get anything out of her, though. The good news is that she's agreed to drive over to Ottercombe when we go on Saturday. She wants to see the Aunts and I've made her promise, otherwise I've said we'll set Flora on her.'

'Well, that's something,' said Hannah reluctantly.

'Will she bring the Bosun?' asked Toby eagerly. 'I do love him. I wish *we* could have a dog.'

'I know you do,' said Hannah. 'You've told us before, actually. Just once or twice.'

'On the hour, every hour. But, yes, Lyddie is bringing the Bosun so you'll be able to take him down to the beach.'

Toby's face was lit with excitement. 'Flora! We're going to the sea.'

'Bistik,' demanded Flora threateningly, drumming on her tray.

'No, Flora, that's enough biscuit,' said Hannah. 'Apple, now. Eat up and we'll walk down to the river. You can ride your bike, Tobes, and Daddy will give you a piggyback, Flora. You like that, don't you?'

Flora, who did indeed feel that there was a certain rightness when her head was higher than anyone else's, began to eat her apple pieces with enthusiasm.

'Thanks,' Jack said. 'There's nothing I love more than having both ears violently twisted.'

'That's all right, then,' she answered equably. 'I like everyone to be happy. I'll get the coats. And don't pinch the last of the chocolate biscuits, Jack. I know exactly how many there are.'

She left the kitchen and there was a silence broken only by Flora eating apple. 'Tell me, Tobes,' Jack asked thoughtfully, 'have you come across the word "witch" yet?'

Nest woke suddenly, heartbeat unsteady, struggling into awareness as she tried to see the clock. Even before she could read its illuminated face she knew that the night was over. The thickness of the curtains could not completely block the light-fingered morning as it groped between the gaps in the heavy folds.

In the first months after the accident, her helplessness had brought nightmares to her waking and sleeping hours. What if the house should catch fire? Or if there should be an intruder? Her inability to move quickly or defend herself manifested itself in sweating terrors, which Jack and Mina had tried hard to allay by practical means: a very good smoke alarm system, bars at her windows. The large morning room, barely used since Lydia's death, was the obvious choice for Nest's quarters. Next door to the kitchen, it had been quite easy to plumb in a small bathroom and equip it for her needs. The fact that it was on the ground floor made access simple for her, yet increased her night-time fears.

'It's so *stupid*,' Nest cried vexedly, almost weeping with frustration. 'I'm OK until I go to bed. It's the dark . . .'

Now, even as she peered at the clock, she stiffened into immobility. Someone was in the room. Tense and alert, she strained to see the darker, denser shape near the door. It waited, motionless, yet, in the breathless silence, Nest's heightened senses detected confusion on the part of the intruder. Then there was a movement: a stealthy turning of a handle, a wedge of light lying across the floor before the door closed again with a tiny but audible click. Instantly Nest was washed in a drenching sweat of relief. She swallowed, and began deliberately to inhale long deep breaths. Presently, she pushed back her covers and began the slow process of dressing, and, later still, wheeled herself into the kitchen for breakfast. She leaned from her chair to stroke Nogood Boyo and wished her sisters 'Good morning'.

Georgie was immersed in a catalogue but Mina folded and put aside the *Spectator*, and smiled at Nest. 'There was an email from Jack last night,' she said. 'They're all coming on Saturday for the whole day. And Lyddie's coming too. Isn't that good news?'

Nest lifted the kettle onto the hot plate, responding to Mina's evident delight with a raising of spirits.

'Great,' she answered cheerfully. 'Isn't it, Georgie? How long is it since you saw Toby and Flora? Flora's baptism, was it?'

'*What* a day that was,' remembered Mina.

'Do you remember, Georgie?' persisted Nest, as Georgie rather fumblingly turned a page, frowning to herself.

'Of course she does,' said Mina anxiously, her happiness evaporating a little in the face of Nest's odd insistence.

'When are they coming?' asked Georgie. 'When . . .?'

She fell into an odd, listening, posture; eyes vacant, head slightly cocked, and Mina looked at Nest in dismay. Nest wheeled herself to Georgie's side and put a hand on her wrist; she saw that there were fresh egg-stains on the brown jersey and her sister's hair was unbrushed.

'Georgie,' she said gently, and shook the flaccid wrist, 'Jack and Hannah are coming on Saturday. Good, isn't it?'

Georgie's glance travelled slowly from her wrist up to Nest's face. 'I know a secret,' she said. She began to smile a little, cunningly. 'I know a secret.' Her voice was stronger now, the old singsong intonation, and Nest knew a tiny stab of fear. She looked at Mina, who was watching Georgie with an expression that mirrored her own sudden anxiety, and she released her sister's wrist abruptly.

Mina pushed back her chair. 'Yes,' she said with forced brightness. 'On Saturday. What fun it will be,' and, calling to the dogs, she went out into the garden. After a moment, Georgie returned to her catalogue as if nothing had happened and Nest wheeled back to the now boiling kettle and, very thoughtfully, began to make herself some coffee.

'It was Georgie,' she said to Mina, some time later when they were alone together in the drawing room. 'You never come into my room without knocking. It was morning. Who else could it have been?'

'She gets confused,' said Mina. 'You know she does. Oh dear . . .'

'But why stand there in the dark without speaking? I was terrified.' Nest's fear was manifesting itself in anger. 'If she's going to start creeping about I shall have to lock my door.'

'Oh, I am so sorry,' said Mina distressfully.

'It's not your fault.' Mina's dismay made Nest feel guilty. 'Obviously it isn't. But I can't cope with this.' Silence. 'Mina. Do you think Georgie might know . . . something?'

The true fear was out in the open now. Mina's eyes met Nest's briefly and slid away. 'I . . . don't know.'

'But no one else knew,' said Nest urgently. 'Only you and me and Mama.'

'I certainly never told Georgie,' said Mina firmly.

Nest stared at her. 'Do you think Mama can have told her?'

'I can't believe that she would have done, but that's not to say that somehow Georgie didn't . . . hear something.'

'Oh my God!'

'Look,' said Mina quickly, 'let's not panic. She's obviously suffering from delusions of some kind. It's probably something she just thinks she knows. After all, there are other secrets.'

'Other secrets?'

'Well, not secrets,' said Mina quickly. 'Not . . . real secrets. This is just Georgie being . . . Georgie.'

Nest turned to stare out into the garden. 'I hope you're right.' She wheeled herself out through the French windows onto the terrace and Mina was left alone. She sat motionless except for one hand which, gently and quite unconsciously, continued to stroke their mother's rosewood sewing box, standing where it had always been, beside her chair.

Timothy manages one more visit to Ottercombe before vanishing again into Europe. Ambrose and Georgie, by now, are firmly fixed in London; each manipulating the other to attain his or her own ends. Petrol rationing and restrictions on travel give them excellent excuses to avoid the long journey to Exmoor but, somehow, Timothy finds the means: travelling by train to Barnstaple, catching the last connection to Parracombe and walking the rest of the way, nearly four miles, across the moor. He arrives late on a wild March evening and only Lydia and Mina are still up to greet him. His skin is burned dark brown by a harsh foreign sun, his hair bleached like straw, so that, to Mina, he seems as exciting and romantic as she has always remembered him.

Lydia is unable to contain her relief and joy, speeding across the hall and into his arms, holding him tightly. Timothy has been trained in a tougher school and is able to smile at Mina, shielding Lydia while he stretches a hand to her daughter.

'Were you anxious?' he asks her, his eyes creasing into a smile. 'Did you fear for me, crossing the moor at night, wondering if I might meet Carver Doone?'

Mina laughs, touched that he remembers how her whole life is a world informed by fictional characters. 'I was worried,' she admits, 'but I told Mama that this was nothing compared to what you're used to.' She smiles indulgently upon her mother, who is calmer now although her eyes are strangely brilliant, her cheeks flushed. 'But we didn't tell the Tinies, did we, Mama, or they'd never have gone to bed at all?'

'I expect you'd like something to eat.' Lydia schools her voice into a steadiness she does not feel and he smiles down at her. Their glances lock and linger, her hand tightens on his sleeve, but Mina is already leading the way into the kitchen.

'We're very lucky,' she calls back to them, 'that we have a farm so close. They give us cream and eggs and cheese. I think it's better to be in the country in wartime although Georgie thinks we're very dull. Did you see Papa and Georgie in London?'

'No.' By now they have joined her in the kitchen. 'No, there was only just time to catch the train. They are well?'

'Oh, yes.' As the kettle boils on the range and she prepares some simple food, Mina chatters happily. 'They survived the Blitz, at least, although Mama tried to make Georgie come home. She thought it was a great adventure and insisted on staying with Papa. She'd like me to go to London but Mama needs me and I teach the children, although Henrietta and Josie are getting too big and they'll be going away to school in the autumn. Timmie goes over to Trentishoe for lessons with the vicar. Papa says he must go away to school soon too . . .'

Her chatter dies away as she becomes aware of the silence behind her. They both smile at her as she glances over her shoulder but she senses a tension. 'You must be terribly tired,' she says to Timothy. 'Why don't you take your supper through on a tray?'

'That's a lovely idea.' Lydia is trembling as she embraces Mina. 'Good night, my dear child. Away you go to bed, now.'

'The house is full.' Mina kisses Timothy too. 'Our cousins are here with their babies. You've had to go into Papa's dressing room next to Mama. It's small but we've made it comfortable, haven't we, Mama?'

'Very,' smiles Lydia. 'Have no fear. He'll sleep well tonight.'

She glances almost mischievously up at Timothy but his face has a brooding, almost impatient expression. Watching them, despite her sharing in Timothy's homecoming, Mina feels suddenly excluded. Lydia picks up the tray and Timothy follows her across the hall; neither of them glance up as Mina climbs the stairs.

The children are wild with delight when he appears at breakfast time. Even Henrietta and Josie, who are trying to outdo each other in the attempt to be sophisticated young women, forget their quarrels and readily resume their familiar relationship with him. He brings each of them a pretty, flowered silk scarf—blue for Henrietta, green for Josie, but otherwise identical.

'How clever of you,' says Mina with relief, 'to give them the same thing, otherwise they would fight.'

She does not see the tender glances Lydia and Timothy exchange, nor does she guess that there has been a certain collusion with regard to the presents. Timmie has a model of a Spitfire, which renders him quite speechless with excitement, and Nest is given a charming rag doll.

'Imagine all those things being in that small holdall,' marvels Mina. It does not occur to her, now that she is grown-up, that she might have a present. Timothy waits until she is alone before he takes his opportunity. 'I have something for you,' he says. He hands her the package and watches her face as she quickly takes the book out of the bag. The mere fact that it is a book, doubly precious in these times, causes her to gasp with delight but when she sees the title, 'Oh, *not* an M. J. Farrell,' she cries. 'Oh, this is the nicest thing you could have given me. Oh, thank you,' and she flings her arms about him and hugs him tightly. 'You've written in it, haven't you?' She checks anxiously and then grins at him again. 'I can't wait to start it.'

'You'll have to wait a little,' he smiles, touched as always by her warmth and her likeness to Lydia. 'I want you to take some photographs for me.'

'Me?' she asks, surprised but flattered. 'I'm not terribly good at it,' she warns him. 'I cut off people's heads and feet, but I'll try.'

'Good girl,' he says. 'Most of the children are down at the beach but Nest and Mama are about. You can practise on them. Come along, before we lose the sunshine,' and she follows him out into the garden.

It is Ambrose who breaks the news, four months later; telephoning from London on a sultry July afternoon when the children are at the beach. Suspecting nothing, he feels that it is *he* who requires sympathy: he has, after all, lost a very good friend.

'One of the best,' he says, over and over, until Lydia feels that she might slam down the receiver. 'Poor old Timothy, I shall miss him.'

When Mina arrives back, Lydia is sitting in the drawing room, dry-eyed, her hands stroking the last letter, which had arrived a week before. She stares at Mina. 'He is dead,' she says almost matter-of-factly.

Mina knows at once that she is speaking of Timothy. She picks up a stool and perches close to her, taking the letter so that she might hold Mama's hands and placing it carefully on the top of the sewing box. They sit together, Mina gently cradling the icy hands, while the sun sinks slowly behind the cliff and the garden is filled with shadows.

No word is spoken: the tears come later.

'Sorry,' said Nest later, when they were clearing up after lunch. 'I had a complete sense-of-humour failure. I'm sure you're right and it's just that she's so confused.'

'I'm sure she meant no harm,' said Mina quickly. 'And you were always overimaginative.'

Nest began to chuckle. 'I think we both were. All those books we read. I can't begin to count how many characters I was in love with.'

'Mr Rochester. Richard Hannay. And Peter Wimsey . . .'

'No.' Nest shook her head. 'No, not Wimsey. He was rather mere.'

Mina grinned at her. ' "Personally I am a bit parshial to mere people",' she quoted and they laughed together, a whole shared past flowing richly between them.

'What's the joke?' Georgie was watching them from the doorway.

'Oh, nothing much.' Nest fought down an unworthy impulse, resisting the temptation to exclude her oldest sister. 'We were talking about all the people we'd been in love with. Just being silly.'

'It's funny you should say that.' Georgie came farther into the kitchen, smiling at them: a sly, knowing smile. 'I was only thinking earlier about Tony Luttrell. Do you remember him, Mina?'

'Yes,' said Mina after a moment. 'Yes, of course I remember him.'

'I think I remember him too.' Nest frowned thoughtfully. 'Although I must have been quite young. How odd! I remember him with Mama, being terribly upset . . .' Too late she caught sight of Mina's face, grim with hurt, and, confused and surprised, hurried to repair the blunder. 'We were thinking of going out, Georgie,' she said. 'We're going to the Valley of Rocks. I wonder if Mother Meldrum's Tea Rooms is still open . . . ?' She could hear herself gabbling, aware of Georgie's watchful, almost amused gaze flicking between them.

'I'm sure it will be.' Mina seemed to have regained her serenity. 'I'll go and find the dogs, Nest, and then we'll get your chair into the camper.'

They drove slowly up the steep drive, turning left, eastwards towards Lynton, over the high road on the edge of the Down, which plunged precipitously into the Channel. This afternoon, the water dazzled in the autumn sunshine, the silky skin of the sea rippling lustrously until it met with the sheer grey cliffs where it broke in gentle creamy foam against the unyielding rock.

As the camper plunged into the narrow lane that led to Trentishoe church, Nest was thinking of the expression on Mina's face. Staring out at the tall bushes of spiky gorse in bright brimstone flower, she still felt as if she had unintentionally pried into something very secret.

Nest thought: Tony Luttrell. I *do* remember him. Images were forming in her head: a young man standing on the terrace, laughing with Mina and Mama, a thin face with a long, mobile mouth. How odd that Georgie should think of him after all these years.

'I'd forgotten how beautiful it is,' said Georgie slowly, as the road dipped into the wooded lanes of the Heddon Valley.

The other two smiled, her appreciation binding them briefly together so that they travelled for a while in a peaceful, harmonious silence, between the stone-faced banks topped with neatly clipped beech hedges, the turning leaves glowing coppery gold.

Unreeling like a silent film, the pictures continued to project onto Nest's inner eye: a young Mina with Tony Luttrell in some kind of uniform, and, once, very smart in a dinner jacket. Nest cudgelled her memory, aware that a sense of affection informed these memories, recalling that she too had liked him. He had been kind, she thought, playing racing demon with her and Timmie and—oh, yes!—he'd owned a little open-topped sports car, so dashing and romantic. They'd taken turns to sit in the driving seat, pretending to drive it.

The camper moved slowly on, past Lee Abbey and into the narrow valley road between the craggy, piled rocks. Watching the wild goats, bearded and horned, playing among the boulders on the gorse-covered slopes, Nest's memory still reeled slowly across nearly sixty years: Tony pleading with Mama, his face tight with despair, and, later, Mina weeping. Why? Had Mama refused to give her approval to the match? Why should she?

The past, however, refused to give up its secrets and, presently, seeing that Mother Meldrum's was open, they stopped to have some tea.

That evening, with Georgie in bed, exhausted by the day's outing, and Nest finally settled, Mina went gladly to her room, the dogs clattering about her feet. There had been no message from Elyot yesterday evening and she was beginning to fear that she might have been too forward in suggesting a visit to Ottercombe. Perhaps he was finding it difficult to frame a refusal that was both polite and convincing?

'Po-po-po,' the air escaped her lips on an outward exhalation of breath as she undressed slowly. Manhandling the camper through the steep countryside was beginning to be an effort for her, and her neck and arms ached alarmingly, yet she dreaded the time when she might be unable to drive. How would they manage, so far from shops, so isolated, if she had to give up driving?

Mina thrust these fears away, comforted as always by her familiar belongings. As she cast off her clothes and reached for the long fleecy wrapper, a tiny flickering excitement fluttered beneath her rib cage. She switched on the computer, eyes fixed on the screen: five unread messages—and one from Elyot. Foolishly weak with relief she opened it.

From: Elyot
To: Mina
Things are not too good here. Yesterday, the carer came in to look after Lavinia while I took a few hours off to get out into the country and stretch my legs. The weather is more like May than October, isn't it? I had a wonderful walk in the hills, so refreshing and uplifting, but unfortunately,

on my way home I clipped a parked car and the owner, a young man, was uncomplimentary about 'old buffers' being allowed on the roads and I felt strangely humiliated. Worse, when I got home, I found that Lavinia had been very difficult and the carer was rather worried about her, suggesting that I might not be able to cope for very much longer.

I can tell you, my dear friend, that once she had gone I was prey to the most terrible depression. What shall I do when I can no longer drive? How could I possibly put Lavinia into a home and walk away from her? I was too low to talk to you last night—I don't sound much better now, do I?—but I needed to make contact. At these moments the only people who can really help are those who are in a similar position and your offer of a few days' holiday has been like a tiny sparkle of light at the end of a very long, dark tunnel. Bless you for it. Even if it never happens, the thought of it is keeping me sane—just.

I hope all is reasonably well with you?

Mina sat for some moments, deep in thought. Presently she began to type, in her careful, two-fingered way.

From: Mina
To: Elyot
How strange, Elyot, that our experiences seem to bear a close comparison of late. Georgie and Lavinia are clearly suffering from the same kind of mental problems and she is beginning to make trouble—well, Georgie always did that! But it's these swings from past to present that unnerve me. Mentally, she's clearly unstable. It's nowhere near as bad as it is for you, I know that, and, anyway, Georgie is not my responsibility. If I insisted, Helena would come and remove her, but she is my sister. The trouble is that she's worrying Nest, talking about a secret. Well, we all have those, don't we? But there is something rather serious here. I only wish I knew which secret Georgie is thinking she knows. Oh dear! How odd that makes us sound but it's such a relief to talk to you about it.

Didn't you tell me that your son was due home from abroad later this year? That's something to hold on to, isn't it? And we have Jack and his family, and Lyddie visiting on Saturday. They will certainly cheer us up. Forgive me if I'm beginning to sound dangerously trite but I know how close to the edge we both are.

Stay in touch, Elyot. You are much in my thoughts.

Earlier that same evening, Lyddie had been hurrying through the narrow streets, hoping to get to The Place before the rain started in earnest. During the last two days, since the row over the letter, a kind of truce had begun to stretch between them and she was finding the strain of behaving like a polite stranger difficult to maintain. She'd been rather shocked—and then frightened—to discover that Liam seemed almost indifferent to the loss of their happy relationship. That evening, after the row, she'd found it impossible to stroll into The Place as if nothing had happened. He'd returned home in the early hours of the morning and had been surprised to find her waiting up for him.

'Why aren't you in bed?' he'd asked, almost irritably—and when she'd gone to him to explain why she'd been unable to come to The Place, he'd said that it was too late for scenes and they'd both best get some sleep. Silenced, humiliated, she'd trailed upstairs behind him. He'd been asleep in minutes, but it was only towards dawn that she'd fallen into a heavy sleep and, when she'd woken, Liam had gone.

His note was on her desk: *It's going to be a busy day—we've got the VAT inspector in the office. See you this evening for supper as usual.*

She'd seen it as an olive branch and, anxious to build on even this small peace offering, had gone, as usual, for supper. Liam, however, had remained in the office for most of the evening. As they'd walked home, it was clear that Liam had been drinking, something he rarely did when he was working, and, although he was more approachable than he had been the previous evening, nevertheless there was an odd indifference, almost a brutality, about him that unnerved her. This time he made love to her with a passion that held no tenderness whatever and yet she still clung to him, determined to break through this stranger's façade to the real Liam, whom she loved.

He brought her a mug of tea in the morning, but the constraint was still there. 'So what time are you away to your cousin Jack?' he'd asked—and, when she'd told him she'd cancelled her visit, he'd looked quite put out.

'How could I go when we're like this?' she'd pleaded. 'Can't you see that it would have been impossible?'

'Mother of God!' he'd exclaimed. 'What a child you are'—but then he had relented and stretched out a hand to her.

'I was going to take the day off to go to Dorset,' she'd said, holding his hand tightly, 'so couldn't we spend some time together?'

'I couldn't possibly,' he told her, looking away from her disappointment, disengaging his hand. 'The VAT inspector's not done with us yet, I'm afraid. I'll be stuck in the office with him. But I'll certainly be able to have supper with you this evening. Is that a date?'

'Oh, yes,' she'd said, grateful for this much at least and responding to his lighter tone. 'I'll be there.'

So here she was, the Bosun padding at her side, hoping to be at her seat in the snug before the wine bar filled up. She knew she was being foolish but she flinched at the thought of facing the glances of the now-familiar clients, who might guess from her expression that all was not well between her and Liam. It came as a tiny unwelcome shock to realise that; no warmth or true friendliness awaited her here; only polite greetings and the knowledge that any fall from grace would delight one or two regulars. Of course, there was Joe . . .

She paused inside the door, glad to see The Place was nearly empty. She looked around her as if for the first time, approving the black-and-white tiled floor, whitewashed rough-stone walls and the large gilt-framed mirrors. Comfortable, cushioned basket-weave chairs were set at the round, black-stained beech tables. The long bar, with its high stools, stretched the length of one wall and the snug was right at the back, just outside the kitchen door. In one corner a narrow staircase curved to an upper floor, where the offices, storerooms and lavatories were situated. Discreet wall lights gave an intimate glow, the place was fresh and clean and inviting.

Passing between the tables, she was nearly at the entrance to the snug when she heard the conversation, low-pitched but tense. The words were not clear but the tone was; she recognised the voices of Joe and Rosie—and they were arguing. The background music made it impossible to hear, or to make her approach heard, and Lyddie paused anxiously, wondering what she should do. The Bosun, however, had no such finer feelings. He shouldered his way past her and wagged cheerfully into the snug, confident of his welcome. The voices ceased abruptly and, by the time Rosie emerged, Lyddie had moved back into the body of the room and was busy taking off her long raincoat.

'Oh, hi!' She smiled at Rosie as if surprised to see her. 'It's beginning to rain quite hard. We only just made it in time.'

Rosie watched her for a moment, not speaking, until Joe came out of the snug behind her. 'Come and sit down,' he said, smiling back at Lyddie. 'Liam's still in the office, but you must have a drink and then I'll go and tell him you're here. I know he wants to eat with you this evening. I've had instructions.'

Her heart was warmed by his words, and by his welcome, and courage flowed once more in her veins. She sat down and waited for her drink.

'So.' Joe put a glass of wine in front of her and slid onto the opposite bench. 'How are you? I didn't have a chance to talk to you last night, we were too preoccupied with the man from the VAT, but I think he's finished with us and we've passed all the tests with flying colours!'

He was friendly, easy in his corner, yet Lyddie still sensed uneasiness beneath the jokey exterior.

'I'm worried about Liam.' She said the words without really thinking; they seemed to jump from her lips like the toads from the princess's mouth, and she watched his expression change.

Joe frowned a little. 'What's to worry about? He seems fine to me.' But he would not look at her.

'I don't know.' She rested her arms on the table. 'I hoped you'd be able to tell me. He keeps the whole business side so private but there's something on his mind.'

She noted that he looked relieved, watched him relax slightly. 'Oh, that's Liam all over,' he said. 'Even I don't know what's going on when it comes to the business. It's his baby, always has been. No good getting upset about it.'

'It's not quite that.' She wondered how much she could confide in Joe. 'The thing is, I've been wondering if the business needs money. If— Oh, I don't know how to put this. We've had a row about it, actually.'

She looked so miserable that Joe faced her directly. 'OK,' he said. 'I know you saw a letter. Liam told me and I think he was over the top about it. You're his wife, after all. He's too obsessed—well, possessive, anyway—about The Place. It's his whole world and you're going to have to try to accept that. But there is no need to worry about the financial side of it. Honestly. We've got to modernise the kitchen and that's the long and short of it. I'm doing the same as him, raising money against my flat, and Rosie's not too thrilled about it, I can tell you.'

'Is that what you were arguing about?' she asked, comforted by his matter-of-factness.

He flushed, clearly embarrassed, and she cursed herself. 'Anyway,' she said quickly, covering the lapse, 'it's simply that I might have some money coming to me, you see, and I wondered if I could help him.'

'Liam's a bit of a control freak,' Joe told her. 'He likes to do everything himself.'

'And who is it taking my name in vain?' Liam appeared in the doorway. 'What lies is he telling you about me?'

'I was just telling her what a mean, arrogant bastard you are.' Joe got up, grinning easily. 'But I'm sure she knows that by now.'

'She does indeed.' Liam took Joe's place, lifting Lyddie's hand to his lips. 'I'm a mean, arrogant bastard. Can you forgive me at all?'

'Oh, Liam.' She was so overjoyed to see him easy and charming, so loving as he looked at her, that she knew she'd forgive him anything. 'I'm really sorry about the letter. It was quite wrong of me—'

'Shall we forget the old letter? The VAT man has gone and I feel like a reprieved man. Could you manage another drink?'

'Yes, please,' she said gratefully. 'Oh, I could.'

Chapter Five

DRIVING TO OTTERCOMBE on Saturday morning, Lyddie still felt all the relief and happiness that making up with Liam had brought her. Within her relationships, Lyddie dealt in absolutes: she was incapable of living with strife, unable to ignore surly tempers or icy silences. She liked open discussion, however painful, and preferred communication to the bottling up of discontent. Now, despite the relief and happiness, she was experiencing the first stirrings of anxiety. She was forced to admit that there was a whole part of Liam's life to which she had no access: a no-go area that was closed to her. Had this been clear from the beginning or had she wilfully misled herself because she'd wanted him so badly? Even now, although Liam was full of apologies for his outburst and the current of love was flowing once more between them, Lyddie was obliged to face the fact that he had not budged an inch from his original position. The Place was his and she had no part or say in it. The subject of the loan to be raised against the house, along with her own offer, had been simply despatched straight back into that no-go area; it was as if these matters had never been raised and, despite her policy of negotia tion at all costs, Lyddie had found herself unable to resurrect them. She knew why: the resumption of their warm, easy-going pattern of life had been too precious to risk. He'd shown her his weapons—withdrawal of love, silence, coldness—and she'd surrendered her own principles.

She told herself that it was early days, that Liam could not be expected to change overnight with regards to his passion for his business. Five years of Liam's life was bound up in the wine bar: it had been his whole world. She needed to make allowances, to give him space to adjust. As the car fled along the A39, leaving Hartland Point and Bude to the west, Lyddie tried to convince herself that Liam would slowly relinquish his grip on the business and allow her to enter into it with him. She must be patient. The fear remained, however; a tiny shadow cast across her happiness.

Both Mina and Nest were aware of it as they watched her playing with Toby and Flora or laughing and talking with Jack and Hannah. There was a febrile quality to her brightness that worried both of them. They guessed that it might have something to do with Liam.

After lunch, however, Georgie was beginning to behave oddly enough to keep them both alert. She'd begun the day well, appearing to have a reasonable grasp on the proceedings. Nest managed to avoid irritating her, reminding herself not to fall into the trap of asking her sister if she remembered Hannah and the children, talking instead with Mina about the little family while the three of them had breakfast. Georgie had not contributed but appeared to be listening and taking it in.

'After all,' said Mina philosophically, as she and Nest cleared up afterwards, 'Jack and Hannah know the score. I doubt they'll be offended if Georgie muddles them with someone else.'

'As long as she doesn't . . .' Nest hesitated, 'you know—blurt something out.'

Anxiety curdled Mina's gut. 'The thing is, we don't know what it is she might blurt out.'

Even as they stared at each other fearfully, a commotion was heard outside: Jack and his family had arrived. The sisters hurried out into the garden. Jack had already released Toby from his seat and he came hurtling round the front of the car to greet the dogs. Jack kissed his aunts and looked tolerantly upon his family. Flora had now fought her way both out of the car and from Hannah's restraining grasp and stood swaying uncertainly on the gravel, her gaze fixed upon the dogs.

'Which is Nogood Boyo?' asked Toby, kneeling among the three of them. He thought the name was exceedingly funny. 'Why is he called Boyo? Why is he no good?'

'Because he's very naughty,' explained Mina, 'and he's Welsh.'

'What's Welsh?' asked Toby, puzzled.

'Don't,' murmured Jack. 'Please, Aunt, just don't. After "no" and one or two other unsavoury words of the moment, "why", "how" and "what" follow in quick succession. Ah, here's Aunt Georgie. Good morning, Aunt, and how are you?'

Georgie allowed herself to be kissed, stared fixedly at Hannah for a moment, then stood watching the proceedings as Flora was whisked upstairs to have her nappies changed. Toby reflected upon the rival merits of orange juice and milk, and Nest and Mina chattered and joked with Jack. In the midst of their jollity, Lyddie and the Bosun arrived.

Lunch passed without too many alarms but now, as they sat drinking coffee in the drawing room with the French windows open to the terrace, Mina grew aware of the change taking place in Georgie. That particular expression, which Mina was learning to dread, was transforming her face. Confused, even anguished, Georgie sat contemplating her family. In the drawing room, the scene of so many family occasions, she seemed to drift in time, staring first at Toby, now at Flora, in puzzlement. She turned her eyes to Jack and saw Timmie sitting talking—but to whom? Was it Nest who sat beside him, leaning towards him, listening intently, as they had so often sat together in the past? Yet here was Nest, wheeling her chair into the circle . . .

A child paused to look up at her, a small, fair-haired boy with Timmie's eyes, puzzled by her unnatural immobility. Georgie stared back at him, remembering. Of course, these two tinies were Timmie and Nest and the other two, the grown-ups, must be Timothy and Mama. She chuckled to herself . . .

'I know a secret,' she said to the child—but, before Toby could take her up on this, Mina turned quickly.

'Toby,' she said, 'take this cup to your mother, darling.'

Distracted, Toby carried the coffee to Hannah and a tiny 'po-po-po' of relief escaped Mina's lips, but she felt tense and fearful, as if awaiting a blow of some kind. She glanced again at Georgie. She had the look of one who had been unfairly thwarted; yet there remained an air almost of triumph; the air of one who wielded a secret power and relished it.

Lyddie was explaining, now, that she didn't work on her computer, that she used it for typing but that she didn't edit on it.

'You should be more flexible,' Jack said teasingly. 'You should be ready to embrace new technology. Look at Aunt Mina and her email.'

'But then, Aunt Mina has always been a trendsetter.' Lyddie smiled affectionately at her aunt.

'Absolutely right,' declared Jack. 'A yes-person.'

'Oh, no.' Georgie had been listening intently, watching for an opportunity. 'Not always, were you, Mina?'

Mina clasped her hands together. 'I don't think I know what any of you mean,' she countered lightly.

'Not always,' insisted Georgie eagerly. 'You didn't say "yes" to Tony Luttrell, did you?' She smiled, watching their faces, seeing surprise fading into anxiety and curiosity, enjoying the sudden, uncomfortable silence.

'Much too long ago to be interesting.' Nest used the voice that had once quelled classes of young students to good effect. 'Aren't you going to take these children down to the sea, Jack?'

'The sea! The sea!' chanted Toby, scrambling to his feet. The party broke up rapidly and Georgie was left alone, still smiling. 'I know a secret,' she murmured, but there was nobody left to hear it.

Early in the evening, after the younger members of the family had gone, Mina, in her turn, walked down to the sea with the dogs. It was rocky underfoot, stepped with roots from the trees that climbed the steep sides of the coomb, and she went carefully. The dogs were well ahead—scrabbling after a squirrel, although Polly Garter trotted back to encourage her mistress onwards. Mina was scarcely aware of her; she was travelling back in time, remembering a springtime fifty-five years before.

It seems contrary to Mina that she should meet Tony Luttrell at a party given by the Goodenoughs; those Sneerwells who she dislikes so much.

'Do come, Mina,' says Enid, having driven over one afternoon in the early spring of 1943 with the faithful Claude. 'It's not a smart event. Just a little get-together with some officers of the SLI. I suppose you've heard of the Somerset Light Infantry?' she says to Lydia, whom she considers almost mentally deficient, buried away at Ottercombe.

'We need some pretty girls,' says Claude with his sneering smile. 'There's a terrible shortage of them, don't you know? We need Mina to swell the ranks.'

'And what about Henrietta and Josie?' asks Enid. 'Surely Henrietta is old enough for parties? Will they be home from school for the holidays?'

'Oh dear.' Lydia grimaces a little. 'It will have to be both or neither, I'm afraid. There is only a year between them, you know, and I simply couldn't stand the fighting if Henrietta goes but not Josie.'

Mina feels a flicker of excitement. 'But how shall we get over to you?' she wonders. 'I suppose we could cycle to Parracombe and catch the train to Lynton.'

'Don't worry about transport,' says Enid kindly. 'We're all clubbing together with our petrol coupons so that one person can do a round trip. It'll be a bit of a squash, but that's part of the fun, isn't it? We've decided that we deserve a bit of excitement. Now, that's settled, then.'

Once they've gone, Mina looks apprehensively at her mother.

'It will be fun,' says Mama comfortingly. 'And you don't get much fun, Mina. I'm only sorry that you'll still have Henrietta and Josie to keep an eye on. You have quite enough of that kind of thing here. Although it's so much quieter, now that Jean and Sarah and the babies have gone.'

'I don't mind them coming. Actually, I'm rather pleased. I should feel terribly shy all on my own. You have to remember that I shall hardly know anyone there.'

'You won't have time to feel shy with Henrietta loose,' predicts Mama. 'And now we must think about something to wear. I have some pretty things that should make up into something nice for you. We'll telephone Georgie and ask her what the latest fashion is in London. Do they still have fashions, I wonder, in wartime?'

Two weeks later, squashed into Claude's roomy, dark green Rover 16, Mina feels almost sick with excitement. Happiness and expectation lift her above the wrangling of her younger sisters, who are still arguing over which of them should have been allowed to wear the most respectable pair of party shoes.

As they put their wraps in the guest bedroom of the Goodenoughs' house, high above the little town of Lynton, and Henrietta and Josie barge each other in an attempt to stand before the glass, Mina catches a glimpse of herself between their elbows. The minimal amount of make-up Mama has allowed lends a glow to her cheeks and emphasises her eyes, which stare back at her, huge in her small, oval face; her long, shining black hair, piled high, gives height and sophistication, and softly falling folds of silk accentuate her slenderness. Her sisters turn away, sweeping her with them, and they hurry down into the wide, brightly lit hall, where some of the other guests are already assembled.

'Ah, here they are at last,' cries Enid Goodenough. 'Now, come along and meet these young men who have all been waiting for you.'

Dazed by so many strange faces and names, Mina smiles, shaking hands again and again, until the young officer who has been part of a small circle of people in the corner turns to meet her. His blue eyes light up, as if she is, indeed, the one for whom he has been waiting, and he takes her hand in his warm fingers.

'Hello,' he says. 'Isn't this fun? I'm Tony Luttrell and you must be one of the beautiful Miss Shaws.'

For all of that April, and for part of May, the cleave and the beach, and the Down high above the Channel, become their private sanctuary. Here they walk, arms entwined, among the uncurling bracken, looking down upon the waves rolling in, driven by a westerly gale, to beat against the tall, grey cliffs. Or, on hot afternoons, they sit close together on one of the flat boulders that edge the beach, watching the sleek otters chasing and rolling in the surf; or, on still, quiet evenings, they stand beneath the trees, the scent of bluebells all about them, locked in long, dizzying embraces that shake them both and make them long for more. The frenzied, urgent needs of wartime lovers, and the changing world beyond this small corner of Exmoor, have left Mina untouched, and Tony, only twenty-one and yet to be in any real danger, is no more experienced than she, so it seems the natural course for him to approach Lydia so as to ask formally for Mina's hand in marriage.

The interview takes place one May evening in the lamp-lit drawing room. Lydia listens gravely to Tony's stammered declaration of love, careful not to smile at his earnestness. During these last four weeks she has grown deeply fond of him, warmed by the sweetness he shows to her beloved daughter. He brings the Tinies little gifts, enters into their games, and the affection with which he treats Lydia goes some way to healing her own unhappy, grieving heart.

'I shall have to speak to my husband,' she tells him, 'but as for me, my dear boy, I think you know how delighted I am.'

'The unit will be going away soon,' he tells her anxiously, 'and we should like to be engaged before I go. Is it possible that you might speak to Mr Shaw soon?'

'Very soon,' she promises him, 'but he will want to meet you, Tony, and it is difficult for him to get away from London. The formal engagement might have to wait a little longer.'

'But we have your blessing?'

Lydia gets up from her chair and goes to him, embracing him as if he were one of her own children. 'You have my blessing,' she tells him. 'As long as you continue to love her as you do now.'

Now, fifty-five years later, down on the beach, Mina sat on a rock watching the dogs playing, thinking of that love and remembering how it transformed her quiet, placid life. His love had been everything that she'd ever dreamed of: the culmination of every romance that she'd read. She'd adored him, investing in his youthful, charming chivalry every last ounce of her love and trust. Only much later could she imagine the irresistible atmosphere that possessed the young men of the newly raised 9th Battalion; the excitement and the urgency as they trained for the invasion of Normandy. The young must boast their way to maturity and, now, she was able to understand how his fall from grace had been simply a part of the whole 'live now, for tomorrow we die' war mentality that she'd experienced for herself only when, finally, she went to London to stay with Georgie.

Mina sat on in the fading light, tears on her wrinkled cheeks, her heart heavy with regret and pain. How could he have lived up to such adoration, such worship? And why, oh, why, when the unit returned in November, on its way to coastal defence in Berwick-upon-Tweed, had he been foolish enough to tell her of his brief affair with an older newly widowed woman in Cornwall?

'It was nothing,' he'd cried, his voice breaking now that he saw her shocked, hurt face. 'Nothing at all. I missed you so much and she'd lost her husband . . . Oh God! Can't you see that I'm telling you because I can't bear for anything to be between us. It's over. Please, Mina . . .'

Unable to understand, with their love debased, ruined, lying in tatters between them, she'd sent him away with a cold, proud face that only just managed to hide her anguish.

As she walked home in the twilight, Mina recalled that last meeting:

their shyness after six months' separation. Nervous as she was, his fool-ish young-man bragging might have been forgiven had she been more experienced, but the thought of the widow in Cornwall stood mock-ingly, triumphantly, between them, destroying confidence and trust.

Mina thought: How strange that it should still hurt.

Lyddie parked the car in the only space left in the narrow road, coaxed the weary Bosun out onto the pavement and went into the house to change. Saturday nights at The Place were rather special: tables had to be reserved and a certain formality of dress was observed, although there was no specific rule. Lyddie enjoyed the opportunity of dressing up and, this evening, chose a soft, velvet, figure-hugging dress in a dark navy blue. She picked up her long, well-worn, wool and cashmere coat, and ran quickly down the stairs and into the windy street.

At The Place Lyddie made her way between the tables to the snug, surprised at how nervous she felt at the thought of seeing Liam again. Despite the reconciliation she felt a fluttering anticipation that was not wholly joyful. Joe was behind the bar and he smiled at her as he pulled a pint, although his greeting was lost in the babble of voices and back-ground music. Lyddie wondered where Liam was, but she didn't have the courage to look for him. During a brief lull, Joe brought her a drink and leaned beside her, looking out over the rapidly filling tables.

'Thanks.' She raised the glass to him. 'Is everything OK? You look a bit fraught.'

'Oh, I'm OK.' He didn't return her smile. 'Liam'll be down in a minute. He's just finishing off in the office.'

She sipped her wine, feeling oddly uneasy. 'It's busy tonight, isn't it? Is Rosie in? I don't see her anywhere.'

'No, she's not in.' A pause. 'She's not working here any more. Didn't Liam tell you?'

'No.' She stared up at him, shocked. 'But why? Has she got a better place somewhere?'

'I don't really know. We've split up. I don't know her plans. She's stay-ing with a friend for a while.'

'But that's awful. I'm so sorry, Joe.' Lyddie remembered the low, furi-ous voices, and reached out to touch his crossed arms.

'Here's Liam.'

Before she could speak to him again Joe moved back behind the bar as Liam reached the snug.

'So here you are. Safely back again. And how are the Aunts? And Jack?' He bent to kiss her.

She was foolishly pleased with such an uncharacteristically public display of affection, aware of the glances of several of the women diners, and tried to think of something sensible to say. 'I'm sorry to hear about Rosie,' was all she could think of. 'It's such a shock. Poor old Joe.'

'Well, that's just life, isn't it? Some you win, some you lose. Could you manage some supper, do you think?'

'Yes. Yes, I could.' He sounded philosophical in the face of Joe's misfortune, and Lyddie was faintly annoyed by his indifference to Joe's plight. 'Unless, of course, it's time for the royal walkabout.'

His eyes narrowed a little, amused, acknowledging her thrust. 'Let 'em wait,' he said, and sat down opposite. 'Tell me about your day while we decide what to eat.'

Later that evening, Nest sat in bed, propped about by pillows, her book lying face downwards on her knees. She'd been unable to concentrate on the book, seeing Mina's face on its pages, hearing her voice.

'We were so cut off here, you see,' she'd said, sitting at the kitchen table, holding her mug of hot tea. 'The war was simply a dreary, boring time of endless shortages. We were often cold and hungry but we were never truly scared. It wasn't until I went up to London, in 1944, that I first experienced the frenzy for extracting the most out of every single minute. Georgie and I talked about Tony. Actually, she was very sweet to me. She was in her element: the town mouse dispensing wisdom and guidance to the newly arrived country mouse.'

'Did she think that you should have forgiven him?'

'Part of her did.' Mina was trying to remember. 'She could sympathise with how it might have been for him. The other chaps egging him on, the pressure and that "I don't want to die before I've had sex" feeling that is so prevalent in times of real danger. But part of her didn't want me to be the first to be married—Georgie always needed to be the first—but, to be fair, she also wanted me to have a good time. She thought that I'd been buried alive down at Ottercombe and she genuinely wanted me to enjoy myself. She felt that I deserved it.'

'Wartime London, just before the invasion, must have come as a fearful shock.'

'Oh, it did. But it was a relief, too, not to have any time to think. And I used it to take my mind off Tony. He'd started to turn up at Ottercombe whenever he could get any kind of pass or leave, and the strain was frightful. I had to get away.'

'That's the bit I could remember,' agreed Nest. 'His pleading with Mama.'

'I didn't understand, you see. I was still living in the thirties. The war made a huge chasm in the world we knew, but I discovered it too late.

And, anyway, I was barely nineteen. The only men I knew were in books; a real flesh-and-blood one was beyond my ken. How priggish I must have been!'

'You were never priggish,' protested Nest. 'Of *course* it was a shock. It was just a pity that you reacted to it so drastically.'

'Ah, yes. You mean Richard?' Mina shook her head. 'Yes, I was a fool. You were much wiser when it was your turn.'

'We were both fools. But Richard Bryce, Mina. Did you really think you were in love with him?'

'Oh, po-po-po . . .' She leaned back in her chair, thinking about it. 'I suppose I felt that it didn't really matter in the circumstances. And Richard was very good for my morale. He fell for me like a ton of bricks and his fellow officers were so excited about it. It was rather as though I were marrying all of them, not just Richard. The wedding and everything was entirely unreal. Wild and romantic and crazy, typical wartime stuff. It was only then that I began to realise a little of what Tony had experienced when he was down in Cornwall. That sense of unreality allows one to behave quite out of character; a game that has nothing to do with real life.'

'And then,' Nest took the story up when Mina fell silent, 'Richard was killed when the King David Hotel in Jerusalem was blown up. It always sounded so odd, it being a hotel. Of course I was only twelve but I overheard Mama talking on the telephone. I never quite understood why Richard was staying in a hotel in Jerusalem.'

'It was the British HQ,' said Mina. 'Jordan had been granted independence. The war was over. How cruel life is.'

'And you came back to Ottercombe,' said Nest, after an even longer silence, 'and in the autumn I went away to school. But you seemed so calm about it all. Not like you were after Tony.'

'I am ashamed to say that there was almost relief at Richard's death.' Mina set the mug back on the table. 'Once he'd gone back to the Middle East I realised what a fool I'd been. He was a stranger, a nice, kind stranger, but a stranger, and the thought of spending the rest of my life with him was terrifying. By his death I was released and because of it I've felt guilty ever since. Stupid, isn't it?'

'Did you ever think of getting in contact with Tony again?'

An almost humorous look smoothed away Mina's expression of self-disgust. 'The Sneerwells went out of their way to tell me that he was happily married,' she said. 'It was too late.'

'Lord,' said Nest at last, 'what fools we mortals be.'

'It's late.' Mina pushed back her chair. 'Away you go to bed.' She bent to kiss Nest, her eyes still shadowed with memories. 'God bless.'

'Is it your turn,' asked Jack hopefully, his voice muffled by pillow, 'to make the Sunday morning coffee?'

A long, low groan issued from the farther side of the bed.

'I think,' Jack said aloud, but as if to himself, 'that that was a "yes". Oh, good.' He settled himself more comfortably but, before Hannah struggled out of her cocoon of quilt to disabuse him of this assumption, a steady, rhythmic roaring could be heard, and, presently, a pattering of feet. Jack instinctively braced himself as the door was flung wide.

'Flora's awake,' announced Toby, 'and she pongs.'

'Tobes is beginning to develop a real flair for the Obvious Remark,' Jack murmured to his wife. 'Have you noticed? Don't let me keep you, though. Hurry away. Oh, and do switch the kettle on before you de-pong our child.'

'It's your turn.' Hannah held on to the quilt. 'You know it is, Jack. Go and do something, for Heaven's sake, before she explodes.'

'It *is* your turn, Daddy,' Toby reassured him. 'Mummy did last Sunday because I was sick in the night from Hamish's birthday and nobody went to church because you didn't want to take Flora on your own.'

Jack struggled into a sitting position and stared at Toby indignantly. 'So much for male solidarity,' he said. 'Thanks, mate. Oh, and don't expect any support from me next time you embark on your "Oh, I wish *we* had a dog" stuff.'

'Jack, just shut up and go and deal with her,' moaned Hannah urgently, burrowing farther into the feather quilt. 'You can argue with Tobes in her bedroom. Go away.'

Jack shrugged himself into a long towelling robe and followed his son across the landing. Flora, her face puce but tearless, stood clinging to her cot-rail, wailing loudly. At the sight of Jack she paused, drew a ragged breath and began to hiccup.

'Uh-oh!' said Toby with dreadful satisfaction. 'She'll have those for ages now. Sometimes they can make her sick.'

Before Jack could think of a suitably quelling reply, he was overcome by the pungent odour emanating, along with the hiccups, from the cot. He closed his eyes, shuddering.

Later, he made coffee while Flora sat contentedly in her highchair with a chocolate biscuit, her hiccups quite abated, and Toby, having finished his biscuit, examined a new plastic dinosaur from the cornflakes box.

'Be a good chap and watch over your sister while I take some coffee up to Mummy. OK? Shan't be long.'

He went out of the kitchen and there was a short silence.

'You've got chocolate all over your face,' Toby told Flora.

She observed him placidly as she carefully licked the chocolate from the biscuit and dropped the soggy crumbs over the side of the chair onto the floor. Toby watched for a moment, imagining his mother's face when she saw the mess later.

'*Not* very helpful, darling,' he said aloud to himself, in Hannah's voice, and set the dinosaur on the table, making growling noises, and Flora chuckled as she watched, stretching sticky fingers towards it.

Upstairs, Jack stood the coffee on the bedside table and looked down on the small piece of Hannah that he could see.

'I'm not asleep,' she said, muffled. 'Are they OK?'

'Quite OK. Coffee's there if you want it.'

'Thanks.' She fought her way out of the quilt and reached for the mug. 'Jack, I've been thinking about us getting a puppy. I didn't want to say anything coming back from Ottercombe yesterday, because of Tobes, but it was such fun seeing the kids with the dogs, wasn't it?'

'It was.' Jack was smiling. 'I have no problem about having a dog, Han, but it's you who'll bear the brunt. Are you sure you haven't got enough on your plate already? I shan't be able to do much about puppy-training during term-time.'

'I thought we might wait until the Christmas holidays,' she told him. 'Then we've got three weeks off to break it in ready for next term. I think it would be good for the boys too; help them settle in and take their minds off being homesick.'

Jack bent to kiss the top of her head. 'I think it's a brilliant idea. Tobes will be out of his mind.'

'We'll have to decide what breed is best for a houseful of children,' she mused, sipping her coffee thoughtfully.

Jack beamed at her. 'I've heard that Dobermans are *very* partial to children,' he said. 'Or is it Rottweilers? You know the joke? What dog has four legs and an arm?'

'Go away and watch over our young,' she said. 'And don't say anything about the puppy yet. I want to see Tobes's face when we tell him.'

Later that same morning, wheeling slowly, Nest progressed from the sunny courtyard along the mossy path that wound through the wild garden. She crossed the small stone bridge, below which the stream flowed, and passed beneath the last of the tall, silky plumes of the pampas grass. Here, where the culvert carried the flow of water down into the valley, the umbrella plant spread its red-and-brown serrated leaves underfoot, and, in a cranny of the cliff hidden by salix and witch hazel, the pied wagtail built her nest. Pausing, turning her chair a little in the autumn sunshine, Nest watched a charm of goldfinches, dipping and fluttering with their dancing flight above a clump of thistles. As she wheeled herself onwards, she recalled the games that she and Timmie had played in this enchanted garden, with its secret places and wild, dramatic setting. Could there possibly have been a more wonderful place on earth for two imaginative children?

It is in the Christmas holidays of 1943 that Timmie is given his first Arthur Ransome, *Swallows and Amazons*, and, after the first reading, the beach is easily transformed into Wild Cat Island, although Mama refuses to let them have a sailing boat. In vain they plead: the currents on this north Somerset coast are much too dangerous to allow two small children to act out their fantasy stories to the limit, and they must be content with the rock pools, in which to swim, and the cliffs to climb. After Christmas, once Mina has gone away to London and Timmie and her sisters have returned to school, Nest is left with Mama. Now, alone for hours at a time, she enters almost completely into the world of make-believe, her vivid imagination fuelled by the stories that Mama reads to her during the children's hour. All through that late winter and early spring she wanders like a small wraith, verses and phrases singing in her ears, images crowding in her mind, dazed by the glory of the English language, groping towards ideas she cannot, at nine years old, hope to understand.

The Easter holidays bring her companionship again in the form of Timmie and, once again, they play out their small dramas, though, this time, they are enacted against the background of a perpetual battle waged between Henrietta and Josie. The two girls are locked in a rivalry that drives their mother to despair and fascinates their two young siblings. At the height of their passions, Henrietta empties a teapot half full of the dregs of cold tea over Josie's freshly set hair and, in retaliation, Josie slashes the skirts of Henrietta's best party frock. Tears and shrieks rend the peaceful cleave, while Mama pleads and remonstrates in turn. Much though she misses Timmie, Nest is almost relieved when the summer term begins and she is alone again with Mama.

'We miss Mina,' says Mama. 'There's something *steady* about her.'

Fifty-five years on, Nest smiled to herself as she wheeled over the lawn and onto the gravel. Yes, beneath Mina's warmth and apparent age-lessness there was a serenity that remained unchanged even when it was challenged by grief or despair. All the family, at one time or another, had leaned against it and drawn strength from it. As Nest had this thought, Mina appeared from the open doorway, Georgie behind her.

'Lovely news!' she cried, making a fearsome face for Nest's benefit which denied the loveliness of the news and made Nest grin privately. 'Helena and Rupert are coming to see us. Won't that be fun?'

Chapter Six

LYDDIE TELEPHONED THE LOCAL OFFICE of the courier service she used, asked for her parcel to be collected, and put the kettle on for a cup of tea. The Bosun watched her hopefully, but she shook her head at him.

'You'll have to wait until he's collected this,' she told him, showing him the package, and he heaved a sigh and settled down outside the door in the hall.

Lyddie huddled a little in her long green knitted coat as she waited for the kettle to boil. Now, with November approaching, her small room was increasingly cold. In fact, the whole house could do with more warmth. As she made her tea, Lyddie had a new idea. Perhaps the money from the house in Iffley could be used to install central heating. It would add to the value of the house and make their lives more comfortable; surely Liam couldn't object to that? She carried her tea into the other room where she could sit at the table and look out into the tiny yard filled with pots and tubs of flowers. The back wall and the woodshed were washed in a creamy pink and, with the chrysanthemums and hebes making a late, colourful display, it was a delightful little scene.

Watching the robin pecking up toast crumbs, Lyddie wondered why she felt this very real need to contribute—apart from her own earnings. Why not just save the money for an emergency? Looking at the situation dispassionately, the truth was that, even after two years in Truro, she had this odd sensation of unreality. Just occasionally she caught herself thinking: What am I doing here? or had an unsettling feeling that she was waiting for something; that this was temporary and something else was going to happen very soon.

Perhaps this feeling of unreality was because of the odd life she and Liam led. It was impossible, with The Place, to live as other young couples did: making supper together; going out for a meal or down to the pub; having an evening at the cinema. She was beginning to realise that the glorious day when Liam and Joe could afford a full-time bar manager, so as to relieve them from their heavy workload, would be long in coming. Liam, at least, had no desire to be free of his work: he loved it; it was his life.

Lyddie sighed. The point was that she'd enjoyed it. Going to The

Place after a long day of isolated concentration, sitting joking with Joe in the snug, eating delicious food she hadn't had to buy, prepare or cook, was a wonderful change from that unhappy year in London after James had left for New York. How well she could remember coming back to the small flat, after a long day and a gruesome journey home, only to find that she was out of food and much too weary to go out again to shop. It was her work as an editor, and the relationships she'd had with her friends at the publishing house that had made life worth while. Now, she still had her work but it was difficult to make new friends when one either had to entertain them alone or take them to The Place, where Liam might—or might not—be available to sit and chat with them.

At this point, however, she shook her head. To be honest, it was not really a lack of friends, it was this inability to come close to Liam that was beginning to affect her. It was as if his inner self were kept inviolate, and, even for her, he was not prepared to make exceptions. His delight-ful charm, his wicked tongue and knowing eye, disguised a depth that even Lyddie could not penetrate.

The difficulty was that Lyddie was beginning to be less able—less willing—to remain passive. Her instinctive reaction to consider Liam's point of view was beginning to crumble in the face of her own needs. This insecurity—a result of James's defection—was not a genetic part of her character and, beneath the fear that she might lose Liam too, her sense of fair play and determination were re-emerging. More, a longing for his child was beginning to possess her. Perhaps Liam's indifference to children, his reluctance to discuss the possibility, was simply due to his obsession with The Place? A new mind-set was needed but how to approach it?

A ringing at the doorbell startled her. She picked up the parcel and hurried out to open the door.

'When is Helena coming?' asked Georgie, for the fourth or fifth time since the telephone call, and Mina answered patiently, 'At the weekend, not long now.'

'And don't forget dear Rupert,' murmured Nest wickedly.

In a corner of the sofa Georgie had already relapsed, as she so often did, toes restlessly tapping, shoulders shrugging, even her face twitch-ing—now frowning, now pouting—as if she could hear a tune in her head, or, rather, as if she were having a long conversation with an unseen adversary. Nest knitted the toys and small garments that she sent to the local Women's Institute for their charity stall, and Mina did the crossword. The wind, howling up in the cleave, rattled at the windows and echoed eerily in the chimney.

'Yes, Rupert's coming too,' agreed Mina absently. 'Who wrote *Of Mice and Men*? Nine letters with a B in it.'

'Steinbeck,' said Nest. 'The thing is that it's rather easy to forget dear old Rupert, though, isn't it?'

'Terribly easy,' said Mina, still absently, then, realising what she'd said, glancing up, first guiltily at Georgie and then reproachfully at Nest.

'Just testing,' grinned Nest. 'Away with the fairies.'

'But not always,' warned Mina.

'No, not always.' Nest put her knitting aside and yawned. 'Bedtime. Would you like a hot drink, Mina?'

'Yes, please.' Mina folded up *The Times*. She raised her voice a little. 'Hot chocolate for you, Georgie?'

Recalled from her inner world, Georgie looked up at her intelligently enough, but Nest could see that, even now, it was still second nature for her to frame her answer carefully. There was seldom, with Georgie, a warm, uncalculated response. 'As long as it's not as milky as last night,' she said.

'Oh dear.' Mina sounded cheerfully apologetic. 'Wasn't it quite right? Would you like to do it yourself?'

This was something of a challenge for all three of them. The last time Georgie had made herself a hot drink, Nest had wheeled herself into the kitchen to find milk boiling over the Esse, no sign of Georgie, and Mina's favourite milk pan ruined.

'Well, if you can't manage to make a cup of hot chocolate . . .' Georgie was struggling to get out of her deep, comfortable corner, while Nest had already gone ahead to begin the night-time preparations. Mina put the guard across the fire, collected her spectacles and her book and shut the door behind them all. By the time she reached the kitchen, Nest was already managing the hot drinks, observed closely by Georgie.

Mina went past them, out into the windy night, watching the dogs disappear into the wild garden. Between the flying racks of cloud, torn apart by sharp gusts, she could see the bright stars, while the music of the tumbling waterfall joined with the roaring of the gale in the trees up on the steep-sided cleave. Invigorated, refreshed, she called to the dogs, and they went back into the sudden hush of the kitchen. Georgie had already gone, carrying her mug of chocolate, and Nest was putting the pan to soak, Mina's mug waiting on the Esse to keep it warm.

'That was naughty of you,' she said, bending to kiss her good night. 'Saying that about Rupert. Very risky.'

'I know,' said Nest unrepentantly, 'but, you know, Mina, there are times when I *want* to do something outrageous. To break out of this damned prison; to dance and run . . .'

She looked away, the passion dying from her flushed face, biting her lips, while Mina watched her helplessly, knowing from past experience that nothing she could say would ease the pain.

'On the other hand,' said Nest, wheeling towards the door, 'I think I'd rather be physically than mentally crippled. I'm not really making fun of Georgie, it's just a kind of letting off steam. Oh God, the frustration! And now, the fear on top of it. Sometimes, I think I might explode with it all. Anyway, none of it's your fault. Sorry, Mina. Good night.'

Distressed, Mina climbed the stairs, but, once the bedroom door was closed behind her, the tension slipped away and she entered into her little sanctuary with hopeful cheerfulness. 'Po-po-po'—each breath dispelled some tiny anxiety as the drink was placed carefully beside her computer and the dogs curled themselves on their beds. Tonight, she hurried herself into her fleecy robe and decided, switching on the computer, that Elyot would not be reserved as a treat. She needed him. Her thin shoulders sagged with relief when she saw that there was a message from him, and she opened it eagerly.

From: Elyot
To: Mina
My dear friend,
    How are you? Not blown away, I hope? We've had a better day, today . . .

Nest could not sleep. The demons, against which she struggled with reasonable success during the day, returned at night to torment her. Frustration, resentment, guilt and despair: these were her night-time companions. As she sat in bed, propped about with pillows, she wondered if Georgie's presence was good for any of them, even for Georgie herself. It seemed to Nest that, back here at Ottercombe, in the home of her youth, Georgie's confusion was increased: she was travelling between the past and the present, trying to make sense of it, and failing. She'd already disinterred Mina's love for Tony Luttrell; what else might she decide to uncover? It was clear that Mina was nervous, although she still denied that Georgie knew as much as she pretended.

'She always enjoyed that sense of power,' she'd said comfortingly. 'Hinting at things and putting us all on edge. But when it came down to it, it was only things she'd imagined or half heard.'

'The trouble is,' Nest had answered, 'if you have a guilty secret then that kind of thing makes you distinctly nervous. People have been murdered for behaving like Georgie.'

The blurting out of Mina's secret had seriously upset Nest. Not only was she furious for Mina's sake—it might have been very embarrassing and distressing for her—it had made her frightened on her own behalf. In Nest's opinion Georgie could not be trusted.

'But what can we do?' Mina had said despairingly. 'I shall ask Helena to take her away if you're really frightened.'

'The trouble is, she might say something to Helena or Rupert. Or to anyone!' Nest had looked wretched. 'I don't think I shall feel safe again.'

'If you feel like that, then I shall talk to Helena at the weekend,' Mina had answered firmly. 'After all, at my age there are limits to how much I can do. She and Rupert must understand that.'

Nest had shaken her head, torn between her own fear and pity for Georgie. 'Let's wait and see,' she'd said.

As she sat in bed she fretted at her inconsistency yet, each time she saw Georgie's vacant, lost expression, her heart contracted with compassion and she knew that she must cope with her own anxiety for a little longer. Knowing that a bad night lay ahead, Nest gave up any attempt at stoicism and took a sleeping tablet. Settling herself as comfortably as she could, she allowed her thoughts to drift, giving way at last to the memories she'd buried for so long.

There are so many changes after the war. Georgie is married, now, to a young man at the Treasury, while Henrietta and Josie, still quarrelling, go to London and find jobs: Josie as a secretary in a department of London University and Henrietta in a small antique shop owned by a very wealthy, titled woman. To begin with, the first floor of the London house is turned into a flat for them but, when Ambrose dies of lung cancer just after his fifty-fourth birthday, the house is divided formally and the rest of it is let. Georgie promises to keep an eye on her two younger sisters and, when Mina returns to Ottercombe after Richard's death, it is clear that Lydia is very happy to sink into a semi-invalidism. Her world has changed: Ambrose dead, Timothy dead, one daughter is married and another a widow. It seems that she no longer has the will or the energy to control the lives of her two strong-minded, single daughters, and she lets them go to make their own way in this new world.

Mina comforts her. 'Georgie will keep an eye,' she tells her.

Lydia is content to believe her; Josie and Henrietta have worn her down during the last years of the war and she is delighted to have Mina home again. They settle down peacefully together to long periods of quiet, only enlivened when Nest and Timmie come home for the school holidays. For these two it seems that the old, happy days have returned. Soon they grow out of their make-believe games and begin to explore farther afield than their beloved cleave: walking inland over the moor;

cycling along the coastal road to Countisbury. They go to the tiny village of Oare and explore the church, where Lorna Doone came to be married to John Ridd, and stand together at the altar where Lorna was shot down by the villainous Carver Doone. They descend from the wild, wind-blown coast road to the sudden, sheltering peace of wooded valleys, and eat their picnic on the banks of the East Lyn or on a sunny, heather-covered slope, watching stonechats and whinchats flitting above the rounded grey stones.

Timmie, it seems, is destined for the army; he has all the eager zest for exploration and adventure that so defined his godfather, and Nest, watching him grow strong and tall, is filled, in turn, by pride and fear.

'Does he have to be a soldier?' she asks Mama one morning just before a new term. 'Supposing there's another war?'

Mama's eyes look beyond her—as they so often do these days—to a far-off summer afternoon when she once stood in the hall, smiling at Timothy as he said, 'I apologise for arriving unannounced . . .'

'There is nothing we can do, my darling,' she says gently. 'He would be unhappy doing anything else.'

Mina understands how she is suffering, and tries to comfort her, but Nest returns to school knowing that there are very few holidays left that she and Timmie will share.

In the autumn of 1951, Timmie goes to Sandhurst and Nest embarks on her last year at school. Now, with Nest at seventeen and Mina at twenty-seven, the two sisters are closer than they've ever been. Occasionally, Georgie visits with baby Helena, or Josie and Henrietta descend. Josie is now engaged to a young nuclear scientist, and Henrietta and she have become rather closer. Henrietta continues to play the field. Glamorous, amusing, confident, she has plenty of admirers but no special one. Despite her air of elegant sophistication she can be wickedly, cruelly funny and she makes Nest and Mina laugh until they cry, with her naughty imitations of Georgie's Tom and Josie's Alec.

'Too yawn-making for words,' she says, wrinkling her nose after one such performance. 'Tom is only interested in the National Debt and Alec is bored by anything that isn't in a test tube. He's only happy in a laboratory. Poor old Josie. They might be off to America, did she tell you?'

Nest is fascinated by her beautiful, modern, older sister and during the Christmas holidays, begins to think that it will be fun, when she leaves school, to go to London and try her wings. When the Easter holidays come, however, the possibility of going to London is postponed. Lydia has a recurrence of her asthmatic troubles and Mina is much preoccupied with looking after her, leaving Nest to deal with mundane jobs about the house and much of the cooking. Nest is quite happy and, one soft, warm afternoon in early April, she wanders down to the beach where she stops, startled by the sight of the figure of a man, lying stretched on a rock, his face turned up to the sunshine. Out in the bay a small boat bobs, and a wooden dinghy is pulled up on the shingle. Once or twice small boats have taken shelter in the cove from sudden squalls, but never before, to her knowledge, has the sailor come ashore. The man raises his head, shielding his eyes against the sun, sees her and slews round on the rock, staring.

She stands still, watching him: his cord trousers are rolled above his ankles, he wears a thick, oiled fisherman's sweater and old sandshoes.

'Hello,' he says, not moving from the rock. 'Have you come to tell me I'm trespassing or are you simply a passing dryad?'

She is transfixed by his light Irish voice and the utter beauty of him, so wild and casual there upon the rock.

'No,' she says at last, foolishly.

'No to which?' he asks teasingly.

She smiles, then, possessed by a sudden glorious upswing of spirits. 'You *are* trespassing,' she says, crossing the beach towards him. 'But I won't tell on you.'

He laughs. His red-brown hair glints in the sunlight and his eyes are a dark, bright blue. 'And me hoping you were a dryad,' he says ruefully. 'So you own this magic place, do you?'

'Well, not me,' she answers, looking at him, confused, breathing fast, already wanting to touch the crisp hair. 'My family own it.'

'Do they so?' His voice is warmly intimate, his glance keen. 'And will you share it with me for this afternoon, lady?'

'Oh, yes,' she answers simply, so sweetly, that he jumps up and makes her an old-fashioned bow.

'My name is Connor Lachlin,' he says.

'And mine is Nest,' she answers, and holds out her hand.

When he takes it—and carries it briefly to his lips—she feels that she might faint with wild, longing joy and, when they sit together on the rock and he retains her hand in his, she knows how, at last, between a moment and a moment, the world can change for ever.

Nest stirred, her dreams disturbed. Drugged with medication, unwilling to wake, yet she was aware of someone standing close to her. Her eyelids, weighted with sleep, fluttered open but it was too dark to see anything clearly. A denser shape detached itself from the shadows and leaned over her; she felt the breath upon her face and did not know whether she still dreamed. Her body, heavy and relaxed, was incapable of movement, yet she knew fear and tried to speak.

The form still hovered above her and she was aware of hands lightly moving upon her. Her skin shrank from the touch, her muscles contracting in horror, but she could not lift her arms or make any sound.

'Mama.' The word was little more than a whisper. 'Why is it dark in here, Mama? Why are you lying down in the morning room?'

Trying to rouse herself, Nest felt herself to be swimming in treacle, and 'No,' she tried to say. 'No, I am not Mama . . .'

'I know a secret, Mama. *Your* secret.' The whispering voice was horrid in its knowing confidentiality. 'Why don't you speak to me? Shall I tell your secret, Mama?'

In an enormous effort of will, Nest raised her arms—oh! how heavy they were—and feebly gripped Georgie's wrists.

'It's me!' she muttered. 'It's me. Nest. Not Mama. It's Nest . . .' Exhausted from the effort, she fell back against her pillows, dimly aware of a new quality of silence: surprise, perhaps, and confusion.

'Nest?' Georgie began to chuckle a little. 'Nest. I know about you too, Nest. I know a secret. Shall I tell?'

'No!' cried Nest—but the shout that rang in her head was merely a whisper and she closed her eyes as a great weariness overtook her, no longer aware of Georgie or of the door opening quietly and then closing.

She dreamed again, her eyelids fluttering as she watched the past replay itself before her.

During that week, while Mina is occupied with Lydia, Connor sails to the cove nearly every day. He is staying in Porlock, at a small cottage owned by a friend, and the boat is part of the deal.

Connor is a professor of history at one of the Oxford colleges and is at least ten years older than Nest is: a fact that worries him a little.

'As if it matters,' she cries. 'Think of Maxim de Winter and the girl in *Rebecca*. Age isn't important.'

She attributes to him all the manly graces which, nearly ten years before, Mina bestowed upon Tony, but Connor is not an impressionable young man with no experience. In fact, his holiday in Porlock is specifically to put distance between himself and a girl who is pursuing him. To be fair, he has not wilfully led her on—nevertheless he has not discouraged her too much either. Connor likes to be loved. With Nest, however, he sees all the responsibility of encouraging a much younger, innocent girl; a girl, moreover, with a respectable family at her back.

'I think I should meet them,' he says, 'Mina and Mama. I'm behaving like a thief, lady, and I feel uncomfortable with myself.'

His principles only serve to make her love him more, yet she postpones the meeting, fearing that somehow the magic will be spoilt. One morning she tells Mina that she is going for a long ride and sneaks away on her bicycle, meeting Connor on the road over Trentishoe Down. He cannot resist the spice of adventure or the romantic secrecy, and the bike is hidden in the furze while they flee away in his old convertible, laughing and singing together. At Brendon they stop for a pint and a sandwich, and afterwards she tells him he must take her to Oare church again so that she might show him the Gothic window, just west of the screen, through which the wicked Carver shot at Lorna. He teases her for living in her books, and kisses her.

Once he returns to Oxford, Nest wishes that she had allowed him to meet Mina and Mama. She sees now that it was childish and, more importantly, it means that there can be no letters or telephone calls. Even Mina would be shocked, or more probably hurt, to think that Nest has been deceiving them for nearly two weeks. If only he'd met them she could now be having the bliss of his letters and of hearing his voice. As it is, they have had to part in a deeply unsatisfactory manner.

Yet, as she sits on the beach on 'his' rock, watching the sun setting into the glowing west, she cannot quite regret it. How could such magic be part of the humdrum world? It is precisely because it is the stuff of fairy tales that it has no place in the ordinariness of daily life. Later, standing at her bedroom window, watching the cleave fill with moon-light, listening to the nightjar, her heart is brimming with joyful hope. Something must occur to make this a true story; miracles, happy endings, *do* happen and it is on such people as her and Connor, who believe that they can, that the grace falls.

So she is not surprised, on her return to school, when she is invited by a friend, Laura, to stay for half-term. Nest is suddenly aware of the opportunity this offers. Mina responds positively to her request: Mama needs to convalesce and it will be nice for Nest to be with young people.

The school is strict: visitors have to be vetted, letters are checked. Going home with Laura for half-term with Mina's permission, however, is quite acceptable and Nest sees that, if she wants to make the most of this opportunity, she must take Laura into her confidence.

Laura is thrilled: it is simply *so* romantic. A letter is smuggled out to Connor and a reply awaits her when she arrives at Laura's home on the outskirts of Gloucester. A meeting is arranged. It is easy for the girls to travel into the city together, where Laura will shop, go to the cinema matinée, and then meet up with Nest again for the journey back.

'Good job it's *Brief Encounter*,' says Nest, on the train. 'I've seen it. Just in case your mother asks questions about it, I mean.'

Laura looks at Nest with envy. 'I can't wait to meet him,' she says.

Nest stares from the train window, biting her lip. This has been the condition of Laura's being party to the deception, and Nest hopes that Connor won't mind. He has been less than fulsome about the plan, and she is alternately beset with nerves and possessed by a fierce, wild excitement. She shivers as she contemplates her actions and imagines her mother's face if she were to find out. Presently, however, courage and high spirits flow back; after all, what can it harm if Laura meets him? Soon Nest will be free of school, in six weeks she will be eighteen, an adult, and this foolish need for secrecy will be over. So she tells herself, as the train rattles into the town, forgetting that she has ever thought that she and Connor could never be part of the humdrum world.

They pass through the barrier into the sunshine outside the station— and he is there; leaning against the car, legs crossed at the ankles.

'Golly gosh!' murmurs Laura, awed by the impact of a mature male, and Nest feels an uprush of pride.

When he stretches a hand to her, however, her pale skin is suddenly stained blood-bright, but he kisses her lightly on the cheek and shakes Laura's hand with a blend of natural courtesy and wicked deference that makes her his slave for ever.

Once they are alone, Nest's shyness continues to rob her of speech. The casual holiday clothes are replaced with a tweed sports coat and flannels. He looks older, more serious; very real indeed. When he stops the car, in a quiet spot overlooking rolling farmland, and turns to her, she stares ahead through the windscreen, unable to meet his eyes.

'Do you not think that this is a bit rash?' he asks gently. 'Not that I'm not delighted to see you, of course.'

She glances at him quickly, made fearful by his question, so clearly anxious for reassurance that he takes her face between his hands and kisses her until the blood hammers in her ears and she clings to him. Gently he takes her hands in his own, folding them quietly together.

'I've brought a picnic,' he tells her, his voice deliberately light, 'made of all the right stuff, believe me, though nectar was in short demand and they were fresh out of lotus . . .'

She is laughing, adoring him, but he hasn't finished with her.

'We'll have a perfect day,' he tells her, more seriously, 'but this is the last one, lady, until I meet your family. You don't do this to me again.'

She promises, too relieved to protest. But even though the picnic is delicious the ease they shared is gone, the holiday magic slightly tarnished, as reality presses in on their idyll. When she suggests that they find somewhere to have some tea, he is not too keen. In the little teashop he withdraws even further; his tone is light, social, amused. She feels that she is still a schoolgirl being given a treat by an older member of her family, a cousin perhaps. Oh, how distant, now, the beach and the moor; how natural and easy their love was, then.

'So,' says Connor, back in the car, unaware of her churning gut and destroyed confidence, 'will you give me an address or a telephone number so that I can meet this family of yours?'

'If you still want to,' she mutters miserably—and he laughs and kisses her.

'For my sins,' he says, 'I do. So now which of them do I drop in on?'

'Mama and Mina.' She feels better now, sitting straighter. He wants it to be above-board and she has been so ready to misjudge him. 'But they're such a long way away.'

'I'm going down to Porlock again for a weekend. I'll drop in.'

'What will you say?' She stares at him, fascinated by his insouciance.

'Oh, that's not a problem. I shall say that I met you through your friend Laura at a party, and you told me to call on them when I was down next. How does that sound?'

'It sounds wonderful.' She is renewed again, full of delight. 'They'll love you, of course.'

He smiles drily. 'Of course. And you could be writing them a letter, just to say you've met this chap who might be passing through. Mention Porlock but keep it light; a coincidence, that kind of thing. But no contact between us until I've done it. Now, do you promise me that?'

'Of course I do.' She melts towards him, yearning for his embrace, weak with longing.

'I'm taking you back,' he says at last, 'and you'll never know what it's costing me. It's a medal I should be getting. Comb your hair and make yourself ready to meet that pop-eyed friend of yours.'

'I love you,' murmurs Nest, trying the words for the first time, but he is busy reversing the car out of the parking space and doesn't hear her.

It was Friday evening before Lyddie summoned up the courage to speak to Liam about her idea for installing central heating. When she arrived, there was already a crush at the bar, but Joe waved to her cheerfully and several regulars stopped the Bosun to make much of him. To her surprise, Liam was already installed in the snug and he stretched out an arm to pull her down beside him. 'What a racket!' he said.

'I like it,' Lyddie said, kissing him. 'It's fun, although it seems busier than usual. Were you waiting for me?'

'I was,' he answered. 'Someone's having a birthday and I think we'll get our order in before they want to eat. That way I can give Joe a bit of a break later on.'

'That's fine by me.' She let him help her out of her coat. 'We've had a very long walk and I'm starving.'

'I feel guilty about giving you that animal,' he said, leaning to stroke the Bosun. 'All this walking you have to do!'

'I need it. I sit down all day, remember? A long walk in the morning and then again in the evening is good for me—as well as him.'

She saw that he was distracted, looking towards the bar, and glanced in the same direction. A pretty blonde girl was working beside Joe and, as they watched, he smiled reassuringly down at her and she pulled a face at him, clowning terror.

'Who's that?' Lyddie turned to Liam, surprised.

'That's our new girl, Zoë. Rosie's replacement. This is her first night so we're keeping an eye on her.'

Lyddie saw Joe give Zoë an approving nod. She asked a question and he bent to show her something below the bar, their heads close together.

'Well,' she said thoughtfully, 'perhaps she'll be taking Rosie's place in more ways than one.'

Liam smiled. 'Always the romantic. So what are you going to eat?'

They sat together, companionably, sometimes talking, sometimes watching the ever-changing scene beyond the snug. After they'd eaten, Liam went to relieve Joe at the bar so that he could have some supper.

'How's Zoë doing?' she asked him, once he was settled on the bench opposite. 'She looks very competent.'

'She's good. She knows the job, it's just a question of getting the hang of the layout, that kind of thing.'

She looked at him as he forked fettucini into his mouth, wondering if he'd heard from Rosie. 'Are you OK? You look tired.'

He raised his eyebrows. 'What's new? I *am* tired. Tired of working fourteen hours a day.'

'But no hope of a bar manager yet?'

He shook his head at her warningly. 'I'm not going down that road. I don't like being caught in the crossfire between a husband and wife. It'll happen one day.'

'I suppose so.' She glanced towards the bar, watching Liam sharing a joke with one of the regulars. They roared with laughter, and Lyddie sighed. 'The thing is that Liam actually never seems to be tired. On the contrary, he seems to thrive on his work; the more he does the more it seems to energise him. Odd, isn't it?'

'There are lots of people like Liam,' he answered. 'It's a kind of genetic instruction. A driving force. If they stop, they die.'

'Don't say that,' she said. 'I don't want us to be like this for the rest of our lives. I want us to spend some time together occasionally, have a holiday, start a family, that kind of thing. Like ordinary people do.'

He looked at her compassionately. 'But Liam's not an ordinary person,' he said gently. 'Something drives him. You must know that by now.'

'Yes,' she said. 'Yes, I know that.'

When Liam came to sit with her again, and Joe disappeared, carrying his plate into the kitchen, his vitality licked over him like a flame; even his hair seemed to tingle with it. He kissed her, glossy with goodwill. 'Did I tell you that you look beautiful tonight?'

Joe brought them some coffee and they sat quietly together, drinking companionably.

'I had an idea earlier,' she said at last, 'about putting in some central heating. You're right about my room getting cold. I know I could use the electric radiator but it's terribly expensive. What about biting the bullet and putting in proper heating? It would increase the value of the house, wouldn't it?'

'It would.' He was staring down at his coffee, stirring it thoughtfully. 'But have you any idea of the cost?'

'No,' she said slowly, 'but we could get an estimate.' A pause. 'I could use the money from the house for it. What do you think?'

'It's a thought,' he said. He took a draught of the coffee and leaned back, stretching, a smile touching his lips. 'Definitely a thought.'

She drew a long breath, feeling herself relax. 'Good,' she said.

'And I must go and talk to the punters,' he said and chuckled suddenly. 'What did you call it? My royal walkabout?' He stood up and then smiled down at her, sending her a little wink. 'I'll be back.'

She settled comfortably, quite weak now that the moment was over, still astonished at his amiability. After pouring some more coffee, she sat quietly, watching him as he moved among his customers; a nod here, a pat on the shoulder there. After a moment she was aware of someone watching her and, glancing across to the bar, she saw Joe looking at her with an odd expression of mingled affection and compassion.

Mina carefully set out the pieces on the backgammon board, put the dice ready in their cups and waited for Nest to position her chair comfortably. In the corner of the room, Inspector Morse, with the faithful Lewis, was solving Oxford's crime, while Georgie watched alertly, muttering excitedly from time to time.

Mina threw a five, Nest a two, and Mina began to move her counters.

'Georgie came into my room again last night.' Nest spoke quietly, knowing that the noise of the television would mask her actual words.

'Oh, no!' Mina fumbled with her dice as she put them back into the cup. 'What happened?'

'I was out for the count.' Nest threw her dice. 'To begin with, I wondered if it was a dream. You know what it's like when you take a sleeping pill? You feel drugged.' She began to move her counters. 'She thought I was Mama, lying down in the morning room.'

'Did she say anything . . . well, anything silly?'

'She said that she knew Mama's secret and asked if she should tell it.'

Mina's hand trembled a little; she moved her counter quickly and then put both hands in her lap.

'And did she?' she asked, quite casually. 'Did she tell this secret?'

Nest made her move, taking one of Mina's undefended counters as she did so. 'No,' she answered. 'I managed to catch hold of her. She was leaning over me, you see, whispering.'

'How horrid for you.'

'It was, rather. I managed to grapple with her, then I said it was me, Nest. There was a bit of a silence. Then she said, "I know a secret about you too," or something like that. "Shall I tell it?" she asked me.'

Nest glanced across the table at her sister. Mina looked old and tired; her frailty filled Nest with love and remorse.

'And did she?' Mina could barely frame the words.

'No.' Nest shook her head. 'I shouted at her. Well, I think I did, it was all so hazy, but perhaps it was stupid of me. I'm beginning to think that it would be more sensible if we confronted her and found out exactly what it is she *does* know. If anything.'

'No,' said Mina quickly. 'No, I don't think so.'

They stared at each other across the forgotten game and, suddenly, the sound of commercials crashed earsplittingly into the room. Nest winced and, just as suddenly, there was silence.

'Sorry,' said Georgie cheerfully. 'I turned the thingy the wrong way.' She got up and came towards them. 'I've seen this one before. It's the don who did it. Funny, isn't it? You'd never expect the things that happen in Oxford, would you? I always thought that Oxford dons were such *respectable* people.' She peered at them, eyes bright. 'Shall I get the tray in while the commercials are on? The coffee's all ready, isn't it? Just pour boiling water in the jug?'

She went away. Nest bit her lip. 'I was dreaming about Connor, you see. Remembering those years after the war and Timmie going off to Sandhurst. Mina, do you remember the day Connor called on you here that very first time?'

Mina took a slow, deep breath, her gaze drifting away from Nest's face, looking back to a long-past June day.

'Yes,' she said gently. 'Yes, of course I do. We were in the garden after lunch. I was putting out some bedding plants and Henrietta was chatting to me. Henrietta was being naughty about Mama disapproving of her slacks. You know how old-fashioned Mama was about things like that? They were beautiful, I have to say, in a delicious navy-blue linen. Superbly cut, of course, and she was wearing a bright yellow shirt . . .'

'Go on,' said Nest grimly. 'I can imagine the scene.'

'Well, Connor came walking down the drive—of course we had no idea who he was—and introduced himself and explained that it had seemed rather pushy to sweep in with the car and so on. He apologised for calling unannounced but said he'd been passing and that he'd met you at a party and you'd told him to drop in.' She paused, thinking back, cudgelling her memory.

'Go *on*,' whispered Nest urgently, listening for Georgie.

'Henrietta was enchanted by him. She got up and said something like, "I didn't know my baby sister had such good sense," and introduced herself. He took her hand and bowed over it but you could see,' Mina's voice was dragging, hesitating—'Go *on*!' said Nest fiercely—'that he was bowled over by her. I have to say that she looked sensational. She was so . . . breathtakingly English. A dark-haired Grace Kelly. It was the true *coup de foudre*—I recognised it because I'd been there once, myself—and he shook my hand in a complete daze. Henrietta carried him off to help her make some tea.' Mina paused. 'You must remember that he was much more our generation than yours.'

'You don't have to remind me,' answered Nest bitterly. 'Once he'd clapped eyes on Henrietta I must have looked like a raw, tongue-tied schoolgirl. That's what he said when he wrote to me, you know? Not in those words but it's what he meant. Oh, he didn't mention that he was dating Henrietta, of course—I found out about that much later—but he talked about the difference in our ages. Cradlesnatching, I think he called it. He took me out to tea first, if you remember? He wanted to do the honourable thing and tell me face to face but, afterwards, he wrote to me, to confirm it, you might say. He wrote that he'd given it a great deal of thought and he'd realised that it would be wrong of him to let our friendship develop any further. He said that the romantic way we'd met had put a whole false impression on it and that I'd soon find that my feelings for him were simply infatuation, a schoolgirl crush. He was very, very kind.' She stared across the neglected backgammon board at Mina. 'I learned that letter by heart,' she said bleakly.

'Here we are!' Georgie was back with them, carrying the tray. 'Oh, it's started again.' Mina and Nest stared guiltily at the silently mouthing Morse. 'You should have shouted.' She looked at them reproachfully.

'Well, if you've seen it before I expect you'll soon pick it up,' said Mina pacifically. 'You get back to Morse and I'll pour the coffee.'

By the time she got back to the board, the moment of confidence was over and they played in silence, each locked in thoughts of the past.

Chapter Seven

HELENA AND RUPERT ARRIVED LATE on Saturday morning, by which time all three sisters were in a state of nervous tension. Georgie was, by turns, either capriciously critical of the arrangements made for their comfort or petulantly indifferent, as if she'd suddenly remembered exactly why she was at Ottercombe in the first place. Nest had slept badly, and looked exhausted. Mina, anxious for Nest, was still trying to come to some decision as to whether or not she should insist that Georgie should be removed.

'Mother!' Helena swung herself enthusiastically out of the car. 'How *are* you? Looking *very* well.'

She beamed tenderly into Georgie's sulky, watchful face and Nest felt an overwhelming urge to burst into hysterical laughter. She caught Mina's eye; Nest knew that she too longed to chuckle. Rupert was approaching, having carefully locked and alarmed the car—'Does he think that there are car thieves hidden in the garden?' asked Mina indignantly, later—and smiled graciously upon them.

'Well, Ma-in-law,' he said jovially, with all the brutal condescension of a senior master to a foolish pupil, 'have you been behaving yourself?'

Georgie stared up at him: humiliation stiffened her jaw and her thin shoulders while the colour flowed into her pale cheeks. She turned away from him.

Mina and Nest looked at one another—'It was at that point,' Nest said, afterwards, 'that I knew we couldn't ask for her to be taken away. My God! He is such a pompous prat of a man!'—and both broke into speech, urging the whole party into the house.

The meeting, having got off to an unfortunate start, continued to deteriorate. It was clear that Helena was ashamed of Rupert's patronising behaviour, though she refused to side against him: she could understand that it was his own past humiliations at her mother's hands that reinforced his own least-likable mannerisms in her presence. Yet she also wanted to restore Georgie's pride. Her desperation to shield her husband, while ameliorating the situation with her mother, became too painful to watch and, after lunch, Mina announced that she was taking the dogs for a walk down to the beach. Nest was truly tempted to break her self-imposed rule and ask to go with her but Mina, not guessing this, added that this was Nest's rest time.

'I expect that the three of you would like to have some time together,' she said brightly and, without waiting for anyone to agree with this optimistic statement, she seized Nest's chair and pushed her firmly out of the drawing room and into her bedroom, closing the door behind them. Nest let out a gasp of relief while Mina collapsed on Nest's bed.

'Do you realise,' asked Nest, presently, 'that we have nearly *twenty-four* more hours of this hell to get through?'

'Don't,' said Mina. 'Just don't. At least you can plead exhaustion or pain, or something, and escape.'

'Poor Georgie,' said Nest. 'Oh, wasn't it horrid? She looked so utterly humiliated.'

'Yes. I think, after all, that she'll be better off in that home.'

'So do I,' agreed Nest at once. 'And she will only be with us for three more weeks.'

They talked together for a little longer but, by the time Mina set out on her walk, the decision had been taken.

Lyddie heard the cathedral bell chime as she passed down Pydar Street. It was a bright, crisp October morning and even after a long walk with the Bosun, she felt full of energy and was enjoying a sense of freedom. An author had been late submitting his manuscript, a long novel, and Lyddie was in the unusual position of having a two-week slot booked and no work. For some reason she couldn't quite define, she hadn't told Liam: she'd decided to chill out a little, to do some shopping and perhaps pop in to The Place at lunchtime: something she very rarely did.

She spent some time in the Body Shop and then headed for the Mounts Bay Trading Company, where she bought a charming silk and wool cropped jersey. Then she hurried out into the bright sunshine, back to Boscawan Street, wondering whether to check out the Jaeger shop in Lemon Street. There was a small queue at the bank and she glanced at her watch as she waited to draw some money: it was nearly half past eleven. Should she have coffee at the patisserie in Lemon Street or go to The Terrace? Lyddie pushed her card into the slot and tapped in her code. Of course, she could have coffee at The Place—but almost instantly she rejected the thought. It was much more likely that Liam would spare half an hour to have lunch with her than to stop for coffee.

For the last few days he'd been on brilliant form: amusing, tender, passionate. She'd begun to believe that the 'No Thoroughfare' sign was beginning to come down. She'd decided that the time was very nearly right to suggest that it was time they started a family. Putting the cash into her purse, peeping at her new jersey, remembering last night, with its long, languorous hours of glorious, heart-stopping love, Lyddie thought: I am *happy*. She paused for a moment, aware of nothing but untinged, pure joy; a few seconds in which nothing else existed but this upward-winging sensation.

She was passing the narrow entrance into Cathedral Lane when she saw them: Liam and Rosie, silhouetted at the other end of the passage. Liam had his hands up, rejectingly, while Rosie seemed to be remonstrating. Lyddie was past, actually looking in the window of Monsoon, when her mind did a kind of double take and she realised what she'd seen. Or had she? She stepped back to look into the lane just as Liam turned away, heading towards The Place, Rosie staring after him. Her stance was defeated, frustrated, and she thrust her hands into her pockets before she glanced round and saw Lyddie. She stiffened, hesitated, and then, ineluctably drawn, each walked to meet the other.

'Rosie,' said Lyddie warmly, 'how good to see you. I was so sorry to hear that you'd . . . left. How's it going?'

Rosie stared at her with that familiar intense, calculating look and then smiled wryly. '*Is* it going?' she asked. 'That's the question.'

'Oh dear.' Lyddie felt both sympathetic and responsible, guessing that Rosie had been asking for her job back and that Liam had refused. 'Look, I was just going to have a coffee. Do you feel like joining me?'

'Why not?' Rosie seemed to be debating with herself as much as with Lyddie. 'Yes, OK. We'll go to The Terrace.'

With white cane furniture and mirrors, and the ivy in its hanging baskets, The Terrace was charming—yet totally unlike The Place.

'I always feel faintly guilty when I come in here,' said Lyddie when they had their coffee in front of them on the small round table. 'It's rather like being unfaithful, if you see what I mean?'

'Well, you needn't let that worry you, need you?' asked Rosie flippantly.

Lyddie was puzzled, sensing some subtle challenge beneath the casually uttered question. 'How do you mean?' she asked.

'I mean why should *you* worry about being unfaithful.' Rosie watched her, still unsmilingly, and then shrugged impatiently. 'I *mean*'—she emphasised the word as if implying that Lyddie were being unnecessarily stupid—'that you're married to the expert.'

'I don't understand you.' Lyddie tried to speak lightly. 'Sorry. Look, you seem a bit upset—'

'No, *you* look.' Rosie leaned forward. 'Open your eyes for once. It's about time, after all. I've always thought that you should know . . .' She sat back again, eyes narrowed, assessing her. 'Perhaps you *do* know that Liam's cheating on you.'

Lyddie smiled disbelievingly. 'Cheating . . . ?'

'Oh, for God's sake!' Rosie looked away for a moment, her hands clasping in an odd wringing movement, and then stared at Lyddie. 'Joe always said you never guessed but I didn't really believe him. Christ, Lyddie! You've seen him with the customers, with the women.'

'Yes,' agreed Lyddie carefully, 'and I *did* wonder if he'd been with one or two of them before we were married—'

'One or two?' Rosie gave a short explosive laugh. 'And the rest!'

'I don't believe you.' Lyddie sounded quite calm, although an icy hand seemed to be twisting and gripping in her gut. 'Oh, not about Liam going with some of the women in the past. He was a free man, after all, why shouldn't he? But I think that all this is because he won't give you your job back—'

'We're *lovers*, Lyddie. Me and Liam. We were lovers long before you blew into The Place on that *bloody* summer's day and turned his head with your class act . . .'

'All the more reason for you to be—'

'Please,' Rosie interrupted wearily, 'oh, *please*, don't let's pretend that I'm doing the woman scorned bit. I left The Place of my own free will. Liam and I have been having it off for the last year—yes, there was a break for a while after he married you—but now there's someone new. Oh, I haven't been given the push, Liam's not like that. The more the merrier where he's concerned. He likes a harem. It lends spice, a bit of competition. Christ! Lyddie, don't look like that. Where the hell did you think he was when he said he was going to the bank every day, or the cash and-carry?'

'And Joe?'

'Joe?' Rosie looked baffled at the question and then shook her head. 'You really want some convincing, don't you? Joe and I were never serious except for a short time after you and Liam got married. When Liam and I started to go to bed together again, Joe kept up the pretence because he didn't want you to be hurt. He was furious but he can't do anything about it. They're partners and that's that. The Place is more important to them than anyone, haven't you found that out yet? I told Joe I was going to tell you before one of those other cows that Liam hangs out with spills the beans but he was very angry with me. That's what we were arguing about that night when you came in out of the rain.' She looked away from Lyddie's white face. 'It's *not* spite,' she said urgently. 'It's just . . . You need to know before someone else decides to drop him in it. He has one hell of a magnetic pull, does Liam, but one of the others might just tug free and decide to get her own back. You're not very popular, you know, waltzing in and pinching him from under our noses.'

Lyddie remained silent; she even drank a little coffee, although her hand trembled and the cup rattled as she replaced it in its saucer. Rosie watched her admiringly, consideringly.

'I'm not sure you believe me, even now,' she said. She leaned forward again. 'Tell me,' she asked casually, 'would you agree if I said that, just these last few days, since Thursday, let's say, Liam's been really sparkling, right up there, know what I mean?' She smiled. 'Yes, I see that you would. Know why? The reason's very close to home and she's called Zoë. You can tell when Liam's pulling someone new. It goes to his head like champagne and he wants everyone to share the bubbles. He was at The Place yesterday afternoon, wasn't he? Right? And he couldn't possibly get home. Right? I bet you haven't seen the set-up in one of the store-rooms upstairs, have you? Just in case someone's ill or has to stay over? No, well, it's bloody useful. And that's where he was yesterday afternoon and I bet you had one hell of a night with him!'

Once again she looked away from Lyddie's shocked, vulnerable expression, biting her lips with frustration.

'Look,' she said at last, 'don't take my word for it. Go there now and see for yourself. He won't be expecting you. I'm sorry, Lyddie. I am, really, because you're a sweet person and he should have left you alone. But I love him too, and he was mine before ever he was yours.' She stood up quickly. 'And now,' she said bleakly, 'you'll never know, will you? You'll look at them all with new eyes. The ones who smile at him and, even worse, the ones he doesn't take too much notice of, and you'll never know.' She gave a bitter laugh. 'Well, join the club.'

She whirled away, out into Boscawan Street, and Lyddie sat on, her hands still trembling, sick to the stomach. Mechanically, she finished her coffee and, presently, she found that she could stand up, pay the bill, and walk out into the sunshine. Her mind a careful blank, she crossed the road and stepped briskly towards The Place. She paused just inside the door. Zoë stood at the entrance to the snug, smiling down at someone hidden from sight inside. As she watched, Lyddie saw the hand that came out to draw a sensual, lingering finger round the bare space between Zoë's jeans and short, cropped T-shirt. She leaned towards the owner of the finger, laughing now, and Lyddie drew back quickly as Liam swung himself into view and, after a swift but even more intimate touch, pushed Zoë affectionately but firmly aside and disappeared into the kitchen.

Some people, coming in for lunch, screened Lyddie's escape and she hurried away, her cheeks burning, her heart knocking in her side. Walking fast she broke every now and again into a stumbling run, until she was safely home with the door closed behind her.

Overnight, the wild westerly gales, driving onshore behind the high tides, piling the sea against the rock-bound coast, had refashioned the beach and scoured the pools. Seaweed had been flung far beyond the usual high-water mark and the dogs ran excitedly among the brown, shiny kelp, examining the spoils. Behind them, Mina moved more slowly, collecting smooth, twisted pieces of bleached, salty wood, which later would sizzle with magical red and green and blue flames when she lit the sitting-room fire. Farther down the beach, Georgie stooped over a pebble, turning it carefully in her fingers before putting it in her pocket. She was beginning to develop a fondness for inanimate things: a stone, a short length of string, an old stub of pencil. These would be placed together in odd, meaningless, still-life patterns that she would touch tenderly from time to time.

Now, as Mina watched her, Georgie's attention was caught by something half buried in the wet sand. She crouched to dig deeper, disinterring the object from which she brushed the gritty shale.

'Look what I've found.'

Mina hastened down the beach curiously. 'What is it?'

'It's a toy car.' Georgie was delighted. 'The rubber wheels are gone, and all the paint, but you can see quite clearly that that's what it is.'

'So it is.' Mina laughed incredulously. 'One of Timmie's, d'you think? Fancy finding it after all this time. I wonder how long it's been buried? Oh, of course, it might be one of Toby's.'

'No.' Georgie shook her head at once. 'It's too old. No, it's Timmie's. I recognise it. Timothy sent it for his birthday when he was about seven, at the beginning of the war. He was quite mad with joy about it. So was Mama. Surely you remember? There was such excitement when the parcel arrived. *She* had a letter, of course.'

Mina felt, quite suddenly, an odd sense of stillness. The shrieking of the gulls overhead, the pounding, rhythmical crash of the insatiable tide upon the shore, the wild barking of the dogs; all these sounds seemed to recede as she looked at Georgie. Her sister's expression was compounded of simple pleasure and a knowing, amused scornfulness as she examined the toy car. Silence stretched between them.

'Did you read her letters?' Mina asked at last. 'Mama's letters from Timothy, I mean. Did you, Georgie?'

Instantly the expression changed: replaced by the bridling motion of the shoulders, the sly face movements, as if she heard another conversation in which she was already justifying herself to an unseen accuser.

'Did you, Georgie?' insisted Mina. 'She kept them in her sewing box, in a little, shallow, secret drawer.' Mina turned to look out across the Channel. 'Odd how the Victorians loved secret drawers, isn't it? I saw her by mistake, putting a letter away. I thought it was the Tinies playing in the drawing room. Do you remember how they'd hide just before lunchtime and one of us would have to find them?' She chuckled. 'I can see them now, standing behind the long curtains with their sandals showing at the bottom. They never *could* guess how I found them so quickly. Did you see Mama putting the letters away too?'

'I heard something.' Georgie was willingly drawn into the remembering game. 'A little, sharp bang. I was lying down on the sofa and she didn't know I was there. I was home from London for a weekend or a holiday during the war. Quite early on, I think it was. After the Blitz, though. I looked over the back of the chair but she was going out of the room.' Georgie paused, thinking about it. 'I was curious,' she admitted, after a moment. 'There was something, you know . . . *furtive* about it. It was so unlike Mama that I felt a little flutter of . . . well, a "What's she up to?" kind of sensation.'

'So you went and had a look?' Mina's voice invited intimacy.

'Well, I did. It wasn't difficult to find the spring-catch. Goodness, I couldn't believe it when I saw them all stacked together. There were dozens of them, weren't there?'

'There were quite a lot,' Mina agreed. 'Most of them were from abroad, of course . . . Did you read them too?'

'Some of them.' Georgie's glance crossed Mina's and slid away. 'Enough of them to see what had been going on between them.'

'But you didn't tell anyone?'

'No.' Georgie sounded defensive, almost as if Mina was accusing her of dereliction of a duty. 'Of course, I was less shocked than I might have been before I went to London but, somehow, this rather old-fashioned love affair was quite in keeping with the times. Timothy off doing his bit, while Mama waited for him at home.'

A pause. 'You didn't feel that Papa should have been told?'

'No, I didn't!' answered Georgie at once, almost indignantly. 'It didn't take me long to discover what had been going on for all those years with that frightful widow while Mama and the rest of us were shuttled off to Ottercombe. He preferred her to *us*, his own family. To be quite honest, I felt a sense of *satisfaction* that Mama had been playing him at his own game, if you want to know.' She looked slyly at Mina. 'Did *you* tell him?'

'I didn't read them until after she'd died,' replied Mina gently. 'And he was long dead himself, by then. He would have made a terrific row, widow or not, so I suspected that, if you'd known about them, you'd kept it to yourself. Anyway, you like to have secrets, don't you?'

Georgie looked down at the toy again, hiding her own secret smile. 'Sometimes,' she said pertly, almost childishly. 'Timmie loved this car,

414

you know. He took it everywhere with him. I hid it once, just to pay him out.' Her smile faded a little. 'He was Mama's favourite. And Papa's. *I* was the eldest. *I* was their first-born but, because he was a boy, they loved him most. Sometimes he needed a lesson.'

'I don't think he was really their favourite.' Mina was dismayed by this relapse. 'I think they loved us all differently.'

She spoke soothingly, trying to hide the tiny spasm of distaste at Georgie's disclosure—a young woman of seventeen or eighteen hiding a child's toy for spite—and her sister looked at her again, her eyes bright.

'What a joke, wasn't it? Timmie, so blond and tall. Not a bit like any of us and Papa so proud of his only son.' She began to laugh. 'Everyone remarking on how *different* he was. But all the time . . .' her laughter was edging out of control, 'but all the time . . .'

'I know,' said Mina quickly. 'I read the letters too, remember.'

Georgie stared at her, tiny bursts of laughter still escaping from her lips, her eyes confused now. 'It's a secret,' she muttered vaguely.

'Yes,' said Mina urgently. '*Our* secret. Nobody else must know.'

Georgie turned away, smoothing the little car with her fingers, mumbling to herself. 'I want to go home,' she said.

She set off, stumping away across the beach, and, sighing with frustration and anxiety, Mina collected her bag of firewood, called to the dogs and followed her on to the path.

It was almost dark before Lyddie realised how cold the house was becoming. She had taken the Bosun out rather earlier than usual, striding purposefully through the streets as though by sheer physical effort she could conquer the numbing horror that pervaded her mind. Walking the lanes, she'd felt scorched by humiliation. She remembered, with shrinking mortification, the looks of those other women and was able to put quite a different interpretation upon them. How blind she'd been!

Now, as she lit the stove, she tried to determine how much of her hurt was pride and how much damaged love. Those women—oh! how many?—like Rosie had colluded with Liam to deceive her and she had gone in and out, happy, sure in her love, despite her twinges of jealousy, while they laughed behind their hands. She knew that she would be quite unable to enter The Place again and wondered, in a moment of panic-stricken despair, where she should go and what she should do.

She made herself some tea, just for the reassurance of doing something ordinary and normal, and drank it sitting at the table. When the telephone rang she didn't answer it. The answering machine and fax were in her study but she made no attempt to listen for a message. When it rang again an hour later she continued to ignore it.

As she crouched beside the Bosun, drawing comfort from his bulky warmth, she heard the key in the lock and, in one short moment, Liam was in the room. She stared up at him, painfully aware of all that she had lost, seeing clearly that nothing could ever be the same again. She stumbled to her feet, and saw that he was furiously angry.

'Why did you not answer the telephone?' he asked abruptly.

Speech seemed impossible, so she continued to stare at him, as if she were learning a whole, new person.

He sighed, his eyes flickering about the room, weighing up what he might say. 'When you didn't come in for supper, and then you didn't answer the telephone, I began to get worried.' He'd decided to get straight to the point. 'Joe told me you had coffee with Rosie?'

'I had rather more than coffee.' She was thankful that her voice sounded quite normal. 'She decided that it was time that I should know that I was living a delusion.'

'I love you. That's no delusion. We're married. That's a fact.'

'Yes.' She couldn't deny it. 'My delusion was in imagining that you were being faithful to me.'

'Oh, Mother of God!' A sigh of weary impatience, his anger dissipating into irritation. 'You have to understand that none of them matter. It's you I love. Do you not see that? I could have married any of them but I married you . . . What's amusing you?'

'It's just that I thought you might be more original. But I'm not really amused. There's nothing at all funny about being told that your husband is a philandering bastard by his chief mistress.'

'But you had no difficulty in believing her?'

The brief descent into hurt innocence didn't sit well on him and Lyddie smiled faintly.

'Oh, but I did,' she assured him. 'Tremendous difficulty. I could believe that you and she had had an affair before we were married—after all, why not? But I thought she was getting her own back, you see, for being given the sack. I didn't realise she'd gone of her own free will.'

'Rosie's a chancer, always has been.'

'Oh, I can believe that. But it doesn't mean that she's a liar.' There was a silence. 'So does that mean that you're denying it?'

In the longer silence that followed her question, Lyddie felt all that had once been confident and secure in her begin to crumble.

'No,' he answered at last. 'There'd be little point in that. I'm saying that it's unimportant. It needn't affect what we have together.'

'But it does!' she cried. 'Do you really think that I can walk into The Place ever again? That I can sit there calmly eating my supper while you slink around the tables mentally screwing whichever female customer takes your fancy and drooling privately over the barmaid you were knocking off earlier up in the storeroom?'

He made a fastidious grimace and she saw that, fantastically, some puritanical streak deep in him hated her outspokenness. A surge of pure anger, untinged with self-pity, rinsed her clean of any insincere emotion.

'I saw you earlier,' she told him. 'I came to The Place at lunchtime and saw your behaviour with Zoë. And her response to you. Do you suggest that I should come along and sit in the snug while she laughs behind her hand as Rosie has done for the last year? Do you really think that I'm that strong, Liam? Or that I'm capable of such heroic acts of humiliation on your behalf? Do you actually think you're worth it?'

He was silent. She could see that the knowledge of her lunchtime visit to The Place had shaken him.

'Do you have any suggestions to make?' he asked at last.

'I gather you're not contemplating changing your ways?' she asked lightly.

'Oh, I might contemplate it,' he said truthfully, 'but it wouldn't last. I did try for a while, after we were married, but . . . No point making promises I mightn't be able to keep.'

'Well, ten out of ten for honesty.'

He looked as if he might try further persuasion, but changed his mind. 'I've got to go back,' he said—'You amaze me!' she said sarcastically—'would you prefer it if I stay the night at The Place? Give you space to decide how you want to play it?'

'Why not?' She shrugged, part relieved, part oddly disappointed. 'I understand you've got very comfortable accommodation.'

'I'll be back in the morning,' he said unemotionally. 'Around ten.' And before she could reply he went out quickly.

'**D**id you remember the car, Nest?' asked Mina, after Georgie had gone to bed. 'So odd, finding it after all these years.'

'Oh, yes.' Nest wheeling across the kitchen, paused to look at it where it stood on the dresser. 'Anything from Timothy was a treat, wasn't it? Those postcards he sent and the unusual presents. I still have a beautiful Peruvian doll he gave me for a birthday. I think we all envied Timmie having him as a godfather. I probably remember him least because I was youngest, but I still have this feeling about him. A sensation of someone special and charismatic that we all loved. Or am I endowing him with childish fantasy?'

'No,' said Mina. 'Oh, no. Timothy was very special indeed. I'm glad you can remember him. After all, you can't have been more than seven when he was killed.'

'It's more this feeling inside than a clear picture.' Nest screwed her eyes tight shut, as if she were trying to summon Timothy up from the past. 'He seemed so tall, taller than Papa, and fair. But I suppose everyone seems tall when you're seven years old. Oh, and I remember Mama writing to him, telling him about Timmie and how he was getting on.'

'Yes,' said Mina, after a moment. 'She wrote to him often, especially during the war. The letters went to a special BFPO address. Anyway, I just wondered . . . about the car.'

'I don't remember Timmie losing it.' Nest's brow furrowed. 'He must have had it for some time when it finally went missing otherwise there would have been a frightful row. He mislaid it not long after he first received it and he was quite distraught. Luckily it turned up.'

Mina, remembering Georgie's confession, said nothing. Nest turned her face up for her good-night kiss and went wheeling away across the hall. Mina switched off the lights and climbed the stairs; as she reached her bedroom door the telephone began to ring. She hurried into her room and snatched up the extension.

'Aunt Mina? It's Lyddie. I've only just realised that it's rather late for you. I'm sorry. Did I wake you?'

'Gracious, no, child,' answered Mina cheerfully. 'I'm about to do my emails. Shan't be in bed for hours yet. How are you?'

'It's . . . um. I'm OK but there's a bit of a problem this end.' A pause. 'Would it be terribly inconvenient if I came over for a few days?'

'Of course it wouldn't, my darling,' said Mina warmly. 'Do you want to talk now or wait until you get here?'

'It's just I've had a bit of a shock.'

Mina could hear that she was near to tears and her heart beat fast with anxiety. 'Oh, darling, are you all right? You don't have to say a word. We shan't pry, but if we can help you only have to say the word. You know that.'

'Yes, I know.' Another pause. 'It seems that Liam's been sleeping around. You met Rosie when you came down, didn't you? Well, she told me. They've been lovers for the last year and there are others. It was she who told me . . . He doesn't deny it and, anyway, I . . . saw him with someone.'

'My poor darling.' Mina was horrified. 'Oh, I *am* so sorry. How perfectly wretched for you. When will you be here?'

'I hope to be with you by about ten o'clock, if that's not too early?'

'Of course not. Come any time you like. We'll be waiting.'

Mina replaced the receiver and stood for some while staring at nothing in particular, her face anxious. Then, in her alcove, she read her e-mails: one from Helena, thanking her for a lovely weekend, which made her grimace, and one from Jack, which made her chuckle. At last she opened Elyot's offering.

From: Elyot
To: Mina

Your account of the weekend was very amusing. And also touching. After a period of peace here, we've had another setback. Lavinia has unaccountably taken against our GP, a thoroughly decent fellow. She seems to suffer from quite horrid delusions about him, which I try to dispel by explaining that she's imagining things. This upsets her even more and she accuses me of siding against her, etc, etc. On top of this, I've had my eye test. Ever since that accident, I've felt quite nervous when driving and now the dreaded word 'cataract' has been used. The foolish thing is that, in losing my confidence, I'm more likely than ever to have another accident. Lavinia, however, hates to be left alone for long, even with friends, so long journeys by public transport aren't really an option. I really fear that the day is approaching when we shall have to give up this place and move into the town, or even into sheltered accommodation. And, as Lavinia's confusion and mistrust grows, so the circle of help I can call on shrinks. Today I might leave her quite happily with a friend who, within five minutes of my departure, Lavinia is unable to recognise. I return to a scene of real drama: Lavinia sobbing, angry with me, frightened: the friend, affronted, indignant, even cross.

It's interesting to see how soon friendship cracks in the face of rejection—even when the one who rejects is so clearly not in her right mind. Sympathy, compassion, attempts to understand, vanish very quickly indeed. And I am just as bad as the others. I want to shout at her—even, in the worst moments, to strike her—simply in order to make her listen to me. Lavinia was always strong-minded, draconian in her views, hot-tempered, and it's rather as if all her other gentler qualities are being squeezed out by these more dominant traits.

My dear old friend, I shouldn't be saying these things, even to you. I can't tell you how much the thought of you soldiering on at Ottercombe sustains me. I feel, from your descriptions of the house and the cleave, not to mention Nest and Georgie, that I know you all, that you are friends to whom I could come in the ultimate despair. But William will be home in a week or so—oh! how much comfort that thought brings!—although he has worries of his own. Anyway, enough of us! Let me know how you are.

Mina read this several times with a growing and quite irrational resentment for the unknown Lavinia. She brooded on her reaction for a while. Clearly her sympathy must be with Elyot, who she 'knew', as it were, rather than with his tiresome wife. It was much *easier* to side with Elyot, who always came over as sane, rational and cheerful in the face of adversity, rather than with Lavinia, who, let's face it, even in her heyday hadn't sounded particularly attractive. Unless, of course, you had a thing about pig-headed, narrow-minded, intolerant bigots . . . 'A good slap would probably do her the world of good,' muttered Mina crossly—and then burst into a fit of giggles. For goodness' sake! Here she was, at the age of seventy-four, behaving like a jealous teenager.

Having pulled herself together, Mina began to compose her reply.

From: Mina
To: Elyot

Oh dear, things sound a bit grim at your end. Not so much the cataracts—beastly, but can be dealt with relatively painlessly, I understand—but more about poor Lavinia. It is utterly wretched for both of you but I wonder if it's wise to try to make her see the truth about her GP and so on. In opposing her, you might well a) make her even more determined to insist upon them and b) undermine her confidence in you. It's important that she feels that you are on her side and, after all, does it matter if you pretend a little? The important thing is to keep hold of the love and confidence that is between you.

Oh dear, Elyot! I've just re-read this and feel that I sound like a rather second-rate cross between Mother Teresa and Mary Whitehouse. Have you noticed how terribly easy it is to moralise about other people's dilemmas? Well, the shoe might well be on the other foot soon. I've just had a telephone call from Lyddie, who is coming home for a few days. Her husband, it seems, has been playing the field and she's in need of a little TLC. The timing couldn't be worse and poor Nest will be in a terrible state. It's the unpredictability of it all. All I can say is, watch this space.

'The timing couldn't be worse,' said Nest, her face drawn and strained. 'And Helena and Rupert are about to go on a week's holiday.'

'Try not to anticipate trouble,' said Mina gently. 'Lyddie is only here for three days. Just a breathing space.'

'That *bloody* man,' cried Nest. 'I never liked him. He's so smooth. Always smiling. One shouldn't trust people who smile all the time.'

'Oh, Nest.' Mina couldn't help chuckling. 'It's too late to do the "I always said his eyes were too close together" thing now, I'm afraid.'

Nest burst out laughing. 'Mama used to say that,' she said, 'do you remember?'—and they laughed again until Georgie came upon them, looking for her breakfast.

'What's the joke?' she asked amiably.

Once again, Nest found herself making the effort not to answer 'Nothing', thereby excluding her sister. Instead she said, 'We were remembering how Mama used to say that you couldn't trust people whose eyes were too close together. So silly, really.'

'But probably true,' said Georgie. 'There's always a grain of truth in the old saws. Is it porridge this morning, Mina?'

Nest and Mina exchanged a glance of relief at this apparently sane approach and prayed that it might last.

'If you like,' said Mina cheerfully. 'Oh, and Lyddie's coming later on this morning for a day or two. Just a little break between books.'

'Oh.' Georgie looked put out. 'But I wanted to go to Lynton this morning to get my new library book. Did I say that it was in?'

'Yes,' said Nest quickly. 'The librarian phoned yesterday afternoon. There's no reason why you shouldn't go to Lynton to get it.'

'Of course not,' agreed Mina. 'I'll drive you over later.'

Her eyes met Nest's—'and keep her out for as long as I can' implicit in the glance—and Nest felt a lessening of tension. As they ate breakfast the dogs began to bark and they heard Lyddie's voice in the hall.

Mina reached her first, hugging her tightly, holding her close. 'How lovely for us,' she said. 'My dear child . . .'

Coming behind her, wheeling slowly, Nest could hardly bear to look at the pain on Lyddie's face. She took the outstretched hand and clasped it tightly until Lyddie bent to kiss her.

'I'm not doing very well,' she muttered, tears threatening again, and Nest swallowed her own pain and anger on Lyddie's behalf and gave the hand a little shake.

'We'll have a chat very soon,' she said, 'if you want to. Can you manage in front of Georgie?'

Lyddie nodded, straightening up, trying to smile, and the two older women looked at her with affection and encouragement, enfolding her in their love, communicating their strength.

'I'm just about to take Georgie off to Lynton,' said Mina, 'and you and Nest will be able to have a coffee and a good old talk or whatever. Georgie, do you need anything else besides your library book?'

'I don't know.' Georgie looked distracted. 'I can't remember . . .'

'It doesn't matter.' Mina was very calm. 'We've got all morning to wander round. Go and get yourself ready while I make a shopping list.'

When Georgie reappeared in her coat and hat, carrying a capacious bag, Mina collected her belongings and hurried her away. There was the usual commotion as the dogs were encouraged into the camper, the engine started up and, finally, there was silence.

Lyddie made some coffee, blew her nose and stared at the kitchen table. 'Did Mina tell you?'

'She said that Liam had been unfaithful with Rosie and probably one or two others.' Nest watched her sympathetically. 'We gained the impression that he didn't deny it.'

'No, he didn't deny it,' said Lyddie bitterly, 'nor did he feel that change was an option. The thing is, we lead such a strange life. I can't just go back to how it was. Rosie's right when she says that I shall never know now which of those women he's been with. I feel so humiliated. How could I walk into The Place again, knowing what I know?'

'How clever of Rosie, wasn't it? Those words were a death knell to your relationship.'

'He didn't bother even to make a stab at protesting. He seems to feel that, because he married me, I shouldn't mind. "None of them matter. It's you I love." I quote.'

'And, as far as he's concerned, that's possibly true. The rest probably come under the same heading as a pint of beer. Necessary at that moment, briefly satisfying, but easily replaceable.'

'But you don't think that I should go along with that, do you?' Lyddie sounded anxious. 'How would *you* feel if the man you adored was having it off with someone else?'

There was a silence. 'I should feel gutted,' Nest said at last. 'I should feel betrayed, sick with jealousy, and utterly gutted. I wouldn't want anyone to see me, I would feel incapable and helpless, but the worst and most humiliating thing of all would be the fact that I still loved him and wanted him more than anything else in the world.'

'That's much too close to be a guess,' said Lyddie, after a while. 'So what did you do when it happened to you?'

'I didn't have too many choices,' answered Nest, 'and we weren't married. It was a different situation but if you're asking if I fought my corner the answer is no. I was too humiliated and I couldn't bear for anyone to know.'

'Well, that's a luxury I don't get,' said Lyddie grimly. 'I feel quite sick when I think of all the nights I've gone bouncing into that bloody wine bar and everyone's been thinking, poor fool, if only she knew, while those women . . .' She swallowed. 'How could he do that to me?'

Nest shook her head. 'It makes you wonder if he thinks the same way as other people, doesn't it?' she asked. 'It's like cruelty to helpless children. It makes you wonder how people's minds actually work. You can see that Liam is driven by some restless urge to achieve and this might be all of a piece with the sexual urge. It explains his passion for The Place and his will to make it succeed. At its best it's amoral rather than immoral. It's utterly tunnel-visioned, and everything and everyone is sacrificed to the greater plan.' Nest glanced at Lyddie and was shocked by her white face and shadowed eyes. 'You look exhausted,' she said. 'My poor darling, could you sleep, do you think?'

'I couldn't sleep last night,' Lyddie admitted, 'and I'm absolutely bushed. My head feels as if it might split open at any moment.'

'Take some paracetamol and go to bed,' suggested Nest. 'If it doesn't work, get up again and we'll think of something else.'

'I might just do that. Am I in my usual room? Great. I'll see you later, then. And, thanks, Nest.' She kissed her cheek. 'You've been brilliant.'

It was only after she'd gone that Nest realised that, for the first time, Lyddie had dropped the prefix 'Aunt'. She smiled a little; perhaps it was a compliment. She sat, thinking about Connor.

It is Mina who, unaware of the real situation, arranges for Connor to take Nest out to tea just before the end of term. His letter to Mina, thanking her for his afternoon at Ottercombe, suggests it—very casually—since he will be near the school during the following weekend.

Nest is relieved to hear that Connor has managed to visit Ottercombe but Mina's letter unconsciously strikes a warning note that makes her uneasy: 'He's great fun. Mama was very taken with him but not as much as he was with Henrietta, who was down for the weekend. Anyway, he's sent a bread-and-butter and asks if you'd like to go out to tea . . .'

'You seem to have been a great success with my family,' she says lightly, once they are settled in the teashop in the little local town. There are other families with their daughters at nearby tables and she is obliged to behave with a decorum that she doesn't feel at all. 'Mina says Mama was very impressed with you.'

'She's a lovely woman.' He seems calm, but she senses his tension. Fear seizes her. 'I can see where you get your looks, you and your sisters.'

'We're all very alike.' She wants to take his hand, touch him, make him look at her properly, but from the corner of her eye she sees little Lettice Crowe's mother watching them, trying to be noticed. 'So what did you think of Mina?'

'Ah, Mina.' He smiles in the old familiar way that twists her heart. 'She's a darling, so she is. A rare soul.'

'And Henrietta? I hear you met her too?'

The arrival of the tea gives Connor a moment in which to rally, but Nest, watching his face, knows that her premonition is a true one. At last he looks at her and the truth is there in his eyes for her to see.

'Yes,' he says. 'I met Henrietta.'

As he picks up the tea-strainer and the pot and fills the two cups, Nest knows that she could never have done it with so steady a hand. The full ten-year age gap stretches its whole length between them: he is controlled, steady: she knows that at any moment she might cry. She thinks of Henrietta, of her beauty, ready wit and sophisticated confidence, and is miserably aware of her own immaturity. He pushes her tea towards her. 'Drink it.'

The quiet, bitten-off command causes her to glance up at him. With a slight jerk of the head, he directs her attention to the other families and she responds, sipping her tea obediently.

'I wanted to see you,' he says gently, 'because I needed to tell you myself, not by a letter. And it's not just to do with Henrietta. I'm too old for you, Nest, and you know that this is something that's worried me from the beginning. When I met your family it underlined it. I'm Mina's contemporary, older than Henrietta even. It never occurred to them, even for a second, that there could possibly be anything but a chance acquaintance between us. They still regard you as a child—oh, yes, I know you're nearly eighteen—but suddenly I saw it with their eyes and I realised what I'd done.'

He leans forward, smiling very slightly, as if telling her a story; deliberately disguising the tension of the moment from her schoolfriends. 'Cradlesnatching, they call it.' His warm, flexible voice makes it sound almost amusing. 'I can't do it, Nest. It was one of those magic interludes which happen out of the real world but shrivel once they're exposed to harsh reality. I knew that when I met your family.'

She takes another sip of tea. If they were alone, she could plead with him, but what can she do here, surrounded by her watchful peers?

'Try not to be too hard on me. It's not easy, Nest, I promise you, letting you go.'

Oddly, it's the plea for sympathy that stiffens her spine. She pushes her cup aside. 'I have the most terrible headache,' she says, quite clearly, so that others might hear if they're listening. 'I'm terribly sorry, Connor, but do you think we might go back now?'

They drive the half a mile to the school in silence. He is too intelligent to risk any further conversation that might lead to tears or appeals or recrimination: he conceals his own sadness, knowing that she needs all her pride and courage to get back inside with her dignity intact.

A few days later, she receives a short letter from him, a repetition of the things he has already said—kind but firm—but still she cannot quite take it all in: she loves him too much. In fact she is back at Ottercombe, more than a month later, before Nest truly believes that it is over, that he will not telephone or suddenly appear, telling her that it was all a dreadful mistake. On the morning of August 15, Mina receives a letter from Henrietta, which she reads aloud.

'"Connor and I are seeing rather a lot of one another"—You remember Connor, Mama? He came to visit us—"and he comes to London quite often. We've discovered one or two mutual friends and he's invited me to a party in Oxford next weekend, which sounds fun . . ."'

Nest is gripped with such agonising jealousy that the rest of the letter passes unheeded. She pictures them together, knowing that now she has no chance at all of regaining his love. Once he has spent time with the most glamorous of all her sisters how could she possibly compete?

Mina finishes the letter, while Nest stares into a bleak emptiness; a future that no longer contains Connor. The rain, beating against the windows, lowers her spirits further.

'I can't remember a wetter summer,' says Lydia. 'The lawn is like a sponge.'

'Lots of the rivers are flooding,' says Mina, 'but surely it can't go on like this? Even our own little stream is over its banks.'

There is some kind of melancholy satisfaction to be had from the walk to the beach, although Nest watches anxiously as a duck with her ducklings is swept at high speed on the current; tumbling against boulders and overhanging branches, they scramble almost comically in their mother's wake, seeking a quiet shelter in a peaceful backwater. Following them, Nest is so preoccupied that it is some time before she truly appreciates the weight of water flowing down from the high moors. All manner of tiny springs gush from the rockface as though, as the locals say, the rocks are being squeezed, the water swelling the stream as it cascades to the beach. To begin with, the drama of the scene, the ceaseless roaring of the water, the crying of the gulls, is in keeping with her mood. Nevertheless, she has on odd sense of foreboding; as if, today, nature's force is too great for her.

When she arrives home, she is relieved to see that Mina has already lit the drawing-room fire.

'Mama is restless,' she tells Nest. 'It's this wretched weather. It's madness to have a fire in August but I think we need it. If only this rain would stop!'

The rain, however, does not stop; it increases as evening wears on and, at about half past eight, there is a cloudburst and five inches of rain fall in one hour. Up on the Chains, no longer able to penetrate the unyielding ground, the torrents of water pour off the moor, gathering all before them as they hurtle towards the sea. Houses and buildings are demolished as though they are cardboard; the West Lyn—changing course, destroying roadways, a chapel, shops—rushes to join the East Lyn River. They swirl violently together, twenty feet deep, bearing along 100,000 tons of boulders, building a dam twenty-five feet high, until the pressure becomes too much and the great tide gives way in a mighty roar, sweeping houses, cars and animals far out to sea.

At Ottercombe, using old sandbags to keep the water out, Mina and Nest are too anxious for their own safety to give too much thought as to what might be happening farther up the coast. It isn't until the morning that the devastation becomes apparent—on Lynmouth Street hotels and houses have disappeared without trace, the road buried deep in silt and strewn with boulders, while half a mile out to sea, hundreds of great trees stand upright supported by their enormous roots, torn from the ground—and the acts of heroism begin to be told, along with the tales of tragedy.

The women at Ottercombe listen, shocked, to their wireless, read the newspapers in horror and give grateful thanks for their own safety. For Nest, her personal grief becomes a part of a larger mourning and, for ever afterwards, the twin disasters of the Lynmouth Flood and losing Connor are inextricably entwined.

Chapter Eight

FROM: MINA
To: Elyot
Dear Elyot,

What a household we are! Lyddie arrived just after breakfast. Things are clearly every bit as bad as we feared. I took Georgie off to Lynton—which is another story!—leaving Lyddie able to talk her problems through with Nest. Nest is finding the whole thing very painful, as you might imagine. You won't know that there has been a long pause between the last sentence and this one. My dear Elyot, it shocks me to think how much I have trusted you. There is no doubt that Georgie has opened Pandora's box and all our skeletons have tumbled out. Or am I mixing my metaphors? First me and Tony Luttrell, then Nest and Connor . . . And I have made a present to you of these secrets, by so doing lifting part of the burden from my shoulders but putting us all into a vulnerable position. The odd thing is how easy it has been to become intimate with someone I have never seen. Would it be as easy by telephone? I don't think so. Or at least, not quite so quickly. I have come to depend on your advice and encouragement. Writing seems to lend a natural familiarity.

Anyway, Nest is finding it difficult. 'How would you feel if the man you adored went off with another woman?' asked Lyddie, or something like that. Well, Nest told her exactly how she'd felt and is now in a fit of anxiety lest Lyddie should question her more closely. Oh, how deceit and self-image does make prisoners of us all! Yet it hasn't been Nest's fault that she's practised deception all these years. It was forced upon her. The thing is, Elyot, I can feel it coming: a kind of nemesis for us all. Nest felt it first, all those weeks ago when Helena telephoned to ask if we could look after Georgie.

As for Georgie . . . Well, you might not believe this, Elyot, but this morning I lost Georgie! Oh, the horror still grips me, although I find I can't help laughing too. We went off very cheerfully, dogs in the back, nice, bright morning. She was sharp too, remembering places very clearly as we went along. Have I said to you that I wonder whether coming to Ottercombe is the worst thing we could have done for Georgie? It seems to me that it is easier for her to drift back, that she remembers things from forty years ago more readily than she can remember what we did yesterday. So we arrive in Lynton, park the camper and set off to the library. We are at the age, dear Elyot, which brings out the best in our nice local people and we are assisted, waited for, smiled upon. And very nice it is too. The shopping is put into the camper but it is not until we get to the café and we are having some coffee that I remember that I need some bread. I tell Georgie that I must dash out to buy some and tell her not to go anywhere until I come back.

I rush away, buy the bread and when I get back—no Georgie. The waitress, rather surprised by my anxiety, said that she'd suddenly remembered something and went off. Now, though I might have been startlingly indiscreet to you, my dear friend, I have not yet made the local people aware of our personal problems so I could do little more than check that she'd paid the bill—she had!—and hurry out onto the pavement. Which way had she gone? I run this way and that, panting along, checking her favourite places. No Georgie. People glance oddly at me and I see myself in a plate-glass window, a bundly old lady, red-cheeked, hat awry, scarf flying. Lynton is not a big town and before too long I have covered all the main streets. I even check the health centre. It is only as I make one last desperate search before going to the police station that I see her, standing on the pavement in a small side road, staring up at a terraced house. She turns, her brow puzzled, sad. 'I've been looking for Jenna,' she says wistfully, 'but I can't find her. They say they don't know her here.' Jenna, the girl who looked after us when we were children, has been dead for more than ten years. She and her husband moved into Lynton in the sixties—into this very house. 'Jenna's moved,' I tell her—it's not altogether a lie although I hope she won't ask where, it's a fair step to the cemetery—'and we must be getting home.' By the time I'd got her settled, and found that Nogood Boyo had gnawed the end off the loaf, I could have burst into tears. As we set off, I saw a mind's-eye image of the pair of us: two potty, white-haired old biddies, wrestling an aged camper round the steep bends— and quite suddenly, I have to say, I began to laugh and laugh. Georgie, bless her, joined in and the dogs barked wildly until I pulled up at Brendon Two Gates to get my breath. 'That was fun,' observed Georgie cheerfully. 'Now, where shall we go next?'

So, Elyot, how has your day been, I wonder?

From: Elyot
To: Mina
Dear Mina

I have to say, dear old friend, that I laughed too, although I felt such a twinge at the picture of Georgie outside Jenna's house. This kind of situation is one with which I can identify only too easily.

However! I have taken your advice and stopped trying to persuade Lavinia that her wild imaginings about our GP are simply not true. I go along with it now, and we drift along in this twilight world but, like you with your nemesis, I fear that something will happen shortly over which I shall have no control. The point I want to make, though, is: yes, you were right about accepting the situation. Lavinia is calmer and, because she no longer has to persuade me to believe these horrors that cloud her mind, she dwells on them less and is more readily distracted from them.

My dear Mina, I too am amazed at the ease with which we've slipped into such comradeship. But we've both managed better in our different situations because of this ability to let off steam. Perhaps it is because we cannot see each other that we are able to confide in each other so openly. Like you, I have wondered about the aspects of dis-loyalty and have decided that what we are doing is no different to being 'counselled'. But I know how you feel. We haven't just told each other about ourselves; we have told about those who are close to us and sometimes we feel we are betraying a trust. Well, so be it. We have done it out of love and concern for them, in an effort to under-stand and to gain strength to continue with the task. So, I offer you a toast: to family life.

'The thing is,' Lyddie said, 'that I still love him.'

Her three-day sabbatical was nearly over and she planned to return to Truro after lunch. Meanwhile she was kneeling on the kitchen floor, brushing the recumbent Bosun.

'Well, of course you do,' agreed Nest. 'It would be odd if you didn't. Love isn't nearly so convenient as that. I've often wondered how it must be for those poor wives of serial murderers, suddenly discovering this whole other side to someone they love. How do they deal with it?'

'I suppose it doesn't have to be a partner.' Lyddie was distracted from her own pain for a moment. 'It might be a parent.'

'Yes,' said Nest, after a moment. 'It might be. Or a child.'

'The helplessness of little children is appalling,' said Lyddie. 'Jack said that he lives in terror of something happening to Toby and Flora. The worst thing is, he said, that you're constantly having to encourage them to do things that might hurt them so that they extend themselves otherwise you would make them prisoners. Having to decide whether they're ready for the next big step. How terrifying!'

'There's something worse than that,' said Nest grimly—and fell silent. Lyddie looked at her curiously. 'What?' she asked.

'Watching other people making those decisions for one's own child,' answered Nest at last.

'That's twice,' Lyddie said. 'First you talked about your lover being unfaithful and now you say that, about children, as if you really know.'

Nest stared at her, as she crouched beside the sleeping dog. Her small face, pale beneath its shining mop, was full of innocent affection—she looked like a child herself—yet Nest knew instinctively that the moment had come at last. Her hands clenched upon her lap in terror but she spoke out bravely. 'I *do* really know,' she said. Her heart seemed to flutter in her throat. 'I had a child, you see, years ago.' She looked away from the expression of surprise on Lyddie's face, concentrating on her story lest she should lose courage. 'It wasn't so simple, in those days, to be a single parent. Apart from the stigma there was none of the financial support that can be claimed now and you had to be very well off to provide child care while you earned a living. I taught English—well, you can remember that—and I worked in the private sector . . .'

'Did they throw you out?' Lyddie sounded so indignant that Nest managed a faint smile.

'No,' she said. 'The headmistress was a very fair woman. And very sensible. She gave me a sabbatical. I became pregnant in the autumn and took the spring and summer terms off. If anyone at the school suspected they never said anything, and I was very glad to have work to go back to the following September.'

'But what did Grandmama say?' Lyddie was sitting back on her heels, the grooming forgotten, shocked but full of sympathy for this beloved aunt. 'And Aunt Mina? Did she know?'

'Oh, yes. Mina knew. Your grandmother was horrified, to begin with, but it was Mina who calmed her down. As much as anything it was the terrible stigma of having an unmarried pregnant daughter. That's probably so difficult for you to imagine in these enlightened days, but even in the middle sixties it was a disgrace . . .'

'But the father,' interrupted Lyddie. 'Couldn't you . . . ? Was he . . . ?'

'He was married.' She spoke so low that Lyddie got up and came closer, sitting down on the chair beside the table.

'Oh, Nest . . .'

Nest looked at her. 'It wasn't an affair,' she said with difficulty. 'Nothing like that. It was just once. But I loved him, you see.'

Her face crumpled a little—and then she smiled again.

'So Grandmama made you have the baby adopted?' Lyddie prompted her gently, full of compassion.

Nest took a deep breath, her eyes looked unseeingly out into the courtyard and she nodded. 'Mmm.' She steadied her voice. 'It was agreed that . . . the baby must be adopted. Even Mina pressed for it. Everyone decided that it was the best thing for . . . the best thing.'

Lyddie got up, dropping the brush, and came to kneel beside Nest's chair. In the face of this pain her own suffering receded. 'How awful.'

'It was awful.' She stared down at Lyddie's hand, warm upon her own, and then into the green-grey eyes that watched her so lovingly.

'But who was "everyone"? Did all the family know?'

'No, not all. Josie and Alec had gone to America by then and Georgie was with Tom in Geneva. Timmie was with the army in Germany, but he knew. Timmie was a great comfort.'

'And Mummy? Did she know?'

Nest stared round the kitchen, out into the courtyard and, at last, back at Lyddie. 'I've thought this through a million times,' she said, 'and there is no way except plain truth. Yes, Henrietta knew because it was she who adopted my baby girl.' She watched confusion give way to realisation and the sudden wash of colour flood into Lyddie's cheeks. 'Forgive me, if you can, for breaking the silence now. It's just—'

'*Your* child?'

'Henrietta had great difficulty in carrying a baby. She had several miscarriages and she couldn't have any more children after Roger.' Nest spoke quickly, as if by words she could alleviate the effect of such a bombshell. 'And she so longed for another baby . . . Oh God! This is awful.' Nest tried out various phrases and rejected them; they were, ultimately, simply pleas for pity. She felt weak and ill but strove to hide it from the girl who still kneeled beside her, her eyes wide with shock.

'I could say all the obvious things: we felt it was the best thing for you; you had a better chance with Henrietta and Connor; you were staying within the family.' She gave a gasp of self-disgust. 'None of it is relevant to how *you* feel, I imagine. The trouble is, I don't *know* how you feel. Utterly shocked, of course. Betrayed?'

'And my father?' asked Lyddie after a moment. 'Was it the man you talked about who left you?'

Nest looked down, surprised to see that Lyddie was still clasping her hands. She rallied herself for this next hurdle.

'Yes,' she said. 'I loved him.' Somehow this was important, terribly important. 'And he . . .' She could see all the pitfalls, knew that Lyddie, in her present raw state, would judge according to her own lights . . .

'And he was married.' Lyddie finished the sentence for her—but almost calmly, as if she were making her own assessments.

'It was Connor.' Nest couldn't bear her guessing. 'Your father is . . . was your father. He and I—' She stopped: how to tell this without condemning Connor as an adulterer? 'He and I . . .'

'Were in love before Henrietta came on the scene.'

They both started as Mina spoke from the doorway behind them, their joined hands clutching convulsively together.

'Georgie's pottering in the garden with the dogs.' This was clearly to reassure them and she smiled at Nest. 'I have a feeling that you've been telling the story the wrong way round. Come, child.' She held a hand out to Lyddie, who climbed stiffly to her feet. She looked dazed. 'Nest needs to rest and I have things to tell you. When you've heard the whole of the story you and Nest shall talk again.'

She slipped an arm about Lyddie's shoulders and led her out of the kitchen and up the stairs.

After a moment Nest wheeled herself across the hall into her own room. As soon as she was alone she began to tremble. That it should happen like this after more than thirty years of silence; after these last few weeks of heightened anxiety and strain. The moment had offered itself and she'd taken it; the relief was enormous. She gulped down great, ragged draughts of air, steadying herself, trying to control the shaking of her limbs. What had Lyddie actually said? How had she reacted? Mina had come to her rescue as she always had; right from the beginning when, in the early days after the flood and the arrival of Henrietta's letter, Nest had taken her fully into her confidence. Mina might be able to make more sense of it to Lyddie just as she had, somehow, made sense of it to Mama all those years ago.

She stands between Nest and the appalled expression on Mama's face. 'It's not the end of the world,' she says firmly. 'Is it, Mama? This happens to all kinds of people. Doesn't it, Mama?'

There is an intensity in the question that slowly penetrates Mama's shock until she blinks. 'Yes,' she says, 'yes, of course; nevertheless . . .'

'We'll deal with it,' Mina says, smiling comfortingly at Nest. 'Let's not panic, shall we?'

Afterwards she says, 'Why did you just come out with it like that, you idiot? Why didn't you warn me first?'

Nest shakes her head, tears threatening, unable to speak. It is Mina who guesses. 'It's Connor's, isn't it?' she asks.

'It was only once, honestly.' Nest shivers uncontrollably like a sick dog. 'It was at Jack's christening. Connor came straight from a conference, remember? Roger was ill and Henrietta couldn't get away.' She cries out in frustration and anguish. 'It was the only time.'

Now, as she edged herself out of her wheelchair and on to her bed, reaching for her medicine, Nest recalled all the meetings and family gatherings; the humiliations and despair. Only Mina had known the whole truth; as Nest attempted to stifle her stubborn love for Connor, Mina had suffered with her, made her laugh, given her courage.

'One more time,' she'd say firmly, regarding a family ordeal involving Connor. 'If you could do the wedding you can do this.'

The wedding had become the bench mark; the reference point.

'But of *course* you must be a bridesmaid,' cries Henrietta. 'Mina's going to be too busy arranging it all with Mama. And Georgie and Josie have the babies to worry about. Anyway, if it hadn't been for you, Connor and I might never have met!' She turns to him with a sparkling look, slipping an arm through his.

'That's true,' he says lightly.

Nest can hardly look at him, unable to bear those possessive gestures that bind him to her sister. She listens, though, to hear by what terms he addresses Henrietta. She calls him 'darling' but he never uses endearments in return. Nest finds some bitter consolation in this, treasuring those moments when he called her 'lady' and bewitched her with his voice. He is careful to raise no expectation in her breast—there are to be no backward glances—but neither does he raise suspicion by ignoring Nest. He treats her with all the casual affection of an elder brother.

The wedding is a different kind of torture. As chief bridesmaid she must be seen to sparkle: to show her delight in her sister's happiness and to listen to Connor's speech, in which he tells the guests how beautiful she looks. She sits smiling brightly, laughing, and only Mina's face shows that *she* understands. The groom's present to her is a silver and coral bracelet, delicate and beautiful—'Like you, lady,' he says quietly, lifting her wrist with the bracelet encircling it and kissing her hand. Henrietta breaks suddenly upon this breathless moment so that Nest's heart hammers violently in her side, although Connor remains cool.

'It's the helplessness,' she says to Mina later. 'How do you learn to stop loving?'

'You don't,' answers Mina grimly—and, not knowing about Tony Luttrell, Nest thinks she's talking of Richard.

Timmie does everything he can to help, inviting her to parties, balls, introducing her to delightful young men who fall gratifyingly in love with her; but all of them seem crude and immature.

She trains to be a teacher, has several brief relationships, but it is during those years of her twenties that she becomes closer to Mina than ever before. To begin with, she teaches at a school in Barnstaple, Mina driving her to Parracombe to catch the train each morning, collecting her each afternoon. They take long rambling walks, work in the garden, look after Lydia.

It is Henrietta who tries to encourage Nest to spread her wings, to move away from Ottercombe.

'It's different for you,' she says privately to Mina. 'You spent those few years in London and married Richard. You had your own life before you buried yourself down here, and to be honest, Mina, I think you're actually quite content. Nest's ten years younger than you are and, apart from her training college, she's never been away. She's twenty-five and soon it will be too late. A friend of ours teaches at a school in Surrey, and she told me that they need an English mistress for the juniors. It's a really good post. Persuade her to try for it. It's not right for her to simply fade away down here. You'll miss her, of course . . .'

It is that last sentence, implying selfishness on Mina's part, that spurs her to talk to Nest. Perhaps she is ready for a change, perhaps she too sees that she might never have a life outside Ottercombe; for whatever reason it is, Nest applies for the job and gets it.

'If you hate it,' says Mina, as the parting draws near, 'you can always come home. And we'll have the holidays . . .'

Once she is in Surrey, Nest inevitably sees more of Henrietta and Connor. They invite her during half-term, introduce her to their friends, and Nest has to struggle against a reopening of the wound of her love. There is still a kind of restraint between them, and very occasionally, as the years pass, she catches his look: a tender, almost puzzled glance, as if he has begun to question his actions. She is afraid, however, of reading too much into it, of destroying her fragile but slowly increasing peace of mind, and she avoids him as much as possible. She manages to deal with family birthday parties, weddings, Christmases, hiding her tenacious love successfully, until the weekend of Jack's christening.

Ten years of wise self-preservation done away with in a single evening!

Timmie's wife, Anthea, has rejected the garrison church for her son's christening and has decided that he shall be baptised in her family's church in the small Herefordshire village where she grew up. Those members of the family who can attend the afternoon service, and the jollities afterwards, book in at the local hotel, apart from Lydia and Mina who are to stay with Anthea's family. When Nest, rather late in the day, tries to reserve a room at the local hotel, they advise her that all their rooms are fully booked but suggest a charming pub a mile or two away, just over the Shropshire border.

It is while she is preparing to go down for her lunch at the pub that she sees Connor's car swing into the car park. She goes down to the bar where she discusses the lunch menu with the landlord, orders an omelette and asks for a whisky. When Connor appears she is still sipping it, sitting at a small table by the window.

'So there you are.' Clearly he expected to see her. 'What are you drinking? Scotch? Yes, I think I'll have one of those. Refill?'

She shakes her head and watches him go to the bar. He looks good in his smart suit and a tense excitement rises in her.

'What a farce it all is!' He is back, looking faintly irritated, partly amused. 'Your family!' he exclaims.

'I thought you and Henrietta were staying at the hotel,' she says calmly.

'We were,' he answers, 'except that Roger has developed some childish ailment and she can't come. When I got to the hotel Georgie and Tom were having conniptions because they hadn't booked, and there was no room for them and dear little Helena at the inn. I offered them our room, at which point the receptionist—grateful, no doubt, to be rescued from Georgie in full spate—sent me along here. She said that one of the party was already booked in and obligingly told me which of them it was.'

'And so here you are.'

It is the whisky, perhaps, that has lifted her into this oddly confident, carefree mood. He looks at her, his smiling eyes narrowed consideringly, so that she feels rather breathless.

'So here I am,' he agrees.

What was it about that afternoon and evening, she is to wonder afterwards, that worked the magic and flung them back headlong, so that ten years of constraint vanished? Well, obviously the absence of Henrietta was a contributory factor—and, just as crucially, the absence of Mina. When Nest and Connor meet up with the party at the hotel, to walk the short distance to the church, they hear that Lydia has had a bad attack of asthma and she and Mina cannot come.

'What a shame,' cries Georgie fretfully. 'And Tom and I are flying to Geneva in a fortnight. I'd counted on seeing them here before we go. Now I shall have to go down to Exmoor, as if I hadn't enough to do . . .'

Nest catches Connor's eye and they laugh secretly, delightedly, together in spirit as they were once before.

'Filial devotion's such a wonderful thing,' he murmurs, cupping his hand around her elbow as they walk up the church path.

'You're a cynic,' she answers, trying not to shiver at his touch.

'Me, lady?' He looks shocked. 'The saints forbid!'

As the afternoon lengthens into evening the game between them changes subtly. Anthea's family are generous hosts and there is much laughter and revelry. It seems perfectly natural for Connor and Nest to spend these hours together. Constraint relaxed by wine and champagne, years of enforced familiarity eased into intimacy, once they are back at the inn the long period of frustration and loneliness resolves itself into one night of passionate release.

Nest was woken by Mina bringing her a cup of tea. She struggled up on her pillows. 'Lyddie,' she said anxiously. 'What did she say?'

Mina stood the tea on the bedside table. 'Lyddie has gone back to Truro. No!' as Nest exclaimed distressfully, 'not in a fit of rejection. She was going anyway. Remember?'

'Yes, of course I remember. What a fool I've been. To burst out with this now when she's got so much on her plate . . . How did she react?'

'She was surprisingly balanced about it,' she answered gently. 'Clearly it's a huge shock but she listened to the whole story, asked sensible questions and said, very reasonably, that it was going to take a while to sink in. To be honest, it would have been difficult for the pair of you to meet over lunch, wouldn't it? This break will be good for both of you. She sent her love to you . . .'

'Did she?' asked Nest eagerly. 'Did she say that?'

'Yes, she did.' Mina looked with compassion at Nest's strained, pain-lined face. 'I wouldn't make up something so important, you know that.'

'No,' said Nest, after a moment. 'No, you wouldn't.'

'You and Lyddie have more than thirty years of loving between you. That can't be discounted. She thought it was very brave of you to tell her. She said, "Everyone has a right to their own history." I think, oddly, her own problems will give her an added insight. It's always those who have never suffered nor failed who are the most intolerant. Lyddie will be fair, but that doesn't mean that it isn't a shock.'

'Of *course* it is!' exclaimed Nest. 'Good grief! Discovering that your mother isn't who you thought she was!' She shook her head. 'How do you come to terms with it? How often I've asked myself that question when I've wondered if I should ever tell her the truth.'

'Mmm.' Mina looked thoughtful. 'And is she right, do you think? That everyone has a right to their own history?'

'Well, I'm very glad *she* thinks so, in which case I hope she won't be upset that I've kept it from her for so long. But in general terms? Well, if I believed it I suppose I would have told her once Connor and Henrietta died. Before then, they'd both made me swear not to tell her. It's a very complex subject with so many implications. It happened now simply because of the strain. And to think that after all that it wasn't Georgie in the end who let the cat out of the bag.' Nest groaned. 'All that terror . . .'

'Georgie was the catalyst,' said Mina. 'She played her part. And now you are going to sleep. You look exhausted. Drink your tea and then try to rest. All is well. The worst is over.'

Lyddie, travelling west, was crossing the Torridge Bridge at Bideford. She was driving automatically, only some small part of her mind concentrating on the traffic.

'This has been the worst week of my life,' she told the Bosun and he turned his head to look at her, listening with pricked ears to her voice.

But was that true? she asked herself. Hadn't it been worse—or at least as bad—when she'd heard the news that her parents had been killed in a car accident? The shock had been cataclysmic, unbearable, yet it was an unpalatable truth that time had eased the pain. It made her feel guilty when she acknowledged this but 'It must be so,' Jack had said once, talking about the death of his own father. 'How else could we function if we continued to bear that kind of loss every hour of our life?' This had comforted her, made her feel less selfish and uncaring as, gradually, she'd learned to live with the sadness and the loneliness.

'And now?' she murmured aloud. 'And now—well, what?'

It seemed impossible not to think of Henrietta in any other light than as her mother: the nurturing and caring; the loving actions that make up a childhood: all this belonged to Henrietta. Yet Nest was her biological mother. The extraordinary thought 'Does it matter?' slipped into her weary mind and she felt a stab of guilt. Perhaps, because Henrietta had been dead for more than ten years, it was possible to let these two images juxtapose: Nest on the one hand, Henrietta on the other. Both the women who had loved and cherished her in their different ways.

'Nest lost everything,' Aunt Mina had said. 'First she lost Connor—and you will be able, now, Lyddie, to really understand what that means—and then she lost you. She had no choices. Mama was absolutely determined that you should be adopted and Connor pressed her hard. Naturally, neither Mama nor Henrietta had any idea that you were Connor's child, but you can imagine what it must have been like for Nest, beleaguered on every side. Connor wanted you desperately and yet what could he do? Should he leave his wife and child so as to support you and Nest? Either way it was an appalling decision to have to take. Someone had to lose and Nest drew the short straw. She paid very heavily for her one moment of need. She never stopped loving him, you know, and I believe that he loved both of them; that to Connor they were opposite sides of the same coin. And, to do Henrietta justice, she was delighted to help Nest by taking you as her own child and she was never less than generous in including Nest in your upbringing—as far as it was reasonable without harming you. There was only once—'

She'd stopped then, and Lyddie, still trying to assimilate all these things, had not pursued it, intent on another line of thought.

'So Daddy wasn't an unfaithful kind of man, not really?'

'No,' she'd answered readily. 'Connor was not in any way a libertine. If he hadn't been so scrupulous over the fact that Nest was ten years younger than he was, and still at school, it's very likely that they would have married. Henrietta was the mature fulfilment of all that Nest promised and he was knocked sideways by her. He made his decision and stood by it. Nest never quite got over him, that was the tragedy.'

Remembering, Lyddie felt another wave of sympathy for Nest. She could imagine all too clearly how hard it might be to recover from loving the one man you adored. How was it to be done? She found herself thinking about Rosie. In an odd way, she'd played Henrietta to Rosie's Nest.

'He was mine before he was ever yours,' Rosie had cried—but Rosie was not prepared to back down: Rosie intended to make a fight of it. Had Liam ever really loved Rosie? Did he love her still? How cold, how sick she'd felt when she'd imagined her father being unfaithful; for a moment she'd thought of Liam and a sense of revulsion had swamped her as she'd imagined her father betraying her mother.

'I can't imagine Nest as my mother,' she'd said desperately. 'It's not . . . not possible. Mummy was my mother. It's not that I don't love Nest. I do, she's been terrific to me, but I can't *do* that.'

'You don't have to,' Aunt Mina had answered firmly. 'Nest won't expect you to change how you feel about either her or Henrietta. It would be impossible. And unnecessary. She is Nest, a person in her own right, and she has her own relationship with you. It would be foolish to say that nothing will change now, but the past is the past, unchangeable. All she will hope is that you can go forward without hating her for the deception and for giving you such a shock.'

'I could never hate Nest,' she'd said after a moment—and had been surprisingly relieved to know that this was the truth. 'She's meant too much to me for that. But I don't want to try to think about her in this new light. It's . . . not right.'

'I agree with you,' Aunt Mina had said at once. 'Henrietta was your mother in all ways except biologically. Nest asks for nothing except that you shouldn't condemn her or, more importantly in her eyes, your father. Why do you think she hasn't told you before? After Henrietta died, for instance?'

'So why now?'

Aunt Mina had drawn a deep, deep breath, letting it out again with the characteristic 'po-po-po'. 'The simple truth is she was afraid someone else might tell you first.'

'Who else knows?' Lyddie had felt an unexpected surge of real fear and anger. 'Who . . .? Does Jack know?'

'Nobody knows,' her aunt had answered calmly. 'I am certain of it. The trouble is that your Aunt Georgie has some inkling of one or two things that happened in the past and is making rather a thing out of it. Nest has convinced herself that Georgie is going to blurt out some secret or other to you.'

'And might Aunt Georgie know?' Lyddie had suddenly realised how much she would hate others knowing while she did not.

'I think it's highly unlikely. Georgie and Josie and Timmie and their families were all abroad during that time. Timmie knew that Nest was pregnant—but not about Connor—and I had to know because Nest came here to be with us. But nobody else knew. Georgie was always a bit of a troublemaker; she liked to ruffle feathers and now, especially, she's very confused. Nest has been carrying this secret for a long time and I think it's simply that the strain had become too much for her.'

'It must have been awful. Such a secret.'

'A terrible weight to carry. If you are not harmed I must admit that I am delighted that the silence has been broken at last.'

'I shall be OK,' Lyddie had answered. 'And I'm glad I know. Everyone has a right to their own history.'

'There's one last thing,' Aunt Mina had said with an effort. 'I think it's important. Do you remember that Henrietta wanted you to join her in that boutique of hers when you left university?'

'Oh, I certainly do. There was a frightful fuss about it. It was crazy.'

'Connor, most unwillingly, took out a big loan against the house to buy the lease and get the shop stocked and, when the business started to lose money, Henrietta was insistent that you should work with her so as to save on wages. Connor and Nest were absolutely against it. It was the first time Nest had ever interfered . . .' She'd paused. 'There's this last thing that you should know. During that final car journey the three of them were arguing strongly about it. Nest has always felt that if she hadn't been so vociferous, so anxious that you should not be coerced into giving up your chosen career, Henrietta might have concentrated harder on her driving and the accident might never have happened.'

Lyddie had stared at her. 'But . . . that's crazy.'

'Possibly. She felt unbearably guilty that she survived and, in the pain and depression that followed, she got it out of all proportion. I mention it to you because you should know that her punishment ever since that day is that she has never once been down to the beach. More than ten years. She always loved the sea so much and she took this form of punishing herself.'

'Poor Nest.' Lyddie had been stricken with compassion. 'But it could have been *anything* that caused the accident. More likely Mummy was trying to light a cigarette. She was always a menace doing that.'

'I felt you should know,' Aunt Mina had repeated. 'You need not mention it to her but if you can show that you forgive her for all the subterfuge, she might at last be able to forgive herself.'

There was a long silence.

'We need to talk, Nest and I,' said Lyddie at last, 'but not just yet. I'd like a little time to digest all this very carefully and adjust to it. But I think I shall go back to Truro now. Give Nest my love, won't you, and tell her I'll be back soon?'

'And Liam?' Aunt Mina had asked gently. 'Have you been able to come to a decision?'

Lyddie had shaken her head rather desperately. 'But I need to see him,' she'd said. And now, here she was, driving back to Truro, wondering what Liam would say to her—and what she would say to him. Her heart contracted with fearful apprehension and, for a while, the thought of the approaching meeting thrust all other more recent revelations from her mind.

He was waiting for her when she finally arrived; sitting at the table by the window, reading the newspaper. 'Well, hello,' he said.

'Hello.' She stood rather awkwardly just inside the door. Liam could cover his awkwardness by ruffling the Bosun's ears and playing with him, but Lyddie had nothing to do. She looked about the room, and at him, and experienced her third shock. He was a stranger: handsome, sexy—but a stranger. Even the room looked changed. It seemed smaller and utterly unfamiliar. She frowned, trying to make sense of it, wondering if her mind was playing tricks. After all, it had been an extraordinary week and she was very tired.

'Would you like some tea? Or something stronger?' He was standing up now, watching her, but he made no move towards her. 'You look bushed.'

'I *am* tired,' she admitted—and realised with another tiny jolt that it would be completely impossible to tell him about Nest's revelation. It would be like exposing one's deep, most private self to a kindly but indifferent acquaintance. She felt a sense of isolation accompanied by a feeble desire to burst into tears. 'Thanks, some tea would be great.'

She listened as he talked to the Bosun, filling his bowl with cold fresh water while making the tea. Liam put the mug before Lyddie on the table and went to sit down again. It occurred to her that they had not embraced; deep down, a secret fear was growing. She looked at him across the table. He looked back at her, a pleasant, unmeaning smile playing round his mouth, his eyes bright and blank.

'So you haven't missed me, then,' she said flatly.

It was a statement rather than an enquiry and his eyes flew wide open in genuine surprise before the mask was dropped again. 'And who told you that?'

'Oh, I'm just guessing. How's . . . everything?'

'*Everything*,' he emphasised the word almost mockingly, 'is just fine.'

'And everyone?'

'Now, who would you be meaning by "everyone"?'

'Oh, well,' she cradled the mug in her hands, pretending to ponder. 'Joe? Rosie? Zoë?'

His smile slipped visibly and his eyes were unfriendly. 'Could that be a leading question?'

'I imagine you've seen them?'

'I work with them, remember? It would be odd if I hadn't.'

'Has Rosie been given her job back, then?'

His expression was hostile now. 'She has not.'

'You haven't seen Rosie, then?' The pause was a shade too long. 'I take it that means "yes". Well, I guessed she wouldn't miss an opportunity.'

'It's you who left,' he reminded her. 'You didn't have to go.'

She looked at him with a kind of smiling disbelief. 'You're saying that it's all my fault?'

He shook his head. 'I'm not saying anything.'

'But you saw Rosie.'

He was losing his carefully controlled patience. 'Yes, I saw Rosie. I've known her for a long time, remember? Long before you came on the scene.'

'So she took pains to tell me. And I have this feeling, Liam, that you wish you'd stuck with her.'

The silence was even longer and, this time, Lyddie did not break it. She sat watching him, the fear blossoming inside her.

'She accepts me for what I am,' he said at last, almost sullenly. 'She takes the package.'

Lyddie swallowed some tea and put the mug carefully on the small round mat. These coasters had been a wedding present: six different cartoons of a shaggy dog. She stared at it, remembering her wedding day, how she'd felt, and was suddenly overwhelmed by a devastating sense of loss.

'I was thinking,' she said, turning the mug round and round on its mat, not looking at him, 'on my way down. Thinking about how it could be done. I'm not like Rosie, you see. I can't just share you around. I can't *do* that. But supposing we were to make a fresh start? Go some-where new to both of us and you were to create another wine bar?'

She looked at him at last and caught his stare of incredulity.

'Mother of God,' he said at last. 'Are you crazy? And what about The Place, do I just walk away from it?'

'Joe could take it over. You could do it again in another town. Why not? It happens all the time. Shops, bars, start with one and then two and then chains of things in the end.' Suddenly she remembered their first conversation and how he'd answered when she asked why he'd called his wine bar The Place. 'You could call it The Next Place or The Best Place.'

For a second, just for a fleeting moment, she watched him catch the vision, saw the glow of it touch his face alight, before it died and his eyes were bleak again.

'We couldn't afford it,' he said, 'even if I wanted to. Joe couldn't run it alone and it wouldn't stand a bar manager's salary yet. Anyway, we'd never get another loan to start a new place.'

'What if we used the money from the house in Iffley for the new place?'

He laughed and shook his head. 'I wondered how long it would be before that was dragged in. A drop in the ocean . . .'

'You could sell this house.'

'Have you forgotten I've got a huge mortgage on it? Forget it.'

Another pause. 'You said "even if I wanted to" just now.' Lyddie spoke slowly. 'That's the whole point, isn't it? You don't want to change, or leave The Place and, if you're really honest, I think you don't want us even to try, do you?'

'I can't see what all the fuss is about. You were perfectly happy before. Nothing's changed.'

'Oh, but it has,' she said quickly. 'Everything's changed.'

'I'm the same person I always was.'

'Oh, yes, but, you see, I didn't really know the person you've always been. I only knew a part of you and I fell in love with that part. But now I know that you lie and cheat, that I'll never know in future whether you really are going to the bank, or the cash-and-carry, or whether you're upstairs in the storeroom with the new waitress. That's quite a change.' She watched him for a moment. 'You really can't see it, can you?'

He shrugged. 'So what do you want to do?'

'I've already told you what I'd like us to do.'

'It's out of the question.'

She was silent, the fear mushrooming, filling her with misery.

'I knew it was over when I came in and saw you,' she said at last. 'It was as if you were a complete stranger. As if, in those three days, you'd changed completely.'

He looked away from her. 'You shouldn't have gone away,' he said.

'What does that mean?' she cried. 'If I'd stayed, would you now be considering my suggestion for a new start?'

'No,' he answered. 'No, I wouldn't. But it gave me time to see . . . .'

He hesitated so long that she guessed his meaning. 'It gave you time to see that you don't need me enough to change for me. For us.'

He nodded, still not looking at her. 'Something like that.'

'And how much input did Rosie contribute to your decision?'

'Rosie's always been there when I needed her.'

It was as if he'd struck her across the face. 'And how many times was that during these last two years?' she asked furiously.

He frowned, almost distastefully, and looked at her at last. 'I've got to go,' he said, and stood up. 'Sorry. I'm really sorry, Lyddie. I made the mistake of falling in love. Oh, I did. You were different, you see. Clever with words. Aloof. Just that bit unattainable and it was a challenge. But I don't need it. I know that now, not if it means arguments and questions. I can't hack all that stuff. Rosie knows me. We're on the same wavelength. She knows how I feel about The Place and puts up with it. She accepts that I need variety now and then. She doesn't like it but she doesn't complain. She knows that I don't want kids and neither does she. She'll go along with what I do and what I want.'

'And what do I do?'

'Well.' He didn't quite shrug it off. 'You've got your work and, after all,' he gave a little laugh, 'there's always the money from the house in Iffley.' Even he seemed to feel the brutality of his quip and he bit his lip. 'Sorry,' he said. 'That was cheap. I'm no good at this stuff, I'm afraid. You've always got the Aunts as a stopgap.'

'Thanks,' she said. 'So I have.'

'I'll be at The Place,' he said, 'if you need me. You'd better speak to your lawyer.' He paused, his jacket hanging over one shoulder, head lowered. 'And thanks, Lyddie.' He looked at her, grimaced. 'It was great while it lasted.'

Chapter Nine

'OF COURSE SHE MUST COME,' said Hannah. 'Of *course* she must. The kids could go to Mum for a couple of days.'

'It's just for two nights and then she's going to Ottercombe until she can sort herself out,' said Jack. 'Apparently she's got to get back to work again by next weekend—she's booked up until Christmas and she doesn't want to let anyone down.'

'She daren't lose her contacts, I can see that,' agreed Hannah. 'She'll need her work. But can she live on it?'

Jack shook his head. 'I've no idea. Roger pays her interest on her share of the house. That should help.'

'Poor Lyddie. It's so devastating to find out that someone you trust has been cheating. It destroys your self-confidence.'

'The trouble is that there is absolutely nothing that one can do to help. Nothing can take away the pain or the reality of it. Why is loving people so damned agonising?'

She smiled at him. 'I had no idea when I married you that you were such a mother hen. I should have guessed when I saw all those little boys trailing after you, "Sir, I've lost this . . ." or, "Sir, I've done that . . .", and you behaving like a dear old nanny.'

'I am nothing like a dear old nanny,' he answered indignantly. 'I'm an absolute brute to the little monsters. Good grief! They're terrified of me.'

'Oh, yes,' she agreed mockingly. 'Scared to death. Like Hobbes the other evening? Reading him a story at ten o'clock at night?'

'He misses his mum,' said Jack defensively, 'and I didn't want him to wake the others'—Hannah snorted disbelievingly—'and he'd had a rotten day.'

'You're a big softy and they all know it,' she said, grinning at him. 'Marshmallow right down to the centre. Flora had you sussed when she was three days old.'

He grinned too. 'Our daughter has an unerring instinct for a weak spot,' he agreed. 'Attila the Hun could take her correspondence course.' A pause. 'Will your mother cope OK?'

'Oh, now *don't* start fussing about that,' cried Hannah, exasperated. 'She manages them brilliantly and they love being with her.'

'Yes, I know they do,' he admitted.

'Well then. I think it would give Lyddie a freer rein to talk things over if we're on our own. There's nothing worse than being interrupted every five minutes when you're feeling like that. The best thing we can do for Lyddie is to concentrate on her. That's quite impossible with Flora in the house.' She paused, looking at him affectionately. 'Did I ever tell you that I have a thing about mother hens?'

'It's too late for soft soap,' he answered with great dignity. 'My feathers are already ruffled.' He flexed his shoulders, as if puffing himself up, and clucked several times like a meditative hen. 'Haven't you noticed?'

'Looks great,' she said admiringly. 'I'll be back later to check out your quills.'

She disappeared and Jack sighed. 'And people ask where Flora gets it from,' he murmured. 'We all know who rules the roost in *this* house.'

At Ottercombe, Mina was preparing for bed. Lyddie had telephoned to tell them that Liam didn't want a reconciliation, and to ask if she could stay with them until she could decide what she should do next. Saddened though they were by the news, Mina and Nest had been deeply relieved that Lyddie wanted to come back to them. It showed, as nothing else could, that she'd accepted her past even if she had not yet had time to assimilate it. She was going to see Jack and Hannah first, just for a few days, she'd said; a plan that her aunts had encouraged.

'Roger simply must get his act together with his mortgage,' Nest had said. 'Thank goodness that the big loan Henrietta took out for her boutique was paid off by the insurance. It was so foolish of Connor to go along with that business.'

'Henrietta wouldn't give in,' Mina remembered. 'She was absolutely set on it. Even to the point of sacrificing Lyddie on its altar.'

Nest had looked at her, suddenly alert. 'Did you tell Lyddie about the accident?'

'I told her,' answered Mina carefully, 'that you'd all been heatedly discussing the question of whether she should work at the boutique and that you'd always feared that it was because of the high feelings that Henrietta wasn't concentrating.'

'But that's not all of the truth,' Nest had said sharply.

'Maybe not,' Mina had felt it necessary to be firm, 'but that's all you can tell her. To tell the whole truth would be self-indulgent.'

Nest had stared at her, almost shocked. 'Self-indulgent?'

'Yes,' she'd cried. 'Can't you see that? It can do no good except to relieve *your* feelings. She'll feel obliged to absolve you and she will simply be left with the burden of the knowledge and all the horror to live through again. It would be cruel. You must continue to live with this part of the story, Nest. If Lyddie is ready to accept all the rest of it, and to move forward, then you must forgive yourself at last and go with her. It's over.'

She'd seen Nest swallow, her hands tighten on the arms of her chair, and, feeling a brute, she'd left her.

Now, as she brushed her hair, a little 'po-po-po' escaping her lips, she wondered if she'd been right. She went into the alcove. She clicked and scrolled, intent upon the screen, and finally opened Elyot's email.

From: Elyot
To: Mina

A good day. William is home! Oh, the relief and joy of having him safely with us. Lavinia has reacted so positively. She recognised him at once, although she seems to have completely forgotten about Marianne, his ex-wife. His unexpected appearance is doing Lavinia so much good. The happy shock seemed to trigger something in her brain so that she is . . . I nearly said 'quite her old self', which is far from true, but she is so bright that it does my heart good.

William looks well and has leave until after Christmas, when he takes up a posting with the Ministry of Defence. It will be good to have him back in the country for a while. Like you, my dear old friend, he has that blessed, happy ability to raise the spirits.

Enough of us. How are things at Ottercombe? Don't imagine for a moment that having William with us makes me any less anxious to hear from you as usual.

Elyot

Mina sat for some moments, considering. It was good to think of him enjoying the company of his son and heartened by Lavinia's new-found brightness; it would be selfish to tell him about Lyddie's predicament quite so quickly. Yet she found herself longing to tell him, rather shocked by her need, realising how much she'd come to rely upon him. She typed quickly lest she should weaken.

From: Mina
To: Elyot
All is well here. I am so pleased to hear how happy William's arrival is making you. You deserve a break, dear Elyot, and it is lovely to think of you all together. Enjoy this time together. We'll talk again tomorrow. Good night.

Mina closed down the computer, took off her long fleecy robe and climbed into bed.

'*Everyone has a right to their own history.*'

She reached for Lydia's rosary and began to pass the smooth, cool beads through her fingers ,but still she found it impossible to sleep.

Nest, too, was lying awake, thinking very carefully about the things Mina had said earlier. She had been right to explain the accident in those terms to Lyddie. Lyddie could not absolve her of her guilt and it would be cruel to put such a burden of knowledge upon her. It was bad enough for her to know that anxiety about her future might have been a factor in Henrietta's momentary loss of concentration.

Nest shut her eyes against the picture of Connor's profile, his head turned towards her. They'd been returning from the house of a mutual friend, Henrietta driving. Nest had agreed to go only because Connor had asked her to plead Lyddie's case with Henrietta. For the first time in more than twenty years he had invoked her support, visiting her at the school in Surrey, asking her to persuade Henrietta out of her scheme.

'Lyddie would be wasted,' he cries. 'She's done well at university and now she's been offered a job with a major publishing house. She's over the moon about it. The real problem is that Henrietta's worried about the repayment of the loan and feels that Lyddie should be prevailed upon to help us out. There's all this talk about loyalty and family ties. Henrietta has this mad idea that Lyddie won't need much in the way of wages, as she'll be able to live at home, and so she'll save on having to pay her full-time assistant. What future is that for Lyddie, I ask you? *Why* was I so crazy as to have gone along with the idea of a boutique in the first place? I won't have her sacrificing Lyddie's future . . .'

She watches him sympathetically, agreeing whole-heartedly that Lyddie should not miss her chance in London, but wondering how it is that the birth of their daughter so effectively killed all her passion for him; as if a sword had fallen, slicing the ties that once bound her to him.

How hard, how very hard it is, to give up her child. And yet, when she finally agrees to 'the terms and conditions', as she bitterly refers to them, that period at Ottercombe is among the happiest of her life. Even Mama, once everything is settled—'once I knuckled under,' says Nest—becomes affectionate and sweet-tempered again.

Perhaps the acceptance, the giving in, is the mainspring of this release of a new kind of contentment. The horror and the fear, the terror for her child's future—and her own—gives way to a calm confidence. At Ottercombe, it is as if she's stepped out of the world, and is able to offer herself wholly to this wonderful new experience. The three women pick up the threads of the life Nest had left five years before, and she sinks contentedly into the warmth of Mina's caring. She walks for miles over the moor and spends hours watching the sea, revelling in the softly stealing, all-pervading sense of peace of its unceasing movement.

Timmie visits as often as he can, bringing Anthea and small Jack, lending his support. He, like Mama, has no idea of the identity of Nest's lover and it is never discussed. He simply offers encouragement and unconditional love, as is Timmie's way. They all adore Jack. When Nest cuddles him, feeling his warm, heavy weight, touching his flushed cheek and feathery hair, it seems impossible that she should not hold her own child like this. Yet some sense of self-preservation refuses to allow such thoughts to develop. It is agreed that she should be allowed to choose her child's name and Nest has no doubts in her mind: if the baby were a boy he is to be named Timothy; if a girl, Lydia.

She remembers how she'd gone away to start a new life five years before, leaving Mina with Lydia isolated at Ottercombe, and she feels a pang of guilt. 'Do you ever get lonely?' she asks one evening.

'Lonely?' Mina considers the thought. 'I don't think so. I have Mama, who requires quite a lot of care and, to be honest, I think I'm a naturally solitary person and I have the house and garden to look after. I've always had this passion for books. I live in them, you see, and the people are quite real to me. They are my friends and I've always found their worlds much more satisfying than the reality outside.'

Yet when the outside world imposes itself upon her, Mina responds with courage and cheerfulness. Nest knows that during her own bad times, first losing Connor, then those empty, agonising weeks—mercifully few before she'd had to start the new term—after Henrietta takes the baby away, and, later again, the months immediately after the accident, it is Mina who holds her firm, instilling the will to go on.

Nest stirred restlessly, glanced at her bedside clock—nearly half past one—and decided that she needed a hot drink. She edged herself out of bed, pulled on her dressing gown and got herself into her chair. Opening the door quietly, she wheeled herself into the kitchen. She was sitting beside the kitchen table drinking tea when Mina came in.

'Oh dear,' she said. 'You too? Not brooding, I hope?'

'I was a bit.' Nest set her mug down. 'Thinking back to the accident, you know. Trying to decide whether Henrietta actually took in what I said. I keep going over it. It was a soaking night, terrible rain, if you remember. The wipers were going and the traffic was quite bad; the tyres swishing on the wet road. I was almost shouting, well, we all were. Henrietta was in a state because she was beginning to see that she might not get her own way. She was cross that I was involved, and she knew that Connor had roped me in to support him. "I may not be Lyddie's mother," she said, very sarcastic, and, quite without thinking, I said, "No, but Connor is her father . . ." I remember clapping my hand over my mouth, and she turned her head very sharply and they looked at each other. And then the car just clipped the lorry coming in the other direction and we were spinning and spinning out of control. I'll never forget the terrible sounds . . .'

Mina had her arm about her, cradling her, rocking her.

'She might never have heard you,' she said. 'Guilt can distort the truth. She might simply have turned her head to hear better.'

'Possibly.' Nest took her hands away from her face. 'Anyway, I agree with you about Lyddie not knowing. You are absolutely right about that. I just wish I knew how she's feeling about . . . the other thing.'

Mina straightened up, pushing her hands into her dressing gown pocket, her fingers encountering the rosary where she'd put it quite unconsciously earlier. She stood for a moment and then took a deep breath, 'po-po-po', and dropped the rosary on the table beside Nest's mug. Nest looked at it.

'That was Mama's, wasn't it?' she asked, momentarily distracted. 'Didn't Timothy give it to her?'

Mina put the kettle on the Esse and chose a mug. 'Not as such,' she said, 'although it *was* Timothy's. It came to Mama with the rest of his things after he died.'

'That was odd, wasn't it?' Nest picked up the rosary and let the beads slip through her fingers. 'Why Mama? Didn't he have a family?'

'Not as far as I know. All her letters to him came back with it and a few other things. The flat he rented in London had been bombed and he hadn't much with him when he died. Just his rosary and the letters and a few photographs.'

'I remember letters arriving from him.' Nest was smiling now, remembering happier times. 'And occasionally presents for us.'

'Timothy had the gift of empathy,' said Mina. 'He grew to know us all and his presents were very distinctive and absolutely right. He was an explorer and a soldier and I think that he was doing Secret Service things in the war. He was Papa's friend and he came home with him one day and stayed for nearly a month. It was the summer before Timmie was born and one of the happiest summers I can remember.' She poured boiling water on her sachet of tea and waited for a moment. 'We all simply adored him. It was Timothy who gave us our names.'

'How do you mean?' Nest looked startled, completely distracted now, as Mina had intended, from the horrors of that ten-year-old accident.

'Before Timmie was born we were called by shortened versions of our names. At least, by Papa we were. Mama tried to prevent it and she called us by our full names but Papa was trying to make a point. I didn't realise at the time but I see it now.' She hesitated a little, stirring the tea thoughtfully. 'There was a little streak of brutality in Papa. He never considered how anyone else might feel. He called us George, Will, Henry and Jo. I can remember that day, you know, when Timothy arrived. We came up from the beach and Papa introduced us. He used to call us the bandar-log, jokingly. "Here are the bandar-log," he said, and then he told Timothy our names. "But why?" Timothy asked. He looked puzzled, almost distressed. "Such pretty children," he said. And Papa said, "It's the next best thing to having boys," or something like that, and I saw Mama's face. So did Timothy. It was as if she had been struck. He began to give us different names, kinder and more feminine.'

'And what did Papa say?' asked Nest, rapt as always by Mina's story spinning.

'The thing was that he loved Timothy too.' Mina came to sit at the table. 'Everyone did. He was irresistible: we all fought to sit next to him or hold his hand. We saved up our treasures to show him and did drawings for him. And he looked so handsome. Do you remember? Very tall and fair with a brown face. He looked as if he spent all his time in the open air. He was very tough and yet there was this kindness.' A little pause. 'You know about Papa's widow in London, of course?' Nest nodded. 'But I was never sure how much Mama knew about her. Nothing in those early days, I'm sure, but I can see that he used her asthma attacks as an excuse to get us out of London whenever possible. Not that this was any punishment to her—she adored Ottercombe—but I wonder if she might have missed Papa, or adult company. She'd had several miscarriages, and she was never very strong, but Timothy warmed her into life. Does that sound silly? She flowered and grew in his company and he was a buffer between all of us and Papa's insensitivity. We were all in love with him, I think, not just Mama.'

Nest glanced up quickly from the rosary, which she was threading through her fingers.

'Not *just* Mama?' she repeated questioningly.

'They fell in love,' said Mina dreamily. 'I didn't understand then, I was too young, but I know it now—and, anyway, I read the letters.'

Nest was wide-eyed. 'Were they love letters?'

'Oh, yes. Once I'd read them everything fell into place. That amazing summer, before Timmie was born . . .'

'Wait a moment,' said Nest slowly. ' "Before Timmie was born." You used that phrase just now. That's it, isn't it? This is the secret that Georgie knows. You said once, "There are other secrets," and then you clammed up. I see it now. A boy after all those girls and Timmie was tall and fair—even his name! Oh, I know that Timothy was his godfather, but even so. I'm right, aren't I? Timothy was Timmie's father. Good grief, fancy Mama—'

'It's not *quite* right,' interrupted Mina gently. 'Although it's what other people believed too. The wretched Sneerwells were always hinting at it. But it wasn't quite like that although there is a tiny truth in it. Timothy relaxed Mama, he made her happy and confident, and I think it was because of that she was able to conceive. But Timmie was Papa's son. It wasn't until the following year that Timothy and Mama became lovers. It's you who are their child, Nest. You were the love child, the baby he adored but couldn't acknowledge.'

She stopped speaking and the silence flowed into the kitchen, filling the spaces.

'*Timothy's* child?'

'She loved him so much.' Mina felt it was important that Nest should know this. 'It's odd how history repeats itself, isn't it? Mama and Timothy. Me and Tony. You and Connor.'

Nest looked at her and Mina saw that there was no horror or distress on her face, only a kind of awed amazement.

'Tell me everything,' she said. 'Start again and tell me everything.'

Lyddie dropped her case on the bed and looked around the small room. 'It's great.' She gazed appreciatively at the vase on the chest, with its arrangement of autumn berries and beech leaves; the folded fluffy towels on top of which lay a new tablet of deliciously scented soap. 'Thanks, Han.'

'Come down when you've got yourself sorted.'

She disappeared and Lyddie unpacked the case, squeezed it between the foot of the bed and the wall, and set her sponge bag beside the mirror on the chest. Before she'd left Truro she'd packed the contents of her office—laptop, reference books, charts—into the car, given her four favourite and most useful editors her mobile telephone number and sorted out her winter clothes. She would have to go back, of course, but she needed to make this a significant break; a new beginning.

As she drove to Dorset she wondered, as she often had in the past, why it should be that she'd been so much closer to Jack than she'd ever been to Roger. She realised that it would be easier to disclose Nest's revelation to her cousin than to her brother, although she'd begun to see that it would be impossible to tell anyone at all. After all, it was not her secret to tell; there were too many people involved. However, there was more to it than that. Although she could imagine the comfort it would be to share it all with Jack, she knew that it was too early; she needed time to digest it, to discover her own feelings about her new identity.

Jack was waiting for her when she'd finished unpacking and came down to the kitchen, sitting on the floor talking to the Bosun, who sat beside him gazing with a blend of amazement and affection into Jack's face. Lyddie burst out laughing and, immediately, the tiny knot of fear and pain in her gut began to unwind and dissolve.

'Caligula upset him,' Jack was explaining. 'Dogs are very sensitive people and Caligula was very rude. Wasn't he?' he asked the Bosun, who licked Jack's nose gratefully.

'Quite mad,' observed Hannah resignedly. 'But don't let it worry you. I suppose you realise that the Bosun is going to cause havoc when the boys get back after supper. Bedtime is going to be a very interesting experience.'

'Oh dear,' agreed Lyddie, 'we'll have to hide him in the garage.'

'You'll do no such thing,' replied Jack indignantly. 'His nerves are quite lacerated enough already. The boys will be delighted. I can't wait to see their faces. Has Hannah told you that we're going to get a dog?'

'No.' Lyddie smiled, delighted at the thought. 'Goodness, Tobes must be out of his mind at the prospect.'

'He doesn't know yet.' Hannah poured Lyddie's tea. 'We decided to wait until the holidays begin.'

Jack gave the Bosun a hug and climbed to his feet. 'You look very tired and rather fraught.' He studied Lyddie closely. 'Later on you shall have a large drink. I'm not really allowed to start until the little darlings are in bed. Not allowed to be drunk in charge of a dormitory.'

'But that doesn't mean that we can't,' said Hannah, nodding encouragingly at Lyddie. 'Anyway, he's only here to say hello before he goes off to supervise prep and then supper. We can't wait for him.'

'Such unselfishness,' observed Jack to nobody in particular.

Lyddie chuckled. 'Sounds good to me. Never mind, Jack. You'll soon catch up.'

'I thought you might walk over to the school with me,' he said.

'Stretch your legs after the drive and give the Bosun a gallop.'

As they paced across the smooth turf beneath the chestnut trees, where each autumn the boys gathered conkers, Lyddie tucked her hand in his arm and he smiled down at her.

'Poor old love,' he said. 'Want to talk?'

'I'll tell you something strange,' she said. 'I feel sick to my stomach when I think how Liam's behaved, and I still want him and feel that it's a tragic waste, but behind all that is a sense of . . . well, almost relief. Oh!' she cried in frustration. 'It's so *difficult* to explain this because it sounds as if I don't care and I do. My heart flips when I think of him, and I feel bereft, but the whole way through, Jack, there was this weird feeling of unreality. Like I was on a holiday where none of the normal rules of daily life applied. Oh, I was working, and that was real enough, but it was odd, working at home all day and then going to The Place every evening and joshing with Joe.'

'I often wondered how you would carry on like that, to be honest. Where did children fit into the scheme of things, for instance? You could have only become more and more isolated. The hours are so anti-social—or, at least, antifamily—that I wondered whether, at fifty, you'd still be working alone all day and then sitting in a wine bar every evening while Liam lived his own life on the side.'

She looked up at him. 'Did you suspect that Liam was cheating?'

He frowned, formulating his thoughts. 'I had this feeling that he was playing a part. You know, all that gliding around chatting to the punters. It's just that he is a bit of a poseur and a very attractive one, by the way. I can imagine that women really fell for him.'

'Well, *I* did.' Lyddie sighed. 'I think you're absolutely right. There was no chance of real family life, no weekends, no holidays. Perhaps that's why, in this very odd way, it's almost a relief. Not that it hurts less.'

'No, but it gives you something to work towards,' said Jack. 'That it was, really, a mistake, I mean. You can hang on to that. I have to say that I did wonder if it was a bit quick after James.'

'I'm beginning to lose my confidence,' said Lyddie. ' "To lose one man might be regarded as a mistake", et cetera.'

'Absolute rubbish,' he said. 'What about third time lucky? I shall insist on vetting the next candidate.'

'So you don't think it's wrong of me to give up on marriage to Liam?' She was surprised at how important his answer was.

'You didn't have much option,' he replied. 'You offered him a way forward and he rejected it. I can't think what else you *could* do.'

'You don't think I should just go along with it?'

'No, I bloody don't,' he said forcibly. 'Good God, Lyddie! Don't be

daft. However much you love him, nobody could expect you to pas-
sively accept such a role. He's put his cards on the table and you have to
take it or leave it. Well, you're leaving it.'

She smiled, hugging his arm. 'Thanks, Jack.'

'I'm not sure why I have your gratitude but you're welcome. Will you
be OK with the Aunts for a bit?'

'I think so.' She hesitated. 'I need time to think it through. I can do
that at Ottercombe.'

'Nowhere better to recuperate than with those two old darlings,' he
said affectionately. 'Look, if you take the way through the shrubbery it'll
take you round the outbuildings, back onto the path home, and it'll give
the Bosun a good run. Will you be OK?'

'Of course I will. Bless you, Jack, you're such a comfort.'

Nest was sitting by the fire in the drawing room. It was a bleak and
dismal November afternoon, a raw wind blowing the drizzle against the
windows, and it was good to turn one's back on it and stare instead at
the comforting flicker of the flames. The dogs and Mina had gone down
to the beach, despite the weather, and Georgie had gone upstairs to rest.
It was good to be alone in this peaceful room to think about all the
things Mina had told her. Was it simply Mina's skill at story spinning
that had enabled her to listen so calmly and, if not immediately accept
this new startling evidence, at least be able to begin to come to terms
with it without anger or fear? Was this how Lyddie might feel? Had
Mina woven her spell there too? Never had Nest been so grateful for
Mina's gift. She'd spun the events of the past into a rich tapestry, threading each strand carefully together so that the characters emerged, vivid
and exciting against the bright, familiar background of the cleave and
sea or moving within the old house as if it might be yesterday.

Nest looked down at the things she held in her lap: some photographs; an Easter card; the rosary. These were the only objects left
behind by her father, except, of course, for his letters. She'd read them
chronologically, remembering as she did so Mama opening his letters at
the breakfast table: the flimsy sheets rustling as she turned them, folding them away in the envelope, and the way her hand had strayed to
touch it as if reassuring herself that it really existed. Given their circumstances, the letters were almost shockingly indiscreet:

'Oh, my darling,' she'd write. 'How can I bear this endless
separation . . .?' and his replies, which always began 'My dearest love,'
and covered sheet after sheet with the outpourings of his love.

'I am expecting your child and I feel nothing but the deepest joy. Oh,
why am I not afraid? I am so happy . . .'

There had been no question that she should leave Ambrose who, as luck would have it, arrived at Ottercombe a few weeks after Timothy's visit so that there was never any doubt in his mind but that this was his own child. It was clear that Lydia, even for Timothy, would never have contemplated leaving her children, and equally clear that he had never demanded it of her:

. . . for what kind of life could I offer you, my heart's love, which could give you the stability and security required for you and your beloved children? How can we take our joy at their expense? They are very dear to me and, if we harmed them in any way, our love would be dust and ashes . . .

She answered him:

. . . to know that this is your child gives me the greatest happiness, and I have your namesake too, your godson. When I look at Timmie, I remember how we first met and how you stood in the hall saying, 'I apologise for arriving unannounced,' and I knew that I would fall in love with you . . .

Nest had been shocked by the naiveté and the simplicity of these letters: they were like two children standing in awe before this amazing gift of their love. At first, Nest had read avidly, gulping the words down as she relearned her own history; later, though, she'd been ashamed.

'I feel as if I've spied on them,' she'd said to Mina. 'It doesn't seem fair, somehow. They were so . . . so *innocent*, if you see what I mean.'

'Oh, I know exactly what you mean,' she'd agreed ruefully. 'I felt it too, but when Mama died I didn't know what should be done with them and by then, you see, I'd begun to guess the truth. Towards the end she began to talk about him, to believe that he was here with her, and it wasn't difficult to work out certain things. It felt wrong to destroy the letters without quite knowing if I had the right. In the end I read them and decided that I should keep them, just in case.'

'I'm so glad you did,' said Nest fervently. 'I feel proud to have been the product of such love. Gosh! That sounds a bit naff, doesn't it . . . ?'

'No, it doesn't,' Mina said quickly. 'It doesn't at all. There isn't one of us who wouldn't have been thrilled to have Timothy as our father. You *should* be proud.'

'I wish,' Nest had said, after a moment, 'that Lyddie could feel the smallest bit of that in her position. And not for any reason except that it would help her, as it's helping me, to accept it.'

'I think you'll find that those thirty-odd years of love and friendship which you have given Lyddie will earn much more than her acceptance.

It makes it easier, too, that Henrietta has been dead for over ten years. Lyddie hasn't got to choose or worry about disloyalty; she simply has to continue to allow herself to receive your love.'

Listening to the wind casting handfuls of cold rain against the window, Nest looked again at the treasures she held. First, a photograph of Lydia and Timothy with seven-year-old Nest standing between them. One sandalled foot resting upon the other, with a rag doll clasped in her arms, Nest watched the person behind the camera, her face eagerly intent; Timothy's hand was placed lightly about Lydia's shoulder; he was laughing, while Lydia looked at Timothy, her face alight with love. On the back of the photograph in faded ink was scrawled: *1941. Lydia and Timothy with Nest at Ottercombe.*

'I probably took it,' Mina had said. 'My guess is that the others had been sent on ahead to the beach so that he and Mama could snatch the opportunity of a photo with just the three of you.'

Nest stared down at it, willing herself to remember the occasion. Words from one of the letters slipped into her mind:

She's such a darling baby only, oh dear, Ambrose insists that she is to be called Ernestina, after his father! Such a ponderous name for such a pretty, tiny scrap of humanity . . .

Nest tried to bring her father to mind but it was difficult; he'd been such a distant figure. Yet she could still recall the presence of Timothy; that aura of excitement that clung to him, the security he represented.

'But I can't have been more than seven or eight when he died,' she'd said to Mina. 'It's odd, isn't it?'

'You can remember the atmosphere, I expect.' Mina had smiled reminiscently. 'When Timothy was here it was like Christmas, Easter and birthdays rolled into one. He was special.'

'Like Timmie. Or Jack?' suggested Nest.

'I know it sounds peculiar but I suppose it's possible that Timmie was *shaped* by their love in some way, which in turn passed on to Jack. To be fair, it would have been easy to believe that Timmie was their child but you only have to read the letters to see that they weren't lovers until the following year.'

Now, alone in the quiet drawing room, Nest passed her fingers gently over the battered photograph and looked at the second one: a portrait of Lydia, beautiful, wistful, her lips curving into a smile. On the back was written: *Lydia—1934.* She would have been thirty-five years old. The last photograph was one with which Nest was familiar: Lydia sitting on a chair just outside the French windows, smiling peacefully, her children gathered about her. On the back was written: *Ottercombe, 1936.*

Strangely moved, sighing a little, Nest placed the photographs together and looked at the Easter card. Beneath a simple colourwash of the empty Cross, bathed in sunshine, were the words: *He is risen.* Inside Lydia had written: *With love from us all at Ottercombe,* and each of them had signed it. She wondered why he'd carried it: was it simply that the card held the love of all of his 'family' within it? As she pondered this, a voice spoke in her ear.

'What have you got?'

It was several seconds before Nest could control the violent shock and the crashing of her heart, so as to look up calmly at Georgie, trying to shield her treasures from that interested stare as she slipped them into the tapestry bag that held her spectacles and book.

'Nothing much.' She tried to keep her voice neutral. 'I didn't hear you come in.'

Georgie edged past Nest's chair and sat down at the end of the sofa.

'I couldn't sleep,' Georgie said. 'The wind is getting up.'

'Mina should be home soon.' Nest took some deep, calming breaths and then, quite suddenly, she relaxed. She'd forgotten that Georgie had no power to harm her now.

'I think you can be quite certain,' Mina had said, when she'd given Nest the letters, 'that Georgie knows nothing about you and Connor and so has no idea about Lyddie. *This* is the secret Georgie knows. She's read these letters too.' She'd given a great gasp of relief. 'Po-po-po. How wonderful to have everything in the open at last.'

Now, Nest looked at Georgie with compassion; her teeth were drawn, her reign of power was over.

'Do you remember Timothy?' she asked quite naturally.

Georgie looked at her slyly and started to perform that strange bridling movement, a smile on her lips, her eyes sharp.

Nest thought: She's like a child who knows she has done something wrong, yet justifies it with this kind of 'see if I care' defiance.

'I know a secret,' Georgie said—and, from nowhere, Nest was caught up in a memory of a hot summer's afternoon: she and Timmie conducting a toys' tea party under the trees on the lawn. Georgie was towering over the table and Timmie was frightened; even when Mina appeared she could not restore the harmony; the happy atmosphere and sunny afternoon were scarred with the ugly stains of anger and cross voices and she, Nest, wept frightened tears wrung out of impotent helplessness and a sense of destruction: the foreshadowing of the transience of childhood and the loss of innocence.

Now, more than sixty years later, she leaned forward and touched Georgie's arm gently. 'So do I,' she said.

Walking back from the sea, Mina was experiencing an unusual blend of light-headedness and light-heartedness. The last few weeks, ever since Georgie's arrival, had taken their toll—dizzy spells and a terrible exhaustion—in a way that nursing Lydia and caring for Nest had never done. It was odd that mental stress should be so much more deeply wearing than sustained physical effort. Towards the end, Lydia had become very demanding in terms of sheet-washing and running up and down the stairs dozens of times a day; she'd required carefully planned meals and a great deal of company, yet she'd rarely been fretful, never critical. She'd loved to have Mina with her—'Oh good, you've brought your coffee up too, we can have it together'—and she'd loved Mina to read aloud to her. Lydia had always been delighted to see her grandchildren, and she'd written regularly to Josie's boys in America. Each winter her asthma attacks and bronchial infections had grown a little worse, yet she'd clung to life with surprising tenacity. She'd been nearly eighty when a series of strokes put an end to her patient suffering.

Mina pulled up the hood of her jacket against the rain. Great beeches, some still retaining their tiny hoard of copper, groaned restlessly above her head while at their feet, among thick bare roots, mallards rested from the hurly-burly of the rushing water. The dogs scampered among the reeds and up the steep sides of the cleave. She walked on, thinking of Lyddie and Nest, praying that all would be well between them, remembering how Nest had worked to hide the pain of watching her daughter being loved and cherished by her sister.

'Sometimes,' Nest had told her privately, desperately, 'I wonder if it would be better if I never saw her at all. I can't explain the longing to seize her and hold her and then, oh God! when Henrietta gives her to me I'm so afraid of breaking down, of simply getting up and running away with her, that I hardly dare think about it and I sit like a dummy, so busy keeping my feelings under control that it's a complete waste. I used to ache for Connor, and now I ache for Lyddie.'

Mina had put an arm about her. '*Used* to ache for Connor?'

'Yes.' Nest had looked at her, distracted for a moment. 'It's odd, isn't it? Once Lyddie was born it was as if a curtain came down on all that. I felt quite detached. Even when I see him with Lyddie I feel nothing but a sense of relief that he loves her so much. It makes me sure that I did the right thing—given that I couldn't keep her.'

Pausing to pick up some twigs and small branches, brought down by the gales and useful for kindling, Mina sighed with relief as she revelled in this new sense of freedom from the weight of secrets. Standing up, suddenly, she felt quite light-headed again, and had to put her hand against a mossy tree trunk to steady herself.

'Isn't it odd,' Nest had cried almost indignantly, once she'd read the letters, 'that Mama should have become pregnant by Timothy and yet was so horrified when it happened to me? So determined that I couldn't keep my baby?'

'I think you have to take several things into consideration,' Mina had answered carefully. 'First, and this is quite important, was the passage of time between your pregnancy and hers. It's amazing how people forget. How, looking back, it seems that it was quite different for them. There was a deeply romantic element that she couldn't see in your case. If you'd been in a long-term relationship, Mama might have reacted more understandingly. As it was, you were obliged to make it all sound rather chancy. Second, and even more importantly, she was a married woman with the protection and status of a husband.'

'Even so,' Nest had said, rather sadly, 'I think she might have been a bit less Victorian about it, given the circumstances.'

'I think she was utterly true to her Victorian upbringing, double standards and hypocrisy.' Mina had tried to make her laugh.

'It's OK,' Nest had grinned at her, 'I'm not going to go all hurt at this late stage, it's just so incredible. I can't see myself breaking this one to Lyddie for a long time, if at all. I think she's got enough on her plate.'

'Well, I agree but it gives you an even stronger bond, doesn't it? And, one day, who knows, you might be able to share it with her.'

Now, Mina opened the kitchen door and she and the dogs went inside. She put the kettle on the hot plate and went through to the drawing room. Nest was nowhere to be seen, but Georgie was sitting at the end of the sofa, slumped a little, her head dropping forward onto her chest. There was a stillness about her, an immobility, and when Mina spoke her name she did not move. Heart in mouth, Mina went forward and bent over her.

'Georgie?' she said huskily, swallowing in a suddenly dry throat.

Her sister opened an eye and looked at her. 'Where on earth have you been?' she asked grumpily. 'It must be long past teatime.'

Mina straightened up and took a deep breath, controlling an urge to smack her hard. 'The kettle's on,' she said. 'It won't be long.'

Only one more week, she told herself grimly.

From: Mina
To: Elyot

. . . afterwards I simply had to laugh. Probably nervous hysteria. Nest came into the kitchen and wondered what on earth was going on, the kettle boiling its head off and me weeping with laughter. For one terrible moment I thought Georgie was dead and, to be honest, I think my reaction was pure relief. Nest made the tea in the end and when we got back to the sitting room Georgie was sitting up, aggressively perky, although I believe that she is beginning another stage of deterioration.

I shall be glad to be free of the responsibility, which sounds terrible because she is my sister, but I am getting too old for all these alarums and excursions. Lyddie will be back soon and poor Nest is very fidgety, but it will be a great treat to have her with us until she's decided what she is going to do. Her money from the house near Oxford could set her up in some small flat—but where? I think that, legally, she's entitled to something from the house in Truro, and even from the business, but I guess that both are in thrall to the bank and Lyddie is not the kind to demand an eye for an eye. She can stay here for as long as she likes, of course . . .

From: Elyot
To: Mina
Take care of yourself, old friend. You deserve a good long rest. Make certain that Lyddie has a good lawyer . . .

'I'm not sure that it's been good for me being with you two,' Lyddie said, as she and Hannah drove into Dorchester to do some shopping. 'You are so right together. It points up everything I've lost.'

'Are you sure?' asked Hannah. 'I mean, did you actually have it in the first place with Liam? That absolute rightness?'

Lyddie stared out through the windscreen at the rain drifting across the gently rounded hills.

'I suppose not,' she said at last. 'Not ever quite like you and Jack—but there were moments . . .'

'Of course there were,' said Hannah remorsefully. 'Sorry. I'm really not trying to belittle what you had. It would be utterly wrong to pretend that Liam is some kind of monster and you were never happy with him.'

'So what did you really think about Liam?'

'Truth?' asked Hannah cautiously.

'Truth,' agreed Lyddie firmly.

'When I first met him I thought, well, lucky old Lyddie! He is, let's face it, a very attractive man, but, after a bit, I began to sense that there was something driving him along a one-way track and that nothing and nobody was going to get in the way of his objective. I was worried that he'd find marriage too demanding and that you'd be abandoned at some wayside station. For instance, I simply couldn't imagine Liam as a father, which would have been fine except that I knew that children were definitely on your agenda, and, anyway, it seemed such an odd way for you to live. You know what I mean? Spending all day working and then going to the wine bar. There was no privacy, no weekends or evenings for you to be yourselves. I worried about that.'

'But Liam himself?'

'Well, I feel this tormented restlessness about him. He's very alive, but there's something desperate about it. Like he's watching himself perform and, underneath it all, a terrible obsession. As long as you're prepared to sacrifice yourself to it you'll be fine. Step out of line and you'll be dumped. I think that in another age he might have conquered worlds, or gone with Scott to the Antarctic, but there again . . .' She paused.

'But there again?' Lyddie prompted.

Hannah bit her lip. 'I was going to say—but there again perhaps not, because there's something *little* about Liam. I suspect that those types whose natural position is leading, conquering, discovering, often have a sexual appetite to match.' She shrugged. 'He has charisma but at the same time I just have this feeling that he will only ever be a big frog in a small pond.' She gave a quick sideways glance. 'Have I upset you?'

'No,' replied Lyddie, remembering Liam's face when she'd spoken about a chain of wine bars: how he'd seen the vision and then instinctively drawn back from it. 'It's a relief, really,' she continued. 'It makes me more sure that I'm doing the right thing. It's not easy, walking away from a marriage.'

'But I thought *he* was doing the walking? He's the one making the rules. And the rules are not fair ones, Lyddie. You can't accept a situation like this where one partner says, "I must have the freedom to do exactly as I please no matter how it hurts or humiliates you." Well, only if you can't live without him.' Another anxious glance. 'Do you feel that might be the case?'

Lyddie took a deep breath. 'Just occasionally,' she admitted, 'I need him so much I almost feel tempted but I only have to think of Rosie or walking into The Place and I know I couldn't do it. I'm going to have to manage somehow.'

'Might you go back to London?'

'I simply don't know. I can't see it somehow; anyway, what would I do with the Bosun?'

'Could you afford to live, doing what you do now?'

'Just about—as long as I get my money from the house and buy my own place, however small.'

'Well, don't make any important decisions until after Christmas,' Hannah suggested. 'We'll come down to Ottercombe to see you all and have some fun. And you could come to us for New Year.'

Chapter Ten

IT WAS SEVERAL DAYS before Mina wrote again to Elyot.

From: Mina
To: Elyot

And so the day is nearly upon us. It seems like several light-years since I told you that Georgie would be arriving—and now it's all over. Although her presence has triggered off so many memories and prised open some of Pandora's boxes, I can honestly say that I think, on the whole, it has been for the good. Nest looks much better—more content, younger—and she and Lyddie seem to be settling down to a new acceptance of their relationship, which is strongly underpinned by the affection they've always shared. For myself, I have been forced to come to terms with a foolish decision I took as a young girl and which has been buried ever since. We've confronted these things together, Nest and I, and we've drawn even closer because of it. I wish I could tell you much more, dear Elyot, but these are not just my secrets. I still feel certain that one day you will come here to see us all.

As for Georgie, well, now that her departure is at hand I feel unusually fond of her! More seriously, much though I feel saddened by the thought of her in a home I know that we couldn't keep her here. Even in these few weeks I've seen a deterioration, and I simply couldn't be responsible for some disaster.

Lyddie seems to be coping remarkably well, although I suspect she misses Liam very much. She works very hard, which occupies her mind and saves her from too much brooding, but if you come upon her unawares you catch a glimpse of the misery she feels deep down. The dogs are learning to live together too! So how are things with you? Lavinia? William?

From: Elyot
To: Mina

I can't tell you how deeply glad I am to receive your sitrep. I can well imagine how your feelings must war together regarding Georgie. Knowing you, my dear old friend, I feel you would be happier if you could gather her in beneath your capacious and comforting wing, but you are right to resist it. You simply can't afford to take the responsibility. If something were to go badly wrong you'd never forgive yourself.

And if you detect a note of serious anxiety—even panic?—in my 'voice' then you are quite right. Quite suddenly, yesterday, Lavinia took a downward turn, which took the form of not knowing who I was, screaming in true terror when I approached her, fighting me. She tried to run away from me, wrenching at the front door in an attempt to open it, fell badly and has had to be taken to the cottage hospital. She has broken her wrist and sprained an ankle and is in an altogether wretched condition. As you know, this lack of recognition has happened before, but it had been possible to calm her down eventually. This truly violent reaction was terrifying for both of us.

From: Mina
To: Elyot
My dear Elyot

I was shocked to read your account of poor Lavinia's lapse and her accident. What a devilish thing this is, isn't it, eating away at the mind, stealing away memory and rationality? I am so pleased that you have William at hand, and how good of you, at such a time, to share your experience so as to strengthen my own hesitant decision. You are right in suggesting that my instinct is to keep Georgie with me, but I see now that it would be wrong to consider it. But never mind me! My thoughts are so much with you. Is there anything I can do?

From: Elyot
To: Mina
Only be there to listen and to make me feel that I have a very good friend close at hand. I'm well aware that this accident has brought us to a new point from which there is no going back and has made me face the fact that we couldn't have continued as we were. Even that state, now that Lavinia is settled in the hospital, seems desirable compared to this loneliness. Thank God for William.

From: Mina
To: Elyot
Of course I am here—you know that. Oh, my very dear friend, how I feel for you. Of course you must be missing Lavinia terribly and I quite understand that you'd rather have gone on as you were with her at home with you. It is even harder when you've been depended on so much. Suddenly everything seems so pointless, a terrible emptiness turns the world grey, and life stretches futilely ahead. And I'm supposed to be comforting you!!! What can I say?

THE CHILDREN'S HOUR

From: Elyot
To: Mina
Your very real understanding is a thousand times more valuable than meaningless banalities. As usual you have given me comfort and made me feel that I am not isolated. God bless you and good night.

From: Mina
To: Elyot
I know you won't read this tonight, and quite right, too. You need rest. I couldn't go to bed, however, without reminding you that we are here if you need us; if you think that a trip to Ottercombe might do you and William some good. I know once you told me that you live near Taunton so it's not too far. I'm sure you're spending a great deal of time with Lavinia at the hospital but the invitation is there.
Good night, dear Elyot.

Helena arrived late in the morning to fetch her mother; for the other three, waiting for her, the hours since breakfast had stretched interminably. 'It's not that I want to see the back of her,' Mina had assured Nest despairingly, 'it's that she looks so wretched. I feel like a traitor.'

Lyddie watched them anxiously. 'Doesn't she want to go?' she asked.

'It's simply that she won't know anyone at the home and it will be so strange for her,' said Mina, her hands winding unconsciously together. 'To be honest, I don't quite know how much she knows. I just feel this sense of reproach emanating from her, as if she feels that this is her home and we're throwing her out. Being here has taken her—well, all of us—so far back into the past that I'm not sure she can remember what happened before she was here.'

'I'm sure she can,' said Lyddie gently. 'She doesn't question who Helena is, does she? Or that she has some right to fetch her?'

'No,' agreed Mina, after a moment. 'No, that's absolutely true, she doesn't. But I still feel that there's been some change.'

Nest bit her lip. She had a horrid feeling that the change had followed the conversation in the sitting room when Georgie had said, 'I know a secret,' and Nest had responded, 'So do I.' After that brief exchange Nest had watched an expression of surprise, confusion and finally a kind of despair pass over her sister's face. The jigging of the shoulders and the sly smile, the tapping foot and inward glee had died away and she'd drooped, slumping into the corner of the sofa. She'd refused to answer or talk to Nest, turning her head from her so that, after a while, Nest had gone away. Yet she'd felt guilty that in confronting Georgie at last, she'd removed her power, defused the vital will to control.

For the remaining days she'd continued in that dull, listless mood;

shuffling about, sitting in corners, unresponsive. When Mina told her that Helena would be coming to take her home—her lips stumbling at the word—Georgie had stared at her rather vacantly, but had been quite ready to go with her upstairs to start the packing.

'The point is,' Lyddie was saying, 'that this is progressive. You're simply not equipped for it here. She could wander off anywhere; up on the moor or down to the beach. You can't be her jailer, Aunt Mina. She'll be very well looked after and we'll go and visit her. Now I'm on the insurance of the camper I'll drive you and Nest up and we'll stay in a hotel somewhere. It'll be fun.'

Mina stared at her, almost weak with gratitude. While she would have vehemently denied any suggestion that she was not perfectly strong enough to care for Nest or to run Ottercombe, nevertheless this infusion of youth and energy was the most tremendous relief. The last few weeks had drained her more than she had realised and Lyddie's strong, practical support was like a tonic. She knew a sudden foolish desire to burst into tears. 'It sounds . . . wonderful.'

'I was wondering . . .' But before Lyddie could tell them her idea the door was pushed open and Georgie came in. She looked round at each of them almost suspiciously.

'Perfect timing, Aunt Georgie,' Lyddie said cheerfully. 'I'm making some coffee and I was just about to come and find you.'

Georgie frowned, looking round the kitchen, not answering, and Mina's spirits sank. Nest wheeled forward touching Mina lightly, comfortingly, on the arm as she passed.

'Are you looking for something?' she asked gently.

Georgie stared at her distrustfully, and turned away to peer along the dresser shelves. Her hands fumbled over the surface, and the other three watched in a kind of breathless, unmoving silence.

'Aaahhh . . .' She let out a long breath of relief.

'Have you found it?' Nest tried to keep her voice light.

Georgie looked at her guardedly for several moments before opening her hand to show what it held. It was Timmie's little car, washed and scoured by a thousand tides.

'I took it from him before,' Georgie said confidingly. 'He is Papa's favourite but I am his first-born. I shall hide it.' Her eyes travelled over Nest—puzzled now, as if surprised to see her in a wheelchair—and beyond her to Lyddie, who watched her compassionately. 'Mama?' she murmured. Her face, confused, even frightened, crumpled suddenly, and Mina came quickly to her, taking her arm.

'Let's go and pack it so that it doesn't get lost again,' she said, 'and then we'll have that coffee.'

They went out together and Lyddie looked at Nest.

'Wow!' she said feelingly. 'That was scary. What was all that about?'

'It was Timmie's car,' said Nest. 'Timothy . . . his godfather sent it to him and Timmie adored it. Georgie found it on the beach. It had lain there for all those years but she remembered it. I was rather hoping to keep it, for various reasons, but there we are . . .'

'Oh, what a shame,' cried Lyddie. 'Was it a kind of keepsake because of you and Timmie being little together?'

'Yes,' said Nest slowly. 'Partly that. Timmie and I were very close and I was very fond of him,' *and*—she wanted to say—*because it was a present from my father and I have so little by which to remember him*—'which is probably why I'm so fond of Jack.'

'Oh, they are such heaven,' said Lyddie warmly, 'Jack and Hannah, but it's good to be here, Nest.'

They looked at each other rather shyly, each remembering acts of love that spanned thirty years, but not confident enough yet to make any great gesture.

'I'm glad you feel comfortable with us,' said Nest. 'You're happy in your little study? That was Timmie's room, you know.'

'I love it,' said Lyddie. 'It's just the right size, and I've fitted all my things in. I've got my proper chair now. It was good of Liam to let me keep the car. I managed to bring back most of my stuff on this last trip.'

'But you didn't see him?'

Lyddie shook her head. 'I told him when I would be arriving and he steered well clear.' She gave a mirthless snort. 'I had a moment's temptation to go into The Place. Just to go in like any ordinary customer and order some coffee, but my nerve failed me.'

Nest chuckled. 'I'm not surprised,' she said. 'Early days for that kind of courage.'

Lyddie looked at her, wondering how she'd managed to meet Connor as her brother-in-law, how she'd hidden her pain and her longing. She felt a surge of respect and fellow feeling for Nest, a sense of grateful recognition, and knew that it was this that truly related people: this deep-down knowing and sharing. They smiled again, reaching tremulously towards this new level of trust and love but, before either could speak again, there was a sudden ringing of the doorbell, a voice halloo-ing in the hall, and Helena was at the kitchen door.

'What excellent timing,' said Nest, pulling herself together. 'The coffee's just made. Did you have a good trip?'

It was clear that Helena expected an unspoken but hinted disapproval, but her fear faded in the feeling of goodwill that pervaded the kitchen and she was able to sit at the table with her coffee, admiring the

Bosun while describing her journey. It was accepted that to drag the moment out would be foolish and, when Georgie appeared with Mina some minutes later, it was tacitly agreed that the two of them would hurry away.

'You must come and visit,' Helena said.

'Oh, we shall,' said Lyddie cheerfully, 'we've got it all planned. You'll have to find a good hotel locally which can deal with wheelchairs, Helena, and send us the details. Goodbye, Aunt Georgie. See you soon.'

Lyddie's positive approach carried them through the painful farewells. Still looking puzzled, Georgie was kissed and hugged, put into the car, and Helena drove away.

The three of them stood together on the drive, staring after the car, suddenly at a loss. Mina, fighting tears, was swallowing hard. 'I just know that I shan't see her again,' she muttered.

'I feel the same,' Nest assured her, 'but we shall. Not here, perhaps, but Lyddie is going to drive us up to visit her.'

She looked helplessly at Lyddie, who smiled and put her arms about them both. 'I certainly am,' she said cheerfully, 'but I'm going to need some practice with that monster you've got, Aunt Mina, so I suggest a trip to Dulverton for lunch. The run over the moor should be wonderful on a day like this.'

'What a lovely idea,' said Mina, still near to tears. 'Oh, *what* a treat it would be. But can you spare the time, my darling?'

'I started work very early,' said Lyddie—who, finding sleep impossible, was tending to work half the night so as to distract herself from her thoughts of Liam—'and I can work this evening. The important thing is to make the most of this glorious day before the light goes.'

They hurried inside to find their coats and, as Nest was shrugging herself into a warm fleecy jacket, Mina appeared.

'I think this is yours,' she said. She opened her hand and there, lying on her outstretched palm, was the little silver car.

Nest stared at it and then looked at Mina. 'How on earth . . .?'

'Never mind,' said Mina briskly. 'Soon it would have no meaning for Georgie, and it's important to you.'

'Yes,' said Nest, close to tears, 'it *is* important to me.'

For a whole week the crisp golden weather held good and excursions became the order of the day: over to Simonsbath for coffee in the little café; lunch at the Hunter's Inn where the wild peacocks frightened the Bosun; a drive along the coast and through the Valley of Rocks. Lyddie, tired as she was with lack of sleep and the pain in her heart, was never-theless glad to be of use, to feel needed and—more than that—she was enjoying herself. Mina and Nest had always been important to her, but now, living with them, she discovered the depth of their humour, the breadth of their courage, and her love for them was informed by this knowledge and grew deeper and wider with the discovery.

'They're terrific fun,' she said to Jack, one weekend not long before Christmas, when he drove his family down to see them.

'An exeat weekend,' he'd said on the telephone, 'the little blighters are going home, the Lord be praised, so we could come down on Sunday, if you can cope with us?'

Their arrival increased the sense of continuity and Lyddie was beginning to be aware of a slow healing.

'Well, of course they're fun!' he'd answered her, almost indignantly. 'We all knew that.'

'Of course we did,' she said, 'but I think I shall stay here for a bit, Jack. It's not just because I feel I can help them by driving them about and doing all the things that Mina probably shouldn't be doing at her age, but quite selfishly because they're helping me.'

'Quite right, too,' said Jack. 'That's the tragedy of this present way of life. We no longer consider that older people have all this to offer. Their courage and wisdom and experience is just brushed to one side. They're probably doing you much more good than you could do them.'

'I agree,' she answered with humility. 'I *do* need them. And you too.'

'Well, naturally,' he said, his voice losing its serious note. 'I'm quite aware of it. It's a gift I have, a burden nobly borne . . .'

'Oh, shut up,' she said, laughing.

'So are you going to let me get you on the Internet like I did Aunt Mina so you can email your friends? Come on, Lydd, take a chance, why not?'

'I might,' she said, laughing. 'I just might at that. Dear old Aunt Mina loves it. She chats to all her friends at night. I see her light on, really late, shining under her door.'

'Lunch is ready,' said Toby, appearing suddenly, 'and Mummy says it will get cold if you don't come *this minute*.'

'A directive I never disobey, do I, Tobes? Mummy's word is the Law and the Prophets rolled into one, especially when food is involved.'

'What's the law and the prophets?' asked Toby predictably.

'Ask your Aunt Lyddie,' answered Jack promptly—and vanished.

Toby beamed up at her. 'We're going down to the beach after lunch,' he told her. 'All of us with the dogs. Well, all except Aunt Nest. She never goes to the sea, does she?'

Lyddie stared down at him, thinking of Mina's words. 'No,' she said slowly. 'No, she never does. I expect she has a little sleep after lunch.'

Later, as the beach party assembled, Lyddie said that she would stay with Nest and do the washing up.

There was a blessed silence, once the door had shut behind them all, and Lyddie smiled at Nest.

'Would you like to rest?' she asked. 'I'm very happy doing this lot on my own, really I am.'

Nest made a little face. 'To tell the truth, I would,' she admitted. 'If you're sure . . . ?'

'Quite sure,' said Lyddie firmly. 'Off you go. I'll bring you a cup of tea later, if you like. Although you'll probably hear them all coming back.'

'I expect I shall,' agreed Nest.

She wheeled away and Lyddie was left in possession of the kitchen. She began to clear up methodically and, after a moment, found herself humming. These small, unexpected manifestations of happiness were still surprising to her and she moved quietly about, grateful that she was granted such a refuge.

By the time the lunch things were washed up and put away, the kitchen tidy and the kettle ready on the Esse, she heard the sounds of the returning party.

'It was the devil of a job getting them away,' said Jack, accepting his cup of tea, 'but we really should be on our way very soon. It's a long drive and the boys will be back this evening.'

Nest was roused and came to join them for the last ten minutes, before the children were packed into the car after tearful farewells to the dogs, and the grown-ups embraced each other with thanks and promises of future jollies.

'We'll get together somehow for Christmas,' Jack said, hugging Lyddie. 'We'll sort something out.' He bent to kiss Nest, holding her hand tightly for a moment, and then turned to Mina. 'Lyddie looks well,' he murmured, under the cover of the others' farewells.

'She does, doesn't she?' she answered eagerly. 'And it's such joy having her here. My dear boy, you are *such* a blessing to us all.'

He looked down into her sweet, old face and bent to kiss her lips gently. 'Love you lots, darling,' he said tenderly.

'God bless you,' she said. 'Drive carefully.'

They went away up the drive, Toby's hand waving furiously at the window. The three standing motionless on the gravel heard the car pull out and accelerate away across the moorland road.

'And now,' said Lyddie, 'you and the dogs have a little rest, Aunt Mina. I've lit the fire in the drawing room.'

'It sounds wonderful,' admitted Mina, 'but what about you?'

'Ah.' Lyddie laid her hands upon the back of Nest's chair. 'Well, *I* think it's time that Nest and I went down to the sea.' She smiled at her. 'What do you think, Nest?'

The silence seemed to engulf them all and Mina realised that she was holding her breath. Then Nest turned to look up into her child's face.

'I think that's a very good idea,' she said.

It was exactly as she'd remembered it, dreamed about it. The steep-sided cleave clothed with larch and oak and tall, noble beech, their bare, twiggy branches reaching to the tender blue sky; great thickets of rhododendron beneath the rocky shoulder of the moor; bright green ferns at the water's edge. The stream ran beside her through the narrow valley, flowing over smooth boulders and under willow, while ducks dabbled among the reeds and the sharp scent of gorse was carried on the breeze. Nest's hands clutched at the arms of her chair as she turned this way and that, each sight furnishing a hundred memories, until at last the cleave widened into the crescent-shaped beach, and the stream travelled onwards to its inexorable meeting with the sea.

The sea. Nest hardly realised that her chair had stopped moving. Voices were carried on the wind:

'We'll live here together when we grow up.'

'Have you come to tell me I'm trespassing or are you simply a passing dryad?'

'We have a new baby brother. Do you think Papa will love us any more?'

She was quite unaware of the searing tears that streamed down her cold cheeks as she listened to the rhythmic beating of the tide and allowed the salty air to wash away her bitterness and pain. Presently she was aware of Lyddie kneeling beside her. Lyddie took her handkerchief and dried Nest's cheeks and kissed her before she straightened up.

'We must go home before it gets dark,' she said gently. 'But we'll come again . . . won't we?'

'Oh, yes,' said Nest, struggling to keep her voice steady. 'We'll come again. And thank you, Lyddie.'

Lyddie tucked the handkerchief away, paused for one last look out to sea, and turned the chair for the journey home.

Mina watched them go, her warm heart full of gratitude: the miracle had happened, the acceptance made. She'd been watching the love between Nest and Lyddie growing steadily and now any reservations she might have had were finally lifted from her. She went into the drawing room, still feeling light-headed with the joy of it all. Unconsciously pressing her fingers to her old, withered lips, holding the kiss Jack had given her, she sat down in the corner of the sofa while the dogs flopped gratefully and wearily upon their beds. She stared at the fire, thinking back over these past few weeks: jaunts in the camper, quiet contented evenings, walks with the dogs; and further back again, seeing scenes among the burning logs and hearing voices in the whispering flames.

'I'll tell you a story,' said the Story Spinner, 'but you mustn't rustle too much, or cough or blow your nose . . .'

'I apologise for arriving unannounced.'

'He is dead.'

'Is it possible that you might speak to Mr Shaw soon?'

Arousing herself suddenly, as if from a dazed sleep, Mina thought first of Timmie, going away to school and then into the army, and then of Jack and his small family. She murmured a prayer for their safety and wellbeing and, as a stronger wave of dizziness engulfed her, she had time to see quite clearly, and with deep joy, Lyddie smiling down at Nest; to hear her saying, 'I think it's time that Nest and I went down to the sea,' and see Nest's answering look of love and trust. It was her last conscious thought.

Walking in the early mornings with the dogs on the moor above the house, looking out to sea, Lyddie tried to come to terms with this new blow. Without Aunt Mina, she felt as if she'd suddenly lost her footing, trodden confidently out onto a step that was not there. In the ambulance, leaving Nest white-faced but determined—'You *must* go! I can't be with her but she mustn't be alone. Please go with her. I'll be all right!'—she'd held Mina's cold, unresponsive hand and stared beseechingly into the calm, serene face. Waiting alone in the hospital, she'd known the truth, already learning to face a future that did not hold Aunt Mina.

The minute Jack had heard the news, telephoning Ottercombe to say that they were safely home, he'd come straight to the hospital and taken the whole terrible business into his hands.

This morning, the fourth after Mina's death, watching a tanker ploughing down the Channel, Lyddie could feel the tears running down the back of her throat.

'It's just that she's always been there,' she'd said to Jack. 'I can't quite imagine life without Aunt Mina.'

'She's left everything to you, Ottercombe, everything,' he'd told her. 'Did you know that I'm an executor? Aunt Nest has the right to live at Ottercombe until she dies, but it's academic, of course. She could never manage there alone.'

'She isn't alone,' Lyddie had said. 'I shall be with her.'

Jack had watched her thoughtfully. 'Shall you stay at Ottercombe?'

'Yes, I shall. Even if I wanted to I couldn't possibly uproot her now. It's been the most terrible shock for Nest. On top of all the other knocks she's taken, it would be the last straw. Anyway, I don't want to leave. I love it here and I can't imagine where else we could go.'

'When you talk of Aunt Nest's "knocks" do you mean the accident?'

'Well, yes . . .' She remembered with a sudden shock that Jack knew nothing of the true relationship between herself and Nest. It was odd to have secrets from Jack. 'Yes, of course. Do you think it's crazy? Us staying at Ottercombe?'

'Of course not,' he'd answered. 'If Aunt Mina could cope with it all, I'm sure you can, although you have to remember that you work full-time. There's money invested, so that should help a bit. No, it's simply that Aunt Mina devoted her life to Grandmama and then to Aunt Nest and I don't want to see you sacrifice your life in the same way.'

'Was it a sacrifice?' she'd wondered. 'I can't think of anyone more content than Aunt Mina. And how wise she was, considering that she only spent a few years outside the cleave. We all turned to her at one time or another, didn't we?'

'Oh, I agree.' Jack had smiled at her. 'Aunt Mina was a communicator and she retained her intellectual integrity. She never shut herself off. I'm delighted that you'll be together, you and Aunt Nest, but I don't want you to forget that there's life outside Ottercombe, that's all.'

'I shan't do that,' she'd promised. 'Perhaps the time might come when we'll want to sell up and move into a town, that kind of thing. It's just that I don't want to do anything in a hurry and I don't want to upset Nest any more than she is now.'

'Fine.' He'd paused. 'Have you noticed,' he'd asked, 'that you don't call her "Aunt" these days?'

'No, I don't, do I?' she'd agreed after a moment. 'Odd, isn't it?'

At Ottercombe, Nest was getting herself up by degrees. She sat on the edge of the bed, pulling on a long, warm flannel skirt in soft blues and red, fighting with the tears that threatened night and day. Mina was everywhere: working in the garden, cooking in the kitchen, reading beside the fire. Nest could still see her, in those dreadful days after the accident, dancing on the terrace, a puppy in her arms, holding up one of its paws elegantly as they swept to and fro; pouring a very necessary drink before dinner; pushing the wheelchair round the supermarket so that Nest could choose something special for her birthday.

'Christ . . . did not cling to equality with God . . . but emptied himself . . .' The verse came unbidden to her mind. Perhaps that was what the attaining to Christ's hard-won peace was about: an emptying of self, cheerfully, willingly . . .

She heard Jack moving about in the kitchen and steadied herself, continuing with the slow dressing process. What would she have done without Lyddie and Jack?

'I'm staying,' Lyddie had said firmly, generously. 'We belong together, you and I. We'll get through this somehow. You'll have to show me the ropes, mind.'

Nest was too grateful, too thankful, to make anything but a token protest about being a burden.

'And where would I go?' Lyddie had demanded. 'I hope you're not intending to throw me out? Anyway, someone's got to look after the dogs.'

Her cheerfulness did not deceive Nest and her heart went out to Lyddie. 'Does Liam know?' she'd asked Jack privately—and he'd nodded.

'Lyddie telephoned to tell him,' he'd said, 'but it's clear that he doesn't give a damn.'

He'd looked unusually angry, for Jack, and Nest had been filled with love for him. He was dealing with every aspect of the funeral and she was relieved to be spared.

'Just let me know anyone you think should be invited,' he'd said. 'And I hope it's OK but I've checked her email correspondence and sent a message out to some of the people in her email address book. It seems wrong, I know, to read her letters but I wondered if there might be someone out there who's wondering what's going on. She had several regulars and one man, especially, called Elyot. Did she ever speak of him?'

Nest had shaken her head, frowning. 'I don't think so. She only ever talked in a general way about them. It was good for her to have people to speak to and I know that some of them were looking after disabled people like me.'

'Well, this chap seemed a bit worried not to have heard from her. His wife is ill in hospital, apparently, so I suspect she met him through some carers' chat room. Looking at their emails it's clear that they've been very good friends. I'm going to print them off for you to read.' He hesitated. 'It probably sounds odd but I think you should read them too. Anyway, all her close contacts know now.'

'It's so good of you,' she'd said, tears threatening again. 'Sorry, what a fool I am!'

'Have a good weep,' he'd advised sympathetically. 'I do, regularly.'

Now, fully dressed and having got herself into her chair, she heard the sound of Lyddie's voice talking to Jack, and Nogood Boyo's high bark. It was Captain Cat who was feeling the loss of his mistress most; he mourned Mina quite heart-rendingly. He'd adopted Nest as his protector, sitting beside her chair and following her about. Oddly, Nest was glad of Captain Cat's companionship, his shared sadness, and she often lifted him onto her lap, murmuring to him, smoothing his warm white head, as Mina had in the past. He would be waiting for her now, with Lyddie and Jack.

Straightening her shoulders, schooling her lips into a smile, she wheeled herself across the hall and into the kitchen.

By the day of the funeral the house had been cleaned from top to bottom. As the family waited for friends to return from the church, Ottercombe seemed ready to welcome them, with its familiar, homely smells of log fires, flowers, beeswax and dog.

Hannah had arrived two days before, having left the children with her mother. 'I could possibly have managed Tobes,' she'd said to Lyddie, 'but not Flora. You need to be able to concentrate at times like these. At least I can get on with the catering part without any distraction. How many are we going to be?'

'I'm not too certain.' Lyddie was trying hard not to burst into tears. It was odd how this grief suddenly came upon one, out of nowhere, twisting the heart. She swallowed the weight of tears in her throat. 'We've got eight of us in the house. Me and Nest; you and Jack; Helena and Rupert; and Aunt Josie is flying over from Philadelphia with her youngest son, Paul. Roger and Teresa are driving down early in the morning. But I don't know how many people might turn up at the church tomorrow and then come back here afterwards.'

Hannah looked at her, noting the shadows beneath the eyes. 'Have you done the beds?' she asked.

Lyddie nodded. 'We're all ready. Only the food to do, and Jack's collecting Josie and Paul from Taunton this afternoon. Helena and Rupert will be down this evening.'

'Then come with me in the kitchen and help me make a shopping list. We'll go into Barnstaple and get everything and then have a quiet cup of coffee somewhere. Jack can keep an eye on Nest.'

'I'd like that,' said Lyddie. Suddenly she longed to be away from Ottercombe, to see that the world was still carrying on as usual, to forget—for a brief moment—that she would never see Aunt Mina's face again. 'Thanks, Hannah.'

Surprisingly, the arrival of Josie and Paul did much to lift the spirits. Josie had been away long enough for her grief to be a gentler affair; a warm recollection of happy times; of, 'Oh! and do you remember . . .?', which seemed to comfort Nest and animate her. She was fascinated by this tiny, thin, vital woman, very smart, very American, who looked so much like Henrietta, and to talk to her youngest son, Paul, who was quiet and good-looking with delightful manners. Jack and Rupert took him off into a corner with a bottle of whisky, while Helena told Lyddie and Hannah how Georgie had settled into the home.

'It was strange at first,' she said, 'well, we expected that, but she was very quiet, a bit bemused. She doesn't bother to answer us much or seem to know what's going on. I really couldn't see any point in bringing her down with us.'

'Oh, no,' said Lyddie quickly. 'It would have been horrid. So confusing for her. At least her memories will be happy ones.'

'Poor Helena,' Hannah said sympathetically. 'I think these terrible times are worse for the carers and the watchers than the ones who have gone beyond anxiety.'

Helena looked at her gratefully. 'But then we don't know what's going on in their heads, do we? They might be suffering in a way we know nothing about.'

Her eyes filled with tears and Lyddie took her hand. 'Don't,' she said, trying to smile. 'Don't you dare, Helena, or we'll all be at it'—and the three of them had laughed, albeit shakily, together.

'**S**o many memories,' Josie was saying to Nest. 'Goodness, when I think back! Me and Henrietta fighting like cat and dog and Mina trying to keep the peace. Poor Mama! Of course, you and Timmie were just babies to us. Remember how we called you the Tinies?' Her face clouded. 'Oh, Nest. Timmie and Henrietta gone, and now Mina. All those years looking after Mama and then . . .'

'And then all those years looking after me?'

Nest was smiling but Josie grimaced. 'Still Miss Big-Mouth,' she said cheerfully. 'That's me! But Mina was a saint. *I* couldn't wait to get away after the war. Stuck down here with nothing to do. Goodness, do you remember those wretched babies that came to stay with cousin Jean . . .?'

'That's right.' Nest pretended to frown too, to cudgel her memory. 'And do you remember Timothy?'

Josie's brow cleared. 'Timothy,' she said gently. 'Of *course* I remember Timothy. He was like a visitor from another world. A fairy godfather. How we envied Timmie, Henrietta and me, his having Timothy as his godfather. Although he was so sweet to all of us, wasn't he? *Much* nicer than Papa. Surely you can remember him, Nest?'

'Yes. Yes, I can. But not so well as you, I expect. Being that much younger, of course . . .'

'Sure. Well, he was something else, I can tell you. So good-looking and romantic. And all those places he went to . . .'

'Mina used to talk about him sometimes,' said Nest mendaciously, 'but she couldn't remember too much.'

'Well,' Josie settled herself more comfortably.. 'Let me see now . . .'

And now here they were, standing awkwardly about, waiting for the first arrivals. The sound of an engine, a car bumping down the drive; Lyddie looked at Nest and they exchanged a reassuring smile, a nod of mutual encouragement, as Jack came through from the kitchen and went to open the front door.

Sitting just outside the drawing-room door, Nest watched them come. She'd been surprised at the numbers in the church: tradespeople from Lynton, some locals from the outlying farms, a few family friends and one or two strangers.

Listening to the familiar words of the service, Lyddie's hand tightly clasping hers, Nest had tried to empty her mind, to keep her eyes away from the coffin. Visions filled her eyes: Mina pushing her in the garden to show her the first primroses; Mina, singing as she drove across the coast road so that Nest could see the sea without feeling guilty; Mina talking to the dogs, her love murmurings followed by the little 'po-po-po' of sighing breath. Nest's throat had ached with the pain of it, her heart was heavy and cold as lead in her breast; only Lyddie's warm clasp had held her firm.

Now she smiled at these dear souls, who had in their own ways loved Mina, as she accepted their gentle commiserations, thanking them for coming. Above the heads of an aged farmer and his wife, who were telling her that they could remember Lydia, she saw two men enter the house. They'd been at the church, right at the back, and, as she'd wheeled out, she'd glanced at them, thinking for a moment that she recognised the younger man. As the farmer and wife turned away, Nest watched the two men look about rather diffidently, saw Lyddie turn to greet them, holding out her hand with a smile.

The younger man took it, smiling down at her. 'I apologise for arriving unannounced,' he said—and Nest felt a tiny shock wave as though the two, standing there together, were locked in some eternal memory.

'*I apologise for arriving unannounced.*'

'My father can't drive at present and he asked me to bring him,' he was saying, still holding Lyddie's hand. 'You won't know who we are.'

As the older man moved forward to stand beside him, Nest wheeled swiftly forward.

'But I do,' she said—and joy lifted her heart, as though Mina had touched her upon her shoulder. She looked from the young face to the older one, and smiled with warm recognition. 'You're Tony Luttrell,' she said, and put out her hand. 'Welcome back to Ottercombe.'

In the days that followed, once Jack and Hannah had returned to Dorset, Josie and Paul to America, Helena and Rupert to Bristol, it was the promise of this new beginning that gave Lyddie and Nest courage to go forward.

'Although it's hardly a new friendship,' Lyddie said. 'After all, it's more than forty years old. Oh, how fantastic it is! I feel that Mina sent them along specially. And you recognising him like that after all those years!'

'Well, I didn't recognise Tony,' Nest reminded Lyddie. 'It was William I recognised.' She chuckled. 'How silly that sounds. The thing is, he looks so much like Tony looked when I first knew him. Quite a bit older, of course—William must be in his thirties—but it's there. When I saw them in the church I felt a sort of flicker, but I was too overwrought to follow it through. It was when I saw him standing there with you . . .'

She fell silent, unwilling to go further, to speak the words that William uttered, which her own father had said to Lydia so many years before. Lyddie was too absorbed to notice her withdrawal, so taken was she by this strange happening. She made Nest tell her Mina's story over and over.

'I'm not doing it as well as she would,' Nest would cry in frustration. 'It was Mina who was the story spinner,' and then Lyddie must hear the other stories, of Nest and Timmie when they were the Tinies, of Henrietta's ongoing feud with Josie, despite their very real affection for one another; of picnics and the games they'd played, and of the stories that Mama had read them during the children's hour.

Lyddie would sigh with pleasure at the end of each telling, the thought of the life in the house stretching back, helping to heal her hurt from Liam and the loss of dear Aunt Mina.

'William might be over tomorrow,' she'd say casually—and she'd take the dogs down to the sea, trying to control the strange lifting of her heart at the thought of seeing him again. 'It's too soon,' she'd tell herself savagely. 'Don't be a fool! You did this with Liam after James . . .' but she knew that William was no Liam. His clear gaze and quiet smile betokened a quite different character, and she felt at peace with him, relaxed and content. Both of them were recovering from broken relationships and neither was in any haste to rush into a new commitment. They were simply happy to spend time together, discovering one another. As they walked together in the woods, listening to the restless hush-hush of the waves on the shore, a quietness stole upon her heart.

Nest, too, was comforted; not only by the sight of Lyddie and William together but by Tony's company. How extraordinary it was that he should reappear now, as a result of Mina's death, to be such a staunch comfort to her. He came with William when he could; Lavinia was failing and he tried to be with her for as long as was practicable each day.

'If only Mina had known who you were,' Nest had mourned when Tony explained how he'd received Jack's email, described how he and Mina had 'talked'.

'I was afraid to tell her,' he'd said, his still-handsome face sad. 'It was so amazing when I first saw her name. She made no attempt to hide it. Why should she? I was more cautious when I started experimenting on the Internet and decided to use a part anagram of Tony Luttrell and call myself Elyot. It wasn't long before she mentioned Ottercombe and you, and then I knew. Oh, Nest, I can't tell you what I felt! How often I longed to tell her the truth. But I didn't know whether she still hated me and I was afraid to take the chance. I needed her too much.'

'She never hated you,' said Nest gently—and found herself telling Mina's story yet again, the whole truth of it, so that Tony was unable to contain his emotion and they sat together in the dusk, comforting each other.

'She needed you too,' she told him. 'You helped her through these last few years. You *must* know that.' She hesitated. 'I have to say that Jack printed off your "conversations" and showed them to me. Forgive me for that, but it meant so much to see that she had all that love and support from you. Perhaps it was better this way, for all sorts of reasons.'

'Perhaps.' He blew his nose. 'I shall never forget that email from Jack. It was exactly as if I'd lost her all over again. I simply had to come, just once, to see this house and you.'

'And now you'll come often, I hope,' she said. 'You and William.'

He looked at her, his eyes bright with unshed tears. 'It would mean so much. Thank you, Nest.'

So now, with Christmas less than a week away, they were waiting for more visitors: for Jack and Hannah and the children, and the puppy.

'I think it's utterly noble of you to have us all,' said Hannah, on the telephone to Lyddie.

'It's really good of you to come, Han,' said Lyddie.'Don't think I can't imagine what it must be like to transport two children and all your Christmas this far.'

'We can't wait,' promised Hannah. 'Once Tobes knew that you had a chimney worthy of Father Christmas he was ecstatic. A Christmas with *five* dogs? I ask you. What more could life hold? Jack's bringing the booze, by the way. Says he doesn't trust you with his delicate palate.' A pause. 'Quite,' agreed Hannah. 'I was silenced too. Then I hit him!'

Lyddie burst out laughing. 'Give them a hug from us. 'Bye.'

Now a peaceful silence hangs over the house. William has arrived and taken Lyddie and the dogs off to the beach; everything is in readiness. Slowly Nest wheels her chair out of the shadows, the rubber tyres rolling softly across the cracked mosaic floor, and pauses outside the drawing room. Brightly wrapped Christmas presents are piled upon the ancient settle and a jar of spindle-berries stands on the oak table beside the lamp, whose light glints on the big copper plate. Silence fills the high spaces of the hall and flows about her as she bends her head to listen, her eyes closed. She can no longer see Georgie and Mina, with Timmie propped between them on the sofa, nor Josie, working at her jigsaw on the floor, while Henrietta leans to look at the pictures in the book. Mama's voice is stilled, the children are gone.

Their story is finished; a new chapter is beginning.

MARCIA WILLETT

Apart from a brief period when she lived in naval towns, Marcia Willett has spent her life in the area in which she was born—between the three moors, Dartmoor, Exmoor and Bodmin. 'I'm extremely lucky to live in this beautiful part of the world,' she says emphatically, and goes on to explain its special appeal for her. 'When my son Charles was nearly a year old—many years ago now, since he was ordained this summer—I was rather unwell and very depressed. I'd caught an infection after he was born, which was very painful but not diagnosed, and it destroyed my chance of having any other children. But the elemental, spiritual quality of the moor healed me more effectively than any medicine. The West Country's beauty is magical and I only hope I do it justice in my novels.'

After the much-deserved success of her previous novel, *A Week in Winter*, Marcia Willett and her husband Rodney were at last able to buy their dream home, a wonderful old Devon longhouse to the north of Dartmoor. 'The Hermitage is a perfect place for peace and inspiration, such necessary tools for a writer,' says Marcia. 'We have needed to do very little to improve it, apart from a new coat of paint to protect the old stone walls from the winter winds. In fact, we have just learned that we are going to be able to rent the adjacent field, which will give a whole new dimension to Trubshawe's walks.' Trubshawe is Marcia's

huge, hairy and much-loved Newfoundland dog.

'My study is the central room of the longhouse. There is a vast inglenook stone fireplace, lots of bookcases, a long oxbow table for my laptop and two lecterns that hold postcards, photographs and paintings of the current book's landscape. The windows look across fields, beyond the wooded valley of the River Wolf, to Dartmoor. It is here that I write each morning, from about nine thirty until two o'clock, and then I like to take Trubshawe on a long walk in the afternoon. He waits patiently in the kitchen, where he likes to lie on the cold slate flagstones, while I'm working, and only disturbs me if he thinks his lunch has been forgotten or Roddy has to go somewhere without him and he gets lonely.'

In every page of *The Children's Hour*, Marcia's love for both the West Country and for literature shines through. 'From the moment I could read I had an absolute passion for books,' she told me. 'When I was a child, a neighbour—an elderly, kindly man—let me loose in his library and I read Dickens and Hardy, Brontë and Austen, as well as history books, long before I could understand them properly. My mother was very musical, and her own reading was of a particularly spiritual variety, but she had a gift for choosing wonderful books, which she would read to us. I loved the imaginary world she introduced me too during the children's hour—a world that, as a novelist, I am still able to inhabit.'

Jane Eastgate

601-023-1